PAST IMPERFECT

As well as being a novelist, John Matthews is an experienced journalist, editor and publishing consultant. He lives in Surrey with his wife and son.

D1637691

PAST IMPERFECT

John Matthews

MICHAEL JOSEPH
LONDON

MICHAEL JOSEPH

Published by the Penguin Group
Penguin Books Ltd, 27 Wrights Lane, London w8 5TZ, England
Penguin Putnam Inc., 375 Hudson Street, New York, New York 10014, USA
Penguin Books Australia Ltd, Ringwood, Victoria, Australia
Penguin Books Canada Ltd, 10 Alcorn Avenue, Toronto, Ontario, Canada M4V 3B2
Penguin Books (NZ) Ltd, Private Bag 102902, NSMC, Auckland, New Zealand

Penguin Books Ltd, Registered Offices: Harmondsworth, Middlesex, England

First published 1999
1 3 5 7 9 10 8 6 4 2

Set in 11.5/13.5pt Monotype Bembo
Typeset by Rowland Phototypesetting Ltd,
Bury St Edmunds, Suffolk
Printed in Great Britain by Clays Ltd, St Ives plc

A CIP catalogue record for this book is available from the British Library

ISBN 0-718-14359 0

For Sean
And for my family close at heart

My thanks go to Robert Kirby, Nicki Kennedy and all the team at PFD for their tremendous enthusiasm on the front line. To Tom Weldon, Lindsey Jordan and everyone at Michael Joseph/Penguin for their tireless commitment and support. And finally to Stephanie Grey, Betty Schwartz, Elspeth Dougall, Corinne Mayhew and Anthony Sheil for early readings and encouragement (it took a while for the rest of the pack to catch up).

PART ONE

Prologue

Provence, June 1995

The three figures walked along the rough track alongside the wheat field. Two men and a boy of eleven.

The older of the men, Dominic Fornier, was in his late fifties. A stocky figure just short of six foot with dark brown hair cropped short and almost totally grey at the sides. Another twenty metres ahead would be the best vantage point, he thought, his eyes scanning the broad expanse of the wheat field. Soft brown eyes with a faint slant at the corner. A slant that somehow made them sharper: knowing eyes, perceptive eyes. Eyes that had seen too much.

The younger man, Stuart Capel, was an inch shorter and slim with light brown, almost blond, hair. Mid thirties, the first faint worry lines showed more prominently as he squinted against the sun and the glare of the bleached-white field. Dominic could see the slight resemblance between Stuart and the young boy, though the boy's hair was a shade lighter and a few freckles showed across his nose and cheeks. Fresh-faced, happy, but Dominic could still sense the slight barrier, a distance and detachment in the boy's eyes that betrayed the pain and scars of the past months.

As they shuffled to a stop, Stuart asked, 'So is this where it happened?'

'Yes, more or less.' Dominic pointed. 'About five metres ahead on the left.'

Stuart looked at the area of wheat, and it told him nothing. Barely knee-high after being cut down to stubble in the early summer, it was silent, eerie. No hint of the events which now brought them to this spot. What had he expected? He looked across, at young eyes and a distant look that now he knew so well; but there was no glimmer of recognition. As usual, little or nothing while the boy was awake. Probably now even the ghostly shadows had finally faded from the edges of his dreams. Acceptance. Stuart wondered.

Six months? It seemed far longer as Stuart's mind flicked through the nightmare odyssey which had finally led them here today. And now with the trial, so much would hinge on the events of the next days and weeks.

Is that what he'd hoped for by asking Dominic Fornier to bring them out here: a final closing of the book, a laying to rest of the ghosts in both their minds?

To the right of the lane were pine trees and thick bushes clinging to an embankment which dipped down sharply towards the small river tributary thirty metres away. Stuart could hear its faint babbling above the gentle wind that played across the field.

He reminded himself that whatever pain and anguish he'd felt, for Dominic Fornier it must have been much worse. The case had plagued Fornier for over thirty years. From a young gendarme to a chief inspector, from a provincial case to now one of the largest and most intriguing in French legal history. 'The trial of the decade', *Le Monde* had apparently headlined it. And it had ripped apart Fornier's own family life.

Dominic lifted his eyes from the field and gazed into the distance, towards the village of Taragnon. *Blood patches dried brown against the bleached sheaves. The small face swollen and disfigured.* Dominic shuddered. The images were still stark and horrific all these years later.

The field and the view had remained constant, thought Dominic, but everything else had changed. Everything. How many times had he stood in this same field the past thirty-odd years, searching for clues and the missing pieces of his own life? One and the same. The last time he'd visited in the spring just past, he'd cried: cried for the lost years, cried for the family and loved ones long departed, cried for his own and Taragnon's lost innocence. One and the same. Cried and cried until there was nothing left inside.

For a moment, he thought he could even hear the goats' bells again. But as he strained his hearing above the soft sway of the wind across the field, he realized that it was the distant church bells of Bauriac, calling morning prayers . . . *the many services through the years: christenings, marriages . . . funerals . . .*

Dominic bit his lip. He could feel the tears welling again with the memories, and turned slightly from Stuart and the boy as he scanned the silent panorama of fields and the rich green Provence hills beyond. And as the pain of the images became too much, he closed his eyes and muttered silently under his breath, 'Oh God, please forgive me.'

1

California, December 1994

Fields of gold. Burnished wheat under the hot sun.

Eyran could feel the warm rush of air against his body as he ran through the sheaves, thrilling to the feeling of speed as they passed in a blur, springing back and lashing lightly at his legs and thighs. It was England. He knew instinctively, even though there were no guideposts in the dream from which he could be sure. The field where he used to play back in England was on a hill, a slow incline which led down to a small copse of trees with some of his favourite hiding places. Another wheat field rose beyond, linking it in turn to fields of cabbages, maize and barley. A colourful and lazy patchwork of green and gold stretching towards the horizon.

But the field in the dream was flat, and Eyran found himself running through frantically looking for those familiar landmarks. The hollowed tree in the copse where he had built a camp, the small brook that ran into the copse from Broadhurst Farm – where Sarah was on some days with her labrador. The field stretching out before him remained obstinately flat, no matter how fast he ran and how many sheaves he pushed past. The line of the blue horizon above the gold stayed the same. Though he knew somehow that if he kept running, the scene would change, he would see the incline towards the copse, and he picked up the pace, a tireless energy driving him on. The contours changed suddenly, he could see what looked like the brow of a hill just ahead. But the position of the sun was also different, shining straight into his eyes and moving closer, closer – blotting out the hill ahead, then the horizon. Fading the golden wheat to stark white and searing his eyes as it became one blinding blanket of brightness.

Eyran awoke abruptly as the light hurt his eyes. Looking from the car window, he could see the car lights shining at them from one side start to swing away, taking a left at the four-way junction. He didn't recognize any landmarks, though he knew they must have driven some way since leaving their friends in Ventura. He heard his father Jeremy mutter something about the junction they should take for joining Highway 5 for Oceanside and San Diego, then the crinkling of paper as his mother in the front passenger seat tried vainly to unfold a large map to the right place. They slowed slightly as his father looked over intermittently at the map.

'Is it junction 3 for Anaheim and Santa Ana? Can you see?' Jeremy asked. 'Maybe I should stop.'

'Maybe you should. I'm no good with these things.' Allison half turned towards the back seat. 'I think Eyran is awake in any case. He's got school tomorrow, it would be good if he slept some more.' Allison gently stroked Eyran's brow.

Eyran slowly closed his eyes again under the soothing touch. But as his mother's hand moved away and he realized she was looking ahead again, his eyes instinctively opened to stare at the back of her head, focusing on her golden blonde hair until it became almost a blur. Willing himself back into the warmth of the wheat field and the dream.

Allison noticed Jeremy gripping the steering wheel hard as he talked about a problem case at work. His eyes blinked as they adjusted to the fast dying dusk light. Signs now for Carlsbad and Escondido.

She stole a glance back at Eyran. He was asleep again, but she saw that his brow was sweating, the neck of his shirt damp. She pulled the blanket covering him lower down to his waist. Early December and the weather was still mild, temperatures in the late sixties, early seventies. Two weeks to school breaking up, with the trip to England to see Stuart and Amanda only days after. Part of her mind was already planning: how many days she should arrange for Helena to visit during their three weeks away, fresh food left in the fridge, clothes, packing, what woollens and coats to take.

'We should be back within an hour,' Jeremy said. 'Shall I give Helena a call on my mobile?'

'Up to you. She's preparing something, but that's only going to make us forty minutes earlier than we said.'

Jeremy looked over as a large double trailer truck sped by, and checked his speed: 57 mph. The truck must be touching seventy. He shook his head briefly. He didn't notice the motorbike change lanes without warning ahead of the truck, nor the sudden swerve the driver in the cabin made to miss the bike. The first thing he noticed was the lazy snake-like undulation at the back of the trailer, twisting abruptly at an angle and into a jack-knife which finally pulled it away from the cabin.

There was a suspended moment as it happened. As if in one blink everything was still: the road, the trees, the roadside signs and hoardings, the grey dusk sky; the landscape rolling past suddenly frozen. And then in the next blink the trailer was rushing towards him.

Jeremy braked hard and turned the wheel sharply away – but the suddenness with which the trailer flew at them made him gasp out loud, 'Oh . . . *Jeez!*' He braked harder, wrenching the wheel frantically away from the large grey steel block that floated inexorably upon them, filling the windscreen and his view as it scythed through the front of the Jeep.

He heard Allison scream as the Jeep tilted sharply with the impact, and felt something jam hard into his stomach and ribs, pushing the air from his body as the windscreen exploded and shards of glass flew past them like blizzard snowdrops. Numbness more than pain hit him as the engine block was shunted back, severing his right leg just below the knee joint, and the first two rolls of the Jeep became a spinning confusion of sky, road, grass verge. Then darkness.

He remembered awakening once later. He could hear voices, though they were muffled and indistinct. When he tried to focus, the people seemed to be far away, though he could see clearly the arm of a man leaning over and touching his body. He found it hard to breathe, as if he was gargling and choking on warm water, and a jarring pain gripped his stomach and one leg. He must have lain there for some while, at times almost succumbing to the welcome release of the darkness, but knowing somehow that the pain was his only tangible link with consciousness and life.

He mouthed the word 'Eyran', but the man by his side didn't respond, nor could Jeremy in fact hear his own voice. As finally they lifted his body, the lights twisting and spinning briefly to one side and away, the voices faded and he drifted back into the darkness.

Stuart Capel looked at his watch: 10.40 p.m. – 2.40 p.m. in California. When he'd tried his brother Jeremy's number earlier it was on the answerphone, so he'd made a note to call again in the afternoon.

Only two or three weeks to go and so much to plan. He hadn't seen Jeremy and his family for almost two years. He had ten days off work over Christmas while they were over, but he couldn't remember if it was the 16th or 23rd when they arrived. All-so-precise Jeremy, phoning him almost a month ago, going painstakingly through flight numbers, dates and times. Somehow he'd ended up with the flight number and the time on his phone pad, but not the date. The problem was, the same flight number left at the same time each week.

If he had to ask Jeremy again, it would probably provoke a comment. A short snub that said it all: I'm organized and you're not, I'm successful because I plan carefully, you've suffered in business because you don't. All-so-precise Jeremy. Each step of his life carefully mapped out and planned. From university at Cambridge, through London chambers, then retaking exams in the US and six months in Boston as a stepping stone to a San Diego law firm.

Stuart's life and career had been in almost complete contrast. A massive rise in the eighties in design work for print media, then the slump. Two partnership break-ups followed and he was almost bust by the late eighties, only crawling his way out the last few years. Methodical planning had never worked for Stuart, and nearly all of his arguments with Jeremy revolved around the same thing: Jeremy trying to suggest some well-staged plan, Stuart telling him at every turn why it wouldn't work, what would probably arise to fuck it up, and finally they'd reach the subject of Eyran.

Stuart would strike back by complaining that Jeremy was trying to structure Eyran's life too carefully, the boy was being stifled. He sensed a kindred spirit in Eyran that was somehow lost on Jeremy, a curiosity and thirst for life that Jeremy so often quelled by trying to map out his son's life to finite extremes. Jeremy loved Eyran, but had little grasp how important it was to allow the child some freedom. Some choice.

The last get-together was almost two years ago when Stuart had taken his family out to California. He'd put his foot in it by mentioning some of Eyran's old friends in England. Could Eyran write them a postcard or perhaps get them a small memento from San Diego Zoo? Jeremy had shot him a dark look, then explained later that they'd had problems with Eyran being homesick and missing his English friends. Only in the last six months had he settled in more and not mentioned them.

Later in the same holiday, Jeremy had poured cold water on Stuart's plans to expand into multi-media production, and they'd had more words. Of course there were risks, Stuart explained. Anything that depended on creative input, market forces and an unpredictable general public was a risk. As usual, Jeremy was blinkered; Stuart might as well try and explain Picasso to a plumber.

Stuart made a mental note: Eyran's friends in England, advice about Eyran's upbringing and future, current business activities which might be viewed as risky. Any other no-go areas for his conversation with Jeremy?

He made the call again, but it was Helena, the visiting Mexican maid, telling him that they were away. 'Hup state till later tonight . . . about nine o'clock. You want I ask them to call you when they get back?'

'No, it's okay. I'll set an alarm call early and phone them back.'

He arranged the call for 6.30 a.m., 10.30 p.m. California time. One finger tapped at the receiver for a second after putting it back. Fleeting unease. He pushed it as quickly away, told himself it was just his nerves settling back from steeling for possible confrontation with Jeremy.

Dr Martin Holman, at thirty-four the youngest of Oceanside's three head ER consultants, heard the babble and commotion of voices a second before the Emergency doors swung open. He was aware of two gurneys heading to different parts of the room, and then his attention fell on the young boy.

'What have we got?'

'Accident victim. Ten or eleven years old. Head injuries, but the chest's the most severe: two cracked ribs, possibly a fractured sternum as well.' The paramedic spat the words out breathlessly as they wheeled the gurney rapidly towards a bed.

'Conscious at any time?' Holman asked.

'No. He's been out since we loaded him. Breathing blocked – so tracheal, respirator, plasma to keep up the volume. The normal. But still his blood pressure and pulse dropped the last few minutes in the ambulance. Last pulse reading was forty-eight.'

'Okay. Let's get him up and attached. One . . . *two*.' They lifted the boy in unison on to the bed. Holman called over two nurses and a junior doctor, Garvin, to attach the monitors: pulse, respiration, central venous and arterial pressure. Within a minute, the readings and a steady pulse bleep were there for Holman. But he was immediately alarmed: blood pressure 98 over 56, and pulse only 42 and dropping . . . *40*. Something was wrong. Seriously wrong.

'More plasma infusion!' Holman snapped at Garvin. 'Do we know the blood type?'

'O positive.'

Holman instructed a nurse to arrange a supply for transfusion, then looked back to the boy. The pulse stayed stable at 40 for a few seconds with the increased plasma, then dropped another notch . . . *38*. Holman began to panic. By the early 30s, it was all over. The boy was dying!

He scanned rapidly – the chest bandaged and blood-soaked, the face and head bruised with heavy contusions – looking for tell-tale signs. Blood loss was heavy, but the plasma infusion should have compensated. He moved around, feeling the boy's skull, shining a penlight into the eyes. No responsiveness. There was probably internal damage, but no alarming swelling to cause the current problem.

'Thirty-six!' Garvin called out with alarm.

Then Holman noticed the unevenness of the boy's chest: one part of his lungs wasn't expanding! Possibly a broken rib puncturing one lung.

He nodded urgently at the remaining nurse: 'Trochal cannula! Set up a plural drainage.'

Holman cut through the chest bandages and then slowly inserted the cannula, a hollow metal pipe with a cutting edge, between Eyran's ribs and into his left lung. He then fed a thin plastic pipe through the cannula, and at his signal the nurse activated the pump. It started sucking out blood from the flooded lung.

Garvin announced: 'Thirty-four!' And Holman muttered under his breath, 'Come on . . . *come on!*' It had been a good day so far, mostly only minor injuries. He'd been hoping to finish his shift unscathed at midnight. *Don't die on me now!*

Holman looked anxiously between the cannula pipe and the pump. It was a race against time. Hoping that enough blood could be pumped from the lungs to restore blood pressure and respiration before the pulse dipped too low. But when blood pressure fell to 92 over 50 and Garvin announced pulse at 32 – then, after only a few seconds' gap, 30 – Holman realized with rising panic that it was a race he was losing.

Garvin's shout of 'bradycardia!' and the boy lapsing into cardiac arrest came almost immediately after. The pulse became a flatline beep.

Holman had already signalled the nurse and now prompted urgently: 'De-frib!'

Garvin put the electroshock pads into position, but Holman held up one hand, counting off the seconds . . . *six . . . seven.* It was a calculated gamble. Holman knew that as soon as the heart started again, fresh blood would be pumped into the lungs. Each extra second gave him more chance of clearing the lungs and stabilization. *Ten . . . eleven . . .* Garvin looked at him anxiously, the flatline beep sounding ominously in the background . . . *thirteen . . . fourteen . . .* 'Okay . . . Clear!'

Holman stepped back as Garvin hit the charge. The shock jolted the boy's small body dramatically.

But there was nothing. The flatline pulse still beeped . . . *nineteen . . .*

Holman's jaw set tight, frantic now that he might have mistimed it, left the de-frib too long. *Twenty-one* seconds now the heart had been stopped! He leant across, put one hand firmly on the boy's chest and started massaging. It was thick with blood, and with the cracked ribs and sternum, Holman feared he couldn't apply the pressure he'd have liked. *Twenty-eight . . . twenty-nine . . .*

Still nothing! The beep a persistent, infuriating reminder. He didn't need to look up. He leapt back, signalling Garvin. 'Hit it again!'

Another shock and jolt. But with still no pulse signal, Holman feared the worst. He leant back over for another massage, his hands now slippery with blood on the small frail chest, trying to feel deep with each push down, silently willing back a spark of life. Beads of sweat massed on his forehead. Only minutes since the boy had been wheeled in, and his nerves were gone, he was fighting now to control the trembling in his hands to hold the massage rhythm . . . *forty-three . . . forty-four.* If he lost the boy now, he doubted he could face another patient the rest of his shift.

But already he knew there was little hope. One more de-frib, and then that was it. By then the boy would have been dead almost a full minute.

Fields of wheat, swaying gently in the breeze.

The incline changed suddenly, without warning. Eyran could see the small copse at the end of the field and ran down the hill towards it, excitement growing as he got closer. Inside the copse, it was dark and damp, the air cooler. He looked for familiar landmarks that would lead him towards the brook, picking his way through the darkness. At one point he thought he was lost, then suddenly the brook appeared ahead from behind a group of trees. He felt uncertain at first, he couldn't remember the brook being in that place before. As he got closer, he could see a small figure hunched over the brook, looking into the water. He thought it might be Sarah, but there was no dog in sight. The figure slowly looked up at him, and it took a second for recognition to dawn: Daniel Fletcher, a young boy from his old school in England whom he hadn't seen for years.

He asked what Daniel was doing there, it wasn't the place where he usually played, and Daniel muttered something about it being peaceful. 'I know,' Eyran agreed. 'That's why I come here. It's so quiet. Sarah comes down here with her dog sometimes as well.' Then he remembered that Daniel lived almost two miles beyond Broadhurst Farm. 'It must have taken you ages to get here. Do your parents know you're here?'

'No, they don't. But it doesn't matter, I haven't seen them in years.'

'In years! Very funny.' Though Eyran could see that Daniel wasn't smiling. He was looking soulfully back into the water, and some small quirk told him that something was wrong, that all of this wasn't real, it was a dream. Then he recalled with a jolt what it was: Daniel had suffered with acute asthma, he'd died at the age of six after a severe bronchitis attack, over a year before Eyran left for California. He remembered now the service of the school chaplain, the whole school tearful, and how all the boys who had picked on Daniel for his frailty had felt suddenly guilty. He could see Daniel's pigeon chest struggling for breath, hear the faint wheezing. Eyran was startled by a rustling among the trees, preparing himself to turn and run before seeing that it was his father walking through.

He felt nervous because he'd never seen his father down by the copse before. He knew instinctively that he must be late returning home or have done something wrong, and mouthed 'I'm sorry', almost as a stock reaction.

His father looked thoughtfully down at Daniel before waving his arm towards Eyran. 'You must go home now, Eyran, you don't belong here.'

Eyran started to move away, then realized his father wasn't following. He was staying by Daniel at the side of the brook. 'Aren't you coming with me now, Daddy?'

His father shook his head slowly, his eyes sad and distant, and Eyran looked out of the copse to find that now it had become dark outside. The darkness was a solid black blanket, the wheat field seeming to stretch endlessly into the distance, as before, with no hills and contours that he recognized. 'But I could get lost,' he pleaded, just before his father turned and disappeared back into the darkness of the woods.

Eyran started to tremble and cry. He sensed that he must do as his father said and try to find his way back home, though he was struggling desperately at the same time to understand why his father had deserted him to fight back through the darkness on his own. If he could just get back home, he knew that all would be well. But the darkness of the field was deep and impenetrable, with no familiar landmarks.

2

Provence, August 1963

Alain Duclos saw the boy a few hundred metres ahead walking at the side of the road. His figure emerged like a mirage from the faint shimmer of the August heat haze.

At first Duclos wasn't going to stop. But there was something about the boy's tired posture and profile that made him slow down. As he drew close, taking in the boy's wavy hair and olive skin, the sweat on his brow and his flustered expression, he decided to stop. The boy was obviously tired and something was troubling him. The side window had been wound down because of the heat. Duclos leant across as he pulled over.

'Can I give you a lift somewhere?'

The boy was hesitant and looked back towards the far ridge of the fields for a second. 'No. No, thank you. It's okay.'

Duclos guessed his age at no more than ten or eleven. He couldn't help noticing how beautiful the boy's eyes were: green with small flecks of hazel, in contrast to his deep olive skin tone. The eyes betrayed the boy's anxiety. 'Are you sure?' Duclos pressed. 'You look as if you've lost somebody.'

The boy looked back towards the ridge again. 'My bike broke down back there just beyond the field. I was walking to my friend's house, Stéphane. His father has a tractor with a trailer to pick it up.'

'How far is it to Stéphane's house?'

'Four or five kilometres. It's the other side of the village. But it's okay, I've done the walk before.'

Duclos nodded knowingly and smiled, pushing the door ajar. 'Come on, you're tired and it's hot. I'll run you there. It's too far for you to walk.'

The boy returned the smile hesitantly. For the first time he looked at the length of Duclos' car, the sudden excitement at the prospect of a ride in a sports car showing. 'If you're sure it's okay.'

Again the reassuring nod and smile as the boy got in. Duclos leant across to shut the door, revved twice quickly as he checked the mirror, and pulled out. They both sat in silence for a moment as the car picked up speed. Duclos noticed the boy looking at the dashboard and leather seats, then lifting up slightly to take in the sloping bonnet. Duclos answered his obvious curiosity.

'It's an Alfa Romeo Giulietta Sprint, 1961. Custom colour, dark green. I wanted one of the classic Italian racing colours – red or dark green, but I thought the red was too loud. I've had it just under two years. Like it?'

The boy nodded enthusiastically, now checking out the small back bench seat and view through the coupé rear window.

'What's your name?' asked Duclos.

'Christian. Christian Rosselot.'

Duclos checked his watch: 12.48 p.m. He'd made good time since leaving Aix-en-Provence. Duclos knew now what had made him stop. The boy reminded him of Jahlep, the young Algerian boy his Marseille pimp had found for him and who had become a favourite on his last few visits. Except more beautiful. The skin colour wasn't as dark as Jahlep's and had a smoother tone like polished cane, and his large green eyes with hazel flecks were striking beyond belief. The boy was wearing shorts, and he found himself looking over at the smooth copper of the boy's legs. They'd already gone a kilometre and a half, Duclos estimated, when he noticed the roadside sign: *Taragnon, 1.3 km*. The friend's house wasn't far past the village. There wouldn't be much time. Duclos glanced again at the boy's legs. His mouth felt suddenly dry. He had to think of a device to get himself alone somewhere with the boy, and quickly. A few hundred metres ahead he saw a roadside farm track. Duclos slowed down and stopped just past it.

'I've had a thought. If we get to Stéphane's and his father's not there or for any reason can't help out – it's a wasted journey. I've got some tools in the back, I'll run you back to the bike, and if we can't fix it I'll rope it into the boot and run you home with it. Where do you live?'

'Almost three kilometres that way from where the bike is now.' Christian pointed behind them and slightly to the east. 'But it's okay. I'm sure they will be there. Stéphane's father is always working on the farm.'

Duclos shrugged. 'The problem is, if they're not there you're going to be stuck.' He backed into the farm track, checked briefly for traffic, then turned out heading back the way they'd come. Just take control, his instincts told him. The boy's protests weren't strong. 'Look, it's no trouble. In any case I've just remembered I should have picked up something at the patisserie back in Varages, so it's not putting me out of my way.'

Duclos wondered if the boy was suspicious. In the wake of his insistence, the boy had finally nodded and smiled, though hesitantly, then hastily looked away through the side window. It could have been his normal awkwardness with strangers, or perhaps he was suspicious. It was hard to tell either way. Duclos was now more concerned of passing anyone who might see them together. After almost a kilometre, a truck came towards them with a company name and MARSEILLE in large letters on the side. With the height of the cab and the speed they'd passed each other, Duclos doubted the driver had paid them any particular attention. For a moment he thought to himself, 'Just drop the boy off, leave him alone, continue on to Salernes.' But the urge driving him on was now too strong. A mixture of excitement, curiosity, anticipation, the thrill of the unknown. He found it impossible to resist. They'd just passed the point where he'd first picked up the boy.

'Is it far now?' Duclos asked.

'No, just under a kilometre more – it's on a rough track between two farms.'

The patchwork of green and gold pastures on each side was faded with the summer heat. After a long flat stretch, the road curved and they were passing a peach orchard, only part of which appeared to be harvested; uneven grass patches grew between the trees on its far side. Christian lifted one arm to indicate the pathway.

Turning in, Duclos could see that a hundred metres ahead the peach orchard verged into woodland. The track then ran between the orchard and the woods, and the grass was long and unkempt closest to the woods. The boy was pointing to where he'd left his bike.

'Just up there on the left, where the grass is long. I tried to hide it so it would be safe until I got back.'

With the bumpiness of the track, Duclos had changed down to second. Those legs. Those eyes. His pulse quickened with expectation. Images of what was to come were already forming in his mind. But at the same time he felt nervous and uncomfortable. With Jahlep it was always pre-arranged, the young Algerian boy a willing participant. Now he was facing the unknown. He wasn't sure how to make the first move, that first contact that would break the barrier. Once he'd touched the boy and his intentions were obvious, he knew it would be impossible just to stop there. The only question then was whether he continued with consent or force.

Duclos pulled the car over to the side of the track and followed the boy out. Only after a few paces and prompted by the boy pointing could Duclos make out the bike lying flat among the tall grass.

'What went wrong with it?' he inquired.

'The back brake locked on the wheel. That's why I couldn't move it.'

Duclos knelt down to examine the wheel, moving it back and forth with difficulty against the locked brake. The boy was by his side, also kneeling and keenly inspecting. Duclos could smell the faint acid sweetness of the boy's sweat mixed with the scent of grass and ripe peaches. It was then that he noticed the graze and bruise on the boy's thigh. It was the chance he'd been looking for. He reached over and touched the graze, gently stroking it.

'That looks bad – you should get some antiseptic on it. And the bruise is going to be a real beauty in the morning. Did you get that when the bike broke down?'

'When the brake jammed, the bike got thrown to the side.' The boy made a dramatic motion with one arm towards the grass. 'My leg got trapped underneath.'

He was so sweet, thought Duclos. The eyes were hauntingly beautiful, green limpid pools in which he could almost swim. The boy had flinched at the initial touch, but hadn't moved. Duclos continued stroking, working slightly higher. It was in that moment that Duclos saw the change in the boy's eyes; the pupils dilated, the eyes suddenly looked darker and more troubled. The boy knew something was wrong. As the boy's body tensed to move, Duclos reached up and gripped his shorts tight.

'There's no point in struggling, you'll only get hurt. I don't really want to hurt you.' Duclos' voice was both soothing and menacing.

The motion was sudden. Christian let out a half-scream, half-gasp as Duclos yanked down his shorts and pushed him face down in the grass.

Duclos gently stroked the boy's back, lifting his shirt higher and running his thumb up and down the ridge of his spine. The boy's sweat eased the motion, and after a few strokes Duclos lowered his stroking to the boy's buttocks and the cleft in between. Duclos became quickly aroused. The boy's skin was so smooth. He could feel the small body trembling beneath his touch, though after a few moments it became more intense then finally verged into gentle quaking as the boy started sobbing.

Duclos found the noise disturbing, the mood was being spoilt. 'Be quiet. For God's sake, be quiet. It will do no good.'

The crying became more muted. Duclos took off his own clothes. He tried to force in other thoughts to distract himself from the crying as he crouched over the boy. Jahlep was beckoning with one finger, smiling back at him and urging on his increasingly urgent thrusts. The Algerian boy's eyes were dancing with mischief and pleasure. He could feel the sun hot on his back, the sweat in the ridge of the boy's back as he ran his hands slowly up and down. Duclos shook his head from side to side. The wind through the nearby treetops momentarily drowned out all other sound, and Duclos felt himself sailing on a wave of pleasure. Jahlep's brown eyes looked at him soulfully, imploring, willing him on to greater heights of pleasure. But the green eyes of the boy beneath him were suddenly superimposed – sullen and haunted, frightened, pleading. He shook his head again to shift the image, but it stayed with him obstinately until his final moment of orgasm, his strangled and guttural cry of pleasure lost among the wind rippling through the treetops.

It took him a moment afterwards to become orientated again. He'd pulled out and ejaculated on the ground and part of his weight was rested on the boy's back, his cheek against the bare skin, suddenly sweaty, sticky. He rolled off.

In the aftermath he lay on his back and stared up at the sky. He could still hear the boy gently crying, though intermittently it merged with and was drowned out by the rustling of the wind. They became one and the same.

Duclos looked over. There was a small trickle of blood running down the boy's inner thigh. He reached over and touched the boy's back, but felt him flinch sharply under the touch. He wanted to say 'I'm sorry,' but it would sound so empty and futile now. He knew that he would have to be stern to warn the boy off. He sat up and gripped the boy's shoulder tight.

'Look at me. Look at me!' Duclos gripped tighter and shook the boy until he looked up. The boy's face was streaked with tears and he made a vain effort to wipe away a fresh tear with the back of one hand. 'What happened today never happened, you understand. It never happened!' Duclos looked at the boy intently, as if by staring and continuing to shake the boy's shoulder he could force his will home. 'It's our secret, and you're to tell nobody. Nobody! If you do, I'll come after you and kill you. I know where you live now, it will be easy for me to get to you.'

The boy nodded after a second. Duclos shook his shoulder once more for emphasis. 'You understand?'

But once again the boy's eyes betrayed him. Mixed with the fear, Duclos could see the uncertainty and confusion. He knew that whatever the boy agreed to now, later he would be faced with awkward and insistent questions from his parents about the afternoon, and he would finally talk. The police would be called. With his distinctive car, he would be easily found, would face a trial, public humiliation and a jail term; his life and career would be ruined. His dreams and plans of becoming Assistant Public Prosecutor in Limoges within three years would be over.

He knew in that moment that he would probably have to kill the boy.

Duclos sat close to the window in the restaurant. From there, he had a clear view of his car at the far side of the car park. It was out of the direct path of people approaching the restaurant, but still he couldn't be too careful.

Having decided what to do, it had taken him almost fifteen minutes to secure the boy, ripping up the boy's shirt and using some rags from his car to tie his hands and feet and gag him. Space in the car boot had been very restricted, and he huddled the boy tightly next to the spare tyre in almost a foetal position, the arms draped over the tyre itself. He warned the boy not to make a sound or move about, otherwise he'd feed in a hosepipe from the exhaust and gas him. The boy had nodded fearfully, his eyes wide. It was the last image he remembered as he shut the boot lid – those eyes staring back at him, questioning, pleading.

At first Duclos wasn't sure why he'd delayed. It had just felt wrong killing the boy then and there on the spot. And he wanted time to think. But was the delay just to steel up courage for what he already knew was inevitable, or was he having second thoughts? In the end what he thought about most was if he had to kill the boy, how best to cover his tracks? He didn't want to take any action hastily.

The effort of tying up the boy and bundling him into the car in the heat had tired him. Duclos' clearest thoughts only came as he drove away, jigsaw pieces matching with how he saw the crime being reconstructed by investigators based on his past experience with forensics. By the time he reached the outskirts of Taragnon, he'd worked out most of the details, and the restaurant was an integral part of that plan. He checked his watch: 1.41 p.m. Timing would be the key. Ideally, he should stay just over an hour.

Duclos had already looked at the menu, and scanned it briefly again as the waiter came over.

'*Plat du jour*, but with the veal cassoulet, please. The mushrooms to start and the *île flottante* to finish.'

'And for the wine?' the waited asked.

'*Vin rouge*, please, and some water. What is the house red with the menu?'

'Château Vernet. It's quite good, fairly full-blooded.'

Duclos didn't ask about the year. The house wines were nearly all nondescript recent vintage. In any case in the hot weather he normally mixed house wines with water, though if it was good he might savour one glass on its own.

The restaurant was the first that he saw after Taragnon with a reasonable car park in front. It was important that he could see the car while he ate. Simple and café style, it was very close to the village, less than a kilometre, and the roadside sign advertising the *plat du jour* at only 3 francs 40 had attracted a reasonable crowd that lunchtime. It was almost half full; Duclos counted another eight cars and two trucks in the car park.

The waiter had put his order into the kitchen and now returned with his wine and water. He poured the wine but left the water for Duclos to help himself. Duclos took a sip; it was full-bodied, but had a slight acid aftertaste. Palatable but unexceptional. Duclos added some water, and noticed the other waiter behind the bar look over briefly. He was more surly and curious than his own waiter, and had been by the front window serving, looking out as Duclos had pulled up and walked in. He could tell what the look meant, he'd seen it a thousand times: young, nice car, nice clothes, *rich kid!* Everything bought and paid for by his parents. The waiter, little more than his own mid twenties, was slaving behind the bar day and night thinking that meanwhile kids like himself whiled away their summers on the coast on their parents' money.

But in Duclos' case, the resentment was misplaced. He'd come from a family probably no better than the waiter's, his father just a simple works foreman in a local pottery factory. It had taken his father years to work up to foreman through various positions on the factory floor. Then three years later a badly stacked crate fell and injured his back. After increasing time off for treatment, he was forced to work part-time, then the company finally wanted to let him go. The company was inadequately insured, the compensation poor, and it was only by involving a lawyer and the threat of a large suit that his father had finally won the day. The company paid for treatment, gave a six-month-pay cash settlement and a full-time office position for his father handling inventory.

The object lesson of how the lawyer had managed to save the family when his father was virtually powerless had stayed strongly with Duclos, only thirteen at the time. The power of being able to wield the law like a heavy sword to get what you wanted from life. He worked hard at school and graduated to take Law and a second in Business Studies at Bordeaux University.

At twenty-one, three months after graduation, he'd joined the Public Prosecutor's office in Limoges. The first year as a *stagiaire*, then two years with case preparation for the Assistant Public Prosecutor and some lesser cases which he handled himself. But in the last year he'd handled a more important caseload, including two landmark cases for the Head of Public Prosecution who was retiring in three years. Everyone would then move up a rung, and he was one of three lawyers in line for Assistant Public Prosecutor. His success rate with cases was higher than the other two and his file preparation was noted for being meticulous. Three more years of hard application and the job was his.

The waiter came up with his mushrooms. He looked over towards his car again as he ate. He'd worked too hard for too long to give it all up now.

The friend that he was staying with in Salernes, Claude Vallon, he'd met at Bordeaux University and they'd stayed in close contact since. This was Duclos' sixth visit in four years, invariably for three weeks in August or ten days at Easter. Claude's family owned one of the area's largest vineyards, the main château had its own grounds and pool, and the Côte d'Azur was just over half an hour's drive away. Idyllic, particularly for summer holidays. Duclos would usually sneak off at least twice to Marseille to see his pimp and Jahlep, making an excuse about visiting an aunt in Aubagne, a boring but necessary social visit. Claude had never been suspicious.

Through the years he'd got used to covering up, had become quite proficient at it. There had been no steady girlfriends, but he was not unattractive and with his position he'd always been able to find girls for special dinner dates or work-related functions. Keeping up appearances.

He finished the mushrooms, and the main course arrived after a few minutes. Duclos checked his watch again. He'd been there twenty-five minutes. He might have to take coffee and brandy to stretch the time.

There was one small element still missing from his plan, and it began to trouble him increasingly. He dwelled on it through the cassoulet. Only as he was close to finishing, topping up his wine with water for the third time, did something strike a chord. He looked thoughtfully at the bottle. He wondered. It could work, but would there be enough water in the bottle? The thought was still gelling when an out-of-place movement in the corner of his eye made him look past the bottle towards the car park. His nerves tensed. Two women who had just left the restaurant were approaching the car next to his. As one went to open the car door, the other appeared to be looking over at his car. Was she just admiring it, or had some sound alerted her? She stood there for a moment, then finally looked towards the fence behind and got in. The car backed out and moved away. Duclos relaxed.

But his peace of mind was short-lived. Minutes later a truck pulled in and took the vacant space, obscuring his view of his car. Duclos felt immediately ill at ease; now he could only see part of the furthest rear tail light.

He found it hard to concentrate on the rest of the meal. When the *île flottante* arrived, he ordered coffee and brandy from the same waiter to save time. Fifteen minutes more. The waiting was infuriating. His nerves had built to fever pitch by the time the brandy arrived. He had to steady his hand as he lifted the glass. He wasn't sure if it was the aftershock of what had already happened, or what he knew he faced. The other waiter was looking over at him again with that same curious expression. Or was he reading too much into it, seeing imaginary demons and problems? He just knew that he had to get out of the café fast. Having steeled his nerves over the past hour, he knew that if he didn't do it soon, he might never be able to. His composure and resolve would be gone.

Mopping his brow, Duclos signalled to the waiter. The waiter finished up an order three tables away and came over.

'The bill, please.' The waiter had turned to go when Duclos realized he'd forgotten something. He pointed to the bottle on the table. 'And some bottled water to take with me.'

The bar was noisy with conversation and the gentle clatter of cutlery. Duclos closed his eyes, fighting to calm himself while he waited for the bill. Had he appeared agitated? Was the timing right? *Had the woman by his car earlier heard something?* Thoughts of what might have already gone wrong and potential pitfalls yet to come jumbled desperately with soul-searching. What might have been if he hadn't gone to Aix-en-Provence that morning? If he had never seen the boy at the roadside? All those years of reading affidavits from people who'd got themselves into hopeless messes, and how he always knew so much better. He shook his head in disbelief.

It took another six minutes to pay and receive his change, and by that time Duclos was trembling uncontrollably. He smiled and tipped generously, hoping that his nervousness wasn't outwardly obvious. He wanted them to remember him, but not in that way.

Getting back into the car, Duclos let out a deep sigh and fought to calm his trembling hands as he gripped the steering wheel. He felt nauseous and his mind was spinning with a thousand conflicting thoughts – and finally the build-up of nerves overtook him and his body slumped defeatedly. He didn't think he could go through with it.

In the dark, the first thing Christian became conscious of was the sound of his own breathing.

He felt hot in the boot, despite being without his shirt. He'd managed to control his tears, but his body still trembled violently. How was he going to explain his shirt being destroyed when he got home, and why did the man have to tie him up and put him in the boot out of sight? He just hoped the man wasn't going to hurt him again. He knew that he would probably have to tell his mother what had happened. She was going to be furious; she had warned him so often about talking to strangers. But the man had reminded him of his cousin François who worked with one of the perfume companies in Grasse – not like the rough men he'd imagined.

Christian began to dwell on the man's threat. *If you tell, I'll come after you and kill you . . . I know where you live now, it will be easy for me to get to you.* Perhaps he could swear his mother to secrecy; though if she still had to tell the police, surely they would protect him. For what the man had done, would he be locked up so that he couldn't get to him, and for how long?

Christian listened to the monotonous drone of the car engine and the wheels spinning on the road. He strained to hear noises beyond. After a moment, there was a faint rushing sound, perhaps a lorry or car passing, then nothing. How far had they gone? It was difficult to judge speed, the only guide changing echo tones when they passed buildings. The echo was there for a while, then gone briefly before returning for a long continuous stretch. They were passing through Taragnon, unless they'd branched off and it was Bauriac. Pontevès was too far.

After a while the echoing stopped, another faint rush of something passing came immediately after, and not long after they slowed; he felt the car turn, then they stopped. And then the long wait.

The heat built up insufferably in the confined space. His body was hunched up tight and he could feel the twinge of cramps in his legs. For a while he wondered if the man had gone off and left him. At moments he could hear distant voices and thought about kicking the side to attract attention, the only action allowed him with the ties and gag. But they were distant enough that they might not hear, and what if the man was still close by? He waited.

With time passing, he became more fearful of what the man might do to him. He found it difficult to breathe with the extreme heat, the hot air rasping uncomfortably at the back of his throat. He started to feel faint. It was then that he remembered the coin in his pocket: the silver twenty lire given him by his Grandpapa André. The luck token he took with him everywhere. It was in his left-hand pocket. With his hands tied, it took a minute to fumble in his pocket and finally have it in his grasp. Moving his arms back over the spare wheel, he grasped the coin tight in his right hand and started a silent prayer: that the man wouldn't hurt him again, that he would be home soon, that the police would find the man and lock him up, and that his mother wouldn't be too annoyed when he told her what had happened.

The heat made him tired. He was on the edge of sleep when some voices snapped him alert. Unlike the other voices they were coming closer, until he could hear them virtually at the side of the car. There was some shuffling and the sound of a car door opening. He pondered on the action only for a moment – then kicked back with his legs against the back metal panel. Then waited, listening. Nothing, except some fumbling and another car door opening. He kicked again, but at that moment everything was smothered by the rushing of a car or truck passing. Then he heard the car doors closing. The engine started. The car backed out and moved away. Christian let out a long sigh and bit his lip.

Shortly after he succumbed to the heat and dozed off. He had started to think about the farm, and it filled his dream. There was a small stone wall in the main back field against which wild strawberries grew. One summer he'd cut down an area of the strawberry brambles and built a small hideaway house against the wall with wood and patched straw. He was in the hideaway when he heard his father Jean-Luc calling. He decided to stay hidden a minute, then leap up and startle his father. On the third call, he jumped up on to the ridge of the wall. But his father kept scanning the horizon; he hadn't seen him. Christian started waving one arm frantically. Once more his father scanned back and forth, more slowly and purposefully this time, calling his name yet again. For a moment more his father stood looking blankly across the fields, then finally turned resignedly and headed back across the farm courtyard to the back-kitchen door.

Christian jumped down from the wall, calling his father's name desperately as he ran towards him. But as he ran, the grass gradually became longer, obscuring his vision of the courtyard and his father. He became confused and lost. He could never remember the grass being that long, and now that he couldn't see the farm he'd lost all direction. He continued running, calling his father's name frantically; but with still no answer, he felt increasingly lost and was becoming tired. It was getting dark and he was frightened. He called his father's name again with no response, then sat down defeatedly among the tall grass. He started crying. He felt deserted by his father. *Why didn't you come and find me?* After a moment the ground seemed to reverberate and shake with the heavy drone of an engine. The noise and movement perplexed Christian, and the only thing he could think of was that his father had brought the tractor out to try and find him.

That hope only quelled his tears slightly; he was still crying as he awoke to the reality of the boot and the rough track they were driving on. They had obviously turned off again from the main road. How far had they gone? He realized with a sinking feeling that he'd completely lost track of time and distance; they might be too far from Taragnon for his father to find them. Suddenly he felt as lost and alone as in the dream. Fear and dread crept over him and his body started trembling again.

Then he noticed with sudden panic that something else was wrong. Grandpapa André's coin was no longer in his hand. His right hand had relaxed slightly open and it had probably slipped from his grasp with the track's bumpiness. He started feeling for it in the dark. It was not on top of the wheel hub; the top of the hub was smooth metal, except for several small oval holes around its rim. They were too small to reach into, especially with his hands tied; if the coin had fallen through one of them, he wouldn't be able to retrieve it. He started feeling around the edge of the tyre.

The car had stopped without Christian noticing. He was still searching for the coin when the boot lid opened and the bright sunlight flooded in, blinding him.

3

Provence, August 1963

Dominic Fornier sat in Café du Verdon and enjoyed his normal breakfast of coffee with hot bread and pâté. The coffee was large, in a cup almost big enough to be a soup bowl, and he always kept one piece of bread without butter or pâté just to dip in it. It was 3.40 p.m. An unusual time for breakfast, but then he had been on all-night duty in the police station and had woken less than an hour ago to return for the afternoon shift.

It was a regular ritual. The café owner Louis knew his order off by heart now, and had almost worked out his sequence of shifts. One large coffee with milk, third of a stick loaf sliced in half, one half plain, the other half with pâté, coffee refill halfway through.

The café overlooked the main square and fountain at Bauriac and the police station was only fifty metres to the right of the square on the road flanking the town hall. The town hall and Louis' café were the most imposing structures overlooking the square. Neoclassical, the town hall should have been far more imposing, but Louis had compensated by putting out striped blue canvas awnings and a row of tables with Martini umbrellas. It was particularly busy in summer and it was only from Louis' pavement frontage that tourists could appreciate the town hall façade and the ornate fountain at the centre of Bauriac's square.

There were a few tourists there that afternoon. Dominic could spot them straight away. Shorts, leather-strap sandals and cameras. Always cameras. Louis grunted his way past Dominic's table as he served some of them. The front doors to the café were wide open and from the jukebox inside came the strains of Stevie Wonder's fingertips. Louis gave a mock bump and grind to it on his way back into the café and twirled his tray in one hand. Dominic smiled. It had been his one contribution to Louis' jukebox: decent music. Tamla, the Drifters on RCA, Stax, Sam Cooke, Ben E. King, Booker T, and now a new artist called Stevie Wonder. All of it American soul brought in through his uncle's export business in Marseille, and practically none of it available in France for at least two to three months. Sometimes never. It was improving now, but when he'd first started getting records through his uncle in the late fifties, only a selected few American soul releases made it to French shores.

None of the tourists on Louis' terrace, unless they were American, would have heard Stevie Wonder's new record yet. They seemed oblivious as they sipped their tea and cokes or ambled off for photos in front of the fountain or town hall. They hadn't come to France to listen to American soul. The records were there just for the benefit of himself and Louis and the growing number of discerning late-nighters. A welcome escape from the syrupy tones of Sacha Distel, Serge Gainsbourg, the Singing Nun and the endless pop rock which filled the French charts and, since Louis had installed the jukebox, it drew an increasing crowd of young locals on their Solexes and Vespas with a sprinkling of 100 and 150 cc bikes. Lightweight rockers. Mostly between the ages of fifteen and twenty, they came in heavier numbers on Friday and Saturday nights. Louis' hunch about installing the jukebox had worked.

Those over twenty mostly had larger bikes or cars and would head off to the clubs or discos in Aix, Draguignan or even Marseille or Toulon. But for local entertainment, apart from the town cinema and one other bar with music near Taragnon, Louis had the market cornered.

Bauriac's population was just over 14,000 and, even with the surrounding villages of Taragnon, Varages, Pontevès, Saint-Martin and La Verdière, which came under the administration of Bauriac's town hall and gendarmerie, overall area population was still under 35,000.

Dominic Fornier was one of eleven gendarmes stationed in Bauriac, and at twenty-six was the youngest of two senior warrant officers there, having transferred from Marseille just the year before. Head of station and the four other area gendarmeries was Captain Olivier Poullain, thirty-seven, locally born but now just biding his time by tending provincial turf; advancement meant transfer to Aix-en-Provence or Marseille and a city administrative position with a shot at Colonel, and Poullain hoped to make it there by forty. Station veteran was Lieutenant Éric Harrault, forty-nine.

Harrault's knowledge of past Bauriac cases and general procedures between the station and the local courts was absolute, and as a result he spent much of his time desk-bound. Without Harrault for reference or procedural advice, the station just didn't run smoothly.

Louis was at the side of his table. 'Coming by tonight?'

'I'm not sure. Depends how heavy my shift is. I might be too tired.'

'Too tired at your age.' Louis waved one arm dismissively. He nodded towards the boulangerie. 'Why don't you ask Odette? Valérie will probably be coming.'

'Maybe.' Odette was a fresh-faced nineteen-year-old serving in the baker's whom Dominic had been dating the past four months. Nothing too serious. Dominic tried to restrict dates to no more than two a week, particularly with his other commitments at home. With him not finishing until midnight it would be too late in any case for a full date, though the sight of Louis fighting to win Valérie's affections was well worth a visit. 'I'll probably come by on my own for a quick brandy, keep you company at the bar.'

On Valérie's last visit, Louis had put on Sam Cooke's 'Another Saturday Night', which Dominic had brought him only a few weeks before. Coming out from behind the bar like a matador, Louis dramatically threw his shirt to one side. Now down to his vest, Louis felt that it showed off his physique, and with his dark and brooding Corsican features he saw himself as another Victor Mature. Dominic teased him that he looked more like Bluto. The wrong side of forty, too much of his own short-order cooking had long ago rounded out most of his muscle definition. Louis' bull-like figure trying gracefully to imitate something between the jive and the tango with Valérie was a sight to behold.

'Should be a good crowd later tonight,' Louis commented.

Dominic nodded. Calling by when his shift finished at midnight was probably good timing. After 11 p.m. the bikers normally thinned out and more young couples came in on their way back from the cinema. *Cleopatra* was showing for a second week. Louis was probably right, the turn-out should be good. 'I'll only stay an hour, though, then I should get home.'

Louis grimaced understandingly. Dominic not wanting to spend too much time away from his sick mother was by now almost common knowledge. Dominic's elder sister lived in Paris with her husband and only visited periodically, so Dominic had shouldered most of the responsibility. Diagnosed just over a year ago, less than two years after they'd buried his father, his mother's cancer had been the main reason for his transfer from Marseille. Why he restricted his dates and tried not to stay out too late. Dominic knew that there wasn't much time left to spend with his mother.

Dominic was distracted. Servan, one of the young station sergeants, was running across the square towards the café. Louis stared as well. The last time he'd seen a gendarme running was when the newly installed alarm had gone off by mistake at the jeweller's around the corner. Something was wrong.

Servan was breathless as he approached Dominic's table. 'A young boy has been attacked out towards Taragnon. Poullain's just radioed in. He's on his way there now. He wants you to assist, and take myself, Levacher and another sergeant. We're to meet him there.'

'Where's Harrault?'

'He was with Poullain at Tourtin's farm when it happened. One of Tourtin's outbuildings was broken into last night. When Poullain got the call, he left Harrault taking the statement.'

'How old is the boy?'

'Anything from nine to twelve years old. We still don't have any firm identification.'

'Is the attack bad? How badly is he hurt?' The surprise came through in Dominic's voice. This was Bauriac. They hardly ever faced anything more serious than a stolen tractor.

Servan was hesitant and looked away slightly. He either didn't know or didn't want to talk too openly in front of Louis. 'I think you should get the details from Poullain.'

The 2CV rattled along the rough track alongside the wheat field. The basic black gendarme squad car, it felt as if it was made from old tin cans and powered by a lawnmower engine and rubber bands. Dominic hated them with a vengeance. The track was on a slight incline, and with three passengers the engine whined in protest.

Servan pointed the way. 'I'm sure this is the right track, the river's to our right. About one hundred and fifty metres up, Poullain said.'

Rounding a curve, they could see the lane cordoned off with rope fifty metres ahead. Poullain's black Citroën DS 19 was parked one side with an ambulance behind.

Poullain was down to his shirt sleeves and his flat gendarme cap was off too. Beads of sweat massed on his receding hairline and he was in the midst of a heated argument with one of the ambulance medics as they parked the car. Poullain was not very tall, but he was quite stocky and in any confrontation fought to make a powerful presence with effusive and rapid arm movements. As they approached, he was almost hitting the medic repeatedly with the back of one hand to emphasize his case.

Poullain looked past Dominic and snapped at Servan. 'Did you bring the camera?'

Servan nodded hastily. 'As you asked.' And ran back the few paces to the car to get it.

Poullain was impatient and flustered. When Servan came back with the camera, an old Leica 35mm with a dented and chipped black frame, Poullain barked, 'Are you any good at taking pictures?' Servan shrugged as if to say 'okay'. 'Then take them yourself so that we can get rid of this prick.' Poullain looked disapprovingly at the medic, then down at the figure of the young boy on a stretcher at the medic's feet. The medic was holding an oxygen mask to the boy's face.

Poullain turned his back and let out a deep sigh as Servan moved around for best position and angle. Dominic was close behind and studied the boy's face as the shutter clicked away. The medics had obviously cleaned much of the blood from the face. But facial bruising and swelling was so intense that the bone structure looked distorted, and blood was still caked thick in his hair. A bandage was wrapped around part of the boy's skull and under his chin. A few paces to the side, Dominic could see a flattened area of wheat sheaves with dried blood patches. A large oval patch with two smaller patches and some spots and splashes radiating out. Dark brown against the bleached-white sheaves. Dominic shuddered.

After five pictures, Poullain waved the medics away with a few curt words about making contact later, and directed Servan's attention to the blood patches, pointing out some suggested positions for two or three close-ups that he would need. The medics loaded the boy aboard the ambulance and backed down the lane. Poullain looked up at Dominic.

'Sorry about that. First the medics say that they can't move the boy, he could choke on his own blood, and they spend time cleaning him up and putting a pipe down his throat. I say, fine, I need some pictures in any case. But as soon as they're finished, they want to move him. By this time I can see you approaching – but they don't want to wait. I end up arguing with them to gain one minute.' Poullain dabbed at his forehead with the back of one sleeve. 'Look, Fornier, I want you to assist in this. There's two reasons. First, there'll be an awful lot of paperwork and notes. Second, we're going to be talking with a lot of outside units, particularly from Marseille. A forensics team are on their way from Marseille now.'

'What about Harrault?' Dominic asked. Harrault's seniority would normally have guaranteed his role in assisting, particularly on a major case.

'Harrault will do what Harrault does best. He'll take our notes and reports and make sure the filing with the Aix *Cour d'Assises* runs smoothly. This will no doubt end up there, particularly if it becomes a murder case.

The medics said that it's going to be a close call whether the boy lives. Harrault's going to spend half his time running reports between us and the examining magistrate and the Public Prosecutor's office in Aix. I want you to assist and take notes, ensure the reports reach Harrault in good shape, and liaise and smooth out any problems with the boys from Marseille. I don't want us to lose control on this one.'

Dominic wondered what was more important, his good shorthand for taking notes or his three years with the Marseille force. Obviously Poullain was worried about getting upstaged by Marseille. The boy wasn't even at the hospital, might not last through the night, and already Poullain was more worried about the politics of the investigation. Afraid of losing a major local case that could boost his career.

'Who's coming from Marseille?' Dominic asked.

'I don't know. I radioed in and was advised that a forensics team would be dispatched. Wasn't given any names.'

Servan was at their side with the camera held limply, waiting for more directions. Warrant Officer Levacher was looking thoughtfully towards the river.

'Have you brought the sticks?' Poullain asked.

'Yes.' It was Levacher who answered. He turned back to the 2 CV to get them. They'd stopped for them at a hardware store on the way, but it was obvious they were still wondering what they were for.

Poullain pointed towards the wheat field. 'Levacher and Servan, start from three metres out from the blood patches and head out across the wheat field keeping two metres apart. Then at the end turn back and cover the next four-metre stretch. Use the sticks to part the sheaves. We're looking for items of clothing, even small fragments of cloth or buttons and sweet wrappers. Any possible clues. And the weapon used in the attack – a heavy stick or iron bar, or perhaps a rock with tell-tale blood stains.' Poullain pointed towards the river. 'Then take the bushes along the river bank. Also, look in the shallows. As I say, *don't* disturb the three metres around the blood stains. Leave that for forensics.'

Poullain surveyed the wheat field as Servan and Levacher headed out with their sticks. He shook his head slowly after a moment. 'Who on earth would do such a thing?' A rhetorical tone, so Dominic merely joined him for a second silently watching their progress tapping across the field like blind men.

'Who discovered the boy?' Dominic asked.

'The man from the farm behind, Marius Caurin. This track provides the only access to his farm. These fields are owned by his friend who is on an engineering contract in Orléans – that's why some of them are untended. Marius just plants the few extra fields he can cope with.'

A light breeze played across the field. As it shifted direction, they heard the sound of a car approaching. It was a large black Citroën C25 pulling in behind Poullain's car with three men inside. Probably the team from Marseille. Poullain greeted them, then introduced Dominic.

They walked towards the blood-stained area. Dominic stayed in the background as Poullain pointed and brought them up to date on events. He explained that the boy might be facing an operation in hospital at Aix-en-Provence, so would be studied by the medical examiner there. They could confer with him later. The main thing now was gaining information from what was left: blood group and some indication of timing for the attack. Were all the stains the same group as the boy, or were any different?

Dominic smiled to himself. In his fifteen years of policing in Bauriac, Poullain had only seen one murder, an almost predictable domestic crime of passion, and two manslaughters: one domestic, one bar fight. Yet he was handling this with all the casual aplomb of a Marseille veteran used to fishing bodies out of the harbour every day, no doubt driven by his fear of being upstaged from outside.

None of them was really prepared for this. He'd seen the shock on Servan's face when he'd leant over the boy to take the first photos. Servan had gone deathly white and looked sick. The other rookies had only managed to maintain some composure by keeping in the background. None of them had come close to the boy and studied his face the way he had. Seen the massive bruising and fractures, seen where his small face had been mashed half to a pulp, part of his skull only held in place by a bandage. This was Bauriac, and if they stayed their distance, perhaps they could still cling to the illusion that things like this just didn't happen in their area.

Even he'd found the sight of the young boy disturbing, despite having been directly involved in five murder cases in Marseille. Perhaps it was because the victim was so young; none of his previous cases had involved children. *Who on earth would do such a thing?* The one moment, staring silently across the wheat field, when Poullain had shown his true emotions. The rest of the time he'd been too busy sparring to try and prove he was in control.

One of the forensics team was walking to his car with a set of small clear polythene bags. Another was crouching, now examining further up the rough track. He looked over at Poullain.

'It's been too dry, and the track is too uneven and dusty. I doubt we'll get any decent imprints.'

Poullain nodded, and asked the team leader Dubrulle about progress. Dubrulle explained that they would probably be at least another thirty or forty minutes, then they would head over to Aix and see the medical examiner. 'It could be he'll have some information by tomorrow morning. Our first lab test results won't be ready till tomorrow afternoon.'

Servan and Levacher were halfway back on their third sweep and Levacher had his jacket unbuttoned with the heat. Poullain's radio crackled with a sudden harsh, distorted voice; he went over to it.

Dominic couldn't hear what was said. He saw Poullain look down thoughtfully after a moment. The conversation appeared quite staccato, apart from a stretch towards the end of the call when Poullain waved his arms in a struggle for emphasis and then checked his watch as he finished.

Poullain was pensive as he approached. 'A call's come in to the station from a woman saying her son's missing. It's the only call of that type they've received today. The boy said that he was going to a friend's house on his bike and should have been there for one-thirty. He never showed up. But it's only four-fifty now, it could be too early to jump to conclusions. You know what kids are like. The boy could have gone to another friend's house or disappeared for sweets or to play somewhere else.'

'How old is her boy?'

'Ten. The age is right.'

On a bad month, the station might get three missing-person alerts, sometimes two months would go by with none. Most were false alarms, but the timing and age of this one narrowed the odds. Dominic could sense Poullain delaying the inevitable. He recalled the incident of a young boy who'd died falling down a disused well the previous autumn. Facing the relatives with the news had unsettled Poullain for days. This time he would probably send someone else.

Dominic looked out thoughtfully across the field. 'What's her name?'

'Monique Rosselot.'

4

Monique Rosselot looked out on to the farm courtyard. From the kitchen, a mass of bougainvillaea covered the wall on one side. Christian had been only six when he'd helped his father, Jean-Luc, plant it; now it was a profusion of pink flowers.

Christian's bike rested on the corner of the wall just past the bougainvillaea. Jean-Luc had come back with it just twenty minutes before, having followed the path Christian normally took to Stéphane's house. At first she'd felt relieved: the bike's brake was jammed. At least that might explain some of the delay, walking would have taken him far longer. But still he should have been there by the latest at 2.30 p.m. It was now 5.45 p.m. Where had he gone? Perhaps he'd stopped off in Taragnon for a drink or sweets, the walk would have tired him and made him hot and thirsty. Though still that would only account for another forty minutes or so. He must have met another friend in Taragnon, gone off to play somewhere else and lost track of time. It was all she could think of.

When Jean-Luc had come back with Christian's bike, their daughter Clarisse had asked, 'Is Christian lost somewhere?' Only four, she'd seen her parents' consternation and picked up on part of their conversation.

'No, it's all right. He's just late seeing his friend because his bike broke down.' Christian was so protective and caring of Clarisse; he was like a second father to her, sharing his own sage past experience of the pitfalls and problems of being five. But she was too young to be worrying along with them.

Monique bit her lip. It was over an hour since she'd called the police. The nearest phone was over a kilometre away, and in the intense heat the walk had been exhausting. On her return she'd felt sick and gone into the bathroom, leaning over the sink. Despite her stomach still churning, in the end nothing came. She'd caught her reflection in the mirror as she looked up; she'd aged five years in the last hour. She felt physically and emotionally drained. *Where was he?* Why hadn't anyone called by? The waiting was killing her nerves. Jean-Luc had headed off on another search and probably wouldn't be back for forty minutes or an hour. She resolved finally that, despite the long walk, if she hadn't heard anything from the police within half an hour, she was going to put through another call.

In the end she was saved the trouble. Just ten minutes before she planned to leave, the black 2CV pulled into their courtyard and two gendarmes got out.

It was almost 1 a.m. Louis' bar had been crowded, but the numbers were beginning to thin out. Louis had been dancing earlier with Valérie, but now she was talking with a friend in the corner while he put away some glasses and had a Pernod with Dominic at the bar. Dominic was out of uniform, in slacks and a short-sleeved polo shirt, nursing a brandy.

'Who saw her?' Louis asked.

'Harrault and Servan. Poullain was going to send me at first, but there were too many notes to take from the afternoon, recording times and early findings from forensics and our own team. In the end he sent Servan to pick up Harrault. He's the most senior. Poullain thought if anything he'd bring the right tone.'

'Where's Monique Rosselot now?'

'Probably still at the hospital. Harrault ran her and the father there and stayed with them the first hour, introduced them to the main doctors, got as much information as possible and tried to console them. The doctors were operating at midnight, the boy's probably still in there now. The father headed back with the daughter, but Monique said she would probably stay the night.'

'What are the boy's chances?'

'Not good. There's a lot of internal cranial bleeding and damage. If he lasts through the operation and the next twenty-four hours, the doctors say his chances will increase. But brain damage is heavy and even if he survives, he could be severely disabled.'

Louis reached for the bottle and topped up his Pernod, swirling it briefly in its narrow glass before tipping it half back. 'God, this must be rough on her. Have you seen her before? She's quite a woman.'

'No, I don't think I know her. Harrault said that she was quite pretty.'

'Quite pretty. Huh! Let me tell you, Monique Rosselot is one of those rare beauties that you only see once in a while. In Bauriac, those once in a whiles are even rarer. Even on the coast she'd stand out – I'm amazed you don't know her. When are you seeing her?'

'Sometime tomorrow. We haven't asked her any questions yet, it

34

seemed inappropriate while she's still grappling with whether or not her son will live. I'll see her with Poullain tomorrow, we'll arrange it around the timing of her hospital visits. If she's at the hospital all day, then we'll go there.'

Louis raised his glass, taking another quick slug. '*Santé*. Let me know what you think when you've seen her. I warn you now, you'll be spoilt for other women.'

Dominic smiled. Louis the lecher. Louis the connoisseur of women. Three tables could be calling for service and Louis would stop to admire at leisure a beautiful woman passing. The fact that Monique Rosselot was married was immaterial, she was still there for the admiring. Harmless voyeurism. But Dominic wondered if Louis' knowledge of Monique Rosselot went deeper than that. 'Do you know her well?'

'Not personally. She's been in a few times and we've spoken briefly once or twice, but that's all. She used to come in more when her boy was younger. But my barman, Joël, is quite friendly with the father Jean-Luc, and Valérie knows one of their neighbours. And you know me, if there's a beautiful woman involved I'll spend half the day talking, I'm not choosy who I speak to. Probably why I spend so much time talking to you.' Louis paused for effect and chuckled. 'No, seriously, you know what Bauriac's like, people talk a lot, and they came here, what, seven or eight years ago – the boy was just a toddler. People are particularly curious about newcomers. Questions were thick and fast the first year they arrived.'

'Did many of them get answered?'

'A few. It seems she had Christian when she was under age, no more than fourteen or fifteen when he was conceived. Nobody knows exactly. Jean-Luc's family gave him a hard time, not only about being careless with an under-age girl, but her background. Her mother's half Moroccan, half Corsican, and her father's French – but the Moroccan and Corsican blood is predominant in her features. His family's prejudice starts to show through. Cheap young Moroccan whore seduced their poor young boy, which is laughable seeing as he's ten years older than her. Don't they have prostitutes at the age of twelve on the streets there? You know the type of comment. In the end they had a bellyful of it and moved. She was more resilient than him, I hear; she could have stayed and put up with it, but he insisted on moving. Cut himself off entirely from his family, had little or no contact with them. When the little girl was born, they just sent a photo, no invitations to the christening, nothing.'

'Where did they come from?'

'Beaune, not far from Dijon. But it was out of the frying pan and into the fire. What with the fact that they were newcomers and with her dusky looks, she attracted more than her fair share of attention. You couldn't really call it prejudice, but it was curiosity so blatant it was almost rude. You know, the way you would expect a lost tribe to react upon seeing their first explorer. I was probably one of the darkest-skinned people in Bauriac until she arrived, and I attracted a fair bit of attention in my time, let me tell you. It took a few years for Monique to be accepted here, for people to look beyond her colour and realize what a nice person she is. And by the time your mother and you arrived, they'd practically been numbed into acceptance.'

So this is what all this was about, thought Dominic. Why Louis had been so inquisitive about Monique Rosselot. It was all Bauriac-newcomers-together time. Battling against the odds of small-town minds and prejudices. It was difficult enough being a newcomer without standing out as one and, true enough, when his parents had arrived four years ago, his mother had encountered a few raised eyebrows. Her lineage was part French Indonesian, part French, and Dominic's father had been pure French Alsace. By the time it reached Dominic, the Indonesian blood had left only a slight almond slant at the corner of his eyes, looking almost out of place with his proud Gallic nose. Girls either found it endearing and mysterious, or they didn't like him at all. It might have caused some problems at the station too, but Dominic could never be sure; the fact that he was newly transferred and enjoyed warrant officer status so young was reason enough for resentment.

Louis had travelled up from Marseille thirteen years ago to be the chef at the Café du Verdon, and when the owner had died four years later and the relatives were keen to sell on, he'd mortgaged his neck between the banks and private bills of exchange to take over. Only in the last few years, having cleared the bills of exchange, had Louis enjoyed the fruits of his labour. Dominic could imagine that the locals had not been too keen on a Corsican owning such a prominent local establishment, especially all those years ago. Marseille was teeming with migrant workers and cosmopolitan mixes, and the tide of invasion by outsiders and foreigners was accepted on the coast fifty kilometres away, but not in Bauriac.

Louis was shaking his head. 'It's hardly believable, something like this. Her and Jean-Luc have been through such a tough time already. They've had to work so hard to make a go of that farm; they were sold a real pig in the poke. Previous owner saw them coming a long way off, as locals often do with people like us from outside. Bastard. Drainage was bad, top soil and yield was poor, it's been a real struggle for them. And she dotes on that boy. I don't know how she'll get over this.'

Dominic nodded thoughtfully. He was still trying to get a picture of Monique Rosselot. She sounded quite exotic, a rare beauty according to Louis; surely he'd have seen her in the past year. He realized then how closeted and predictable his life had become the past seven months, his time spent between the gendarmerie, home with his sick mother, and the occasional drink at Louis'. Even on his dates with Odette, they always went to the same places: the cinema, the Café du Verdon or, on the rare occasions they felt more adventurous, on his bike to a favourite club in Saint-Maximin.

Valérie was up at the bar, ordering drinks for herself and her friend. A Marie Brizard and soda and a glass of red wine. 'You having another dance soon, Louis?'

'Maybe later. I'm not as young as I used to be.' He smiled as he watched her walk back to the table with the drinks. 'How's Odette these days?'

'Okay. A bit too demanding. Wants to go out every night. I just don't have the time, even if I did have the energy and the inclination.'

'What first attracted you to her?' Louis leant forward slightly. He lowered his voice conspiratorially. 'Come on, you must remember that. That first flush of romance.'

Dominic thought for a moment. 'I think it was when we first went on a picnic. The way she wrapped her mouth around a bread-stick sandwich. I knew then she was the girl for me.'

Louis smiled broadly. 'Is that the only qualification your girls need?'

'No. I quite like it if they're good at yoga and can put their ankles behind their ears.'

Louis guffawed so loudly that Valérie and her friend looked over briefly. Still chuckling, Louis poured another Pernod. 'You're a card, Dominic. An absolute fucking card. Excuse me.' He swept out from behind the bar and, half kneeling with a bar towel draped across one arm, asked Valérie to dance. Ray Charles's 'Take These Chains From My Heart' was playing on the jukebox.

Dominic took a quick slug of brandy and smiled to himself. Normally, he was quite considerate and romantic with women. But that wasn't what Louis wanted to hear. Louis would probably have been happier to hear he'd split up with Odette, back to how he was the first five months in Bauriac: a different date every other week, screwing his way endlessly through the local girls in search of nirvana. That at least was the idyllic, swashbuckling image in Louis' mind. In reality, half of the dates had been a disaster; Dominic didn't know it was possible to go out with so many girls and still feel so lonely. The only consolation had been, editing the dates down to just the highlights, that he'd kept up his stock of bar-stool stories for Louis.

Dominic watched Louis and Valérie dancing, smiling as one of Louis' rogue hands drifted down towards her bottom in the clinches. After Ray Charles came the Crystals' 'Da Doo Ron Ron'. Louis' attempt at the jive looked more like a flamenco dancer in the grips of epilepsy, and Dominic fought to keep a straight face. Louis thought of himself as a good dancer and Dominic didn't want to spoil a good friendship by shattering that illusion. After a moment his thoughts took over and the dancing and music faded into the background.

Tomorrow would be a big day. They would have the first forensics report, plus the findings of the medical examiner. They should know the timing of the attack, the exact weapon used, any other blood groups found and any irregularities. They would hopefully get the first responses to appeals for witnesses in the area, and he would meet Monique Rosselot for the first main interview to learn the boy's last movements before the attack.

They should also know if her son was going to live.

Dominic wasn't sure if it was the events of the day or the two brandies at Louis', but it took him a long while to get to sleep. He'd checked on his mother on coming in; she was already fast asleep. Often, if she was awake, he would bring her a hot chocolate and they would talk for ten minutes. Her weight loss in the past four months had been more dramatic, but her mind was still lucid, so Dominic grabbed whatever conversations he could. He knew that any day now her mind could slip.

If the day hadn't been too eventful, they would reminisce: the days from his childhood in Louviers near Paris were the most memorable. Some of the memories jumbled with the events of the day as he tried to get some sleep. Images of the young boy, the dark blood against the bleached-white wheat, preparing himself for the interview with Monique

Rosselot, flashes from his own childhood and thinking of his own mother as she was then, how she could have possibly coped with anything so horrific. It was the closest he could come to trying to understand how Monique Rosselot felt.

His bedroom's french windows led on to a small first-floor patio overlooking the garden. They were left partly open because of the summer heat, and the sound of the wind through the trees outside wafted gently in. After a while, he finally drifted off to sleep.

The dream came three hours later. He was a boy again in Louviers, and the wheat fields stretched out endlessly before him. The sheaves seemed so tall, he could hide among them and nobody would find him. He walked ten paces into the field and crouched down, holding his breath as he hid; the sheaves were at least an arm's length above his head.

Then suddenly he was looking down at the field. He could see the gendarmes tapping across the field with their sticks to find him. He felt that he'd done something wrong, but didn't know what, and he wasn't sure whether to leap up and let them find him. But in the end he stayed crouched and hidden. He could hear them tapping closer, closer, and his heart pounded with the sound of their nearby movement, though looking down from above, he could see that they'd already passed him.

A gentle breeze across the field suddenly became more violent, bending the sheaves almost at a right angle. Their threshing with the sticks was drowned out by the sound. He stood up after a moment and was clearly exposed. But the gendarmes were looking away, holding on to their caps and shielding their faces from the harsh wind stinging their eyes. He called to them, but his voice was lost among the wind and the wild rustling of the sheaves . . .

Dominic woke up with a start. He was sweating profusely. Outside, the wind had risen and the branches of the trees close by his window whipped back and forth. He got up and walked to the small balcony, looking down on to the garden. There was a tall jacaranda tree close by, and its branches and leaves moved like surf rising and falling with the wind. It could be the first stages of a mistral, Dominic thought, or hopefully a small summer storm that would blow over by the morning.

Dominic's heart was pounding. He wasn't sure if it was the dream or something else that he suddenly remembered would happen the next day. A reporter from *Le Provençal*, the area's main newspaper, had called

39

the station that evening. Two hours later Poullain had released a statement that would no doubt appear in the paper the next morning.

The attacker would know then that the boy he had left for dead was still alive. He would feel threatened; the boy could possibly later talk and identify him.

5

When the phone call came about the accident, at first Stuart thought it was his alarm call, but it was Helena. Stuart's clock showed 6.08 a.m.

She was babbling and incoherent, and 'Is terrible . . . so sorry,' was repeated among the jumble, along with a number he should ring for the Oceanside police who had called her just ten minutes before. Emerging from his drowsiness, Stuart tried to clarify some points, but Helena was not very forthcoming, as if she either didn't know much or didn't want to be the messenger of bad tidings. The tears and the trembling in her voice betrayed the worst.

When Stuart got through to the Oceanside police, he was asked to call back in ten minutes. 'Lieutenant Carlson has all the details for that. He should be finished with his interview then.'

After confirming his relationship as Jeremy's elder brother and Eyran's uncle and godparent, Stuart felt himself go numb as Carlson went through the catalogue of horror, as if it was a routine shopping list: 'We have one female, Caucasian, pronounced D O A at Oceanside County General. The other two occupants of the jeep, a Caucasian male and a young boy, are both still in emergency. The boy was critical at one point, but he's more stable now. We're waiting on more updates. Can I ask, sir, do you know of any other relatives the victims might have here in California whom we can contact?'

'No, I can't think of anyone. We're all here . . . here in England. We've got an uncle in Toronto, but we haven't seen him in years.' Stuart felt lame and helpless due to the distance, an image of Jeremy and Eyran cut off and alone. He knew he should be there with them.

'Can I rely on you then to make contact with your sister-in-law's relatives in England?'

'Yes, yes . . . of course.' Stuart was still numb, trying desperately to work out how he could get out to California quickly. He'd never actually met Allison's parents, only a sister over six years ago at one of Jeremy's parties. At his side Amanda was stirring, squinting over at him quizzically.

'From identification found in the car, we have your brother's age, thirty-eight, but not that of your sister-in-law or the boy.'

'Allison was thirty-five, I think. Eyran was just ten years old last April.'

'What number can we reach you on to inform you of any developments?'

Stuart gave Carlson his home number then, as an afterthought, said, 'I'll give you my work number as well, just in case you don't hear anything from the hospital before tonight.'

But as he said the words, it suddenly hit Stuart that he couldn't possibly just sit there through those hours waiting for the phone to ring, knowing that Eyran and Jeremy were lying in hospital beds ten thousand miles away. He made the decision. 'I'm coming out there. I've been thinking about it as we've spoken. I've got to be there with them.'

'That's your prerogative, sir, but with all due respect, we might know something within the next hour or so from the hospital. They're both in Emergency right now.

'That's okay, I'll book the ticket and phone you before I leave for the airport, then again just before the flight leaves. But I've got to start making my way out there.' Amanda was sitting up now, following every word of the conversation.

'I fully understand, sir. I'll wait to hear from you.'

It took Stuart only half an hour to make all his travel arrangements, part of which was explaining the situation to an incredulous Amanda and leaving her a few vital numbers to contact. All San Diego flights routed through LA, but with the average four hours' delay between connecting flights, the quickest way would be to take a bus or a train straight from LAX down to Oceanside, sixty-five miles south of LA.

On the flight out, Stuart tried to read a magazine or a book, anything to distract him. But he just couldn't concentrate, he found himself scanning the words blindly, his thoughts still with Eyran and Jeremy, trying to read something into Carlson's bland status report on the call he'd put through just before the flight announcement. The news from the hospital was that Eyran was out of Emergency and had been transferred to intensive care, and that Jeremy was still in Emergency.

Stuart put down the magazine and closed his eyes briefly, knowing that sleep was hopeless, but trying to force some calm into his nerve-wracked body. He let the images wash over him slowly: the night they celebrated Jeremy passing his bar exams, Jeremy helping him to unload some antique timbers for the cottage, Eyran asking for a ride in the sports car he'd bought to celebrate the first major account of his new agency, the surprise on Jeremy's face when he turned up in the hospital with a half-bottle of scotch in his coat pocket the night Eyran was born. 'What, no cigars?'

Eyran. So much of their lives had revolved around Eyran. He remembered now that it had been almost eight months since he'd seen Jeremy when Eyran was born; yet another futile argument that had forged a divide. As the first-born of the two families, Eyran had created a bond that just wasn't there before. A simple focus of love and affection which crossed over any boundaries and past differences between himself and Jeremy. The petty arguments continued, but suddenly Eyran was an overriding force pushing them into the background.

Probably even Jeremy sensed he had become more than just an uncle, he'd stepped into the role of a second father to Eyran. The fact that he'd been unable to have children with Amanda, despite numerous tests and clinics, had intensified that bond. Eyran became like the son he could never have.

After another year of trying vainly with Amanda to have a child, they'd applied for adoption, taking Tessa as a two-year-old eight months later. Amanda had suggested a boy, admitting in the end that she thought Stuart had wanted a boy because of Eyran. He said that he wanted a girl because he didn't want their child seen as some sort of replacement for Eyran. They'd both told only half the truth. Stuart didn't want a child that might eclipse Eyran, perhaps dilute or distract his affection for the boy. A girl could be seen as a separate entity. Amanda had wanted *any* child that would return Stuart's focus to his own family, breaking what she felt had become an unnaturally close tie between himself and Eyran. He remembered Amanda's anger brimming over one day, as not for the first time he brought home two toys, suggesting that they drive over later to give Eyran his. 'Is this your idea of the perfect family, Stuart? A girl in our family and a boy in your brother's?'

Throughout, Jeremy had never shut Eyran out of their lives. He could have become jealous and guarded about the relationship, fearing that Stuart might steal some of the limelight of Eyran's love and affection. Yet he seemed to welcome it, as if he understood that somehow it fulfilled something he himself could not provide: a kinship of free spirit and shared likes and dislikes. Jeremy appeared happy in his role as guardian angel of *both* of them: warning Stuart about bad business deals and investments in the same way that he would warn Eyran about climbing too high or not going near the electrical sockets. Jeremy didn't feel threatened because he saw them just as two boys playing together, one small, one big.

With the excuse that he lacked time to organize everything, Stuart left Amanda to phone his partner at work and his father in Wales; but the truth was, he just couldn't face phoning their father and telling him this news. Jeremy had always been his favourite. Only their mother, when she was alive, had any time for Stuart; she'd died of a brain haemorrhage two years before Eyran was born, and their father, at the age of sixty-two, had then decided to take early retirement and move back from London to his native Wales. Each month either he or Jeremy had dutifully gone up to Wales to visit. But when Jeremy went to California, Stuart sensed that his own family visits were little compensation.

Stuart tried to sleep, but found it impossible until much later, almost three hours after he'd washed down lunch with half a bottle of wine. The sleep was fitful, images of Eyran, Jeremy and their father all jumbled together. Eyran was playing, but the image quickly changed to himself as a child. He was with Jeremy in the derelict warehouse where they played hide and seek, but couldn't find him – and in the end decided that Jeremy must have sneaked out and headed home. But when Stuart got home, their father David asked where Jeremy was. He didn't want to say he didn't know in case his father worried that Jeremy was lost. So he said that he would go and get him, and ran back to the warehouse.

He went looking for Jeremy again along the rows of dusty shelves and empty crates, telling him that their father wanted to see them; but he knew that Jeremy was purposely staying hidden, thinking it was just a trick. He called out Jeremy's name repeatedly, starting to plead, but only the empty echoes of his voice returned. He started to cry, but the tears weren't for Jeremy but for himself, for what he felt certain was some dreadful trick being played on him. *How could Jeremy do this, stay lost and let him go home alone to face their father?*

Stuart awoke bathed in sweat. The dream had disturbed him, combining so much of the shock and anguish of the day's events. It washed over him without warning, gentle sobbing shaking his body as he turned away towards the plane window to hide his tears. Guilt compounded his sorrow; so many of his thoughts about Jeremy the past few years had been ungenerous. Anger at him for taking Eyran so far away. After a few moments he snapped out of it, telling himself it was only a dream.

Though four hours later, all of Stuart's worst fears were realized as he phoned Carlson from LAX to hear that his brother had died just over an hour beforehand. And, knowing that he couldn't possibly ask Amanda to do this duty, he had to call their father in Wales and, above the noise and activity of the crowded terminal, tell him that his favourite son was dead.

6

Dominic drove the DS19 so that Poullain could absorb the teleprinter message which had just arrived headed 'Palais de Justice, Aix', from the nominated prosecutor, Pierre Bouteille – declaring that Poullain's jurisdiction had been granted prime investigative control over the case, but he should liaise with Marseille on items such as forensics. Bouteille had already notified an examining magistrate, Frédéric Naugier, and a *commission rogatoire générale* had been signed off to empower Poullain for the initial investigative stages. A meeting had been arranged for the following Thursday at 11.30 a.m., in two days' time, to establish the full procedural process. The brief teleprinter message gave no options on time: Poullain was being summoned.

Dominic parked at the far end of the courtyard. The air-cushioned suspension settled back as they got out of the car. The Rosselots' farmhouse formed an L-shape around the courtyard, with the garage and some farm store rooms at an angle to the main house. Dominic could see a child's bike resting against the wall of the garage. Pink bougainvillaea grew profusely on the same wall, and, positioned equidistant between there and the front door was a small wrought-iron table and four chairs. Two palm trees at the end of the courtyard separated the house from the broad expanse of the fields beyond, and a mixture of elm and pine bordered the main road and the short approach to the house. The sound of cicadas was heavy in the air. It was 10.30 a.m. and the temperature was already over 80°F.

Variegated ivy grew up and around the front door frame. As they rang the bell, they could hear a faint clanking sound coming from the garage, competing with the rhythm of the cicadas. They waited only a moment before Monique Rosselot opened the door.

At first she was in half-shadow as she greeted them and asked them in. Dominic only got a quick impression of dark wavy ringlets, large eyes and a simple beige floral-pattern dress – but it was enough for him to catch his breath slightly. Her eyes looked particularly large and striking in the half-light of the porch. They followed her into the kitchen. There was hot coffee on the stove which she offered to them.

'It's freshly made just minutes ago.'

Poullain thanked her and said that he would have black coffee, and Dominic followed suit and said yes, but with milk. The kitchen was large, with a small fireplace in the far corner. A large rough wooden table with chairs was close to the fireplace, making up a breakfast area. Monique waved one hand towards the table. 'Please.' Poullain and Dominic took seats on its far side. Dominic observed her closer as she prepared the coffees.

Louis had been right about Monique Rosselot. A rare beauty. Despite the fact that he should have been prepared by Louis' description, he'd still found himself taken aback, his mouth suddenly dry. Her wavy dark hair hung halfway down her back, her eyes were an intriguing blend of green and hazel, and her mouth was full and generous. It was an open, expressive face with an almost childlike innocence tempering its sensuality, making her look younger than the twenty-six years mentioned by Louis. Dominic would have guessed her age at no more than nineteen or twenty, despite the faint dark circles no doubt brought on by the past night of worry. He'd heard that she'd stayed at the hospital till past 4 a.m. Her skin tone was smooth mocha, the outline of her full breasts pushing against the cotton print dress with her movements. She glanced over at him and Poullain as she poured the coffees, and Dominic looked hastily away. He felt a momentary flush of embarrassment, as if he'd been an unwelcome voyeur.

Monique brought their cups over and set them down, then looked towards the garage and the continuing clanking sound. 'I'd better ask Jean-Luc in now. He probably doesn't realize you're here.' She went out and crossed the courtyard.

It struck Dominic that he'd only half believed Louis, whose ratings of women's beauty had become increasingly suspect through the years. That was why he'd been caught by surprise. But he felt immediately uncomfortable with those thoughts. He was here to take notes about her son who was barely clinging to life; the last thing she wanted was some gendarme ogling her.

Jean-Luc came into the room ahead of Monique and she made the introductions. By the way she faltered, it was obvious she hadn't remembered their names, and Poullain filled the gaps. Jean-Luc took a chair at the far end of the table while Monique poured a coffee for him. His light brown curly hair was deeply receding on both sides, and he was perspiring from his work outside. Some freckles showed on his forehead and arms from the summer sun, his shoulders and forearms were broad from the years of farm work, and there were calluses on his rough hands. But there the farm labourer ended: his eyes were soft and inquisitive and he had a vaguely intellectual air, as if he was an accountant or lecturer who farmed just at the weekends. According to Louis he was in his mid thirties, but the receding hairline made him look closer to forty, thought Dominic. The contrast in age between him and Monique looked more marked than it was; they could be father and daughter.

Poullain looked up expectantly at Monique and waited for her to set down her cup and join them. Dominic flipped over to a fresh page in his notebook as Poullain started speaking.

'First of all, my condolences. On my own part and on behalf of the gendarmerie. I understand, Madame Rosselot, that you stayed with your son until the early hours of the morning.' Poullain looked pointedly towards Monique. 'To bring you up to date, I managed to check with the hospital just before leaving, and your boy has rallied well after the operation of last night. Though the doctors won't know the full extent of just how successful the operation has been until this afternoon. We can only pray for some improvement.'

Monique nodded appreciatively. She had gone with Jean-Luc to the nearby phone kiosk only half an hour before their arrival to call the hospital, but it was hardly worth mentioning. Poullain realized she was some distance from a phone and therefore checking was difficult. No point in dampening the good intent of his gesture.

Poullain placed one hand firmly on the table top, as if he might reach out to Monique's hand for comfort, but stopped halfway short. 'Now, as painful as this might be for both of you, we need to go through the times you last saw your son before the attack. When you first realized there might be a problem, and the timing of you finding the bike.' Poullain looked at Jean-Luc. 'We will also need you to show us afterwards exactly where you found the bike. But for now we are trying to establish the timing of events.'

Monique and Jean-Luc glanced at each other briefly, as if deciding who should be main spokesperson. Jean-Luc shrugged and held out one hand. 'You first. I was in the fields for much of the time.'

Monique drew a breath and glanced for a moment out of the window towards the courtyard and Christian's bike. 'I let Christian out to play at about quarter past eleven. He took his bike because he was visiting his friend Stéphane who lives five kilometres away on the other side of Taragnon.'

'What route does he normally take to Stéphane's house?' Poullain asked.

'About six hundred metres down the road, a track cuts between our neighbour and the next farm. It goes between two more farms for half a kilometre, then comes out on the main Taragnon–Bauriac road. He goes along the main road through Taragnon village, and the farm is just over a kilometre past.'

'Which side of the road?'

'On the left as you come out of Taragnon. It's set back a few hundred metres from the road. From the roadside you can see mainly vines, though they also have some fields for grazing.'

'What is the family name?'

'Maillot.'

'And your son never arrived there.'

Monique looked down and bit her lip. Dominic noticed that she looked at them directly only at intervals, the rest of the time she looked down at the table or at the notepad as he recorded the interview in shorthand. 'We didn't know straight away. We're not on the phone, nor are they. I finally called Jean-Luc in from the fields at just past four. We had expected Christian back by three, and normally he's very good with coming back on time. Jean-Luc went over to Stéphane's house and checked. They hadn't seen Christian. That was when Jean-Luc checked back along the route Christian normally took and found the bike. At first we thought that with the bike broken down he'd decided to walk the rest, which would have taken him far longer – then perhaps he'd got distracted and stopped off in the village.'

'How far away was the bike?'

Monique looked at Jean-Luc. Jean Luc answered, 'Almost towards the end of the track down the road. Not far from where it joins the Taragnon road – a few hundred metres at most.'

'So it looked to you as if Christian had walked the rest of the distance to the main road, then the two kilometres to the village.'

Jean-Luc nodded. Poullain paused for a moment, looking over at Dominic's notes and taking stock of the information so far. Christian had been found on a farm track a little more than half a kilometre from the Maillots' farm, but on the other side of the road bordering the river. But somehow the boy had made it through the village. Poullain voiced the thought. 'The first thing to find out is who in the village might have seen your boy between midday and three. Because we will then at least know if he walked through the village or was transported through by someone he met at the roadside.'

Monique and Jean-Luc looked at each other for a second. Something troubled them about this comment. Jean-Luc was the first to speak. 'If he was on foot, the problem is he could have cut through the fields behind the village. On his bike it's not possible, but on foot there's only a few stone walls and small fences to negotiate.'

'Is it likely he cut across?' asked Poullain.

Jean-Luc shrugged. 'It's a possibility. It's something he's done before. In any case, he would probably cut down and walk the last hundred metres of the village heading for Stéphane's house. There's another track there.'

A hundred metres at the end of the village, Poullain considered. It was quiet, the main village establishments petering out. If the one or two shopkeepers there hadn't seen the boy, it proved nothing. Yet if the boy had walked through the entire village, past boulangeries, patisseries, the main square and cafés, without being seen, it would be a different matter. He'd already assigned three men to call on village shops from early that morning, and had been hopeful of their findings. Now he wasn't so sure. Poullain couldn't even remember what shops there were in those last hundred metres. The disappointment showed on his face.

On a fresh page Dominic had been making a small diagram of Taragnon: the path from the Rosselots to the main road, the Maillots' farm, and the track by the river. It was a simple triangular drawing, with distances in metres between Xs marking where the bike was left and the boy was found. While his pen hovered for Poullain to speak again, he took a quick scan of the kitchen: dried flowers, ornaments, flour and spice jars, a plate wall clock with 'Portofino' in scrawly black loops below a background harbour scene, no photos. Little in the kitchen said anything about the Rosselots' lives. Though the kitchen was where the coffee was, Dominic couldn't help wondering if they hadn't been asked into the sitting room for another reason. The Rosselots didn't want too deep an intrusion into their lives.

'So finally you made the call to the police station just before five that afternoon, when it was clear that your son had not turned up at the Maillots' farm and you had found the bike abandoned.' Monique muttered yes, and Jean-Luc merely nodded. Poullain glanced briefly at Dominic's crude diagram, as if for inspiration. He voiced his thoughts in staccato fashion as they came to him, as if he was at the same time refreshing his own memory. 'Your son was originally discovered at about three-fifteen by a neighbouring farmer, just half a kilometre from the Maillots' farm. We arrived on the crime scene within forty minutes and received your call almost an hour later. We subsequently made some confirmations of identity, to be sure the boy was yours – and two officers were sent to you an hour and a quarter after you called. We suspect – although we cannot be totally sure until all the medical reports are in – that your son was attacked within an hour of being discovered.' Poullain looked keenly between Monique and Jean-Luc as he related the sequence of events. This was the first time they were hearing this information, and he wanted to see their reactions.

Jean-Luc stared back blandly, and Monique looked mildly expectant, as if she sensed Poullain wanted to add something vital. Dominic noticed Poullain unclench one hand and wave it to one side. The difficult part was coming, and he was struggling for emphasis before the words were even formed. 'I want you to think about this for a moment before you answer. But are there any relatives, any cousins or uncles, or any friends or neighbours, who have shown a special interest in Christian? In a way that perhaps might be described as a bit over-friendly or unusual.'

Poullain was doing this by the book, thought Dominic. Most child molesters were found close to home and turned out to be a relative or a friend. Often the dividing line between a natural fondness for children and an 'unnatural' interest was impossible to determine.

Monique appeared nonplussed at first. Then finally it dawned on her what Poullain was aiming at and her face clouded. But as she spoke, her voice faltered, as if she was still struggling to comprehend. 'I don't think there's anyone we know like that.' She looked hastily towards Jean-Luc for support. 'But I don't understand. Why do you ask this?'

Poullain smoothed back his crown. Faint beads of perspiration had broken out on his forehead and he looked uncomfortable. 'Believe me, I'm sorry to have to ask you this. But we suspected that your son was sexually assaulted before he was beaten, and when I checked this morning with the medical examiner, this was unfortunately confirmed. We know only a little about the timing of the attack or the sexual assault, the full details will come out later from forensics and blood sampling. But we do know at this stage that a sexual assault took place.' Poullain exhaled slightly; a part-sigh, part-release of tension. 'I'm sorry to have to bring you this news.'

Monique's lip trembled as she stared at Poullain. It took a moment for what he'd said to sink in. Then she turned sharply away, got up and walked over to the window, her back to them. Her shoulders slumped and she cradled her head in one hand, shaking it slowly. Her jaw line tensed as she fought back the tears.

Jean-Luc stared at his wife's back for a moment, unsure whether to get up and comfort her. There was some awkwardness, some tension between them. In the end he stayed where he was and looked down at the table, smoothing it with one hand. His face was slightly flushed, a mixture of anger at Poullain's news and frustration. He wasn't there to save his son, and now he even felt too impotent to comfort his own wife.

Dominic noticed the muscles' tensing in Jean-Luc's neck and thick forearms as he struggled for fresh resolve. There was silence for a moment. The sound of cicadas from outside was broken only by the crackling of Poullain's radio.

Finally, Jean-Luc commented, 'As my wife said, I'm sure we don't know anyone like that. Christian is a very loving, trusting child – but we know nobody who has taken advantage of that trust, or would do so.'

Poullain grimaced understandingly. 'I'm sorry I had to ask. But as you appreciate, we have to explore every possibility.' As the radio crackled again, Poullain asked Dominic to answer it.

Dominic left the main door open as he crossed the courtyard to the car. It was Harrault from the gendarmerie. He brought Dominic up to date on progress. Three gendarmes had been out calling on shops in Taragnon since 8.30 a.m., and the item appearing in the morning's *Le Provençal* had also attracted some calls. Harrault felt that Poullain should know about one lead in particular. 'Madame Veillan from the charcuterie was driving out towards Pontevès yesterday and saw Gaston Machanaud on his moped, coming out of the lane where we found the boy. It looks like we might have struck gold quickly.'

Dominic knew Machanaud. He was a casual farm labourer who filled in with some local poaching. 'What time was this?'

'Just after three. Madame Veillan aimed to be in Pontevès for three-fifteen, so she was quite sure of the time. About fifteen or twenty minutes before the boy was found.'

Dominic confirmed that they would be returning to the station before heading out to see the medical examiner, so they should have time to go through the call notes. Hanging up, he noticed Monique Rosselot still by the window. She had stopped crying and was staring at him resolutely. Large, soulful eyes which seemed to look right through him.

Alain Duclos left the Vallon estate early to buy a morning paper, deciding to head to Brignoles for his morning coffee. He wanted to look through the paper in private, not with Claude or his father looking over his shoulder.

He picked up a copy of *Le Provençal* at a news kiosk close to the café, took a seat at one of five outside tables, and folded out the paper. He scanned the front page: Khrushchev and the nuclear-test ban treaty in Moscow; four dead in floods in Tournin; Marseille warehouse fire, two dead; French Navy aids 6,000 stranded cruise passengers. Nothing there. He felt a twinge of anxiety. A murder should have taken precedence over the warehouse fire – it should have been there. He flicked over the page, and was rapidly scanning page two when the item caught his eye on page three: BOY SAVAGELY ATTACKED IN TARAGNON.

It was a sixth of a page entry describing the discovery of the boy by a local farm worker and the police questioning of people in the village. Two-thirds of the way down, Duclos froze; he had to read the paragraph over again before it sank in: *The boy suffered severe head injuries and is now in hospital. The police and the family are awaiting news from doctors as to the extent of the injuries.* The name of the hospital wasn't mentioned. Duclos felt numb and stared blankly at the same paragraph, the text fading out of focus. He felt suddenly faint, an icy chill gripping him. *The boy wasn't dead!*

He'd found the lane only three minutes from the restaurant, his resolve rebuilding on the way. Everything had gone well, except in the final moments he'd been disturbed by the tinkling bells of a shepherd's goat flock being moved into the adjacent field. But he was sure he'd felt the skull crush, the blood spilling out. Another few seconds and he'd have been able to check the pulse in the neck or wrist. *Check that . . .*

'Monsieur. What can I get you?'

It took a moment for Duclos to detach himself from the paper and register the waiter's presence. His voice broke slightly as he answered. 'An orange juice, coffee with milk and a croissant.'

The waiter nodded and moved away. Duclos' hands shook as he closed the paper and folded it on the table. How could he have made such a mistake? The boy could have already identified his car; in no time the police could trace it back to Limoges. A few more phone calls and they would know he was on holiday and where he was staying. The police could be at the Vallon estate that same day, they might even be there on his return. He shivered involuntarily, his stomach churning with fear. Suddenly he felt very alone and vulnerable. He couldn't go back to the estate, and he would also have to change his car. Perhaps he would head for Monte Carlo and the Italian border, or the other direction, to Spain. Then what?

He wiped the sweat from his brow. He realized he wasn't thinking rationally. Closing his eyes, he fought to calm his nerves and think clearly. His own breathing seemed louder in the self-imposed darkness, his heartbeat pounding a solid tattoo through his head along with the sounds of passing traffic; he had to concentrate to filter any clear thoughts through. A few minutes passed before the faint background shuffle and rattle of the tray of the waiter returning made him look up again. Some ideas had started forming.

As the waiter set down his breakfast, Duclos asked if he had a telephone.

'Yes, at the back of the café.' The waiter pointed.

The bar was narrow and busy, and Duclos had to edge and push past the workmen and truck drivers having early morning coffees with brandy and Pernod chasers. The large directory on the shelf beneath the phone was the first thing Duclos reached for. He leafed through it rapidly. There were only two hospitals he could think of in Aix-en-Provence where it was likely the boy could have been taken, and one in Aubagne. The name of the second large hospital in Aix had momentarily escaped him, he had to call out to the barman to be reminded. Duclos took a pen from his shirt pocket and grabbed a serviette from the counter to write on as the barman mouthed the word above the noise of the bar: Montperrin.

Duclos noted the telephone numbers of the three hospitals on the same serviette, then made his way back to the tables out front. He didn't want to call from the bar – too many people close by who could listen in. He took a quick sip of orange juice and coffee, put down enough money to cover the bill, and left. Turning the corner, he found a phone kiosk. He dialled the Montperrin first.

'I wondered if you could help me. I understand you have a young boy at your hospital by the name of Christian Rosselot. He would have been brought in just yesterday.'

'One moment.' Duclos could hear the flicking of paper. It went on a long time, as if the receptionist was checking twice. Finally: 'I'm sorry, I don't see anyone registered by that name.'

'Thank you.' Duclos called the second Aix-en-Provence hospital.

'Centre Hospitalier.'

'I'm sorry to trouble you. I understand you have a young boy registered at the hospital, brought in yesterday. Christian Rosselot.'

'And who may I ask is inquiring?'

'He's a friend of my son Michel from school, Michel Bourdin. I wondered what room he might be staying in – we would like to send some flowers and perhaps visit.'

'*Ne quittez pas.* One moment.'

Duclos was nervous during the wait. He had no idea if she was suspicious or what instructions she was receiving at the other end. It was a full minute before she returned.

'The boy is still in intensive care. But when he can be moved, he will be in one of the five private annexe rooms of Bénat Ward.'

'When will that be?'

'It could be tonight, tomorrow, or even two days or a week from now. He's still in a coma now and can't be moved. Until he's conscious, there are strict instructions in any case for no visitors but family. But if you still want to send some flowers, they'll be put in his room.'

'Yes. Thank you. That's a good idea.'

Duclos felt a twinge of relief as he hung up. But he knew it could be short-lived. At any time the boy might regain consciousness and talk. He just couldn't sit back and let that happen.

7

The light of a single candle was reflected against the glass. Monique Rosselot's concerned profile was caught in its glow, looking through the large glass partition towards her son in intensive care. The partition separated the small preparation and observation room, no more than two and a half square metres, from the main intensive care room. Monique Rosselot sat in one of three chairs close to the glass. She'd been allowed to bring in a candle, only one, and light it as part of her daily bedside vigil, two to three hours each visit.

The attending nurse had been gone for a full minute. Monique decided to go inside the intensive care room. There was no chair, so she knelt at Christian's side.

After a second of studying his features thoughtfully, she reached out and started tracing one finger gently down his face. Memories flooded back of the many times she had stroked his face, of him smiling back at her at bedtime, asking her to read him a story.

His skin had been warmer then, and it felt strange and somehow remote stroking his skin with no response. No smile. No bright eyes turning towards her. She had to be careful as she ran her finger down not to disturb any of the tubes feeding and monitoring. The story read, she would reach out and ruffle his hair. Only now, his head had been shaved clean, his skull marked out for the tests they'd made. Stitches marked a grotesque gash to one side.

Monique closed her eyes and gripped Christian's hand. But it felt even cooler than his face, and suddenly a pang of fear gripped her inside. Oh God, *please . . . please don't let him die!* Her eyes scrunched tight at the unthinkable, Christian's prone figure blurred through tears as they slowly opened again.

She tried to push from her mind what had been done to him, the cold hard details from the two visiting gendarmes: the sexual assault . . . the repeated blows which had left him for dead. Her tears had mostly been in private – but then that had reflected how she'd felt almost throughout her vigil. Alone. Jean-Luc had merely absorbed himself more in his farm work to cope. He'd only visited the hospital once with her.

Now, gripping Christian's small hand in hers, she wouldn't have wanted it any other way. She probably wouldn't have grabbed this moment of intimacy if Jean-Luc had been with her. She'd only done this once before – and then too had felt like a thief sneaking in and stealing something she shouldn't. Stealing a few minutes of intimacy with her son. Perhaps their last . . .

She shook her head. *No!* That wasn't going to happen! She would see Christian smile again . . . *feel the warmth of his embrace.* She gripped the small hand tighter, willing the message home. Willing Christian to awake.

The candle burning reminded her of birthdays, and she remembered then that it would be Christian's birthday soon – her mind flashing back to past birthdays with him smiling in the glow of the candles. Unwrapping presents expectantly. The Topo Gigio doll. A model car racetrack. His bicycle only last birthday. The house filled with joy and laughter. And suddenly she felt more assured: *his coming birthday!* Something close and real on which she could focus, could actually picture Christian's presence. 'It's your birthday soon, Christian,' she muttered. 'There'll be some great presents for you. I'll bake a cake. Bigger and better than you've ever seen before.' In her mind's eye, she could imagine Christian looking on with wide eyes and smiling at the oversized cake. And in that brief moment, she felt sure that Christian would awaken, was able to ignore the coldness of the small hand in her grasp. 'We'll all be there . . .'

'Now let us see what we have here.' Dr Besnard, the chief medical examiner, had a manila folder already opened in front of him, as if he'd been studying it before they entered. A duty nurse ushered Dominic and Poullain to upright seats opposite his large mahogany desk. Poullain knew Besnard from four previous cases, mostly car accidents.

'. . . Young boy, Christian Yves Rosselot. Ten years old. Eleven on 4 September – just over two weeks from now. Admitted on 18 August at 4.38 p.m.' Besnard flicked forward a page and then back again. In his early fifties, he was bald except for some long wisps of greying brown hair. He cradled his head for a moment, smoothing the wisps across as he looked up again. 'So. The medics recorded arriving on the scene at 4.03 p.m. The boy was wearing shorts but no shirt, and he was lying face down, his back exposed. There was blood visible on his head and shoulder, quite thick, obviously from a wound to the head. Some smaller blood spots were noted on the boy's back – from the same wound – and also a blood trail, mostly coagulated, on the boy's inside thigh. This was obviously from a separate wound. The shorts were therefore cut with surgical scissors, and the blood flow was discovered to have come from the rectal passage. The wound was not active, there was no fresh blood, so their efforts were concentrated on the head wound.' Besnard looked up at Poullain periodically, marking off his position in the file with one finger as he glanced at Dominic, as if waiting for his notes to keep pace.

X-rays, complex fractures, haematomas, somatosensory cortex. The pages of Dominic's notepad were already filled with notes from the surgeon who'd operated on Christian the night before. Medical notes in shorthand were a nightmare. Effectively only the conjoining words could be shortened. Poullain had arranged for Dominic to take the notes, then wait on him for the meeting with Besnard. But there had been a spare thirty minutes for Dominic in between.

Pale green tiling and cream–emulsion walls. The clatter of heels and voices along bare and stark corridors. Dominic found the atmosphere unsettling. He'd spent far too much of the past year in hospitals. *Images of the doctor approaching, footsteps echoing ominously, telling him the results of his mother's biopsy. A year, two years if she was lucky. No, unfortunately there wasn't much they could do except administer morphine in the closing stages to ease the pain. Check-ups every three months, but let us know if the pain becomes too much in between . . .*

'. . . Clearing the airway of any residual blood was a priority, so a tracheal tube was inserted.' Besnard's finger ran quickly down the page. 'Fortunately, the boy was face down, otherwise he would have probably choked on his own blood before they arrived. The wound was cleaned and the source of the blood flow as a ruptured blood vessel was discovered, as was a likely skull fracture – though not immediately the extent of the fracture. That showed up later on X-ray. Badly bruised and broken skin also on the right cheekbone, blood by then coagulated, possible fracture beneath. The patient was therefore bandaged both to stem the blood flow and support the skull; oxygen was administered once the airway was cleared, then he was transported here to the hospital – from which point on Verthuy in Emergency attended. Conclusions from the medics' report and Dr Verthuy? First of all, time of the attack.' Besnard looked up pointedly. 'From the extent of blood coagulation around the main wound and rate of new blood seepage, their estimate was that the attack took place any time between an hour and an hour and a half before they arrived. As for the other injury – to the boy's rectal passage – this was more or less the same time, possibly only minutes beforehand. But probably the most interesting factor was from Verthuy's note on the boy's sexual assault. He discovered varying degrees of rectal inflammation and damage – suggesting that in fact *two* attacks had taken place at entirely separate intervals.'

Besnard's pause for emphasis had the desired effect on Poullain. He sat forward keenly. 'Two attacks? How far apart?'

'Thirty minutes, forty minutes – one hour at most. But definitely two separate assaults. One area at the neck of the rectal canal which had been bleeding had almost completely coagulated by the time the second attack was made.'

Dominic could sense that Poullain was still grappling with the timing of the attack when he was hit with this new information. Dominic had already written on his pad: *Attack, 1–1½ hours before medics arrive: 2.33–3.03 p.m. Anything from 12–42 minutes before discovery. Sexual assault minutes beforehand.* Now Dominic wrote: *Separate sexual attack, 30–60 minutes prior to final assault.* That meant that at the outside estimate the attacker had stayed close to the path up to an hour and a half, resting a full hour in between the assaults; and at the least, he had stayed there almost forty-five minutes, resting for half an hour. Surely someone else would have come along the path in the time. Where had he hidden?

'Any semen detected on either attack?' asked Poullain.

'No, none. Verthuy found nothing in the rectal passage apart from blood and inflamed tissue. All the blood is also of one type, B positive, the boy's blood group. Our attacker obviously was careful and pulled out to ejaculate. Did forensics find anything?'

Poullain pictured the succession of polythene-bagged samples taken from the wheat field by the Marseille team. Their report was due the next day. But they didn't know till now that the attacker had probably ejaculated on the ground. Would they have looked for that as a matter of course? A few droplets of semen among the wheat, probably by then hopelessly dried and crystallized by the heat of the sun. If not, by now it had probably been washed away with the previous night's rain. 'I'm not sure yet,' Poullain commented. 'I'll know tomorrow.'

'Other points of interest in Verthuy's report . . .' Besnard's finger skipped a few paragraphs. 'Instrument of attack, a rock or large stone, determined from rock particles found in the boy's hair and embedded in skull tissue. Four blows in total, one breaking the skull and rupturing a blood vessel. Another blow tore heavily through the skin and shattered the right cheekbone. Bone fragments were removed, though constructive surgery will later be required for the cheekbone. Eleven sutures were required for the skull wound, eighteen for the cheek. Suspecting internal cranial haematomas, Verthuy ordered a series of X-rays at 5.32 p.m. – fifty-four minutes after the boy's entry into Emergency. The boy was comatose throughout – and still remains so – with the only break from intensive care for surgery last night, at the hands of Dr Trichot . . . notes of which you already have.' Besnard nodded towards Dominic. 'Trichot's full report is expected sometime tomorrow. But I can let you have a copy of Verthuy's report now. You might find something small that I haven't covered in summary.' He passed across a carbon copy.

While Poullain flicked through, Dominic asked, 'Any estimates for how long for each sexual assault?'

Besnard looked forward, then back a page. 'No longer than a few minutes for each one, though Verthuy suggests the second was perhaps shorter purely because it was less forceful.'

They were silent for a second as Poullain continued looking through the folder. Finally he looked up. 'Possibly there'll be some questions when I read it in more detail back at the gendarmerie, but that's fine for now. Thank you. You've been most helpful.'

Besnard came out from behind his desk to show them out, making small talk about the continuing August heat and how it slowed work. Doctors and gendarmes were probably the only city officials not to disappear for the month *en masse* to the coast. 'Call of duty or foolhardiness, you tell me?'

The corridor was quiet as they made their way along and down the stairway. Activity increased as they approached the first floor.

'What arrangements for Machanaud's interview tomorrow?' Dominic inquired. Poullain had decided earlier they would interview Machanaud the next day, but the time and place hadn't been fixed.

'I think we should go out to visit him initially, try not to make it look too official and serious. If a second interview is necessary, we'll ask him in. Apparently he's working at Raulin's farm most of tomorrow, but we should try and get to him by midday, before he has a chance to hit the bars.'

'And the other leads that came in today?'

Poullain looked at Dominic pointedly. 'Let's not lose sight of the fact that at present Machanaud is our main suspect.'

A curt reminder that earlier that afternoon they'd had words for the first time on the investigation. Machanaud was a drunkard, a part-time poacher and vagabond, and, with his wild stories and bar-room antics when drunk, was viewed as odd by at least half of Taragnon . . . *but a murderer?* It was ridiculous, and Dominic had made the mistake of voicing that thought. But what was the alternative? The inquiries had centred on anything out of place. In Taragnon, imbued strongly with the belief that nobody local could do anything so atrocious, this had translated into *people* out of place. The only other leads were a van with Lyon markings and a traveller passing through.

As if atoning for his previous sharp tone, Poullain commented, 'You'll probably be pleased to hear that another lead came up late this afternoon. Café Font-du-Roux, just over a kilometre from where the boy was found. Barman saw a green Alfa Romeo coupé he hadn't seen before; its driver had lunch there.'

But Dominic wasn't particularly pleased. It was too simplistic: *misfits.* Machanaud because of his oddball nature at times, and now three others purely because they were strangers. Village thinking was one track, and Poullain and his merry men lacked the imagination to push it that one stage further.

Ahead a crowd at the reception caused a small bottle jam for people entering and exiting the hospital. Doctors and nurses criss-crossed the passage from the main admittance hall to Emergency. A face among the crowd stared at them briefly, startled and concerned. But among the milling confusion of people it hardly registered, and the figure turned and was lost again in the crowd as it made its way swiftly out of the hospital.

Alain Duclos headed for the coast. At first, he had decided on Cannes and Juan-les-Pins, but then he realized he just couldn't face the people and frenetic activity. He headed instead for Saint-Tropez. The village was quiet and the beach wasn't too crowded; because of its expanse, there were wide-open areas where Duclos could walk and think or sit in solitude away from the groups of sunbathers.

He wondered if the gendarmes had noticed him at the hospital. He kicked himself now for taking such a risk. But he'd found it difficult to think clearly or function since reading the newspaper and phoning the hospital. Leaving the bar that morning, he'd headed out of Brignoles towards Castellane and the mountains. He stopped close to the Point Sublime and looked out over the Canyon du Verdon. The view was breathtaking, the wind sweeping up sharply from the valley floor, ruffling his hair. He closed his eyes and let the refreshing coolness play over his skin. But it did little to clear his thoughts: *the wind playing through the treetops in his final moment of pleasure, the rustle of wheat sheaves as he brought the rock down repeatedly on the boy's skull. Shifting wheat, rising and falling on the wind . . . white noise merging with the sound of waves gently breaking.*

He opened his eyes. Slowly he scanned the horizon of Saint-Tropez bay: two distant yachts and a fisherman's boat showed as white flecks against a deep blue canvas. Children played in the shallows. The view was different now, but the images in his mind remained the same. Perhaps he hoped the grandeur of the vistas would override the images in his mind, or was he simply seeking solitude? Space to think clearly. In the end, none of it touched his soul. He still felt desperately empty inside and confused.

After the mountains he'd headed back to the Vallon estate for lunch. Claude and his father had hardly seen him in the past twenty-four hours. He'd picked at his food through lunch, struggling even to make small talk, and he was sure they'd noticed his preoccupation. The obsession haunted every spare moment when his thoughts were free; respites though outside distractions were brief.

The sun was weak now above the bay. It was almost 7.30. He hoped to make a better show of it that night for dinner at the estate, and headed back.

Dinner was impressive: *caviar d'aubergines, daurade cuite sur litière* and *gelée d'amande aux fruits frais*, served by the estate chef. There was vintage '55 red wine from the Vallon cellars, and cheeses, coffee and cognac to finish. The conversation was animated, Claude talking about arranging a day on one of the Camargue ranches, and Duclos even managed his own anecdote about one of his first disastrous experiences riding a Brittany seaside donkey; though later his conversation petered out, the images resurging to plague him, and he excused himself early and went to bed.

It was difficult getting to sleep. He kept replaying in his mind entering the hospital, pushing past the crowd by the reception – then seeing the two gendarmes and turning quickly away. He could have milled with the crowd for a moment, kept his back turned until they'd gone, then continued along the corridor. If only he'd kept his head.

The night was hot, humidity high, and he turned incessantly to get comfortable. Sleep finally came after almost two hours. The dream was confusing. The boy's eyes were looking back at him from the darkness of the boot, haunting, pleading. Then the boy was playing in the shallows at Saint-Tropez, and Duclos was hovering above him with the rock, silently willing him to move away from the crowds. But when the boy looked up at him directly, he was smiling, his eyes suddenly mischievous and defiant. He was mouthing some words softly, and Duclos had to move closer to hear what he was saying. The words were a tease, whispers almost lost among the wash of the surf. Thin red strands appeared like spider webbing, slowly thickening, seeping across the clear blue shallows, blood that at any minute others on the beach would see. 'As soon as I open my mouth, they will know . . . *they will know!*'

Duclos awoke with a jolt, almost knocking the clock off his small side table as he grappled to look at the time: 5.10 a.m. His hands were shaking. He knew it would be impossible to get back to sleep, so he went down to the kitchen to make coffee. He decided to sit on the château's back terrace overlooking the pool and watch the sunrise. He was on his second cup of coffee just over an hour later when Claude joined him.

After a few attempts at small talk, Claude sensed his consternation and asked what was wrong. Knowing that he might get the same questions over the following days, he answered that it was a girl he'd met two days ago at Juan-les-Pins. He'd arranged to meet her on the same stretch of beach the afternoon before, but she hadn't shown up.

Claude half smiled. 'She must have got to you badly. You look quite ill.'

Quite ill? In different circumstances, Duclos would have burst out laughing. Claude could be such a prat at times. In the end all he managed was a weak smile in return. But at least the past torturous hours had strengthened his resolve. The obsession was destroying him, the constant fight to keep hiding it fraying his nerves, and he just couldn't cope any longer. There was only one way to end it. He would have to return to the hospital.

Dominic opened the door slowly. The first thing he saw was Monique Rosselot's profile reflected in candlelight against the glass screen. Shapes beyond the glass were more indistinct with the reflections.

Monique didn't notice him immediately, and Dominic gave a small nod of acknowledgement as she finally looked up. Then he looked towards the prone figure of Christian beyond the partition. The wires and intravenous feed tubes looked somehow obscene on such a small body. Desecration. Apart from the tubes, the harsh reminder that doctors

63

were fighting for his life, the boy looked like one of Botticelli's gently sleeping angels, though his burnished curls had gone, shaved off for the operation the night before.

The pain of the ordeal, the daily waiting without knowing, was etched on Monique's face. Her anguish was almost tangible, pervading the small room – though he knew that the full depth of her pain was beyond him. He could understand it and feel desperately sorry for her without really feeling it himself. Would it make him deal with the investigation more effectively if he had? Make the battle he feared was brewing with Poullain over charges against Machanaud any easier?

Dominic eased the door shut. Monique looked up again fleetingly, a faint pained grimace of thanks or goodbye through the closing gap. He didn't want to disturb her. He'd had to call back to the hospital to pick up the final surgical report, so decided to look in for a moment. Some visual reference to match with the medical descriptions. In answer to his concern about the boy's safety, they'd only been able to allocate a gendarme two hours each day, though when Monique Rosselot wasn't visiting, Besnard had assured him that a nurse would always be in attendance.

Dominic shook his head as he made his way down the corridor. Poullain. Machanaud. The interview with Machanaud hadn't gone well. Still, it had only been a casual visit to the farm where Machanaud had been working that morning, the true test would come tomorrow with the official interview in the gendarmerie. But why would Machanaud lie about his whereabouts? Dominic had no ready answers to that when Poullain posed the question, and Poullain's keenness had been sickeningly transparent in his own answer: 'Other than to shield his own guilt.' Suddenly the question was rhetorical; Dominic's opinion was superfluous. He could imagine Poullain already preparing the charge statement in his mind, one hand playing distractedly with his handcuffs. The glory of the case solved early.

Dominic made his way out of the hospital and started up his bike. Evening traffic in Aix was light, and within minutes he was on the N7 heading for Bauriac. Officially, his duty shift had ended half an hour ago, the hospital had been his last call after picking up the forensics report from Marseille. But Poullain wanted summary notes on both reports by 7 a.m., so he would have to do them later that night.

The day had been busy: the meeting with Pierre Bouteille had taken over an hour and a half in the morning. While a prominent case for Bauriac, filed under *grievous assault*, it was probably just one of many such regional cases on Bouteille's desk. Court clerks with files and the telephone interrupted at intervals throughout. Bouteille would now determine the best point of crossover: general to official inquiry and handing over to the examining magistrate, Frédéric Naugier.

Dominic panned back again through the meeting and the events of the day, trying to pick up on small details that might be significant; but his thoughts were dulled by overload. He found it impossible to focus.

He pulled back on the throttle. The wind rush was fresh, exhilarating.

Alain Duclos circled the hospital for the third time. Each time he took a different street a block further away, until he felt sure he'd covered all the streets within reasonable walking distance of the hospital. He didn't want to make the same mistake as the day before, almost walk into two gendarmes.

The black 2CVs and DS19s were practically standard police issue. He saw only one black 2CV two blocks away; stopping briefly and looking inside, he saw that it had no police radio. He turned the corner and went another 200 metres before parking. The hospital was now four blocks away; he was conscious too of his conspicuous car, of it not being seen too close to the hospital.

Duclos kept close to the buildings as he walked along, turning his head from the road as cars approached. It was relatively quiet that time of night: 8.16 p.m. Only three cars passed in the first two streets. Turning the corner, he passed a busy restaurant with a large picture window looking out on to the street: a babble of voices, some muted laughter and merriment, a lone face catching his eye as he scurried past. It brought home stronger the solitude of his mission now. He should be with Claude and some friends at a restaurant on the coast; instead, he was sneaking through the back streets like a thief, his nerves at fever pitch. His eyes had probably looked wild and startled to the people he'd passed in the restaurant.

At least this time he'd planned more thoroughly. With the story that his son went to the same school as Christian Rosselet and that he wanted to ensure that flowers arrived while Madame Rosselot was there, the receptionist informed him that she normally visited every day, arriving at any time between four and five and staying two or three hours. 'Though on two occasions, she also visited in the morning for an hour or so.'

He had timed to arrive just after the evening visit. Rounding the next corner, he faced the hospital entrance fifty metres ahead. He paused for a second, taking a deep breath, then continued at a steady pace; he didn't want to look hesitant, be stopped at reception and asked what he wanted.

There was a small crowd at the reception desk, and the two nurses behind hardly noticed him. One had her head down, studying something in the register, the other was deep in conversation. Duclos only gave them a brief sideways glance, not wanting to attract undue attention as he made his way quickly through the main hallway to the stairway and lift.

He waited only a second before deciding on the stairs. Too many prying eyes close by in the lift, people who might talk to him, ask him which way for so-and-so ward, notice on which floor he got off. On the stairs he would be far more anonymous. Second floor, far end of corridor, room 4A. His heartbeat seemed to pulse through to his head, its rhythm almost matching the stark echo of his footsteps as he made his way along the second-floor corridor. It split at one end into a T-junction, with markings and arrows indicating the different departments. It looked like 4A was close to the end. Duclos shortened his step as he got close to the door. Almost unconsciously he held his breath for the last few steps, reaching one hand out for the door handle.

His hand hovered by the handle for a second – then he retracted it, wiping the sweat that had built up on his palm on his trouser leg. The plan was straight in his mind: if anyone was there or he was confronted, he would say that he'd arranged to meet Madame Rosselot. Had he missed her?

Another breath, forcing the air deep into his lungs to calm his nerves – he reached for the handle, turning it . . .

The room opened out before him: a woman's profile, dark hair, a candle glowing . . . a bed and instruments through a glass partition. A split-second impression. The woman started to look up – Duclos closed the door again swiftly. A sudden exhalation, release of tension, then he headed quickly away – afraid that the woman might come to the door and open it, look out to see who had been there. Not daring to look back he listened intently for sounds behind him. None came. He turned the corner of the T. Safety again.

He was sure the woman hadn't seen him. It was probably the boy's mother, Madame Rosselot. He cursed his bad luck – she should have left at least fifteen minutes ago. Suddenly a door to his side opened, startling him; he almost jumped out of his skin as a nurse and hospital porter came out. Duclos covered hastily with a sheepish grin, but they hardly paid him any attention as they headed towards the stairs.

Duclos thought about giving up, heading back out of the hospital, coming back another day. His nerves were shot; there was a trembling deep in his stomach and his body was weak from lack of sleep and nervous anticipation. But he knew that if he left now, he would never come back, he wouldn't be able to face the same ordeal again. He went across to a bench a few paces to one side with a clear view of the stairway and, when he leant across, the full length of the corridor and room 4A at its end. Perhaps he could wait it out. She was already fifteen minutes late, how much longer could she stay?

He fought to relax again, breathing deeply and steadily. But with each passing minute he became increasingly agitated. Two fresh sets of heels he'd heard, only to lean over and see people coming out of other rooms. False alarms. Only a few minutes had passed, but it seemed like a lifetime.

Another set of heels, faint at first, started their echoing clipping. He leant across half expecting another false alarm – then pulled back quickly, catching his breath. *At last!* His pulse raced, counting each beat of the slowly receding footsteps.

He waited a full twenty seconds after they had faded down the stairway, then concentrated on the sounds around for a moment. No fresh footsteps on the stairway or in the corridor.

He got up and made his way along, covering the distance steadily, half of his senses attuned to the sounds around, the rest focused on what lay ahead: *the door* . . . approaching closer, reaching out for the handle, listening for a brief second for any sounds beyond. Nothing. The corridor was empty, no fresh footsteps approaching. Slowly he turned the handle; the door opened, the view steadily expanding . . . *nobody inside!* A quick release of breath. Then he looked through the glass screen to the larger room beyond, stepping fully into the small anteroom, closing the door quickly behind him.

The boy lay beyond the glass partition, his skin pallid like yellow porcelain, wires and tubes connected and monitoring. It was certainly the boy from the day before, and there was nobody else in the room. Duclos' mouth was dry with anticipation. The boy's breathing was probably so shallow that all he would have to do was reach out and cover his nose and mouth for a minute to finish him. But he would have to be quick – at any moment somebody could come back in the room.

His nerves were racing, his palm suddenly clammy on the handle of the door to the main room. His whole body trembled and he felt cold, even though the night air was close to 80°F. With a final deep breath, he opened the partition door and stepped inside.

'When this old world starts getting me down, and people are just too much for me to face . . . I climb right up to the top of the stairs and all my cares just drift right into space. On the roof, the only place I know . . . where you just have to wish to make it so . . .'

Dominic lay on his back on his bedroom terrace, staring up at the star-lit sky above Bauriac, the Drifters on his record player soothing his thoughts. It was one of the best songs of the year, his favourite. The record had been in his collection and on Louis' jukebox since early January, just as it was climbing up the American *Billboard* charts. Files and notes lay scattered over his bedroom floor. He'd finished his summary report for Poullain – all but the last paragraph. He'd searched for the right tone, that key phrase which neatly encapsulated everything, before finally giving up after half an hour and deciding on a break to clear his thoughts.

His mother had gone to bed over an hour before with some hot chocolate and biscuits, just after ten. The day's basic household activities seemed to tire her earlier by the day. He'd positioned his record player close to the double terrace doors so that it didn't disturb her asleep downstairs.

His mind drifted back to Algeria. The Foreign Legion, where he'd first found the habit of lying on his back staring up at the stars. The desert sky had been even more spectacular, crystal-clear skies of deep blue velvet sprinkled with a snowstorm of stars. After a few months, the idea had caught on with half the platoon. Somebody would light a camp fire, he'd spend a while rigging up his record player to a car battery and would put on some Ray Charles or Sam Cooke, and on occasions some hashish would appear that somebody had picked up at a souk. It was easier to get hashish than alcohol in Algeria. The sessions made him popular with comrades. The fact that they were lying in the middle of the desert, cut off from civilization and all they knew, yet listening to the very latest sounds courtesy of Dominic's uncle almost two months before the rest of France had the privilege somehow made them feel in touch, in tune. Compensated for the isolation.

The Legion had left its scars. Not so much on him personally – he'd been a back-room radio and communications sergeant and had hardly seen any fighting – but on his present career. The gendarmerie treated ex-Foreign Legion recruits with an air of suspicion, as if they were all unarmed combat experts or reformed cut-throat murderers. At the end of the last century with uprisings in Morocco and Algeria, many recruits had come from the French prison system, an alternative to jail or Devil's Island – but not in the last few decades.

Dominic didn't trouble to put them right, tell them he'd hardly seen any action during the Algerian war. Sometimes the tough-guy image had its benefits; colleagues were careful not to tread on his toes. Local prejudices could be used to advantage – but he feared that they might work against Machanaud if the interview didn't go well tomorrow.

The forensics report revealed little. The blood tested was the boy's group, no semen deposits were found, and there were no startling fibre discoveries. Rock particles found in the blood confirmed the medical examiner's suspicion about the murder weapon, though no blood-stained rock had been found by the search team, nor the boy's shirt, and the few items of paper from the field and a man's torn jacket and shoe by the river bank looked too weathered to be connected. Still they'd been passed to forensics for checking.

With little or no forensics findings, the police investigation became more reliant on the timing of the attack and on eyewitnesses – which pointed back to Machanaud. But in spite of his protest to Poullain the day before that it was ridiculous to suspect Machanaud, he was just a troublesome drunkard and poacher – if Poullain's look of thunderous reproach was any gauge – Dominic feared that public opinion could rise swiftly against Machanaud. Like himself and Louis, Machanaud was from the outside, originally from the foothills of the Pyrenees, and had been in Bauriac less than three years. More than a few times, Dominic or others from the gendarmerie had been called to a local bar because of Machanaud's drunken antics. Machanaud would usually either want to sing or fight, or both, having warmed up for the evening's renditions with stories of his wartime exploits, how as a young lad of eighteen in the Resistance he tried to blow up a Nazi truck with vital supplies – but the truck had spun off the road and hit him and he'd ended up with a metal plate in his head. Most villagers thought he was half mad and treated him with a mixture of suspicion and contempt.

Perhaps the other leads would prove fruitful and divert attention away from Machanaud. When he'd phoned the gendarmerie earlier, Servan brought him up to date on progress: a green Alpha Romeo had been seen in Pourrières, the number taken, and they were now putting through a trace request with vehicle registration in Paris. The Lyon van was seen sixty kilometres away about the time of the attack, and no news yet on the passing traveller.

Dominic sat up. Filtering down through his thoughts, his summary notes finally gelled. He went back to the folder before the thought flow went, and wrote: *Distinct lack of forensic evidence. No other blood groups other than the boy's, no semen, no fibres. The weapon cannot be found, nor the boy's shirt. Whoever committed this crime was extremely careful. If we are to suspect Machanaud, then we also have to ask ourselves, 'Is he really the type to be this careful and meticulous?'*

Dominic scanned quickly back over the report. The time gap between the two attacks had introduced a new, puzzling perspective, but with no specific relevance to suspicion of Machanaud. Whoever had made the attack, the question was the same: where had they been in that time? No other area of flattened wheat had been discovered, and from the strength of body imprints where the attack was finally made, the Marseille team's view was that it had been occupied for no more than ten minutes. The supposition was therefore that beforehand the boy and his assailant had been by the riverbank, mostly obscured by trees and bushes from the bordering farm lane, or somewhere else.

The record had finished without Dominic noticing, the needle clicking repeatedly on the inner circle. Dominic took it off and put on Sam Cooke's 'Another Saturday Night', then came back on to the terrace. He closed his eyes for a moment as he lay down on the floor, then opened them again, letting the broad blanket of the sky and the mass of stars sink slowly through his consciousness, suffuse through his body until it touched every nerve end. Touched his soul. Solitude.

A single candle flickered at the back of his mind. Monique Rosselot's profile, partly in shadow against the dancing light, a raw essence of beauty and motherhood hoping and praying that her only son would live. He remembered in Algeria a woman at the souk in El Asnam. He never normally paid much attention to the local women, generally a nondescript lot covered from nose to toe in black sheets. This woman had been dressed the same, except that her eyes above her face mask had been large and captivating – and she'd met his stare for a second longer than was probably considered discreet. Her eyes laughed at him provocatively, hazel with green flecks, soulful, bright. Then she was gone, disappearing quickly among the market stalls and back-street warrens of the souk. Many times since he had wondered what her face looked like, images forming in the flames of the campfire or from the starry depths of the velvet sky during those long and lonely desert nights. But the image that was superimposed now, as the face veil was gently removed, was that of Monique Rosselot. He shook the image away.

Sam Cooke was wailing about finding a girl to help spend his money or else leaving town. It reminded Dominic of one of his last dates with Odette; the song had been playing at a fairground they'd visited in Draguignan. Another Saturday night. Bright lights, candyfloss, a fluffy baby-blue toy cat he'd won for her at the rifle range. But the single candle burned through, the sullen but proud profile half in shadow reflected against the glass. He found it hard to get the image of Monique Rosselot out of his mind.

8

Session 1. London, 16 February 1995

Stuart Capel looked anxiously at the door ahead. Through it he could hear only muted mumbling; only the occasional word could be picked up clearly. He leant forward keenly, his arms resting on his knees.

Around him were a mixture of diplomas – Dr David Lambourne, PhD, MR Psych – and theatre posters. A collection of magazines on a small coffee table. No receptionist, just an answerphone that would kick in. Only two calls the past fifteen minutes.

But despite Stuart's posture – every nerve and muscle tense, his jaw set tight – his eyes were dull and unfocused. Dulled by the nightmare of the past two months. Clinging to one last chance as his hands clasped and unclasped. Oh God, I hope this will help. *I hope this will help . . .*

'. . . and so you'll be twelve soon, Eyran. Is that right?'

'Yes, in April. The fifteenth.'

'And what would you like for your birthday?' David Lambourne asked. 'Any thoughts?'

'I don't know, really. I was going to get a surf board in San Diego.' Eyran drifted off for a second, scanning the ceiling. The couch he was lying on was old and overstuffed, with a fading floral print. It would have looked more at home in a country cottage than a psychiatrist's office in Holborn. 'Perhaps a new bike. Some more computer games.'

'Have you thought of asking for a pet? A dog, maybe?'

'No, not really. But the boy two doors away has got a red setter. We went playing in the fields with it a few days back.'

'Did you get on well with the boy?'

'Yes, sort of. His name's Kevin. He's two years older than me. He was asking a lot about San Diego, said that he'd like to go there.'

Fresh-faced, light brown hair. A few faint freckles across the bridge of his nose. It was difficult for Lambourne to relate the boy before him to what he knew from the report on his desk: *Accident victim. Nineteen-day coma. Temporal- and parietal-lobe trauma. Both parents lost in the same accident.* And now possible psychological discordance: increasingly violent dreams and development of a secondary character to push away acceptance of his parents' death.

'Have you ever had a pet before?' asked Lambourne.

'No. But I like them, dogs more than cats.'

'Maybe you should ask your uncle for one. With all of those fields around, it could be fun. The perfect place for a dog.' It had come out of his discussion with Stuart Capel the day before: new object attachments to help diminish what Eyran had lost. 'And at school. Any friends yet? I understand that you started at the beginning of last week.'

'Only one. Simon. He was at my primary school from before in England. I didn't know him so well then, but we're becoming friendlier now.'

'And how are you getting on with Tessa?'

'Okay. But she's a few years younger than me. She has her own friends.'

Lambourne looked down at his notes briefly, was about to ask another question about home or school, trying to gauge how Eyran was settling in, when Eyran continued.

'My other old friends from before are too far away. Though I went over to Broadhurst Farm the other day with Kevin. Being there with his dog reminded me of Sarah and Salman, her labrador. We used to play there years ago, before I went to America. They were in one of my first dreams.'

Too early. Lambourne didn't want to explore the dreams yet. His first aim was to put Eyran at ease, establish comfortable ground: birthday, presents, friends, possibly a pet. From his two-hour meeting with Stuart Capel the previous day, he'd planned his guideposts well: he knew that the mention of a pet would trigger Eyran mentioning one friend, school another. But the past kept interjecting – San Diego, old friends and memories – spoiling the rhythm.

'How are you settling in at your uncle's house? I understand you're right out in the country. It must be nice.'

'Yes, it's very nice. My room looks over fields at the back.'

'So, they've given you one of the best rooms in the house.'

Faint smile from Eyran. The first so far. Stuart Capel had told him Eyran smiled rarely, uneasily, was generally slow to respond. It was one of Stuart's main areas of concern. 'And you've got all your favourite things around you . . .'

Lambourne continued building on areas of familiarity – but the answers gradually became more stilted and relied on past reference. Understand-able. Eyran had only been in the house six weeks; his main memory of it was from when he lived with his parents nearby. Eyran was more preoccupied with the old house, its position and distance from his uncle's house.

'It's only four or five miles away, and Broadhurst Farm is just at the back. When I look out of my bedroom window now, there's a hill in the distance. It's not too far on the other side of that.'

'And that's where you went with Kevin the other day? That's quite a distance to walk.'

'It wasn't too bad. I wanted to see how it had changed from before. Perhaps I might have bumped into some of my old friends there. It was strange, the pond was much smaller than I remembered. And in one of my dreams, it was enormous.'

Present. Past. And now the dreams again. It was a hopscotch. Each time Lambourne dragged him to the present, Eyran leapt back.

'The week before, I drove past there with Uncle Stuart. But we just looked up from the field behind that leads up to the copse. We didn't go in.'

'I see.' Stuart Capel had mentioned the significance of the copse, that at least two of Eyran's dreams had taken place there. But Lambourne didn't want to let on that he knew. It was important that Eyran revealed the significance in his own words. Although Lambourne had planned to delay exploring the dreams until the second session, one area of them might be worth exploring now.

'In the dreams, who do you see most? Your mother or your father – or do they both appear equally?'

'My father appears more. In the first two dreams, my mother didn't appear at all. Then when I did finally see her, she was distant, out of reach. In another dream, I wasn't even sure whether I saw her or not. It was misty, and I thought she was just ahead of my father, but I might have just been imagining it. It wasn't very clear.'

'And do either of them speak to you in the dreams?'

'My father has twice, my mother never. On the one occasion I was sure I saw her, she was turned from me, walking away. And I was trying to catch up.'

'I see.' Lambourne glanced at his notes. One area where the dreams offered a convenient allegory; it would have been awkward to ask straight out which parent Eyran felt closest to.

'Did you catch up with your parents in any of the dreams?'

'No. My father was closest, but he always remained just out of reach.'

'Do you think there's any reason why your father appears more than your mother in the dreams? Were you closer to him?'

'When I was younger, no. But as I got older, I felt I could talk to him more. You know, if I was having trouble with someone picking a fight, some problem with my bike, or selection for the school football team. I just felt he'd know more about those things than my mum.'

'So you went to him for help, confided in him more. But you felt equally close to both of them?'

'Yes.'

'And did you love them both equally – Mum and Dad?' Stupid question, but it was necessary to have Eyran say it, admit the attachment before he started suggesting other object attachments.

'Yes.'

'And do you miss them?'

Longer pause this time; Eyran's brow was slightly furrowed. 'Yes, of course . . .'

Clasping. Unclasping.

The muted voices through the door after a while made Stuart's mind drift. Back through the nightmare which had finally brought him to David Lambourne's office.

Hands clasped behind his back as he looked out at the view: two large palm trees like sentinels on either side of the garden. A faint mist rising from the swimming pool. December in Southern California.

Moment's break from packing boxes with Jeremy's personal papers and mementoes. Behind him, Helena, Jeremy's Mexican maid, saying something he didn't quite catch. On arrival, she'd grasped his hand extended in greeting in both of hers as she looked deep into his eyes and expressed her sorrow. He could tell that she had been crying, and as she kept grip a second longer, willing home her emotions with eyes brimming with watery compassion, she burst into tears again. He'd cried too much on the flight over and since, identifying the bodies of his brother and Allison in the morgue – seeing Eyran lying helpless and prostrate in the hospital bed – to be able to join her.

Death. The morning mist somehow mirrored his mood. Looking through the sliding windows towards the pool and patio; happier times. Jeremy at the barbecue, Eyran and Tessa swimming. Allison and Amanda sipping Long Island iced teas and preparing a salad. He snapped himself away, back to packing boxes. Another minefield of memories: Jeremy's diplomas from Cambridge and his bar exams, photos with his old rugby team in Hertfordshire, him and Jeremy sitting at a restaurant table in Mykonos, one of their few holidays together. They'd been in their early twenties and Stuart couldn't even remember the name of Jeremy's girlfriend at the time who had taken the picture. Two boxes had already been filled with a mixture of photos, papers, mementoes and small ornaments. How long did it take to tidy away the personal effects of a lifetime? Leave the room neat and tidy, so no memories, no trace, remained?

The day before had been a nightmare, a blizzard of paperwork and officialdom. Forms to be filled out at the police station and morgue, more at the hospital, then on to Jeremy's employers, Hassler and Gertz, to deal with Jeremy's probate and insurance details.

It seemed that all he'd done since arriving in California was sign papers, autograph his brother's aftermath. Perhaps it was all part of the grieving process. 'You've now witnessed and signed fifteen papers relating to your brother's death, surely you can now finally accept that he is dead.' Hadn't he read somewhere that the grieving process didn't start until *after* acceptance?

Then when Stuart went finally into Eyran's room, the thought of Eyran at that moment in the hospital deep in coma, barely clinging to life, gripped him hard. Posters of Pamela Anderson, the Power Rangers, *Jurassic Park*, the Daytona racetrack. It was amazing how quickly they grew up. Had he started thinking of girls when he'd been eleven? From the stereo and a small stack of CDs to one side, he picked out four: Janet Jackson, Seal, Madonna, UB40. Quick scan of the rest of the room – probably the last time he would see it: a semi-precious rocks and minerals collection, some model sports cars, an SX25 computer with a small box of disks, a signed baseball bat, a model dolphin from San Diego SeaWorld, a large corner box full of assorted toys – many obviously from when Eyran was much younger.

Stuart bit his lip as he packed. But at least this duty carried with it a bit more hope. Mementoes for the living.

Hands clasping.

Clutched tight to the report as Eyran's surgeon in California, Dr Torrens, delivered his stark prognosis.

Traumatic intracranial haematomas. Two small parietal-lobe haematomas. Larger temporal-lobe haematoma. Risk of oedema. Irregular EEG recording.

But which one had carried the possibility of later psychological disturbance? thought Stuart. *Which one?*

At the time, all he'd hoped and prayed for had been Eyran awakening; he hadn't looked beyond. Torrens had mentioned only the possibility of later disorientation of direction, topography and shapes due to the temporal-lobe haematoma. Usually hardly noticeable outside of reading detailed maps or directions, or sorting out complex puzzles. 'If that's all we're facing, be thankful.'

In the end there had been two EEG activity recordings – ninety-four hours and seventeen hours respectively – before Eyran finally waking up. In answer to his key questions – chances of survival, how long the coma might last and degrees of damage that might persist if and when Eyran finally awoke – Dr Torrens seemed reluctant to speculate, hiding mainly behind textbook statistics from a cross-section of American hospitals. Stuart recalled that 14 per cent of coma victims made a full recovery and another 14 per cent made recoveries with impairments so slight as to be unnoticeable, though a daunting 49 per cent did not survive at all, the mid ground taken up by cases ranging from moderate disablement to complete vegetative states.

Easy to get lost in the medical terminology, Stuart thought. Acceptance by conditioning. Concern and grief, all so real when focused on a loved one, swallowed up as part of the grander scale of general statistics affecting all coma patients. The first shock had come when learning that Eyran's heart had stopped for fifty-four seconds when he was first admitted. Stuart had asked if that might have contributed to the coma but Torrens felt that the direct head injuries and cranial haematomas were likely to be the prime causes.

Clasping – as a nurse had led him finally to Eyran's bedside, an image to match with Torrens' stark report. Tubes and wires feeding and monitoring, Eyran's face grey and wan. He found it hard to relate to the Eyran he remembered, so full of curiosity and enthusiasm – and suddenly a day out in his sports car came to mind, Eyran at his side, cheeks rosy with the crisp air.

Eyran had been only six, and they were driving up Highgate Hill. Stuart pointed theatrically towards the cemetery. 'Do you know who's buried there? Karl Marx!' To which Eyran's eyes lit up with enthusiasm. 'Was he one of the Marx brothers?' It had remained part of Stuart's dinner-party repertoire for almost two years.

Talk to him, Torrens had said. Familiar voices, shared memories. Stuart started with the Karl Marx incident, then went on to relate another story from when Eyran had been seven and asked him what was the rudest word. At first, he'd tried to avoid it by saying he didn't know, but Eyran was persistent. 'But you must know lots of rude words at your age, Uncle Stuart.' Knowing that he couldn't easily escape, but not wishing to get into trouble with Jeremy for teaching Eyran rude words, he'd finally offered 'codswollop'.

'Is that the rudest word?'

'Yes, absolutely. It's a terrible swear-word – never to be used.'

'But is it the rudest, rudest?'

'Yes, it's the rudest, rudest. You must never, *ever* say codswollop.'

A moment's thought as Eyran compared with what he'd heard in the school playground. 'Is it ruder than fuck?'

Jeremy had burst out laughing when Stuart'd told him, finding Stuart's vain attempt to preserve his son's already tainted innocence particularly amusing; yet another dinner-party anecdote. Eyran too had been let in on the joke later when he was old enough. But Stuart found relating the story to Eyran, hearing only the echo of his own voice, unsettling. Like a comedian on stage with no audience.

And so half an hour later when his one-man dialogue ran out of steam, he turned to the CDs he'd brought from Eyran's room and let Janet Jackson take over. *Familiar voices, familiar music.* Torrens had arranged for a player.

But now listening to the muted mumbling beyond Lambourne's door, he recalled with clarity the feeling that had crept over him in that instant. Dreading the moment – if and when his tearful wishes of Eyran awakening were fulfilled – when he would have to tell Eyran his parents were dead.

And when that moment did finally come, the haunted, lost look in Eyran's eyes – still lingering days and even weeks later. He should have guessed then that a part of Eyran would always cling on, refuse to accept.

David Lambourne flicked back through Torrens' report. So, what did he know after the first session? The first aim had been to judge Eyran's responsiveness.

Made just four days after Eyran had revived from his coma, the report showed 10 to 15 per cent impairment on conventional thought and speech response. If anything, there had been improvement since then; Eyran's response had been slow to very few questions. Though perhaps when he entered the more complex and problematical areas of Eyran's dreams, responsiveness would drop. The barriers would go back up.

Thirty-eight per cent below average on IQ puzzles. Lambourne couldn't help much there: the best indicators would come from maths results at his new school. Or perhaps he could get some standard tests from St Bart's for the Capels to do at home.

But the main problem was Eyran's increasingly violent dreams, and the key question: were they a by-product of the accident and the coma, some chemical imbalance causing dementia, or a defence mechanism of Eyran's subconscious, unwilling to accept that his parents were dead?

With the first, Lambourne realized he'd have limited control, swept along on the changing tide of the condition, leaving him little range within which to wield influence. Damage limitation. But if it was the latter, he'd have far more control, and at first glance the analysis was straightforward: Eyran couldn't accept that his parents were dead, so his subconscious had manifested various scenarios, played out through his dreams, where he could find them alive. Textbook Freud denial/mourning/object attachment.

Though Lambourne had conducted his main studies in the Freudian school, he liked to think that he'd kept an open mind on later theories and papers – some of them contradictory to Freud's principles. Jung, Winnicott, Adler, Eysenck, and then the later radicals Lacan, Laing and Rollo May. Twenty-two years in practice, seventeen of them at St Bart's, Lambourne prided himself on keeping up to date with his papers and readings, felt that he was better equipped than most to pick and choose at the smorgasbord of psychoanalysis, return with the plate most suited to his patient.

Lambourne looked around his office. The furniture had hardly changed since St Bart's. The same old floral-pattern sofa, his upright padded-seat chair, a rolled-top walnut desk, the dark oak coffee table with a few magazines strategically scattered. Stuffy, country-cottage atmosphere which he felt put patients at ease.

Or perhaps it was all just a replica, a home away from home modelled on the Buckinghamshire country house he'd left his wife in their divorce settlement six years previously. Now he was just a weekend father to their two daughters. He'd learnt more about object loss during the divorce than through the years of study and practice; for the first time he'd actually felt what his patients fought to describe in bland monotones. He could help solve their problems, but not his own.

He'd left St Bart's a year after the divorce and decided to combine costs by living in. He loved the theatre, and the main theatre areas and Covent Garden were a short stroll away, past old book, stamp and curio shops, and one in particular he'd discovered specializing in old theatre posters.

He never used the armchair, always the straight-backed chair. The armchair made him appear too relaxed, distant from his patients; while in the hard-back chair, he invariably ended up leaning forward. He looked more interested in them. Throughout the first fourteen years of his practice, he'd smoked a pipe, but, with the more responsible age of doctors taking the lead with non-smoking, he had given up. He immediately found his pipe hand, his left, at a complete loss, and so sucked at an empty pipe during sessions for another three years, felt that chewing on the mouthpiece helped him concentrate – until one woman patient had been bold enough to question what he was doing. As he'd explained, her puzzled look had made it clear just who of the two of them should be on the couch. So now there was no more pipe, just one orphaned hand.

Jojo? Eyran's imaginary dream friend who always promised he could find Eyran's parents. A simple invention to support non-acceptance of their death, or a possibly threatening secondary personality? Lambourne wondered.

One of the key factors was going to be separation from reality, if any illusions in the dreams started crossing over into Eyran's thoughts while awake. And if they did, to what extent might Eyran accept or adopt them. At present, they were at arm's length. But Jojo trampling through Eyran's conscious thoughts could be disastrous.

There was also the maze of object attachments to fight through: not just Eyran's loss of his parents, but attachments and memories about the house in San Diego, their previous house in England and old play areas – which perhaps due to their closeness to his uncle's house were resurging strongly.

Finding his way through was not going to be easy. He would need to follow the threads carefully in order to draw out Eyran's perception of Jojo in the right way, then press hard to break Eyran away from Jojo's subconscious influence. Yet too hard and all trust and patient transference would be lost.

It was going to be a delicate tightrope, and Eyran would probably resist him all the way. No child wanted to face that their parents were dead, and the dreams and Jojo were probably the only sanctuary Eyran had left.

9

The courtyard was in Moorish style, in the Panier quarter of Marseille. Two sides framing the courtyard were the house itself on three floors, the third the blank wall of the adjacent building. The fourth, and the entrance to the courtyard, were large solid-wood double gates studded with black iron, with a small door with buzzer inset in one side: the brothel's main entrance and all that was visible from the narrow street. Émile Vacheret's establishment was discreet, its façade anonymous, as its many regulars preferred.

The centrepiece of the courtyard was a small fountain edged with blue and white mosaic tiling, and window sills throughout the building had the same pattern edging. Some white doves played and strutted in and around the fountain. While he waited, Alain Duclos looked out through the ground-floor french windows towards the fountain and courtyard.

Prostitution was legal, so the anonymity of the building was for the benefit of clients and for the small side-attractions offered to clients which weren't so legal. The rooms' cleaners, servants and the waiters in the bar were all young boys, mostly from Morocco and Algeria, between the ages of twelve and nineteen – though the youngest age on any identity card was sixteen, in the event of a police raid. Vacheret paid heavily to the local police each month. The boys' functions as waiters and room cleaners were mostly a cover; they were also there for the clients' pleasure, if so required. For heterosexual clients, which were indeed 70 per cent of Vacheret's trade, a choice of girls would be paraded in, and the boys just served drinks and made the beds afterwards.

Duclos sat on the bed as Vacheret introduced two new boys who had arrived in the last week, as possible alternatives to his favourite of the last few visits, Jahlep. The two boys wore claret-red baggy harem trousers and round-necked white shirts. One was very young, possibly twelve, while the other was closer to fourteen or fifteen. Duclos concentrated on the younger one as Vacheret explained that he was a mulatto from Martinique, exquisite light brown eyes, delicate complexion, brand new the last week, hardly touched. Vacheret might as well have been trying to sell him a used car, Duclos thought. True, the boy was exquisite, cream-brown skin, just the age he liked. But he just couldn't concentrate and get up any enthusiasm.

Noticing his hesitancy, Vacheret commented, 'What's wrong, you want a drink while you decide, or is there something private you want to ask me about them? Shall I send the boys away?'

'I'm not sure. Perhaps. Give me a minute.'

Vacheret ushered the boys away and sat down beside Duclos. 'Have you decided on Jahlep again, but you didn't want to say so in front of those two? Or are you just undecided between Jahlep and this new boy? Perhaps you could try the two together?' Vacheret raised his eyebrows hopefully.

Beads of sweat stood out on Duclos' forehead and he looked troubled, his eyes darting as he contemplated the floor. 'Look, I'm sorry. I can't think clearly about the boys for the moment. Maybe later. But there's something on my mind, something I'd like to ask you about first.'

Vacheret nodded, suddenly pensive, barely containing a half-smile; he was sure that Duclos was about to inquire about some bizarre practice or fantasy, something he'd been too coy to mention before. It always tickled him, this part, clients admitting their secret sexual desires; it was almost like being a psychiatrist or priest, finally clients got around to what was *really* troubling them.

But as Duclos explained what he wanted, Vacheret's expression became slowly graver. This wasn't what he expected.

Crossing the courtyard as he left twenty minutes later, Duclos could see the misty shape of a girl rolling up one black stocking through the net curtains at a window to one side. She had wild red hair and was naked except for a garter belt and the one stocking, and was sitting on the edge of the bed facing the window. Because she was close to the window, she saw him and smiled, gradually parting her legs wider. Duclos turned away and headed for the courtyard door. If he'd stayed, she would probably have put on a little show for him, but he wasn't interested.

He phoned Vacheret that night and, as arranged, Vacheret gave him a name and a time and place to make contact.

The room where Machanaud was taken to was at the back of the gendarmerie. The main window was open with the heat, its grey wooden shutters closed. Only faint slats of sunlight filtered in, so the main light, a football-sized glass sphere screwed to the ceiling, had been switched on. The rooms at the back, away from the traffic and looking on to a car park shared with the town hall, were quiet.

Machanaud had arrived at 11.30 a.m., as scheduled. But Poullain had made him wait in the room on his own for almost twenty minutes. Dominic timed and dated an interview form and made notes as Poullain started with Machanaud's main background details. Age: thirty-nine; town of birth: Saint-Girons; place of residence: Seillons; occupation: farm labourer. Past convictions? Machanaud could recall two past convictions, but not the dates, so Dominic took the details from the past charge sheets: drunk and disorderly in March of that year and poaching the previous October.

Machanaud looked older than his age, Dominic always thought: closer to mid or late forties. His skin was weathered and pitted; his thick brown hair long and unkempt and heavily greased back in an effort to make it look tidier, though all too often a lank forelock would break loose and hang across his face. When drunk and in one of his more rebellious moods, the one eye that wasn't covered by hair gave the impression of leering wildly.

Poullain waited for Dominic to stop writing, then started with a general summary of Machanaud's activities on 18 August, most of it purely skimming details from their interview of the day before. Then Poullain went back to the beginning, going into more specific timings. 'So you left after finishing work at Raulin's farm at about eleven, is that right?'

'No, closer to twelve.'

Poullain was testing. Machanaud had told them twice before that it was twelve. Eleven was closer to the time they thought he had left from their interviews the day before both with Raulin and Henri at Bar Fontainouille, who seemed to remember Machanaud calling in and leaving earlier. 'And you went straight on to Bar Fontainouille from there?'

'Yes, that's right.'

'How long would that take, do you think?'

'About fifteen, twenty minutes.'

Poullain spent the next ten minutes running through Machanaud's movements: Bar Fontainouille at 12.15 p.m., leaving just before 2 p.m. for Gilbert Albrieux's farm where he'd planted some vines the February past. Albrieux apparently hadn't been there to see him, but after a quick check of the vines Machanaud claimed he sat on a stone wall and had a sandwich. After half an hour, he then headed off to Léon's.

Dominic felt the tension building with each question, or maybe it was

83

because he knew what was coming: Poullain was slowly circling in for the kill.

'So, it's what – only ten or twelve minutes from Albrieux's to Léon's bar. What time did you arrive there?'

'About two-thirty-five, two-forty. But I only stayed about an hour, because I had to be back at Raulin's for the late shift at four o'clock.'

Dominic looked at his notes. Effectively all that Machanaud admitted to was being on his own for about half an hour after two o'clock. Their various interviews from the day before told a different story. Raulin didn't recall seeing him after 11 a.m. and, although Henri at Bar Fontainouille wasn't sure what time Machanaud had arrived, he was certain of the time he'd left, at about 1 p.m., because of when he started serving set lunches that day. Léon too wasn't sure what time Machanaud had called in, but they had the firm sighting from Madame Veillan which would have put Machanaud at Léon's at about 3.15 p.m. That left almost two hours unaccounted for between 1 p.m. and 3 p.m.

'Did you go anywhere on the way back to Raulin's?'

'Just to pick up some tobacco, but that's just a few doors from Léon's. It only took minutes.'

'And in all of your travels on that day, did you happen to see a young boy?'

The question threw Machanaud. All of his answers had been carefully thought out to defend their suspicion of him poaching. Why else would the questions be angled so insistently around the two hours he'd been by the river? The continued questioning, the fact that they seemed to be taking the issue so seriously, for the first time started him wondering. 'A boy? What has that got to do with anything?'

'I don't know, you tell us.' Poullain's easy manner, asking questions at a steady pace, suddenly went. 'What time did you meet him – half past one, two o'clock? Where was it you first picked him up: in the village, or near the lane?'

Machanaud was perplexed. He ruffled his hair uneasily. 'I was at Bar Fontainouille, I had at least two drinks with Henri himself serving at the bar. I couldn't possibly have met anyone then.'

'Except that you left the Fontainouille an hour earlier, at one o'clock. And yes, you went to have lunch with your knapsack. But instead of going to Albrieux's place, you went down to the river by Breuille's land. And on the way there, you met the boy.'

Machanaud blinked nervously and looked down, then across briefly towards Dominic's notes. So they knew he'd been down by the river at Breuille's, probably guessed that he'd been poaching. But why the insistence about this boy? 'I don't understand why you're asking all this. I don't know anything about a boy.'

'Oh, but I think you do.' Poullain went in for the kill; he leant forward, his body rigid with intent. 'Your account of the entire day is complete fabrication. Not one bit of it is true. The only thing we know for sure is that you were seen at three o'clock by Madame Veillan coming out of the lane at Breuille's farm.' Poullain's voice was rising feverishly. 'The same place where, minutes beforehand, a young boy was left for dead with his skull smashed in!'

With a sickening sensation, it suddenly dawned on Machanaud why Poullain had been asking about the boy. He'd heard about the attack, it was the talk of the village, but there had been no mention of where. 'Are you trying to tell me that this boy was found on the lane to Breuille's farm?'

Machanaud's tone of incredulity only served to anger Poullain deeper. 'You know he was, because that's where you left him – just after you smashed his head in with a rock!'

Machanaud shook his head wildly. 'No! I told you. I had nothing to do with that boy, I never touched him.'

'So are you now trying to say that you were there and saw the boy – but you never touched him?'

Machanaud was confused, his voice breaking with exasperation. 'No, no. I *never* saw the boy. I know nothing about him. I went from the Fontainouille, a short break for lunch, then straight on to Léon's.'

'Léon doesn't remember seeing you until at least three-fifteen.' It was a bluff, but Poullain was more confident of Madame Veillan's time-keeping than Léon's. 'And Henri says that you arrived at eleven and left about one.'

'That's impossible,' Machanaud spluttered desperately. 'I was at Raulin's until twelve.'

'Raulin says that he didn't see you after eleven, and that's the time he has entered in his book for you finishing that day.'

'There was some extra work on the bottom land. He probably didn't see me there.'

Poullain ignored it. 'Henri knows for sure you left at one o'clock, because that's when he starts preparing lunches. And between then and

Madame Veillan seeing you leave the lane – that's almost two hours.' He leant closer to Machanaud, his tone low and menacing. 'Two hours in which you calmly took your pleasure with this boy, before deciding that you'd have to kill him. What did you do to keep him quiet in the meantime – tie him up?'

Machanaud was cold with fear. He had been shaking his head at Poullain's bombardment, stunned by the sudden turnaround of events; surely they couldn't really believe that *he* had attacked this boy. If it was just a ploy to get him to admit to poaching, they'd succeeded. He was so frightened, he'd run for any sanctuary. 'Okay, I admit it, I was there. But I know nothing about the boy – I was poaching.'

'I see.' Poullain looked down thoughtfully, drawing a deep breath before looking up again. 'And how long were you there?'

'Two hours.'

'And have you been to that stretch of river before?'

'Yes, two or three times, I don't remember exactly.'

'Any particular reason why you favour there?'

'The fish are no better than elsewhere – but Breuille is away. Less chance of getting caught, and even if I am, he's not around to press charges.' Machanaud risked a hesitant smile.

Poullain considered this for a moment. 'So now you're trying to tell us that all of this morning's subterfuge, all of this lying, was purely to cover up the fact that you were poaching. Even though you know Breuille's away and therefore charges can't be pressed.' Poullain looked disgustedly towards Dominic. He waved one hand dramatically. 'Pah! It is not even remotely believable.'

A swathe of hair had fallen across Machanaud's face. He cut a sad picture, like a lost and bewildered animal. A lamb to Poullain's slaughter. His eyes darted frantically. 'But Marius Caurin is still around caretaking the land – I even saw him head out at one point on his tractor. He could have seen me.'

'Even if we accept this ridiculous story that you were poaching, you expect us to believe that you spent two hours calmly fishing while a young boy was savagely raped and assaulted not metres away – and you saw absolutely *nothing*?'

Machanaud looked pleadingly towards Dominic, clutching for any possible support. Dominic looked away and back to his notes. Whatever misgivings he might have about Poullain's interviewing tactics, it was the first golden rule: unless a two-pronged assault had been previously agreed, the interview witness remained silent. He had already made his thoughts clear to Poullain about suspicion of Machanaud. Any comment about what arose in the interview itself would have to wait till later.

Machanaud was desperate, spluttering. 'The river bank dips down at points. The lane is partly obscured by trees and bushes. Somebody else could have come along without me seeing.'

'Yes, they could. But that same person couldn't possibly have stayed on the lane for all that time without the risk of someone coming along and seeing them. And yet if they hid in the only place possible – down by the riverbank – you would have seen them. But the real reason that you saw nobody else is that there was only one person down by the river bank – *you*.'

'No . . . no . . .'

'And it was there that you chose as your hiding place, a place you know well from past visits, while you molested the boy. Concealed from anyone passing. Twice you sexually assaulted him; then later, to cover your tracks, afraid that he would talk, you picked up a rock and –'

'*No!* . . .' Machanaud rose to his feet, slamming one hand on the table. His head had been shaking slowly, his low and repeated groans of 'no' finally rising to a crescendo.

Poullain let out a final exasperated breath, looking towards Dominic. 'Just take him away, I'm sick of hearing his lies.'

'What do you want me to do with him?'

'Put him in the holding cell for a few hours, let him cool his heels. Perhaps he'll remember something with a bit more sense. We'll decide then if we're going to hold him longer.'

The arrangement was that Duclos meet the man in front of the Fort Saint-Nicolas in Marseille. From there, they could walk across Boulevard Charles-Livon and into the Parc du Pharo to discuss their business. At dusk, the number of park strollers would be thinning out; it should be quite private.

The time and place had been arranged through Vacheret, and the man was known as Chapeau, obviously not his real name. Duclos had already waited ten minutes, gradually becoming more anxious, dwelling stronger on what he was waiting there for. Conscious suddenly of every small sound and movement around – the wind ruffling a flag on the fort, a stray cat tugging at a bag in a nearby bush, the shuffle of people approaching and walking by – uncomfortable if someone looked at him as they passed, catching his eye. For God's sake, hurry up. He couldn't take much more of this waiting.

While he was distracted for a moment by a coach that had pulled up in front, collecting a stream of tourists shepherded aboard by their guide, a man was suddenly at his side. He seemed to emerge from nowhere among the throng leaving the fort, and Duclos was slightly startled. He hadn't seen him approach.

'Your name is Alain?' the man inquired.

'Yes.'

'We have some business to discuss, I believe.'

Duclos merely nodded. It was obviously Chapeau. There was something familiar about him, but Duclos wasn't totally sure. 'Were you across the road a moment ago, looking over?'

'Yes, I was.' Chapeau didn't offer to explain why, which unsettled Duclos further. They walked in silence towards the park. Duclos took the opportunity to study him closer. No more than thirty, skin quite dark, tight-knit curly dark hair, heavy-set and jowly; probably Corsican judging by the accent, Duclos guessed. One eye was slightly bloodshot and yellowed in the corner, as if he'd been hit close to it. Or perhaps it was a permanent ailment. The nickname intrigued Duclos; the man wasn't wearing a hat.

'What is it your friend wants done?' asked Chapeau.

At the mention of a friend Duclos was wary just how much had already been discussed. 'What did Vacheret tell you? Did he explain the problem and what needed to be done?'

'No. Just that you had a friend with a problem, nothing more. You know what Vacheret is like, afraid of his own shadow. Doesn't like to get involved.'

Duclos grimaced weakly. Good. He had spun a story to Vacheret of a married friend who played both sides getting into trouble with a rent boy and his pimp. The pimp was threatening blackmail by informing his friend's wife. Some muscle was required to warn him off. Duclos knew that Vacheret had *milieu* contacts and would be able to recommend someone. The pimp was streetwise, so it should also be someone with a reasonable reputation, perhaps a few hits to his credit, otherwise the warning would carry no weight. Thankfully, Vacheret had been worried about complicity, didn't want to know too many details. '*I'll just give you a number, the rest is up to you.*' For the same reason, Vacheret had obviously said little to Chapeau. If any details had conflicted, Duclos would have covered by claiming that for obvious reasons he hadn't wanted Vacheret to know everything. Now none of that was necessary, except to maintain the subterfuge that the boy who was lying in hospital in Aix-en-Provence was a rent boy, and that his friend was responsible for the attack.

'Why did your friend attack him in the first place?' Chapeau asked.

'Blackmail. My friend is married; this is one of his little indulgences on the side that he tells me he's only given in to a few times and was trying to get over. But this time he got caught out – the boy was threatening to tell.'

'And your friend didn't finish the boy off?'

'No.'

Chapeau pondered over this information. 'So now he's afraid the boy will wake up and tell?'

Duclos nodded. They'd walked almost 200 metres into the park. A few evening strollers passed, staccato breaks in a conversation they were both being careful to keep out of anyone else's earshot. At times, the pauses were unsettling; Chapeau left long gaps after people had passed.

'Why the hospital at Aix?' Chapeau asked.

'They were driving out of Marseille into the country, and they got into an argument. It just happened that Aix was the nearest town – so the boy was taken to the main hospital on Avenue des Tamaris.'

'What's the boy's name?'

'Javi. But it's just a nickname. I don't think my friend knows the boy's real name.'

'And has he known him long?'

'I don't think so. Just a few months, at most.'

Another silence. Something didn't add up, thought Chapeau. Though he thought he knew what it was. As usual, Vacheret had been tight-lipped, except in answer to two simple questions: how was this Alain known to him? A client. For the girls or boys? Boys! And now Alain was talking about problems with a rent boy and a friend. It could be just a case of all queers together, but it was too much of a coincidence for comfort. Chapeau was sure the friend was pure invention – it was this Alain himself who had the problem with the boy and now wanted him killed. But there was no point in confronting him and possibly frightening off a good paying client. More fun to see, if pushed, if he still clung to the story. 'Your friend likes fucking young boys, does he? What's wrong – can't he get it up for his wife any more?'

'I don't know, you'd have to ask him yourself.' The irritation in Duclos' voice was barely concealed. He bit back, hoping to pique Chapeau a little. 'How did you get the nickname? I don't see a hat.'

'No, that's true, you don't.' Chapeau smiled wryly, as if he was about to elaborate, then had suddenly decided against it. They walked in silence for a second. Chapeau let out a long breath. 'Hospitals are risky. It's going to cost extra – 7,000 francs.'

Duclos went pale. Even at what Vacheret had estimated 5,000–6,000 francs, it had been a fortune: over half a year's salary and a third of his savings. Now it was going to cost more. 'I'm not sure if my friend can afford that. He was expecting it to be less.'

'There's people around in a hospital, more risk of being seen, some sort of diversion will probably have to be created. I'll have to visit at least once beforehand to work out what that diversion might be. It's not worth doing under 7,000'.

'But the boy's half dead already. All you have to do is sneak in and cut off his life support, or put a hand over his mouth. My friend even knows the room he's in and the layout.'

Chapeau's brow furrowed. 'So your friend has actually been there?'

Duclos faltered, looking away for a second as a young couple passed. The memories of the day before came flooding back. He'd known from the outset that it would be hard to skirt around the issue; it was vital to pass on detailed information so that Chapeau didn't start phoning the hospital. The only way his imaginary friend would know that information was if he'd actually been in the room. 'Yes – at first he thought he might be able to deal with the problem himself.'

'How close did he get?'

Heartbeats. The nightmare was still vivid. The sound of his own heartbeat and pulse almost in time with the bleep from the life support machine. Stepping closer . . . reaching out. *Sounds in the corridor. A moment's pause as he went to put his hand over the boy's mouth. Voices outside getting closer, louder.* 'He was actually inside the room when he got disturbed.'

Chapeau's tone was slightly incredulous. 'What? Your friend gets a second chance at it – and still he can't manage to finish the boy off?'

Fighting to control the trembling as his hand closed in, feeling for a second the boy's shallow breath on his palm. Warm vapour, cool against his sweat. Indecision. Then quickly retracted . . . sudden panic as he heard voices almost upon him . . . 'I told you, he was disturbed. What else could he do?' Duclos stammered.

'I don't know. You tell me.' Chapeau half smiled. 'Sounds to me as if your friend's a bit of a gutless shit.'

90

Duclos didn't answer, turned away, biting at his lip. Coming out of the room, the worst part had been realizing that the people outside had already passed; he could have stayed a moment longer. He even thought for a moment of going back inside – but his nerve had gone. He had been close, *so close*.

Chapeau savoured his discomfort for a moment before commenting more philosophically, 'Still, I suppose if it wasn't for friends like that, there'd be no need for people like me. Shall we conclude matters?'

It took another ten minutes for them to run through the other details: room number, position and floor, best timing, payment arrangements. Chapeau took the point of the urgency of the situation; at any moment the boy could wake up. He would try and make a reconnaissance of the hospital, work out a diversion and hopefully execute the plan all in the same day: tomorrow.

They were coming to a point in the park where both the marina and the old harbour could be viewed: a succession of white masts speared the skyline, stretching back towards the town. Again it reminded Duclos that this was his holiday; he should have been out sailing on the Vallons' Jonquet '42, the wind in his hair, then afterwards grilled sea bream or swordfish washed down with a glass of chilled white wine in a café overlooking the old harbour. Instead he was negotiating murder and being taunted by this Neanderthal prick, who was also going to take almost half his savings for the privilege. But hopefully the whole sad saga would soon be over. That was what he was paying for. The thought of the freedom ahead, of not having to go through this nightmare again, made it all worthwhile. Means to an end. He took a deep, refreshing breath of the salty air of the harbour.

As they concluded, Duclos asked how the boy was going to be killed, but Chapeau said that he wouldn't know till after the first visit. Chapeau had given nothing away. Twenty minutes of conversation and Duclos knew nothing about the man; he was still the same shadowy figure as when they'd entered the park.

Chapeau asked if he was heading back towards the fort, but Duclos said he wanted to enjoy the last rays of sunset over the harbour. Truth was, he couldn't bear to stay in Chapeau's company a moment longer. The man made his skin crawl. Duclos found a bench near the apex of the harbour walk as Chapeau headed back. A part of him felt relieved at the action he'd taken, but yet another felt strangely uneasy.

Had Chapeau suspected him of lying? He'd kept everything as remote as possible: the friend, a disagreement with a rent boy, the nickname. It was unlikely Chapeau would tie anything in with the recent newspaper article, even if he had seen it. And with the depth of detail provided about the room's position and best timing, he doubted Chapeau would call the hospital. Surely it was unlikely that all his precautions would collapse? The thought of what Chapeau might do in response sent a shiver through his body.

Duclos looked away from the harbour view for a moment, watching Chapeau's figure as it receded into the distance, faintly silhouetted against the dying light. And for a while his strong will to believe he'd taken the right action fought hard against the fear of what new horrors he might have introduced.

Dominic was called to the teleprinter as soon as the message came through. It was from the gendarmerie in south Limoges, and read:

Your inquiry regarding Alain Lucien Duclos. Not at the Limoges address you supplied from vehicle registration. However, Monsieur Duclos is known to us. He is an assistant prosecutor attached to the main Cour d'Assises *in Limoges. According to work colleagues, he is currently holidaying with friends at the Vallon estate near Cotignac, Provence. Trust this is helpful.*

Head of station, Captain Rabellienne

Dominic ripped the message from the printer. The corridor and reception were busy, and he found Poullain in the back mess room having coffee with Harrault. He handed the message across and waited a moment as Poullain read it.

'Do you want me to make initial inquiries?' Dominic asked.

Poullain was hesitant as he lifted his attention from the message. 'No, no – it's okay. I think I'd better phone first – then we'll probably go out there together.' It looked like a waste of time, a complete mismatch, thought Poullain. An assistant prosecutor staying with one of the area's largest landowners and most highly regarded citizens: Marcel Vallon. It would need personal kid-glove treatment; Vallon was good friends with the Mayor, they played golf together and belonged to the same Masonic lodge. Poullain looked at his watch. They had a meeting about the Rosselot case scheduled for the next day with Bouteille, the prosecutor in Aix-en-Provence. 'If we can see this Duclos late morning or at lunchtime, since we pass through here again on our way to Aix, do you think you could have the notes typed up and put in some semblance of order before tomorrow's meeting?'

'Yes, I think so.' Dominic faltered only for a second; another lunchtime with a rushed sandwich.

'Good. Let's plan for then. I'll phone within half an hour. Anything new from Machanaud?'

'No, not really. Apart from the car sighting he mentioned. As you requested, we got him to sign the forms and hand over his identity card, then let him go just before eleven last night.'

Without sufficient evidence to hold Machanaud, it was all they'd been able to do: a standard 'local police to be notified if moving' form, and holding his identity card. Without it, new housing, jobs or any form of social registration for Machanaud would be practically impossible.

Poullain had already half discounted the car sighting. It had been so vague: a dark car, perhaps blue or dark grey, sloping at the back, possibly a Citroën DS. When pressed, Machanaud admitted he'd only caught a quick flash of it between the bushes – but what he was sure of was that it had left only minutes before him. How convenient! Machanaud knew that if he didn't come up with another possible scapegoat things were looking grim for him, and after a couple of hours alone in the jail cell, he'd come up with one. *Quelle surprise!*

Poullain glanced again at the brief message. It looked like it would come to nothing, but you never knew. If nothing else, it would at least demonstrate they were being thorough and exploring all options. A bit of dressing for when they laid Machanaud's head on a plate for Bouteille and Naugier.

10

The car tyres of the Citroën DS19 crunched on the gravel driveway. The front of the building was an imposing but flat-fronted three-storey Provençal *mas*, its line broken only by frequent window boxes and a long terrace at one end running above the garage. A row of neatly manicured cypress firs framed the semi-circular sweep of the driveway, with two smaller trees in large pots on each side of the entrance.

A servant came out to greet them and showed them through the house, along a wide main hallway then into a narrower corridor towards the door at its end: the library. Marcel Vallon was nowhere to be seen. He'd ascertained on the phone with Poullain that his presence wouldn't be required. While Poullain had assured him that it was nothing too serious, something just to help with their other inquiries, Vallon had made it patently clear their visit was an intrusion, a favour granted only by his good nature. Don't take advantage was the silent undertone. Poullain was therefore already nervous about the visit, complaining on the drive over that it would be a waste of time, would serve no purpose other than to upset Vallon. He'd probably get a call from the Mayor in a day or so.

While they waited in the library, Dominic could sense Poullain's unease returning. Poullain had taken one of three seats by a low round coffee table, while Dominic sat at a small drop-leaf desk by the window. A room six metres by five, two walls lined with books, the atmosphere austere, stuffy. This was old Provence, old money and power. A gentle reminder. They waited almost five minutes before Duclos walked into the room.

A taut smile upon introduction to Poullain, a brief nod towards Dominic. He was only slightly taller than Poullain, and slim, Dominic noted: short black hair swept neatly across, a rounded almost baby face, eyes so dark green they were almost black. Some women liked that sort of soft, innocent look, thought Dominic; someone to mother. But he couldn't help thinking that some men liked it too.

Poullain started with the niceties of thanking Duclos for seeing them at such short notice and apologizing for the intrusion; it was just a general inquiry regarding visitors to Taragnon five days ago, on the eighteenth.

A young boy had been attacked then. No attempt at subterfuge, Dominic noted; no trap for Duclos by drawing him out before mentioning the main purpose of their visit.

'We are as a result talking to anyone in the area at the time for information. Your car was seen at the Café Font-du-Roux during lunchtime that day. I wondered, Monsieur Duclos, do you remember your movements then, last Thursday, particularly before and after your visit to the Font-du-Roux?'

A moment's thought from Duclos, a slow blink. 'Well, I remember stopping at the café. I'd been to Aix-en-Provence for the morning and was on my way back. What exactly did you want to know?'

'Let's start with the time you arrived at the café, if you remember.'

Duclos looked down, feigning deep thought. A hundred times over he'd worked out his timing and what he'd say if questioned; but coming straight out with it would seem unnatural, pre-prepared. How much hesitance was normal to recall something that'd happened five days earlier? 'It would have been quite late in the lunch period, one-thirty, maybe quarter to two. I remember stopping because I knew I wouldn't make it back for normal lunchtime here at the estate, and the chef Maurice can be quite strict. He doesn't like preparing separately for latecomers.' He forced a smile. 'Yes, it would have been about then.'

'And did you stay long?'

'Maybe an hour or so. Service was a bit slow when I arrived, they were quite busy. And I had coffee and brandy to finish.'

'So, you left at what – half past two or so?'

'No, it was closer to three when I asked for the bill. I remember looking at my watch then, because I'd planned to head to Juan-les-Pins for the afternoon and started to get a bit anxious about being too late. Perhaps five minutes to settle the bill, so about three when I left.'

'Had you arranged to meet someone in Juan-les-Pins?'

'Nothing particular planned. But I'd seen someone on the beach the day before that I hoped to bump into again. A girl. So I wanted to be there more or less at the same time.'

Poullain looked towards Dominic. 'For our notes, then: you arrived at Café Font-du-Roux at a quarter to two and left at three. More or less.'

'Yes, I suppose it must have been closer to a quarter to when I arrived. I don't think I stayed as long as an hour and a half.'

A moment's silence. The sound of Dominic's pen scratching on paper. Some distant splashing from the swimming pool in the rear garden, which

Dominic could just see at an angle if he looked through the window at his side.

Duclos' heart pounded. The timing was etched on his mind: *arrived at 1.41, left at 2.51, three minutes' drive to the farm lane, eight minutes off the road with the boy, heading off again at 3.02.* Hopefully he'd buried the eleven minutes without them noticing. Surely the barman wouldn't remember the *exact* time he left? He fought to control his nerves; it was vital he appeared calm.

'And after the café, did you head straight for Juan-les-Pins?' Poullain asked.

'Yes.'

'Did you stop anywhere or see anyone on the way?'

'No.' A moment's afterthought: 'Oh, except I stopped off at a garage near Le Muy, filled up with petrol, had an oil check.' *Speeds of 110–140 kmph nearly all the way hopefully to bury the eight minutes he'd been off the road with the boy.*

'Do you remember the name of the garage?'

'No. It was a few kilometres before Le Muy, on the right.' It was the only garage for fifteen kilometres, thought Duclos; they were bound to find it if they bothered to check.

'And what time did you get to Juan-les-Pins?'

'About a quarter to five, maybe five. I don't remember exactly.' Duclos felt small beads of sweat pop on his forehead, but then it was quite hot in the room. *Pulse racing, palms clammy as he'd stopped by a bin in a deserted alley at the back of town, pushing deep inside the rock and the boy's shirt wrapped in a large rag from the car.*

'In Juan-les-Pins, did you go anywhere in particular, perhaps meet the girl you'd hoped to?'

'No, she didn't show up. But the café I went to on the beach is one I've been to a few times before. Claude Vallon and I had lunch there just a week ago. The owner knows us.' *If the garage didn't remember him stopping, he was sure at least the café owner would.* Inside his nerves were racing, but it was hopefully going well: pauses at the right juncture, the afterthought of the garage, remembering the timing of leaving the Taragnon café but guessing at the arrival time: accurate details, but not too glib too quickly. Though now he sensed, as the questions became more direct and personal, that perhaps he was being too compliant. 'But what has my visit to Juan-les-Pins got to do with this? I thought you were interested in events around Taragnon and the Font-du-Roux?'

Quick retreat and apology from Poullain. 'Yes, yes – I'm sorry. We just need to ascertain people's general movements. We're quite happy to accept that you were not in Taragnon later on. So, earlier, on the way *into* Taragnon, did you see or meet anyone?'

A barely perceptible flinch from Duclos. Poullain didn't notice it, only Dominic; though it could have been the sudden jump in timing and mood, from hours after the event to before, defensive to offensive.

'Such as this young boy? No, I'm afraid not,' said Duclos. *The final masterstroke to throw forensics: inserting a finger in the boy's rectum and working it brusquely around. Hopefully interpreted as a second attack.* 'There were people walking about in the main street of Taragnon, but I don't remember anyone in particular.'

'You stopped nowhere in or near Taragnon except the café?'

'No.' *The bottle taken from the café. Stripping down to his underpants before striking the boy with the rock. Then washing down with the bottled water and dressing again. No bloodstains.*

Poullain waited for Dominic's note-taking to catch up with them, using the gap to collect his thoughts. Then he recapped on a few points, mainly clarifying times. At one point he asked Dominic, 'What do you have noted for the time that Monsieur Duclos arrived at Juan-les-Pins?'

'Five or a quarter to.' Dominic was sure Poullain remembered the time; normally statement recaps were purely to see if the suspect said something different the second time around.

'And the time you stopped at the garage, Monsieur Duclos?' asked Poullain. 'I don't believe we covered that before.'

Duclos shrugged slightly. 'I don't know, what is it? Just over halfway there. About four o'clock, I suppose.'

Poullain nodded slowly, as if still preoccupied with all the prior in-formation. Then he suddenly went off at a tangent. 'Do you visit your friends here, the Vallons, very often?'

'At least once a year. Nearly always in the summer months. Claude Vallon and I went to the same university, Bordeaux.' A slight frown from Duclos. 'Why do you ask?'

Poullain shook his head hastily. 'No particular reason. It's just that your car was reported in response to our request for any strangers to the area – when in fact it appears you're almost an honorary local.' Poullain grimaced weakly. He could hardly admit that he wanted to know the strength of association between Duclos and the Vallons in case of later problems with his own Mayor. He sighed faintly, bracing his hands on his thighs with an audible slap. 'Well, I think that's just about it, Monsieur Duclos. Thank you for your time.' Poullain stood up, nodded curtly, and shook hands with Duclos. Heading for the door, he turned. 'Oh, I forgot. One thing I meant to ask. You mentioned that when you went through Taragnon, you were on your way from Aix-en-Provence. What time did you leave there?'

Duclos' hammering nerves had settled slightly with the questioning trailing off, but his keen prosecutor's nose made him suddenly alert again. The throw-away question: he'd seen them so often catch defendants out. *The boy's stark green eyes struggling to look back at him as he pushed his face flat down to the earth, raising one arm with the rock . . .* 'Twelve-fifteenish, I suppose. It was just a quick shopping trip. I was there probably no more than an hour and a half.'

'Pick up anything interesting?'

'There's a cheese shop and delicatessen I always visit, on Rue Clemenceau. While there I picked up a few other bits and pieces, some olives and pistachios and some aged brandy to take back for my uncle.'

Poullain nodded and smiled. 'Once again, thank you, Monsieur Duclos. And sorry for the intrusion.'

Started with an apology and finished with one, thought Dominic. No surprise tactics, no ambush; the nature of their inquiry explained clearly. Quite a contrast to the tactics used with Machanaud. The only thing Poullain had pushed for was trying to get Duclos to say he'd left the restaurant half an hour earlier. The vital half-hour in which the boy was attacked. Perhaps Poullain was going to wait until they'd checked some of the details from Duclos, then hit him harder on a second interview.

They were led out to the main hallway by Duclos, then the servant reappeared from the adjoining drawing room and took over.

Duclos went into the drawing room and watched through the window as they crossed the gravel driveway. Overall, he'd been quite convincing, he thought. Controlled his nerves well. Poullain had been easy to handle, had accepted his account of events readily, was almost apologetic; a true system man, obviously daunted by the association with Marcel Vallon. The younger one had looked more surly and doubting, but had stayed silently in the background. A junior with no real power, he would present no problem. There was only one thing left to worry about, but hopefully Chapeau would be visiting the hospital soon, if he hadn't already done so. *Screaming, pistoning crescendo, hot white light stabbing his mind as he brought the rock down repeatedly . . . the tinkle of goats' bells from the next field barely*

98

breaking through his frenzy and the gentle sough of wind through the trees . . .

A slow exhalation of breath; sudden relief and letting loose the overflow of built-up tension. But deep in his stomach the butterfly contortions he'd been fighting to control during the past hour finally got the better of him. He headed for the bathroom to be sick.

Chapeau visited the hospital twice within three hours before a plan started to take shape, the time in between filled in with a leisurely lunch and an afternoon stroll along Aix's Cours Mirabeau.

The hat he wore was a nondescript brown trilby, a habit acquired from a spell working as a bouncer in a Marseille nightclub, Borsalino's, where he had to wear a bright, wide-brimmed trilby. The hat was a distraction, it covered his tight-knit curly hair and could be tilted to shade his discoloured eye; the eye could be noticed only up close, but it was a strong distinguishing feature. He always wore a hat while working, never when not.

On the first visit, he'd walked along the second-floor corridor twice, then sat on a bench at its end for a while, watching the movements of people back and forth. From viewing a hospital porter a few doors down from 4A exit laden with towels, he guessed it was a store room. He didn't notice the porter open or lock the door, so Chapeau waited for a quiet moment when the corridor was empty, then went to check: it was three metres long and a metre wide with one side stacked with linen, towels, cotton swabs; there was a bucket with a mop in the corner, floor cleaner and bleach. No uniforms.

The room gave him an idea, the rest of it slotting into place over lunch. He would have to get a uniform, lighter fluid and a syringe. He returned to walk the corridor again, rechecking positions between the store room and 4A, the distance from the fire alarm and the main wards. Then he sat down on the bench again, one last run-through of the plan in his mind.

He looked up; the door to room 4A had clicked open. He watched a woman walk out, long dark hair in ringlets, pale beige dress.

As she lifted her eyes towards him, he leant forward, resting his elbows on his knees while he contemplated his shoes. All she would see was an apparently concerned trilby, waiting for news from one of the nearby rooms. As she went from view, he headed for the stairs and made his exit.

When they'd gone through best timing, Alain had mentioned that his friend had seen a woman visiting the room – probably a girlfriend or relative of the boy's pimp. Quite a beauty, thought Chapeau; at least partly Arab, but dressed simply and understated, not the gold hoop earrings, heavy make-up and high heels of a pimp's girlfriend. So, she was just a 'friend', though probably her main role was as caretaker and guardian for his various boys, as many as twelve or fifteen under the same roof, a surrogate 'auntie'. With pimps mostly male, women invariably took care of the domestics: cooking, cleaning, shopping.

Over the next few hours he visited three shops in Marseille specializing in hotel and industrial uniforms before finding one close to that of the porters at the hospital. Lighter fluid he picked up at a nearby tobacco shop, the syringe at a pharmacy.

Now, sitting at a Panier bar, he sipped at a brandy and ran through again the projected sequence in his mind.

The only thing still to decide was whether he went back that night or waited till the next morning.

Dominic headed out straight after their meeting with Pierre Bouteille, with Poullain suddenly eager to progress to the next stage: alibi verification for *all* possible suspects, not just Machanaud.

He made it to the garage near Le Muy by 7.54 p.m., then made the deduction from the time he had passed Café Font-du-Roux: sixty-eight minutes. That meant that if Duclos had left the café at just after three, he would have been at the garage by 4.08–4.10 p.m.

The garage attendant remembered Duclos' car, not only because of the rarity of Giulietta Sprints, but because Duclos had asked for an oil change and whether he might make it to Juan-les-Pins by 4.30. 'Impossible. I told him it would take at least forty minutes – he'd be lucky to make it by four-fifty. So it must have been about five past four then.'

Dominic asked if he'd noticed anything unusual, any bloodstains or clothing in disarray – but no on each count. Dominic headed off on his bike for Juan-les-Pins.

The attendant was right. The road was winding for part of the route, and it took him forty-eight minutes. He parked close to the sea front and walked along the promenade, past the pavement artists and makeshift souvenir stands. The promenade was raised so that he was looking over the rooftops of the bars and restaurants tucked in below at beach level.

As Dominic came to the third set of steps leading down, he saw the sign for the Rififi to the left. Part bar, part restaurant, at nearly nine o'clock it was busy with diners. The evening air was still hot, so stepping off the bike he'd taken off his leather jacket. Underneath was his white epaulette shirt, and he put his gendarme cap back on. A waiter asked how he could help, or did Monsieur wish to dine?

Dominic explained the purpose of his visit and was shown to the bar to await the owner, a short, stocky man with bushy grey hair in his early fifties who introduced himself as Pierre Malgarin. He looked slightly flustered at the interruption during the busy dining period.

Dominic explained the background and confirmed that Malgarin knew the Vallons. 'Apparently, they dined here about what, twelve days ago or so?'

'About that, yes.'

'Claude Vallon, the son, had a friend with him – an Alain Duclos. Mid twenties, slim, black hair. Did he come in here about six days ago on his own? It would have been late afternoon, about five o'clock.'

'I don't know. I'm not usually here then, I come in lunchtimes and evenings. But possibly my head waiter will know.' Malgarin beckoned the waiter who had shown Dominic to the bar. As Malgarin repeated the question, the waiter nodded.

'Young friend of the Vallons. Yes, I remember him coming in for about half an hour or so five or six days ago.'

'Do you remember what time it was?'

'Not really. Just that it was well after lunchtime, because we'd cleared up by then. But for all I remember, it could have been any time between four and six-thirty. Maybe Gilbert will know.' He leant across and involved the barman in the conversation, but the barman shrugged.

'I don't remember exactly. Only what he drank – Campari and lemon. And he asked me if I'd seen a girl: long dark hair, Italian-looking, early twenties. She was wearing an orange bikini when he'd seen her on the beach the day before. We get so many girls, I told him, it was hard to place one just like that. I couldn't remember her.'

'Did he call into the bar the day before when he saw the girl for the first time?'

'No. Or at least I don't remember seeing him. Perhaps he saw her from the promenade or from one of the adjoining bars.'

'Anything unusual about his dress or his manner?'

'No. Not really. Just that he seemed bothered that he might not see her.'

Dominic couldn't think of any more immediate questions. In the conversation lull, the waiter excused himself. The owner asked, 'Has that been useful? Would you like to stay for a quick drink – on the house?'

Dominic was about to decline, then ordered a beer on an afterthought and offered his thanks. Perhaps one of them might remember something else while he waited. He was close to the end of the bar, with only three lines of tables between there and the beach edge. Two sets of large glass windows had been drawn back so that the front of the bar was mostly open to the beach.

Dominic sipped at his beer. The sound of gently lapping surf wafted in above the babble of voices and clatter of cutlery. Deep into the bay, Dominic could see the lights of four or five fishing boats; and behind him, from an open-air restaurant with a live group by the town square, drifted '*Quando caliente el sol . . .*'

A sordid investigation with a young boy sexually assaulted and battered? It seemed a world away from this. Could Duclos really have battered the boy half to death, then come down here and calmly sipped at Campari and lemon while looking for this girl, *if* she existed? Where had he seen her from the day before? It struck Dominic as a rather convenient underlining of heterosexuality. And if Duclos had been so worried he might miss her, why stop for an oil change and to confirm the time? What was more important: that the attendant remembered him, or to get to see the girl on time?

But despite the inconsistencies, *time* would be the deciding factor. And there simply was not enough of it for Duclos to have committed the crime. Even at excessive speeds, he might have had ten or fifteen spare minutes at most. The minimum estimate covering both attacks was forty minutes. Given the background of his debates with Poullain over Machanaud, even mentioning the inconsistencies would be seen by Poullain as obstructive and pointless unless something new came up about Duclos' timing.

Dominic wished now he hadn't made the trip; he felt deflated. He had set out in hope of deflecting Poullain's one-track case against Machanaud, and instead would be returning with information which would help to further seal his fate.

Chapeau poured the lighter fluid generously on the cotton sheet, then bundled it into the corner with some other sheets and thick towels.

He listened for a second to sounds outside on the corridor: nothing audible. It was important that nobody saw him come out of the small store room. Once the sheets were lit, there was no turning back, he would have to exit immediately. The small room would fill with smoke in seconds.

He lit the sheet and stepped back hastily as the flames leapt. He watched for only a second to ensure the sheets beneath had caught – then exited. The corridor was empty, and he headed past room 4A towards where the corridor angled off at an L, at the end of which was the fire alarm. A few paces past 4A he heard footsteps close to the top of the stairs. He'd been lucky; two seconds more and he'd have been trapped inside the store room. But it was important also that he wasn't seen rushing away from the store room, and he picked up pace – only just making it behind the angle of the L before they reached the top of the stairs.

The corridor ahead was twenty-five metres long with two doors at its end, three on its right flank and one on the left past a window. The fire alarm was close to the end, just before the two final doors.

Suddenly, the middle of the three doors on his right opened. A doctor stepped out.

Merde! From the sound of their footsteps, the people who had come up the stairs were also heading in his direction, just about to turn into the corridor. But there were no cries of alarm, obviously the smoke hadn't yet started seeping through the door.

Noticing Chapeau hesitate and look around as if he was lost for a moment, the doctor asked, 'Looking for someone?'

'Dr Durrand,' Chapeau answered, hastily recalling a name he'd seen on the resident doctors' list by the reception. Chapeau fought to control his agitation, appear calm.

'You won't find him up here, I don't think. First floor, ophthalmology.'

The two people, an elderly couple heading for a door at the end, passed them. His porter's uniform shouldn't raise suspicions; it was an almost exact match. *Ophthalmology?* His mind spun, panning frantically for options. His eyes fixed on the number of the furthest door. 'I've just come from ophthalmology, and they said I might find him in 6C.'

'What's the patient's name?'

'They didn't say.'

The doctor shrugged. 'There's nobody in 6C right now. New patient isn't coming in till tonight, and the old patient was moved back to the general ward yesterday.'

'Okay. I'll try there.' Chapeau headed back the way he'd come. Pacing, calming his breath. He silently cursed: crucial seconds had been lost, and the doctor might later remember him. Behind him, at the end of the corridor, the couple had already disappeared. *Calming.* The sound of the doctor's footsteps receded beyond his own rapid, shallow breaths. But ahead now, at the angle of the L, he could see the first trails of smoke drifting across, misty grey suffused with stark sunlight from the window. And he begged that the doctor wouldn't turn around suddenly and see it. He listened intently to the sounds of the doctor's fading footsteps between his own, a faint shuffle, a door opening . . . slowly closing. All too slowly.

Chapeau let out a long breath as it finally shut, then ran the last few steps towards the smoke. A nurse had come out from the general ward at the far end, looking equally startled as she noticed the smoke. Chapeau lifted one arm in acknowledgement and ran back towards the alarm. Halfway along, he heard the plaintive cry of *'Fire!'* from the nurse.

He took the small brass hammer on a chain at the side of the alarm and swung it sharply, smashing the glass and releasing the alarm button.

The bell was deafening, echoing from the stark walls and floor. Chapeau ran back swiftly towards the smoke and room 4A. He heard a door open behind him, some muttering, a sudden startled voice – but he didn't look back. As he turned the L and came back into the main corridor, five or six people had come out of their rooms.

'Is it another fire drill?' someone asked.

Faint babble of replies, more startled voices rising above, the final realization – as the build-up of smoke became evident – that this was the real thing. Sudden mobilization, more people starting to spill out of the rooms, most of them from the large general ward at the end. Some were now heading for the stairs and the five or six quickly grew to over twenty. Panic, confusion.

Chapeau suddenly felt more secure among the milling crowd; hardly anyone was paying him any attention. He took the syringe from his pocket. The needle was already attached, and he slipped off the plastic protection cap. Room 4A was only a few metres to one side. He tucked the syringe neatly up inside his sleeve, and reached out for the door.

A quick intake of breath, but he felt confident. His adrenalin was racing because of the fire and activity around, not nerves. The scenario was perfect. It would all be over within a minute.

It didn't strike him as odd that he'd seen nobody run from 4A until he opened the door wide. No nurse or doctor, nobody in attendance. A split-second elation that he'd been lucky and chosen a totally unguarded moment before realizing – as he looked through the glass screen – that there was no boy either.

'Shit . . . *Shiiit!*' He stood transfixed, staring at the empty space. Around him, pandemonium was building. He was the only person on the second floor not in motion. A steady stream was now heading for the stairs, and a medic with a fire extinguisher was spraying the inside of the store room while a porter rushed for another extinguisher.

It took a moment for Chapeau to break himself out of his trance and ask someone passing where the boy had gone. He'd stopped three nurses before finding someone who knew. 'He was taken into the operating theatre over an hour ago.'

'Thanks.' Chapeau merged with the throng heading down the stairs. The porter had joined the medic with a second fire extinguisher. They would probably have the fire out within a few minutes.

In the first-floor operating theatre, the alarm bell rang ominously in the background. The chief surgeon, Dr Trichot, asked one of the nurses to find out what was wrong.

She came back in after a moment. 'Fire on the second floor, apparently.'

'Is it confined to there?'

'I don't know, I didn't ask.'

Trichot nodded for his assisting nurse to dab his forehead, and silently cursed. 'Let's assume that there's no immediate danger, or at least that someone will come running in when there is, and continue. *Please!*'

The assisting nurse took the scalpel from him as he held it out tersely. She thrust a self-retaining retractor into the same hand.

The boy, Christian Rosselot, had been on the operating table over thirty minutes now, but they'd lost vital time getting X-rays and angiograms and preparing for an anaesthetic. In that time, the temporal skull section by the boy's ear had bulged alarmingly with an active clot.

But two nights ago he'd operated on the boy for a similar clot in the parietal lobe, snatched him within minutes from the jaws of death – and he was determined not to be defeated now. Fire or no fire. The clanging bell was infuriating, grating at his nerves. It couldn't have come at a worse time. He needed all his concentration at this point. Implements were placed in his hand and taken back without him looking up, the last an electric burr drill. Its high-pitched drone lowered as Trichot cut into the bone of the skull.

The extradural cortex was exposed. There was no sign of haematoma, and Trichot began to worry. He would have to go deeper. 'We must go into the subdural.'

Trichot sliced through the partly gelatinous dura easily with the scalpel, pulled back with a hook and prompted his assistant to shine a penlight into the aperture.

Grey and white tissue and vessels reflected brightly under the light; the dark matter of the blood clot only showed up as Trichot widened the arc of the penlight. It was in the upper portion of the temporal. He wouldn't be able to judge its size or remove all of it without a larger incision.

A nod, a dab. Trichot passed back the penlight. 'I'll have to go higher.'

The attending anaesthetist announced, 'Pulse rate sixty to sixty-five,' as the sound of the drill cut in again.

From seventy, seventy-five just a few minutes ago, thought Trichot. He looked across briefly at the blood-pressure gauge. It had dropped twenty points to 116 over 67 in the same period. The burr hole made, he started sawing. The bleep rate dropped still further.

'Fifty-four, fifty-one.' Now with a note of urgency.

Trichot was sweating profusely. Another dab. It was going to be a race against time. Another ten seconds of sawing, fifteen or twenty seconds to cut through the dura and widen the aperture. Then the time needed to suck away the clot itself would depend on how large it was. How much more would the pulse have dropped by then?

Trichot finished sawing, and pulled back with the hook. All but a small portion of the clot was now visible. The air-pressure sucker was passed across.

'Forty-five . . . three . . . dropping fast! *Forty!*'

Trichot felt a twinge of panic. Once the pulse rate fell to thirty, thirty-two, it was effectively all over. He'd fought too hard for the boy to let him go now.

The air sucker ate into the congealed dark red mass of the clot. Within twenty seconds, Trichot had removed almost a third of it.

'. . . Thirty-eight . . . *seven.*'

The rate of pulse drop had slowed, but part of the clot was still out of sight. Trichot glanced up at the blood-pressure gauge: 104 over 61. It was going to be a close call. If the rupture was behind the last portion of the clot; if it was difficult to reach to cauterize; if the pulse rate dropped more rapidly; if there was more than one rupture . . . Any one factor meant that he wouldn't make it in time. Beads of sweat massed on his forehead, and his own pulse drummed a double beat to the bleep from the monitor. Trichot moved his way upward with the sucker, praying that the ruptured vessel would soon come into view.

'Thirty-six . . . *thirty-five!*'

Outside, the alarm bell suddenly stopped ringing. Only the sound of the bleep remained, slowly counting down the seconds Trichot had left to save his patient's life.

Chapeau found a bar three blocks from the hospital and sat over a Pernod while he pondered what to do. How long would the boy be in the operating theatre: two hours, three? Probably he would be returned to the same intensive care room, but then what? He couldn't use the same fire distraction again; he would have to think of something else.

Nothing came to mind quickly, and Chapeau sharply knocked back another slug of Pernod. He should have made the hit the night before rather than wait till the morning. His best shot had probably now gone; he was going to be hard pushed to come up with an alternative plan that would be so effective and carry such low risk. Worse still, if the boy died on the operating table, there would be no more chances. He finished his drink, paid, and headed out. He needed a walk to clear his mind.

Nine-forty in the morning, the streets of Aix were coming to life. But Chapeau was in his own world, oblivious to passers-by: planning, scheming, weighing options. He'd walked for almost twenty minutes, blindly window-shopping between his thoughts, when a smile slowly crossed his face. It was cheeky and audacious, but why not? He'd always liked a gamble, and the prospect of shafting that little paedophile prick, Alain, somehow appealed to him. He thought it through once more for possible pitfalls, but it was perfect: the timing matched almost exactly.

But he would have to wait over two hours to deliver the news: two prearranged phone kiosks and times. One in Le Luc for the midday call, one in Brignoles for the ten o'clock call. Chapeau decided to drive back to Marseille to make the call. At one point on the drive, the audacity of what he was about to do tickled him again, and he burst out laughing.

By the time he made the call, he'd managed to control his mirth. It rang only twice before Duclos answered. 'It's done,' said Chapeau.

'When was this?'

'Just this morning. I created a diversion, pumped the boy with a syringe, and last thing I knew they were in the operating theatre trying to save him.'

'Are you sure he's finished?'

'Don't worry, he won't make it. Also, they won't suspect anything: it will look like he died from complications arising from his coma and the initial injuries.'

They made arrangements to meet and settle payment at six o'clock the next day at Parc du Pharo. Chapeau was sure Alain would probably phone the hospital that afternoon to check, but it was a reasonable set of odds. If the boy made it, he would just have to come up with another plan. If not, for once he'd get paid without having any blood on his hands.

11

Session 3

'. . . And when you fell back asleep, did the dream return?'

'Yes. But the wheat field had changed, it was different . . .'

A large-reel tape whirred silently in the background. Eyran's eyelids pulsed gently as the memories drifted across. The second session had been disappointing, details of the dreams scant, so Lambourne had decided on hypnosis. The practice had become increasingly outmoded in his profession, and he used hypnosis on less than 4 per cent of his patients: only in the case of deeply repressed thoughts or where normal transference was poor or non-existent. And hardly ever on children.

But with the main clues buried in Eyran's dreams and so much either faded or selectively erased, he'd seen little other choice. He hadn't expected anything significant from the dreams until Jojo appeared after the coma – then suddenly sat up sharply as Eyran started describing a dream just before the accident: his mother folding out a map and Eyran staring at the back of her hair, willing himself back into a previous dream.

'In which way was it different when you went back?' Lambourne pressed.

'It was flat, not on a slope how I remembered. And suddenly it got dark, I couldn't find my way back. Everything was too flat – I couldn't pick out anything to tell me which way was home.'

'Was it important that you reached home?'

'Yes. I had the feeling that if I didn't make it back, something terrible would happen. I might die. Finding my way out of the darkness and home was my way of staying alive.'

Lambourne clenched one hand tight. If there was a significant gap between the two dreams, the accident could have already taken place by the second dream! Its later corruption after the coma and the introduction of Jojo could speak volumes. 'When did you first start dreaming about the wheat field?'

'I don't remember exactly. Quite a few years back.'

'Was it when you first went to California and started missing your friends?'

'No, I'd dreamt of it before. When we first moved into the house in

East Grinstead and I walked into the field, it felt familiar. I had the feeling I'd been there before.'

'And did the dreams always feature the wheat fields?'

'No, sometimes it was the copse and the pond they led to, sometimes the woods at the back of the old house that led to the field.'

'Did you ever dream of the house itself?'

'I don't remember exactly. Perhaps once before. Then the dream recently where I was looking out of the back-kitchen window and saw my parents, and met Jojo again in the woods.'

So, the wheat field and the copse were more significant than the house itself: his own private play areas, whereas in the house his parents were dominant. The house started to feature again only when he was trying to find them; he took the search partly to their territory. 'In the dream about the time of the accident, when you feared you couldn't make your way back home – how long did you feel had passed since the last moment in the car when you remembered being awake?'

'It seemed to come almost straight after. But I don't know. The other dreams seemed to come with little gap, yet they told me when I awoke that I'd been in a coma for three weeks.'

Lambourne scribbled a quick note: *Timing inconclusive. First significant dream could have occurred before or after the accident.* Probably they would never know. 'And was there anyone else in the dream, any of your old friends from the copse?'

'There was someone, but not really a friend. It was a boy from my old school, Daniel Fletcher. He died just a year before we left for California. And then my father appeared, saying that I didn't belong there, that I should start making my way back. But it was suddenly dark and I couldn't make out anything familiar; and then he disappeared and left me to find my way back on my own.'

'What was the stronger emotion? Anger that he'd deserted you, or fear that you were suddenly alone and lost?'

'I don't know, I felt both. Maybe more confused than angry. I just couldn't work out why he'd left.'

'And was your fear just because you were alone and it was dark, or was it also because you felt you should do as your father said – you were equally afraid to disobey him?'

Eyran frowned; he looked vaguely uncomfortable. 'It was because I was alone. I wouldn't purposely disobey my father and upset him, but I wasn't afraid of him. He was a very good father.'

'I know.' Lambourne noted the defensive tone; he changed track. 'Which was the first dream that Jojo appeared in?'

Moment's silence. Eyran's eyelids pulsed. 'It was the dream straight after that, again in the same place. The small pond in the copse.'

'And in that dream, tell me what you saw. What happened?'

Eyran's eyelids pulsed more rapidly. Only grey outline at first, hazy. But gradually the images sharpened, became clear . . .

Eyran could only just make out the brook in the darkness of the copse at first. A faint mist lingered across its surface. He moved forward cautiously, a figure on the far side becoming gradually clearer as he got closer. It wasn't Sarah or Daniel, it was a boy of about his age that he hadn't seen before, though the trees and mist cast a shadow over part of his face, so he couldn't be sure. He knew that the boy had seen him because he waved and called out to Eyran, his voice echoing slightly across the water.

'Who are you?' Eyran asked. 'I haven't seen you here before.'

'Yes, I know, I don't normally come here. But we have met before, don't you remember?'

Eyran looked hard into the face. It was still indistinct. He felt suddenly uncomfortable admitting that he couldn't remember, the boy seemed so certain they had met before. 'It's the mist . . . I can't see very clearly across the brook.'

'Then you should come over this side with me.'

Eyran peered through the mist, but as part of it cleared, the expanse of water between them appeared to be much wider, a dark and fathomless lake. All the familiar landmarks of the brook were now far away, out of reach across the murky depths. 'I'm looking for my parents,' Eyran said. 'My father was here earlier. Have you seen him?'

'No, I haven't. I lost my parents as well. Though it was many years ago – I can hardly remember it now.'

Eyran tried hard to make out the boy's features, tried to remember him, but the shadow across his face and the mist of the lake robbed him of any chance of recognition. 'What's your name?'

'Gigio.' Though the faint echo that came across the lake sounded more like 'Jojo' to Eyran. The boy looked straight across for a moment in silence. The air was cold, his breath misty. 'You don't remember me, do you?'

Eyran could see a tear on the boy's cheek, though he couldn't believe he was that upset at not being remembered; it must have been the memory of losing his parents. Which reminded Eyran again of why he'd returned to the brook. 'I must find my father. He was here only a short while ago.'

'I told you, you won't find him over that side. If you cross over, I'll help you find him.'

Eyran looked down and across at the water. It was jet black, murky. He felt afraid of what might lie beneath the surface, imagining water snakes and all manner of creatures, tree roots like tentacles trapping him and dragging him down, thick mud and slime like quicksand. Cold with fear, he shook his head hastily. 'No, I can't come over there. It's too dangerous.'

The boy smiled warmly, raising one arm, beckoning. 'But you must come over. Otherwise you will never find your father.'

Eyran closed his eyes, steeling himself against what he knew he had to do, feeling the cold of the water as first he put his feet in. He stopped for a second, looking imploringly to the boy. 'Are you sure? Are you sure I have to do this?'

The boy was now openly crying. 'I can't promise you'll find your father, Eyran – I looked for my parents and never found them. But I had to be on this side of the lake, and you belong here with me. Then at least if you don't find them, you're not alone.'

'But I must find them,' Eyran pleaded.

'I know, I know. I'll help you. If they are here, we'll find them, don't worry.'

Eyran waded slowly deeper, trying to walk as far as he could before swimming. The cold of the water penetrated deep into his body as it came up above his waist. The mist was moving on the surface of the water, partly obscuring the boy on the far side, then clearing. As the water came up to his chest, Eyran started swimming. The mist became denser towards the centre of the lake and Eyran lost sight of the boy completely for a while – then suddenly he was there again. But he still appeared the same distance away. Eyran didn't feel that he was getting any closer, or perhaps he was losing direction with the mist. Fixing the boy's position when it cleared, Eyran tried to make sure that he stayed swimming in a direct line. During the blind periods he was never sure, and when it cleared again the boy still seemed to be the same distance away. He started to despair and called out 'Jojo,' seeing clearly the boy's reassuring smile and his beckoning wave before his figure was swallowed up once more in the mist.

At that moment he was conscious of the weight in his legs, thick clinging mud and tree roots pulling at his ankles, holding him back. Or perhaps they had been there all along, which was why he hadn't been getting any closer. He fought to break free, but the roots slowly raised like tentacles higher up his legs – pulling at him harder. In blind panic he screamed Jojo's name again, the roots dragging him inexorably downward as he struggled vainly to raise his head . . . the first icy water filling his mouth.

'*Break away! . . .*'

He fought hard, thrashing out with his arms, coughing and spluttering as his lungs began to fill, but the grip of the tree roots on his legs was impossible to break.

He felt tricked, cheated by the boy, led into the cold depths of the lake to die. But as he slid deeper into the watery blackness, the vision of Jojo stayed with him, still smiling reassuringly and beckoning, reaching out a hand towards him . . .

'Slipping deeper . . . I . . . I . . .'

'Break away . . . Break away! . . .'

'I . . . Can't breathe . . . can't . . .'

'Eyran! . . . Eyran! . . . Break away . . .'

The rapid pulsing beneath Eyran's eyelids slowly settled. His tortured breathing eased.

Lambourne's mouth was dry, there was a film of sweat on his forehead. He cursed himself: he should have seen it coming! Cut everything short as soon as Eyran started wading into the pond. He could feel his nerves still racing. He waited a few seconds more, watching each beat of Eyran's slowly settling expression.

He swallowed slowly. 'So. Outside of the dreams, when you're awake, has Jojo ever spoken to you?' Switch to generalities, thought Lambourne. Avoid specifics.

Eyran's brow knitted slightly; obviously he found it an odd question. 'No.'

'And how do you feel immediately after waking from the dreams? Are you able to believe just for a moment that your parents might be alive?'

Long pause from Eyran. 'I don't know. Just confused, I suppose. And afraid.'

But Lambourne could tell that Eyran was holding back. 'Yet they're enough to convince you that the next time Jojo might succeed and catch up with your parents. You're willing to trade that for the horrors the dreams might bring.'

Eyran shook his head. 'I don't know. When they start, I don't seem to think about how they might end. I'm just happy that for a few moments I'm somewhere where I might see my parents again.'

'But do you consciously welcome them - knowing that you might see your parents?'

'I don't know. No, I don't think so.'

Lambourne eased back. It was the closest he was likely to get. 'Do most of your dreams occur by the old house in England?'

Eyran took a second to catch up with the shift in questioning. 'Yes.'

'Do you know why?'

Eyran paused, as if for a moment unsure whether the question was rhetorical and Lambourne would suddenly answer. 'I'm not sure. Perhaps in the dreams that's where I think I have most chance of finding them. Or perhaps I don't think I can do it alone, I need Jojo's help – and I know I can find him there.'

'Are your memories of that particular house stronger than those of your other house in San Diego? Is that where you recall your happiest times – with your parents, with your friends?'

Eyran's expression relaxed. Lambourne watched the self-realization sweep slowly across; at least one small piece of the puzzle had slotted in place. 'Yes, I suppose so. I was happier there.'

Lambourne made a final note: *Main object attachments: father, mother, house in England, old play areas, old friends (possibly now represented through Jojo), house in San Diego.* A quick distillation from the sessions so far; he might change the order later and add to the list, but it was a start.

The session had taken an hour and ten minutes. When he went into the waiting area with Eyran, Stuart and Amanda Capel were already there. Before they left, he arranged and pencilled in the time for the next session.

Lambourne was pleased with progress so far. Eyran was quite bright and more open and communicative than he'd at first feared, his recall of detail in the dreams strong under hypnosis. But Stuart was right: the smiles were rare. Apart from the dreams, perhaps this was the only outward sign that Eyran was deeply disturbed.

But the dreams were becoming more of a refuge where Eyran could believe his parents were alive. Jojo was also becoming bolder – in two recent dreams introducing Eyran's father again to maintain the illusion. Lambourne was convinced it was only a matter of time before Jojo crossed over. Eyran would awake one day to find Jojo's voice still with him. From there, his own core character – and everyone in the outside world telling him his parents were dead – would regress, and Jojo would gain dominance.

The only way was to confront Jojo now, drag him from the dark recesses of Eyran's dreams and strip him bare, let Eyran face the truth, accept: his parents were dead. Only then would he be able to start mourning, adjust to whatever his new life held without them.

But it wouldn't be easy, Lambourne reflected. His nerves were still rattled from the session just past. Like Faust with the devil, he could find himself trading all the way through: a truth for a nightmare.

12

The news that Christian Rosselot had died reached the Bauriac gendarmerie mid morning.

The call came from Dr Besnard, the chief medical examiner at the hospital. Poullain wasn't there at the time, so Harrault took the message. Dr Trichot had fought hard to save the boy, but an oedema from an active clot had caused unforeseen complications. After more than two hours in the operating theatre and three attempts to restart the boy's heart, all procedures were finally terminated at 10.52 a.m., and the boy pronounced dead. 'Could you please try and make arrangements to inform his mother straight away, as she normally plans a hospital visit for the afternoon? Thank you. And I'm so sorry to have to bring this news.'

Harrault was in the small room directly behind the main entrance desk. He fell silent as he put down the phone. It was a moment before he got up and looked for Fornier who, as the main assisting investigator, was the first person he felt should know. Fornier was in the general administration office, typing. In the same room was Levacher and a secretary.

After confirming some details of the call, Dominic looked down thoughtfully at his typewriter. He exhaled audibly; suddenly his body lacked any strength to punch the black metal keys. Levacher mumbled the obvious about how awful it was, then after a brief pause asked who was going to tell the family. When no answers came, everyone wrapped in their own thoughts, he added, 'I suppose we'll have to wait for Poullain to decide.'

And the secretary, who had stopped typing, felt she had her emotions under control until the silence and constrained atmosphere suddenly got the better of her and, shielding part of her face, she hurriedly left the room.

Hushed voices in the corridor, questions, muted surprise then finally, again, silence. The pall spread through the small gendarmerie as if by osmosis, whispers of death seeping through the cream plaster walls.

Within five minutes, the full complement of nine gendarmes and two secretaries on duty knew. From there, it started spreading through the town. A young sergeant went out to buy some cigarettes; there were two other people in the shop at the time who heard that the Rosselot boy had died. One of the shoppers' next call was the boulangerie, where five more heard the news. It ricocheted through the main town shops.

Echoes of death which, by the time Dominic had fired up a Solex and started heading out towards Taragnon and the Rosselots, had already changed the atmosphere in the town centre. Or was he just imagining it? A nod of acknowledgement from Marc Tauvel restacking his front display of vegetables, but then a look that lingered slightly. Madame Houillon following his progress around the square, staring; she was over-inquisitive at the best of times, but now her head was slightly bowed, as if he was a passing hearse. Respect for the dead.

Dominic felt that he couldn't wait any longer before heading out. Poullain was expected back soon, but that could be an hour or more, by which time Monique Rosselot could have started making her way to the hospital. Or worse still, by the way the news was spreading through the village, she could hear it clumsily from a neighbour or tradesman calling by. 'My condolences, I'm so sorry to hear.' Hear what?

Dominic didn't want it to happen that way; after a quick consultation with Harrault, they'd jointly agreed to break protocol by not waiting for Poullain, and Harrault signed out a Solex.

Nothing in his past had prepared him for this. All those years stuck in back radio and communications rooms both in the Legion and the Marseille gendarmerie, he'd had so little 'people' contact. Between the code and call signature manuals, the gun range and procedural guides for arrest, filing and administration, there had been no special training on consoling grieving relatives. How should he phrase it? How would he even start?

On the edge of town, Dominic passed the tannery and leather work-shops tucked into a hillside rock outcrop where the road was cut away. Dyes and acids for stripping and treating the skins were heavy in the air, piquant sauce for the smells of death.

Dominic's eyes watered slightly; he wasn't sure whether they were sensitive with emotions or it was a combination of the fumes and the wind rush on the bike. Eighty metres past, he was clear of the fumes and the smells of the fields took over: ripening vines, lemons, almonds and olives, grass and wheat burnished almost white by the sun. He breathed deeply, but still his eyes watered.

Images flashed before him – the dark brown blood patches against the wheat, the boy being carried to the ambulance, the gendarmes tapping through the field with their canes, Monique Rosselot opening the door to him on that first visit and the single candle in her daily bedside vigil of begging and praying to God to spare her son. *How could he possibly bring her this news?* The well of his emotions finally ebbed, a gentle catharsis washing through him without warning, his body trembling against the vibrations of the bike. He bit at his lip and swallowed back the sobs at the back of his throat; no sound emanated, his steadily watering eyes and his trembling body the only release valves.

His reaction confused him. He'd witnessed murder before, battle-hardened by his years in Marseille. Was it the age of the boy or Monique Rosselot's strongly displayed devotion for her son bringing him closer to her emotions, *too close? Her saddened face in half-shadow reflected in the glass against the candlelight, tears streaming down her cheeks as he told her that her son was dead. Dead!* 'No! Oh God, no!' As he uttered the words breathlessly, what lay ahead of him suddenly seemed impossibly daunting: in one simple sentence destroying Monique Rosselot's life, tearing down any remaining vestige of hope. His grip on the throttle relaxed, the bike slowing slightly, apprehension gripping him full force. His conflict was absolute: he knew he had to go. He cared too much to risk her hearing it casually from someone else passing. But he dreaded having to utter the words himself.

And so he switched off part of his mind driving the last few kilometres. *Cared for her?* He hardly knew her. Pushed the thoughts back as he turned his Solex into the Rosselots' driveway, parked, dismounted. Words shaped in his mind, almost on the edge of his lips, all of them sounding so inept, inadequate. *The messenger?* Was that what worried him, being the messenger? Always being remembered as the man who brought the news that her son had died?

As he approached the door, he noticed the boy's bike still against the garage wall, waiting in expectation. His mouth was dry. He took a last deep breath to calm his nerves as he reached for the door knocker and flipped it down twice.

But it did little good. His nerves built to a crescendo, blood pounding through his head as the door opened and she stood there, her young daughter Clarisse in the shadows behind.

He fumbled, the words seeming to catch in his throat, but from the quickly distraught look that came back from her, she seemed to already half know, perhaps from his expression and awkwardness, and he only managed to say, 'I'm sorry, I have bad news. I wanted to make sure I caught you before you headed for the hospital . . .' before she started pleading.

'No, no, no, no, *no* . . . *No!*' A repetitive and steadily rising mantra hopefully to drive the inevitable away, her eyes imploring him as she slowly collapsed to her knees and, her body finally giving way to convulsive sobbing, she let out a single wailing cry.

The cry, painful and desperate, pierced the still morning air, echoing from the walls of the small courtyard and rising up the gentle slope of the fields beyond. Jean-Luc Rosselot had been working in the west field out of sight of the courtyard for over an hour, digging to find the leak in an irrigation pipe. He didn't see or hear the Solex approaching; the cry was the first thing he heard. He dropped his spade and started running the fifty metres that would bring him in sight of the courtyard. Halfway, another wailing cry arose; a gap, then another.

And already he feared what was the cause before he'd thrashed his way through the last of the dried grass in the almond orchard and the courtyard came into view. It was like a frozen tableau: the gendarme trying to stand proud with his wife on her knees before him, one hand clutching out and almost touching his ankles. As another cry of anguish drifted up across the field, he saw the gendarme reach out towards her shoulder as if to reassure, but the hand hovered just above without connecting.

Each of them stood alone, grief unshared, though Jean-Luc felt even more distanced and awkward, looking on. He tried not to accept what the tableau told him, to force it from his mind in search of other explanations; but in the end the imagery was too strong, left nothing to interpretation. His son was dead.

His first instinct was to rush towards his wife, comfort her – but after a few paces he stopped. His legs felt weak and he was strangely dizzy, the field seeming to tilt slowly away from him, the light oddly dim in hues of dull grey. And suddenly it seemed ridiculous for him to bound down the hillside, waving, even if his legs still had the strength to carry him, and so he resigned himself and slowly sank down, gave way to the buckle in his knees until he was sitting.

They hadn't seen him; they were facing away and he was still too distant. And so he watched from a distance through the grey haze, through eyes stinging with tears, watched his life and all he loved, all that he had prayed these past days for God to save, slowly slip away with the tilt of the grey field into nothingness.

★

The death intensified the investigation and the mood in Taragnon and the surrounding villages. Questions and speculation peppered much of village conversation. It was in part a nervous reaction; there were few other escape valves. New snippets of information about possible suspects and growing expectation of an impending arrest replaced the normal daily routines and pleasures. In a village where local gossip and drama were a large part of the daily fare, this indeed was a lavish banquet. But in the lulls, moods were dark and sullen, silent. It was either feast or famine.

The first main change in the case came in a call from Pierre Bouteille notifying Poullain that he had passed over his file to Alexandre Perrimond, Aix chief prosecutor. 'The main reason is workload. With this now a murder investigation, I'm afraid I wouldn't be able to devote the time it deserves. I've brought Perrimond up to date on everything. No doubt he'll make contact soon.'

The morning after, *Le Provençal* carried the news in a three-column band at the bottom of its front page, carrying over on to page two. It was the most complete story they'd carried yet of the Rosselot case, going over the initial assault, its impact on the small village of Taragnon, and police progress. The police were quoted as having a few possible suspects and hoping to 'conclude the investigation and press charges within the week'. Poullain had spent almost twenty minutes on the phone the previous afternoon with the reporter. The end of the article went back over other notable child disappearances and murders in Provence over the past decade, mostly from the Marseille and Nice areas, underlining the rareness of such incidents in inland villages.

Perrimond made his mark on the case early. Within an hour of being on morning duty, Poullain received a call from his office in Aix. 'I see from this item in the paper that you have a *few* possible suspects. That is news to me. From the information I was passed by Pierre Bouteille, I understood there was only one.'

'It is still only one. The other suspect mentioned to Prosecutor Bouteille, a certain Alain Duclos, was fully interviewed and later my assistant Fornier checked his details. He's a non-runner. We're still left only with the main suspect in the file, Machanaud.'

'Bouteille might handle things differently, but I like to be informed *before* having to read it in the newspapers.' The phone was put down abruptly.

'Headline chaser,' Poullain muttered to the dead phone. The call put Poullain in a bad mood for the rest of the day. He pressed and niggled at

Dominic about small details in their final report, making him retype it twice before he was satisfied. Most of it went over Dominic's head. He typed mechanically, the words little more than a blur. He was still preoccupied with how the Rosselots were coping.

Most of the news had come from Louis, whose girlfriend Valérie was friendly with the Rosselots' neighbours, the Fiévets. They were the Rosselots' closest friends in Taragnon. Clarisse Rosselot had stayed with the Fiévets during Monique's daily hospital vigils so that Jean-Luc's farm work wasn't too heavily disrupted.

Monique Rosselot had hardly left the farm since receiving the news, asking the Fiévets to get whatever shopping and essentials were needed. Jean-Luc had meanwhile buried himself back in his farm work, was out in the fields much of the day. The one time she'd left the house was to use the Fiévets' phone when she'd finally summoned up the courage to call her mother in Beaune to break the tragic news. The mother was going to travel down to console her the next day, a day before the funeral. But, according to Valérie, at the same time Jean-Luc was talking about visiting his parents straight after the funeral; he'd had no contact whatsoever with them in twelve years, but just couldn't break news like this to them over the phone. He had to see them. Monique had complained to the Fiévets that while she understood Jean-Luc's reasoning, the timing was bad; she felt as if she was being deserted when she needed him most.

Louis' message was clear: she was coping, but except for her mother and some neighbourly support from the Fiévets, she was coping *alone*.

Dominic sipped thoughtfully at a beer Louis had poured for him. The first day back at the bar after having seen the Rosselots, Louis had teased and pressed him until he'd finally admitted, yes, she's very pretty. Now the bonhomie had gone, replaced by sullen camaraderie, trying to understand, through pieces of second-hand information, the grief and pain of someone they hardly knew. Dominic wasn't even sure what drove his curiosity: pity for Monique Rosselot, or a desire to assuage his guilt at having brought her the news?

Late that afternoon, Dominic had his worst argument yet with Poullain over Machanaud. The emotions of the day before, the relentless funnelling of evidence now aimed at Machanaud, the words he'd blindly typed that morning – as the mist of his preoccupation with Monique Rosselot lifted – all converged; and it dawned on him that they were delivering little more than a death warrant for Machanaud. He once again raised doubts about him.

'But you were the one who drove out and actually gained corroboration of Duclos' movements that afternoon,' Poullain defended. 'We know he was in the restaurant when the boy was attacked, and he had little or no spare time after he left. It's all in the report – and half of the facts you gained yourself.'

'I know. But some of his alibis fall into place too conveniently, almost planned, and something about Duclos makes me uncomfortable. Also, I'm not convinced about Machanaud. Even if Machanaud was accused of raping a woman, I would be doubtful – but a young boy! We have nothing on him in the past more serious than some poaching and drunk and disorderly.'

'And you're saying that Duclos *is* the type?'

'Possibly. Let's face it, we know nothing about him. At least with Machanaud, we have something to go by on past form. And based on that, it just doesn't sit right with me.'

'Yes, I suppose you're right, we don't know much about him. When they telexed through from Limoges and told us he was an assistant in the prosecutor's office, they forgot to mention that, oh, by the way our friendly local assistant prosecutor has a history of buggering young boys. Hope that is useful, but as you appreciate we like to keep that sort of thing quiet with public officials. Maybe that will follow in their next communication.' Poullain smiled cynically. 'You think that Duclos *looks* the type, don't you?'

Dominic ignored the barb for the second time. 'No, it's more than that. I mean why stop for oil when you're in a rush to see a particular girl and you're worried about being late? Why spend over an hour in a café when time is tight?'

'He probably only remembered the girl and hoped to see her on a whim when he left the restaurant, or perhaps not even until he was at the garage, which is why he asked about timing. There was no specific meeting arranged; as he told us, he just hoped she might still be on the beach that time of day. I don't see anything suspicious.'

'I don't know, it's almost as if he wanted people to remember him visiting at specific times that day. And the girl was just thrown in to underline heterosexuality. Some of the facts are just too convenient, the way that –'

'But they *are* the facts, and you seem to be ignoring that,' Poullain cut in. 'Or perhaps you can give us your alternative dissertation on how to prosecute, based on type and looks. He's a bit of a pretty boy, a bit soft and erudite in manner – he looks the type who would bugger young boys. So let's sweep aside all the facts for a moment, especially the fact that he was in a restaurant when the attack happened, and aim for him. Perhaps you could explain your thinking to Perrimond. He works with assistant prosecutors all day, he might be able to spot the type quickly. Marvellous! Why didn't we consult you earlier, Fornier?'

Dominic bit at his lip and went back to his desk. He should have bided his time; only the day before he'd reflected on just this reaction from Poullain. But he realized now that the boy's death had changed everything, changed the mood and pace of the investigation, that the keen scent of Machanaud's blood could soon drive a hungry pack, a fast rising tide of panic that said 'cry halt early' and swept away his previous resolve.

Bauriac's church bell sounded in the square, calling the faithful to evening mass. It reminded him that there was a memorial service for Christian Rosselot in three days. Flowers. Incense. Candles burning. *Monique Rosselot on her knees before him . . . her heart-rending cry seeming to pierce right through him and drift, unheeded, over the fields and hills beyond.* Still the memory of that moment sent a shiver through his body. How much longer before that was him, grieving the loss of his mother? Six months, a year? The bell tolled ominously in the background, and he found himself looking towards the window and the sound filtering in with the muted shuttered dusk light. He felt very alone, cold and distanced from the gendarmerie activities around him, and he tried to escape the fast descending gloom that the bell was striking for the inevitable, for that which he would be helpless to change.

It was about 6.30 p.m. when Machanaud called by the gendarmerie. Briant was on desk duty. Machanaud asked to see Poullain and Briant said that he wasn't there and looked at his watch, adding, 'But if you want to come back in forty minutes or an hour, he should be back then.'

'Or Fornier, Warrant Officer Fornier, is he here? He would do.'

'No, I'm afraid that he's with Captain Poullain in Aix-en-Provence.' Briant noticed Machanaud sway for a moment uncertainly as he took in this information. He'd obviously been drinking and mixing this now with deep thought didn't go well together. 'Is there anything I can help with?'

A slow blink through bleary eyes, then finally, 'Yes, you can take a note for them.' Machanaud shuffled closer and leant on the counter. 'You can tell them I've now remembered the car that passed. You might want to write it down.' Machanaud waited for Briant to grab a pad and pen from the side, then said the words very slowly, the last part in pronounced syllables. 'It was very low, dark green, a sports coupé. Probably an Alfa Romeo. An AL-FA RO-ME-O COU-PÉ. Have you got that?'

'Yes, okay. But you realize that this is only a note. If you want to make this part of any official statement, you'll have to return and speak to Captain Poullain.'

'Okay, okay, I understand. You have your procedures.' Machanaud held up one hand defensively as he stepped back from the counter. 'I just thought it important that they have that note while I remember.'

'Yes, certainly. I'll make sure they get it.' Briant watched thoughtfully as Machanaud shuffled back out, probably back to the same bar where he'd found inspiration to suddenly remember the car.

They'd walked for almost a minute in virtual silence through Parc du Pharo, waiting for the groups of tourists to thin out before the package was handed over. It was a large manila envelope. Chapeau looked briefly inside and saw the small bundles of cash.

'It went well,' he commented. 'Your friend should be pleased.'

'Yes, he was.' Duclos looked back at Chapeau directly for the first time. It had been his main worry: that Chapeau would have read the papers and discovered his lie. It had been quite prominent in *Le Provençal*, but still easily missed by someone only half paying attention, wedged in at the bottom of the front page with no accompanying pictures. He breathed an inner sigh of relief; obviously Chapeau hadn't seen it. Probably was illiterate or only read comics and gun manuals, he thought cynically. 'I think you'll find it's all there.'

Chapeau walked to the nearest bench, sat down and, partly shielding the envelope, counted one of the bundles. Then he measured its depth against the others: three bundles each of 2,000 francs, one half-size. Chapeau shut the envelope, folded it over by the flap and stood up with the closest he'd come to a smile in all of their meetings. 'Hopefully your friend can rest easy now.' And with a curt nod, he headed back the way they'd come, leaving Duclos on the bench.

Chapeau's car, a Peugeot 403, was parked fifty metres back from the main entrance to the park. He'd arrived ten minutes early so that he could see Duclos arrive, get the registration number of his car. It'd arrived punctually, just two minutes before six: a dark green Alfa Romeo coupé. A neat compact car for a neat compact man. Everything in his life was probably neatly compartmentalized, thought Chapeau. He watched Duclos get out and enter the park and then waited a minute before following.

Chapeau flipped over the newspaper on his passenger seat and glanced again at the report at the bottom of the front page. He'd already read it twice earlier that day, pondering what to do. The last person to cross him so blatantly he'd left with his throat cut in a Marseille back alley.

But with this Alain he wanted to bide his time, learn a bit more about him before taking any action. At one point earlier, he'd laughed out loud at the double dupe; in return getting payment for nothing somehow seemed divine justice. But he couldn't get out of his mind the bad intent that had been there, the possible repercussions if he had killed the boy: a high-profile murder case with a whole station of rural gendarmes with little else to do but catch the murderer, he'd probably have had to move to Paris for a few years until things had quietened down.

Ahead, he could now see Duclos getting back into his car. He decided to follow.

13

'. . . And in that dream, did you recognize it immediately?'

'Yes. It was the pond at Broadhurst Farm. It only turned into a lake later.'

'And you said that Jojo was already there. Could you see him clearly? What did he look like?'

Stuart Capel tensed as the tape rolled, leaning forward. Lambourne had told him one of the key objectives had been to get a clearer picture of Jojo. Lambourne's notes were in his hand, headed 'Session 4: 28 February 1995'. He knew how the notes and the tape slotted together from the last tape sent.

'I couldn't see clearly . . . it was too misty, and he was too far away.' Then, after a second: 'I only saw him clearly when I was closer . . . looking up through the water . . .'

Silence. Background drone of London traffic. Brief cough from Lambourne.

Stuart could imagine Eyran struggling for a clearer image. Finally: 'His hair was dark, slightly curly, and his eyes were bright blue or dark green. I'm not sure.'

'Does he remind you of someone you know perhaps? An old friend or someone from school?'

Longer pause this time. Eyran's low, regular breathing came over clearly for a second. 'No. But there's something familiar about him – yet I don't know why.'

'Note one.' Lambourne's voice came across in a deeper timbre. Stuart dutifully followed the instruction and read the note: *An initial assumption was that Jojo might be modelled on an old friend, someone from Eyran's past. If that's now to be discounted – why the familiarity?* After the 'Note one' announcement, an eight-second silence, then: 'Continues.' In transferring the initial session recording to cassette, Lambourne had put in the break points. It reminded Stuart of Linguaphone tapes with gaps left for student repetition.

'Did Jojo tell you where you'd met before?'

'No. I told him I was looking for my parents, and that was when he first offered to help.'

'And you went back because in the previous dream, you'd seen them there.'

'Only my father.' Another long silence. Faint rustling of papers. 'That was when Jojo wanted me to cross over . . . told me that he'd lost his parents as well and hadn't been able to find them until he crossed over.'

'Did he tell you what happened with them?'

'Nothing then . . .' Eyran swallowing, clearing his throat. 'Only in another dream . . . later. But he said it was years ago – he could hardly remember it.'

'Note two.' *Shared grief, yet Jojo conveniently has no memory of his loss. Eyran's loss is the main focus. Crossing over could symbolize to Jojo that Eyran trusts him, is siding with him. Yet we know from a later dream that they are together in their search – the barrier has by then been crossed.*

Lambourne's voice on tape reminded Stuart of their first meeting: '*When did you first realize there was a problem?*'

And he'd told Lambourne everything. The nineteen-day coma. The hospital. *The nightmares.* Everything except how much he'd resisted bringing Eyran to see him. Clinging to the Eyran he remembered.

Eyran had awoken finally from his coma four days before Christmas.

When did you first realize . . . ? Had it been when he'd first told Eyran his parents were dead? The hospital staff had been briefed just to say his parents were ill, in another ward – until Stuart arrived. But then Stuart remembered seeing that same look in that first moment of greeting Eyran: something distant and lost in his eyes, almost as if Stuart was someone he knew only vaguely who couldn't be placed for a moment.

Yet it remained through those first hours, that split-second delay in recognition and response. At first, the explanation in Stuart's mind had been the shock and grief and Eyran struggling to come to terms with the unbelievable, the unacceptable. But by the late evening, as Eyran prepared to sleep, Stuart was keen to know Torrens' assessment. How much of Eyran's slowness of reaction was due to the coma, how much could be attributed to shock and grief? Was he under any drugs or medication that might cause such an effect? How long might the condition prevail and, most importantly, might it be permanent?

Torrens started with the obvious: it's too soon to tell, he's only been out of a coma a day; yes there has been some recent medication, promethazine, to cool his body temperature down – though that shouldn't delay his reaction rate. But possibly the shock of his parents' death could cause such a reaction. 'His mind might be numbed by the collection of recent events. It's just awoken, electrical and chemical connections are flexing their muscles for the first time in almost three weeks, and suddenly it has to deal with the fact that his parents are dead. The numbness, the slowness of reaction, could be a form of protection. I doubt if it's all sunk in yet. Did he cry much when you told him?'

'Yes, a bit.' But what had struck Stuart the most was Eyran's eyes looking so lost, desolate. He'd hugged Eyran, expecting a catharsis of sobbing which in the end had never come; just the same sad, distant gaze through watery eyes as they broke the embrace.

'I don't think we should read too much into it for a few days. I'll run some detailed responsiveness checks then.'

A few days? Stuart had always assumed he'd be flying back with Eyran the next day in time for Christmas.

Impossible. Apart from the necessary tests and monitoring, there were Eyran's other injuries to consider. 'The cracked rib has a way to go yet, and we'd want to restrap that and run another X-ray before okaying him for a long flight. Don't reckon on him being able to leave before five or six days.'

Staying over Christmas? He knew he couldn't possibly leave Eyran alone in hospital over those days, but he wasn't relishing the call to Amanda to tell her he wouldn't be back with her and Tessa for Christmas.

As it was, it had taken him over a week to talk openly about his grief with Amanda. So many years' sparring with Jeremy, fighting over stupid, inconsequential things – it all seemed such a waste now, so pointless. No opportunity left for amends, except to whisper emptily, 'I love you,' vapoured breath on the chill air as they'd lowered Jeremy into the ground. The only thing to keep them close the past ten years had been Eyran. If it hadn't been for Eyran, he'd have had the same relationship with Jeremy as he had with his father.

It was the nearest he'd ever come to explaining to Amanda his affinity with Eyran. He'd lived part of his life through Eyran, the childhood he felt he had lost, the mistakes and barriers between his father and himself that he could see being repeated between Eyran and Jeremy. But, at times, he'd taken it a step too far, kidded himself he knew better about Eyran's upbringing, tried to be an alternative father. And he felt guilt for that now: in forging his own close bond with Eyran, trying to be honest broker, perhaps he had stolen some limelight from Jeremy; precious years that now couldn't be replaced.

After explaining Torrens' prognosis, brief silence from Amanda. Finally: 'I understand. You have to stay with him.'

But the silence and the tone said it all: *You should be here with us, your family, but how can I possibly protest about favouritism for Eyran, appear heartless by suggesting that you leave him alone in hospital over Christmas?*

'Thanks for understanding. I'll phone Christmas Eve, then again Christmas Day. I can have a long session with Tessa then.'

Christmas at the hospital was a strange affair. On Christmas morning everyone gathered in the canteen for a small show, the highlight of which was one of Torrens' colleagues, Walowski, playing Father Christmas with a heavy Germanic accent. It was like some exaggerated Robin Williams sketch, with a couple of curvy nurses in short red skirts and black stockings playing his little helpers. Eyran smiled at intervals, but was still too remote and withdrawn for full laughter. Even the first half-smiles had only come that morning, opening his presents from Stuart.

Christmas lunch had been laid on for later, but Stuart wanted something less organized, more personal. He got permission from Torrens to take Eyran into town, and they found a lively restaurant a block back from the sea front. The menu was a curious mix of Tex-Mex and Italian with a sprinkling of Christmas turkey specials. But the atmosphere was wonderfully raucous and joyous, party streamers and cheering, and a small Mexican combo in the corner played a range of Tijuana, Christmas favourites, Tony Orlando, Gloria Estefan and Santana.

They had Taco dips to start and turkey for the main course. Stuart finished off with brandy pudding, Eyran with pecan and maple syrup ice-cream. They found it difficult to talk above the music and background noise and had to shout Merry Christmas as they'd pulled two crackers. But Eyran enjoyed the atmosphere regardless. At least they could lose their emotions within it, rather than feel obliged to speak to fill a silent void; especially when Stuart knew he'd have to do most of the talking, tiptoeing around an emotional minefield. He'd already done it for three days at the hospital and was fast running out of safe footholds.

He noticed Eyran's fingers tapping to the band's version of '*Oye Como Va*'. *Good,* something at least breaking through the barriers built by the coma, a part of him getting back into the rhythm of life. But the smiles were still infrequent, stilted. Stuart had a Southern Comfort with his coffee, Eyran an elaborate butterscotch-flavoured milkshake. As they left, half the restaurant was singing along to 'Knock Three Times'. Outside, the fresh salt air hit them even a block back from the beach.

'Let's go down there, walk along for a bit,' Stuart suggested on impulse. Eyran merely nodded, a faint smile threatening to escape.

On the front, the air was bracing. A fresh westerly breeze was struggling to clear some cloud build-up, the air warm and moist with salt spray. As they walked, Stuart talked of Tessa looking forward to seeing Eyran. They'd plan something special for New Year's Day when they were all together.

And it was there, walking with the warm Pacific breeze buffeting them from one side, ruffling their hair, that the dam of Eyran's emotions finally broke and he started weeping. He mumbled, 'I miss my mum and dad,' as Stuart pulled him into an embrace. Then something about remembering Mission Beach where they all used to go for the day together, the words partly muffled against Stuart's chest and then finally lost among the sobbing and the noise of the surf.

'I miss them too. Terribly,' Stuart said, but it sounded so lame; empty consolation. Stuart felt the small body quaking and trembling against him, and inside he felt his own sorrow rising again, tears welling; but this time it wasn't just for Jeremy, but for the strength of spirit and zest for life in Eyran that now also seemed lost. Bitter tears and silent prayers on the mist of the Pacific surf rolling in, willing that the next days and weeks might see some improvement, bring back the Eyran he remembered.

Eyran awoke in the middle of the night, eyes blinking, adjusting, consciousness searching in that first moment for a reason.

Had he dreamt again, or had a noise perhaps disturbed him? He didn't remember any dream, and no sounds came except the faint swish and sway of trees outside his window as he held his breath and listened intently. He tried to judge if the wind was rising, a storm brewing; but the movement of the branches remained gentle and steady, soothing and swaying, white noise to lull him back to sleep again.

Was he still in the hospital or at his uncle Stuart's house? He looked at the light coming in through the window and tried to pick out shapes in the room. Faint light from a watery moon: the hospital room had been brighter from street lamps outside, the window larger, and the two large trees his side of the hospital he could never hear moving for the thickness of the glazing. Sometimes the days in the hospital and those in England seemed to merge, then suddenly he would be back once again in his room in San Diego, joy and surprise momentarily leaping inside that everything in between had been a bad dream – before the shapes and shadows in the room slowly fell into place.

The nightmares and the time awake had sometimes been difficult to separate: the friendly face of his uncle Stuart, voice echoing, telling him his parents were dead, doctors with tests and monitors, smiling faces telling him that everything was going to be all right, his uncle was coming to see him, explain. '*You'll stay with us now, we'll take care of you. Everything's going to be fine, Tessa's looking forward to seeing you.*' The rhythm of the band pumping through his body, people cheering, smiling as they clinked glasses; everyone seemed so happy except him. And so the sleep became a welcome release, transported him back where he wanted to be: the warmth of the wheat field where he might meet Jojo and they could look for his parents again.

The first dream had been two nights after awakening from the coma. The doctors said that he'd been asleep for nineteen days, but he couldn't recall anything, not even the accident; the last thing he remembered was his mother reaching back to soothe his brow, and staring at her blonde hair as he sank back into sleep.

Only when he saw Jojo in the dream did fragments of the other dreams start coming back to him, and he remembered that they'd been on this adventure before of trying to find his parents. After the dream by the pond, there had been another with him and Jojo pushing their way uphill through thick woodland and bracken. Jojo had said there was a clearing towards the brow ahead, and from there they would see his parents waiting for him in the valley below. After thrashing through, a light had shone ahead and Eyran could see the trees and bracken thinning, see the clearing, and he ran expectantly towards it, hardly feeling the barbs of the bracken pricking his legs. But as he finally burst free into the light, he awoke.

Since that night, he'd willed himself back into the dream each time before sleep to try and reach the brow and find his parents – though there had been no more dreams with Jojo, only one with him alone sitting in a stark hospital corridor waiting for news of his parents from one of the rooms, expecting Jojo to come out at any minute and say that he'd finally found them. But in the end it was Uncle Stuart and a doctor, faces forlorn, eyes sad, saying there was nothing that could be done, the doctors tried their best . . . but your parents are dead. *Dead!* He'd hidden his face and his tears momentarily in his hands, and when he'd looked up again the corridor was empty, his uncle and the doctor had gone. He began to fear the entire hospital was empty – that he was the only one there. The last thing he remembered was calling out for Jojo, but no answer came except the hollow echo of his own voice from the corridor walls.

And so all he was left with was the stark solitude of those waking hours; and sometimes those hours seemed like the nightmare, and the hours asleep and his dreams – the possibility of meeting Jojo and being able to find his parents – became a welcoming and warm reality.

Familiar objects had been placed in his room – his computer, the Daytona racetrack and *Baywatch* posters – to make him feel at home, as if nothing too much had changed. But unless they could tell him that they'd made a mistake, that his parents were alive and had survived the accident, none of it held any meaning for him. Uncle Stuart and his wife Amanda and Tessa – who tried so hard to play with him and cheer him up – became little more than vague, background voices. He was always trying to remember, play vivid scenes in his mind of how it was: picnics on Mission Beach, a visit to DisneyWorld, hot dogs at the Chargers game, going fishing on his father's boat. Sometimes he could hear his father or mother speaking, recall whole phrases and sentences. The other voices around became an intrusion.

Eyran wondered how far it was to Broadhurst Farm. Four miles, five? He got up and walked towards the window. He left the light off so that the faint moonlight might pick out objects in the garden and the field beyond. A large oak and two elms had lost nearly all their leaves; only two large fir trees at the end of the garden moved with the wind. The hedgerow separating the garden from the farmer's field beyond, Tessa's climbing frame, the rockery and pond – even small objects became clear as his eyes adjusted. The field beyond was still indistinct, except for the faint silhouette of the line of trees on its brow. He wondered if – if he closed his eyes and willed it hard – in his mind he could sail across the farm fields to Broadhurst Farm, form an image, so that when he went back to sleep his dreams might take him there again. But he wasn't even sure which way it was. Was it over the ridge ahead, or over more to the west?

The moon was a watery half through faint mist and cloud. For a moment he thought he saw the dull shapes of figures moving beyond the garden – but as he looked more intently, they were no longer there. It was just the shadow of tree branches moving on the breeze. He closed his eyes and tried to imagine the wheat field beyond the hill, let his mind drift until it was before him. But he'd never been there at night, felt too frightened to let the image linger, and he tried to cast his mind back to how he remembered the wheat field in daylight, running through the sheaves with the warm sun on his back.

But the image never came, it remained dark and cool, shades of grey under the pale moon. And the field for him in that moment became yet another symbol of death, something that could only serve a purpose in his dreams if he could recall it in daylight. Perhaps he would ask his uncle Stuart to drive past Broadhurst Farm the next day.

The first dream Stuart became aware of was six days into the new year. Eyran had awoken screaming, bathed in sweat. Stuart asked him if he'd dreamt like that before and he'd said yes, but they hadn't turned bad like this one. 'What happened in the dreams?'

'Different things. It was confusing. Some of it was at the hospital, some at the farm where I used to play.'

'Is that the farm we drove past the other day, just down from your old house?'

'Yes.'

Stuart thought it was quite a normal request that Eyran had wanted to see the old house. Relive old and fond memories. They'd stopped while Eyran studied the front of the house, saw the changes, the different colours on the window frames and doors, along with the familiar: the basketball hoop that Jeremy had put up still above the garage door. Stuart had a quick flash of Jeremy and him playing basketball, showing off for the kids. Jeremy had twisted his ankle, sending the kids into guffaws of laughter as he'd hobbled off. They thought it was all part of the act: Abbott and Costello do the Harlem Globetrotters. They'd been quite close then, lived only five miles apart; in fact Stuart had been drawn to the area on Jeremy's recommendation. And then after only two years, Jeremy had left for America.

As they drove off, Eyran asked him to turn right at the end of the road. It was a narrow country lane, and after another two hundred yards or so, Eyran asked him to stop again. Stuart pulled into the first available farm-gate entrance. This time they got out of the car and stood, misty breath showing on the crisp air, looking out across the fields. Stuart asked him if that was where they used to play.

'Yes, there's a small pond in the copse over there.' Eyran pointed towards a wooded area in a dip between the fields, oval in shape, no more than a hundred yards at its widest point. 'Then the wheat field on the other side rises up towards the woods at the back of the house.'

Little more than stubble now, Stuart noted, looking bleak in the cold, misty air. The sun was weak and low in the sky, hardly penetrating a faint mist which obscured its far end. Two crows suddenly cawing loudly and flapping away from a nearby tree broke them out of their moment's reverie.

It was almost a week ago they'd made the drive. 'What frightened you in the dream?'

'There was a ledge and a drop I didn't see until too late. I started falling.'

'Is there a ledge like that in the field?'

'No, just in the dream.' Eyran blinked slowly. 'Even the pond in the woods is very shallow, at most up to my chest.'

'Are you all right now?'

Brief pause for thought. 'Yes.'

Stuart playfully ruffled Eyran's hair and forced a smile. A vague smile returned. Nothing too harmful, thought Stuart. Just some old memories jumbling, trying to sort themselves out. Probably driving by the old house and the farm fields had sparked it off.

But over the following two weeks, there were three more dreams, increasingly violent and disturbing, and Stuart began to worry. Two took place in the fields by the old house or at the hospital, the other was at the house in San Diego, at night with the pool lights on, mist rising from the warm water. Eyran thought he heard voices coming out of the ghostly mist and moved towards it; but it spread quickly and drifted in billows until it engulfed the entire garden and the house, and he couldn't find his way through. Hopelessly lost and frightened, the warm mist clinging all around him, suffocating, he awoke. Stuart asked him if any of the other dreams had involved him looking for his parents, and after a moment's hesitation he'd answered yes, in the hospital dream.

When Stuart'd discussed it with Amanda, she'd immediately opted for them taking Eyran to the psychiatrist Torrens had recommended. Stuart wanted to wait, see what the next week or so brought. It had been five days after his return before he'd even mentioned the psychiatrist to Amanda.

Stuart remembered twirling Lambourne's card in his hand without really reading it as Torrens explained: 'Some electrical activity within the brain concerned me. It occurred on two different occasions, but only on the last did it finally reach any motor senses and lead to Eyran awakening.

Which meant for the remainder it was largely confined to the subconscious. It could be nothing, but it warrants keeping in check. Given the tremendous grief Eyran has suffered, and to help him come to terms with the loss of his parents, counselling is advisable in any case.'

'I don't think we should delay,' urged Amanda. 'These dreams are beginning to worry me. Why wait another week or so?'

'I want to give Eyran some natural period of grieving, some time for him to come to terms with the loss in his own way, before sending a psychiatrist into the fray to force the issue.'

'I just don't see any dramatic change coming quickly. He's not the same bushy-tailed, bright-eyed Eyran we remember, and the sooner we accept that and try and do something about it, the better. I don't think delaying will help. With the dreams he's having, it could even do more harm.'

Stuart was insistent. 'We don't know yet if his unresponsiveness is a result of his grief and loss, or a by-product of his injuries and the coma. And I'm not sure a psychiatrist would be able to tell that. Only time will tell. Some time for his grieving to subside.'

Amanda held his gaze for a moment with her best 'you can't be serious' expression. Then slowly shook her head and went into the kitchen. For the next five minutes, he could hear plates and cups moved and stacked and kitchen cupboard doors closed with more gusto than normal.

Perhaps she was right, delaying was unreasonable. Behind her annoyance, he could almost hear the words she was biting back: *You don't want to face it because you're unwilling to accept anything less than the Eyran you remember. Only a miracle recovery will do for the golden boy.* But she'd spared him the barb, or perhaps wished to avoid what was now a stale and unnecessary argument between them: absorption with Eyran over and above his own family. But that thin line was probably close to being crossed, and she was painfully close to the truth. Part of him couldn't accept Eyran's current condition, perhaps never would be able to. The psychiatrist was the last line of defence, the final throwing in of the towel: admittance that Eyran was psychologically disturbed and needed help.

'. . . *There was nobody there, just rows of old weed-killers and pesticides . . . and I recognized it as the shed from our garden. My father warned me when we first moved in not to go in the shed until he'd fixed it . . . the floor was rotten and the old jars of weed-killers were dangerous. I was confused . . . I remembered him clearing them away that summer . . . and now they were back.'*

'*Did Jojo say anything? Explain.*'

'*No. I felt the floor shaky beneath my feet . . . and he held one hand out to me. But as I stepped forward, I felt the floor give way . . . and I . . . I . . .*'

'*It's okay, Eyran. Step back . . . back! . . .*'

Stuart was yanked back to the tape. Sharp reminder of the dream after which he'd finally relented to Eyran seeing Lambourne. Eyran screaming and Amanda's rapid footsteps on the landing.

'*. . . I was falling . . . falling . . . everything spinning . . .*'

'*Back . . . Break away. Away!*'

Stuart sat forward. His pulse was pounding hard as it had been that night when he was running towards Eyran's room. Lambourne had mentioned the danger area of the dream endings; that as much as possible he would generalize or pick out random details. But still he'd been caught out: Eyran in that moment reliving falling, spinning down helplessly.

Silence finally. Only Eyran's rapid, fractured breathing came across.

Lambourne waited a few seconds more. 'You must have been disappointed when you didn't see your parents – Jojo let you down. And has he let you down in other dreams?'

Eyran's breathing easing more. A faint swallow.

Stuart picked up on Lambourne's tactic: generalities to shift Eyran's focus. But the sudden leap seemed to have caught Eyran by surprise. Stuart could feel the tension coming across with each beat of silence on the tape; could imagine Eyran struggling to extricate himself from one set of horrors, sifting frantically through time and misty images, probably only to find himself facing still more. A simple consent, and now he'd put Eyran through this! A pang of guilt gripped him, one hand clutching tight at Lambourne's report.

'I don't remember exactly . . . *I* . . .'

Eyran either still struggling for images or pushing away acceptance.

'Do most of the dreams end abruptly in the same way?' Lambourne prompted. 'Yet with the hope you'll find your parents right up until the last moment?'

At length a slow exhalation. Final admittance. '. . . Yes.'

'Note five.' *No explanation is offered by Jojo for his failures from one dream to the next. Each one starts anew, Eyran filled with fresh trust and hope. Like an incurable gambler, Eyran conveniently blots past form from his mind, and Jojo is there to convince him that this time they'll hit gold.*

Lambourne went back to the early sequence of dreams, before and after the coma, then: 'And during those dreams – the first of running through the wheat field directly after the car accident and the last you remember before awakening in the hospital from the coma – do any other voices reach you? Did you hear anything from outside?'

'I don't know . . . I'm not sure.' Eyran sounded flustered, uncertain.

'Try to concentrate. Take yourself back, and try to remember if you heard anything.'

Stuart saw immediately where Lambourne was aiming. After the last session Lambourne had commented that what went against the theory of Eyran creating Jojo through non-acceptance of his parents' death was him appearing *before* Eyran awoke and knew they were dead. Lambourne was digging for subliminal reference. Stuart felt for Eyran in that moment, wished that he'd been alongside him to hold his hand as he delved back through the darkness of his nineteen-day coma.

At length a low, almost indiscernible muttering: 'There was something . . . a man's voice.' Stuart felt his skin tingle.

'What did it say?' Eagerness in Lambourne's voice; fear that at any second the images would slip from Eyran's mind.

'That . . . that the woman was gone, nothing could be done . . . but there was still some hope for the other two.' Staccato breathing, the words mumbled in between. 'There was the sound of traffic in the background . . . then I was being lifted, moved to one side.'

'Was there anything else?'

'Some other voices, more distant . . . Someone I thought called my name, but I couldn't be sure.' For Stuart, the images were suddenly too clear, too painful. He was still in his mind gripping Eyran's hand, only now he was by the roadside while Eyran's shattered and bloodied body struggled for life. Gasps for life now no more than gasps for words. 'Then a lot of movement . . . some lights passing which hurt my eyes. A voice closer saying that it looked like another late shift, but he hoped to make it up the next day. And another voice, more muffled . . . speaking on a radio phone. It was answering and crackling. And the siren . . . the siren again . . . the siren and the crackling made me feel sleepy.'

'Any more voices?'

Brief pause. 'Only the wheat field then. And Jojo.'

'Note six.' *Memory of medics and police attending and first few minutes in ambulance. Nothing after that. But it appears there was some subliminal reference for Eyran to draw upon. The fact that he knew his mother was already dead might explain why in the dreams she either doesn't feature or is more distant.*

Stuart recalled from the Oceanside medical report that Eyran's coma hadn't been caused immediately by the accident injuries but by the fast accumulating blood clots and the oedema soon after. And while the cranial pressure was still building, *before* . . . Stuart bit at his lip. *Oh God.* Eyran had been conscious for a few moments then, and while he was struggling for his own life, had learnt of his parents' fate. Stuart could hardly think of a worse scenario.

Stuart's hand was trembling as he came to Lambourne's summary: *Unless we can confront Jojo directly in future sessions, progress could be slow. Working second hand, scant additional light, I feel, can be thrown on Jojo's core character and motives. My plan would therefore be to side with Eyran over specific questions, instil in him a strong need to know the answers from Jojo – then switch over and try and ask them directly.*

Yet part of that process is in conflict: all other voices are telling Eyran his parents are dead, and Jojo is probably the only crutch supporting that part of Eyran's psyche still clinging on, refusing to accept. The bridge between the two has to be crossed cautiously. Remove it too hastily, destroy the illusion, and Eyran either falls into the void or has to leap towards full acceptance before he is ready. Yet if we don't act quickly, Jojo could become increasingly dominant - it would then be that much harder to wean Eyran away. The threat of schizophrenia would be a stage closer.

Stuart shook his head. Forty minutes of hell approved by a single signature and now another consent slip was before him: approving Lambourne's foray to confront Jojo. When he'd finally assented to the sessions, he'd told himself that it was for Eyran's own good – but now he wasn't so sure. He found himself wrestling with the nagging doubt that his own desire to have back the Eyran he remembered might have played a part. This time he wanted to be sure the decision was purely for Eyran's benefit: the pitfalls and dangers set against the advantages. Lambourne saw Jojo as a threat, and no doubt he was right; yet in Eyran's troubled mind, with his parents gone, Jojo was probably one of the few friends he felt he had left in this world. And now Lambourne wanted rid of Jojo with another simple signature.

Stuart picked up a pen, then put it down again. He flicked back through Lambourne's notes for more guidance. But suddenly he found himself biting back tears, and slumped dejectedly, cradling his head in one hand.

14

The small back room was insufferably hot. A ceiling fan swirled slowly, but Poullain could still feel his shirt sticking to his back. He adjusted a small swivelling desk fan so that its sweep cut across him more directly. The telephone rang.

It was Perrimond, the Aix chief prosecutor. 'I've had a chance now to think about this new information from Machanaud, and I think your assessment is right. It's a little too convenient that he should suddenly now remember an accurate description of the car. Has there been much mention of the car in Taragnon or Bauriac?'

'Not so much in Bauriac. But we visited quite a few shops in Taragnon and then the restaurant just outside where Duclos had lunch. The village is small, news spreads quickly, and Machanaud hits the bars heavily, spends half his time leaning on the counter swapping stories with barmen. I think that's how he picked up the description of the car.'

'Yes, yes. I would agree.'

A brief pause, flicking of papers from Perrimond's end. 'So what do you want me to do?' Poullain asked.

'It's up to you. But if you should decide not to ask Machanaud in to make the statement official on the basis that the description has been manufactured from local gossip, I'd support that assessment.'

'I understand.' But he suddenly realized the decision was back with him; he'd hoped merely to provide background and let Perrimond decide. The desk fan cut a cool swathe of air across his chest. More papers turning, then, 'Oh, I had a call from Bayet, the Aix Mayor yesterday. Apparently, Marcel Vallon is quite a close friend of his. Vallon expressed concern about the police questioning of one of his house guests, this Duclos character. Of course, this came a day before this new information, so I felt quite safe assuring that Monsieur Duclos had merely assisted with some information and was not in any way a suspect.'

The message was clear to Poullain: if they made the statement official, they would be duty-bound to question Duclos again. Perrimond would have to backtrack on what he'd said and call the Mayor, the Mayor would have to call Vallon, and he'd have to go cap in hand when he phoned Vallon again to arrange a second interview, this time under far less hospitable circumstances. But he felt uncomfortable making the decision without more support from Perrimond. 'So you think it might be awkward to suddenly put Duclos back under the spotlight?'

'The awkwardness I can argue with the Mayor. This is a murder case and we have to do what's right and damn the awkwardness. But I would like at least to be armed with a good reason. If at the end of the day it couldn't possibly be Duclos because he was in a restaurant at the time, and if you're already suspicious that Machanaud has merely picked up on the car description from town gossip, I'd rather not make the call. I'd sound foolish. You just phone Vallon directly yourself for a second interview and be prepared for a cold blast of air, and I'll wait for the Mayor to phone again. And if and when he does, I'll tell him it's something routine regarding a sighting of Duclos' car. Nothing to worry about. Really, Poullain, it's up to you what you do.'

'I see.' It would be awkward. It would be foolish. It would serve absolutely no purpose because the person concerned was somewhere else at the time. There was only *one* sensible decision to be made, and it was now entirely his to make. No more clues or guidance. 'I think I made my views clear at the outset.'

'Yes, you did. Now I've given you my input. I can only deliberate on details you present to me for prosecution, not how or why those details should be gained. While the case is still under a *commission rogatoire générale* and not yet passed to the examining magistrate – it's an investigative matter. Your jurisdiction.'

Whichever way it went, he would never be able to say, 'Perrimond made the recommendation.' He was on his own. 'I understand. If I should decide to pursue the matter, I'll call you first as a matter of courtesy. Let you know whether or not to expect another call from the Mayor.'

Perrimond mentioned that the warrant for Machanaud would be ready the next day and that he would be requesting a pre-trial for only three weeks' time. 'Machanaud's defence – probably a standard state appointee – will no doubt try and push for anything up to two months. We'll end up somewhere in between. How's the statement from this woman he used to live with coming along?'

'It will be typed up later, delivered tomorrow when we pick up the warrant.' Through Machanaud's old work place on the Camargue they'd tracked down a divorcee with four children in Le Beausset with whom he'd had a relationship. She'd had a child by him, a girl, but he'd disappeared when she was three. She hadn't heard from him since, nor had a penny been sent for the child. The tale of bitter desertion, of his hard drinking and violent temper tantrums, lashing out at her and sometimes the children, had been an important breakthrough. Built a picture that Machanaud was not just a harmless oddball vagabond; he had a temper, was unpredictable and violent when drunk. 'It's quite a strong statement. I think she'll make a good witness on the stand.'

'Good.' The case against Machanaud was looking stronger by the day. That was where their energies should be concentrated; not wild goose chases with this Duclos and him having to fend off calls from the Mayor.

They arranged the time for collecting the arrest warrant for Machanaud, and Poullain commented, 'I should also by then have decided if there'll be any follow-up on the car description and Duclos.'

'Very good. I'll see you tomorrow.' Perrimond bit lightly at his lip just after he hung up. The call had gone well, except at the end he realized he'd sounded too nonchalant, already confident of the decision Poullain would make.

Dominic finished his shift at 7.00 p.m. He changed at home, fried two veal steaks, tossed some salad and fifty minutes later sat with his mother on the back porch, sipping some chilled white Bordeaux in the fading evening light. Pale pink, then crimson streaks along the skyline, finally ochre. In the last of the light, his mother asked if he was going to cut back the mimosa in the next few days.

He did most of the gardening now, she'd become too frail, and they'd talked about the mimosa the week before. But he'd just been too busy recently with the investigation; workload should be lighter soon. How was it going? she asked. He made light of it, didn't want to burden her with his disasters: that they were probably charging the wrong suspect and there was little he could do about it. He just said there were two strong suspects, but that evidence was light on the one he suspected the most. Difficult.

They talked about his older sister Janine and her husband possibly visiting from Paris at Christmas; she'd missed the previous Christmas and had come out at Easter instead. Her boy Pascal was now nine, her younger daughter, Céleste, just six. His mother surveyed the garden fondly, probably remembering her grandchildren running around playing earlier in the year. Then her eyes fell back to the tree and the mimosa. 'It's starting to get strangled. We shouldn't leave it too long.'

'Don't worry, this weekend or next I'll see to it.' The tree. As far as she was concerned, it might as well be the only one in the garden. A young tangerine tree now a bushy two metres high, planted by his father two years before he died. He saw its first blossom, but died before the November when it fruited. His mother viewed it now as a symbol: she'd seen two years of full fruit; how many more would she witness from what her dear departed had planted? And now a nearby overgrown mimosa was threatening its continuing blossom and fruit, and she was too weak to cut it back.

It somehow seemed unjust that after a lifetime's work and struggle, they'd moved to this quiet backwater in expectation of a long and peaceful retirement, and within four years his father was dead. Another two, and his mother was gravely ill.

Dominic lit a night light on the table as it became too dark and they sat like two lovers on their first date. Except that the stories swapped were old and familiar, fond memories. Perhaps one of the last chances.

Fading light. His mother's skin had a pale yellow translucency to it, looking now even more ghostly under the flickering candlelight. He drank faster than normal, swilled away the unwanted thoughts; he was on his third glass to his mother's one before he even noticed. He started to mellow. The sound of cicadas and crickets added rhythm to the night, pulsed gently through his veins.

When his mother finally announced that she was tired and headed for bed, he felt suddenly restless. He sat only five minutes on the empty terrace before resolving to head back into town. She hardly made it past nine these days; the medication sapped her strength as much as the illness. *Was this what it would be like when she was finally gone? Empty terraces by candlelight, Odette or some other simple shop girl with the right face and the right smile sat opposite just to fill the void?* He needed another drink.

Louis' was half full. He sat up at the bar and Louis, after pouring a beer, asked if he'd seen Monique Rosselot again. Louis' interest was somewhere between the healthy curiosity he showed in any good-looking village woman and genuine concern for how she was coping with her grief. Dominic hadn't seen her, nor had anyone else from the gendarmerie as far as he knew. 'We probably won't now until the memorial service. There's been nothing new.' Somebody would probably have to see her straight after arresting Machanaud, tell her that a suspect had been arrested.

But he couldn't tell Louis: news could too easily reach Machanaud on the village grapevine.

'I think a lot of people will be going to the service,' Louis commented.

'I know.' Originally shunned, now, at least in her worst hour, the village would be there for her. It took time to be accepted in Taragnon.

Louis gave him the latest from Valérie through the neighbours. Jean-Luc wasn't coming back from seeing his family for another day or so, might not even make it for the memorial service. Monique was distraught, awkward that she might have to be alone in front of the village. Tongues would wag: either they were having problems or he didn't care about his son's service. Both were far from the truth, Monique had protested to the Fiévets, but that might be the impression given. Louis shook his head. His distant, slightly glazed expression said it all: if Louis had a woman like that, he certainly wouldn't desert her at a moment like this.

They indulged in small talk, and it quickly came around to Odette and his love life. He had only seen Odette once since the investigation had started, had been too busy. But Louis was a master at reading between the lines when it came to romance, was astute enough to realize things weren't going well. The glazed look was back, broken prematurely by a renewed throng at the bar. Louis excused himself to serve. The cinema had just emptied out, and two tables in the corner had also filled. Louis was obviously going to be rushed, little time for more talk. After a few minutes Dominic knocked back his drink and said his goodbyes to a suddenly harried Louis.

His first intention was to head home, but as the night air hit him, he decided on another drink. He aimed his bike for the Maison des Arcs bar two kilometres out of town. It was almost empty, just a few die-hards clustered at the bar. He stayed only for a quick beer and a play on their fruit machine, then went on to the Bar Fontainouille near Taragnon.

Just past 11.30 when he arrived, this time he ordered a brandy. It was busy, though most of the noise and activity was towards the end of the room with a group of ten or eleven, mostly men, egging on whichever contestant they'd backed in a table football game. Among the noise and throng, it was a moment before he noticed Machanaud; though Machanaud was already staring at him, and he had the uneasy feeling that he probably had been doing so on and off from when he'd walked in. Machanaud raised his glass. Dominic nodded back and smiled.

He looked just as quickly away from Machanaud, as if he was partly listening in on a conversation of Henri the barman with a customer two bar stools away. In the corner of his eye he could tell that Machanaud was still looking over at intervals. He wondered if unconsciously he'd sought out Machanaud; he knew this bar was one of his regular haunts. See the suspect on his last night of freedom. Reconcile the image in his mind of the harmless vagabond and poacher with how Perrimond would soon portray him before a jury: woman and child beater, child molester, *murderer*.

Dominic wasn't convinced by the ex-girlfriend's statement, felt that Poullain had prompted too conveniently. She had a hard face, lined and worn and looking ten years beyond her thirty-five years. She was struggling between absent fathers, state aid and part-time cleaning jobs to keep food on the table for four children, and the bitterness and scars showed in her mannerisms and speech. With Machanaud's illegitimate child she'd probably been unable to get aid. Then suddenly came the chance of pay-back: *'We can't get you money, but we can get you retribution. Just say the right thing and we'll nail the bastard.'* How often did a woman like that get the system working on her side?

The table football game was breaking up: money was changing hands, coins and notes being slapped on the table side, back-patting and jovial abuse, someone suggesting that the loser join the paraplegics' league. Machanaud started singing a ribald version of 'Lili Marlene' to the cheers of some colleagues.

Perhaps he would simply whisper in Machanaud's ear, 'Go and go now. Get far away. Come tomorrow afternoon there'll be no more chances. They're out to get you and there's nothing I can do to stop them.' Dominic wished now he hadn't come. He felt awkward, could hardly look Machanaud in the eye knowing what was coming the next day. He swilled the last of the brandy in his glass and knocked it back, was suddenly eager to get out. But it was already too late. Machanaud's voice had trailed off mid chorus, he was peeling away from his group and coming across. A swathe of black hair fell across his face, and he tilted his head as if to see better.

'And how is young Monsieur Fornier this evening?'

'Fine. I was just leaving. But can I get you one before I go?' He held out a five-franc note to get Henri's attention.

In the same hand as a Gauloise, Machanaud held up a small tumbler with a finger of pale amber spirit in the bottom. He passed the tumbler across the bar. 'I'll have another eau-de-vie, if that's okay.'

Dominic ordered and paid, and Henri poured in his normal elaborate style of pulling the bottle gradually further from the glass.

After taking the first swig, Machanaud commented, 'I suppose you'll all be over the moon with this new information.'

Dominic squinted quizzically at Machanaud. Surely the gossip network didn't work that quickly for him to already know about his ex-girlfriend's statement. And was he drunk enough to be sarcastic about his own downfall? 'I don't understand. What information?'

'The car. The car. I suddenly remembered what that car passing looked like. I came into the station two days ago and told your desk sergeant.'

'Who was that?'

'Didn't catch his name. Young chap, brown hair, slightly wavy.'

Briant or Levacher, thought Dominic. Why hadn't Poullain mentioned it?

'Can't be many Alfa Romeos like that, at least not in this area. You've probably tracked it down already, but don't want to say much. *Santé.*' Machanaud took a quick slug, knocked back half his eau-de-vie. Then he was suddenly thoughtful. 'Isn't that why you've asked me in tomorrow? To make the statement on the car official?'

Dominic's mind was still reeling. *Duclos' car!* 'Yes, yes,' he answered hastily. Perhaps in all the confusion Poullain had overlooked mentioning it. The past days had been a nightmare of notes, typing statements, reports and filing for the arrest warrant. Or perhaps Poullain intended to mention it only once he had the full statement from Machanaud. Perhaps. It had been Dominic's suggestion to serve the warrant on Machanaud by asking him in to make another statement, rather than trying to serve it outside and risk a scene, fighting to subdue a handcuffed Machanaud all the way back in the car. Now he knew why Poullain had been so keen on the suggestion: Machanaud had expected to be asked in to make his car statement official.

Machanaud noticed Dominic's consternation and leant over, whispering conspiratorially, 'It's okay, if it's awkward to talk about it, I understand.'

Machanaud cut a pathetic image, smiling, probably thinking that half the local gendarmerie were busily tracking down the car that would solve their largest case in years, and *he'd* provided the vital clue. Totally unaware of the sword of Damocles hovering over his own head. Dominic felt a pang of guilt at aiding Poullain's false pretence with the statement. Or was he missing something with Machanaud that Poullain and others saw?

Machanaud put one reassuring hand on Dominic's shoulder, smiling, the harmless poacher. Dominic smiled in return. Tinker, tailor, poacher, *murderer*. Machanaud leering, one hand raised with the rock to smash down on the boy's skull. *Which was the right image?* From the end of the room came renewed shouting and cheering. Two new contestants had stepped up to the table football machine. Beyond a plume of Gauloise smoke, Dominic could smell the eau-de-vie on Machanaud's breath. *Eau-de-mort. Water of death.* Machanaud swilling down the boy's blood-stains from his clothing. Dominic shook the images away. The atmosphere in the bar was suddenly claustrophobic, suffocating. He stood up.

'Are you all right?' asked Machanaud.

'Yes, yes. Fine. It's just someone I should have seen, and I suddenly realized I might now be too late.' He looked at his watch: 12.06 a.m. Officially, Poullain finished today's shift at midnight, but often he was still there up to half an hour afterwards.

Chapeau backed into a side farm track a hundred metres along from the main gates of the château on the opposite side of the road. Some trees and foliage mostly concealed his car, though he had a clear view of its main gates through a small gap. Two days before, when he'd first made the drive, he'd kept at a discreet distance from the Alfa Romeo all the way from Marseille, especially on the quieter country roads. On that first occasion he waited across from the château fifteen minutes.

He then spent the next day checking with the land registry and vehicle registration in Paris: the château was owned by one Marcel Vallon, one of the area's largest vineyard owners and wine producers. But the car was registered to Alain Duclos with a Limoges address. So this wasn't Duclos' family house, he was probably a family friend or business associate visiting.

Chapeau decided to return, see if Duclos was staying with the Vallons or whether two days ago had been just a one-off visit. After half an hour he saw a Bentley leave, then a delivery van arrive fifteen minutes later. Then nothing for over twenty minutes. Chapeau was getting impatient, it was late morning and the heat was building up – he longed to get moving and get some air rushing through the car's interior – when finally the green Alfa Romeo appeared. It was heading towards him!

He quickly ducked down out of sight, heard the engine drone past, and raised his head again. He counted three seconds, fired up his engine, waited for a Renault Dauphine to pass heading in the same direction, and pulled out.

*

Harrault was on desk duty and confirmed that Poullain was still in his office, getting ready to leave. Dominic decided to look through the desk register first, then talk to Poullain. Harrault flicked back the page, then stood to one side as Dominic ran one finger down the entries. Nothing. He was halfway through checking back the entries when Poullain came out of his office.

He looked between Harrault and Dominic. 'I thought you'd finished a few hours back, Fornier. Looking for anything interesting?'

'Yes. I just bumped into Machanaud. He asked how our inquiries were going after his statement about the car.'

Poullain met his stare for a moment, then nodded towards his office. It was obviously going to be awkward discussing this openly in front of Harrault. As soon as the door was shut behind him, he questioned, 'So. What is the problem?'

'I don't see anything entered in the register.'

'And you won't. Not until I've discussed the development fully with Perrimond.'

'But Machanaud came in two days ago.'

'If he'd come in five or six days ago, or mentioned it on one of our first interviews, it might have been different.' Poullain walked around his desk, stood to one side of his seat. 'Think about it, Fornier. We've been asking about sightings of this car at bars and shops throughout Taragnon. Half the village have probably heard about it. And suddenly, miraculously, Machanaud remembers what it looked like. Don't be so naïve! Machanaud has picked up on the description from village gossip.'

'Is that what Perrimond thinks?'

'No, it's what we have both discussed at length as a distinct possibility. He'll no doubt tell me what he thinks tomorrow.'

Dominic shook his head. 'Regardless of what we think, it should be taken as a full statement and entered in the register. We can interpret it any way we wish after that.'

Poullain was keen to keep some distance in the argument, a pending decision from Perrimond gave him someone detached to blame. 'I have to take Perrimond's guidance as prosecutor. If the statement is so obviously false, is not heading anywhere concrete, there's no point. I can't force him to pursue it. Also, we would probably then have to question Duclos again – an additional waste of investigative time we can ill afford.'

'Perhaps it wouldn't be such a waste of time. If we mention his car has been sighted, put him on the spot, his story might change. Something new might come to light.'

Poullain stared dully at Fornier. So they were back again to Fornier's groundless suspicion of Duclos. When he thought about Perrimond's concern about the Mayor's call, the whole messy background he was stealthily avoiding mentioning, the eagerness in Fornier's voice was almost laughable. 'And what is going to change? All the waiters who saw Duclos while the attack took place are suddenly going to say they were all wrong? They didn't see Duclos? Or is Duclos going to do it all for us and just say that the waiters were all lying? He wasn't in the restaurant at the time? Wake up! It's not going to happen. There's no point in us even going through the exercise.'

'Is that your assessment or Perrimond's?'

Poullain stared back icily. 'Both!'

It was already clear what answer would be coming the next day, thought Dominic. The statement wouldn't be made. 'Then I don't agree with it.'

Dominic noticed Poullain openly flinch; then he cocked his head slightly, as if he hadn't heard properly, his eyes darting fleetingly across the desk top for explanations before looking up again. The surprise showed in his face. In their previous disagreements over Duclos, Dominic had always given way.

For a moment Poullain looked undecided as to how to rise to this new challenge. Then at length he exhaled audibly and waved a hand to one side. A dismissive gesture, as if the whole affair was suddenly unworthy of his emotions. 'And what exactly do you propose to do?'

'If the decision is made not to take the statement, then as the assisting investigative officer, I would like my disagreement of that action recorded.'

'Are you sure that's what you wish to do? You're aware of the seriousness of such an action?'

Dominic felt uncomfortable under Poullain's intense glare, his heart pounding heavily. But he'd gone too far to back down again now. His mouth was dry as he stammered, 'Yes.'

Poullain stared at him a moment longer, then sat down and rubbed his forehead with one hand. Fornier obviously wasn't going to budge, was forcing the issue to its limit. The procedure, normally used only in extreme cases, was to protect officers who felt that a line pursued in an investigation might later reflect badly on their career records; once filed, the complaint would no doubt end up on his area commanding colonel's desk in Aix.

All manner of awkward questions and complications could arise. Faced with that, perhaps it would be easier to take Machanaud's statement and visit Duclos again, regardless of the fact that it was all a waste of time. Do everything by the book. Perrimond would just have to put up with another call from the Mayor. Poullain sighed. 'Is there anything else?' He looked up only fleetingly, his annoyance evident.

'No.'

'Then I'll make your thoughts known to Perrimond when I visit him tomorrow and pick up the arrest warrant. You stay here in case I'm not back before Machanaud arrives.'

'What shall I tell him if you're not back by then?'

'Tell him you think it's for a statement, but you won't know for sure until I arrive.' Poullain forced a tight smile. 'If you get your way, you'll be partly telling the truth.'

Chapeau sat in a café in a side street just off Marseille's Rue Saint-Ferréol. Duclos' car was parked twenty metres along in the same road; he could just see its back bumper, was ready to mobilize quickly if it moved, coins already on the table for the black coffee and brandy chaser he was drinking.

At one point, following Duclos from the Vallon estate, he thought of giving up. The road headed towards Aix and Marseille, but most interesting of all it went through Taragnon, the village where the boy was found. For a while he toyed with the enticing possibility that Duclos might stop in Taragnon, perhaps even revisit the old crime scene – but Duclos headed straight through the village. Shortly after, when Duclos took the Marseille rather than the Aix road, it struck him that Duclos might be visiting Vacheret's for one of his young boys. He decided to continue following.

They were parked close to the main shopping area, and the Panier district and Vacheret's establishment were over a kilometre away. He'd followed to the corner and seen Duclos head in the opposite direction towards the Opéra and the Palais de Justice, before deciding to find himself a café in the small side street and car-sit. He'd been there now forty minutes and this was his second coffee and brandy.

Where was Duclos? Shopping no doubt: buying designer shirts and silk underpants, or whatever queer paedophiles liked wearing. Or perhaps a quick stroll in the Puget gardens, sitting on a park bench and feeding the pigeons while surreptitiously getting his jollies by watching young boys in shorts play with a football. People like Duclos made him sick. Clean on the outside, dirty inside, and with the cheek to look down their noses at people like himself. He might be a thug and a killer for hire, but there was no pretence. What you saw, you got. No false labelling.

He sharply knocked back another slug of brandy to quell his growing anger. Little shit. Feeding him a false line to commit a murder that would have had half the gendarmes in the region hunting him down. The irony and sheer joy of stiffing Duclos for the 7,000 francs was already waning. He wanted more, much more. If he'd actually gone through with the murder, he would have probably killed Duclos straight after collecting the money, followed him out into the country lanes beyond Aubagne, pulled up alongside at the first deserted crossroads, pumped two bullets through Duclos' head, and driven on. Bliss.

It had still been a tempting proposition following Duclos to the Vallon estate that first time. But he was glad now he'd shown restraint. If he was patient, nurtured it well, this could turn out to be a long and profitable association. A meaningful relationship. No point in fucking Duclos on the first date. He had been disappointed to discover that he wasn't part of the Vallon family, that would have been a remarkable pot of gold to strike so quickly. But he was obviously a family friend, perhaps came from a similar moneyed background. Waiting and watching, he would soon know.

Chapeau suddenly pushed back from the table, almost spilling his coffee. Duclos was passing! Heading for his car. Chapeau was poised to stand up and head out, and pointed to the coins on the table for the benefit of the concerned waiter looking over.

Duclos put a shopping bag in his car, leant over, rearranged something in the back seat for a moment, then straightened up and locked the door again. He started heading back down past the café. Chapeau turned away from the window, looked back towards the bar until Duclos was past, then got up and went out. He hovered by the doorway for a few seconds, until Duclos was about eighty metres ahead and almost at the end of the road, then followed.

He saw him turn right this time, heading towards La Canebière and the Vieux Port, with the Panier not much further on. Perhaps Duclos would end up at Vacheret's after all. Along Rue Saint-Ferréol towards La Canebière, the shops gradually became smaller and seedier. Cheap souvenirs and cards, carved wood and ivory, beads and caftans, goat-skin drums, a delicatessen with goat's cheese and couscous. They might as well be in the kasbah. Half the shopkeepers and people passing were North African.

At La Canebière, Duclos turned left past the quayside cafés and the Hôtel de Ville. A brief respite of nice cafés and shops, people dining out and looking out over the kaleidoscope of brightly painted fishing boats in the harbour. Then they turned into the winding Panier back lanes: dark and narrow cobblestone streets, washing strung at intervals between the dank stone buildings to catch what few shafts of sunlight filtered through. Some yorrelling in the distance, a radio playing the latest hit from Morocco: wavering pipes and strings that sounded like cats being strangled.

An old man in a black djellaba passed Chapeau and, on the corner, in front of a small café with a beaded-curtain entrance, a young Moroccan was trying to sell lottery tickets. He was wearing a stained pale blue shirt, black trousers and flip-flops, his watery eyes behind dark glasses staring distractedly at the corner gable of the house across the street. Chapeau doubted that he was really blind, and listened hard beyond his repetitive sales chant for Duclos' footsteps in the next street. Finally he picked it up: to the left, thirty, forty metres down. He waited a second before following.

As Duclos took the next right-hand turn, Chapeau realized he was heading for Vacheret's. At the end was a short street that wound up some steps, with Vacheret's not far along in the next street. Chapeau kept a block behind, hidden around the corner, waiting until Duclos had receded deeper into the street before entering it. By the time Chapeau reached the start of the steps, Duclos was already at its top, turning left towards Vacheret's. The short street was deserted: one side was a half-demolished building, the other the blank stone wall of a building plastered with posters. Two cats scavenged around a group of rubbish bins at the top of the steps. Now that he knew where Duclos was going, he might as well head back. But he was suddenly curious to see how long Duclos stayed. Twenty minutes, it could be a simple business meeting. Forty or fifty minutes and he was probably with one of the young boys.

Chapeau decided to wait it out, found a bar not far around the corner with Vacheret's a hundred metres further up on the opposite side. It was a small and seedy bar, sawdust over cream and terracotta patch tiling. The barman was fat and wearing an orange T-shirt two sizes too small. From his accent, he was a Marseillais, though over half the bar were North Africans: two men playing draughts in the corner, two at the bar, and a group of local workmen in blue overalls at another table. The radio was playing Tony Bennett. The barman poured the brandy Chapeau ordered.

Chapeau waited.

An easy-listening station. Edith Piaf, Bert Kaempfert and Frank Sinatra followed. A minah bird in the corner chirped in on every other chorus. Chapeau wondered how the Moroccans liked Frank Sinatra: after cats being strangled, it must sound like golden syrup. It was his kind of music, but the accompanying minah bird and the sounds of draught pieces being banged down to grunts and shouts started to grate on his nerves. Half the afternoon he'd spent tracking this prick Duclos. And now Duclos was probably in some lavish back room with potted palms, being sponged down by one pre-pubescent boy while getting his rocks off with another, while he sat in a bar surrounded by grunting Moroccans and a minah bird singing along to Frank Sinatra. Great. His hand gripped tightly at his glass. He looked at his watch: almost thirty minutes. Ten minutes more and he'd leave.

But minutes later, already thinking ahead to the other pieces of the puzzle he'd like to put into place with Duclos, an idea struck him, a smile slowly crossing his face. Perfect. His initial gloating gradually gave way to the worry that it was almost too good, too cheeky, it must somehow be flawed; but after chewing it over some more between brandy slugs, he saw few pitfalls. At the same time it might also get rid of some of his pent-up anger and frustration with the little turd. All he had to do was keep close to the end of the bar, look out at an angle until he saw Duclos emerge, then head out a moment beforehand. He put some change on the bar to cover the brandy, ready for a quick exit.

Chapeau sat through Billie Holliday, Maurice Chevalier, Mario Lanza and Brenda Lee, with minah bird accompaniment and draught-piece-slapping percussion, before Duclos finally emerged.

He stepped out briskly, he was at least eighty metres ahead of Duclos, and hoped and prayed that Duclos wouldn't suddenly recognize his profile from behind. Ten metres more, six, *two* . . . He ducked around the corner sharply, taking the steps almost two at a time, now at a half-run. He stopped thirty metres down, eyeing up an open doorway in the derelict building for suitability a second before stepping inside. He went two metres in, stepping over the rubbish piled up. And waited.

The sound of Duclos' footsteps came after a minute. The short street was deserted; Chapeau prayed that nobody else would suddenly come into it. A sudden sound from behind. Chapeau jumped, wheeling sharply around to see a cat pulling at a rubbish bag. Its eyes met his for a second in the semi-darkness, then it scampered off. Chapeau's nerves settled back.

Duclos was close. Very close. His footsteps almost upon him.

Chapeau held his breath low, shallow – and as soon as Duclos' profile came into view, he stepped deftly from the shadows and struck out quickly. A right-fisted blow to Duclos' cheek. Duclos hadn't seen him, had only started to turn towards the approaching sound as Chapeau's ham fist connected.

Chapeau swung again, hitting Duclos' nose from the side this time, feeling the bone crunch and seeing the blood spurt as Duclos crumpled and fell. This felt good. Chapeau got in a quick left to the stomach as Duclos was going down, then as Duclos hit the ground and lay prostrate on his side, all that was left was to kick. He managed one to Duclos' groin before Duclos rolled over and put his hands down, then made do with two swift kicks to his kidneys.

Duclos started to look back up towards his attacker, so Chapeau pushed one hand against the side of Duclos' face, jamming it hard against the ground. Half kneeling now, he took out his gun, a Heckler & Koch 9 mm, and slid it next to his hand against Duclos' cheek. Duclos' eyes shut tight as the cold steel of the barrel pressed home. Chapeau cocked the chamber. The eyes scrunched tighter, a breathless *'non'* escaping. Chapeau savoured Duclos' fear a moment longer before uncocking and releasing the pressure, then deftly flipped the gun in the same motion and swung the butt twice sharply against the side of Duclos' ribs, and again lower to his kidneys and stomach. It was a measured attack. He didn't want to kill Duclos: just enough to make him walk like an old man for a week and piss blood.

Chapeau reached across and took out Duclos' wallet from his inside pocket. Straightening up, he gave one farewell kick to his groin. Keep him away from the young boys for a few weeks. Then he slipped his gun back inside his jacket and scampered off down the steps to the receding groans from Duclos, which brought a smile to his face.

15

'We've got a problem.'

Poullain was in Perrimond's office. The arrest warrant for Machanaud had been duly signed, notarized and stamped. Perrimond passed it across. 'Tell me.'

Poullain started by explaining that he'd already reached the decision not to make Machanaud's statement official for the reasons they'd discussed the other day, when the problem arose: his assistant Fornier had been told about the car sighting by Machanaud while off duty, and was now of a different mind. So much so that if it wasn't entered officially, he was threatening to file a complaint with the commanding area gendarmerie colonel. 'Though it might be a complete waste of time pursuing the statement, perhaps under the circumstances it will be less awkward if it is made.'

'Perhaps. Where did this Fornier meet up with Machanaud?'

'In a bar in Taragnon.'

'I see.' Perrimond's nostrils flared and pinched back as if an odious smell had just hit him, though it was unclear whether his disdain was directed at Fornier or Poullain's lack of control over his staff. 'Leaving aside the implications for a moment, before this happened with Fornier you personally had made the decision *not* to make the statement official.'

'No point. It's very obviously fabricated, and interviewing Duclos again would serve absolutely no purpose. At least two people saw him at the time of the boy's attack. His alibi is solid.'

So now it was down to varying degrees of awkwardness, thought Perrimond: another call from the Mayor or questions from the area gendarmerie colonel. 'Tell me about this Fornier. What's his background?'

'Young, twenty-six years old. Was with the Foreign Legion in Algeria for four years, then joined the gendarmerie in Marseille.'

'Did he see any combat action in Algeria?'

'None that I know of. His work was mainly with radio and communications, back-room logistics stuff. He took a similar position with the Marseille gendarmerie.'

'What made him move to Bauriac from Marseille?'

'His mother's ill, dying from cancer. He wanted to be close to her, and he put in a request for transfer through Marseille. We had no communications or logistics department, just purely street-pounding work, but he took it. He was pretty desperate, feared she might have only six months left, and so was willing to take whatever was offered.'

'So he has sacrificed career advancement in order to take care of his dying mother. Very noble.' Though from Perrimond's half-smile it was difficult to tell if he thought it was noble or just foolish. Then he became more thoughtful. 'Why did you specifically use him to assist on this investigation?'

'My main assistant, Harrault, was in the middle of another investigation. Plus I thought Fornier's past experience with Marseille might come in useful. A fair degree of liaison with Marseille was necessary, particularly with forensics.'

'The complaint, if it's made, will probably end up with Colonel Houillon here in Aix, is that correct?'

'Yes. I get one copy, it's noted and filed, and another goes to Colonel Houillon.'

'I have quite good contact with Houillon.' Perrimond glanced down, brooded for a second, as if his ink blotter might inspire him. He was slow in looking up. 'Look. Say nothing to Fornier for the time being. Tell him the issue is still being decided and you'll know something tomorrow. But I think I have an idea.'

'Anything reported for your area?' Chapeau's voice was husky and muted, as if people unseen might be listening in.

'No. Nothing yet.'

'When did you check last?'

'Just before seven when I finished duty.'

It was over twenty-four hours since the attack, thought Chapeau. It was unlikely the report had been made. His police contact, Jaquin, was a detective inspector stationed in the Panier. Revenge against a client who had beaten a club girl was the story Chapeau invented; Jaquin would have little sympathy for such a client. The club wanted to be forewarned of being named in any police statement, or perhaps the incident might be reported simply as a mugging. He'd asked Jaquin to check the station nearest the attack. Nothing filed yet. Not even for a mugging.

'I'll phone again at the same time tomorrow, just in case. Thanks.' But

Chapeau knew that most reports were made within hours and had certainly filtered down within twenty-four hours, even if made from another station. The ploy had confirmed what he'd suspected: Duclos had something to hide, didn't want to report the mugging and risk contact with the police.

Giving Duclos a beating had put him on a high for several hours. But it was nothing to what he experienced now, as he thought over the information gathered during the day. Duclos' wallet had been a veritable treasure chest: identity card, credit card for Banque Nationale de Paris, business cards – mostly lawyers from the Limoges area – and a recent pay-slip. It was from a provincial government office in Limoges, Department E4. Four phone calls later he'd ascertained what Department E4 dealt with and, from scale pay rates, Duclos' position.

He'd dropped the credit card in a Panier back street a block away. Hopefully someone deserving would pick it up, go on a spending spree. Perhaps the supposedly blind lottery-ticket seller: next time by, he'd be wearing crocodile-skin shoes and sporting a Rolex. Duclos would have to report the card lost or stolen to the bank, and if it was used fraudulently he would be duty-bound to make a police report or be liable for the expense. Hassle with the bank *and* the police. Perhaps Duclos would just eat the expenditure. Oh, this was fun.

And he felt sure that the best was to come: Department E4, 15,400 francs per annum. Duclos was an assistant prosecutor!

Chapeau had been to jail only once. For twenty-seven months at the age of eighteen. He'd been a club bouncer since sixteen, and one night threw out three students who were getting out of hand with the bar girls. One of them landed badly as he was thrown out and broke his collar bone. The boy's father was a leading businessman, a member of the Chamber of Commerce and the golfing partner of a local prosecutor. Charges for grievous bodily harm were pressed and a three-year sentence called for. The trial was a farce, a one-track railroad. Chapeau served all but nine months due to good behaviour.

But one vision had stayed with him strongly through the years: the prosecutor and his assistant huddled in conspiracy through the *instruction* process and the final trial, then smug and elated as the sentence was pronounced. The boy's father had come over and congratulated the prosecutor. Another triumph plotted on the golf course.

It had been Chapeau's first taste of the system at work. He'd vowed then that if he was to continue making his living from physical enforcement, it would be done in the shadows and with the buffer of an organization that knew how to work the system. Fifteen months out of jail he became a *milieu* enforcer. At first it was just low-key strong arm work: intimidation and threats, the occasional limb broken. The work ranged from small-time gambling, protection and loan debts, to non-payment on street-level drug packets. But within three years he'd progressed to the big league and made his first hit: an area dealer had pocketed heroin with a street value of almost 300,000 francs, claiming it had been seized in a police raid. Through an inside police contact the *milieu* discovered that wasn't true. It couldn't go unpunished.

He thought again now of the two smug prosecutors, smiling, congratulating themselves. Slowly he twirled Duclos' identity card between his fingers, and smiled to himself. A queer paedophile assistant prosecutor, his entire life and future now resting in his hands. The circle of revenge could hardly be more poetic. This was going to be much more fun than he first thought.

The memorial service for Christian Rosselot was held at the Church of Saint-Nicolas, fifty metres back from the main Bauriac square. The inside of the church was a microcosm of village life and social strata.

The first row nearest the altar was taken up with the Rosselots and immediate neighbours and friends. A dark-complexioned woman in her sixties to Monique Rosselot's left, Dominic assumed to be her mother. She was dressed fashionably and well: dark Pierre Cardin blouse and matching pleated skirt, though perhaps a little too much jewellery. Dominic was surprised; when Louis had mentioned Monique's mother visiting, he'd imagined her shrouded in a black djellaba, like the drab old widows he remembered from the streets of Algeria.

Jean-Luc had made it back in time, and had also brought his brother and his mother. His father had been too ill to travel. These had been the latest updates from Louis through Valérie as they'd filed into the church. They stood to the right of Jean-Luc with the Fiévets immediately alongside.

The next few rows were taken up with village people who had an acquaintance or vague connection with the Rosselots: various shopkeepers Monique visited regularly, Jean-Luc's farm-equipment and seed suppliers, the family doctor, Louis and Valérie.

The gendarmerie was represented five rows back, with an assortment of mostly unconnected villagers who wished to pay their respects filling another four rows behind. The murder had touched Taragnon deeply: sorrow and gentle weeping alongside those who were just curious or open-mouthed, trying to catch a glimpse of the Rosselots in the front row.

Four days earlier, Father Pierre Bergoin had held a small funeral service for Christian Rosselot at the burial ground chapel between Bauriac and Saint-Maximin. Only Jean-Luc, Monique, her mother and the Fiévets were present. The family had wanted a private affair, and the brunt of their grief had already been spent away from onlookers.

The memorial service started with the *Requiem æternam*. Dominic looked up as Father Bergoin's voice echoed around the church: '. . . *Te decet hymnus, Deus, in Sion; et tibi reddétur votum in Jerúsalem*: hear my prayer; all flesh shall come to thee. Eternal rest. Oh, God, creator and redeemer of all the faithful, grant to the souls of all thy servants and handmaids departed, the remission of their sins; that through pious supplications . . .'

There were six of them from the gendarmerie: Harrault, Poullain, Servan, Briant, Levacher and himself. Dominic wondered if the division in their ranks was obvious; Poullain and he were at opposite ends of the group. Since the call late in the day before, they'd hardly spoken.

It had come from Colonel Gastine, his old commanding officer in Marseille. After the preamble of how Dominic was settling in Bauriac, Gastine quickly came to the subject of the call he'd had from Colonel Houillon in Aix. 'He might call me once in four months, if I'm lucky. So although he tried to make light of it, the fact that he should trouble to call at all over such a matter made me realize there was something much more serious in the background. Apparently, there's some sort of disagreement between you and your commanding officer over an investigation now in progress. Is that correct?'

So, Poullain had got to Houillon before him. 'Yes. It's a murder investigation. I don't think the captain heading the investigation here is looking fully at all the possibilities.'

'You might have very good cause, Dominic, it's not my position to question. And that's not the problem. Though it hasn't been said directly, only intimated, if anything lands on Houillon's desk, Captain Poullain is going to request your transfer. He'll argue that he only took you in as a departmental favour to accommodate the fact that your mother was sick and you needed to be close to her. He saw your main usefulness as liaison where Marseille might be involved, such as the investigation in progress;

but that if he can't use you effectively, if your working styles clash, there is really nowhere else in the gendarmerie he can deploy you effectively. You'll be surplus to requirement.'

'Where would they transfer me?' Dominic asked meekly. Perhaps if it wasn't too far away, he could commute.

'Rouen is one suggestion, Brest another, or possibly Nancy.'

Dominic felt as if a trap-door had opened. All were at least 800 kilometres away. The message was clear: if he didn't tow the line, he'd be sent into exile. His mother would die alone.

'I'm sorry to bring you this news, Dominic. The way Houillon put it, it was almost as if they were doing you a favour by using me as honest broker, warning you. Giving you the option. If you'd filed the complaint, they'd have just shipped you out.'

'They?'

'Houillon was slightly apologetic, as if he felt a bit uncomfortable with all of this as well. So I read into it that someone with far stronger influence than Poullain was involved. Poullain couldn't risk directly asking Houillon to get involved like this.'

Perrimond. So in the end they'd all ganged up together to get their way over Machanaud. Put the lowly gendarme in his place, make sure he didn't cause any waves. It had probably all been done with a few quick phone calls, and now he was powerless. A bloodless coup.

'*Fratres, ece mystérium vobis dico . . .*' Father Bergoin's voice cut through some stifled sobbing from the front rows. 'In a moment, in the twinkling of an eye, at the last trumpet: for the trumpet shall sound, and the dead shall rise again incorruptible, and we shall be changed. For this corruptible must put on incorruption, and this mortal put on immortality. And when this mortal hath put on immortality, then shall come to pass the saying that is written: death is swallowed up in victory. O death, where is thy victory? O death, where is thy sting? Now the sting of death is sin; and the strength of sin . . .'

Death? His mother's pale yellow face before him, smiling softly: 'Don't worry, I understand if you have to go. You're young and you have your work and your career.' And him protesting: '*No!* I can't leave you at a time like this. I promised!'

Machanaud screaming at him as he was being dragged from the inter-view room by Servan and Harrault: 'You betrayed me! I was meant to be here for a statement about the car. I trusted you!' Probably Poullain had planned it, left him alone for over an hour with Machanaud before he'd returned with the warrant, knowing fully that Machanaud would get edgy without some reassurance. Busily basting their sacrificial lamb while Poullain and Perrimond cemented the final stages of their coup.

With the arrest warrant served and Machanaud's rights read out as he was dragged off to the cells, for the first time it struck Dominic what Machanaud faced. If convicted, he would get the death penalty or life imprisonment. With the brutality of the crime and the victim so young, the death penalty looked the most likely. From his cell window, Machanaud had probably even heard the church bells announcing the memorial service, rallying the emotions of the village against him.

It was a daunting, impossible choice: leave his mother alone to die, or stay silent and allow a man whose guilt he questioned to be condemned.

'. . . *Teste David cum Sibylla.*' Muted weeping now also from an unknown woman towards the back of the church. '. . . *Quantus tremor est futúrus.* The last loud trumpet's spreading tone, shall thro' the place of tombs be blown – to summon all before the Throne. Nature and death with fixed eyes, shall see the trembling creature rise – to plead before the last assize. The written book shall be outspread, and all that it contains be read. To try the living and the dead.'

Father Bergoin offered little guidance.

16

'. . . Or perhaps you're concerned that if we confront Jojo, ask him questions, we'll frighten him off? He won't appear in the dreams to help you again?'

'I don't know . . . perhaps a bit.'

'The dreams are special between you – and you don't want to spoil it?'

'It's not knowing what to do.' Eyran's head lolled, as if asking consent of an unseen figure.

Lambourne let the moment ride, let the thought sink deeper home. He'd spent the last twenty minutes setting the mood to draw out Jojo directly, and finally he sensed he was close. 'I think you're a lot surer of his friendship than you make out. You don't think he'd frighten off easily, do you?'

After a few seconds, Eyran exhaled slowly; reluctant acceptance. 'No.'

'But while you might like to know the answers – know how Jojo lost his parents and where, see just how much you have in common – you're not sure how to ask the questions. But that's where I can help you.' Lambourne left a long silence, watching Eyran's reaction: his brow furrowed then relaxed, his tongue lightly moistening his lips. The suggestion was fully there now; all he had to do was fill in the gaps. 'You don't need to worry about confronting him – because we can go back to the past dreams and I can talk to Jojo directly.'

Lambourne could see that Eyran was teetering on the brink, fighting between what he'd like to believe – being able to ask Jojo questions, guide some events for once rather than be just a passenger – and what his senses told him was real: the dreams were over, they were in the past. If he could change the past . . . *the first thing he'd do was bring his parents back alive.* Like a boxer with his opponent reeling, Lambourne knew that if he didn't keep up the momentum, he could lose Eyran at any moment.

'But I'll need your help, Eyran. Jojo is with you, he's part of you – part of your dreams. If you really want to know the answers, Jojo will talk to me. Of that I'm sure. Will you help me?'

'I don't know . . . *how* would I help?'

'By wanting to know the answers as much as me. You do want to know about Jojo, don't you . . . know why he's a friend, know what happened to him so that you can better understand why he's there to help you?' Lambourne watched each tick of expression on Eyran's face as the messages went home. Eyran was close to coming to terms with it. 'If you really want to know those things – then I'm sure it will work.'

Eyran swallowed slowly. 'Yes . . . I would like to know.'

But Lambourne could read the uncertainty still in Eyran's face. 'If it doesn't work, if Jojo doesn't want to speak to us – then we'll soon know. There'll be nothing lost. We'll just continue as before.'

And for the first time there was a glimmer of acceptance, an easing in Eyran's expression as the portent of failure was lifted. It wasn't the full acceptance he'd have liked, but probably the best he'd get. He pushed the advantage before the moment was lost. '. . . So let's go back to the last dream you had . . . try and find Jojo. Tell me, what's the first thing you see?'

The sudden leap caught Eyran by surprise, and Lambourne could see that Eyran was suddenly perplexed, fighting for images just out of reach. 'It's okay . . . take your time,' Lambourne soothed. He counted off the seconds as Eyran's breathing slowly settled back.

'It was dark, the light was fading fast . . . I was approaching the copse.'

The dreams were always a tease, thought Lambourne: images not clear, mist that obscured reality, fading light that meant he would be lost in the darkness if he didn't find his parents soon. Jojo always had him on a tight treadmill.

'There was a figure on the edge of the wheat field, just before the copse, looking back at me . . . But I couldn't see clearly who it was.'

'Did you think that the figure might be your father – or Jojo perhaps?'

'I wasn't sure . . . but as I started to run closer to get a clear view, I came into a clearing of wheat which looked like it had been cut neatly away – and Jojo was sitting there, looking down. He looked sad at first, lost . . . but as he saw me, he smiled and stood up.'

Lambourne saw an opportunity. 'Did you ask Jojo what was wrong, why he looked so sad?'

'No . . . no, I didn't. When he smiled and stood up, I was sure then it was my father ahead – and I was keen to point him out to Jojo.'

Lambourne could see the mixture of doubt and elation on Eyran's face. Doubt that once again he might have ignored Jojo's emotions and feelings

– battling with his elation that it might be his father. He would need to deal with the father's sighting first to get Eyran fully focused.

Jojo quickly took control. Eyran described the distant shape fading into the shadows as Jojo looked up, saying that Eyran's father had probably gone deeper into the copse. Jojo started to lead the way. Lambourne tensed as the descriptions rolled, tapping his pencil on his notes. Over a week's delay before Stuart Capel finally signed the consent slip, and only then because there'd been another bad dream. Lambourne knew that if he didn't succeed in drawing out Jojo now, there might not be another chance.

As Eyran described them in pursuit, heading across the field and through the trees towards the brook, Lambourne's nerves bristled – fearing another dream ending. But this time they headed out of the woods and into an open field on the other side, and he was lulled into complacency by the setting and his preoccupation with returning Eyran to where he first met Jojo. He was only alerted by Eyran's sudden change in breathing – suddenly more laboured, his eyelids flickering rapidly. 'Does the dream end badly there?'

'Yes . . . we . . . there was a dip . . . *I* . . . *I*' Fractured breathing, Eyran swallowing on his words.

'It's okay . . . It's *okay!* You don't need to go there again. Step back from the clearing . . . *Step back!*'

Eyran looked startled for a moment. Lambourne realized then that he'd shouted. He quickly introduced a calmer, more soothing tone. 'Let's go back . . . back away from the clearing. Yes – that's it . . . you're away from any danger now . . .'

Lambourne left a few seconds' gap between each comment, as if waiting for Eyran to catch up with him. 'We're going back to the beginning – back to where you first met Jojo in the first field. He was sitting then in another clearing of wheat. You mentioned that he looked very sad. But we never found out why he was so sad.'

Eyran's breathing gradually eased. He looked more settled.

'You thought perhaps that you should have asked, that he might have been upset that you didn't ask. But it doesn't matter – we can ask him now.'

'I don't know . . . I'm not sure, I . . .' Doubt and uncertainty returned, swept across Eyran's face like rising storm clouds.

Lambourne could see Eyran retreating, a moment more and the chance would be gone completely. 'But you need to know more about Jojo.

You never ask him anything, yet he's put in so much time helping you, trying to find your parents. Don't you think it's only fair? He'll be upset if you never ask. One night you'll be dreaming, you'll return to the copse expecting him to be there to help you find your parents . . . and you'll be all alone. He won't be there!'

Lambourne saw Eyran visibly flinch. But as his expression settled back, Lambourne could see that a glimmer of acceptance had returned. It had been the right ploy: remind Eyran that there was just as much risk in *not* talking to Jojo. It wasn't all one way.

Lambourne spent the next minutes cajoling and reassuring, one minute enticing and luring, hoping that Eyran would make the decision, then suddenly once again storm-trooping, before Eyran finally relented and he broke through. Entered the elusive world of Jojo.

Lambourne spent the first minutes getting accustomed to Jojo's voice. The intonation was slightly different, slower and more purposeful, but apart from that it was Eyran's voice. Lambourne asked if he was Eyran's friend, where he knew Eyran from, but Jojo was vague *'From before . . . it was a long time back.'* He got a similar answer when he asked Jojo about losing his parents. Distant memories, obscured by a haze of time. Lambourne wanted to stay for the moment with the present and the recent dreams.

'Did you lose your parents by the copse where you first met Eyran? You mentioned that you'd had the same experience as Eyran – that he wouldn't be able to find his parents unless he crossed over.'

'I only wanted to help. I was over the far side . . . I couldn't help him unless he crossed over.'

'Did you see him crossing over as a sign that he trusted you? That he wanted your help?' Lambourne knew that he'd have to be more patient talking to Jojo; each response was being fed in turn through Eyran.

'Yes.'

'But why the copse? Was it familiar – reminded you of where you lost your parents?'

'There was something about it, I couldn't be sure . . . but I had the feeling stronger in the wheat field. It was a long time ago, though . . . I couldn't remember clearly.'

'The same wheat field where you were with Eyran in the last dream?'

'Yes. But Eyran was running through the wheat field in the first dream . . . it was that which made me look up and see him from the copse.'

Eyran too had mentioned that when he first moved in the house the wheat field had seemed familiar . . . *'as if I'd been there before'*. 'You could see him between the trees – running towards you?'

'Yes, and I . . . I . . . felt his concern, his worry as he was running through. I knew that something was wrong.'

'The same concern that you felt when you lost your parents?'

'Yes – I'd felt the same.'

'And that was what first made you feel close to Eyran, made you feel you could help find his parents?' A small nod and a mumble of 'yes' from Jojo. 'Was that the first time you saw Eyran?'

'Yes – *then*. But I knew him from before . . .'

The past again. 'When was that?'

'I don't know – it was a while . . . a while ago. It's not clear.'

How far back? Lambourne wondered. How many years did it take for events to fade from an eleven-year-old's memory? Five, six? Even in the unlikely event they had met as children and the memory had now gone – Jojo's memory of losing his parents wouldn't so easily fade. In inventing Jojo, Eyran had simply buried the details in the past – hopefully out of reach.

Lambourne picked his way through some other dreams to get Jojo's interpretation, matching symbolism to a list he'd made earlier. *The brook and the wheat field: familiarity, home. Loss of parents: shared experience. Crossing the pond and entering the woodland shed: trust.* Now he added: *Wheat clearing.* Mirror images, Jojo filling the gaps that Eyran didn't want to face. But trust had quickly given way to dominance – Jojo always led, Eyran followed.

Lambourne tried to draw Jojo out on the failure of the dreams, but Jojo seemed as surprised and disappointed as Eyran. Even as Jojo submitted to the reality he knew Eyran would have to face, relinquished control, his sense of failure mirrored Eyran's disappointment. 'Do the failures in the dreams make you despair – wonder if each time you might face the same disappointment?'

'Yes, sometimes . . . but when I see Eyran, I feel hopeful again. And I feel I can't let him down.'

'You feel that he expects it of you – expects you to be able to find his parents?'

'Yes.'

'But how do *you* feel? Do you feel you can really find his parents?'

Eyran's head lolled slightly, then turned slowly back until he was again facing the ceiling. 'I don't know . . . but Eyran feels sure I can find them. And he needs a friend to help him. I couldn't leave him on his own.'

Lambourne wondered if that was going to be the pattern: Jojo side-stepping, passing the main responsibility back to Eyran. 'And you think that your own experience with losing your parents will help?'

'Yes . . . at least I know how he feels. It seems so . . . so unfair that it has happened twice.'

Twice? 'You mean – with you and now Eyran? You both experiencing losing your parents?'

'Yes.'

'But you remember so little about your own loss – you said that it was too long ago for you to recall. So how will you be able to help Eyran?' Create doubt, start chipping away at Jojo's dominance, thought Lambourne. He watched intently as Eyran grappled with the thought. Eyran's expression was taut; a muscle pulsed momentarily by his left eye.

'If I went back . . . perhaps I would remember clearer. Maybe I hope I'll find my parents at the same time . . . that's why I've returned. Why I want to help Eyran.'

'So you were unable to find your parents when you were there before?'

'Yes . . . I never found them.'

The first small admittance of defeat. If he could build on that, get Jojo to admit that he might fail again, then he would be halfway to breaking his hold. 'Do you fear that you might fail with Eyran as well? That you won't be able to find them?'

'Yes . . . sometimes. But I can't just leave him on his own – give up.'

Lambourne sensed a chink of uncertainty. 'But what if you can't help Eyran find them, in the same way that you have never been able to find your own parents? Eyran believes they're alive – but do you?'

Eyran shook his head, struggling with images he didn't want to accept. 'I don't know . . . he needs a friend He's all alone when he's looking for them. I was alone before – I know how he feels. I must be there to help him.'

Lambourne retreated; a direct assault wasn't going to work. Eyran was still clinging, resisting. Jojo continuing to hide behind Eyran's desire to find his parents and take the passive role as just a helping friend. 'What was it that felt familiar about the wheat field? Eyran said that when he saw you in the field in the last dream, you looked sad. Can you remember why?'

'I'm not sure. I just felt alone – deserted.'

'Who had deserted you?'

'I don't remember . . . it was just a feeling. The wheat field, the water running in the nearby brook . . . it reminded me of something.'

'Did it remind you of losing your parents? Is that why you were sad?'

'Yes . . . but I wasn't sure. It was somehow different. I tried to get a clear picture . . . but it was too far back.'

Again the convenient shield. 'If you went back, do you think you'd remember, the images would become clearer?'

'Yes . . . I think so.'

The answer threw Lambourne; he'd expected more hesitance and resistance. Why bury the events conveniently in the past, then invite their exposure? Surely the last thing Eyran wanted was him delving back; yet Jojo seemed to be encouraging it. One area where they were in conflict. Lambourne wanted to stay with the present a big longer, continue exploring the dreams – but he realized the opportunity to go back might not arise again easily. He decided to take the bait, call what he was certain was a bluff. 'So let's go back, Jojo . . . back to where the memories might be clearer.'

Lambourne started by taking Jojo back just over three years, to when Eyran was almost eight: the last months at the old house in England. Nothing. No recall, no memories. The process was slow; Eyran left long gaps as he mentally jumped time frames and surfaced again. Lambourne prompted by mentioning their play areas by the old house: the copse and the woods at the back, the wheat field at Broadhurst Farm. But nothing triggered a memory. He decided to make the invitation more open. 'Take me back to when you first met Eyran. Was it when Eyran first moved into the house there? Were you friends together then?'

'No . . . it was from before.'

'Then go back further . . . back to when you first met.'

Only Eyran's breathing and the faint whirring of the tape reel punctuated the silence. Lambourne tapped his pen softly on his pad with the passing seconds. As Jojo panned frantically back in his mind through past events and images and almost two minutes had passed with only the sound of Eyran's breathing, now slightly more laboured, Lambourne became sure that nothing would surface. Or that Jojo's recollections would only be vague, the painful memory of losing his parents selectively erased. In the same way that Eyran didn't want to accept his parents were dead – Jojo would have no recall of his.

When Eyran finally surfaced and Jojo's voice returned, it startled

Lambourne. He felt numbed, his mouth suddenly dry, and he had to consciously snap himself out, quickly adjust to the new situation and break the silence by asking the next question.

He knew that he sounded inept, hesitant – hadn't fully made the leap to what he now confronted. His palms were sticky and he was stumbling as he continued with a few rudimentary questions. For the first time he was eager to end the session, and minutes later he stopped the tape recorder and counted Eyran back awake. He needed time to himself, time to think. He didn't mention anything to Eyran or the Capels as they confirmed arrangements for the next session and said their goodbyes.

Lambourne sat back and closed his eyes, easing out a slow sigh. Now looking back, the signs had been there clearly: *'It seems so unfair that it has happened twice'* . . . *'From before . . . a long time'* . . . *'If I went back . . . perhaps I would remember clearer.'* As much as he suspected Eyran had buried events in the past and so wouldn't want them uncovered, Jojo had been enticing him to go back throughout. Intent on only one track, he'd missed the signals.

But as the implications sank home, he realized he was out of his depth; he'd need help. Even the few closing questions had made him feel awkward: fishing in areas of psychoanalysis he'd barely touched upon. He looked at his watch. Almost three hours before he could put through a call to the University of Virginia.

17

The warrant holding Machanaud was an initial detention order signed off by Perrimond for four days, the maximum any suspect could be held without an official arraignment before an examining magistrate.

On the fourth day, Machanaud was transported from his cell in Bauriac for a ten o'clock hearing at the Palais de Justice in Aix. Frédéric Naugier was presiding, though informally dressed in a dark grey suit; his gown would be worn at later hearings. Perrimond was to one side of the room, Briant as police escort behind Machanaud, and a *greffier* – court clerk – sat alongside Naugier.

A young duty lawyer was dragged from the floor below to brief Machanaud on what would await him in the proceedings. During a thirty-eight-minute hearing, Machanaud provided his main details for the court file, Naugier read the charges against him, and a decision on bail was held over to the next hearing in ten days, by which time a state lawyer would have been appointed through the Bar Council.

At the close of the proceedings, Naugier summarily signed off a four-month detention order. In that time, he had to complete the *instruction* process and pass the case to full trial. On murder cases, it was not uncommon for him to sign off two or three such orders. The duty lawyer had already made it clear to Machanaud that bail was unlikely given the combination of the charge and his transient background. Whether found guilty or not at the final trial, unless dramatic new evidence came up during the *instruction*, Machanaud was going to spend much of the next year in prison.

Dominic had bought a TV for his mother four months previously. TVs were expensive, luxury items, but it was something to keep her company, especially during his long evening shifts.

He remembered the first time he saw *Perry Mason*. French national programming was poor, and slicker American productions predominated. The popular courtroom drama, however, took time to catch on in France, mainly because the proceedings depicted were alien, bore no semblance to the justice system familiar to the French.

The quick changing drama of different witnesses, surprises, change of pleas and sudden admissions would in France be spread over several months of the *instruction* process. Witnesses were grouped and called in different sessions, and testimony from the victim's family, the police, forensics and expert witnesses such as psychiatrists was heard in continuing separate sessions. With usually no more than two *instruction* hearings in any one month, the process was long and arduous, and complex cases could drag on seven to ten months before presentation to full trial.

But by that time, evidence and testimony had been boiled down to just the essential facts necessary for a jury and three judges to deliberate upon. Witnesses could be recalled, but their answers were now no more than distillations of their previous testimony during *instruction*. No rambling, no surprises, no dramatics or sudden about-turn admissions. Just the core evidence the prosecution and defence wished showcased for the jury. As a result, even murder trials lasted only a day or two.

Dominic had followed the early stages of Machanaud's *instruction* hearings. Two weeks after a second hearing at which bail was refused, Naugier summoned the Rosselots. Apart from confirming vital details about the last time they saw Christian, what he was wearing and who he had headed out to see that afternoon, Naugier had to ask them formally if they wished to press charges against the suspect held. Almost redundant, since if they had answered 'No', the state would have continued with the prosecution regardless – but it had to be recorded. Jean-Luc responded 'Of course' while Monique just nodded.

The next hearing almost a month later was to clarify police and forensic findings at the initial crime scene. Dominic was concerned the subject of Machanaud's car sighting might be raised, but the hearings were strictly structured: Naugier conducted all questioning directly and any questions proposed by the defence and prosecution had to be presented to Naugier two weeks in advance, with a full schedule of topics to be raised then made available to both sides two days before the hearing. Perrimond had gone rigorously through the schedule with Poullain and Dominic. There was nothing about the car sighting, though in two or three hearings' time Dominic knew that they would start to cover Machanaud's later statements, and the subject could come up. He was dreading it: having to face Machanaud and his counsel and change his story for Naugier.

Four days after the call from Houillon in Marseille, he'd decided to throw in the towel and told Poullain that he wouldn't be proceeding with a complaint. Poullain wasted no time in sequestering him and Briant into his back office, closing ranks tightly by ensuring their stories matched. Poullain suggested that they both admit the meetings, but modify the details discussed. 'From what I understand, Machanaud was drunk on both occasions. I'd be surprised if he remembers exactly what was said.'

Dominic agreed numbly along with Briant, but part of him remained uncertain. Hopefully the subject just wouldn't come up.

From what he heard about Machanaud's lawyer over the following weeks, that hope began to fade. Only twenty-six, Léonard Molet had been in full practice just over three years and divided his time between a private firm and state-aid cases. Machanaud had shown alarm at their first meeting that this would be Molet's first murder trial, without fully appreciating how much worse his representation could have been: most state-aid lawyers were inexperienced *stagiaires* still in pupilage, with invariably little or no courtroom experience. Over the weeks, Molet showed his paces and gained Machanaud's confidence, making Perrimond and Naugier at the same time sit up and take notice. Unlike the usual state-aid fodder, he gained preliminary notes on time, saw his client regularly, and rebutted with sensible defence-angled questions for Naugier to pose at *instruction*. The case was going to be tightly contested.

While reading from his notes in testimony about the initial crime scene, Dominic felt Molet staring at him intently at one point, felt uncomfortable that Molet was perhaps measuring him for a confrontation. Later, towards the end of Poullain's testimony, Naugier cut in, admitting his confusion at the various positions of Machanaud supposedly fishing, the lane and the wheat field, and where the boy was finally found. Naugier had already gone over the details twice without being fully satisfied, and suggested that everything be re-examined at the scene itself. Perrimond and Molet showed scant surprise. Examining magistrates often visited crime scenes to question suspects and witnesses. The theory was that suspects found it harder to reconstruct an invented story at the scene itself. Discrepancies started to show.

Looking at his diary, Naugier saw that the next *instruction* in sixteen days was for witnesses who had sighted Machanaud on the day of the attack; at that hearing, he would notify both Perrimond and Molet of the date set for a reconstruction.

Facing Molet had unsettled Dominic. He felt somehow vulnerable, that his guilt about covering up showed. He thought seriously about going back on his agreement with Poullain. His mother's condition had worsened the week before and she'd gone in for more tests: if the prognosis was bad, she might only make it another few months. The *instruction* covering the police statements and later car references wouldn't be for at least six weeks. If he filed the complaint a few days before the hearing and only then warned Poullain of his upcoming change in testimony, it could take them almost two months to manipulate his transfer. *Longer if* . . . Dominic stopped himself abruptly, shaking his head, could hardly believe that he was actually weighing the timing of his mother's death just so that he could come clean and salvage his own guilt.

In the days after giving in to Poullain, he was haunted by images of Machanaud. In one dream Machanaud was alone in the wheat field, calling out as Dominic turned his back and walked away. *'You're deserting me just like the others . . . Why?'* But as he turned and looked back at Machanaud, only then did he notice one of Machanaud's hands covered with blood, could see where it had run down his arm, *the bloodied rock discarded at his feet . . .* and he awoke in a cold sweat, catching at his breath. Even in his dreams he was trying to assuage his concern, convince himself that Machanaud was guilty, he was doing the right thing. But it was little consolation knowing that he was merely joining Poullain and the rabble, and Machanaud's plea about desertion lingered stronger than any other image.

The session with witnesses went smoothly, most repetitions of their earlier police statements. Confronted by Naugier with the various witness statements, Machanaud admitted that he'd lied in his own statements only because he thought the police questioning was aimed at his poaching that day. Naugier didn't pursue the mention of cars or go deeper into Machanaud's police statements: one he would tackle at the reconstruction, the other at the session following. Naugier summarized the proceedings and looked at his diary. The next hearing was the reconstruction to take place at Breuille's farm: present should be the suspect, defence and prosecution, and all relevant police and medics who attended at the original scene. Date set was in nineteen days' time, on 22 November.

Chapeau tried the main Palais de Justice number in Limoges again. When he'd phoned two hours earlier, he was told that 'Monsieur Duclos was in a meeting, but should be free at twelve.' He'd left his name as Émile Vacheret, but no number. He would call back. Originally, he had planned to call closer to the final trial date, but during those months Duclos' memory could have started to fade.

The second time he was put straight through. 'Monsieur Vacheret, yes. One moment. *Ne quittez pas.*'

Then Duclos' voice in hushed tones. 'Émile . . . why on earth are you phoning me here at work, you know that . . .'

'Be quiet,' Chapeau cut in. 'I used Vacheret's name to get through.'

'Who is this? I don't understand,' Duclos spluttered. But it was a stock reaction; suddenly he did know who it was and understood fully. 'Why are you phoning me? How did you get this number? I'm quite sure Émile wouldn't be so stupid as to give it to you.'

Chapeau chuckled. 'No, you're right. But your wallet was a treasure chest of information.' Silence from the other end: only the background clatter of typewriters came through to Chapeau for a few seconds.

'It was *you* the other month,' Duclos hissed.

God, this was fun. Chapeau wasn't sure what was more joyous: the outrage in Duclos' voice or the sudden flashback of the incident itself. 'Ah, you guessed. And I wanted so much for it to stay a mystery.'

'Look, I just can't talk here.' Duclos' voice was muted, edgy. 'I'll phone you straight back from outside. Give me a number.'

Chapeau looked down at the number on the dial and read it out. 'Five minutes, no more. Or I'll be phoning your office back again.' He hung up.

Duclos made a quick excuse to his secretary about seeing a client on the third floor, he wouldn't be longer than twenty minutes. He headed out along the long corridor, then skipped down instead of up. By the time he reached the main Palais de Justice steps, he was practically at a run.

Chapeau picked up the phone on the second ring. Less than three minutes: impressive. Duclos was even keener than he thought.

'Okay, what do you want?' Duclos' voice came breathlessly.

Obviously no patience left for preamble or politeness, thought Chapeau. What was the world coming to? 'Luckily for you, it looks like they're nailing some poor local poacher for what you did to that young boy.' Chapeau listened intently over the static on the line for Duclos' reaction.

A short intake of breath. 'I don't know what you're talking about.'

Chapeau had no time for fencing. 'Look, I know all about the boy in Taragnon. I saw the whole story in the papers. And I know that there's no friend. It was you – *you* attacked him, and that was why you wanted me to finish him off in the hospital. You were afraid he'd awaken and identify you.'

'You're wrong. It was for my friend. And I know nothing about Taragnon – my friend told me the boy was from Marseille.'

Chapeau read the bluff, could pick up on the tremor at the back of Duclos' voice. If there was any slight doubt remaining, now he was certain. There was no friend: Duclos had killed the boy. But he would have to push hard to get Duclos to admit it. 'Come on, Duclos. You've got a weakness for the young boys, you're a regular customer at Vacheret's. You want me to believe that this *friend* of yours has got exactly the same problem? And you drive straight through Taragnon on your way from the Vallon estate to Aix.'

'So does my friend. Whether you believe me or not doesn't really concern me.' Flatter, calmer voice now. 'You seem to be forgetting along the way that the boy was still alive in the hospital. You're the one who killed him. You can't tell your little theory to anyone without incriminating yourself.'

Chapeau allowed Duclos his glorious moment's gloating before dropping the bombshell. 'That's the beauty of it – I never touched the boy. When I got to his room, he was already in Emergency, they were fighting to save his life. I was annoyed at first that I'd missed him; and then it struck me that if the boy died that night, you'd have no way of knowing I hadn't made the hit. So I decided to claim the kill and stiff you for the money anyway. I don't think I've ever had so much fun.' Chapeau sniggered. 'Except, that is, for beating the shit out of you a week later.'

Longer, deeper silence this time. Chapeau could almost feel the waves of panic at the other end. Duclos' mind racing, wondering whether to continue denying, question or retreat. A slow exhalation. 'Why should I believe you now?'

It was a weak protest, more grudging acceptance than doubt. 'You don't have to. Why don't I call the police and tell them about you hiring me to kill the boy, let them work out if the boy died on the operating table or not? After all, they have access to all the hospital records. And then when they turn up to arrest you, you can tell them all about your little friend. As an accomplice, and seeing as the murder you hired me for never took place, you'd probably only get a few years.'

'No, *no*. Don't do that.'

Chapeau savoured the panic in Duclos' voice before commenting, 'So whether it's you or your friend, at least we've established one thing. You don't want me to go to the police.'

Duclos was slow to answer, his voice subdued, barely audible. 'No.'

'That's a shame, because I had such a strong urge to do my citizen's duty this time. The story of that poor poacher in the paper really touched me. So unfair. You know, I probably have a lot more in common with someone like that than . . . than someone like yourself, Monsieur Prosecutor. It would feel almost like I'm betraying one of my own. I think it would take quite a lot to persuade me to do something like that.'

'What do you want?' Duclos had no energy left to spar with Chapeau. As it dawned on him that Chapeau was probably telling the truth about not killing the boy and he realized how vulnerable he was, a sinking sensation gripped his stomach. In the past weeks of work, he'd finally started to free his thoughts from the nightmare of Taragnon, but now it was back with him in full force. Bleak years of the incident rekindled with each demand from Chapeau stretched out ahead. He felt physically sick.

Chapeau paused for breath; like a lion circling his prey, now he had Duclos exactly where he wanted him, and was ready for the kill. But it was too soon. Besides, only a couple of months had passed since he'd probably cleaned Duclos out. 'I don't know yet. I'll have to think about that one. I'll probably call you again when the date for the final trial for this fellow has been set. There'll still be time then for them to haul someone else in for questioning and acquit him if they get new information.'

'When will that be?' Flat monotone, defeated, washed along on whatever Chapeau suggested. It had taken him almost a month to get fully over the injuries from the beating in the Marseille alley; he was still haunted by the image of the cold steel barrel sliding against his cheek, sure in that moment he was going to die. Duclos shuddered; now once again he felt powerless and afraid.

'Two months – maybe as much as four or five. You know probably better than me how slow the wheels of justice turn in France. Why don't I send you regular press clippings, keep you up to date?'

'No, no, it's okay.' The thought of regular reminders through the post made Duclos' blood run cold. Surely Chapeau wasn't serious? 'Just phone me when you're ready.'

'I will. In the meantime I suggest you're a good boy and start saving up for when I call. Have you got a piggy bank?'

'You bastard. You slimy *fucking* bastard!'

'Oh, I do love it when you're angry. It gets me *so* excited.' Chapeau blew an exaggerated kiss close to the mouthpiece and hung up.

18

Voices from the rooms, running feet in the courtyard, a ball bouncing, laughter, crying. Christian biting back the tears after being stung by a bee, Jean-Luc running down the field with Christian on his shoulders and her worrying about them falling, Christian at six holding up his favourite puppet doll, Topo Gigio: he'd left it in the courtyard and some chickens had pecked the stuffing out and an arm was almost falling off. She'd restuffed it and sewn the arm that night, tucked it back in alongside him while he was asleep. Christian running out of the surf at Le Lavandou, helping Jean-Luc by measuring the boules for a local village game, Christian blowing out the candles at his tenth birthday party.

Fragments of memories, some old pictures on the shelves and in albums, Christian's old clothes and toys. All that was left.

Monique had promised herself each time that the next day she'd clear them away . . . the *next day*. Each time she looked at his room – with each toy and item of clothing in exactly the same place he'd left them that afternoon – it was easy in that moment to believe that he was simply away, a school trip or summer camp, and soon would return.

But as the images flooded back – the police drawing up in the courtyard that first day, her candlelight vigil in the hospital, the young gendarme at her door saying he was sorry . . . *so sorry* – a cold steel hand of reality reached deep inside her and ripped out her emotions, her very soul, stripped bare every fibre and nerve ending until her pain was rendered down to no more than pitiful numbness, a grey void . . . whispers in the first empty dawn after his death . . . *'Oh Christian . . . Christian.'* Knowing in that moment that there would be no more answer, no kisses like soft butterflies on her cheek, no more embraces and feeling the warmth of his body . . . clinging now only to the memory, hugging the top cover of his bed around her and rocking gently as her emotions flooded over and once again her body sank into uncontrollable sobbing.

Most of her crying had been done alone, sitting in Christian's room. Now it had come to symbolize catharsis, the only place in the house where she felt comfortable venting her grief. The rest of the house was for cooking, cleaning, sewing, all the day-to-day mechanical chores to help push her grief into the background. When she cried, it was just her and Christian, alone. A last vestige of intimacy.

Only once had she been caught, just over a month after Christian's death; Clarisse had been at the door, half hiding behind the door frame, perplexed. Monique had quickly stifled her tears and rushed to comfort her, feeling guilty.

Clarisse was probably suffering even more than her, struggling at only five to truly grasp what had happened, let alone come to terms with it. Asking questions about where Christian was now, would he be happy, was it nice in heaven? Drawing pictures of Christian sitting among floating clouds, his Topo Gigio doll at one side, his favourite tree from the garden – an old spreading carob which he used to climb – the other. Clarisse's idea of Christian's heaven.

All they had was each other for consolation, Jean-Luc had been distant, remote. When they'd lost Christian, they'd lost most of Jean-Luc as well. She had shared her affections equally between the children, but Jean-Luc had always shown more affection for Christian, and now it was more marked. It was as if he was saying: *'I've lost what I care about most in this family, there's little for me here now.'*

Long, blank stares straight through them at the dining table. Little or no interest in any of their activities; whenever any personal involvement threatened, he would make an excuse about cleaning tools or the tractor and head out to the garage. And when his emotions became too much and Monique tried to hug and console him, he'd shrug her off. During the summer evenings he stayed out late in the fields, but as the evenings drew in he'd make an excuse and head for a local bar. It was as if he could no longer bear to be in their company, or perhaps it was the house itself, both reminders of Christian.

Many a time when he was working in the fields, she would look up from the kitchen window and see him sitting on the stone wall at the ridge of the field, staring emptily into space. She would busy herself with chores for a while, and sometimes as much as forty minutes later he would still be in the same position when she looked out.

The Fiévets had been helpful and supportive, but they weren't close enough for her to share her innermost thoughts about Christian's death or the worry of Jean-Luc's increasing emotional distance from her and Clarisse. The town had rallied well behind her, she'd been particularly touched by the memorial service – but for some time afterwards she felt unable to face another village shopkeeper, another sympathetic face and heartfelt condolence. For over a month after the service, she had hardly ventured out; the Fiévets did her shopping.

Outside the church, Captain Poullain had approached and said that someone was in custody, 'a local vagabond. Justice will soon be done.' A satisfied, firm statement, as if he felt assured the news would salve her pain. She'd hardly remembered him from the first interview; the only gendarme she recognized from the line in the church was the one who had called to tell her Christian was dead. He stayed in the background cap in hand. Most of what had happened outside the church had been sympathy at arm's length – pats on the shoulder, heads hung in sorrow, muttered condolences with eyes downcast, trite offers of help from people she hardly knew. She'd grimaced afterwards at the irony: it had taken the death of her son to make her feel truly accepted in the village.

Apart from the week when her mother had visited, there had been nobody to share her grief – until she looked up and saw Clarisse at the doorway. So for the past long weeks she'd shared small stories, comforts and hugs with her daughter, fighting to come to terms with the unacceptable partly through the innocent eyes of a five-year-old – fill the sickening void with whatever vestiges of love and affection remained in her house.

The only thing Jean-Luc had shown any interest in was the investigation, seeing justice done. While she'd been still too blind with tears and numb to react to Poullain's statement outside the church, Jean-Luc had nodded enthusiastically, asking several questions before they'd parted. For the first time since Christian's death, he appeared animated, drawing hard on each word for comfort, solace. Each week he phoned the police station and was brought up to date on the latest stages of the *instruction*. 'Next week, they're all going out to the scene of the crime to re-enact it,' he commented one morning at breakfast, but she'd hardly been listening.

Jean-Luc mentioned it again the morning of the re-enactment, and only then did she pay attention: two mentions, and again a rare show of eagerness – it must be important. Heading out, he said that he would be working in the west pasture. But half an hour later the rising wind made her think about how exposed the west field was, and when she looked to see if Jean-Luc might have moved to the more sheltered fields at the back, she noticed the car was gone.

As the wind rose, it bent the wheat at an angle. But not evenly: one swathe would be cut sharply at an angle while another remained upright, the path of the wind undulating, weaving patterns through the field like rolling golden surf. The morning air was cool, the wind gusting intermittently, and patches of brief sunshine broke through between the shifting grey clouds, bathing them momentarily in light and warmth.

Dominic looked thoughtfully at the figures ahead as the light shifted. The shadow of a large cloud floated down the bordering hillside like a giant valkyrie until it hung over them, bathing them in grey, matching the intensity of their mood. Thirteen men in a lonely windswept field, linked only by the death of a ten-year-old boy. With the shifting light, the wheat sheaves undulating with each pulse of the wind, it was almost as if the field was protesting, trying to evade them and keep its secrets.

The figures huddled close together to be heard. Naugier was going over information with the attending medics, forensics and Poullain, in no particular order. Servan, Levacher and Harrault were just behind closest to Dominic. A *greffier* constantly at Naugier's side made notes in shorthand.

Machanaud stood beyond, handcuffed to an Aix prison warden. His turn would come next. Perrimond was to one side of Naugier, Molet to the other by the *greffier*. Dominic noticed Machanaud glancing towards the riverbank, his eyes bleary and distant. Perhaps stung by the wind, or was he still in a daze with it all, hardly believing that he was back in the same spot three months later charged with murder, pleading for his life? He'd had a lot of time to contemplate his story. Naugier looked up at Machanaud sharply at intervals as he went over the forensic details.

Naugier then clarified with Machanaud which part of the river he was at that day, and directed Servan to remain standing where the attack took place. Everyone else was then directed down to the riverside.

'Two hours? And in all of that time, did you see or meet a young boy?'

Naugier's question cut through the air crisply. The assembled group stood silent, expectant. Naugier had spent the first minutes by the river confirming that Machanaud had been fishing, what he caught, and the time he was there – ten past one to just after three – before coming to the key question.

'No,' Machanaud said, with stronger emphasis than his previous answers. Even the furthest in the group heard his denial.

Naugier looked pointedly in both directions. 'Did you see or meet *anyone* in that time?' Foliage further down the riverbank was thin, the view virtually clear; most of the foliage and trees were clustered along the bank's ridge bordering the farm track.

'No.'

Following Naugier's gaze towards the flat bridge a hundred metres downstream, Molet suddenly picked up on the significance. The small bridge connecting the neighbouring farm to Breuille's wheat field was in the police report as *'where we think the boy crossed'*, mainly because there were no sightings of him walking through the village itself. But he hadn't realized it would be so visible.

Naugier pointed. 'You are aware that is the only connecting bridge for some distance. Can you see it clearly from here?'

Molet prayed for Machanaud to suddenly plead short-sightedness, but his 'yes' came crisply.

'And you saw nobody crossing that bridge throughout your time here that afternoon?'

'No.'

Naugier looked thoughtfully in the other direction, upstream; then he slowly scanned up the river bank towards the path, as if he was following an imagery line towards where the attack had taken place. 'Monsieur Machanaud. Can you see the gendarme we left standing on the path?'

'No. I can't see him.'

'And the afternoon you were fishing – did you see or hear anything from the position where the gendarme is now standing?'

'No.'

Naugier nodded. This made sense. The river bank dipped down sharply. The only part of the lane visible was lower down as it sloped towards the road. 'Now let us return to your sighting of vehicles passing that afternoon, starting with the first vehicle. What time would that have been?'

'Maybe forty minutes after I arrived.'

'What sort of car was that?'

'I didn't see. I only heard the noise and the direction it was travelling – up towards Caurin's farm.'

Caurin? Naugier flicked back a few pages in his file for the reference. Marius Caurin owned the farm behind and was the first to discover the boy. He'd been quickly eliminated: his tractor had been seen by at least three people going through Taragnon at the time of the assault, and Machanaud too had mentioned his tractor leaving in his first statement. 'The same Caurin whose tractor you saw heading down the track. What time would that have been?'

'Perhaps forty or fifty minutes before I left.'

Naugier ran through with Machanaud the remaining car sightings and timings, then flicked forward to some blank pages in his file and started writing: *First car: up at 1.45−50. Second car: down at 2.15 (not heard by Machanaud). Third car: Caurin's tractor, down at 2.25. Fourth car: up at 2.45−50 (heard by Machanaud). Fifth car: down at 3.00, just minutes before Machanaud leaves himself (heard and seen by Machanaud). 3.03−5: Machanaud leaves on his Solex, is sighted by . . .* Naugier looked up towards Poullain. 'What is the name of the woman who saw Machanaud leaving?'

'Madame Veillan.'

Naugier wrote in the name, and added: *3.16−18: Caurin returns to his farm and discovers boy. Estimated duration of attack: 40−60 minutes. Time of attack: 1.30−3.00.* So certainly Caurin's tractor had passed while the attack was in progress, but possibly the first and second cars as well. He took out and lit a Gitane and blew out the first fumes hesitantly. With the various cars passing, if indeed there was someone else there that afternoon, they couldn't possibly have stayed on the lane. The final attack must have been a few minutes at most; any longer exposure in that position would have been too risky. For the rest of the time, they must have . . .

Machanaud's voice cut in. 'But it wasn't till later that I remembered that final car clearly. It was an Alfa Romeo.'

It took a second for Naugier to detach himself from his previous thoughts. He noticed Molet glaring at Machanaud; probably he had pre-warned his client about making uninvited comments during *instruction*. 'From your statement, I thought that it was a Citroën you saw?'

Molet stepped in before Machanaud put his foot completely in his mouth. 'It *was* − on my client's original statement. But later he went into the police station and advised of the change, which from checking I believe has never been recorded. He also later mentioned the same revised sighting to a gendarme in a local Taragnon bar. We expected this to be covered at a later *instruction*, at which stage my questions would have been put forward for you to pose to the gendarmes in question.'

'A bit late for that, isn't it?' Naugier barked. 'Your client seems to have brought the subject up himself.'

Molet duly nodded and looked down. One of the great inadequacies of the *instruction* process was that the examining magistrate could freely divert, while the lawyers were restricted by the schedule provided two days in advance of each hearing. Diversions were unchartered territory, to be avoided at all costs. The only consolation was that it also worked against the prosecution: Perrimond looked equally as uncomfortable.

Dominic's heart was in his mouth at the sudden change in questioning. He'd resigned himself to prepare for the later *instruction* and tie his answers in with Poullain's. But now with rising panic he realized that Naugier could turn on him at any second and he wouldn't know what to say.

Naugier turned towards Poullain. 'I understand, Captain Poullain, you were the officer who took the original statement regarding the Citroën. To your knowledge, was this at any later stage changed?'

Poullain fleetingly caught Perrimond's and Dominic's eye, but hid his concern quickly. 'Yes . . . I believe so.' He nodded back in the direction of Briant. 'A few days after his initial statement, Machanaud came into the station and saw one of my officers, Sergeant Briant, and he –'

Perrimond interrupted. 'Sir, along with the defence counsel I would like to protest. This was something scheduled to go into in more depth at a later meeting. We are therefore – as with Monsieur Molet – totally unprepared with any questions that could add valuable light. I see neither the prosecution nor the defence case benefiting.'

'That isn't quite how I feel,' Molet countered. 'I see my client benefiting from pursuit of this line of questioning. It's just that I feel he would benefit *more* with prepared questions, as is his right.'

Naugier held up one hand sharply. '*Gentlemen*. In case you both need reminding, I, and I alone, will decide the benefit of any line of questioning at this or any future *instruction* hearing at which you are both present. You may still prepare your questions regarding this subject and propose them at a later date, as originally planned. But this now is for my curiosity.' Naugier pulled hard on his Gitane. 'Captain Poullain – I suggest you finish your answer.'

'Monsieur Molet was correct to mention inconsistencies, because that is exactly why no record was made of the change in statement.' Poullain was more confident, firm. The few seconds' interruption had allowed him to regain his composure. 'Machanaud came into the gendarmerie a few days after his initial statement. It was late in the evening and he was very drunk. He advised that he now remembered more clearly the car that passed – it was an Alfa Romeo sports. An open-top sports. In checking, there were no other sightings of such a car, but in any case we were about to ask Machanaud in to make his statement official when a day or so later he met one of my other men in a local bar. This time he said that it was an Alfa Romeo coupé that he saw.'

182

Molet exhaled audibly. He could see already where it was heading; his worst fears at the issue being tackled early were being realized.

Naugier gave him a sharp look, warning off any possible interruption, and turned back to Poullain. 'Well, surely one or the other should have been entered.'

'Possibly. But with Machanaud changing his description to an Alfa coupé, we started to have doubts. We had already fully investigated the driver of such a car and eliminated him from our inquiry. He was in a local restaurant at the time of the attack – at least three waiters saw him.' Poullain waved one arm. 'With us asking about the Alfa coupé in the village, there was a lot of local talk. It looked as if Machanaud had simply changed his description to suit. And because the car in question had been eliminated, we thought such a change in statement could only further incriminate Machanaud. He'd been drinking on both occasions – so we decided, as much for his benefit as for ours, to stick with the original statement. That was the one we trusted most, free from corruption by village gossip.'

Molet shook his head, lifting his eyes skyward as if for divine help. 'So now we are supposed to believe that all of this was done for my client's benefit. Ridiculous! My client's later description of the car was consistent on both occasions. I went over this with him several times.'

'Nice to know *you* are so certain, Monsieur Molet.' Naugier raised a sharp eyebrow. 'Especially when it appears your client was probably drunk.' He turned to Machanaud. 'How much had you drunk the night you went into the gendarmerie to change your statement?'

'I don't know exactly . . . perhaps a few eau-de-vies, some beers.'

'A few . . . *some?* Try to be more precise,' Naugier pressed. 'Did you have more than normal?'

'Yes . . . yes, probably. I met with a friend I hadn't seen since we worked together in the spring.'

Naugier looked between Poullain and Molet, as if pressing home a final seal of understanding. Machanaud was a known drunkard and bar slouch. A 'few more than normal' meant that he was ratted. 'Hopefully this has cleared up this misunderstanding. You may, as I mentioned earlier, Monsieur Molet, pursue this line of questioning at a later *instruction* when we go back over previous statements. And Captain Poullain, I would suggest that in future you put *everything* in files you present to me – and let me decide whether or not they should be disregarded.'

The noise of the trees swaying in the breeze seemed much louder in the silence following. Poullain muttered 'I understand', while Molet merely nodded and contemplated some dried leaves floating past.

That was it, thought Dominic. He felt a sudden wave of relief wash over him. Weeks of worry, and in the end hardly any blood had been shed. The fact that the file entry had been buried equally to avoid local hierarchical awkwardness had never even surfaced, and now looked unlikely to at any later date. Dominic had worried halfway through that Naugier would suddenly wheel around on him. Only now were the knots in his stomach easing. A low sigh escaped, lost among the wind rush through the trees.

And as quickly Dominic was swept with guilt. How could he be relieved at just avoiding some awkward questions, when what he had witnessed had probably quashed one of Machanaud's last chances of salvation? He followed Molet's contemplative gaze towards the river: some sunshine broke briefly through the trees, flickering off its surface. Glimmers of hope, fading just as quickly as the clouds again rolled across. He had built up a wariness and fear of Molet, and now found himself empathizing with him.

Naugier drew on the last of his Gitane and stubbed it out. He looked upstream again, his thoughts returning to where someone might have hidden . . . *if* there was someone else. No possible refuge on the lane with the cars passing, no other area of flattened or disturbed wheat – so *where?* The view along for the most part looked clear, but he needed a marker to be able to judge distance. Picking out Levacher, he asked him to go up to where his colleague stood. 'Then walk in a straight line until you are halfway down the river bank.'

As Levacher walked up the river bank, forty metres beyond, Dominic thought he saw a figure peering through the bushes bordering the lane. He was sure it wasn't Servan, he hadn't noticed a gendarme's uniform . . . but just as quickly the figure was gone.

Levacher reappeared after a moment. Naugier waved one arm, directing Levacher until he stood halfway down the bank. 'Can you see the gendarme now standing on the river bank?'

Slight pause from Machanaud, then, 'Yes.'

Naugier waved back, shouting, 'Go twenty metres further along and stop.' He asked the same question of Machanaud with Levacher in two more positions further back and received a 'yes' on each one. There were few obstacles along the river bank, the bushes low and sparse.

Naugier instructed the *greffier*. 'Let the record show that the suspect could see a figure clearly along the river bank up to sixty metres past a point running parallel with where the attack took place.'

Molet looked down and slowly closed his eyes, recalling one of the key *greffier* entries from the last *instruction*: *No other area of flattened or disturbed wheat was discovered other than that where the boy was finally found. Due to the risk of exposure of that position, directly beside the lane where cars passed, it has been concluded by the police and attending forensics that the first attack probably took place at some point down the river bank, obscured from the lane.*

Now the two entries would be linked in the jury's mind and would effectively seal his client's fate.

He had started the morning with some optimism, but bit by bit it had evaporated. First the car discrepancies dismissed out of hand, now the image of Levacher standing in clear sight of all present. Levacher could have moved another twenty metres back and still been visible. The image had burned home strongly. His client was now on record as being in clear view of where they thought the boy had crossed the river *and* where it was presumed the first attack took place. Any hopes he'd harboured of sowing strong doubts about Machanaud's guilt had gone in that moment. Molet knew now that it would take nothing short of a miracle to save his client from being convicted.

As they made their way back up the river bank to the lane, Dominic noticed a figure in the distance towards Breuille's farm. It took him a moment, squinting against the sting of the strong wind, to recognize that it was Jean-Luc Rosselot. A sad and lonely figure among the shifting blanket of wheat, watching them play out, like markers on a draught board, the scenes that led to his son's death.

19

'What makes you think it's a case for me?'

'Mainly the boy's use of French.'

'How fluent is his French?' asked Marinella Calvan.

'I only asked a few questions . . . I got a bit flustered. When he started talking in French, it caught me completely by surprise. I just asked a few rudimentary questions, went about as far as my pidgin French would take me – then stopped the session. What few answers there were sounded pretty fluent, but I couldn't be sure. I just didn't ask enough questions.'

Marinella was flattered that Lambourne had called her. They'd met three years previously at a medical convention in Atlanta, and on average he'd called her three times a year since. But this was the first real professional consultation. The rest had been just minor points of reference, do you know such and such professor, someone who'd usually published a paper Stateside about which he thought she might have better knowledge than him. Then invariably he'd get around to how she was, how was work, life in general? She had the feeling that if she said on one of the calls, 'I got married the other month' or 'I just met this great guy', the calls would suddenly stop. Except that when there had been the occasional great guy, she hadn't told him; she obviously didn't want him to stop calling.

At their first meeting, a quick coffee between lectures at the Atlanta convention, they discovered they had a lot in common: he was divorced, she had separated from a common-law husband. She was just coming up to forty, he was forty-four. Light banter, a few quips, some one-liners that belonged more to Seinfeld than Freud. Questions and general background, but no hard and fast answers. Two psychiatrists fencing with each other, both knowing that what had partly spoilt their respective relationships was being too deep, too questioning, not fully switching off when home. Keep it light and simple this time.

They'd snatched a couple more coffees together during the convention, then spent two hours at a cocktail bar on the evening it had closed. But their only real date together had been almost eighteen months later, December 1993. She'd come over to the UK for five days to handle a case in Norfolk and had managed to grab an evening in London. He showed her his office and they went to dinner and the theatre nearby. They'd also been able to find out a lot more about each other, not just personally but professionally: their respective views on psychology. She'd felt guilty at one point that she seemed to be hogging most of the conversation purely because her background with past-life therapy (PLT) was more unconventional, though Lambourne had admitted his fascination and seemed to be egging her on.

In contrast, he'd only had a few cases involving PLT, mostly conventional cures for phobia: regressing a patient initially back to childhood in search of textbook, Freud-induced phobia, discovering nothing, so heading back even further. Patients with inexplicable fears of fire, drowning or enclosed spaces were often found to have had alarming experiences in past lives which explained their phobias. A recent survey showed that 22 per cent of American psychiatrists used PLT alongside standard therapy, though she had no idea of figures for the UK and Europe.

'What made you initially regress the boy?' she asked. 'Did you think that part of your problem might lie further back?'

'Yes, but in early childhood – not in a past life. That was totally unexpected.' Lambourne had already explained the main background to the case: the accident, the coma, the dreams with Eyran clinging to non-acceptance of his parents' death through a secondary character who claimed he could find them. Now he explained that much of the secondary character's memory seemed to be buried in the past; it was impossible to determine if Jojo was a friend from Eyran's infancy who had since faded from conventional memory or a complete invention. 'Jojo also has no specific recall of losing his parents – the main shared experience linking the two characters. He said it was "long ago . . . from before" – seemed almost to be inviting me to go further back.'

'My son's almost that age now,' she commented thoughtfully. Sebastian would be ten next September. But the children she had regressed over the past years, now well over a hundred cases, would no doubt provide the strongest points of reference; very little of it did she relate to her own life. 'When the boy surfaced again and started speaking in French, do you know what year it was?'

'Not exactly. I asked him what he saw on the TV, but he said that they didn't have one, just a radio. I was about to change tack – my

187

knowledge of French radio is non-existent – when he said, "but they have one in the local café". So perhaps late fifties, sixties.'

'Or later if they were very poor or extremely religious – thought T V was a bad influence.'

'Possibly. The only thing I managed to find out was where he lived: a place called Taragnon. I looked it up on the map. It's a small village in the South. Provence.'

'Well, at least some ground can be gained by verifying his regional accent.'

They were both silent for a second: only the sound of faint crackles on the line between London and Virginia. Why did she feel hesitant? Was it just her current workload, the nightmare of arranging a week away and leaving Sebastian with her father, or a concentrated period of working close to David Lambourne when she wasn't really sure what she felt about him? She immediately pinched herself for even having the thought, realized she'd fallen into the trap of thinking that all his calls were just excuses to talk with her masked by a thin professional veneer. This was surely different. Though she was one of the main recognized experts, how many cases of true xenoglossy had she experienced in all her years? Her last paper published claimed twenty-three, but only nine did she count as significant, four of which had been with children. Out of almost 300 regressive sessions. Xenoglossy: use of a foreign language unknown to the main subject. Parapsychological gold dust: rare and one of the strongest proofs for real regressions, particularly where children were concerned. She should be grateful Lambourne had called her.

'Tell me something about Eyran's parents and his godparents. Is the current family environment strong? Are they supportive?'

'Yes, very.' Lambourne gave her the background: Eyran's parents living in California at the time of the accident, the closeness with his uncle Stuart and memories of England. 'Particularly there's a past period which features in most of Eyran's dreams and is only a few miles from where they now live.' Upper-middle class. Thirty-something. Advertising executive. Nice house in the country. One child, a daughter, now just seven. Four-wheel drive. Solid.

'Sounds ideal.' Probably no dysfunctionality stemming from that quarter, she thought. *But are they going to let us tap dance through Eyran's brain while we explore this past life?* 'The only problem I've got right now, David, is workload. It sounds exciting and I'd love to jump on the first flight – but I just don't think I'm going to be able to get out of here for almost a week.'

'If that's the earliest, fine.' But his voice carried a trace of disappointment. 'I don't really want to do any more sessions with you not here, so I'll cancel next week with the boy and hold the week after. Do you think you'll be over by then?'

'Yes, I think so.' She was already thinking ahead to preparation for the first session. 'We're going to need that time anyway. For a start we'll need a French interpreter, preferably a native Francophone who can also tell us if the regional accent is correct. And some method of transcription between us so that too many voices don't start interfering with the patient's concentration. There's also a number of things we'll need to know from the boy's godparents. Look – keep the next session date, but use it to counsel the godparents. At this stage, inform them that the secondary voice has spoken in French and your next session will hopefully find out exactly why. But don't tell them or even infer that it might be a voice from the past – after all, we're not even sure of that ourselves.' Only seconds ago the case had started to feel tangible, and already the adrenalin was running: she was afraid of losing it.

'How many sessions should I schedule initially?'

'Try and plan two within five days. That at least should get us to the first stage: finding out if the regression and its central character are real.'

From her room, if she looked out of the window at an angle, Marinella Calvan could see the University of Virginia rotunda in the distance, the half-scale copy of Rome's Pantheon which, in the spring and summer, attracted a steady stream of tourists. The centrepiece of the seat of learning founded by Thomas Jefferson, which at the US Bicentennial was voted 'one of the proudest achievements of American architecture in the past 200 years'. This was old, grass-roots America, hallowed learning halls to some of the founding fathers of the Constitution, and one of the last places you'd expect a department of parapsychology. Yet the University of Virginia had for the past thirty years, largely under the guidance of Dr Emmett Donaldson, been one of the leading centres for the study of parapsychology in America.

Real? Strange term, given that nearly all their time was spent bringing some texture and colour to the unreal, the unexplained, to convince not only themselves within the department, but the army of sceptics faced with each case paper published. In the end, so many of their questions mirrored those of the sceptics: was the regression's central character somebody famous, somebody with a well-documented life? Accessibility of general historical data about the period and area depicted, patient's interest in the same, possible input from relatives or friends? In the case of xenoglossy, because the most startling characteristic was use of a foreign language, most of her questions for Lambourne to pose the Capels revolved around Eyran's prior knowledge of the language: normal school grades in French, school trips to France, any French friends, past family holidays in France, French study books or Linguaphone tapes . . . general dexterity with the language? From hearing Eyran finally speaking as Jojo, hopefully the interpreter would know whether it was not only fluent but also accurate for the region and period described.

Xenoglossy and conducting sessions under hypnosis had been the main area where her work differed from that of Emmett Donaldson's, her professor and mentor through the years. Donaldson had built up a reputation as one of America's leading parapsychologists, a fountainhead of knowledge in past-life regressions (PLRs) backed by over 1,400 case histories, many of them published, and to date five books. Her contribution paled by comparison: 284 case studies, 178 published, one book. Though one area she had overtaken him already was the talk-show stakes, mainly because Donaldson hated personal appearances. One radio, and two TV: one local, the other a cable science channel. The Oprah Winfreys and Donahues were but distant dreams.

She had been working with Donaldson on and off since 1979. She'd gained her degree and doctorate at Piedmont College and went into private practice for three years before realizing it didn't suit her and joined Donaldson. She'd admired Donaldson's papers and work with PLR even while at Piedmont. Three years later she'd started living with a local architect, but much to her father's disappointment – except for the compensation that she kept the family name – they never married. After a first miscarriage, Sebastian was finally born in 1985. Donaldson was particularly understanding, allowing her three years off until Sebastian was at pre-school. But the more intensive period of work when she returned put extra pressure on an already strained relationship and within another two years she was separated.

It was only during that period that she gained her main focus of where she wanted her work to head. Donaldson's work had concentrated almost exclusively on regressions while awake, conventional question-and-answer sessions. This meant that he could normally only work with children up to seven or eight, beyond that age conventional memory of past lives was invariably erased. Sometimes the memories faded earlier, particularly in societies where reincarnation was not accepted; all too often past recalls were labelled as merely infantile fantasy. Much of Donaldson's work had therefore taken place in India and Asia where reincarnation was fully accepted, children with recall were not stifled by their parents.

Apart from the restrictions of conducting conventional sessions, did she really just want to follow in Donaldson's footsteps? The answer was no, but where to find her own niche? While she was attracted to the broader parameters of age and culture that hypnotic regressions allowed, Donaldson had pointed out that so many practising regressionists used hypnotism: how would she be different?

Donaldson had also built up one of the most impressive bodies of PLR work ever recorded with children, and she didn't want to turn her back on that legacy totally. In the end she chose what she hoped was the ideal compromise: hypnotic regressions, but with a high quota of children and a specific focus on xenoglossy.

Most practitioners of hypnotic regressions had quotas of no more than 12 per cent with children, largely due to the difficulties of gaining parental approval for hypnosis. She hoped to raise that quota to at least 30 per cent. The occurrence of xenoglossy also had stronger significance with children: opportunity to learn the language adopted was far less likely.

In the middle of battling through one of her most difficult cases, Donaldson had commented, 'Just satisfy yourself, Marinella. If in doing so you also satisfy the doubters and critics, then so be it. Set out just to please the critics and you'll be lost. They'll sense your vulnerability, know that you're just playing to the gallery, and have you for breakfast. Why do you think I never do live appearances?'

The case had looked ideal at first: the nine-year-old son of a Cincinnati doctor, originally regressed to cure agoraphobia, fear of wide open spaces. A past life as a conquistador in Mexico was uncovered. He had become detached from an expedition due to a lame horse and spent days roaming in the Coahuila Desert before dying of heat exhaustion and exposure. The Spanish was convincing, and she was already arranging additional sessions to prove the other areas of authenticity – geography, period events, customs and dialect – when the boy's father had phoned. His son's main phobia had been cured, he didn't want to risk his son being disturbed with continuing sessions.

She was destroyed. No Oprahs or Donahues this time either. Donaldson was right: she'd invited the let-down, played too much to the gallery.

But it was difficult not to be influenced by the years of scepticism. Seeing Donaldson's predominance of regressions in Asia dismissed by one critic as having 'scant relevance. There is far too much suggestion within the society of reincarnation. Young children, already with over-fertile imaginations, could too easily be led.'

It had been one of her main reasons for avoiding cases from that region. They were less accepted by the gallery. The university would have swallowed any lame excuse: case studies in the US and Europe were less draining on research funds. She knew that one good mainstream case – such as the Cincinnati boy – would not only boost her career but throw fresh light on the whole profession. PLR for the masses. The kid next door with average grades suddenly speaking fluently in a foreign tongue, with a linguistic expert and historian riding shotgun for authentication. Okay, *now* we believe you!

Marinella Calvan wondered whimsically if Eyran Capel might be her ticket to Oprah. Probably not. She'd become excited before and been disappointed. Too much could go wrong: the boy's godparents could refuse continuing sessions, the boy could suddenly claim to be Marshal Pétain or Maurice Chevalier, his French could turn out to be no better than phrase-book rudimentary, or he could have holidayed or gone on school exchanges regularly in France. It was too early to get excited.

20

After the reconstruction, Molet's hopes of being able to clear his client had sunk, and the witness *instruction* before Christmas if anything lowered them still further. Madame Veillan was very sure of the time she saw Machanaud coming out of the lane: 'Just after three o'clock.' Marius Caurin was next with the time he found the boy, and then the other people who had seen Machanaud that day: Raulin where he was working that morning and the various bar keepers; Henri from Bar Fontainouille and Léon who had seen him from 3.15 onwards. Repeats of the main testimonies which had ripped apart Machanaud's original police statement. Now all officially recorded for full trial.

Molet could imagine what would be built up at full trial for the jury. A day in the life of a low-life vagabond: some casual farm labour followed by a few swift eau-de-vies, then heading out half drunk for some poaching. Only he sees the boy and decides to spice up his lunch hour with a bit of buggery and murder. Then back to the bars again, to what: celebrate? Drown his regrets, steady his hands again . . . *or perhaps blot out the horror of the bloodied images still with him?* Or was it that Léon's at 3.15 was part of his regular routine and he wanted to make sure everything appeared as normal?

Molet knew that the statistics for people cleared at the final trial, having gone completely through *instruction*, were grim: less than 8 per cent. The best chances of acquittal were during *instruction* with the examining magistrate; but that now looked unlikely with Machanaud. He would go the full course.

The only way to introduce a lesser charge was if Machanaud admitted the assault, said that he'd only hit the boy to knock him out, there had been no intention to kill; try to get a manslaughter charge introduced which normally carried a five- to eight-year sentence. He'd mentioned it one day to Machanaud, tried to make him realize how heavily all the prosecution evidence weighed against him, but again Machanaud protested his innocence, was almost outraged at the suggestion. *'I'd rather that they did hang or imprison me than admit to something I didn't do.'*

In February, the *instruction* hearings started to involve witnesses more as character assessments of Machanaud. Molet watched Machanaud's ex-girlfriend give evidence of his unpredictable and sometimes violent nature, then a succession of townspeople testifying to his drinking habits and his oddball nature – and Molet was suddenly struck with an idea. Perhaps he'd be able to save his client's neck after all.

Each Christmas Dominic spent with his mother, he wondered if it would be her last. Six months to a year, the doctors had said; already seventeen months had passed. Clinking glasses over the Christmas table, was it just seasonal celebration, or partly because they knew she was cheating death? Another year.

His elder sister Janine, her husband and two children had come down from Paris for the week and for once the house was full. Janine and Guy took the spare room with their daughter Céleste, while their boy Pascal, now just nine, slept on a mattress in Dominic's room.

When his sister got a moment alone with him, she inquired about the latest round of hospital tests. The message was clear: they could visit only once or twice a year; was mother still going to be around when they visited in the summer? Dominic didn't know either way. There were times when he counted her time left in weeks, others when it seemed she might soldier on for months.

Dominic's uncle had sent him another package of the latest sounds from the States: 'Sugar Shack' and two recent hits from a new producer called Phil Spector: 'Then He Kissed Me' and 'Be My Baby'. Edith Piaf had died two months previously and his mother, not yet satiated by the many commemorative Piaf hours on the radio, was still playing some of her tracks – so Dominic ended up playing the records for himself and Pascal up in his room.

Pascal particularly liked Phil Spector. The boy had never heard such a powerful sound system, and the strong orchestral background and echoing beat were quite awe-inspiring. Dominic warmed more to the records as he edged up the volume. As the music suffused the room and he felt its rhythm washing through him, he found himself smiling. God knows what the neighbours would think if they could hear Phil Spector upstairs and Edith Piaf downstairs. Dominic turned it down a bit.

Seeing young Pascal's excitement over Christmas – opening presents, getting drunk on wine sneaked from his father's glass, and now bouncing up and down on his bed to Phil Spector – brought home even more to

Dominic how terrible it must be to lose a child. What Monique Rosselot must have suffered, must still be going through.

Dominic had seen her only once in the village since the memorial service. Louis had mentioned that she'd only started to venture out a month before Christmas, and then only rarely. If she could avoid going out, she would – but she felt guilty continuing to rely so heavily on the Fiévets. Dominic thought she looked better than at the memorial service, the dark circles beneath her eyes had mostly gone and a faint glimmer of life was back in her eyes. She didn't notice him, and he was careful not to look too long; her beauty he found somehow intimidating, and he didn't want to make her feel awkward.

Village life in Bauriac and Taragnon had settled back, though news from each *instruction* filtered through via the various witnesses called. Dominic started to worry about details of Machanaud's car state-ment arising again at the *instruction* in January, but it passed without incident.

The *instruction* process was due to finish in late April, but at the last moment Molet introduced a new element which kept it going through May – calling character witnesses *for* Machanaud in the same way that Perrimond had paraded an assortment against. The resultant coup by Molet, probably the main turning point of the case, had Dominic smiling as much as Poullain had been cursing when he brought news of it back to the gendarmerie. Molet was giving Perrimond a run for his money.

The *instruction* process ended in early June and twenty-two days later both Perrimond and Molet received notification from the Palais de Justice that the case would be presented to full trial at the *Cour d'Assises* in Aix, and the date set: 18th of October. By then, fourteen months would have passed since the attack on Christian Rosselot.

'What makes you think I can afford that?'

'Okay, I'll be generous. One half now and the other in two months' time, just two weeks before the trial starts.' They'd done the same as before: Chapeau put a call through to the general Limoges office and Duclos went out and called him back minutes later.

It was still 5,000 francs, thought Duclos. Outrageous! Almost as much as he'd paid Chapeau in the first place. 'I don't think I can manage more than four. Even splitting it in two parts.' And even that would mean taking a small overdraft from his bank.

Chapeau sniggered. 'You know, I should ask you for 6,000 for being so cheeky. I'll accept it this time – but next time you try and bargain, I'll put the figure up.'

'What do you mean – *next* time? If I pay you this now, I don't want to hear from you again.'

Chapeau sighed, his shoulders sagging. 'And just when we were getting on so well. You think I phone you just for the money – had it never occurred to you that I might like to hear the sound of your voice?'

'Oh, fuck off!'

'It's true. Practically no family left except my brother, and he's away at sea most of the time. Apart from killing people every now and then and phoning you, there's few pleasures left in my life. You think I'm going to pass up on that?' Chapeau smiled slyly and let the silence ride a second, let it sink home that he would be calling regularly. Duclos didn't respond. 'Don't worry, I'm sensible enough to realize that I'll have cleaned you out for now. I know your salary, everything about you – so I also know when best to phone. You won't hear from me for a while.'

'How long's that?' Duclos asked cynically. 'Six months, a year – two years?'

'I don't know. It depends how quickly I think you can save – or how well you do. But just think, when you get that pay rise or promotion – I could be the first one calling to congratulate you!'

Duclos didn't rise to the bait this time, sensed the pure joy Chapeau was deriving from his anger. 'Let's just settle the business at hand. When and where?'

Chapeau said that he'd make a small concession by driving in Duclos' direction to Nîmes, but no further. He suggested a roadside bar on the A9 heading west out of town, Eau du Gard.

'I don't want to do this in a crowded bar,' Duclos protested.

'It's okay – the few times I've been there it's not been that crowded. But if you feel uncomfortable, they have a large car park in front. We can stay there. When you see my car, come over and get in.'

They arranged to meet the following Saturday at 6.15 p.m.

The three judges filed in: the presiding judge in a red robe and the two assessing judges in black robes who took up seats each side of him, the *pots de fleurs*. The nine jurors were then chosen by picking names out of a pot of thirty-five by the presiding judge, Hervé Griervaut, and his *greffier*. The nine selected took their seats flanking the judges.

Molet had advised Machanaud of his right to challenge up to five jurors, but cautioned that often it aggravated and unsettled the rest of the jury. The defence made no challenges, the prosecution made only one: Perrimond singled out an old man in a crumpled suit and beret. Looked like a farm worker out for the day, thought Molet. Perrimond probably feared he might identify too readily with Machanaud. A replacement juror was picked out of the pot.

Machanaud was first on the stand. He was asked by Judge Griervaut first of all to provide an account of his activities on the day in question, then was questioned by Griervaut on specific points. This was mainly for clarification rather than angled at areas which might cast suspicion. That would come later with Perrimond, thought Molet. For now Griervaut was merely setting the scene for himself and the jury. The only contentious point he raised was Machanaud lying in earlier statements, confirming if Machanaud considered his final statement and later testimony at *instruction* to be correct. Hesitant 'Yes.'

Perrimond was next. He made much of the earlier lies and changes in police statements, sewing a strong opening image in the jury's mind of Machanaud desperately lying to cover up his dark deeds that day. He then focused on Machanaud's claim of not seeing the boy or seeing or hearing an attack, confronting him with the earlier police *instruction* entry that 'the boy was not seen at any time in the town centre, so must have reached the river by crossing the fields behind'.

Molet cringed as Perrimond took Machanaud through each stage of the gendarme's position at the reconstruction. Molet tapped his fingers impatiently to each reluctant 'yes' to twenty metres back, forty . . . *sixty*.

'So you saw absolutely nothing, Monsieur Machanaud,' Perrimond concluded. 'A boy was attacked and killed not metres away, and you had a clear view of the only point where he could have crossed the river. And yet you saw nothing?'

Perrimond kept Machanaud on the stand for another thirty minutes, ripping apart his earlier statements, magnifying the inconsistencies, and planting clearly in the jury's mind that not only was Machanaud at the scene of the crime, but it was stretching credulity that anyone else could have possibly been there. Machanaud would have seen them. Perrimond closed with the equipment that Machanaud used when fishing. 'Apart from your rod and bait – you had a bucket with water for the fish, and what else?'

'Some waders if I have to walk into the shallows.'

'Anything else? Any other sort of plastic protective clothing?'

197

'Oh yes, a plastic front apron to go over my shirt or overalls.'

'And what is that for?'

'If I have to gut my fish, it stops the blood getting on my clothing.'

Perrimond passed the floor. 'Thank you.'

A more complete legal bombardment Molet had hardly witnessed. Machanaud was clearly rattled, his few weak protests and arguments laying in tatters. But Molet wondered why Perrimond had finished with details of Machanaud's fishing equipment; surely a stronger image to close on would have been Machanaud standing in clear sight of where it was suggested the attack took place.

'Monsieur Fornier, when you realized that the car description given to Briant was different to the one mentioned to you, were you surprised?'

'I don't know. I didn't really think about it.'

Molet looked down thoughtfully. The first hour after recess had been taken up with police testimony, dominated by Perrimond asking Poullain carefully weighted questions to support his earlier arguments.

Molet had gone over the same points with Poullain for almost twenty minutes without finding a significant flaw to build on – then came to Machanaud's car statements and the later changes. After a gruelling quick-fire session, Poullain finally conceded that it was incorrect of him not to have passed on the changed statement to *instruction*, then added hastily 'But as the investigating officer it is my duty to enter the information that I trust the most and feel is accurate.' All early advantages were lost.

Molet had dismissed him shortly after and called Dominic Fornier. After the first few minutes with Fornier, he had the feeling Fornier was more nervous about the car incident, might be easier to crack than Poullain – *if* he knew anything.

'When Machanaud mentioned changing his car statement to you in the bar that evening, you apparently showed surprise. Is that correct?'

'Yes.'

'So that was the first time that you had heard about the change in car description?'

'Yes, it was.'

'Quite a few surprises and changes that evening, it seems,' Molet commented cynically. Perrimond looked as if he was about to object, then changed his mind. 'As the assistant investigating officer, would it not be normal for you to be advised of such a change in statement the moment it was made?'

Dominic's hands sweated profusely on the lectern. His chest felt tight, constricted. 'No, not necessarily.'

'So tell me – what would the circumstances be under which you might *not* be informed?'

'As perhaps in this case, where my commanding officer has already determined the information was false.'

'And when did he share this information with you?'

'A day or so later perhaps.'

'Was that the reason for him not entering the change in the file?'

Dominic was sure his face looked flushed as the blood rushed to his head. He glanced across briefly at Machanaud, but his mother's image was stronger . . . *reaching out to him. Poullain and him being questioned, charged with perjury for their earlier false statements. What price for Machanaud's life?* He just couldn't lie! But in the end, as the images receded and he saw Molet staring concernedly and about to prompt, he did the next best thing and only told half the truth. 'Yes, it was – from what he told me later.'

Molet looked down at his file and flicked back a page.

If just asked one more question, thought Dominic – *'Was that the only reason?'* – he was sure in that moment he would have told him everything, told him about Duclos and the call from Marcel Vallon relayed through Perrimond, the pressure from Poullain to cover up – the whole sorry mess that would probably ruin his career along with Poullain's, yet might at least save Machanaud's neck. And he realized then that he was almost willing it, hoping that Molet would look up and ask the question.

But Molet nodded to the bench and resumed his seat while Griervaut dismissed Fornier. Molet was still thoughtful. There had been a glimmer of recognition in Fornier's eyes, almost a look of apology as he'd glanced towards Machanaud. But then just as quickly it was gone. What was it that Fornier knew? The thought preyed on his mind for a while afterwards, through the remainder of the police testimony and the start of forensic evidence.

When Perrimond came on to the gap between the two attacks estimated at forty minutes and Dubrulle pointed out that this had been determined mostly by the hospital medical examiner, not forensics – Perrimond ended the session abruptly.

Molet noted that Perrimond's questioning of Dubrulle, head of the Marseille forensics team, was scant, but put this down to the fact that Griervaut had already covered most of the key points. He took the floor.

'Monsieur Dubrulle. You had the benefit of blood samples for matching supplied by my client, I believe. Is that correct?'

'Yes. We were supplied with samples after he had been detained.'

'And did Monsieur Machanaud's blood match any of that found at the crime scene?'

'No. We found only the victim's blood present. Type B positive. That of Christian Rosselot.'

Molet flinched slightly at the mention of the boy's name and blood together: too vivid an image for the jury. 'Items of clothing were also taken from Monsieur Machanaud's house and tested for any fibre matches and blood deposits from the boy. Is that correct?'

'Yes.'

'Were any fibre deposits found that matched that of my client's, or any blood deposits on his clothing that matched the boy's blood group?'

'No, we found no such matches. But in this case, there were no significant –'

'Is it in fact not the case,' Molet cut in sharply, 'that you found absolutely nothing at the crime scene or after – no deposits left by my client or stains on his clothing – that could have possibly linked him in any way with the crime?'

'That is so. We found nothing.'

Dubrulle was more subdued. But as Molet concluded, expecting Griervaut to dismiss him, Perrimond requested a re-examination. Only the second time he had done so.

'Monsieur Dubrulle. You were about to comment that there were no "significant" somethings or other, when my colleague interrupted. I wonder if you'd be so kind to now complete your comment.'

'Well, it was just that we found no significant fibres of any type at the scene of the crime.'

'Any blood or semen deposits or indeed anything at all linking to any individual?'

'No, we found nothing.'

'So the fact that nothing was found linked to Monsieur Machanaud was not particularly significant?'

'No, not particularly.'

'But in one area of blood stains, I understand you did find something significant. An area of stains that was weaker and pinker than other areas. How do you think this occurred?'

Molet tensed, sat forward keenly. He'd known the information would come up at some point. He should have caught on when Perrimond didn't cover it earlier with Dubrulle. Perrimond's earlier tactic of grandstanding the fishing apron suddenly made sense, and now again he'd carefully engineered everything to make it a closing point.

'It looked as if someone had washed down with water, perhaps from the murder implement or their body. Washed away the boy's blood. It was the same group as the boy's, but had been mixed with water.'

'Now, if somebody in normal apparel,' Perrimond ran one hand down inside his suit lapel, 'say standard cotton shirt and trousers, had tried to swill off bloodstains in this fashion – would the blood have washed off successfully or left stains?'

'Very little of it would have washed off. Most of it would have soaked into the clothing.'

'But if this person was wearing some sort of protective waterproof clothing – say a plastic apron or bib of some type – would it have washed off in this fashion then?'

'Yes, probably.'

'And such a bib would also have protected their clothing from stains, I presume?'

'Yes, obviously.'

'Thank you.' Perrimond sat down and Griervaut dismissed Dubrulle from the stand.

Molet's spirits sank. Scanning the jury, he saw that the impact of the point had gone home strongly.

Testimony from attending medics and doctors was next. Looking at his watch, Molet realized that part of it was probably going to spill over to the next morning. Little arose as the day's events drew to a close to raise his spirits again. Now that Perrimond had stolen his thunder over forensics, there were precious few ace cards left to play. Any chance of clearing Machanaud had probably gone. All that remained was the testimony of an ageing Resistance fighter, an army doctor, and his own closing arguments to be able to save his client's life.

'And how long were you practising at the Military Hospital in Aubagne, Dr Lanquetin?'

'Over twenty years. Though I'm retired now – since just four years ago.'

'During that time, what did you specialize in?'

'In treatment of cranial injuries. I was a practising surgeon who dealt almost exclusively with head injuries incurred by soldiers or legionnaires in active service.'

'I see.' Molet looked down thoughtfully. It was an idea he'd struck on late in the *instruction* process, seeing the procession of character witnesses from Perrimond testifying to Machanaud's strange and oddball character. One of them had commented, 'I believe he even has a metal plate in his head from a sabotage operation that went wrong while in the Resistance.' Machanaud had originally fought the idea, felt that playing on his old injuries was merely supporting the opposition's case that he was mad and had done something strange that afternoon. Molet admitted then that he thought his chances of clearing Machanaud were remote, and this was probably their only hope of getting a lesser manslaughter charge introduced. Reluctantly, Machanaud had given him the name of the hospital where he was treated.

His old doctor had since died, but Molet managed to find a retired army doctor, Lanquetin, who was an expert in head injuries. He introduced him along with an old Resistance colleague at a later *instruction* and argued strongly that a lesser charge of manslaughter should be introduced. 'Half of the prosecution case rests on the fact that Machanaud is slightly odd. Yet he has never done anything like this before, and after months of talking with my client, I can say that if indeed he has done this, he clearly has no memory of it. This is an old Resistance fighter, one with a metal plate holding his head together. And we are going to argue on one hand that he is odd and slightly mad, yet on the other hand claim that he knew exactly what he was doing and condemn him to be hanged. Ridiculous! I move for a lesser charge of manslaughter to be introduced on the grounds of diminished responsibility, and will produce the medical evidence to strongly support it.' Predictably, Perrimond opposed the suggestion. Naugier accepted it reluctantly, but only as an alternative charge. The manslaughter charge would ride alongside that of premeditated murder. It would be up to the jury to decide of which they thought Machanaud was guilty.

'So your knowledge in the area of cranial injuries is quite extensive?'
'Yes.'

'And during this period, have you had experience with metal plates and their effects on patients?'

'Yes, I have. Quite a bit.' Molet merely looked at him expectantly. Lanquetin continued. 'The effects can vary, but the plate is no more than a drastic, emergency solution to hold together two parts of the cranium that could possibly shift. As such, they may be affected by cold or hot weather, or even sudden movement. Electrical and chemical imbalances can be sparked off.'

'What would be the effect of such imbalances?'

'It varies enormously. It could be nothing more than a mild headache, slightly irritable behaviour or anxiety. Or at the other extreme, quite irrational, even violent behaviour.'

'So it is quite conceivable, Dr Lanquetin, that someone with a metal plate – given the right conditions – could suffer a temporary memory loss, have absolutely no recall whatsoever?'

'Yes, it is.'

Molet produced the X-rays Lanquetin had viewed earlier, and Lanquetin confirmed that Machanaud's was quite an extensive implant and that indeed, because of its proximity to the parietal lobe which controlled both some motor and behavioural functions, given the right conditions there could be adverse affects.

'Thank you, Dr Lanquetin.'

Perrimond spent very little time cross-examining Lanquetin, his main thrust was an attempt to discredit Lanquetin's grasp of 'modern medicine' due to the fact that he had now retired. But the ploy partly backfired when Lanquetin reminded him that metal-plate implants were not particularly akin to modern surgery, and indeed the practice was fast dying out.

The conclusion of medical testimony and the various incidental and character witnesses had taken up most of the morning. There was only one witness left to call, Machanaud's old colleague from the Resistance, Vincent Arnaud. Molet realized that the closing arguments would probably now have to follow after lunch; there wouldn't be time before.

Arnaud's testimony transported them back to another age: 1943. He and Machanaud were both in their late twenties, colleagues in the Resistance fighting the Germans near Tours. A ragtag bunch with limited resources doing the best they could. Arnaud described the dynamite set one day so that they could stop and ambush an ammunition truck. But the dynamite was damp, it went off late and the truck veered off the road, striking Machanaud.

'And was it this that caused your colleague Gaston Machanaud to be hospitalized and have a metal plate inserted?'

'Yes, it was. It was days before we even knew whether he'd live or not.'

Whatever was decided later, thought Molet, with Arnaud on the stand it was once again Machanaud's finest hour. Machanaud's eyes welled with emotion. Old colleagues, old memories. And confirmation at last for all his doubters and detractors that his day of glory, the story he had spun over so many bar counters, had not just been drunken ramblings. Perhaps now everyone would believe him.

The first fifteen minutes of Perrimond's closing arguments were predictable. How Machanaud was the only person present, his extensive lying when first questioned, the reconstruction which had proved conclusively that he was within sight of not only where the boy had crossed the river but also where the first attack had taken place, and the forensic evidence which had demonstrated that blood had been swilled away with water. 'Who else but Machanaud would have been equipped with not only waders and a plastic apron, but also a bucket of water for such an exercise?'

Perrimond swung around dramatically, surveying each juror in turn. 'Make no mistake, this was a very measured and deliberate act. Machanaud knew that if the boy was found on the lane and it looked like the assault took place there, then if by chance it was discovered he was down by the river that day, he could claim that it was somebody else who committed this atrocity.' Perrimond looked down thoughtfully, giving the jury due time for consideration. 'And lo and behold, when he is confronted with being by the river that day, this is exactly what he claims.'

Perrimond then started to pre-empt the arguments Molet might propose. 'You will probably hear from the defence that their client was just some poor misfortunate who happened to be in the wrong place on that dark day. That the first attack might have even taken place elsewhere and the child was transported to the lane for the second attack. But how?' Perrimond scanned the jury. 'Each car that passed up and down the lane while Machanaud was there was accounted for. One of the drivers was in a restaurant for over an hour just beforehand with his car in full sight in the car park. A friend visiting spent all his time speaking with Marius Caurin, and Caurin himself when leaving was seen at various places in town.'

Perrimond looked imperiously at the bench. 'This was Taragnon, a small rural village, and it was the middle of the day. The streets were busy. The police spent painstaking weeks and months questioning, and with only one conclusion: Christian Rosselot did not pass through the town. Nor did he pass through from the farm behind, it was too far out of his way – and besides Marius Caurin would have seen him. So desperate are the defence that they would have you believe anything. Anything but the facts.'

Perrimond shrugged and smiled caustically, then quickly became grave again. 'No, the boy crossed at only one point – the small bridge down-river fully in sight of where the accused was fishing. It was there that their fatal meeting took place – and it was also there that the accused relentlessly assaulted the boy and left him for dead. A cold, merciless act perpetrated by only one person, who sits before you now – the accused, Gaston Machanaud.'

Perrimond finished by asking for the harshest possible sentence, saying that it was ridiculous to consider anything but a guilty verdict on premeditated murder, anything less would not be doing a service to themselves, justice, or to the memory of the young boy 'who can now only beg for justice silently from the grave. And trust that in your hearts and souls you will make the right decision.'

Perrimond closed his eyes briefly, nodding as he sat down, as if concluding a prayer, and left the floor to Molet.

'No blood. No fibres. No semen. Not a single thing that links my client to the crime scene itself. I just want you to remember that when you sentence him to be hanged!' Molet surveyed the jury, audibly drawing breath. 'Except the fact that he was there. There at the time fishing, poaching – as he had been so many times in the past. And yes, the prosecution are right – I am going to suggest that someone else came along and committed this crime. Because that is exactly what happened.'

Molet paced to one side. 'A thorough police investigation that discounted all other possibilities? This is the same investigative team that could not even enter a change in car description accurately from one day to the next. That, when confronted, started clinging to the excuse that my client was drunk to hide their error. A vital change, not even entered at *instruction*, which the examining magistrate openly admonished them over. Yet we are supposed to believe that they conducted a *thorough* investigation, one that eliminated all other possibilities, when they could not even pass a bit of vital evidence from one stage to the next when it was laid on a plate before them!

'I think the police merely latched on to the first obvious target, my client, and have been constructing a case out of thin air ever since. One built on a single circumstance – that he was there. And not a single fact or piece of concrete evidence to support this circumstance. What are we all doing here? How could we all have been dragged this far on such a pitiful illusion? A harmless poacher and local drunkard who one day, suddenly, decides to molest and kill a young boy. No history of molesting young boys, no sexual predilections in that area whatsoever – yet we are supposed to believe that this day, this *one* day, all reason and normal instincts were suddenly thrown to the wind. Unbelievable! How did the prosecution even raise the audacity to try and get us to swallow such a ridiculous story.

'So let us think afresh – what are we left with? Let us strip away all the ridiculous coincidences slotted into place by the police and the prosecution, and see what we are left with. A simple man with a long history of poaching and *no* history whatsoever of harming young boys. We ask him what he was doing that day? What do you think is the most likely explanation? That, as he claims, he was poaching, or – the more ludicrous suggestion that then starts to stretch all precepts of credible thinking – that he suddenly broke with past form and harmed this young boy? Because that, exactly that, is what is being suggested today.'

Molet waved one arm dramatically. 'Even what the prosecution are asking for here today and the evidence they are providing in support are at odds. On one hand, they want you to believe that this was a cold-blooded, premeditated murder. On the other, they would have you believe – from the various witnesses they have produced – that the accused is mad half the time and drunk the rest. A complete oddball and misfit. A village idiot who can hardly premeditate his life from one day to the next, let alone plan a murder like this – so meticulously in fact that the police and a whole team of forensics could not find a single trace of evidence.' Molet slowly shook his head. 'The two just don't go together. The only honesty you have seen here today was just before lunch: Gaston Machanaud's old Resistance colleague and the army doctor. That is the real Gaston Machanaud. The Resistance fighter who fought bravely for his country, suffered a horrific injury that still plagues him as a consequence, and is now just left with a few fond tales to tell in the local bars. This is the man that the prosecution want you to hang. Pathetic!'

Molet drew a long and tired breath. 'Yet I had to fight with my client to bring them here today and to the earlier *instruction* – even though it was the only way to bring some honesty to this whole charade – and introduce the charge that, if anything at all, my client should be facing: manslaughter. Manslaughter due to diminished responsibility.

It is outrageous that any other charge should have even been discussed today.'

Molet looked down; reluctant dismay. 'But in doing so, I have partly turned my back on what I believe: that my client is innocent. That only one thing is true about the prosecution's claim – he was there. Nothing more. No blood. No semen. No fibres. No scheming individual who could successfully hide those elements. And no reasonable explanation from the prosecution of what he was doing there that afternoon – except the one he gave himself. That he was there fishing. As he had been so many afternoons before.'

Molet nodded in turn to the jury and the three judges and sat down.

The jury returned after almost two hours. Between the nine jurors and three judges, the votes – counted painstakingly by the *greffier* and then passed to Griervaut to announce – were seven to five not guilty of premeditated murder, nine to three guilty of manslaughter.

Molet felt a twinge of disappointment at no acquittal, followed quickly by relief: it could have been worse. Much worse. But Machanaud looked destroyed. Molet knew from the earlier *instruction* when he fought with Machanaud over getting the lesser charge introduced that Machanaud would probably never comprehend or accept. Understandable for some-one who was probably innocent. Despite his closing arguments, Molet knew how strongly the jury had been swayed by much of the prosecution's presentation and witnesses, and that without the mid ground of the lesser charge they would probably have found Machanaud guilty of premeditated murder.

Because the charge for manslaughter partly hinged on diminished responsibility, Judge Griervaut raised the subject of medical and psychiatric assessment. Molet argued for private assessment, while Perrimond pre-dictably argued for state assessment. After consultation with his two assessing judges, Griervaut cleared his throat summarily and looked up to pass final sentence: that Machanaud be detained in prison for no less than six years, and that he be treated and assessed twice each year by a state psychiatrist. 'At the end of that period, if not deemed to be mentally fit, he should be released to the care of a state psychiatric hospital where he would undergo suitable treatment until fit for release.'

At the outside Machanaud would do the full six with maybe another year in an institution, Molet considered. If things went well, he could get parole in four years and be cleared to leave immediately. What

Molet hadn't noticed was the look that passed between Perrimond and one of the assessing judges when they were deliberating on the issue of state or private psychiatric assessment. All that struck him as odd was Perrimond's slight smile when the final judgment was passed down. A strange reaction to what surely must have been considered mostly a defeat by him.

21

Marinella Calvan was still adjusting after the long flight, and the wine had made her feel sleepy. She held one hand up to indicate half a glass more was enough as David Lambourne poured. 'Where did you find Philippe?' she asked.

'London School of Economics, just down the road. He's not an official interpreter – just a French student on a social sciences course. But his English is almost word perfect and he's all I could find at such short notice with a South of France background.'

'How old is he?'

'Twenty-four. He's from a small village in the Alpes-Maritimes: Valderoure.'

They'd spent just over an hour in Lambourne's office going over the case before retiring to a small bistro close by. They'd already agreed the only French spoken would be between the patient and the interpreter. One voice with questions. Marinella would tap them out to appear on a computer screen; Philippe would then pose the questions and tap out the answers in English on the same screen. The session for them would be a series of on-screen questions and answers in English. It was the only way to avoid distraction and confusion.

'Will his knowledge of accents and dialects from the fifties and sixties for that region be good enough?'

'It hasn't changed that much according to him. Especially in the inland villages.'

Marinella nodded and sipped her wine. Earlier they'd discussed what Lambourne had discovered through the Capels: Eyran's grades for French were average, there had been one or two holidays to France, but no school exchanges or long stays. Eyran's French was at '*la plume de ma tante*' stage. She'd already gained the main background of the Capels, and now filled the gaps. Some details, such as how long they'd been married, Lambourne didn't know. The only thing to cause a chink of concern was Lambourne's flippant remark that the area where they lived, East Grinstead, was 'home to more fringe religious groups than any other part of the country'. When pressed, Lambourne assured her that they were normal. 'Lapsed Church of England.'

Still, she asked the obvious. 'Do you think they could have staged all this?' She knew that it was one of the first questions she'd be asked by sceptics. Advertising executive. Vivid imagination. From an area noted for fringe religions. In no time the media would have them taped as weirdos from some obscure cult which not only believed in reincarnation, but that we all live concurrent lives in different dimensions.

'No, I don't think so. If anything, they were reluctant to enter Eyran into the sessions. Certainly Stuart Capel at least. He admitted that he should have taken Torrens' advice earlier and entered Eyran into coun-selling almost straight away. He delayed, hoping that Eyran might improve in his own time.'

'Torrens?' The name struck a faint chord, but Marinella couldn't recall from where.

'The doctor from California who operated on Eyran and treated him during his coma. He made an initial report recommending Eyran should have psychiatric counselling. Not only due to the loss of his parents, but for assessment of impairment after the coma. The boy was under almost three weeks.'

'Have you got a copy of Torrens' report?'

'Yes.'

'Good, good. That will help enormously.' Couldn't be better. Coun-selling initially recommended by a Stateside doctor.

'Us or the boy?'

Marinella calmed her enthusiasm and bit her lip lightly at Lambourne's frown. 'I'm sorry. That probably sounded a bit callous.' Their aims were at odds, she realized. His was to cure the boy, hers was to prove an authentic regression. Only where the regression might help the main subject did they coincide. But grandstanding her own aims above his had been insensitive. She smiled. 'You know, Donaldson always warned me about playing to the gallery. That each time it would land me in trouble. But it's unbelievable what we have to put up with when we get things wrong.' She went on to explain how their critics, many of them from within the profession, sat on the sideline like vultures waiting for them to foot-fault. 'One bad case, one falsehood we fail to uncover before them, and our credibility can be set back years. Suddenly *everything* we're doing is false. Questions at each corner, the threat of departmental budget cuts . . ."Why didn't you find that out before? Is your next case going to be like the so-and-so fiasco?" It's no wonder we become paranoid, lose sight of other objectives. I'm sorry.'

Lambourne nodded. He'd put her at ease earlier about their respective objectives by assuring her that he couldn't continue with conventional therapy until a regression uncovered more about Jojo. But there was still a gap. To her this was just another research paper; to him, it was an extension of PLT: Eyran's current problems and obsessions partly stemming from his past as Jojo. But there was no point in underlining that gap, spoiling the mood of their association before it had started. 'If we can each get only 30 per cent of what we initially hoped for out of this, then we'll at least be doing better than my normal sessions. Cheers.'

They spent a while talking about the structure of the next day's session, then the conversation became more general, the mood lighter.

'Anything notable come up since we last met?' he asked.

'You mean, like the conquistador boy?'

Lambourne looked down, toying with his dessert. He knew how frustrating the case had been for her, but why the reference now? Was it a warning shot: *don't cut me short on this one, put me through that again.* 'I was hoping you might have had something more fruitful.'

'Not really. Lots of conventional regressions, but only two with xeno-glossy – both adults. But use of language wasn't exceptional; in both cases it could be argued that the subjects would have been able to learn the language used, especially at that level of proficiency.'

Beneath Lambourne's look of concern, she noticed a half-smile. A smile that said: *perhaps tomorrow will change your run of luck.* He was obviously more hopeful than he'd made out. The early signs looked promising, she conceded; but her long years of battling with sceptics had made her fear the worst. Even if the first stages of authentication were satisfied, would the Capels agree to continuing sessions, and for how long would Lambourne remain convinced that their aims coincided?

Session 6

'It's dark and warm inside. Outside I can hear the wind through the trees and the birds . . . or sometimes my father working in the fields nearby.'

The session had been under way forty minutes and already Marinella Calvan was exhausted. The start had been slow, the rhythm staccato, heightened by the gap waiting for Philippe to type the translated answers on screen and then pose Marinella's typed questions in response. The only words spoken in the room were in French. While the on-screen version in English would provide a useful typescript, they'd decided to run a tape as well; nuances or possible language misinterpretations could be gone back over later. David Lambourne was at her side.

Parts had been rambling, the boy spending a long time describing a visit to the beach at Le Lavandou, the seagulls overhead, making a sandcastle with a rivulet for the sea to wash in and form a moat. She'd been eager to move on, but Lambourne felt it might be better to introduce a more relaxing tone and mood. Minutes before, when they'd asked him about being separated from his parents, his breathing had become rapid and hesitant. He'd mumbled something about a bright light, not being able to see, then lying flat in a wheat field, his face against the sheaves – but by that time his breathing had become too fractured, words little more than spluttered monosyllables in the gaps. She quickly prompted Philippe to interrupt. Whatever had separated him from his parents had obviously been deeply disturbing. They'd return to it later.

She guided him towards fonder, more relaxed memories.

Recall of the day at the beach had been one, and now, describing his favourite hideaway camp in the field at the back of the family farmhouse, another. In between the rambling passages, in the moments Marinella had been able to impose some structure to the session, she'd been able to find out the names of both his mother and father and how far the farm was from the local village, Taragnon. Jojo had been a nickname; two or three corrections passed back and forth with Philippe before they had it right: Ji-jo, Gigot, then finally Gigio, after one of his favourite puppet characters. Asking Gigio what he heard on the radio at home, they'd also identified the period: the early sixties.

'Sometimes I jump up from my hiding place and surprise my father.'

'Does your father spend a lot of time in the fields?'

'Yes . . . and in the garage at the side of the house. All his tools are in there.'

'Is it a big farm?'

'Yes. At least four hectares.'

Almost ten acres, thought Marinella. Small holding. But to a young boy it was probably large. 'And from your hideaway, can you see the house? What does it look like?'

'The field slopes down . . . and there's a courtyard before the kitchen door. Sometimes when it's getting dark, I can see my mother working in the kitchen and I know then that it's time to come in. I know if my father is in the garage, because he always has the light on – the window there's small.'

'Do you have other favourite places in the house where you like to hide? What about your bedroom – do you like your bedroom?'

'Yes . . . but I prefer my hideaway. My sister always comes into my bedroom and plays with my toys . . . She broke one of my toys once, it was a favourite car . . .'

Marinella watched patiently as the tale unfolded on screen: Gigio describing how upset he was, how the car had been for his birthday just a few weeks before. He'd shouted and she started crying, his mother took his sister's side and made him even more upset. She was about to interrupt with another question – she felt that Gigio was starting to ramble again – when he suddenly became more thoughtful.

'I shouldn't have become so angry with her, made her cry. I loved her really . . . I always helped her if I could. I missed her so much later, as I did my parents.'

Marinella's skin bristled. Often with regressions accurate detail could be gained only by taking the person back to a specific time and place – a room, a fond memory, an event that stuck out in their mind. But sometimes the patients would jump time frames and generalize periods and feelings. 'Did you become separated from your sister as well – and was it at the same time as your parents?'

'Yes.'

Either Gigio had lost his entire family, or he had become separated from them. She asked.

Eyran's head lolled, his breathing suddenly more erratic as his eyelids pulsed, struggling with the images. 'It was me – I became lost from them . . . I remember thinking how worried they would be. And my father . . . my father . . . why didn't he come and try to find me? There was a bright light . . . so bright . . . I couldn't see anything. And the field . . . I recognized it . . . I thought I might see my father there looking for me any minute, when . . . *when . . . I . . . I . . .*' Eyran's head started shaking, beads of sweat on his brow, the words subsiding into guttural gasps on fragments of breath.

Lambourne put one hand on Marinella's shoulder, but she misread the signal, tapped out, *Did you blame your father for not finding you – think that it was partly his fault?*

Eyran swallowed, fighting to control his erratic breathing. 'Yes – partly . . . but it was more me . . . I blamed myself. I kept thinking how they couldn't face that I'd become lost from them – that I'd somehow let them down . . . their sorrow. My mother's face, so sad . . . *so, so sad* . . . her eyes full of tears, crying . . . no, it couldn't be real – it couldn't have happened . . . no, couldn't . . . *not real* . . . *No* . . . *No!*' Eyran's head started rocking more wildly this time, his eyes scrunched tight. His laboured breathing rasped in his throat.

Lambourne reached over frantically to the keyboard, tapped out, *(Stop it. Stop it now! Move Gigio on from the incident.)*

Marinella looked up quizzically. They'd arranged a code whereby any message between them should be typed in brackets so that Philippe knew not to translate. She'd pushed for Lambourne's benefit, would have been happy just to ask limp questions about Gigio's background and let him ramble at will, build up her research paper – but Lambourne's objective was to find and exorcize the link of shared loss between Eyran and Gigio. It seemed crazy to give up now, just when they might be on the brink. She was about to tap out, *(We're so close to proving the link – just a few more questions)*, when, reading the intensity of Lambourne's expression she thought better of it. She typed, *When you were in your hideaway by the old house – how old were you?* Return Gigio to a calmer, happier period.

They waited over twenty seconds for Eyran to make the leap, for his breathing to settle back and his answer. 'I was ten years old then.'

Marinella knew that Gigio was nine at the time of his day out at Le Lavandou, his sister four. 'Do you have any memories from when you were older – eleven or twelve?' Marinella was aware of Lambourne's slight intake of breath and of him staring intently at her as she waited for an answer. If she could have spoken, she would have explained that general overviews usually posed no danger, didn't get subjects wrapped up as intently as specific recall of incidents.

'No . . . after the light and the field, there was nothing . . . I . . . uh . . .' Eyran's head tilted, as if he was grappling for images just out of reach. 'Everything grey . . . grey behind my eyes . . . then another light – things distant . . . too far . . . can't hear . . . can't . . .' Some mumbling, words and thoughts trailing off.

Lambourne's nerves tensed. This was the second time that *field* had been mentioned. On impulse, he reached forward and tapped out, *Was it a wheat field?*

Short pause as Philippe translated and the answer came. 'Yes . . . yes, it was.'

Marinella sensed that it was significant by Lambourne's sudden urgency, but he just gave her a wide-eyed shrug. An 'It's interesting, but I'll tell you later' look. Now that she knew Lambourne wouldn't expect her to push more on the shared-loss link between the two boys, she relaxed and returned to general information, filled in gaps from what they'd learned so far: how often Gigio went to the local village, his full name, his school, the name of the street by their farm, and friends and neighbours.

At only one point did Gigio start rambling again, describing stopping off from school at the local boulangerie, and how the woman there, Madame Baudert, when her husband wasn't in the shop would often give him some free '*pan chocolat*'. They were stale, from one or two days before, and would soon be thrown out, but her husband was too mean to give them away, she confided one day. It became their little secret, the husband probably puzzled by this young boy coming in his shop so often and browsing without buying anything, and the wife winking at Gigio as soon as she thought her husband's back was turned.

Marinella let Gigio ramble: it was providing some useful extra details to check, and for the first time during the session Eyran had actually smiled. She could feel a stronger bond and trust developing with the lighter mood. If she built on that rapport, by the next session they might have more success breaking through the barriers Gigio had erected and could start tackling the core grief that linked the two boys.

Marinella was aware of Lambourne checking his watch and nodding at her. She checked the time: an hour and twelve minutes. More than enough for a first session. She gradually wound things down, let Gigio finish his description of discovering an old car tyre one day on his way home from school with a friend, and how they rolled it back to the farm – then brought Eyran back out of hypnosis.

While Lambourne escorted Eyran out and she heard him talking with the Capels in the waiting area, she scrolled back on the computer screen. Apart from Lambourne's *stop it* command, the only other item in brackets was where she'd asked Philippe if the regional French was accurate. She asked him now to elaborate on the basic *yes* on screen. 'Was it accurate for the time period as well as the region?'

'Yes, pretty much. As I said to David, it hasn't really changed through the years. Only on the coast has it been corrupted because of the massive influx of visitors and residents from other parts. Fifty kilometres inland, it's a different world.'

'Is it the sort of accent that would be easy for someone to copy or affect?'

Philippe shrugged. 'Not that easy. Perhaps someone from Paris or Dijon could attempt a reasonable mimicry, but they would still be caught out on some words. But somebody English, already struggling with French as a second language — I don't think so.'

Marinella clicked the print command. The printer was on the second sheet as Lambourne came back in. Marinella asked him about the wheat field. 'I remember you mentioning a wheat field from one of Eyran's earlier dreams. Is that why you thought it might be significant?'

'Yes, that, and Eyran mentioning that when he first moved to the old house in England, the wheat field at the back seemed somehow familiar.'

'Well, at least the main prognosis seems to have been supported,' Marinella commented. Earlier she speculated that if a real regression was proved, probably some memory of loss or grief in the past life had been sparked off by the accident and Eyran's loss. In the same way that many PLT-uncovered phobias lay dormant until woken by a similar incident. 'I think we'll find that if there was much memory or link between the two before the accident, it was mostly subliminal — little more than fragments of *déjà vu*.'

'Possibly. But we won't know for sure until we've gone back in more detail through the transcript and compared it with the transcripts from previous sessions.'

Marinella noticed Lambourne glance towards Philippe and picked up on the signal. Either he didn't want to talk openly in front of Philippe, or he wanted more time to consider his prognosis. She too would probably benefit from a few hours to collect her thoughts. 'Of course, we're jumping the gun a bit. The first thing we need to know is if the regression and its main character are real. If not, then we can focus again on the original theory of a secondary character invented by Eyran.' She turned to Philippe. 'How would you like to earn some extra money?'

Philippe smiled slyly. 'The last time an older attractive woman asked me that, I got into trouble.'

Marinella explained her problem. They had various names and details from the session, all of which would have to be checked. This would involve a number of calls to town hall registrars and clerks in France, and her French was practically non-existent. Marinella circled the names on the transcript. 'The Rosselots. The boy Christian and his parents Monique and Jean-Luc. Sister named Clarisse. From Taragnon. Early sixties. Shouldn't be too hard to find — *if* they exist.'

The boy had probably died when he was only ten years old. Everything should therefore start with registration of the death certificate, she explained. Then perhaps they could begin piecing together the details of his life. 'See if those pieces match his descriptions.'

22

Jean-Luc Rosselot sat on the small stone wall and looked down the slope of the field towards the courtyard and the house. It was summer again, eight months after the trial. The scent of the fields reminded him of the day he'd found Christian's bike, of days they'd spent together working on the farm . . . *of the bleak wheat field with the gendarmes placed like markers.*

Christian's small makeshift camp on the far side of the wall he'd dismantled just a few months before. The winter winds had made it look dishevelled, no longer a pleasant reminder of the days when Christian used it.

The images too were fading. Many times before he'd sat on the wall and looked down, imagined Christian running up towards him, waving, calling his name. Now when he summoned up the image, he could see a figure running, but it was indistinct – it could have been any boy. The features were faded, hazy, little more than a Cézanne impression. He wondered whether it was because his eyes were watering with the pain of the memory, blurring his vision – then would suddenly realize his eyes had slowly closed, the images were playing only in his mind.

The only images that remained clearly, *too clearly*, were those he'd fought to blot out: the young gendarme in the courtyard with Monique collapsed at his feet, the photos of when Christian was found which he and Monique had to view at *instruction*, part of the process of official identification before the almost ludicrous question, 'Is it your wish that charges are proceeded with?' The two days in court, his outrage as the defence tactics became clear, and then the judge's final sentence: six years? Six years for the life of his son: not even a semblance of justice. Diminished responsibility? Metal plates, army doctors and old Resistance fighters. The whole thing had been a pathetic sham.

All that he'd clung to all along was justice being done. Everything else had already been stripped away. Pride, hope, some reason to explain the ridiculous, the unacceptable fact that he'd lost Christian. Was that what he'd hoped for that day in court? Some explanation of *why* it had happened to lay the ghosts to rest? In the end, reason had been as lacking as justice.

What were they saying in the end: that the man *had* murdered his son, but it was partly excusable because he had a metal plate due to being hit by a Nazi truck twenty years ago?

Jean-Luc shook his head. He felt tired, very tired. The land, the fight to make the farm work, had been sapping him dry the last few years. Christian's death and the ensuing investigation and court case had taken whatever strength and resolve remained. He felt increasingly awkward in Monique's and Clarisse's company, could hardly look them in the eye, knew that they might see what lay beneath: that he just couldn't love them the way he loved Christian. And he was ashamed that he'd let them down, failed them. The last two letters from the bank he'd stuffed in a drawer without opening them. He knew already what they would say.

He rose slowly, clearing the welled tears from his eyes as he started down the field towards the courtyard. If he saw Christian now, saw a clear image again waving and calling to him, perhaps that would stop him, make him think again. But there was nothing, only the empty field. Empty and dry under the summer sun, unyielding. Nothing left to cling to any more, not even the memory. As he got closer to the house, he saw a faint flicker behind the kitchen window. Monique was busy in the kitchen, but she hadn't noticed him and didn't look up as he crossed the courtyard to the garage.

14 December 1969

Monique Rosselot tried to make out shapes in the room. Everything was misty, as if she was looking through a sheet of muslin. The figures moving around were indistinct, blurred, except the nurse when she leant close, asking her again if she could feel anything below her waist?

'Yes . . . yes,' she answered between fractured breaths, now slightly indignant at the nurse's doubting tone.

Feel was such a lame word for the terrible pain that gripped her, starting deep in her stomach and spreading like a firestorm through her thighs and lower back. She'd never before experienced such intense pain, didn't know it was possible for any human to endure such agony.

'I don't think the epidural has taken,' she heard a man's voice say. 'We might have to give her another shot.'

'I don't think we can at this stage,' came another.

And then the nurse leaning over again. 'Can you feel your body relaxing now?'

'Yes . . . yes.'

'But can you still feel the pain from lower down?'

Monique exhaled the 'yes' between clenched teeth, her breathing now little more than short bursts as she tensed against the pain.

Dr Jouanard contemplated the dilemma. The patient had been given the epidural almost thirty minutes ago. After twenty minutes, when it became obvious it hadn't taken because of the patient's continuing pain, the baby was engaged in the birth canal. It would be almost impossible for the patient to bend forward to get the right curvature in the spine for a fresh epidural. And the risks of trying to administer it without full curvature were too high. A half-centimetre off target and the patient could be paralysed. In the end he'd ordered a mild general anaesthetic, something to calm and relax nerves, but leave the patient awake so that there was some response muscle control to push with.

At least that had now taken, but the continuing pain and the fact that the baby didn't seem to have progressed any further in the birth canal, despite concentrated pushes from the patient, began to worry Jouanard. He'd read the patient's history thoroughly: two previous natural births without complications, her pelvic girth was obviously sufficiently large, why the problems now?

With one hand on the abdomen, he could feel the baby lodged deep in the birth canal; with the other he spread back the vulva to get a clearer view. He thought he saw what looked like the baby's head, and something else – though he couldn't immediately make out what. There was also too much blood; he began to worry that something might have ruptured internally. He felt inside, trying to identify by touch what he thought was the head.

He worked his hand around, moulding to the shape of the smooth damp flesh: it was a shoulder straight ahead that he'd seen, further down he could feel the thorax and arm, and the head . . . the head was pushed sharply to one side. And something in between. Jouanard ran his hand around once more to make sure. He looked up sharply.

'Dr Floirat. Administer the patient immediately with full anaesthetic for surgery.'

Floirat started issuing instructions: ECG monitor and oscillatometer to be wheeled forward, doses for the thiopentone.

Jouanard stepped back, supervising the laying out of instruments by his assistant. The blood loss worried him. Three or four minutes to set up the monitors, another minute for the thiopentone to take effect. How much more would she have lost by then? He directed a nurse to keep swabbing the flow. He noticed the patient's eyes darting, taking in the renewed activity.

'It's okay ... it's okay,' he soothed. 'The epidural hasn't taken fully. We're giving you a general anaesthetic. It will all be over soon. Just relax.'

Stock phrases. Inside he was panicking. Breach birth with part of the umbilical cord wrapped around the baby's neck. Pushing against the obstruction had obviously caused an internal rupture, and the baby might already be strangled. If the placenta had ruptured, the baby would soon be dead, *if* it was still alive. If it was the uterus or womb, he could lose the patient as well. And he wouldn't even know where the rupture was until he opened up.

The nurses were making the last connections on the monitors. Floirat stepped forward and administered the thiopentone. Jouanard looked at his watch, almost counting down the seconds. The blood loss was heavy. Fresh swabs were being dumped in the dish ever ten or fifteen seconds. The patient was still alert, responding to the nurse who was talking to check when she was fully under.

As the questions became totally mundane, Monique began to panic, bringing her anxiety at the renewed activity and the doctors' sudden urgent orders to a peak. She asked the nurse, 'What's happening?', only to receive a trite smile in response.

'Nothing. Don't worry. Just relax.'

Which only made her panic all the more. She reached one hand up. 'I'd like to see my husband. Please ... I'd like him here by me. To help me.'

'Yes ... don't worry. We'll get him.' The same practised smile from the nurse, knowing that the patient would be fully under any second.

Waves of euphoria started to descend, and suddenly the nurse was right. There was nothing to worry about. Her body felt as if it was floating, drifting away on the echoes and voices around her.

'You see ... my husband will know just what to do,' she offered pathetically, her last words before drifting completely into the darkness.

In the first moments of darkness, she saw Christian's face. He was running through a field, waving and smiling to her. But it wasn't the field by their house, it was one she didn't recognize: a wheat field, the sheaves blowing gently in the wind. And she thought: yes, it would be nice if it was a boy. Another Christian. She'd take care of him this time, love him, keep him close to her side and never let him be harmed. Oh God, please, *please* . . . just one more chance.

Floirat checked the patient's pupils for responsiveness with a penlight and nodded after a second. Jouanard made the first incision. He'd already resigned himself to the fact that he'd probably lost the baby. The challenge remaining was to save his patient's life.

28 April 1974

Dominic Fornier swung the black Citroën through the narrow Panier lanes, beeping his horn to move some people aside as he negotiated a tight turn. As he picked up speed, the wind rush reverberated from the buildings close on each side. Ahead, he could now see the crowd. Most people were congregated on the far side. He parked behind two black Citroëns already there. He recognized Lasnel from forensics and Detective Inspector Bennacer, busy taking notes among the crowd.

Lasnel looked up from examining the body, grabbed his attention first. 'Inspector Fornier. Just in time. Another few minutes and the meat wagon might have taken him away.'

Dominic knelt beside Lasnel. 'Been here long?'

'Four or five minutes. Quite straightforward, though. Looks as if the first blow was made here, a straight lunge, quite deep, almost reaching the trachea, then the blade was run across, severing the jugular.'

'So we know at least it was a knife rather than a razor. That'll narrow it down.' Dominic smiled and patted Lasnel's shoulder.

The man's body lay face down, the blood from his neck wound spreading out and now a dark maroon, almost brown. He'd been dead almost an hour. Dominic straightened up and Lasnel too shifted to one side for a moment as a detective moved in and took some photos using flash; though it was afternoon and the sun was shining brightly, the buildings on each side heavily shaded the narrow lane. Dominic went over to Bennacer.

'Any witnesses?'

Bennacer shook his head and pointed to a middle-aged woman, quite dark, probably Moroccan or Algerian. 'She was the first to find him; two other men came up quickly afterwards, one of them went to the nearest phone to make the initial emergency call, the other's here.' Bennacer pointed to an old man not far behind the woman. 'But nobody actually saw the attack.'

Dominic clarified with Bennacer that the other man, in his twenties, hadn't appeared again but probably wasn't significant. The victim's wallet was missing, there was no available identification, but Bennacer knew him: a local club owner called Émile Vacheret. The attack had been made to look like a robbery, but Bennacer had his doubts. It was probably a *milieu* hit.

Dominic nodded. Now that Bennacer had mentioned the name, Dominic remembered the file. Their main informant on *milieu* activities, Forterre, had reported moves to set up stronger drug distribution networks using Marseille clubs. Vacheret was one of the club owners in the file. Vacheret had for years used his clubs as fronts for packets of marijuana, but there was pressure for him to start handling heroin as well. Émile Vacheret was against the idea, but his son François, now in his early thirties, was known to be in favour. 'So it looks as if they didn't want to wait the fifteen years for the old man to retire,' Dominic commented sourly. 'Do you think his son might have actually been involved in the hit?'

'No, I don't think so. He might have disagreed with his father, but he wouldn't have gone this far. With Émile out of the way, they'd get what they wanted anyway with François – so no need to implicate him. It also serves as a warning: what better way to make sure the son tows the line?'

The inner politics of the *milieu*, thought Dominic. Essential knowledge for much of his past nine years in Marseille. As the drugs market had burgeoned, with Marseille one of the main distillation and shipment centres for Europe, the incidence of *règlements de compte* – settling of accounts – had increased. As with so many other similar cases, there would be no murder weapon found, no fingerprints, no witnesses. Just the usual list of suspects bounced between departmental files and computers.

'Are any of his clubs near here?'

'The nearest is at least three blocks away. Nothing in the immediate streets.'

Dominic scanned the street beyond the small crowd. Eleven days! Eleven days before he cleared his desk in Marseille and started his two-year posting with Interpol in Paris. The case wouldn't have progressed much in that time, would no doubt end up with his chief inspector, Isnard, where it would fester in one of his two usual piles: unsolved cases and internal admin overload. If he wanted some movement on the case, some strong legwork while he was gone, his best chance lay with Bennacer.

Dominic flicked back through his notepad. Too many loose ends to tie up in just eleven days: cases in progress, reminders of things to do before he left, now he was adding more. Any work breaks had been filled with organizing packing and moving and rent contracts for their house in Aubagne and their new house in Corbeil, thirty kilometres south of Paris.

No doubt there would be a goodbye drink with his department and, if there was time, a last meal at Pierre T'être in Cannes with his wife and son. They'd dined there the night he proposed to her, then again six years back when he'd received his final exam results and his move from the Marseille gendarmerie to the National Police had become official. The two years at Interpol were voluntary and his current ranking would remain the same, but it would broaden his work experience and help his progress to chief inspector: two or three years after he returned at most. Without clinking glasses first at Pierre T'être, the move to Paris would seem somehow incomplete.

Dominic looked up. The ambulance was approaching, forcing the crowds close to the walls on each side of the narrow lane. He wrote on a scrap of paper and handed it to Bennacer. 'I'm not sure how much I'll be able to do on this before I leave. But don't just let the case rot on Isnard's desk. Do the legwork yourself and work your *milieu* contact as best you can. This will be my number in Paris. Call me directly if anything comes up.'

As Dominic closed his notepad, he saw the word *Machanaud?* written on the second to last page. A year after gaining his inspectorate with the National Police, he'd been driving through Taragnon and was reminded of the case. Machanaud should have been released two years before, might have even been paroled earlier. He tried to contact Molet through the Palais de Justice and his old law firm, only to discover that he had moved practice to Nice; four phone calls later, he gave up on tracking down a phone number. He decided to try finding out what had happened to Machanaud through Perrimond's office. After three calls to Perrimond's secretary and none of them returned within a week, a snowstorm of work pushed the Taragnon case into the background and it was forgotten.

It sprang to mind again a year ago when he saw a press cutting about Alain Duclos. He'd seen nothing about Duclos in the ten years since the murder. It was a small sidebar talking about the new candidate for the RPR – *Rassemblement pour la République* party – in Limoges, Alain Duclos, and mentioned his position as chief prosecutor the past five years and some notable successes against companies for labour-contract infringements, mostly sweat-shop use of illegal immigrants, with Duclos quoted as saying that 'It not only imprisoned the immigrant in a cycle of modern-day slavery, but also robbed the French people of their workright.' Champion of the People, Dominic thought cynically. Duclos and politics were obviously made for each other.

He'd made a mental note then to try Perrimond again but had forgotten about it. Then just the week before he'd made the entry in his notepad along with the other loose ends of his life he wanted to deal with before leaving. No doubt he was worrying for nothing. Machanaud had probably been paroled after four years and spent at most another year in an institution receiving therapy. He would try Perrimond again as soon as he got back to his office.

4 February 1976

Rain pattered against the side window of the car. Duclos looked anxiously at his watch. Chapeau was already five minutes late. Perhaps he was having trouble finding the new meeting place.

The idea had been forming slowly during the past year, though subconsciously it had probably been there far longer. Almost three years ago an old uncle of his had died and, together with his cousin, he'd handled the house clearance. Duclos knew a local antiques dealer, but they'd decided to go through the house first to identify the curios, be sure of their ground for when the dealer arrived. In an old attic trunk, together with a uniform, brocade and medals, Duclos'd found an old service revolver, an SACM 7.6 mm.

His uncle had been an army officer during the Vichy government regime, but it wasn't the sort of thing the family would make public, nor did Vichy-period army memorabilia have strong resale value. The trunk's contents would probably not be passed to the dealer and he doubted that his uncle had even made them known to his family. Yet the gun looked in surprisingly good condition, had obviously been regularly oiled and cleaned, and was now tucked away neatly with a box of ammunition at its side. Duclos looked up and listened for a second – his cousin was still busy downstairs – before pocketing the gun and the shells.

The thought of what he might want it for didn't hit him in that moment, but in retrospect he recalled his eagerness to pocket the gun, his worry that his cousin might come up and prevent him being able to take it. Perhaps the intent and purpose had been there subliminally all along.

But it wasn't until almost eighteen months later, with the next demand from Chapeau, that the significance of the gun really struck him. The demands came almost every year, had worn him down bit by bit. Each step up the ladder, each pay rise or increase in stature, and Chapeau would phone. Congratulations!

He'd come almost to resent his own success, felt physically sick with each press flashbulb and item printed, knowing that Chapeau would read the clipping and the phone would ring. He began even to question his own motives for striving for such heights of ambition, wondering if he secretly wanted Chapeau to call, as if only the continuing punishment might somehow rid him of the nightmares that still haunted him periodically – waking up in a cold sweat as he saw the small boy's piercing green eyes staring back, pleading with him . . . *please don't kill me!*

In the dreams, the car boot and the final moments of attack had become one and the same, the eyes shining back at him from the boot's darkness just before he swung the rock down. The first dream had come six months after the attack and sometimes he would get quick flashbacks as he opened the boot. He'd sold the car shortly after.

But at other times he'd feel that he'd suffered enough, that the dreams were only still haunting him because each call from Chapeau would remind him, bring the incident alive again. And in those moments he'd want it all ended, the nightmare of the continuing calls and demands, the worry, with his career progressing, that each year he had more to lose. The price on his head increased.

And he knew then why he'd picked up the gun, knew that there was only . . .

Duclos' thoughts were broken. Chapeau's car had pulled up to one side. Duclos got out hastily, it was vital they weren't inside his car when he pulled the trigger. He felt light rain spots touch his face, and prayed that Chapeau wouldn't find it strange that he was standing outside.

Chapeau got out and walked over. New car, Duclos noticed: Citroën CX Pallas. With the money he'd been paying to Chapeau over the past years, hardly any wonder he could afford a better car than him. He put one hand in his coat pocket, touched the cool metal of the gun butt.

'I didn't know you were a country lover,' Chapeau commented, his breath showing on the cool damp air.

The weather was ideal. He'd purposely delayed the meeting until it turned damp and cool. He could wear a coat without Chapeau being suspicious.

Chapeau's feet crunched on loose shale as he shuffled close. The track ran between a small area of woodland twenty kilometres north of Nîmes. It led to a picnic area further down which in summer would be busy; at this time of year it was deserted. Duclos had made the excuse of not wanting to meet at the usual restaurant car park: 'A waiter was looking out at intervals during our last meeting.' Chapeau said he hadn't noticed, but had agreed to the new meeting place.

Chapeau's features had become heavier with the years. His neck had thickened and the bags under his eyes gave him the appearance of a sad, malevolent bulldog. He often wore dark or tinted glasses to hide his bad eye, but today there were none: the weather was too dull.

'It's cold out here,' Chapeau said. 'Has the heater been on inside your car?'

Duclos glanced at the car, thinking quickly before his hesitance gave him away. 'Probably. But I wanted a bit of fresh air. We'll be finished soon.'

Chapeau held his gaze for a second. Duclos' hand tensed on the gun butt in his pocket. Was Chapeau already suspicious about the rendezvous, wondering now why he wanted some fresh air when it was misty and raining?

Chapeau looked down thoughtfully, then to one side. 'No worry of any nosy waiters here. Good choice if you like privacy.' Then his gaze swivelled back until it rested on Duclos.

Duclos felt a faint trembling start to grip his legs. He took the hand hastily out of his pocket.

'You must be quite proud. An MP? I read that recent press clipping. Impressive stuff. If I didn't know you so well, I'd be tempted to vote for you myself. Amazing how your private life can be so different to your public image.'

Through the years, Duclos had become used to reading behind Chapeau's comments. What he meant was: *Now your public profile has been elevated yet again, is even more polarized from your private life, the threat of downfall has far higher value. I can charge you more.*

'What a surprise they'd all get if they realized what a prick you really were.' Chapeau laughed. 'No more invites to boy-scout or youth-club hall openings!'

Then always he ended on a rebuke, a tease. *Christ*, for that alone it was going to feel good to kill him. Duclos sneaked his hand back on the gun, snaked one finger around until it was on the trigger. No more teasing and mocking. No more having to look into Chapeau's sad fish eye to see that the only thing to bring some life into it, some mirth, was his own discomfort.

The first thought of killing Chapeau had come as much as five years ago, but getting someone else to do it; then he quickly thought again. That was what had landed him in this cycle of blackmail in the first place. He could end up just replacing one blackmailer with another. Yet in that first moment of discovering his uncle's gun, he'd never dreamt that years later he would be standing on a damp and desolate lane with his own finger on the trigger.

Each meeting, each rubuke and insult, each payment, the fear of discovery and downfall stronger with each year, had bit by bit sewn a patchwork quilt of hatred and resolve. He would *have* to do it himself; there was nobody else.

'Are you okay?' asked Chapeau.

'Yes . . . yes. Fine.' Duclos stuttered. He could feel his nerves returning as he steeled himself, the trembling was back in his legs. 'Let's get it over with. As you say, it's cold out here.' He passed the envelope to Chapeau.

The gun and ammunition would be untraceable. Nobody had seen him come into the lane, and the location was remote to both of them. There would be no possible connection. He would have to make the first shot count, hitting the chest or stomach, with two or three in quick succession after. A superficial wound or a miss and Chapeau would start firing back.

Chapeau was opening the envelope, starting to count the money.

With Vacheret now dead, the last link between the two of them had also gone. The last traces of 1963 would die with Chapeau. He'd got away with it once, he could do it again. He tightened his grip, felt his palm sweating on the gun butt. The best moment was while Chapeau was looking down, distracted with counting the money.

'Thirty thousand, wasn't it?' Chapeau confirmed. But he hardly looked up from counting.

'Yes.' Twelve years focused into a single moment. His legs were trembling uncontrollably and there was a tight constriction in his chest. He swallowed to try and ease it. He'd thought initially of shooting Chapeau through the coat pocket, but then realized that with the mark and powder burns he'd have to dump the coat; it could be traced. But now he began to worry that as he lifted the gun out, Chapeau would see it. A flicker in the corner of his eye while he was counting, making him reach for his own gun.

Chapeau was two-thirds through counting the first bundle. Duclos knew the routine: Chapeau would count the first bundle fully, then would flick quickly through the other bundles and measure them against the first. There were six bundles in all: 5,000 francs each made up of 100-franc notes.

All the months of preparation, and now the moment was upon him, he felt frozen into inaction. He'd even gone out to a deserted field near Limoges one weekend to fire off a few rounds: make sure the ammunition wasn't damp or faulty and get used to the feel of the gun. But what use was that now? This was no longer cardboard targets, but pumping bullets through flesh and bone! His nerves were racing, his whole body starting to shake. Perhaps he should wait until Chapeau had finished counting, started to walk away. Shoot him in the back.

Chapeau was finishing the second bundle.

But what if Chapeau suddenly looked up and read into his expression that something was wrong? Chapeau would see that he was in a cold sweat with panic, would reach for his gun before he even had the chance. Chapeau was flicking rapidly through the bundles . . . starting on the fourth. Any second he could look up and the chance would be gone.

With one last silent prayer into the misty air, Duclos started to ease the gun from his pocket.

PART TWO

23

Heartbeats. Their own pulses marking time. All the three men in the car could hear as they waited for the full cover of darkness. They watched as two more people left the bar.

'How many would that leave now inside, Tomi?' the man behind the wheel asked.

'Maybe nine or ten.' Twenty minutes earlier Tomi had gone in the bar for a quick reconnaissance, downed a pastis and left. 'I doubt if we'll find a time with fewer people inside. Later on, it will start filling up again.'

The driver, Jacques, took out the 11.43 mm automatic from his shoulder holster. In the back, Tomi's fingers tapped nervously on the barrel of a pump-action shotgun. Heartbeats. It had all been agreed earlier: they couldn't leave any possible witnesses. When they'd been handed the photos and half the payment two days before, they'd been told that this was the only place they'd find all three at the same time. Tomi had already checked that all three targets were there.

The sign 'Bar du Téléphone' was only partly visible between the trees which shadowed their car. Jacques looked ahead and in his mirror: there was nobody approaching. He nodded and they pulled on the stocking masks. No more words were spoken between them as they followed him briskly into the bar.

Only two people turned and stared as they walked in and raised their guns to fire. Surprise had hardly registered on their faces as the first volleys rang out, deafening in the confined space. Tomi saw one of the targets towards the far end of the bar and picked him off quickly with a chest shot, then swung to his right and fired at a man diving for cover. Jacques quickly found their second target and picked off two bystanders trying to escape.

Among the pandemonium of chairs and tables overturning and glasses breaking as people tried frantically to escape the relentless volley of fire, the three went through the bar as if it was a routine military exercise. It had all been agreed beforehand: chest shots, floor as many people as

233

possible quickly, then finish off with head shots. Cries and screams mingled with the groans of those already wounded, and the air was thick with smoke and the smell of burning cordite.

At one point Jacques held one hand up, in the few seconds' lull taking stock of who was left to fell. A small movement in the corner – Tomi swung and fired. Everyone else was already gravely wounded or dead. Jacques nodded and they moved in to finish off the wounded.

One man in his late twenties looked up and pleaded as Jacques levelled his gun at him. 'Monsieur, please, no . . . no!'

'*Pardon.*' Jacques pressed the gun barrel into the soft flesh below the man's ear and fired.

Within another fifty seconds, they'd delivered a head or neck shot to everyone in the bar. Jacques grimaced disdainfully; with the carnage, the tile floor was slippery with blood. He'd almost fallen over twice. He signalled and they headed out. Less than three minutes had passed since they'd entered.

Shortly after them leaving, a faint liquid wheezing came from a man by the bar counter. He'd been shot twice in the neck, but miraculously had survived. The gunmen had also failed to notice a faint flicker of movement on the stairway at the back of the bar as they'd entered.

Nicole Léoni, wife of the bar's owner, saw the lead gunman as she was walking downstairs – quickly heading back up again and barricading herself in an upstairs bedroom. She was unsure whether or not the gunman had seen her, and stared nervously at the door as the shots rang out below, fearful of it bursting open at any moment. She stayed in that position for almost three minutes after the last shots were fired, still trembling as she finally ventured close to the door and listened, afraid that it might be a trick and they were creeping up the stairs to surprise her.

Five days since the shooting. The main division responsible for the investigation was in north Marseille where the incident took place, but then quickly involved divisions covering the Vieux Port and Panier districts where most of the interviews for suspects were centred; and finally Chief Inspector Fornier's division in west Marseille for liaison with Paris, due to his past experience as an inspector in the Panier district.

Co-ordinating the investigation was Divisional Police Commissioner Pierre Chatelain. Dominic had received calls practically every day from Chatelain, anxious that liaison with Paris went smoothly.

Dominic was keenly aware of the background. Gangland battles between rivals in Nice and Marseille had left almost sixty dead over the past two years. Not a blink from the politicians and police officials in the North. But this was different. Along with three known criminals, six innocents had also been killed. Nine dead: two more than the St Valentine's Day massacre. Apart from the obvious comparisons to Chicago, suddenly it was a concern that tourists might get cut down in a hail of bullets while sampling some local pastis. Holidays were cancelled or re-arranged for the south-west coast, Italy or Spain. With tourism dropping, foreign exchange would be affected too. Suddenly it was a national issue. Ministers and police commissioners wanted results. Fast.

The local crime network, the *milieu*, felt one of the coldest investigative draughts in years. The message was clear: kill each other by all means but never let it spread outside of that fraternity.

Dominic and most of his division had been working virtually round the clock since being brought into the investigation, and now a more concentrated vigil lay ahead. Phones and teleprinters went almost constantly and files arrived at regular intervals by messenger. Towards the end of the second night, as a stack of files shifted and almost knocked the smiling family photo of his wife and two sons off his desk, he was reminded to phone home. 'Just a couple of hours more, I'll be finished then.'

His wife reminded him that it was their younger son Jérôme's birthday in just three days, he'd be six. 'Try and leave at least some time over the next two days to put thought towards his present.'

'Don't worry, once I've filed this report tomorrow, things will be easier.'

The two hours turned into four by the time he'd run the report through a phone preview with Chatelain before sending it to Commissioner Aimeblanc.

The final report was sixteen pages long, a complex and sordid saga of two rival gangs vying for control of casinos, clubs, race-tracks and profitable extortion and prostitution rackets. Background and texture to the final massacre: *milieu* revenge for the hijacking of a shipment of fake Omega, Cartier and Piaget watches from Italy by three men: André Léoni, the Bar du Téléphone's owner, and two associates present that fateful night. All others killed were incidental.

Details of the killings were gruesome. All the victims had been hit first with chest or stomach shots, then finished off executioner style. Miraculously, one man, Francis Fernandez, was shot twice in the throat but survived. But he was purely a casual visitor to the bar, his descriptions of the three killers were vague, apart from the fact that 'They all wore stocking masks and one had a beard.' Three different calibre bullets were found at the scene: 9 mm, 11.43 mm and 12 mm, the last probably from a shotgun.

Aimeblanc came back within three hours of viewing the report: he wanted the suspect list narrowed. With little firm evidence, successful prosecution might hinge purely on confessions: a more workable interview list was essential. By late the same day, Dominic had narrowed it to just twelve names. Aimeblanc added his own two-page summary and passed the file to Interior Minister Bonnet. With an additional foreword summary, Bonnet had the file copied and duly distributed.

Fourteen ministerial departments were on his direct distribution list, and another eighteen requests had been made. Some were due to ministerial involvement in regional or national crime commissions, or because of the incident's grave reflection on overall crime trends. Others simply because of the concern of constituents who had business interests or holiday homes or holidayed regularly in the area. On the request list was the MP for Limoges, Alain Duclos.

24

'Was there much in the press about it?'

'A fair bit. Two or three clippings in *Le Provençal*, at least. It probably even hit *Le Figaro* or *Le Monde* at one stage – though possibly lumped together with coverage of other child murders.'

'When will you know for sure?' Marinella asked. The concern had come through in her voice, she sensed; perhaps she even sounded how she felt: desperate, deflated.

Philippe described being bounced between libraries and news agencies half the morning. 'But I think I've finally found a couple of reliable sources. I've left them my fax number at the LSE. I should get the results of a search and copies from microfiche records within the next few hours.'

There was nothing she could do but sit it out, wait for Philippe to receive his faxes. David Lambourne was in with a patient, and she felt ill at ease sitting by the phone in his waiting area. She wanted to bounce thoughts off him straight away. Though was it purely to vent some of her frustrations, or to get an alternative viewpoint?

She glanced at the phone. If it was later in the day, she could have at least put through a call to Sebastian and her father – but it was only 5.10 a.m. in Charlottesville. Besides, she'd called them just the day before. Her father had been preparing red snapper with peppers and bean rice for later and the night previous they'd had chicken *arroz brut*; it was like a restaurant waiter reading out the menu. Sebastian would have been happy to stay with her father for a month. And to phone the university – catch up on activities during the last few days and perhaps get some feedback from Donaldson – she'd have to wait even longer, almost four hours. She decided on a walk to burn off some of her restlessness.

She walked for almost half a mile and found herself on the edge of Covent Garden. She decided to have a coffee in the piazza and found a deli with outside tables. A string quartet played Vivaldi while she sipped her cappuccino.

Just the day before she'd been excited about the case. A genuine rush at the first bit of tangible information. Philippe had traced the death certificate in the Bauriac town hall register: Christian Yves Rosselot. Death registered at 9.54 p.m., 23 August 1963. Parents Monique and Jean-Luc. Address: Rue des Rigouards, Taragnon. The boy not only existed, some of the main details had been confirmed!

But the registrar had mentioned a coroner's note on the certificate. Marinella asked Philippe to check. Coroners' notes were not in themselves unusual, present in all manner of accidental deaths, so she was not immediately alarmed. Towards the end of the same day, having followed the trail through the coroner's office and the ministère public which had ordered the report, Philippe phoned her and dropped the bombshell: the boy had been the victim of a murder, quite a notable case in the region at the time. It was too late for Philippe to do any more checking that day, libraries and town halls in France were already closed; she'd have to wait till the morning for the confirmations she feared were looming.

On the edge of the piazza, a mime artist juggled with three red balls, making them disappear dramatically behind his white-gloved hands. A bit like this case, she thought: now you see it, now you don't. If she continued and published a paper, they would laugh at her back at Virginia. A prominent murder case that had been splashed across the press. Almost as bad as the boy claiming to be Maurice Chevalier or Joan of Arc. All the details were there for him to regurgitate.

Stock lines of defence rolled through her mind about the age of the press articles and the family's lack of knowledge of France. But she knew that the sceptics' barrage would be relentless: old newspapers perhaps kept by relatives who had holidayed in the region, current books with prominent murder cases from bygone years, fresh news stories that reflected back to past cases. She knew she couldn't even start to defend her corner until she'd seen the news items from Philippe, weighed the full extent of damage.

She felt deflated, despondent. Brought to the edge of what looked like an exciting case only for it to evaporate before her eyes yet again. Was this to be the pattern of her life? Each case that looked like it had real promise ending in disappointment? Perhaps she should just get the first flight back to Virginia, erase this case quickly, a fresh workload and new cases to occupy her mind? She checked her watch: Lambourne's session would have ended a few minutes ago. She headed back.

Lambourne was sipping at a freshly made tea as she walked back in. He offered her one, but she declined with thanks. 'I've just had coffee.'

She'd flagged her concerns the evening before and now fleshed out the details: as she feared, the case had been reported heavily – she'd know just how heavily by early afternoon. They'd have to start thinking in terms of the case being completely fabricated or, at best, subliminally influenced. If they didn't adopt that stance, the critics certainly would. The case and any resultant study papers were heading nowhere. 'Sorry, David – but if the news from Philippe supports what I fear, I'm bailing out. I've already been four days away from my family; there's no point in my staying on just to face another disappointment.'

Lambourne held one hand up, trying to slow her down. 'Wait a minute. Putting aside the sceptics' view – what do *you* think? Do you think the boy's fabricating?'

'I don't know.' She thought of the frail, lost voice, how convincing it had seemed. She shook her head. 'I'm not sure either way. It looks suspicious, that's all. But I have to take a safe stance, look at the downside. If I don't, someone else will – they'll rap me over the head, beat me senseless with it. Make me look foolish.'

Lambourne was about to comment, 'Is that the most important thing, that you don't look foolish?' then thought better of it. Too harsh. 'Are you sure you're not reading too prematurely into the view the critics might, only *might*, take on this? As Donaldson commented – playing too much to the gallery?'

'It's okay for Donaldson, he never faces the critics like me. Never does personal interviews. Just goes on his jaunts to India or wherever, compiles his papers and books, and if they don't like his findings – fine. He just lets them stew in their own juices. He's in his own little cocooned academic netherworld, protected from it all. Unlike me, he doesn't have to sit on panels and face Professor Novision, a special study team of nerds from Sceptics Incorporated and flat-earth preachers who conveniently forget that over half the world's religions believe in reincarnation. It's okay for Donaldson to pontificate about the gallery, because he has absolutely no idea what –' Marinella cut herself short as she read Lambourne's expression: shocked at the strength of her feelings, or uncomfortable at her mention of ambivalence about Donaldson? She let out a long, tired breath and apologized, admitted that the stress of another promising case curtailed abruptly had got to her. She hung her head slightly in submission. 'Donaldson has built up a body of work and a reputation within the profession that I can only but hope to emulate. It was wrong of me to criticize. I'm sorry.'

Lambourne held his palms out. 'So, what do you want to do? Anticipate the flak you might receive from sceptics and give up now – or battle on?'

'I don't know.' Marinella was thoughtful. Then suddenly she smiled. 'You should worry. If it's all a scam, at least your patient's not ill. Misguided by some inventive, headline-seeking weirdo godparents, perhaps – but not psychologically disturbed.'

Lambourne grimaced meekly. 'Except for one thing. I happen to believe the boy. And I'm fully committed to trying to help him through this problem.'

Marinella nodded slowly. 'For what it's worth – I believe him too. Despite how it might all end up looking to the sceptics.'

While the mood was right, Lambourne tried to buoy her spirits. Assured her that her concern about critics was both premature and probably unfounded. There was the weight of evidence from his own sessions and the initial report from Dr Torrens. A fair body of people to all be wrong. 'What did the Capels do – fake the accident and the coma as well?' The statistics would probably also stack up on her side. 'How many regressions have you experienced before where people have been murdered?'

'Only one. Victim of a carpetbaggers' raid just after the American Civil War. No records. But I believe Donaldson has had one or two cases.'

'I bet if you check the records, you'll find that regressions involving murder reflect almost exactly its incidence in real life compared with other forms of death. One in 500, one in 1,000 – whatever.'

Marinella knew that previous studies had shown that regressions accurately reflected real life: 51 per cent women, 49 per cent men, regardless of the sex of the subject; most were from meagre or mundane backgrounds, with very few rich or notable figures. She didn't recall any specific studies for murder victims.

'And most murders since the turn of the century would have hit the press, so it's not that unusual.' Lambourne raised an eyebrow. 'Have you ever heard of or read the *East Kent Gazette*? Or perhaps a Mexican newspaper?'

'No.'

'Well, the Capels would have had just about as much chance of seeing provincial newspapers from the South of France. And from thirty years ago – forget it!'

'But it might have also been in *Le Monde*, perhaps even a small item in the British press. And then there's the possibility of books compiling various murder cases through the years.'

'For *Le Monde* you'll have to wait on news from Philippe. But the rest you could check yourself. There's a good library not far away on Chancery Lane. In a couple of hours, you could have done a full search.'

Marinella bit lightly at her lip. 'It's not just for them – it's also convincing myself. Building back the confidence and enthusiasm to continue.'

Lambourne wasn't sure whether he'd convinced her or not. When he went into his next session, she was still there: perhaps waiting for Philippe's call, perhaps still balancing everything out in her mind.

Though when he came out of the session, she was gone. Two hours later, just twenty minutes after Philippe had called and left a message, she phoned from the library.

'You were right – there's nothing in the British press. I've searched everything.' The enthusiasm was back in her voice. 'I'm just checking through books now. I'll know for sure in an hour or so.'

Lambourne gave her the message that Philippe had called and Marinella asked if he had mentioned *Le Monde*. 'No, he just left his number.'

'Okay, thanks. I'll call him.' She rang off abruptly.

Lambourne didn't see her again until early evening. She was in high spirits and brought him up to date quickly: *Le Monde* did have an entry, but it was only five lines on page twelve the day after the attack and mentioned only the boy's name and the village. No parents' names, no trimmings. 'The boy was alive apparently for five days after that and his later death didn't appear in *Le Monde*. Three articles in *Le Provençal*, one large, two small. And nothing at all in the British press or books.'

'You look relieved.'

'I'm ecstatic. I'm also starving – let's go eat.'

Over dinner, Lambourne could hardly keep pace. This was the Marinella he remembered: confident, optimistic, energetic, *eyes sparkling*. He felt glad now that he'd calmed her earlier doubts. Though as she talked about the remaining steps ahead of finding the Rosselots or close past friends who could corroborate Eyran's account as Christian Rosselot, he felt the first pang of uncertainty.

Marinella was talking as if she was suddenly on an open freeway, had been lost for a while on some annoying side road, but now was full speed ahead, not an obstacle in sight. And he began to worry that he might have fired her up too much, that if she suddenly hit an obstacle and was deflated again, he'd feel partly responsible. Having rekindled her enthusiasm, it would seem heartless suddenly to pull the plug if in a few sessions' time he decided that continuing regressions were not in his patient's interests.

That enthusiasm carried Marinella through the next two days. The first stumbling block was that the Rosselots could no longer be traced in the area. One of the town hall clerks recommended Philippe to the Bauriac gendarmerie. 'They conducted much of the investigation and someone there might know.' Philippe could only find one person at the gendarmerie who remembered the investigation, Captain Levacher. While Levacher personally had no knowledge of the Rosselots or their current whereabouts, he had another number for someone who might be able to help. 'Dominic Fornier, he assisted in the investigation thirty years ago.' He had a number also for Captain Poullain, who'd headed the investigation, but Levacher explained why he thought Dominic Fornier might be more useful. 'Here it is, National Police, Panier district, Marseille. Nineteen seventy-four. That's the last number we have for him.'

Philippe phoned the number and they gave him another number for a division in west Marseille. The people in west Marseille were more circumspect and gave no information, merely asked his name, logged his call, and promised that someone would call back. Philippe didn't get the return call until the next morning, a girl named Thérèse giving him a number in Lyon. Philippe phoned to be informed: 'Chief Inspector Fornier is in a meeting right now. He'll be free probably about midday.'

Philippe brought Marinella up to date straight away.

She checked her watch: 9.20 a.m. France was an hour ahead, so Philippe planned to try again in almost two hours. 'Great. I'll be sitting by the phone waiting for news.'

Two more hours and they could hopefully piece together Christian Rosselot's life. But along with the excitement, she suddenly felt restless, ill at ease. The last days of research and Philippe's paper chase across France had obviously told on her nerves. Though as she tried to settle the rising butterflies in her stomach, it struck her that it might also be something else: the portent of possible failure was suddenly there once again. Only two hours away.

25

8 December 1978

'What is this – hitman of the year nomination list?'

'Close. It's the suspect list for the Bar du Téléphone killings.' Duclos watched Brossard's expression keenly as he scanned down and saw his own name on the list. Hardly a flicker of recognition. 'You know what this means?'

'Yes, it means the police are going to waste their valuable time with nine suspects – and I'm one of them.'

'It also means that your life will be difficult for the next month or so. You'll be watched, perhaps brought in for questioning whenever it suits the police. Your life will be disrupted – and it will be bad for business. People won't go near you for a while with contracts.'

'Except one thing. I'm the only one on the list for whom the police have no firm identity. Just a vague photokit and an alias I once used. They won't know where to start.'

Duclos nodded. He knew the history. It was partly why he thought Brossard would be ideal. It had taken him almost a week to set up the meeting through François Vacheret. It was over three years since his last visit to Vacheret's, not long after the death of his father. Vacheret had been keen to offer him a new boy from Martinique, but Duclos had wanted to get straight down to business. He showed Vacheret the same list and asked him to pick out the ones he knew. Vacheret came up with three names. 'Forget Antoine Jaumard,' Duclos prompted. He didn't explain why: that he'd had an association with Jaumard through his father, Émile Vacheret. 'Of the other two, who would you recommend?'

The quick biography sounded ideal: early thirties, no arrests or convictions, master of disguises, little or nothing on police files except an identikit picture, description and *modus operandi*: Brossard invariably wore different wigs and glasses to change his appearance. The supposition was therefore that his normal hairstyle was short. Eugène Brossard was a false name from a door-buzzer tag for a flat Brossard had vacated two days before a police raid. He was always one step ahead.

Duclos was sure the Brossard before him was also heavily disguised:

thick blond wig cut in Beatles style, rounded glasses with a mottled burgundy frame. He looked like a David Hockney caricature.

The only thing which had initially made Brossard uncomfortable was the tape recorder running. Duclos explained why: that any minute he was going to offer Brossard 100,000 francs to have someone killed. The reason for the hit was the blackmailing of a close friend. Duclos wanted to be sure that the blackmail wasn't repeated, so the tape would serve as an insurance policy – for *both* of them. 'Now that I've admitted a dark secret, it's your turn. Tell me about one of your hits.'

Brossard laughed at the suggestion at first, but Duclos was insistent. 'The tape will never go out of my possession; after all, it would incriminate me as much as you. What have you got to lose? If you don't want to do it, fine. Me and my 100,000 will walk out of the room.'

Duclos listened as Brossard described in bland monotones the murder of a chief planning regulator in Nice three years previously. Duclos remembered the case: a planning officer implicated in a *milieu* bribes scandal. The *milieu* got to him before the State Prosecutor. He couldn't help wondering why Brossard had chosen this particular story. Was it partly a warning not to misuse the tape? *I've already killed one government official. Fuck with me and one more won't make that much difference.*

Brossard stared coldly at Duclos. Duclos could hardly see his eyes behind the dark glasses except when he blinked. He felt an involuntary shiver run up his spine. He hadn't felt this uncomfortable in someone's presence since . . . *since* . . .

The memory of his palm sweating on the gun butt was still vivid, lifting it, *so slowly* . . . the birds suddenly alighting from a nearby tree, making Chapeau look up. He'd feared for a minute that Chapeau had seen the gun – had thrust it quickly back in his pocket. In the last seconds of their meeting, that fear had stayed with him, that Chapeau would suddenly wheel around, level his gun and fire. He stayed vigilant as Chapeau walked away, but the moment to take the initiative had gone. He said lamely that he wanted to stay in the lane for a bit more fresh air as Chapeau drove off. Truth was, he was shaking too much to be able to drive. Almost as soon as Chapeau had disappeared from view, he was physically sick. He couldn't face going through that again. It had taken him another eighteen months of suffering Chapeau's blackmail and insults even to be able to summon up the courage to arrange this meeting.

But despite the precautions – looking at Brossard's lips curled in a slight smile at his description of murder, his deeply hooded eyes blinking behind dark glasses – he couldn't help fearing that he might just be replacing one nightmare with another. The room they were in smelt of pine disinfectant fighting hard to disguise the odour of musky bed linen and bad plumbing. A seedy back-street hotel which Vacheret had recommended where clients took hookers. Thirty francs to a cleaning lady for a room for an hour, no questions asked. She'd just raised an eyebrow and grunted at the sight of two men entering, one wearing a strange blond wig. Duclos was eager to get out.

Brossard looked back at the list. 'So is the 100,000 supposed to make me feel better about having my name on this list?'

'By the time you get it, hopefully your name won't be on the list. I'm paying Vacheret another 50,000 to spread the right noises in the right places that you were in a friend's restaurant the night of the attack. It happened too early for you to be in one of his clubs. Within a few weeks it should spread on the *milieu* network and hopefully your name will come off the list.'

Brossard's eyes flickered. He was impressed. Clients' plans were normally clumsy; most planning had to come from his own quarter to compensate. 'So who is it you want hit, and when?'

'That's another reason for the list. He's there, sixth name down. You probably know him: Antoine Jaumard.'

Brossard's eyes flickered more rapidly. Hopefully he'd disguised his initial flinch. Antoine Jaumard, alias Chapeau. One of the old reliable *milieu* die-hards. It wouldn't be the first time someone had tried to have Jaumard killed. Of the last two hired guns sent, one died instantly with a bullet through the head, the other was shot in the stomach and groin and spent four hours with surgeons piecing together what was left of his manhood. Jaumard escaped from the fray with only a shoulder wound. 'Jaumard is a high-risk target. For that type of hit, it will cost more. It's not worth doing under 150,000 francs.'

Duclos stared back. 'Is that because of allegiances, possibly upsetting others within the *milieu*?'

'No. I take work from the *milieu* strictly as an independent – I owe no allegiances on any side. It's because of the extra risk. Jaumard is one of the few men on this list I have some professional respect for. It will take more to set up.'

Duclos nodded. Strong allegiances with the *milieu* had been the one remaining area to concern him. Brossard asked where and when.

'Two months, give some time for your name to come off this list,' said

Duclos. 'So you're not quite so hot. The where is up to you. Set it up the way you want.'

They made the final arrangements and set the time for their next meeting. By then Brossard would have the outline of a plan and Duclos would give him the first payment. Brossard left the room first and asked Duclos not to leave for at least a few minutes after. Duclos assumed it was part of Brossard's obsession with protecting his identity, but Brossard offered no explanation.

Walking down the corridor, Brossard thought: a total of 200,000 francs to drop Jaumard, including the payment to Vacheret, and the client had hardly blinked. Almost twice what he'd been paid to hit the Nice city planner. Jaumard had obviously stepped on some important toes. Poor old Chapeau. A sly smile crossed Brossard's face after a moment. At least it was nice to know people in his profession were so highly valued. *More than a city planner.* He could think of worse tombstone epitaphs.

Alone in the dank room, Duclos started to feel uncomfortable after only a minute. A sudden shiver of desolation reminded him just how far he'd sunk to be rid of Chapeau. He packed up the tape recorder and left the room.

Marseille, 12 February 1979

The motorbike messenger bopped with the music on his Walkman as he got off his bike, kicked it on its stand and entered the café. Bob Marley's 'Jammin''. Its jolting reggae beat filled his head, though already his thoughts were elsewhere.

The package he was carrying was his arm's length and half as wide. The café was almost an exact ten metre square. There were about fourteen or fifteen people inside, four at the bar and the rest scattered at tables. The messenger's eyes behind dark motorcycle goggles scanned the room quickly. He could see the two people he expected in the far corner, but didn't dwell – his attention shifted quickly to the approaching barman. He lifted out his earpiece.

'Monsieur Charot?'

The barman pulled a face and shrugged.

The messenger tilted the package and read from the label. 'Monsieur Charot. Thirty-eight, Rue Baussenque.'

Puzzlement from the barman. 'The address is right, but I don't know a Charot. Let me check with my wife.' The barman disappeared behind a bead curtain at the end of the bar.

Brossard put back the earpiece. Behind the motorcycle goggles, he let his eyes scan slowly across again. He was interested only in one position – the table in the corner with Chapeau and Marichel, the local pimp he'd paid to set things up. He wanted it to look like a casual surveillance. The bored messenger waiting to see if he had the right address, head bobbing lightly to the rhythm on his Walkman, fingers tapping on the package.

Bob Marley wailed and jammed about rights and uniting, drowning out the clatter of the room. Brossard's pulse pumped a small muscle in his neck almost in time with the beat.

The barman was back by the bead curtain, now with his wife. The barman pointed, his wife shrugged and returned to the back. As the barman returned, in the corner of his eye Brossard could tell that Marichel was looking over briefly. *Don't look!* Brossard silently screamed. *Just let me blend in, don't bring Chapeau's attention to me.*

He'd made the arrangements with Marichel just the week before. Ten thousand francs to set up the meeting with Chapeau, act as if he was a go-between for a hit contract. Brossard had given Marichel all the details, had practically written the script for him. With a contract on offer, what better way to guarantee Chapeau's attention. But Marichel was probably watching for the timing of the package being opened, the moment he would have to suddenly jump aside.

Brossard swivelled back the earpiece until it rested on his neck. The barman was explaining that his wife didn't know the name either. Brossard pointed to the corner and asked if he could use the phone. 'Check back with my office to see what's happened.'

The barman nodded, turned to the end of the bar by the door to serve another customer.

With the package under his arm, Brossard went towards the pay phone on the wall. It was almost directly opposite Chapeau and Marichel's table. He noticed Chapeau look up as he started across, but he couldn't tell if Chapeau's gaze had stayed with him as he approached the phone – couldn't risk turning or glancing back to see.

He started to worry: was there something in his disguise that didn't fit? Some small detail that Chapeau might have picked up on? He'd tried on several long curly wigs, but most were too bushy to fit comfortably under a crash helmet. Finally he found one that was slightly flatter on top with ringlet curls starting further down, spilling out of the base of the helmet and on to his shoulders. Just another rockin' messenger with some sounds to blot out the drone of city traffic.

Brossard's fingers tapped on the package as he set it down by the phone. Bob Marley's voice was tinnier, higher-pitched with the earpiece pulled away.

He reached for the receiver, his hand slightly damp as he imagined Chapeau's eyes still burning into his back. He started dialling, fluffing the first numbers so that only the last three counted: the speaking clock. As it rang, he turned and casually surveyed the room. Chapeau was looking back at Marichel, deep in conversation. Marichel drew hard on a cigarette, exhaling smoke in staccato bursts as he talked.

It was then that Brossard noticed the girl directly in line behind Chapeau and cursed. He'd told Marichel to choose seats by a wall. The wall was behind them from the bar view, but not from this angle. The girl was fully obscured only when Chapeau leant forward.

Bob Marley pulsed against his neck, a few centimetres below his earlobe as he listened to the talking clock. *'It will be nine-twelve and twenty . . .'*

With the sweep of the gun, it was going to be difficult not to hit her at the same time. Brossard wanted the hit to be clean. For a moment, he tensed, a quick window of opportunity appearing as Chapeau leant forward – then just as quickly it was gone. Chapeau relaxed back again. It was a tease. Brossard considered the possibility of stepping to one side as he fired, sharpening the angle so that the wall was behind. But would that split-second delay make him more vulnerable?

Chapeau was listening intently to Marichel explain the hit. It appeared straightforward enough, but some of the details from Marichel were becoming repetitive and he seemed slightly nervous. He'd noticed Marichel look up at the motorcycle messenger at the bar, and had glanced up briefly himself as the messenger had crossed to the phone – before bringing his attention back to the business at hand. But now he noticed that at intervals Marichel would give the messenger a sideways glance, as if trying to judge his position without staring overtly. And he was suddenly conscious of the messenger looking across, his attention shifting between them and the table behind.

All the other small signals suddenly gelled in that instant. Chapeau tried not to give away the sudden realization, would have averted his eyes to give him a moment more to think – but by the messenger's reaction, he knew it was already too late. The alarm in his eyes had shown.

The messenger reached for the package as Marichel leapt aside.

Chapeau's impulse reaction was to raise one hand as he stood, the other reaching inside his jacket for his gun. He saw the package open, the compact Uzi machine-gun swing up as the package was tossed aside. But he was sure he'd be able to level his gun first.

Brossard knew he'd passed the point of no return as soon as Chapeau looked up. He saw the hand raising in a 'stop' motion, a distraction from the other hand reaching for the gun – but he'd already committed himself to swing the arc of the Uzi from the right. The girl behind was suddenly forgotten. He saw the first shots rip through Chapeau's outstretched hand, but the other hand was rising rapidly, the gun barrel almost pointing straight at him.

Chapeau could see the black leather figure clearly in his sights as the stinging pain hit with the top part of his hand ripped away. He squeezed off his shot virtually at the same time – wondering for a moment why the recoil was so heavy, had tilted him sharply back until he was facing the ceiling.

The arc of Brossard's fire swung across and caught Chapeau squarely in the chest, throwing off his aim so that his bullet missed Brossard by more than a metre. Marichel was now two metres clear of the table, leering wildly with a mixture of surprise and raw excitement.

Brossard paused only briefly, then swung across again, continuing the arc – enjoying the moment's total bewilderment that crossed Marichel's face. The hail of bullets shattered Marichel's breastbone and removed the top part of one shoulder. No witnesses or knowledge of the set-up. It was safer. Brossard had decided on the action shortly after hiring Marichel.

Most people in the bar had dived for cover on the floor or behind tables and chairs. Hysterical screaming rose from somewhere near the door. Brossard moved closer to the sprawled bodies. Chapeau was still breathing faintly. Brossard could see his chest moving as it struggled for air from lungs filling rapidly with blood. Chapeau's shattered fingers lay a couple of metres away. Brossard fired a quick final burst to Chapeau's head, then to Marichel's, and ran out.

26

Dominic looked anxiously at the map. Eight or nine kilometres past Bourgoin-Jallieu, the motorway branched into two: the A43 to Chambéry and the A48 branching off to Grenoble. Radio messages crackled back and forth to two operators to his side.

It had been one of those mornings. He'd seen the message to phone Marinella Calvan as soon as he came out of an early morning meeting. A number in England, he wondered whether it was something to do with his previous Interpol work, though the name didn't strike a chord. But there were other, more pressing, emergencies: there had been a bank robbery in the La Guillotière area of Lyon, and after a sighting a chase had ensued with three police cars on the A43 heading east.

Already events had gone tragically wrong. Bullets fired from the robbers' car had struck one of the pursuing cars, shattering its windscreen and causing it to career into the central barrier; two of the three officers inside had been seriously injured. The only way to avoid more mayhem was to set up a road block, preferably at a turn-off *péage*.

'Looks like they're heading for Grenoble!' one of the radio operators, Morand, called out.

Dominic looked up from the map. 'We need a quiet junction, next three turn-offs. Somewhere where the *péage* won't be too busy. Suggestions?'

'Eleven or twelve could be good,' said Morand.

Dominic checked the distances: sixteen kilometres and thirty-four. 'It will have to be twelve. We'll need time to put everything into place.'

It took another nine minutes: three police cars ahead took up all three lanes, gradually slowing so that a visible jam built up just ahead of junction 12. At the junction 12 *péage*, three slots would be blocked by queues of at least two vehicles, a mixture of unmarked police cars and an old green van with CRS guards in the back. The fourth *péage* slot would be left empty.

All other traffic turning off meanwhile would be waved rapidly through the vacant *péage* slot without paying. As the robbers' car approached the empty slot, at the last second the barrier would come down to slow them;

and as they burst through, two teams of CRS guards with rifles would put out the tyres.

Dominic looked across sharply as the phone rang on his desk. It could be news on the injured officers; he'd asked for anything urgent to be put through on his private line. He picked it up. The girl on desk duty informed him that it was Marinella Calvan phoning again from England, and that she said it was urgent.

'Okay, put her through.' He'd probably have a spare two minutes.

As Marinella introduced herself apologetically and started explaining the reason for her call, it was as if the rest of the room and the activities in it had suddenly receded, become little more than incidental background.

Only the imperatives broke through. At one point, Morand raising a thumb up and shouting: 'They've gone for it! They've taken the bait and turned off. They're coming up to the *péage*.'

On the far side of the *péage*, four CRS guards with flak jackets aimed their rifles at the empty slot, ready for the car as it burst through.

When Morand leapt into the air and a quick cheer went up from the radio desk, Dominic knew that everything had gone well.

He said, 'One moment' apologetically to Marinella Calvan as he hit the secrecy button and looked towards Morand. 'So?'

'One injured. The others came out arms up, no resistance. No injuries our side.'

Dominic nodded and smiled, but Morand could tell that his attention was fractured. Dominic wasn't sure if he was more distracted through struggling to make sense of what Calvan was saying – a young boy in England, hypnotic sessions and a possible link with Christian Rosselot – or through his suspended belief, the painful nostalgia as the years were stripped away. Dark and hazy memories which he thought had been long buried.

Dominic unclicked the secrecy button. 'Sorry. Yes, I think I'll be able to help. I do know someone who could verify Christian Rosselot's background.'

But having made the arrangements, though intrigued as he put down the phone, he was uncertain what ghosts might be unlocked by helping. Reawakening memories he'd spent so much of his life struggling to forget. He shook his head. Thirty years? Perhaps they had never been truly free of the events of 1963.

27

Provence, July 1965

In the two months after Jean-Luc Rosselot died, once again Monique stayed on the farm, hid away from the world. The Fiévets helped out with her shopping and Dominic didn't see her in the village.

The investigation into his death was short, the post-mortem over in ten days: verdict of suicide. Jean-Luc had started the tractor and then purposely shut the garage door, had stayed inside until overcome by fumes. The first thing to alert Monique in the kitchen at the time was the throbbing sound of the motor through the walls. As it continued without the tractor emerging from the garage, she went into the courtyard and saw that the doors were closed. Clarisse had run out behind, had seen her father slumped dead over the tractor steering wheel as the doors were swung open.

Monique tried in vain for a few minutes to revive him, then ran to the Fiévets to use their phone and call an ambulance. Running back, seeing Clarisse standing thoughtfully over the prone figure of her father, hugging tight a small doll as tears ran down her cheek, had been the image to linger most with Monique. The doll. Practically all she had left.

Dominic hadn't been involved directly in the investigation. Harrault went with Servan assisting. Dominic was thankful, he didn't want to be remembered as the friendly face from the gendarmerie always associated with death in her family. Calling at the door to tell her that her son was dead, then twenty months later taking notes on her husband's suicide. He'd have hardly been able to face her.

When a few months later she did finally start venturing into the village, Dominic had his own crisis to cope with. His mother had been in hospital for the past two weeks, her condition had deteriorated so much that the doctors felt sure she wouldn't last more than another week. She knew that she was dying too, had begged Dominic to take her home again, said that she didn't want to die surrounded by 'old and ill people'. She'd even managed a taut smile at the irony. She wanted to be surrounded by some life and that which she held fondest: the garden, the sounds of the birds in the trees, and her son close by her side. The doctors argued that she might last longer where they could care for her better, but Dominic was insistent. A few extra days to be surrounded by bedpans and the smell of disinfectant? She was going home.

She lasted almost three weeks more. It was almost as if she didn't want to leave the beauty and tranquillity of the garden. September temperatures were still in the eighties, bright sunshine practically every day, and Dominic watered the plants early each morning and sat her on the back covered porch with her favourite coffee: Javanese with a hint of chicory and cinnamon. It reminded her of her childhood. She needed to be surrounded by the symbols marking the stages of her life – the coffee, the tangerine tree that her husband had planted, her son – before she could truly feel at ease in leaving it all behind. Everything was in place. It felt right.

The funeral had been a small ceremony. Dominic's sister had travelled down just a few days before his mother's death and stayed for the funeral preparations. Her husband and children joined her for the funeral and Dominic's uncle on his mother's side was also there. He lived in Bordeaux and Dominic had only seen him a handful of times in the past decade.

Not long after, he saw Monique in a Bauriac café. She looked across and acknowledged him with a small nod, eyes downcast. Perhaps she didn't want to greet him with anything nearing a smile, thought it might seem inappropriate. But he had the feeling in that fleeting second that she knew. That her look said: 'I've heard and I'm sorry. Nobody knows better than me how you feel. We've both lost someone we love.'

Dominic wouldn't have been too surprised if she knew. He'd heard so much about her own plight through Louis, via Valérie and the Fiévets. One point he'd picked up on had been problems with a local bank, though details were sketchy from Louis at first. All the Fiévets knew was that Jean-Luc had taken a bank loan for farm improvements and to buy equipment and had fallen behind with the payments. They didn't know how far behind, only that Monique had become increasingly concerned about it. It was also mooted as another possible reason behind Jean-Luc's suicide.

Marc Fiévet helped out on Monique's land when he could and they shared the profits at market, but with him only being able to manage working it at less than 30 per cent capacity, only half the monthly bank repayments were covered with no possibility of making a dent on the back payments. With each update from Louis, the situation seemed to get more desperate. She'd put the farm up for sale as soon as she was aware of problems at the bank, but three months had passed with still no takers.

Listening to Louis explain Monique's dilemma one day, Dominic was struck with an idea. He remembered a farmer he'd reprimanded a month or so back for parking badly on a narrow Taragnon lane. It transpired that he was a tenant farmer and the cottage he'd rented was separated from the land. Because there were no tracks or pull-ins for his car along one side of the land, he was forced to stay on the road.

Dominic tracked him down over the next week to find out if the proposition of renting a farm with residence adjoining would appeal. A few details were exchanged and the answer was 'yes'. Dominic checked with Louis and some others in the gendarmerie for character reference: it appeared the farmer, Croignon, was diligent, worked the land efficiently and always paid his rent on time.

A few days later, Dominic missed the opportunity of broaching the subject with Monique. She was just inside the doorway of the local boulangerie as he was passing, and he wasn't sure if it was because there were other people within earshot, or because the subject was delicate and she might be embarrassed that he knew about her personal problems. Or because, as before, he found her beauty intimidating. He felt awkward and shy in her presence. By the time he'd thought about it, the moment had gone.

Afterwards, he even questioned his motives: was he really trying to help, or was he just looking for an opportunity to speak to her? After a few too many drinks at Louis' one night, with Louis teasing and goading him, he finally admitted with a sly smile that perhaps it was a bit of both. Louis offered to break the ice by getting a message through Valérie and the Fiévets. 'She's so desperate, she's probably past caring where help comes from,' Louis ribbed. Dominic smiled and spun a beer mat across the bar counter.

Despite the ground-laying through the Fiévets, Dominic was still nervous when they met. He needn't have worried. After some initial stumbling and condolences exchanged, it went well. Dominic felt at ease, it was almost as if he was talking to a long lost sister. They traded some background and details as he explained the proposition, and it suddenly struck him how lonely she was. Not just now with the loss of her son and husband, but that she had always been lonely in the village. He could tell from the way she asked about his mother, whether she'd found it difficult at times in the village. It wasn't easy for outsiders to be accepted, he agreed. Shortly after she asked how he had found settling down in the area. He explained that his mother was only half Indonesian, and by the time it reached him her Asian blood was barely perceptible. But yes, it had been difficult the first year or so, purely because he was from outside. Others in the gendarmerie also resented him because of his past Foreign Legion and Marseille experience. He wasn't and never could be completely 'one of them'.

Monique nodded in understanding, her eyes warm and compassionate. She looked down after a second, having met the steadiness of his gaze, toying nervously with her coffee spoon. Perhaps that was how she viewed him, he thought. Another outsider battling against the hostilities of the close-knit village community, the two of them now also bonded by grief. They'd both lost someone they loved.

She went back over some of the details of the proposition. 'If this Croignon rents my farm in its entirety, are you sure about my staying at your mother's house?'

Dominic assured her that it was too big for him and, besides, he'd prefer not to stay with the memories it held. 'You probably feel the same way about your place.' They'd already discussed most of the main details. She would move into his mother's house and he would stay in a small apartment above Louis'. The only initial stumbling block had been that Louis' current tenant wouldn't vacate for another four months. In the end the Croignons suggested that Dominic stay temporarily in the fourth bedroom above the garage. Repayment for brokering the deal. Dominic wouldn't charge Monique anything the first year; then they'd discuss a peppercorn rent to cover his basic costs at Louis'.

Monique reached out and clasped his hand with a smile. 'Thank you.' She was deeply appreciative of the help, but had put up a bit of a fight arguing that she should pay him something straight away before seeing how strongly he was resolved. He wouldn't hear of accepting anything the first year. Dominic flinched a little at the electricity of her touch, felt his face flush slightly.

She was excited by the proposition: not only was the farmer paying a good rent, for the first two years he would share 30 per cent of the profits on the fields already fully planted and cultivated. She could cover the bank payments and start getting her life back in order; a new house would also remove some of the memories and emotional burden. But she wanted to sleep on it overnight and speak briefly with the Fiévets. Could they meet again the next day at the same time and place?

It took another two meetings to arrange everything: the loan details were complex and although the rent would easily cover the fresh payments, the back payments would need rescheduling. Dominic showed her a couple of rescheduling options, but still Monique looked slightly lost and awkward. 'Jean-Luck always dealt with the accounts.' She asked Dominic if he would mind coming to the bank with her to help explain everything to the manager. So much of it had been his plan anyway, and he would be better equipped to propose the rescheduling options. She might fumble or leave out something vital.

Dominic was eager to help, contemplating a diary busy with reasons to see Monique stretching out ahead. By the next day, he had an appointment arranged with the manager at Banque Agricole du Var, Bertrand Entienne. Monique gripped his hand again and this time kissed him on both cheeks.

A handful of meetings and already his feelings for her were running strong. Not only was she beautiful, but warm and compassionate, sincere. He hadn't met a woman like her before. He wondered if she had any of the same feelings for him – then quickly shook his head. He was being ridiculous. He hardly knew her, nor she him. It was a relationship so far based entirely on reliance and help. If he failed with the bank manager and his little scheme evaporated, there would hardly be any reason for her to see him again, he reminded himself soberly.

Bertrand Entienne was in his early forties with dark brown hair greased back and a rounded, slightly ruddied face. He smoked a pipe and his gestures were curt and formal as he showed them into his office. But at least he was smiling, looked eager to help, Dominic thought hopefully.

It didn't take long for the smile to disappear as Dominic explained the proposition.

'I'm sorry, we appear to be at cross purposes,' Entienne commented. 'I thought you were here with a proposition to clear the loan in full. Some sort of sale or other arrangement going through. I would have thought my last letters were quite clear that that is all the bank would be able to accept at this stage.'

Dominic ignored the rebuff and pressed on, explaining politely that Monique Rosselot had tried for four months to sell the property with no success. The market was severely depressed; it could be many months before a buyer was found, if at all. 'Surely it's better to get something secure now, get a rescheduled loan on track with the sure knowledge that all the future repayments will be met.'

Entienne rested his pipe in an ashtray to one side. He opened his hands out. 'I would if I could, but it's impossible. The papers went through to our legal department a few weeks ago. My last letter, I thought, explained very clearly that this action was impending. Once the papers are with them, there's nothing I can do. It's out of my hands.' Arms folded again, hands interclasped. A closed gesture.

Dominic was sure it was still just an opening gambit. That Entienne would soften his stance once he'd seen some figures. 'I managed to work everything out.' Dominic passed across the folder he'd worked on earlier. 'As you will see, all of the fresh payments are covered, plus the back payments are amortized in either three or four years. I suppose that could be adjusted to two years in the bank's favour if need be.' But Dominic could tell that Entienne was paying scant attention as he pointed out the key figures on the schedule.

Entienne shook his head. 'I'm sorry, but the intervention by the legal department makes consideration of this sort of suggestion out of the question. Once the file is with them, the loan is due in full as part of the preparation for court action. Also, there's far higher interest accruing to cover the extra costs of the legal department's action. So these figures are already inaccurate, I'm afraid.'

Dominic asked what sort of levels of interest. Entienne opened a file before him and perched some glasses on the end of his nose as he scanned down the columns. He picked up his pipe for another few pulls as he read out some figures.

Dominic added them together and felt his stomach sink. It was outrageous: 42 per cent per annum. Almost as bad as a Marseille loan shark. 'And what other options are there, apart from paying the loan in full before the papers are passed through for court action?'

'Hardly any, I'm afraid. If all the back money and accrued higher interest are cleared straight away, a continuance on the existing schedule might be possible. But it will still have to go before the bank's loan committee, with no guarantees. And a week or so from now, even that option will probably be gone. The papers will be too far advanced. You see, in any court papers the bank is obliged to press for the full amount.'

Dominic was outraged. But he remained outwardly calm, explained that it would be virtually impossible for Madame Rosselot to find that sort of money at such short notice. He tried yet again to sell the virtue of the rental and a rescheduled loan. 'The tenant is extremely reliable. It would give the bank a firm schedule now, she could probably clear two back payments straight away from the deposit as a gesture of good faith, and everything would roll forward cleanly from that point.'

Entienne wouldn't budge. Clearly he wasn't bluffing. 'I'm really sorry. But there's nothing I can do. Perhaps if you'd come here one or two months back, things would have been different.'

Dominic felt deflated. Monique was glancing down at the floor, embarrassed at the exchange. He'd let her down. He tried one last desperate plea. 'Surely even from the bank's point of view, what I am suggesting is far better than waiting on for a sale in such an uncertain market. There would be no guarantee at all of a buyer materializing before the due court date.'

Entienne's face flushed slightly, showing impatience now at Dominic's persistence. His hands unfolded and quickly clasped back again. 'That, I'm afraid, will be a problem to be resolved between Madame Rosselot and the bank's legal department. As I've explained to you already, Monsieur Fornier, quite clearly I thought, it really is all out of my hands now.'

Dominic saw red. Entienne's smug attitude, the pipe, the glasses, the hands clasped over the folder – all defences against confrontation with real life and humanity. How to ruin lives without getting involved. He felt like leaping across and burying his fist in the middle of Entienne's smug little face.

He took a long breath. 'Let me explain something to you, Monsieur Entienne – hopefully equally as clearly. Probably you know of the Rosselots, or at least as much as your little folder will tell you. What you might or might not know is that two years ago Monique Rosselot lost her only son – victim of a murder. I was one of the investigating officers. Then, just a few months ago, she lost her husband to suicide. Either he couldn't face life without his beloved son, or perhaps the demand letters you kept sending him pushed him over the brink.'

'I am quite aware of the situ –'

Dominic held one hand up sharply. 'Yes, yes – I'm quite sure that you are, Monsieur Entienne. That is obvious by your attitude today.' Entienne, already uncomfortable at the path the conversation was taking, glowered at the sarcasm. 'Monsieur Rosselot made a loan agreement with this bank almost three years ago. But he is no longer here and his commitments have fallen behind. And faced with that, Madame Rosselot has summoned both the bravery and the good faith to come here today. Not only her first visit but her first proposal to this bank. A very clear and straightforward offer, I might add. With what she has suffered, with the loss of her son and her husband, she has had to make a lot of adjustments with her life – and all that she is asking today is that the bank make some small adjustments and meet her halfway.'

Entienne continued glowering. His hands were clasped even tighter than before. 'I'm sorry. As I've already explained, there really is nothing I can do.'

'You put everything forward to the legal department, what – three or four weeks ago? Are you really trying to tell me that you don't have the power to reverse what you enacted in the first place?'

'It's not as simple as that. I would have to argue a strong case to get the file back from them and have it approved by the loan committee. As I mentioned to you before – if *all* the money and penalty interest were cleared almost immediately –'

'And don't you think this is a strong enough case to argue: a young mother who has lost her son and her husband?'

Entienne shrugged uncomfortably. 'It's difficult to introduce such personal situations at this level with other departments. Behind every file there's a story, some sort of tragedy.'

'Oh, so now we're getting closer to the truth. It's not impossible, it's just awkward. You're willing to sacrifice what's left of a family's life so that you're not faced with any awkwardness – anything that might look bad on your future record – in front of the legal department and the loan committee.'

Entienne's glower had turned to abject hatred. He smiled tightly. 'As with you, Monsieur Fornier, I am just a functionary. As you are bound to impose the rules of French law, I have to follow the rules of the bank. I'm sorry. I wish things were different.'

No options left, thought Dominic. He'd tried being nice, both gentle and harsh cajolement, the candy bar and the sledgehammer. Entienne wasn't going to shift. They left.

'*Shithead!*' Dominic spluttered under his breath once they were outside. 'I'm sorry. I probably did more harm than good in there.'

Monique gripped his hands and pecked him on each cheek, said that she was touched by how he had stood up for her. 'Don't feel so bad. You did your best.'

But in the end it had all been impotent bravado, he thought; none of it had done any good. Worse still, he'd probably alienated Entienne so strongly that he'd block any chances of later compromises over the loan, if they arose.

As Monique walked away, he wondered how on earth she was going to cope with this new crisis on top of all else. It also struck him with a sinking feeling that he'd messed up so badly, she might not want to see him again.

'Fucking shits! All of them. Especially at the Agricole du Var. And that Entienne's a prize dry prick. I could have told you that for nothing before you went to see him.'

Louis' insight into the world of local banking. Bauriac's regular *Standard and Poors*, expletive version. Just what Dominic needed to make him feel good, especially since three beers and two brandy chasers had so far failed miserably. His anger at Entienne burnt with a vengeance, and Louis happily stoked it with stories about banks in general and the Agricole du Var and Entienne in particular.

'I wouldn't be too surprised if one of the Var bank directors has his eye on the property. They know she's a widow, won't be able to find a lump sum easily.' Louis had seen it all before. It had happened to a friend of his. The director after the property ensures it's pushed into the legal department early, high interest mounts up, the court fees add even more – in the end it's an impossible mountain of cash to find. The prices at auction are rock bottom and the bank director picks it up at little more than half price. 'It's a legal racket. What with the high interest and the court fees, my friend was left with virtually nothing from the auction.'

Dominic looked into his drink for inspiration. He could see practically the same scenario rolling out ahead for Monique, with nothing but an outright sale of the farm to stop it. 'What's the average time for a farm to sell in this area?'

'The market's never been worse. Eight, ten months – sometimes a lot longer. People have them on the market with no takers as much as two years before giving up and taking them back off again.'

Louis returned to his diatribe about the banks, in particular Entienne's hypocrisy because of his current situation with a young mistress. Dominic was only half listening. Eight months? Four had gone already. Could Monique make it in the four remaining? Dominic suddenly snapped himself back to Louis' conversation. 'What was that you said?'

'What – about the girl, or about Entienne being a fucking hypocrite?'

'The girl. How long has it been going on?'

'Practically a year now.'

'And does his wife know? How many people *do* know?'

'His wife certainly has no idea. The rest's just a few guarded whispers around the village. Maybe it will get back to his wife eventually, maybe it won't.'

'Do they have any particular meeting places, or does it change every time?'

'She works at the jeweller's not far away from him, but she walks around the opposite block from the bank and he usually picks her up there.' Louis leant slightly across the bar. 'Apparently they head to the Espigoulier hotel on the way to Aubagne. He makes the excuse of having a long lunch with clients.'

'Which days?'

'Mondays and Thursdays.'

The following Thursday lunchtime, Dominic turned his Solex into the car park of the Espigoulier. He had already identified Entienne's Citroën from in front of the bank and, sure enough, it was there. Dominic swung the Solex out of the car park and fifty metres along to the first turn-off. And waited.

It was a small slip road and very few cars passed him. Those that did probably thought he was checking for cars speeding. It was over forty minutes before Entienne's car emerged.

Dominic revved up the Solex. He would have to time his exit perfectly – too soon and he could go under Entienne's wheels.

Entienne's car turned out, was starting to pick up speed. *Okay . . . now!*

Dominic flew out of the slip road and into the side of Entienne's car. In the end, his worry about being too early had made him time it slightly too late – instead of sprawling across the bonnet, he hit the windshield, one knee smashing through the passenger window as he spun dramatically over the top of the car and down the far side.

The fall looked good and Dominic broke it with his hands the far side. But he'd connected badly with the windshield, one shoulder felt stiff and his nose had banged against the glass; it was bleeding profusely, soaking his shirt. Still, all the better for effect, he thought as he straightened up.

Dominic feigned dizziness for the first thirty seconds, as if he was having trouble realizing what had happened and where he was. Entienne was in shock at first before turning his attention to the girl beside him. Her initial hysterical screams had subsided into sobbing.

Entienne got out slowly as Dominic took out a pad and started making notes. In that instant, beyond the blood and the dishevelled appearance, he recognized Dominic and mouthed, 'Oh, it's . . .' Then quickly bit his tongue and fumbled into 'Are you all right? I'm sorry, I just didn't see you. You came out of nowhere.' Apology quickly turned to anger. 'What on earth were you thinking of, coming out suddenly like that?'

'I could ask you the same question,' Dominic said coldly. Dominic noted the registration and asked Entienne for the car's papers.

'What do you mean?'

'I mean that when I looked both ways from my turning, the road was clear. And then you came out suddenly from nowhere and hit me!'

'But that wasn't how it happened at all. It was all clear ahead of me – then suddenly you shot out. I didn't even see you, only heard the thud as you hit me.'

Dominic grimaced. 'Well – you'll get the opportunity of putting your side across in court. Papers, *please!*'

Entienne's face glowed red. 'This is outrageous! You know full well that's not how it happened,' he spluttered. But his tone was now more hesitant and uncertain.

'I know nothing of the sort. Only that you're a menace on the roads and I could have been killed. I'm laying charges for dangerous driving. And if I don't have your papers in my hand in thirty seconds, I'll add obstruction of justice to the charge sheet!'

Entienne scampered back to the car and dug them out of the glove compartment. Suddenly he was not on familiar territory, not in control. Unprotected by his office walls, bank files, his pipe and glasses, he was vulnerable. A little flustered boy. Dominic was enjoying every minute. He leant over menacingly as Entienne passed the papers out.

Dominic noted the details and then asked Entienne's full name and address. Entienne enunciated the last words between clenched teeth, then said, 'I know why you're doing this, and you won't get away with it. I have a witness.'

Dominic looked across to the girl, now dabbing at her eyes with a handkerchief, trying not to smudge more eye make-up. 'Oh yes, I forgot. Your *witness*. Of course. Name and address, please?'

The girl and Entienne exchanged glances. Entienne's face was now bright puce. 'Look – does she really need to be involved in all this?'

'But she's your witness, Monsieur Entienne. She's the one person who can stand up in court and support your account of the accident. Why on earth wouldn't you want her to be involved?' Dominic smiled.

'It's awkward, that's all.' Entienne's hands fumbled in his lap. 'If she didn't appear in court on my behalf, what would happen?'

'I would give my account, you'd give yours. Because I'm an officer of the law, my account would no doubt stand and you'd be charged with dangerous driving and vehicular assault. A three-year driving ban and possibly an additional three to six months' jail term – depends on the judge. I'm not sure how the bank would view such a charge.' Dominic watched each word strike home. Mallets of realization and then finally acceptance as Entienne's head slumped. In the same way that Entienne's words had beaten Monique into submission just days before. Retribution at its most divine. 'Oh, and I forgot one thing. Even though your *friend* wouldn't be speaking on your behalf as a witness, I'd still need to take her details. Along with the time and the hotel you were driving away from. Essential background for the hearing. I daresay some local reporter could also be arranged to cover the court case. So, Mademoiselle – your details, please?'

Entienne slowly shook his head, his voice low and dejected. 'I don't think that will be necessary.' His eyes lifted up only fleetingly. 'Can we come to some other arrangement? I'm sure that having gone to all this trouble, you have something in mind.'

Dominic looked sharply at Entienne. 'Are we talking about bending the rules now, Monsieur Entienne? The very same rules which you told me just the other day in your bank couldn't be bent?'

'Yes, yes. We are.' Total defeat.

'Well, I suppose we could have a meeting later this afternoon in your office to discuss the relative rules of our two professions. I will still need to take all the girl's details. But if we reach agreement, my file won't be going anywhere. And I'm sure, Monsieur Entienne, you have a similar file.'

Entienne nodded without looking up. They arranged to meet at 4.30.

Dominic let them drive off first, and on the way back to Bauriac on his Solex he ignored the occasional stares from passing cars – curious as to why the gendarme was smiling with such a badly bloodied nose.

The new loan schedule was approved within ten days. Dominic even managed to tweak the final conditions to allow five years on the back money and get the penalty interest struck off. Entienne totally erased the legal department period; it was as if the file had never gone there.

They celebrated with a bottle of champagne at Louis'. Dominic had made light of it when he told Monique, mentioned only that Entienne had a small skeleton in his closet which he used to advantage. But as the drink flowed, Louis couldn't resist telling the full story.

Monique looked horrified at Louis' dramatic account of Dominic spinning over Entienne's car bonnet. 'You shouldn't have, Dominic. You could have been seriously hurt.' He basked momentarily in the glory as she gripped his arm and kissed him. The third time in as many weeks.

Croignon moved in a few days later, the day before taken up with moving suitcases of clothes and personal items between their homes, with Louis helping out with his van.

When they came to the room above the garage with Christian's clothes and toys piled on the bed, Monique looked on awkwardly. 'Do you mind if I take them to your place, put them in one of the rooms?'

'No, not at all. There's three bedrooms. It's up to you how you use them.' Dominic was more concerned by the way she was still clinging to the memory. Not just one or two personal items – the room had been left practically as a shrine. He also hadn't realized till that moment that the room he would be occupying temporarily had previously been Christian's.

Two weeks later, Monique invited him over to dinner. Symbols of two cultures: lamb and aubergine cassoulet with couscous. He brought a bottle of Châteauneuf and a Pinocchio colouring book for Clarisse. As things mellowed over dinner, she mentioned that she still felt guilty about not paying him any rent the first year and wanted to make a contribution by inviting him over to dinner once every week. It would also, she pointed out, compensate for the fact that his own cooking arrangements were far from ideal, having to fit in for those first months around the Croignons. It was the least she could do.

He initially shrugged off the need for any return gesture, but she was insistent and, besides, it was an opportunity to see her regularly. He accepted with gracious reluctance.

The dinners were every Friday night or the first free weekend night if he had a Friday-night duty. It was difficult to mark the exact time when their friendship transformed first to strong affection, then finally to love. For him, it was probably much earlier than her.

At first it was just small signs. A look in her eyes, a smile, light kisses of thanks on his cheek for the wine or presents he brought. Even when her eyes seemed to openly invite him, he could see the hurt and pain beneath, and he held back. Felt suddenly fearful that he might be taking advantage, was reminded of how damaged and frail she might still be.

Even the night when they first made love, five months after the regular dinners started, couldn't be taken as the main point of transition in their relationship. She'd had more to drink than normal that night, was more affectionate. After the meal, over coffee and brandy when Clarisse had gone to bed, she sat on his lap and kissed him, said that she'd like to show him what she'd done to his room.

She led him upstairs and, before opening his door, asked him to close his eyes and wait a second. He opened his eyes to the soft glow of five night lights burning. Their flickering picked out a flokati rug on the floor and ikat fabric draped on the wall above the bed as his eyes adjusted. She kissed him and they tumbled on to the bed, his mumbled 'It's beautiful' quickly lost.

She broke off only to ask him to close his eyes again – and when she prompted him to open them, she was standing at the foot of the bed naked, mocha and cream skin beneath the soft candlelight. She leant across and started taking off his clothes, planting soft butterfly kisses on his skin – then finally rolled her body on top of his. Her body slithered easily against him, glistening with the scented oil she'd applied, a slow and sensuous movement until he was fully aroused.

Their love-making was slow and gentle at first, gradually becoming more urgent. Her eyes were deep and soulful, and he traced their contour, the gentle almond slant at their corner, running the same finger slowly down her cheek and her neck. But there was something else in her eyes beyond the joy and abandon, a faint flicker of ghosts from the past that seemed to be holding her back – as if the sudden urgency of her frenzy was as much to exorcize them as to lose herself in joyous oblivion. A race between the two.

And as his own climax came, his head lolling breathlessly to one side, the image of the night lights and the soft tears of ecstasy on her cheeks reminded him again of the hospital. Of her long nightly vigils praying that Christian might live.

Some look in his eye – or perhaps the new tension she felt in his body – made her roll away suddenly. She too stared thoughtfully at the night lights, one finger at her lips in contemplation. 'I'm sorry,' she murmured.

Later that night back with the Croignons in Christian's old room, the wind rose steadily. Dominic could hear it rustling through the trees and the field at the back of the house. He thought of the day that they were down by the river and the wind was high, the gendarmes placed like markers in the field. Uncomfortable, ghostly reminders; it took him a while to get to sleep.

For the next three weeks, Monique came up with an excuse for each of their regular dinner dates. On the fourth, she phoned and said that she wanted him to come over, but that it should be with them just as good friends, as it was before. 'I'm sorry. I shouldn't have done what I did that night. I wasn't ready – and it wasn't fair on you. I'd perfectly understand if you didn't want to see me again.'

He came over. It was a lesson that the ghosts from her past would sometimes stand between them; and perhaps if he'd read the signals deeply, he'd have realized that that would always be the case. Part of her heart, her soul, would forever be buried with Christian and Jean-Luc.

It was another three months before they became lovers again. Monique promised that this time she wouldn't leave his bed. But over the coming months, as spring arrived, there would still be times when she felt she just couldn't go on with it. She would suddenly be cocooned again in the past, the ghosts and memories ripping her apart – and she would feel that she had nothing to give to the present, to him and Clarisse.

Dominic was always understanding when those times came, would phone her the next day to see if she was better. Her grey moods usually didn't last long, a few days at most.

As the summer arrived, they took to eating outside at night on the back patio. Monique had also found a babysitter nearby and they started to go out more. He took her to see *Lawrence of Arabia* and they held hands and kissed in the back row like two teenagers. On her birthday, he took her to a new restaurant in Cannes he'd discovered: Pierre T'être. It was on a narrow lane full of restaurants that meandered gently down to Cannes harbour with small candle-lit tables on each staged terrace. Monique found the atmosphere magical.

It was late summer when he finally proposed. She looked concerned. She reminded him not only that she had a daughter but that she still bore the scars of the past. Part of her heart might always be dragged back there. Could he live with that?

He said that he could, but deep down he was thinking that she would gradually get better – he had seen marked improvement already in the past months – until finally the ghosts and the pain of her memories faded to insignificance or went completely. And he felt very close to Clarisse; with gifts every few visits and occasional hugs, if he was still some way from becoming a surrogate father, he was at least a favourite uncle.

Monique made him wait two months before she answered; to be sure that any impulsiveness on his part had mellowed. They were married the next February, 1967. Louis was best man and looked comical in a dress suit. The small reception was also held at Louis', and he had trouble totally escaping from his proprietary role, occasionally barking orders at the waiters. Harrault and Levacher were the only ones present from the gendarmerie.

And Dominic was right, the ghosts from the past did subside – until their first-born. A son. Apart from it being a horrific breach birth which could have cost Monique's and the baby's life, Dominic realized he should have read the warnings when she first mentioned during pregnancy that she hoped for a boy.

The second sign that she might see the baby somehow as a replacement for Christian was when she asked, if it was a boy, if they could call him Yves – Christian's middle name. He began to wish that it would be a girl purely to avoid any possible complications. A gain to replace a past loss: a macabre tangle of emotions that could only lead to problems.

But in the end he resigned himself to fate, consoled himself that, if it was a boy and somehow managed to bury Monique's reliance on the past, it might in an obscure way be a godsend.

He didn't know how wrong he would be.

Monique didn't tell him about the dream until two months after the birth. That moments after urging the nurses that she'd like her husband by her side, when she was fully under the anaesthetic and the doctors were fighting to save her life, she'd seen Christian.

In the dream, they were dining at Pierre T'être. Dominic had taken her there the night she'd announced she was pregnant; perhaps that was what had made the connection, he thought. She saw Christian in the distance as she looked up the street. As she left the table and walked towards Christian, the other people and the tables in the street seemed to fade into the background – only the steps and the lit candles from the tables remained visible, guide lights marking the path to the solitary figure of Christian ahead, the harbour a misty silhouette far behind her. She'd seen his face clearly, seen the gentle tears in his clear green eyes. As she came closer, she thought she heard him say, 'It's all right . . . it's all right' – but it was barely a whisper. And in that moment she had reached out to touch him – though their hands never quite connected. She'd awoken then. A nurse was leaning over and telling her that everything was all right. 'You have a little boy.'

She hadn't mentioned the dream earlier, she explained, because at the time the joy of having Yves had consumed all else.

For the first few years, her absorption with Yves seemed natural: the love and affection of a doting mother for her new-born child. But as the years progressed, he began to notice how fearful and protective she was. It became an obsession: never letting Yves out of her sight, ensuring that there was never an unguarded moment in his life. Dominic railed against it. It wasn't a natural childhood, he argued: Yves was unable to have any freedom, could not play with his friends out of sight of her for any length of time.

Monique promised repeatedly that she would change, but any easing in her protectiveness was minimal. The only thing to help was the birth of Jérôme a few years later – though mainly when Jérôme was old enough to play with Yves, keep him company. They could partly watch and protect each other.

Her intense protectiveness became a recurring argument through their years together. She was well aware that it was a fault: 'But I could never again go through the trauma of losing a child.' She and Jean-Luc had partly blamed themselves for Christian's death. Felt they'd allowed him too much freedom, he'd been let loose to play in the fields or with friends most days. Only natural, Dominic supported; he himself had enjoyed such a childhood in Louviers. She had stifled Yves terribly and now Jérôme too was under her heavily protective wing.

In turn, Monique's advice with his career was incisive. Drawing it out of him that he'd only stayed in Bauriac because of his ailing mother, she pushed him to take a transfer a year after they were married. Careerwise, he was stagnating in Bauriac. At heart, part of him had recognized that fact, but he'd become numbed into acceptance by routine. It had taken Monique to bring it to the surface.

It was also Monique's encouragement that led him to take his inspectorate exams not long after, and she had advised on many of his career moves since. Her style was gentle, no more than a series of questions, so that in the end he felt he had all but arrived at the decision himself.

It was ironic, Dominic thought. In the same way that she had intuitive views about his career, he could see the errors she was making as a mother – a clear picture only gained by being detached from the problem, taking an overview. But in the case of Yves, he wished he'd been wrong.

In his teens came the backlash effect of Monique's protectiveness. At fifteen he left home and got in with the wrong crowd. He started off with sporadic promotional work for a chain of clubs and discothèques, handing out cards on street corners. He would turn up at the clubs late evening and start on some heavy drinking, peppered later with drugs – marijuana at first, then cocaine. He started free-basing and took extra work as a drugs packet 'runner' to some of the clubs to pay for his habit. Often he was paid half in cash, half in cocaine. Dominic picked him up one night after one of the clubs had been raided.

Yves had been lost to them for almost two years. Throughout, Monique had been inconsolable. Where had she gone wrong? She'd done everything to shield him, to guide him on the right path, but still he'd drifted away. Not once did Dominic say, 'I told you so', or suggest that her obsessive protectiveness might have caused the problem, made Yves crave freedom and rebel.

Dominic kept Yves' name clear of any charge sheets, but added a condition: that he remain with them at least six months and attempt to dry out before deciding what he wanted to do with his life. In the end he stayed ten months – a painful period of adjustment and regular visits to a drugs counsellor – before embarking on his national service with the French navy.

The two years of discipline combined with the *frisson* of travel broadened Yves' outlook. He came back a changed person and enrolled for another year, taking a special course in maritime communications. When he returned, he joined the National Police in Marseille as a sergeant. History was repeating itself.

Within two years, he was covering the Vieux Port area attached to narcotics. His maritime communications background and his knowledge of the drugs trade were invaluable in an area where most shipments came in by sea. Jérôme was at Nice University, studying pure maths with a second in IT software architecture, hoping later for a career in computer programming. He had never been a problem.

Monique had long ago ceased to view either of them as any form of replacement for Christian, but she still worried about Yves, especially with his current work. She worried that one day he might swing open the wrong warehouse door to face a *milieu* gun in the shadows.

Throughout the years of arguing against her unreasonable protectiveness, a recurring fear for Dominic had been that one day he might be proved wrong. That, having urged her to loosen the reins, told her not to worry, that nothing would happen, against all odds something might. He'd often contemplated how he'd face her given such a circumstance. For it to happen twice and him feel that he was partly to blame: it was unthinkable.

When Marinella Calvan's call caught up with Dominic in Lyon, Yves was a DI still stationed in Marseille and Jérôme was working for a computer company in Sophia Antipolis. Clarisse was married with three children – two girls and a boy – and lived with her husband, a sales manager for an agricultural feed company, near Alès.

Dominic maintained an apartment for himself and Monique in Lyon, but six years ago had bought a four-bedroom farmhouse just north of Vidauban, only thirty-five kilometres from Taragnon. Jérôme stayed there and commuted to work, and they came down at least every other weekend. Some weekends Yves would also join them and Clarisse and her family would visit every few months.

The words echoed in his mind. *'Yes . . . I do know someone who could verify Christian Rosselot's background.'* But apart from the ghosts that might be awoken in Monique's mind, he had also buried his own secrets through the years: he'd never told Monique that he had doubted Machanaud's guilt. Since the light sentence had been so controversial and Monique felt that it was partly at the root of Jean-Luc's suicide, it would have been insensitive and mocking. It would have hinted that Jean-Luc's suicide was completely in vain rather than just misguided. He couldn't do that to her.

For the same reason, when years later he discovered just how long Machanaud had been incarcerated – fourteen years between prison and mental institutions – he didn't tell Monique. The fact that Jean-Luc would have smiled from his grave because Machanaud had received just punishment would have been scant compensation. The overriding message would be that his suicide had been pointless.

Marinella Calvan had said that she would send over a tape and accompany transcript by messenger. It would be with him early the following day. His first reaction had been that it was all nonsense, would probably all quickly evaporate and prove of no avail. Though he wondered if his underlying curiosity was because of the terrible injustice he suspected might have been wielded against Machanaud, compounded by his own guilt at discovering later, *too late*, the severity of that injustice. But how many ghosts and secrets from the past would he need to trade to discover the truth?

28

Limoges, May 1982

Alain Duclos picked up the smoked salmon on a small octagonal wedge of bread and popped it in his mouth. The waiter paused to see if he'd choose another: caviar, prawns or pâté with chives. Duclos just nodded and the waiter moved on.

RPR celebrations for victory at the local elections. The last bash two years previously had been held in a grand downtown civic hall, replete with marble columns, ornate chandeliers and rococo plaster ceilings. But parking had been atrocious, so they'd opted for a modern hotel function room on the edge of town. The waiters with their liveried costumes and silver trays looked somehow out of place in this room with its low ceilings and suffused fluorescent lighting.

For the first forty minutes of the reception, Duclos had done little more than nod like a toy dog on a car's back shelf at the incessant chain of congratulations. 'Thank you. I'm so glad that you could make it. And thank you for your support during our campaign.' Once or twice, he'd even made the mistake of asking, 'And how's business?' – only to be caught up in endless tales of corporate woe that invariably ended: 'Perhaps there might be some influence you could bring to bear.'

Trite smiles in response. 'I'll see what I can do', but thought: *arseholes*. Even if he could affect entire industry sectors at the local level, invariably an opposing sector would start whingeing and lobbying. Just smile, convince them they're your friends, look concerned, really, *really* concerned; and if pressed, tell them how theirs is an industry and an issue with the highest possible priority on your list. But in the end do fuck all. It was safer. Fewer friends and votes were lost keeping the status quo as it was.

He was glad now of a moment alone at last. A chance to survey the room fully rather than just surreptitious sweeps between nods and smiles at some fawning local businessman or Chamber of Commerce represent-ative. His wife was not far away, just visible beyond a small group towards the bar, talking to one of his main PR aides – friends from before he had married her, when the two girls worked together in his offices. She'd made few friends since.

Eighteen months of marriage. No euphoria or bliss, that had certainly never even been expected by him; and, if he'd troubled to ask, possibly her too. Just convenient. Useful. Cut the right image for the electorate. They looked good together, and he had become increasingly aware that as he approached his mid forties and still wasn't married, questions were beginning to get asked.

She'd been working in his offices almost fifteen months before he really noticed her and started asking about her; before he'd been too preoccupied with his problems with Chapeau to think about anything else. Her application file also helped provide some background: Bettina Canadet. Thirty-two years old. Single. Studied and gained a degree in social economics from the Sorbonne. Worked mainly in civic offices in Rouen where her family originally lived. Joined the RPR in 1976 and applied to the Limoges party offices in late 1979 when her family moved to the area.

The rest he discovered from one of his main aides, Thierry: 'What, the ice maiden?' Duclos was intrigued. Thierry was a mine of information on office gossip and politics. Two people in the office had already tried their luck and struck out. Thierry covered the obvious quickly: no, she wasn't a lesbian, and certainly one of the men she'd liked. 'Went out with him for three months before coming clean with her problem.' She just didn't like sex. Tragic case: victim of a date rape in her early twenties, it was many years before she could even bear to be in the company of men, let alone start feeling comfortable with them or, God forbid, actually touching them. Had to give her time; be gentle with her. The relationship only lasted another six weeks. 'Who has time to spend as an emotional counsellor in the hope that after a year or so she might, just *might*, come in from the cold? Maybe she never will. Who knows?'

Duclos started dating her a month later. 'What is this, the ultimate challenge?' Thierry teased him. 'It's not enough just to swing the electorate, now the challenge is the ice maiden – see if you can succeed where all others have failed?'

Duclos' droll smile in return hinted that the North Pole had already been conquered. 'All it took was the right man to hit the defrost button. Some have it, some don't.'

In reality, it was a relationship built almost entirely on her veneration of his political stature and power and his patience with her sexual and emotional instability. She had never met anyone so patient and understanding.

He looked across at her now and she gave him a tight little smile. She'd hardly changed in the two years: somewhere between Twiggy and Piaf, with large blue eyes that pleaded 'Help me, save me, I'm frail.'

It was far from love. It had been like taking some frightened little deer in from the forest, making her feel comfortable and secure. He'd become her protection from the world outside, from all those nasty, grabbing men and their demands. Yet she carried guilt too, was worried that she wasn't pleasing him the way she should, despite his countless reassurances: he didn't see her like that. She shouldn't worry. He loved her for her soul, her character, her kindness and vulnerability – the sex was far less important. When she was ready, it was okay with him.

She would literally be tearful at his patience, his understanding. And between her summoning the effort, the work that made him tired or him pleading that he felt uncomfortable because he sensed she was forcing herself just for him – they made love at best once every other month. He could manage that, and from certain angles she even had a slight boyish quality. Perhaps that was what had made him first notice her. And, to cap it all, his work colleagues were slightly in awe at his sexual prowess in melting the 'ice maiden', succeeding where they had failed, bringing out the woman in her.

His only worry was that one day she would thaw out. She would look at him with those big eyes suddenly brimming with passion rather than vulnerability and uncertainty. That as she became more insistent and demanding and he was still reluctant, making excuses, she would finally guess his secret. The lie would be out.

He shook off a faint shiver. That wasn't now or even in the near future; hopefully it would never happen. And he'd had three years now out of the shadow of Chapeau. No calls or demands in the dead of night, the constant bleeding him dry, no goading smile and sly humour.

Three years? It felt as if ankle chains and a yoke had suddenly been removed. He'd never known such freedom. Or happiness. He looked back towards his wife and smiled.

Lyon, March 1995

Muffled sounds of the city. Faint drone of traffic, the occasional car horn beeping. Somewhere in the distance, a siren wailing. Dominic was more intent on the words on the tape that drifted through the half-open door into the hallway.

'. . . *Madame Baudert usually gives me some* pan chocolat, *if her husband isn't there.*'

'*How many times a week do you call by there?*'

'*Maybe two or three times. But sometimes he's there, and she doesn't give me any. Just winks when he's not looking as if to say, "Next time", and nods sideways. Madame Baudert explained once that he was too mean, she'd get into trouble if she gave it away while he was there. He'd rather feed it to the chickens or let it rot.*'

'*And the boulangerie is on your way from school to the farm?*'

'*Yes. It's only a few hundred metres from the school. I have to walk almost another half kilometre to the farm. But usually I have a friend with me.*'

Monique was two-thirds of the way through listening to the tape sent by Calvan. Dominic had played it twice as soon as it arrived at the station, then replayed some selected segments. Except for the main, obvious details, little of it meant anything to him – and it struck him, listening to the tape, how little he'd really known about Christian. He'd dealt with the investigation, typed up endless reports about the attack and murder – had eaten, slept and dreamt little but the case for months. But really, at heart, he had known little or nothing about the boy. He'd been dealing with his death, not his life.

Christian's life had taken up ten whole years of his wife's existence – from her mid teens to mid twenties – and as he became immersed in the voice on the tape, he realized how little he knew about those ten years. Ridiculous, *pathetic.* Married to the same woman for nearly thirty years and yet whole segments of her life were still strange to him.

And through the years, he'd never asked. Always thought it would be too painful, too awkward, something to be swept away and relegated to the past, to history, where it belonged. Yet this ten-year-old boy – this boy whose last hours on earth he knew almost everything about, every last shocking, gory detail, yet whose life was a complete void to him, a tome of blank pages – had always been with them. At the birth of their first son, Yves. At Jérôme's birth. At the two christenings. At the moments they might drive past a field and Monique would survey the shifting wheat thoughtfully. In her gaze across a candle-lit dinner table, when she would suddenly focus on the flickering flame and he would be lost beyond it. Her eyes would water and he knew in that moment that the memory had drifted back.

Each time it showed in her eyes as the years were stripped away. A look burdened with pain and anguish, yet with just a dash of joy and irony – a thick emotional soup sieved through misty veils of time. Then finally serenity, acceptance mellowing the sorrow. A look that said: *Of course I remember. How could I forget?* Sad, lost memories. The few pathetic tokens remaining of the love that was.

A love that Dominic had never witnessed, never been party to, never asked about. Never been able to put flesh and blood and words and actions to – except those looks in his wife's eyes through the years. Sudden, threatening grey clouds that invariably as quickly drifted away.

Until the tape. And he thought: Oh God. *God.* Could that really be the voice? Substance suddenly put to the ghost, the memory that had lurked in the shadows of his life the past thirty years? Or was it just a hoax? Conflicting emotions wrenched at his gut, made him feel empty inside yet strangely excited at the same time. *Taragnon. The village shops. The farm.* At least those parts seemed accurate. Playing, rewinding, playing again – agonizing over small nuances and phrases before finally settling back. How could he be sure? *How could he possibly know?* He hardly knew anything about the boy. He was nothing but a shadow, a shadow of memory that only flickered alive again now and then in his wife's eyes.

But at least he'd answered the main question: it seemed real enough to be given a hearing by Monique. The main details were accurate, it wasn't some ridiculous account which had fallen at the first hurdle over inaccurate village descriptions or the boy heading in the wrong direction back to the farm.

Dominic wondered if deep down that was what he'd hoped for. Something that meant he could pack the tape back to London without even troubling Monique. Consign it back to history where he'd so far safely corralled everything by not asking questions, by not raising the issue, by never mentioning the police investigation or the trial and its aftermath, Jean-Luc or Machanaud. Safe.

But another part of him wanted desperately for it to be real. For what? To know what really happened in 1963? To assuage his own guilt over Machanaud? Was that the trade-off? Satisfying his own guilt at the expense of Monique's peace of mind? Reawakening the ghosts after all these years, bringing the pain and shadows back to her eyes? He sweated and agonized over the tape as it played, was tempted to rip it out and send it back at one point, before the weight of detail and the small lost voice got to him, grabbed hard at his insides and fired an intense, burning curiosity. He wanted to know. He wanted desperately to know if it was real.

And that was when he started convincing himself that he was doing it equally for Monique. She would want to know too. How would she feel if she discovered that he'd covered up? That he'd sent the tape back without even letting her hear it? To protect her from the horrors of memories past? She would see only that she had been robbed of the opportunity of some link with her long lost son, however tenuous and remote. Too many buried secrets. It would be almost as bad as staying silent, not speaking out in court on behalf of Machanaud. Almost.

The tape was rewinding. A button clicked. A segment was being played over again.

'. . . when we finally did take the rubber ring to the beach, it was so big I almost fell through the hole.'

'Where was that?'

'La Nartelle beach . . . near Sainte-Maxime.'

When he'd first handed the tape to Monique, she'd hit him with a deluge of questions: Where? When? Who? *Which psychiatrists?* He'd answered mainly with stock terminology from Marinella Calvan; he'd called her back shortly after the first playing to clarify key points: *Past-life regressions. University of Virginia. Started as a standard psychiatric session. Young English boy of a similar age to Christian's – lost both his parents in a car accident. Xenoglossy: use of a foreign language unknown to the main subject. The regional accent has already been authenticated, but now they need to know about the main details on the tape.* As he spoke, he could see Monique become increasingly perplexed and confused, staring at the tape blankly – and in the end his shoulders slumped in exasperation. He held his arms out. 'Look – I know it sounds strange. I have no idea if it's real or just a hoax either. But details of the village are at least accurate. Play the tape and let's talk afterwards, we'll go into the details and background then. If necessary, you can phone this woman in England yourself – let her explain everything directly.'

Click. Stop. Rewind. Click again.

'. . . the tyre was quite big . . . as if it belonged to a van or truck. My friend and me decided to pick it up and roll it home. It took two of us to roll it home.'

'What was your friend's name?'

'Grégoire.'

'And he went to the same school?'

'Yes.' A pause. The boy swallowing, his throat clearing. 'When we finally got it home to the farm, the inner tube only had one puncture. My father was able to fix it easily so that we could take it to the beach one day. I could use it as a big rubber ring . . .'

Dominic hovered halfway between the hallway and the kitchen, listening. He wanted to leave Monique alone while she listened to the tape. Alone with her thoughts and emotions. Hadn't wanted to see the expression on her face or look on expectantly like some eager schoolboy waiting for exam results. So? *So?* He'd made an excuse about making a snack in the kitchen – had got as far as spotting some Brie in the fridge and some rye biscuits in the biscuit tin – but had been drawn back into the hallway by the sound of the tape playing before putting the two together.

Click. Stop. Rewind. Play.

'. . . *The camp's one of my favourite places. I built it against the back of a stone wall in the field at the back of the house.*'

'*How far away from the house is it?*'

'*A hundred metres or so. From there, I can clearly see the back courtyard and the front door, see if anyone . . .*'

Ring, ring. Ring, ring. The sudden loud jangling of the telephone in the hallway crashed abruptly into Dominic's thoughts, made him jump. He suddenly remembered he'd asked to be phoned at home for any news of the motorway-chase police officers. One was out of danger, but the other was still critical.

He picked it up, nodding numbly to the first words, his mind still on the tape and his wife. 'I see. I see. When was this? I see. Crippled, you say?' He realized his voice sounded bland; detached, disinterested. He injected more enthusiasm. 'When will they know for sure the damage done by the shattered vertebrae?'

'. . . *can see my mother working in the kitchen and I know then that it's time to come in. I know if my father is in the garage, because he always has the light on . . .*'

'They're doing more X-rays now. Then as soon as they have those apparently they're scheduling another operation. They should know more soon after that.'

'I see. So, how long? Six hours, twelve?'

'Ten or twelve probably. I doubt we'll know much more till tomorrow morning.'

'. . . *I always helped her if I could. I missed her so much later, as I did my parents.*'

'I see.' Dominic's skin bristled. Distracted. Trying to take in the two voices together.

'But don't expect any miracles. They're pretty sure he won't get the use of his legs back. They just don't know yet how bad the rest might be.'

'. . . and I remembered thinking how worried they would be. And my father . . . my father . . . why didn't he come and try to find me . . .'

'I understand.' Scant relief. No tricolours on coffins, but a home visit nevertheless. A hospital visit. A meeting with his wife and close relatives. Stumbling condolences.

'. . . kept thinking how they couldn't face that I'd become lost from them — that I'd somehow let them down . . . their sorrow. My mother's face, so sad . . . so, so sad . . . her –'

Click. Stop. Silence.

Dominic listened out for the machine clicking again, but there was nothing. Monique had obviously finished with the tape.

'. . . That's all there's left to know now. Whether the rest of his body will also be affected. Arms and upper body.'

'I see. I understand.' Attention completely gone now. Only one thing he wanted to know. 'Let's talk again tomorrow morning – hopefully more will be known then.' Dominic rang off.

As he walked back into the lounge to confront Monique, despite his wish not to pressure her or make her feel awkward in any way, his impatience, he was sure, came through – he probably did look like a schoolboy anxious for his exam results. Not saying anything, but his eyes saying it all, and thinking: So? *So?*

Monique didn't answer for a moment, looked down and away before finally lifting her gaze to speak. But the words themselves were secondary, he had already read everything in her eyes. The storm clouds, the grey shadows, had returned. And this time he feared that they would take far, far longer to drift away.

29

Marseille, October 1982

MARC JAUMARD, brother of ANTOINE JAUMARD, alias 'Chapeau'. Would the aforementioned, or anyone with knowledge of the aforementioned or his current whereabouts, please contact as a matter of urgency the offices of FOURCOT & GAUTHEREAU, 3°, 19, Rue André Isaia, 13 Marseille. Tél.: 69 85 64.

Marcel Gauthereau checked the small entry in the personal column of *Le Provençal*, as he had done every six months for the past three and a half years. He wondered why he bothered sometimes. The copy was exactly the same as the first entry, they were obviously just printing from the first plate. Still he found himself mechanically checking the address and phone number. Particularly the phone number. Then he would consider its position on the page – see if it was placed well and didn't get lost too much among the heavier box adverts and the mass of pleas for instant romance.

The envelope had been signed, sealed and left with the notary for six years now. He had been the lawyer witnessing on behalf of his client, Antoine Jaumard, and it had also fallen to him to carry out Jaumard's instructions regarding the envelope in the event of his death. Antoine's brother Marc was to be notified and he, Marcel Gauthereau, would then accompany Marc to the notary's office where, upon due presentation of identification and signing of a receipt, Marc would be handed the envelope left by his brother. Simple.

Except that when he originally sent out the notification, Marc Jaumard had moved. His letter was returned with no forwarding address. Gauthereau sent a clerk by the building a week later to discover that Marc had gone back to sea, but not with his old company. After phoning his old company and another number they recommended, the trail petered out with a past work colleague and an old flatmate. The only faint light that could be thrown on his whereabouts was that he might have joined up with a merchant company sailing out of Genoa. 'Perhaps he maintains a place there when he's back on shore.'

There were still some funds from the retainer Antoine Jaumard had left him to execute his will. The will simply couldn't be executed without Marc Jaumard; no other relatives were named. Gauthereau started placing the adverts. Once every six months in Marseille, once a year in a Genoa paper in Italian. There was enough cash to cover a total of twelve insertions. Gauthereau was intrigued by what might be in the envelope. Names, dates and vital contacts? Drug routes and stashes, details of Chapeau's account in Switzerland perhaps? Could he have earned that much as a *milieu* button man?

Le Provençal had peppered the account of his death with his nickname. They seemed to all have nicknames: Tomi 'The Wall' Boisset, Jacques 'Tomcat' Imbert, Pierre 'The Priest' Cattaneo. It somehow added to the mystique and fear. Chapeau? The newspapers hadn't explained, nor had he ever asked. Getting through their few brief business meetings had been tortuous enough; he'd always found himself clock-watching towards the end, too uneasy under Jaumard's slow fish eye to ask superfluous questions.

Two more insertions to go in Marseille, one in Genoa, before the retainer was finished. After that the envelope would stay gathering dust in the notary's office, with little chance of anyone knowing its contents.

Session 7

Marinella Calvan listened to David Lambourne's voice in the background as he induced Eyran Capel into hypnosis. The three questions Dominic Fornier wanted asked were on a piece of paper before her.

As before, Lambourne would spend the first ten minutes or so getting Eyran comfortable and asking general, everyday questions – then would slowly regress Eyran back and draw out Gigio.

Then Philippe would take over in French and Marinella would tap out her first question on the screen. Though Fornier's English was good, the questions had originally been in French and Philippe had translated. She would start with her own questions first, get Christian Rosselot settled more naturally into the mood and period, then lead into Fornier's questions.

Though Fornier was sat at the back of the room just as a casual observer, his presence created an added tension. Was it because of what he represented: someone who had been close to, had feelings for Christian Rosselot? What was before just a detached voice was suddenly tangible, real. A young boy whom people once cared about, loved, just as her with

Sebastian. Fornier's presence and the background he'd explained with his wife, the boy's mother, brought it all suddenly home to her.

Or was her concern that the voice and the details wouldn't stand up as real, and in a few questions' time she would know? Nothing left but to pack her bags and fly back to Virginia that evening. Another disappointment. Perhaps it was just the number of them cramped in the small room, hanging on each word of a young boy long since dead, each laboured syllable, not speaking themselves, subduing even the faintest cough or sigh. And all of them, except Philippe, with different hopes and ambitions of what might be gained from the session.

The difference between Lambourne's aims and hers had been underlined acutely at their meeting over dinner the night before, a discussion previously avoided; it'd seemed pointless to air their respective views on the link between Eyran and Christian until they knew whether the regression was real. Fornier had called the previous morning and told them that the details on the tape seemed accurate both to him and his wife, but there were a few extra questions to be totally sure: 'These are more personal, things which only Christian would know.'

Lambourne was particularly anxious after his recent conversation with Stuart Capel. 'Eyran is still having his dreams, though not as intensely or frequently as before – at most maybe one every other week. But Stuart Capel is asking some pretty pointed questions about how we think putting an explanation to this regression will help Eyran.'

'Does Gigio still feature as prominently in them?' Marinella asked.

'Maybe not quite as much – he's only in half of the dreams. But Eyran claims to be equally as distressed and frightened with Gigio not there. He doesn't have a friend to keep him company, face the dangers and pitfalls alongside him.'

'Or lead him astray, lead him into danger.'

Lambourne shrugged. 'The point is, Stuart Capel is starting to question our exploration of the link between the two boys. Suggesting that it might not be helping.'

'I see.' Amateur armchair analysis; all they needed to add to the already contrasted principles between herself and Lambourne. The chasm between standard psychiatry and parapsychology – with Lambourne's brief dabbling with PLT as a rickety rope bridge between the two. And in addition Fornier was now asking oddly angled questions.

Fornier had seemed particularly curious to find out if more accurate descriptions around the time of the murder might be gained beyond the sketchy and fractured details on the tape. Marinella explained that – as Fornier had no doubt gauged from the reaction on the tape – it was an area which obviously disturbed Christian the most and had therefore been almost totally blotted out. 'As a result it would probably be one of the hardest areas in which to gain more information. Why?'

Fornier brushed it aside with an offhand, 'Nothing in particular.' But his tone and the way he'd been hanging on her answer made Marinella wonder. They discussed briefly some of the general circumstances surrounding the murder: sexual assault before the final attack; blunt instrument, probably a rock; wheat field by a river; coma for five days.

Wheat field?

Lambourne held the view that the coma and even the brief fifty-four-second period of death had fired the connection between the two boys. These explained why Eyran had no recall of Gigio/Christian until after then. 'They were major physical events that linked both lives. Object loss opened the door, was a shared emotional experience, but the coma was the shared physical experience to swing it wide.'

Marinella agreed, but felt that subliminally the link had been there long before. 'Eyran had a sense of *déjà vu* with the wheat field when they first moved to the house in England. He didn't dream of those fields purely due to fond memories of England or because he truly felt he might find his parents there – but because of Christian. Eyran knows deep down he's lost his parents on a Californian highway – whether he accepts it or not – but the wheat field is clearly Christian Rosselot territory. It's Christian who can't accept separation from his parents. Eyran's merely aboard for the ride.'

Lambourne shook his head. He disagreed. Their respective views started to head in different directions. Lambourne threw at her the obvious point that Christian's parents hadn't featured in any of the dreams, Eyran's had, and that both boys focused only on finding Eyran's parents, whereas she felt this supported the theory that of the two boys, Christian's non-acceptance of loss was strongest. In his case, it had been pushed further away. Eyran's had been tackled head-on in practically every dream.

But with Lambourne's reluctance to accept her view, at one point she'd blurted out: 'What's wrong? Are you afraid that accepting the theory pushes you further away from what you know best – conventional analysis?' And immediately regretted it, saw clearly that she'd hit a raw nerve. It threw too stark a spotlight on what they both knew: as soon as Gigio had been identified as Christian Rosselot – a tangible past existence rather than a protective figment of Eyran's psyche – most of Lambourne's conventional theories had gone out of the window. This was her territory. Past-life regression versus Freud. The irreconcilable divide: psychiatrists branding parapsychologists as hardly better than tribal witchdoctors, and parapsychologists retaliating by labelling psychiatrists as 'too conventional and myopic'. Far too many of her and Donaldson's critics through the years had been 'conventionalists' – but it was unfair to start taking it out now purely on Lambourne. She softened quickly with: 'Are you afraid that if I'm right, I might be camping out in your office a bit longer?'

Lambourne raised his glass and smiled. 'Now that, as you know, I would never complain about.'

Perhaps it was her. She was drawing the lines of divide too simplistically: she dealt with the past, Lambourne with the present. Each of them sought the explanation where their knowledge was strongest. But Lambourne's smile and comment brought uncomfortably close what she'd feared at the outset: that their views were poles apart and Lambourne had only picked up the phone because he was suddenly out of his depth and it was a good excuse to see her again. He liked her company. But as soon as that novelty wore off, the differences would start to show again. It hadn't taken long, she thought: eight days.

But she was glad nevertheless that he'd called. She could be only three questions away from compiling one of the strongest case studies and papers of her career. For that, David Lambourne could smile and ingratiate himself to her as much as he pleased.

She brought her attention back to the session as Lambourne's voice trailed off and he nodded towards her. Philippe leant forward and she tapped out the first question on the PC screen.

Dominic wasn't sure of the precise moment when the thought first struck him of being able to use information from the tapes to re-examine the details surrounding Christian Rosselot's murder. His initial thoughts – shortly after the first call from Marinella Calvan – had been so fleeting and indistinct, he'd hardly paid them attention. *Possibly a hoax; obscure or unsubstantiated information* – with still the hurdles of *insufficient detail to support a renewed investigation and legal complexities* in the far distance and only paid scant consideration. That consideration only arrived in full force after seeing Monique's reaction to the tape.

But after his last conversation with Marinella Calvan, those hurdles appeared suddenly to have been raised and were now almost insurmountable: *'Due to it being an area which has obviously disturbed Christian the most, the murder has been largely blotted out.'* Details would be difficult to gain.

He'd replayed those segments of tape the most: *'And then there was a bright light . . . so bright . . . I couldn't see anything. And the field . . . I recognized it . . .'* What could have caused a sudden, blinding light? It was a bright, sunny day. Perhaps Christian had been heavily concealed in bushes down the river bank, then had suddenly emerged into the brightness of the lane and the wheat field? Or perhaps he'd been blindfolded as well as tied up and it had suddenly been taken off.

There had also been an earlier reference to the light 'hurting his eyes' not long before he was face down on the ground. *'. . . the sheaves were against the side of my face . . . my own breathing against it. All I could hear . . . nothing else . . . nothing . . .'* The voice trailed off as breathing became heavier, more sporadic. *'. . . I struggled to look back, but couldn't . . . couldn't . . . I . . .'* After that the voice became increasingly catatonic and garbled. Philippe's voice broke him quickly away. It wasn't even clear if Christian had fallen in the wheat or been pushed over, whether he'd already been struck or the blows were still to come.

Calvan was right. Recall of the murder had been heavily erased. Dominic couldn't see how pressing on subsequent sessions would reveal anything more than the same garbled, disjointed account. Someone with passing knowledge of the case, primed by a handful of newspaper articles, could have constructed a more detailed account. Even the few details that were fresh – such as the sudden light – were vague and could be interpreted any number of ways. A re-examination of the case based on fresh information wasn't even a remote possibility. And from a boy dead these past thirty years, his voice speaking from the grave through another boy who had entered therapy because he was psychologically disturbed? The first prosecutor he took it to would laugh him clean out of the room.

But the intense curiosity to know still nagged at him, so in the end he removed that final hurdle: blotted out consideration of a renewed official investigation. Convinced himself that he was eager to know for his own sake; for the curiosity of an old police officer who wants to know the truth before he retires. A final closing of the book. And for Machanaud, or at least for –

Philippe's voice broke abruptly into his thoughts. *'C'est l'été. C'est le mois de mai.* The year is nineteen sixty-one. You are eight years old. You worked with your father Jean-Luc towards the end of that month. What did you help him with?'

Monique's first question. Dominic looked on expectantly, felt his mouth dry with anticipation, the atmosphere tense in the small room.

A frown, a creasing of the boy's brow, as if he was scanning frantically back through images and memories long past. The boy looked very different to how he remembered Christian: wavy light brown hair, a few freckles across the bridge of his nose, his eyes pale brown. Christian's hair had been darker and wavier, his skin tone olive, his eyes a piercing green. It was difficult to relate the two.

The thought lines in his forehead slowly eased. 'We were clearing some long grass from the grapevines my father had planted at the beginning of the year.'

Marinella picked up on the frown, wondered if Eyran was thrown by the questions being suddenly more specific, rather than the very generalized questions of the last session.

'And what happened while you were helping your father in the field?'

Faint lines returned; uncertainty with the question. After a moment: 'It was very hot. I er . . . I became worried at one point that I wasn't being of much help. My father was working very fast, I wasn't keeping up with him very well.'

'But something happened that day to make you finally stop working,' Philippe prompted. 'What was it?'

Gradual realization, the lines easing again. 'I was stung by a bee.' A pause. Marinella tapping at the keyboard. Philippe was about to prompt when Eyran continued. 'But my mother didn't have a plaster or any antiseptic. She applied some vinegar, then some baking powder on cotton wool. It took out a lot of the sting. She said that it was something she'd learnt from her mother.'

Dominic felt the back of his neck tingle. When he'd gone through the questions with Monique, she'd mentioned Christian helping Jean-Luc and getting stung by a bee. Her applying vinegar and baking soda because they had no antiseptic. He shivered involuntarily as the tingle spread down through his body. It was Christian's voice. There remained little doubt.

Listening first hand was dramatically different to just hearing the detached voice on the tape, he thought, seeing the small face struggling with thoughts and images, the brow knitted, tongue gently moistening his lips as the words were finally found. The words of another boy from another era. The description of Christian and Jean-Luc working side by side in the fields, father and son, both dead these past thirty years, cut a powerful and poignant image. Dominic's hand clenched, emotions of sadness and nostalgia gripping him hard.

He'd arranged to fax the transcript to Monique and wait in London for her to answer; if her response was positive, he wanted to stay to talk with Marinella in more depth. But if little additional information surrounding the murder could be gained, what would be the point?

The second question was about a game of boules in the village square one Sunday. Christian was nine, it was only a couple of months after his birthday. Philippe pinpointed the day: Christian had gone with Jean-Luc to watch the village boules games on several occasions. But this particular Sunday something had occurred.

'There was an accident.' Eyran's eyes flickered, the right image finally falling into place. 'Nothing serious. But two cars going around the square, one went into the other. The two drivers, both men, were very angry, shouting loudly at each other. Most of the men playing were distracted, it looked like any minute a fight might break out.'

'And what happened then?'

Eyran had settled into the rhythm of the more specific, narrowly targeted questions. Pauses were now less marked. 'One of the players, Alguine, when he thought that everyone was looking towards the road, moved to stand by his own boule, then nudged it closer to the *cochonnet* with one foot.'

'What did you do?'

'Looking around, I realized that nobody had noticed but me. Alguine had moved quickly away from his boule, so I moved gradually towards it and, as the other players' attention drifted back, I looked down suddenly and apologized: "Sorry. I must have kicked this boule while I was looking at the accident. I'll put it back where it was." I could see Alguine glaring at me, but he said nothing. Later, when I told my father, he couldn't stop laughing.'

Jean-Luc had told Monique, Dominic reflected, then in turn Monique had told him just the other day when she'd prepared the questions. Batons passed down through the years. A few faint brushstrokes depicting an era of Monique's life previously strange to him.

Thirty years? Machanaud had died over ten years previously. Fourteen years in prison. Only six years of freedom in between. A handful of twilight years to swill back some eau-de-vies and spin stories of his long

287

forgotten glory days in the Resistance, poach a last few rivers. Rough justice.

If four years earlier he hadn't bumped into Molet, Machanaud's lawyer, in the recess halls at the Lyon Palais de Justice, he might never have known. Molet was there on a hearing for a Nice-based client. They both recognized each other straight away – but it took some prompting from Dominic for Molet finally to recall from where and when. After some initial pleasantries, they turned to the subject of Machanaud. Molet did most of the talking while Dominic registered in turn surprise, guilt and, finally, outrage.

Molet obviously read his guilt, because he commented that he himself had not realized Machanaud was still being held under psychiatric care until year eleven. 'I thought he would have been released ages ago. But it still took three years to press for his release. There was a review only once a year.'

Molet went on to describe Perrimond's undue influence with hospital governors and state psychiatrists to ensure Machanaud was not released. Provence establishment favour-swapping – at the golf club or Masonic lodge – at its very worst. 'Each time a negative psychiatric report came through. Machanaud wasn't finally released until a year after Perrimond's death.'

'. . . I got a boule close to the white, only a few centimetres away. My father was quite surprised. Only one of the other players got so close – and in the end they had to measure to see who had won.'

Dominic looked down. It wasn't part of the prepared question sheet. Marinella had obviously let him ramble; perhaps happy of a diversion allowing Christian to relax and establish a more natural rhythm. It was obviously also an incident he remembered with fondness.

The boy's faint smile. Dominic found it vaguely disturbing. A reminder of lost happiness, lost years.

Molet had looked sharply at Dominic, as if perhaps expecting a reciprocal disclosure of guilt. But Dominic said nothing. What could he say? That year seven had been the first time it had occurred to him to check on Machanaud, and when he couldn't trace Molet's number he had finally called Perrimond's office. Three calls later with no reply, his workload had quickly swamped his concern. And on the few occasions since that the thought had arisen, he'd convinced himself that Machanaud had probably been released years back? He had never troubled to pick up the phone and check. Too busy.

And even if he had explained all that, Molet would have questioned his concern. And he would have felt inclined to explain the rest: his past doubts about Machanaud's guilt, the police cover-up over the car description, how he had been pushed into going along with everything because of the veiled threat of being shipped off to a gendarmerie in northern France. That his mother would have been left to die alone. He could explain none of that – so in the end he said nothing.

But Dominic was sure that in that moment Molet had seen it all in his face, seen the quickly rising burden of guilt and shock as it struck him just how long Machanaud had spent locked away.

'. . . it was on a trip to Alassio. We went there for a weekend.'

'And that was where you bought it?'

'Yes. I had some pocket money, but it wasn't enough. So I talked my parents into letting me have the rest of the money to buy it.'

The third question, Dominic noted. A trip to Alassio in northern Italy. Alassio. Portofino. He remembered seeing a wall plaque for Portofino on his first trip to the Rosselots', while sitting in their kitchen and asking questions about the last time they'd seen their son.

'How did you talk them into it?'

'I told them I'd read more. That if I had a bedside lamp like that, so nice, I'd promise to read more. Every night.'

'What did the lamp look like?'

'It was made of shell, in the shape of an old galleon. The light inside made the shell almost luminescent and direct light would also shine through the portholes. It was beautiful.'

'So in the end that promise convinced your parents to give you the extra money for it?'

'Yes, it did.'

'And did you keep your promise and read more?'

'Yes. Practically every night in bed I did some reading before going to sleep.'

Dominic looked down and bit his lip. He could hardly bear it. He didn't realize that sitting in on the session would have such a profound effect on him. Christian's voice, all these years later, telling them what a good boy he'd been. As if it was still somehow important to him.

30

Dominic was staying at the Meridien Waldorf, half a mile from David Lambourne's office in Holborn. He'd stayed over the previous night, but hoped to leave without spending a second night. He was therefore in hotel limbo: bags packed and in a store room, though still using the facilities. Particularly the hotel fax.

It had taken Philippe almost two hours to put the transcript back in its original French from the on-screen English, and another fifty minutes for it to arrive by messenger at his hotel. He scanned it through for any obvious errors and faxed it straight to Monique in Lyon. He'd already phoned her to announce its arrival, could imagine her standing by the fax machine in his office at home, practically ripping the pages out as they hummed through.

Beep. Dominic waited a few minutes by the machine for a reply. Then, telling the clerk where he would be if one came through, he went to the bar downstairs and ordered an armagnac.

As the drink hit his stomach, warming it, soothing his nerves, he started thinking about the transcript he'd just read through. The depth of detail came through even more than in the session itself. The contrast with the fractured, garbled descriptions around the murder itself was absolute. He took another quick slug, feeling it cut a warm path. Just his luck: marvellous detail about games of boules, eating *pan chocolat* and the trip to Alassio – but little or nothing of use about the murder itself.

Almost twenty minutes had passed when the office clerk came down with a fax. Dominic was on his second armagnac. Handwritten, it read simply:

> *I'm convinced it's Christian's voice. Nobody else could possibly know those personal details. I don't know how or why – but it's his voice.*

Twenty minutes? Reading through the transcript would have taken only five minutes. Had Monique cried, caught up in a wave of emotions that stopped her putting pen to paper immediately? Or had she sat and laboured over the brief message she was going to send back, eager not to show sentimentality or the mixture of suspicion and outrage she'd voiced immediately after playing the tape. That had now been boiled down to simply, 'I don't know how or why'. When she'd initially prepared the questions, she'd commented in a subdued, almost acid tone, 'I don't profess to understand the tape that has been sent. But if these questions are answered correctly, Dominic, for God's sake don't expect me to believe that this strange English boy is Christian reborn. Some vague, unexplained psychic link perhaps. But that's as far as I'll go.'

Dominic checked his watch, timing: phone through to Marinella Calvan and give her the news, arrange a meeting, forty minutes or so for the meeting itself, then back to the hotel to collect his luggage and out to Heathrow Airport for 6.35 p.m. It was going to be tight.

Dominic wondered whether to forget the meeting with Calvan. Just fax through Monique's message, a brief follow-up phone call, and head out to the airport. When he'd originally thought of a meeting, it had been inspired by the foolhardy idea that he might be able to use the information to reopen the case. Now it was just his own curiosity. But Calvan would probably still insist that details surrounding the murder were too scant. Even that last vestige he'd clung to – salving whether all those years of doubt and guilt had been misplaced – wouldn't be satisfied. The meeting would have no purpose.

The decision made, in a way Dominic felt relieved. He knocked back the last of his armagnac. Fine. No meeting. Perhaps as well. Even if Marinella Calvan had complied, he'd have had to face Monique and explain. Explain everything he'd kept hidden the past thirty years. He'd been dreading that part, and at least that would now also remain buried.

'I don't understand. A suspect was found, charged and sentenced – at least that's what came out of the few newspaper articles Philippe translated for me. I thought the case was closed all those years back.'

'You're right. It was. But there were discrepancies with the case that I was never happy with.' Calvan was staring sharply at him, still getting to grips with his suggestion of using information from the session to reopen the murder investigation. *Discrepancies?* What could he say to this woman he hardly knew? That he'd been press-ganged into joining a cover-up so that he could stay with his dying mother, the resultant years of guilt redoubling when he'd learnt how long a possibly innocent man had spent imprisoned? Yet proving Machanaud's innocence would only heighten that guilt, and then his wife would know his part in the cover-up and that her last husband's suicide had been in vain. Marinella Calvan's eyebrow would merely arch more acutely. What *did* he want out of it all? Perhaps proving Machanaud's guilt: closing the door once and for all on that chink of doubt. In the end, the only other useful thing he could find to say was: 'I was very young then, merely assisting in the investigation. I had very little influence on the way it was conducted. To me, this is like a second chance. How many of us really get a second chance?'

Second chance? The poignancy of the phrase stung Marinella for a second. 'I can appreciate how much you would like to get to the truth, even after all these years. If I can, I would love to help. But you've listened to the tape of that first session when we stumbled on those final moments of the murder. Eyran's almost catatonic. Apart from the obvious risk of dragging him back through recall of the murder – I just don't think we'll gain anything of any use. Most of it has been pushed away. He doesn't want to think about it.'

Clatter of cutlery from two tables away, a waitress with an Australian accent talking to one of her colleagues. Dominic was distracted briefly. When he'd phoned at four o'clock and spoken to Calvan, David Lambourne had just started a fresh session. He'd mentioned how tight he was for time with his flight out, and they'd arranged to meet twenty minutes later at Café Opera in Covent Garden.

Detail? The contrast between the depth of detail in the transcript and the vague garbled accounts surrounding the murder was what first gave Dominic the clue. What had made him suddenly change his mind and arrange the meeting with Marinella Calvan: Christian expanded, detail was stronger relating stories where he felt more relaxed, at ease. This in turn explained why the murder account was so vague and fractured. But forty minutes to an hour earlier, when Christian first met his murderer, before either of the sexual attacks, before Christian even realized he might be in danger – he would have been more at ease. Now, explaining these thoughts to Calvan, words he had already spun over in his mind on the way to the café – he watched her expression closely. 'If nothing else, he would hopefully be able to give a clear, accurate account of those moments. The moments when he first met his murderer.' A chink of acceptance halfway through, then something else: doubt or intrigue, Dominic wasn't sure.

Marinella shook her head. 'I don't know, it's a possibility, I suppose.' She felt her emotions tugged sharply. An image of a young inexperienced gendarme on the edge of an investigation, unable to wield any real influence yet harbouring a strong doubt nevertheless. A doubt carefully tended through the years, intensified and brought uncomfortably close to home by his marrying the dead boy's mother. Like Javert in *Les Misérables*, never entirely giving up on the investigation – until finally, a generation later, the opportunity arises to uncover the truth. *Second chance?* Wasn't that how she felt about the case: a chance to prove herself after the Cincinnati case and the other failures?

Then reality hit. Simple and unequivocal. David Lambourne would never go for it. Let alone Stuart Capel. Unless she could build a strong case to convince them. Intrigue and her desire to help started to bite back. But apart from Fornier's thumbnail account the day before, to her the murder was just a chain of breathless, disjointed words sifted through the decades via Eyran Capel. 'Tell me more about the investigation. All I know so far is from the newspaper coverage and what you told us the other day: the wheat field, sexual assault, blunt instrument, and that Christian was in a coma for five days before dying. The man convicted – what makes you doubt his guilt?'

'Too circumstantial. He was just a local casual farm labourer and poacher who happened to be there at the time. No history of sexual assault or incidents with young boys. But the prosecution nevertheless built a convincing case out of that circumstance.'

'But I understand from the newspaper coverage that he wasn't convicted of murder. In the end he got off with manslaughter.'

' "Got off with", I'm afraid, is not the most appropriate phrase given what finally happened to Machanaud.' Dominic related the sorry tale of Perrimond playing favours with hospital governors and state psychiatrists. 'Machanaud ended up spending a total of fourteen years imprisoned.'

Between sips of coffee, Marinella breathed in sharply. 'God. That's ludicrous. I'm sorry. Sounds almost like a personal vendetta.' And immediately wondered why she was saying sorry to Fornier, except that he seemed to care what had happened to Machanaud.

'It practically was.' Dominic explained how it had quickly developed into an establishment protection case. That the person he suspected was a young assistant prosecutor staying with one of the area's largest landowners. 'A personal friend of the Mayor. It was unthinkable that such a person could possibly commit such an atrocity. Whereas Machanaud was a low-life poacher and village drunkard. He was seen as a far easier target, less troublesome – and the weight of circumstantial evidence built up strongly against him.'

'What happened with the assistant prosecutor?'

'He was questioned only once. The timing of his car being seen in a restaurant appeared to give him an alibi. He went on to become a leading politician, RPR MP for Limoges.' Dominic raised his coffee cup as if saying *Santé*, and smiled. 'Now he's one of France's illustrious representatives in Brussels. An MEP. He's done very well has our dear Monsieur Alain Duclos.'

Images of Javert were back. Relentlessly pursuing through the decades. And now a name had been attached: Alain Duclos. But Marinella felt uncomfortable with Dominic's suddenly maudlin tone. A lifetime of battling the odds against the police *and* the establishment, and now she too might let him down. What was she hoping for, what niche to prise open the barricades she knew would confront her if she requested more sessions? 'And Machanaud. What happened to him after he was finally let out.'

'He died eight years ago. Had only six years of freedom in between.'

Marinella grimaced, her eyes flickering down slightly. But she began to worry that, like Javert, Fornier's pursuit of Duclos might be equally unfounded. 'If this Duclos' car was seen somewhere that supposedly gave him an alibi, then what makes you suspect him?'

Dominic ran one finger absently down the side of his coffee cup. How could he explain? A look, a glimmer in the eye from thirty-two years ago? Something that told him Duclos was nervous, had something to hide? His supercilious, pretty-boy appearance – or the fact that he *looked* like the type who might molest young boys? Calvan would just laugh at him in the same way Poullain had all those years back. In the end all he said was: 'There were discrepancies with the car sightings. Some of the details I wasn't happy with.' *Discrepancies* again. His standard trench when shots were fired. Stumbling through an account of the car-sighting cover-up – even if Marinella Calvan might feel sympathy with the motive of his ailing mother – he was sure overall wouldn't aid his cause.

'Do you think the people who saw Duclos' car were lying?'

'No. But Machanaud said that he saw it passing on the lane while he was poaching – just minutes before he left himself.'

'But he could have been lying to save his own neck.'

'Yes. That's what the prosecution said.'

Marinella forced a wan smile. 'I see. Sorry.' She sensed there was more, but Dominic looked away awkwardly after a second. They were silent, the clatter of the café imposing. Whatever it was, he obviously found it still worth keeping to himself after thirty-two years. If Dominic Fornier truly believed that more information could be gained by avoiding the murder and keeping to when Christian Rosselot first met his attacker – then when and where? All Fornier had mentioned so far was 'forty minutes to an hour beforehand'. 'Where do you think Christian first met his attacker: by the lane and the wheat field, or somewhere else?'

'Probably close by, at least. The supposition was that whoever he met, they probably hid down by the river bank for most of the time. A few cars passed on the lane. If they'd stayed for any length of time in the wheat field, they'd have been seen.'

'Is that where the sexual assault also took place – down by the river bank?'

'Yes. There were two assaults, with a gap of anything from thirty to fifty minutes in between. Certainly the second took place by the lane, and possibly the first close by.'

'If it was Duclos, not Machanaud – is that where you think Christian met him?'

'I don't know. That's one of the details I hoped further sessions might uncover.' Faint shadows from a ceiling fan moved across the floor. Dominic glanced down, memories of the reconstruction drifting. Storm clouds across the shifting white wheat. 'Machanaud admitted poaching in that same position for almost two hours. That became one of the prosecution's strongest arguments. If Christian had met someone else there, Mechanaud would have seen them.'

Two assaults? Thirty to fifty minutes' gap in between? Marinella was trying to assimilate the rest of the sequence of events, get a clearer picture. 'You realize that details regarding either of the sexual assaults would probably be equally as vague. As with the murder, Christian has very likely blotted it out.'

'Yes.'

'Apart from the fact that they would have been deeply disturbing in their own right, Christian might have already suspected that his attacker would later kill him.'

'I understand.'

'Probably the only clear detail we'll get, as you have suggested, is from when Christian first met his attacker. Before he realized that anything might happen. But that might only be a few minutes at most.'

'Then you'll help?'

'I don't know. As I say, it's difficult.' Marinella bit at her lip. The possible obstacles loomed back: Lambourne's and Stuart Capel's reaction to the sessions suddenly becoming an appendage to a murder investigation. She would be lucky to get to first base. 'If it was just up to me, fine. I'd help. But it's not. My colleague David Lambourne has been given charge to cure Eyran Capel's current condition. And Eyran's stepfather Stuart probably wouldn't be too pleased knowing that Eyran's course of therapy has been suddenly hijacked to head somewhere else. But I'll do what I can.'

She could have added, 'Don't hold your breath,' but Dominic's shoulders had already slumped, the eagerness in his eyes suddenly dulled. She studied his face for a moment. The dark hair, greying heavily at the sides, the enticing, almost imperceptible slant at the corner of his eyes. Laughter lines as he'd first greeted her now etching the pain of those long years. It couldn't have been easy, she thought, marrying the dead boy's mother and still harbouring the doubt through all those years. 'I'll do my best. I promise.'

'Thank you.'

Marinella flinched slightly as Dominic touched her hand fleetingly in thanks. It wasn't the touch itself, but something she wasn't able to define until they'd parted and she watched him walk away – shoulders still slumped, or perhaps buoyed by her parting promise? But it hit her then how much Dominic was depending on her, and again the worry came that she might end up letting him down.

There was only one session left to fill in some of the remaining details of Christian Rosselot's life before her flight back to Virginia and Sebastian. But even armed with this incredible story – the quest of a man still searching for the truth in a murder from over thirty years ago – with both Lambourne and Stuart Capel already railing against continued probing in the past, she feared their reaction was a foregone conclusion.

Fornier's quest had touched her deeply, but how was she even going to start to convince them?

Genoa, January 1983

Marc Jaumard looked at the brief entry in the newspaper personal column. He'd already read it twice and now read it through again, trying to measure each word, judge any hidden intent. He only had the single page with the personals, ripped out from *Le Provençal* and sent by a friend in Marseille.

Jaumard had been with the same Genoa-based company now for over four years. Away at sea when his brother died, he hadn't even known until six weeks later when he returned to Genoa. Folded clippings in an envelope from the same friend in Marseille: 'CAFÉ SLAYING'; 'MILIEU WAR HOTS UP'; 'CAFÉ AU SANGUIN'. The main report in Le Provençal described his brother as a 'known milieu associate'. Quite flattering considering that he had mainly killed people for money.

And now this new clipping almost four years later. Jaumard wondered if it really was what it appeared on face value: connected somehow with his brother's death. He'd left Marseille in something of a rush: rent unpaid for three months, a bank loan on a car he'd taken with him left hanging, and his ex-wife screaming for maintenance. The advert could be just a ruse by the bank or his wife's lawyer to flush him out. Create the illusion that it was somehow connected with his brother's death, a small inheritance from blood money stashed away perhaps. Then slap an injunction on him.

A bit extreme for the bank, playing on sympathies with his long-buried brother – but he'd put nothing past his ex-wife. He wondered. He contemplated the nearby phone briefly before his eyes fell back to the entry. Dissecting sentences and then individual words, trying to imagine his ex-wife across a lawyer's desk as it was worded.

31

Shallow breathing. Half-light from the hallway spilling across Eyran's profile as he slept. Stuart Capel stood over the bed, contemplating. In some lights, at some angles, he could see Jeremy's features in Eyran's face, remember Jeremy as he was as a child, the two of them playing together. Eyran was the last link with those memories.

Lost now, all so distant – and pushed away even further by the confusion and nightmares running riot in Eyran's mind. Still the Eyran he remembered – the carefree smiling boy from their trip to California before the accident – was out of reach.

Seven sessions in five weeks. Had Eyran's state of mind improved? Certainly, the frequency of dreams had diminished. Two a week had been the average before the sessions, now they were at least a week or ten days apart and less violent and upsetting. Of the four dreams over those five weeks, two dreams had been with Gigio, two without.

The latest development Stuart found hardest to accept. Past-life regressions? Gigio no longer an invented, protective character from that part of Eyran's psyche refusing to accept the loss of his parents – but a real life in its own right? A life that Eyran had supposedly lived in France from 1953 to 1963? Christian Rosselot. He shook his head. It was unreal, ludicrous, another turn-off along the nightmarish road they'd been led down since Jeremy's death. Yet this one had no familiar landmarks, no signposts, dragged him abruptly away from the only tangible element of Eyran's condition he'd clung to: Eyran's non-acceptance of his parents' death. He could relate to that. He had felt the emotion strongly himself, had spent the last long weeks struggling to come to terms with Jeremy's death and had barely succeeded. A friendly face in his dreams taking him to see Jeremy, he imagined could be quite reassuring, soothing. Make him feel somehow that Jeremy hadn't completely gone.

But his reservations about entering Eyran into therapy had lingered until the second session, when David Lambourne had brought up the possible danger of a predominant character pushing Eyran over the edge into schizophrenia. Only then did he feel assured he'd made the right decision. His earlier fears were allayed.

Now with that premise thrown out of the window, Stuart's doubts were back. Before the final session with Marinella Calvan, he'd voiced his concerns to Lambourne about continued probing into Eyran's past. Lambourne had defended that because the past real character of Gigio/Christian had also experienced sudden separation from his parents, secondary influence was still significant. And even apart from that core shared experience of loss, there were other elements linking the two lives: a period of coma in both boys, Eyran's brief death, the wheat field in Eyran's dreams which was also the last place to feature in Christian's life. By knowing more about Christian Rosselot, they would be better armed to tackle Eyran's current condition.

Stuart had only been partially swayed, and perhaps it had shown in his face because Lambourne added, 'With this one final session with Dr Calvan, the main forays into the past will be complete. We can then assess afresh where we want future sessions to head.'

Though Stuart didn't totally agree with Calvan's views, he appreciated her courage of conviction. After the last session, she'd thanked him and Amanda for allowing her to delve into Eyran's past and explained how she hoped it might help, in that it wasn't only a question of symbols, it was determining where they had stronger relevance, in which life there was stronger non-acceptance of loss and separation. Hopefully the two sessions and the notes and transcripts would provide the answers to that. Provide a stronger framework for continuing conventional therapy.

Calvan had nodded towards Lambourne at that point, but Stuart noted a slight clouding in Lambourne's eyes, as if he disagreed or previously had had words with her on the subject. But Lambourne made no comment. Just smiled tightly at Calvan's nod.

The only time Stuart had spoken with Calvan before was for twenty minutes after her first session with Eyran, when she'd provided some of her background with regressions, children and xenoglossy. She preferred cases of xenoglossy in children because of the unlikelihood of them having learnt the language by other means. Fluent Spanish, medieval German, Phoenician, obscure regional dialects – hundreds of authenticated case studies and papers had been compiled between herself and her mentor, Dr Emmett Donaldson.

Impressive stuff, incredible. Somehow too incredible to be real. Stuart hadn't voiced any doubt, but Calvan somehow sensed it, had suddenly asked him if, apart from Eyran, he knew anyone who had been in a coma. No, he hadn't. But, she pressed, he had probably heard of people who after being in a coma had suffered amnesia. Memory loss. 'Yes,' he'd answered. Calvan had succinctly pointed out that if a period of coma had the ability to wipe out memory, then a death certainly would. 'People tend not to believe in past lives simply because they themselves have no personal recall of a past life. Nothing tangible to which to relate. But that doesn't mean they haven't occurred. Most people under hypnosis do in fact recall past lives. And my colleague Dr Donaldson has had great success in sessions with young boys up to the age of seven while awake. After that, the ability to recall diminishes.'

Stuart could just imagine Calvan back in Virginia, pacing in front of first-year students, dazzling the class with the same graphic examples. Why was he still so sceptical?

Her parting words after the last session still rang in his mind: 'At least now we know it's a real past life, the danger of possible schizophrenia has gone. No more worries about a secondary character taking over.'

But Stuart hadn't felt any relief. Replacing something tangible – something to which he could strongly relate – with a concept he still couldn't quite grasp, just didn't sit right. Regardless of the obvious benefits stressed by Calvan.

When he'd first mentioned his doubts to Amanda about the continuing sessions, she'd quickly thrown in his face that he'd never been keen on them, and now at the first obstacle, the first turn in the road with which he didn't agree, he was ready to throw in the towel. 'Leave it to the experts, Stuart. It's their problem – why their walls are full of diplomas in psychoanalysis and yours aren't. You're never going to second-guess them at their own game.'

So that was how she saw it. The age-old argument. While it was *their* problem, he wasn't so obsessed with Eyran, he had more time to devote to his own family. To Tessa and herself. Eyran had conveniently been shoved off to the sidelines: someone else's problem. If Stuart called an end to the sessions, the problem of Eyran was back fully in their laps.

But Amanda's comment, however misguided, threw a starker light on his own doubt. He had originally hoped that the sessions would break down the barriers and imaginary characters in Eyran's mind. He would feel closer to Eyran again. The Eyran he remembered. But now the character was real, not imaginary. Not one that would be shifted by a few couch-side questions from Lambourne. And apart from worrying about where the future sessions with Eyran might now head, he wondered whether at heart it wasn't scepticism, but more that he didn't *want* to believe. Accept the reality of a secondary character who would always be with Eyran, however deeply buried in his subconscious. Yet again he would be sharing Eyran.

Time was too tight for the evening flight to Lyon, so Dominic decided to stay over another night at the Meridien Waldorf. He opted for an afternoon flight the next day so that he would be readily available through the morning for any news from Marinella Calvan. They had the final session at eleven o'clock, and he imagined that she would broach what he'd proposed either directly before or after the session, while both the Capels and Lambourne were present.

Though she'd voiced caution and doubt, her questions and keen interest had also displayed strong eagerness to help. Dominic was hopeful.

No call by eleven. Either she hadn't yet broached the subject, or it was too awkward to hold up the session or make the call while the Capels were still there. Or, if she got agreement, she might even plough straight in and ask some pertinent questions straight away. Another hour or so to wait.

Dominic felt at a loose end. He'd earlier phoned his Lyon office and gained an update on activities while he was away from Inspector Guidier, his second in command. He now phoned Guidier back and asked him to make contact with the Lyon Public Prosecutor's office. 'Try Verfraigne. It's just a hypothetical situation at this stage.' Dominic explained what he wanted: the likely prosecution procedure for a murder case reopened after over thirty years, any obvious pitfalls and obstacles. 'It wouldn't come under Lyon's jurisdiction, but Aix-en-Provence's. So the names of prosecutors and any likely chains of command for such a scenario there would also be helpful.'

Guidier was curious. 'Anything interesting?'

'Could be. Could be.' Dominic didn't want to say anything until Marinella Calvan had called, didn't want to tempt fate. But by starting the process, at least he had the feeling something was in motion. 'I'm leaving here at one-forty. But I won't be back in the office in Lyon until probably six or seven. Just time to pick up some files before I head down to Vidauban for the weekend.' He gave the hotel telephone number for any immediate news.

Dominic's second call was to Pierre Lepoille at Interpol. Lepoille was one of the best Interpol intelligence officers he knew. A researcher in his early twenties when they'd worked together at Interpol in Paris, now at forty-two Lepoille was a true scion of the electronic age – a walking encyclopaedia of random knowledge, with whatever he didn't know a few keystrokes away: Interpol's own secure network, the FBI's AIS program, Minitel or surfing the Internet.

Lepoille was part of the permanent backbone of intelligence staff who supported the shifting quotas of officers, like himself, on two-year assignments with Interpol, or liaised with the myriad of police forces worldwide. Gaining access, breaking codes, smashing deftly through virgin cyberspace barriers – few secrets could be safely cocooned from Lepoille's probing keystrokes. The thought of a criminal being apprehended in Kuala Lumpur from an initial inquiry from a backwater police station in Tupelo, Mississippi, all through a succession of quick-fire keystrokes, Lepoille found addictive.

His only other addiction was Gauloises, but since smoking was not allowed in the computer room, Lepoille's two vices were in serious conflict. Lepoille would grasp at any excuse to head to the canteen, lighting up as soon as he was out of the computer room, then would chain smoke, practically lighting one cigarette from the embers of another. But at some stage his withdrawal symptoms of being away from his computers would become stronger and he'd be eager to return. Dominic recalled many a chain-smoking canteen meeting with Lepoille.

'Dominic. Nice to hear from you. Been a while.'

They spent a few minutes catching up on the eight months since their last meeting before Dominic got to what he wanted: 'Psychics. Cases proven through psychic phenomena, as well as failed cases involving the same. With the latter, any obvious legal obstacles that came out of why the cases failed.'

'In France or beyond?'

'Mainly France. But any big landmark cases outside might also be useful.'

'Okay.' Lepoille didn't ask what it was for. Countless intelligence inquiries every week had numbed him to the unusual. He had become used to not asking.

Dominic left Lepoille his number at Vidauban for anything that might come through in the next day or two, then took a long deep breath and sat back. It was done. Everything put in motion. Nothing left but to see what came back in. He looked at his watch: 11:52 a.m. Calvan would be finished in just eight minutes. The phone could ring and he would know whether his efforts of the last fifty minutes had been wasted or not.

By twelve-fifteen, when there was still no call from Marinella Calvan, Dominic's nerves were frazzled and his doubts had returned in full force. He realized he'd probably been foolish, allowed his blind enthusiasm to take control, burying the doubts Calvan had flagged. Blotted them out in the same way that Christian didn't want to recall the murder. Alternative, mostly lame, excuses started to spring to mind as to why she hadn't yet called – and finally Dominic picked up the phone. The thought of another hour's phone-watching before he headed off for his flight, waiting anxiously to know, was unbearable.

'I'm afraid she's not here.' David Lambourne's voice. 'She's gone shopping. Some bits and pieces she needed to pick up apparently before her flight back to Virginia.'

'When is she preparing to leave?'

'Later this evening. Six-thirty, seven o'clock.' Brief silence. 'Anything I can help with, Inspector Fornier?'

'It was just that she mentioned she might call me.' If Lambourne knew anything, hopefully he'd speak up. But he just responded blandly, 'I see.' Dominic didn't want to prompt by asking, Didn't she discuss the matter with you? Too clumsy. 'Do you expect to see her later, or will she go straight back to her hotel?'

'She said that she'd probably call by for half an hour or so between three and four; there's some final notes she'd like to go over with me before leaving.'

Final notes? Dominic wondered if that was when she'd chosen to raise the subject with Lambourne, perhaps explained why she hadn't called so far. But by then he realized he'd either be waiting himself to board a flight or mid air on his way to Lyon. 'Can you tell her I called? It's very important. I'm flying out myself soon, but she could leave a message at my office or reach me over the weekend on this number.' Dominic gave Lambourne his Lyon HQ and Vidauban numbers and rang off.

Over the next twenty-four hours, Dominic see-sawed hopelessly between doubt and hope over what news might come from Calvan.

There was no news or message when he arrived at his office in Lyon at 6.40 p.m., only an urgent file on his desk from Guidier which needed to be checked before an *instruction* hearing Monday, and a note:

Verfraigne is in court until Monday. More information then. But his assistant knew the name of the Aix chief prosecutor: Henri Corbeix.

Dominic picked up the file and the note and phoned Monique to tell her he was on his way. He'd already phoned her once before boarding his flight, warned her they would be heading down to Vidauban for the weekend. Hopefully she would already have most things packed and prepared.

When he arrived, the suitcases were by the door, but she'd pan-fried some sea bass with peppers and dill on a bed of rice. His favourite. A glass of white Bordeaux was at its side. She'd already had hers, but she thought he might want something before the drive.

He grimaced apologetically. 'I'm sorry. I already ate on the flight. I'm not that hungry,' he lied. 'I should have told you when I phoned.'

Monique looked back towards the food. He wasn't sure if she was put out by his refusal, or simply working out what to do with the fish. He was eager to get away, see if there was a message on his Vidauban answerphone from Marinella Calvan – but now he felt guilty. 'How long will you be?'

'Five or six minutes. I just need to finish my make-up and throw a few more things in the overnight bag.'

'Well, now that you've prepared it, it looks too good to go to waste. I'll see what I can manage.'

By the time Monique was ready, he'd finished all of the fish, two-thirds of the rice, and downed the last gulp of Bordeaux as he picked up the first bags.

'Fire somewhere?' Monique asked halfway through the drive.

Dominic didn't realize till that moment how fast he'd been driving: 168 kmph, when his normal average was 130–140 kmph. He eased back to just over 150 kmph.

After the flight and the day's events, Dominic was tired. The oncoming headlights stung his eyes towards the end of the journey, particularly their stark glare on the unlit roads approaching Vidauban and the farmhouse. The drive had taken two hours twenty minutes rather than the normal two hours fifty.

But when he pressed the replay button on the answerphone, there were no messages from Calvan. Only one from Lepoille: 'Psychics. Interesting subject. Nothing much has come up in France yet, but I'm still trying. Quite a lot from America though, some of them big cases.

I'm on a short shift tomorrow – four hours starting at midday. We'll speak then.'

Monique caught his expression as he looked up from the machine. 'Anything wrong?'

'No, nothing. Nothing.' She'd probably picked up more on his anxiety than the short taped message. Calvan would be in the middle of a long flight back to Virginia, no more messages would come through that night. And with the time difference, the earliest he could now receive a call would be early afternoon the next day.

Monique sensed his restlessness the next morning. Conversation was stilted over coffee and hot bread. If it was warm enough, Monique usually served up outside, but with this morning's early crispness she wore a thick towelling robe over a T-shirt and jeans. Dominic wore a sweatshirt.

She wondered whether his tension was connected with the tape and transcript she'd read and his trip to London. Analysts, past-life regressionists, voices from the past, and now a message on their answerphone about psychics. Possibly it was all as strange to him as to her.

With the first tape, she'd pushed whatever emotions she might have had away, harboured doubts and used the mechanical exercise of preparing the questions both as a shield and to throw it back quickly in the lap of whoever had sent it: analysts, hoaxers, or whatever they were.

But with the transcript, she'd found herself wrestling with a fast-changing range of emotions: disbelief, anger, outrage that it might be a hoax, rereading segments over and over and searching for fault or possible invention, not *wanting* to believe – before final acceptance; an acceptance that cut through her and chilled her to the bone. It was Christian's voice. There was no doubt. She didn't know how or why, or even pretend to comprehend. But it was him. She did her duty; after three attempts to express her thoughts in a few lines without rambling or being too sentimental, she had faxed the short note back to London.

There had been no tears, then. They hadn't come till the next morning when she read back through the transcript. The first time she'd read it purely clinically, objectively: *Is this Christian's voice?* As if she was an expert character or voice analyst. But the second time, she actually attached Christian's voice, recalled its soft tones, its joy and vibrance, so open and innocent: *'It was made of shell, in the shape of an old galleon. The light inside made the shell almost transparent and direct light would also shine through the portholes. It was beautiful.'* And in that moment, she recalled Christian's face clearly, full of joy as Jean–Luc paid the rest of the money and the shopkeeper took the galleon down from the shelf and handed it to him. And all the other moments of him smiling suddenly flooded back: looking up at her with pride with one of his first drawings from school, her sewing the arm back on his Topo Gigio doll and his kiss of thanks, him asking for a story as she tucked him in bed, bright green eyes sparkling up at her. The soft touch of his small hands against her cheek. All gone now. *Gone.* Gone for so many years. So many.

The tears convulsed her in a sudden tidal wave, heavy racking sobs that shook her whole body uncontrollably. And she'd rocked slightly with their rhythm, muttering 'so many' at intervals, as if it was a mantra that would finally return some control, some normality. Sudden grief rising up and mugging her after so many years felt strange to her. She hadn't cried for Christian for fourteen years, since Jérôme's tenth birthday party, when she'd suddenly recalled a similar party for Christian, his last. But that didn't help, the recalled shame of not having grieved for so many years merely added poignancy.

Perhaps to cover her tears and confusion, she'd prepared one of Dominic's favourite dishes for when he arrived. There. See. Everything's fine. Normal.

She didn't say much on the drive, not wishing to bring up the subject in case her emotions and the tears welled up again. She'd read the transcript and identified the voice. She'd sent her fax back to London. She'd cried. It was over.

But then she became aware that Dominic wasn't saying much either and he seemed tense and anxious, was driving faster than normal. Now, sitting next to him while he sipped his coffee, she could feel the same tension.

'Did something happen in London? You seem anxious, as if you're waiting on some news.'

'Just tired.' Dominic forced a smile. 'And now having to face catching up on work. You know what it's like whenever I go away. Things pile up.'

'I thought it might have been something to do with the tapes and transcripts. That they'd somehow upset you.'

Dominic looked back at her. The stark morning light caught the lines of pain etched in her face. Lines he'd hoped had mellowed years ago. She was still incredibly beautiful, a dusky Sophia Loren with just a fleck of salt in her dark pepper hair. And if he smiled, she would smile in return, and they became laughter lines . . . the pain and sad memories would suddenly melt away. But he sensed she was speaking more for how she felt than for him: the tapes and transcripts had upset her. He reached one hand out and touched hers.

'Of course I was upset by them. But it was more concern for the effect they might have on you.'

'I cried a bit. But I'm okay now.' She forced a smile, felt her eyes welling slightly again. She'd planned not to mention her crying; some quick sympathy and a smile from Dominic and suddenly the words were out. He had that effect on her.

'Are you sure?'

She just nodded, looked down and sipped at her coffee.

Dominic wondered whether he'd done the right thing coming down to Vidauban for the weekend. It had seemed a good idea to get away, both for him and Monique. But now, having left his number with half the world, hoping to just sit back and relax while the calls flooded back in, he felt suddenly cut off, restless. Four hours to wait before Lepoille made contact, five or six for anything from Calvan. He could start on Guidier's file to kill the time, but he wasn't sure he'd be able to apply his mind effectively. He was too preoccupied.

And for Monique, he wondered whether Vidauban might be too nostalgic coming straight after her reading the transcript. The thought hadn't hit him until the night before as he turned into the driveway, as the farmhouse and its small courtyard were caught in the headlamps.

When they'd bought the farmhouse six years earlier, time enough seemed to have passed since Christian and Taragnon for it not to be a reminder. It was just a nostalgic link with an area they loved. It had also looked different to the Taragnon farmhouse – the front façade was flat. But three years ago he'd added a small office that jutted out into the courtyard, and from that moment it held a far stronger resemblance to it. Except that instead of the blank wall on the side of Jean-Luc's garage, a large window looked from his office on to the courtyard. And instead of open fields, it looked out across a small rockery garden sloping up to a few pine trees and a half stone wall twenty metres away, which separated them from the property next door. The only open fields were beyond the garden on the other side of the house.

After breakfast, Dominic retired to his office for lack of anything else to do. He shuffled some papers and files and glanced through the first pages of Guidier's file without them really grabbing his attention. Just after ten o'clock, Jérôme appeared on the patio for breakfast and Dominic came back out to say hello. Work was fine. Jacqueline, his girlfriend, was fine, Jérôme grimaced. She hadn't come over because he was heading off to see a friend in Montpellier. He would be staying overnight in Montpellier and would see them about midday the next day. 'A couple of hours' work on the computer and then I'm off.'

Computer. Dominic thought again of Lepoille. Three hours before he was in his office.

Dominic finally got into Guidier's file: motorbike mugging spree. Two youths on a bike averaging nine muggings a week over seven months had caused practically a mini crime wave. When they were finally apprehended, reported drive-by muggings dropped to no more than five a month.

When the phone rang at 1.10 p.m., he was fully immersed in the report, and it broke his attention abruptly. It was Lepoille. His enthusiasm was infectious, but Dominic found it hard to take it all in just over the phone: several cases in America tracked down through psychics, many of them notable – the 'Son of Sam' killings, the Yorkshire Ripper, the case of Mona Tinsley, Manson/Bugliosi: proving psychic influence over others to commit a murder. Some departments even had regulars they went to when everything else failed: Gerard Croiset and Peter Hurkos were the names that came up the most. But very little so far in France – 'except relatives in the Petit Grégory case contacting a psychic early on to discover if the boy was dead or just missing. The police here hardly ever seem to involve psychics; it's usually only instigated by relatives or sometimes the press. And rarely does it feature in official police filing or trial evidence. I'm tracking down a couple of leads in Paris; I'll know more on Monday. There's a stack of Interpol print-outs and e-mails on my desk. Some arrived late yesterday, but most of it came through this morning. I'll bike it over to you Monday.'

'Great. I'll look forward to going through it.' Hopefully in the reading something would leap out; nothing immediately had from Lepoille's quick-fire descriptions. 'And thanks for the help, Pierre.'

Six hours later, however, when there was still no call from Marinella Calvan, Dominic's excitement had dissipated, doubt set in again. Though this time, unlike before, it was set in concrete. Midday now in Virginia, his urgent messages left with Lambourne. She wasn't going to call. Perhaps she'd even been by the phone when he'd called Lambourne, signalling to make an excuse. When the package arrived from Lepoille, he'd probably just throw it straight in the bin. He'd been foolish to build up his hopes.

Marinella Calvan was on a United Airlines 19.50 flight back to Virginia. In the next seat was an overweight and over-friendly sales manager named Bob returning to Richmond, who she'd finally managed to extricate herself from with a few curt smiles to get back into the file on her lap.

She made notes on a fresh sheet of paper as she scanned back through the transcripts. Depth of detail had been remarkable. They effectively knew everything about Christian Rosselot's life: where he lived, went to school, daily and weekly habits, and a variety of rich recollections, some of which only the boy himself could have possibly known.

The last session she'd used mostly to fill in any gaps. But at one point she'd sat up sharply, her skin bristling as Christian talked about his best friend Stéphane. 'He also went to my school, but he lived on the far side of the village. It was Stéphane I was going to see the day I became lost in the wheat field . . . I never made it to his house.'

'And did you ever see Stéphane again?'

'No . . . no.'

Marinella was about to tap out: *'Tell me more about that day. Did you meet someone else? What stopped you from reaching Stéphane's house?'* But Lambourne was looking across sharply, and even Eyran's simple 'No' had been nervous and hesitant, his breathing more rapid. She could almost feel Fornier at her shoulder, pushing, urging. But even if she got past the first question without Lambourne cutting in, any upset to Eyran's mood and she might get nothing more the rest of the session. Her last opportunity. She moved Eyran away, back to earlier, happier times when he'd played with Stéphane.

Now she wrote: *The wheat field is not just a symbol for Christian's separation from his parents, but also perhaps his best friend. Christian might see Eyran as a replacement for that best friend – the friend he never got to see that fateful day.*

She'd tried to broach the subject of Fornier's quest at first gently, mentioning only that there might be a few more questions. But Lambourne looked immediately dismayed, mentioned that after the last tape Stuart Capel had complained about the pointed, angled questions making Eyran hesitant, almost defensive. 'I assured him that this last session would be far more open, allow Eyran freer range. What questions?' And she'd fluffed that they were nothing important: 'They'll wait.' With Lambourne and Stuart Capel concerned about even a few pointed questions, trying to derail into a full murder investigation was hopeless. At least she'd tried.

Shortly after the last session she'd been struck by another link: *There was a river running close to where Christian Rosselot's body was found, and in one of Eyran's dreams the brook by Broadhurst Farm featured, expanding into a large lake. Perhaps Christian believed somehow that if he'd have been able to cross that river, he would have escaped his attacker and avoided his fate. And in Eyran's dream the lake symbolized separation from his parents. But it is obviously Christian's separation which has the strongest connection with water.*

The debate with Lambourne over whose sense of separation was stronger – Christian's or Eyran's, past or present – was irrelevant. The links were all there. The Freud–devotees and conventionalists were going to love it. Object-loss symbols were classic.

And if they started to wriggle and defend, she had more than enough information with which to bury them: Dr Torrens' initial recommendation for therapy, his earlier EEGs recording brain-wave disturbance, Lambourne's sessions – his concern about dominance of the secondary character and schizophrenia – then finally Eyran speaking in French under hypnosis and her being called in. Over sixty pages of notes even before the three tapes and forty-six pages of transcript from her own sessions – now fully corroborated by a French chief inspector and his wife, not some fringe new-wave religion fanatics who'd named their children Rainbow or Stardust.

It was going to be a good paper, one of her strongest yet. Correction, it was going to be a *great* paper.

Marinella put on the headphones and flicked through the pop and comedy channels until she found some classical music: Offenbach's 'Barcarolle' was playing.

When she'd got back to Lambourne's from shopping, she'd heard that Dominic Fornier had called. She'd felt guilty about not phoning him back. The image of him walking away from their meeting, the die-hard detective shouldering the doubt through all those years, now clinging to one last hope, had stuck in her mind. She'd reached tentatively for the phone just before leaving her hotel for the airport – then decided against it. She'd call him tomorrow. Not sure immediately if she was just delaying facing his disappointment, or hoping for better words of explanation to settle in the meantime.

Grieg's 'Morning'. Soothing, relaxing. Hopefully she'd doze off soon. To her side, Bob was flicking through the in-flight magazine. But the next tunes – Brahms' Hungarian Dance No. 5 and Tchaikovsky's 'Marche

Slave' – broke her slightly out of her half-slumber, roused her spirits. She found herself tapping the armrest to the rhythm of 'Marche Slave' as she imagined the key points of her final paper being pounded home to the army of sceptics who had plagued her through the years.

Only when Mozart's Piano Concerto No. 2 came on could she feel waves of calm and relaxation again descend, sleep once more in sight.

But at the start of the third movement, the thought hit: *politician*.

The man Fornier had suspected was now a prominent politician! An MEP. Murder case. Reopened after more than thirty years. Implicating one of the country's leading politicians! If Fornier's suspicions were right, then it was going to be a big case. *Enormous case!* And one of the first ever proved through a past-life regression. The thoughts hit her in such quick-fire succession that it took her breath away.

She could see it all rolling out ahead: Oprah Winfrey was a given; she was already reading clippings from *The New York Times* and *Washington Post* in between make-up for Maury Povich and Larry King: *'I understand that in France this case is as big as OJ Simpson. But the added factor of core evidence coming from a past-life regression has literally split the French legal establishment in two.'*

The case was already great, but now within her grasp was the opportunity to make it phenomenal. If Fornier's hunch was correct and she played it right, it could dominate the American media throughout the trial. Eight months, a year? It would do more to aid the acceptance of PLR than anything previously conceived. The thoughts and images hit like so many cluster bombs: speeches, increased department funding, books, chat shows . . . *Newsweek* . . .

She felt breathless as they pounded home, suspended belief battling helplessly against the audaciousness, the ridiculous magnitude of it all – a laugh suddenly burst free. A laugh that quickly lost its hesitancy and became more raucous.

Bob was looking over and mouthing something. She pulled off her headphones.

'Is that the Bill Cosby?' he asked. 'Funny, isn't he?'

'Yeah. But not half as funny as Mozart.'

He looked puzzled and quickly buried his face back into the flight magazine. That should keep him quiet for a while, she thought.

Marinella put back the headphones and sank back into Mozart, slowly closing her eyes. Even if it turned out not to be the politician Fornier suspected, proving the guilt or innocence of the person already charged would still grab a few good headlines, be something of a first. She had to at least try. She'd for ever punish herself over the possibly lost opportunity if she didn't. It was probably best to phone Fornier after she'd spoken with Lambourne and Stuart Capel; she'd already raised his hopes once and let him down.

It wasn't going to be easy. All the obstacles with Lambourne and Capel that had made her finally step back from a hard push with Fornier's proposal still held true. She would need to be convincing.

32

Marc Jaumard followed close behind Marcel Gauthereau. If it was to happen at all, it would be inside, thought Jaumard. He would sign everything, Gauthereau and the notary would nod courteously, and then someone would slip from the shadows and slap down the summons. Stepping through the notary's door, he glanced back to check that Gauthereau didn't lock the door behind him. He'd also checked the brass plaque downstairs before following Gauthereau up two flights: Patrice Roussel, Notaire.

Roussel was in his late fifties, wispy greying hair, thin, pinched features and tight economical gestures. Polite nods, quick half-smiles without showing teeth as he took details, the same meaningless smile as he handed Jaumard's identity card back.

It was taking far longer than Jaumard had expected. The door to the reception had been half open at the beginning, he'd been able to keep one eye on the receptionist, see if she made a move to lock the door. See if anyone else suddenly came in. But she'd shut the connecting door on her way out from dropping a file on Roussel's desk halfway through.

The blood pounded through Jaumard's head as the papers were passed back and forth between him and the notary. Another question, another line filled in. Another stamp and seal with the notary's elaborate signature on top. Jaumard found himself half looking at the closed doors in between – expecting it to burst open at any second and the summons be served. He wiped the sweat from his palms on his trouser legs.

And suddenly the envelope was being passed across. Though maybe this was the summons, he thought with a jolt. He studied its front cautiously. Just his name and 'c/o Patrice Roussel' underneath. It certainly looked like his brother's handwriting. He hesitated – suddenly deciding against opening it in front of these two sets of prying eyes. He wanted to get out and away as fast as possible. Slipping it quickly into his back pocket, he stood up. 'Thank you, gentlemen.'

'I thought you might want to open it in my presence,' Gauthereau invited. 'In case there's something that needs my attention straight away.'

'No . . . no. It's okay.' Jaumard backed away to the door. 'I'll call you if there's anything. Thank you.' He opened the door and was out, quick smile to the receptionist, another door, and he was on the stairs – taking them two and three at a time, bounding frantically down the last flight until he was out on the street.

Gauthereau stared bemusedly after Jaumard for a second before saying his own goodbyes to Roussel. All those years of waiting, contact not made until a year after his last advert, and then all over in minutes. Gauthereau's curiosity had grown over those years as to what was inside the envelope: details of a hidden stash, a secret bank account, drugs routes, black book with key *milieu* contacts? Now he would probably never know.

Only once sixty metres clear, around the next corner, did Jaumard pause, let out a long deep breath as he rested his back against a wall. His nerves were still racing. He decided not to risk opening the envelope even there, and didn't do so until he was sequestered at the back of a small café almost half a kilometre away.

Apart from the barman, only three people were in the café, the lunchtime rush hadn't yet started. Jaumard felt safe from prying eyes as he opened the envelope. He had to read it twice before its significance really hit him. A smile slowly crossed his face. Quite a legacy his brother had left him. Alain Duclos, RPR MP for Limoges. Child murder case from 1963. A hit contract that was never fulfilled. Incredible. The three-page letter even suggested two possible courses of action, though he thought he knew already which he would take.

Marinella Calvan had been on the phone for over ten minutes to Stuart Capel, and whatever hopes she'd had earlier in the call she felt suddenly slipping away.

Her thoughts had gelled over the weekend on how best to broach the subject. Telling the truth wouldn't work. Eyran's therapy diverted to aid a murder investigation just wouldn't be accepted. But if she kept close to what she at heart believed, that Christian's non-acceptance of separation was far stronger than Eyran's, she might succeed. The sincerity and enthusiasm would come through in her voice. Following this belief also did much to bury her initial apprehension over her motives. By the time she'd worked up the story in her mind, adding embellishment from her notes, it had become the lead chariot, helping the murder investigation was merely tagging along behind.

But despite the strong case she put forward now to Stuart Capel – Christian's almost total erasure of the last hour of his life, the symbols in Eyran's dreams of the lake and the wheat field having far stronger relevance in Christian's life than Eyran's, that before they could fully get to grips with Eyran's acceptance of loss and detachment, they first had to tackle Christian's – he wasn't convinced. He hadn't said no, only that he wanted to think it over, 'we should speak again tomorrow'. But she had the feeling that he was merely delaying so that he could let her down softly.

She needed to add support to her argument. 'This isn't just my view, but also that of my previous department head, Dr Donaldson. He's had more years of experience in this than myself and David Lambourne put together.' Donaldson might well support her view, but during their earlier meeting he had merely nodded thoughtfully and passed a few minor comments. She wouldn't know his full opinion for probably a few days when he'd had a chance to study her notes and transcripts in more detail.

Silence from the other end. Perhaps he was becoming swayed. She pushed the advantage. 'Look – it would just be for two weeks. Four sessions at the most. I think that should do it. Then Eyran would be back to conventional therapy with David Lambourne.'

'It was actually David Lambourne I wanted to speak to before I decided,' Stuart commented. 'Have you spoken to him already?'

'No, I haven't.' If she had phoned Lambourne, he'd have said no. If Stuart Capel now contacted him, put out by the fact that she'd gone behind his back, that 'no' would be even stronger. Lambourne had given her Stuart Capel's number after the last session purely for her to verify some of Eyran's personal details for her paper. Last-ditch hope: brutal honesty. 'I didn't speak to him because I already know his point of view. He doesn't agree with my prognosis. That's why I called you directly. If you phone him, he'll only tell you the same.'

'I see.'

Swaying again, or perturbed by her sleight of hand? At least the ball was back between them. The main excuse for delay had gone.

Stuart recalled the look that Lambourne had fired Calvan when she'd broached the subject after the last session; he'd thought then they'd previously had words. At least she was telling the truth about that. 'Since you seem to know already what Lambourne's objections are, why don't you tell me?'

'It's simple. He thinks the solution is with Eyran in the present, I think it's with Christian in the past. Difference is, I have a stronger case to back up my argument. David's direction was floundering when I arrived, and all we've discovered since is that the imaginary character is a real life. Nothing more. Where's David going to head from here? He doesn't even have the secondary character to explore any more – conventional Freud is out of the window, and his expertise with PLT is limited. He's at a dead-end.'

'What if you're wrong?'

'There's always that possibility. But what is there to lose? Four sessions over two weeks and then I'm gone. David Lambourne has Eyran back to pursue whatever he wants to pursue. But if I'm right, it could be the breakthrough we've been looking for.' Hearing her own voice, its enthusiasm, she felt a sudden twinge of shame.

Two weeks? Stuart reflected. Eyran had already been in therapy five weeks and they were virtually back to square one. It didn't seem a lot to ask, and Calvan's arguments were convincing. But still he held strong reservations – partly his reluctance to accept this past character, partly the problems that might be caused with Lambourne – when another thought suddenly hit him: Amanda. If she learnt he'd said no, she would probably see it as just another prime example of him being obstructive, trying to be an armchair psychiatrist and map out what was best for Eyran despite expert advice to the contrary. 'Okay – I'll agree to the sessions. But just the four. That's it. And you'll have to phone Lambourne yourself and smooth the way with him. If he phones me afterwards, I'll confirm what we've agreed – but I don't want to get in the middle of any conflict between you.'

Stuart could tell by the brief pause at the other end that Marinella Calvan had been caught off guard by the sudden turn around.

'Yes . . . yes. Certainly. I'll call him.' One more obstacle to go. But Marinella was sure that Lambourne wouldn't roll over nearly so easily.

12.14 p.m. in Lyon. The session in London would already have started.

When the call had finally come through on Tuesday, Dominic had practically given up on hearing from Marinella Calvan. He'd phoned Lambourne's office on Monday only to get an answerphone. He didn't leave a message.

Marinella had started by apologizing for the delay. She'd wanted to work out what she was going to say, develop a particular theory in her mind before approaching Lambourne or Stuart Capel. She explained the theory and the agreement that had resulted to Dominic.

Surprise suddenly tempered his enthusiasm. 'They don't know it's to aid a murder investigation?'

'No. They'd never have agreed. But I'd already been partly exploring this theory for the benefit of Eyran's therapy anyway. It was something I'd voiced previously to Dr Lambourne, and later discussed with my colleague Dr Donaldson. He agreed with my prognosis: the main key lies with Christian in the past, not with Eyran. As much as I was keen to help you at the outset, I'm sure you can appreciate that ethically it would have been wrong to put your case before Eyran Capel's mental stability and health. It's just fortunate that in the end those aims coincide.'

Calvan went on to explain that if it got out that at the same time a murder investigation was being aided, it would cause problems. Dr Lambourne, in particular, had been difficult to persuade; he would no doubt quickly claim the investigation had been the prime aim all along, and try and halt the sessions. Later, particularly if anything worthwhile was uncovered from the sessions, details of the murder investigation would obviously come out – though by then hopefully the sessions would either be over or far progressed. 'Even then it should be admitted to only as a by-product of these extra sessions rather than the main feast. That you only saw the possibility of a renewed investigation when you saw the first transcripts. That is, *if* anything is uncovered.'

If. If. If. Dominic stared at the fax machine in the corner. The arrangement was that she'd fax through the transcript straight after the session. Thirty years of wanting to know and now only an hour remained. While he understood the reasoning, the duplicity of his little agreement with Calvan somehow added to his nerves. Only the two of them knew. It was almost incestuous. In the same way that he was keeping the secret from his wife, she in turn was duping Lambourne and Capel. So many secrets. Something was bound to go wrong.

Like two conspiratorial children playing hide and seek, hunting cloak-and-dagger style through the shadows of memories from thirty years ago. Excited by their little secret as much as the adventure. Unable to tell the adults who would say that they knew better and stop their little game.

The night before he'd had a clear opportunity to tell Monique – but still he put it off. If nothing was uncovered by Calvan or if it merely supported Machanaud's guilt, there was no point. If. If. If.

To support the theory Calvan had sold, he should be absent from the first sessions. Perhaps he could turn up at the third or fourth. They'd discuss it later. Meanwhile she'd fax transcripts through and would readily admit to doing so to Lambourne and Stuart Capel on the pretext of authentication and gaining 'advice on questions for future sessions'. How to guide Christian in the right direction. If Dominic then showed up for later sessions, it wouldn't seem strange; it would follow more naturally that he had by then 'stumbled' on information which might help the investigation.

But the forced detachment, his purposely being kept away from the activities in London, only made him more anxious, his nerve ends bristling because something was happening in a small room over 600 kilometres away over which he had no control. Christian's frail voice at that moment telling them the secrets of over thirty years ago and he wouldn't know for an hour. Or they would be close to finding out when Christian suddenly headed off at a tangent, and if he was there he could whisper sharply in Calvan's ear. 'No, no . . . take him back! Ask him this!'

The squad room was hectic: phones ringing, people calling across the room, typewriters clattering. Dominic had shut his door to concentrate on the normal morning's mountain of papers that required his quick attention: final approval of files to go to the prosecutor's office, an inquiry from Saint-Étienne over a pattern of regional car thefts, a medical report on a rape case. The noise of the squad room was muffled beyond his door, but still Dominic couldn't concentrate. The most he'd manage was a half-page before his thoughts once again drifted, wondering what was happening at that moment in London. And he would glance back at the fax machine: frustration because it symbolized his detachment and impotence at that moment, yet also hope. It was his *only* link with what was happening.

In the two days since Marinella Calvan's call, he'd received even more papers from Lepoille on cases involving psychics to add to Monday's package. He'd hardly looked at them. The last four days he'd been through enough of a ridiculous see-saw of hope and disappointment without putting himself through it again to no avail. Verfraigne from the Lyon prosecutor's office had called and given him the prosecution pecking order in Aix-en-Provence together with some names. He'd written them down, but hadn't called anyone. The list was tucked into the front of Lepoille's top file at the edge of his desk.

A stack of papers and thirty years of doubt waiting on one fax.

'Did you play much by the river with Stéphane?'

'Yes, quite a bit.'

'What sort of games did you play – did you ever swim in it?'

'No. It was too cold. But we used to play on the river bank.'

River bank. Where the police thought the boy was probably held between the sexual assaults. The memories from before open, carefree, not yet linked in Christian's mind. Only minutes before he'd mentioned the field close by. Marinella knew from her last session that Stéphane was one of his closest friends. It seemed as good a place to start as any.

The first ten minutes of the session had been spent with Lambourne taking Eyran back and then she had taken over. Perhaps it was her imagination, but Lambourne seemed to be taking longer than normal. Showing his resentment in the only way left to him.

She'd started with other times he'd played with Stéphane, their favourite places and games, introducing a general, relaxed mood. Christian was free to ramble, no constraints. But ever so slowly she circled in like a cat stalking its prey. The trick was that hopefully Christian was never aware of it. Already she'd struck out once and missed her target. Thinking that she'd asked enough general questions, she'd asked what had happened the day he headed off to see Stéphane but never made it. 'Did you meet up with someone else? What happened?'

Again Christian mentioned a searing bright light after a period of darkness, knowing in that moment that he was close to Stéphane's house as he recognized the field – but as recall of the attack flooded back, he quickly became incoherent. Eyran's head lolled, his breathing becoming laboured. She'd sensed Lambourne about to reach over to the keyboard as she broke Christian hastily away.

She circled more warily now. River bank? She didn't want to pounce too early this time. 'What sort of games did you play on the river bank?'

'We used to build a dam. There was a small stream higher up that flowed down from the hillside and into the river. In the summer it was usually dried up, but in the spring it used to flow in quite fast.'

'How did you and Stéphane make the dam?'

'We would get sticks and leaves and pack them in with mud. Stéphane would bring a spade with him so that we could dig a hollow. One day we dug an enormous hole to one side, then diverted the stream into it by blocking the way with sticks and leaves.' A fond memory, speech

319

animated, excited. Eyran's eyes glistened. 'The water built up and built up, until finally it started overflowing. It was incredible . . . almost like a small lake.'

Marinella remembered a segment from one of Lambourne's earlier taped sessions: *'The pond seemed suddenly to be much larger – like a huge black lake.'* She shot a meaningful glance at Lambourne. His face remained bland. Reluctance to admit any breakthrough, or perhaps he simply hadn't picked up on the connection.

'We would leave a narrow passage leading out, then block it with sticks and mud. Then, when it was full and almost overflowing, we would break the dam and run down alongside the sudden torrent until it hit the river.' A pause, excitement ebbing slightly. Eyran's expression more thoughtful. 'My mother didn't like me playing there. I would come back too muddy and dirty.'

Marinella let the moment settle. 'Did you ever play lower down the river bank?'

'Only a few times.'

'Were you often lower down the river bank on your own? For instance, when you cut across the fields and had to cross the bridge there?'

'Yes, sometimes.'

Gently. Gently. 'And at any time, did you meet anyone else there – at the lower part of the river?'

'No . . . no, I don't think so.' Eyran's brow creased. 'I don't remember.'

'The day you left to meet Stéphane but never made it, the day your bike broke down, did you meet someone lower down the river that day?'

'No . . . I didn't meet anyone there. I didn't cross the river there . . . I . . . I . . . there was . . .' Eyran broke off, swallowing hastily. He looked for a moment as if he was about to say more, but then the thought was lost.

Strike two. Marinella could almost feel Lambourne gloating behind her. When he'd discovered she'd gone behind his back, they'd had the worst argument yet. She said a lot of things she immediately regretted: too staid, limited P L T experience, merely clinging to what he knew for safety's sake, not for the patient's. Confirming his conventional status or perhaps his Englishness, Lambourne had been far less personal, kept mainly to patient/therapist ethics: it was his patient, he should have been consulted first, made the main decision. It had been wrong of her to contact Stuart Capel directly to sell her theory.

Fait accompli. The argument about what was already done predictably headed nowhere. She quickly put Lambourne on the spot by asking pointedly where he planned for the sessions to head next, then – in the face of a faltering and hesitant reply – rammed in with her own solution. 'If I'm wrong, what have you lost? Two weeks. After that, you've got the patient back to explore what you like.' She wasn't doing this for her health: she already had what she wanted, more than enough to compile a paper. And she'd been away from her son now for a week. 'I need another two weeks away like a hole in the head. I'm only doing this because I strongly believe it will work.'

Gradual teetering with each blow. Lambourne was stuck for an answer. But it was a reluctant submission with a cautionary note. He was still far from convinced about her theory. 'One foot-fault, one hint that you're getting close to an area that might adversely affect my patient, and I'll stop the sessions.'

She could feel Lambourne hovering now. Gloating that he hadn't even needed to intervene. She'd made her own foot-fault. The session wasn't heading where she wanted. He'd been right, she'd been wrong.

She suddenly felt the pressure of the small room closing in on her. Lambourne's gloating, Fornier waiting in a squad room in the middle of France for her fax, the ridiculous chess game of secrets they were both playing, Philippe waiting expectantly to translate her next question, her own ambitions . . . now slipping away again by the second.

She'd followed Dominic's cue to go back to when Christian first met someone, before the boy sensed any danger. But all she'd discovered was that Dominic was right: it probably wasn't Machanaud, unless Christian met him later. Christian hadn't met anyone by the river. But if not there, where?

'When your bike broke down, did you cut across the fields behind the village? Where did you go?'

'I hid my bike in some long grass, then I headed down towards the road.'

'Then where?'

'I started walking along the road towards the village.'

Fornier had mentioned that nobody in the village had seen the boy. 'Did you reach the village? Did you see or meet anyone there?'

'No . . . a car stopped. A man offered me a lift.'

Marinella controlled her hands from shaking on the keys. The information had in the end come up suddenly, like a mugger in a dark alley. She quickly hid her surprise. Lambourne wouldn't expect the information in itself to be particularly alarming; it was only her, what she knew it would signify to Fornier.

'What sort of car was he driving?'

'It was a sports car. A green sports car.'

'What make was it?'

'I don't remember. The man told me . . . but I forgot.'

Marinella's hands paused on the keys. Perhaps she would return later. The information was there somewhere. 'And what did the man look like?'

'He was quite thin with dark hair.'

'Was he young or old?' Marinella noted Eyran's brow creasing as Philippe translated. Remembering that to a ten-year-old everyone seems old, she added: 'Was he younger or older than your father?'

'Younger. At least five years younger.'

'What happened then? Did you drive through the village?'

'No. He offered to drive me back to where the bike had broken down. I told him it was all right – but he insisted. He stopped at the side, turned, and started driving back.'

As Christian described heading back along the road, then them turning into the rough farm track which led to his bike, Marinella tried to imagine herself in the car alongside him, this young boy from over thirty years ago who had less than an hour to live. *What did he see or notice that might now help?* Faint beads of sweat had broken out on Eyran's top lip. She could sense his nervousness. She asked him what the car was like inside.

'The dashboard was wood, and there was hardly any back seat – just a narrow bench.'

'As you went up the lane, did you see anyone else – even in the distance?'

'No . . . the field was empty. I pointed to where to stop . . . where my bike was . . . was hidden in the long grass.'

Tension was thick in the small room. Eyran's breathing was laboured, his eyes flickering slightly, anticipation and fear of what lay ahead starting to grip him harder.

She feared that at any second Lambourne would reach forward and stop her. Knew that if she pushed too hard – pushed Eyran over the edge into a catatonic state – it could be the last session. But the desire to know what happened next was too compelling. Like an incurable gambler, she couldn't resist one last bet, one last question. 'When you reached the bike – what happened?'

'The brake was jammed on the wheel. The man tried to free it – then suddenly he reached out and touched me . . . then he . . . he . . . gripped me . . . me haaarrd . . . pulling . . . I . . . th . . . theerrr –'

Marinella could see Christian's panic descending like an express elevator – and went to break him away before Lambourne intervened. But Christian's expression suddenly changed, settling slightly.

'Theerre was . . . something . . . something from before . . . before we turned into the lane. A truck passed us.'

It took Marinella a second to catch up with the sudden leap. 'Did the driver see you?'

'I don't know . . . I'm not sure.'

'What did the truck look like? What did it say on the side?'

'It was grey, very long. It had MARSEILLE on the side . . . and the letters V-A-R . . . N.'

'Anything else? Can you see anything else?'

'No, just Marseille . . . Marseille. I remember going there once with my father. We went to the harbour and watched the fish being landed . . . the fishermen with their nets . . .'

Marinella lost Christian at that moment. A day out in Marseille with his father. Bright-coloured fishing boats. Bouillabaisse in a harbourside café. A pleasant, rambling story: happy memories again. She was happy for a break in mood from the clawing tension – but frustrated minutes later when, letting the story run its course, she wasn't able to get Christian back again to the lane. The thread had gone.

Quite a move. Christian had shifted to where he knew she would be keen for more information, jumped back a question – then deftly skipped to where he felt more comfortable. His influence over the direction of questions was stronger than she'd given him credit for.

Though twenty minutes later when she faxed the transcript to Dominic Fornier, as pleased as she was with the information gained, it struck her that between weaving around threatening chasms of panic and Christian shifting scenes to suit, it might be the only information they would get.

The transcript had arrived only minutes before and Dominic was scanning it frantically. A short handwritten note from Marinella Calvan was at the front:

Breakthrough! You were right – it wasn't the poacher Machanaud. Or at least it doesn't sound like him. Hope it's helpful.

Dominic was eager to get to the part that revealed it wasn't Machanaud – but his attention was wavering. He could see Guidier standing by the door expectantly.

'It's just the report from Saint-Étienne,' Guidier said. 'There's some urgency involved because they already have someone in custody. They've either got to file and charge him quickly or release him. They need the comparison report on car thefts back from us straight away.'

'The day your bike broke down, did you meet someone lower down the river that day?'

'No . . . I didn't meet anyone there. I didn't cross the river there . . .'

Dominic looked up sharply. Only 'Saint-Étienne', 'urgency' and 'custody' had registered. 'Yes, yes . . . I know. I'll deal with it. But I need ten minutes alone. Ten minutes!' Dominic made a pushing gesture with one hand. 'Shut the door behind you and make sure nobody else disturbs me. And no calls.'

Dominic looked straight back to the transcript, his mind screaming *where? who?* He hardly heard the click as Guidier shut the door, one finger tracing rapidly down the page . . . *Christian walking down the road from where he left his bike* – they'd been wrong, he *hadn't* cut across the fields – until a few lines later the words hit him like a hammer blow: sports car; *green car*; slim, dark hair; *Duclos!* Duclos had picked up Christian before he even reached the village!

Dominic closed his eyes for a second. He'd always suspected, though now it struck him that it had never been more than that. He'd buried his suspicion, his doubt, in the *instruction* and trial process, with the witnesses who had said they'd seen Duclos in the restaurant, in the general throng pushing towards Machanaud and away from Duclos. And the thirty years since had buried it still further. Amazing that any glimmer of doubt had survived, he thought sourly. Just enough to occupy his mind for a few minutes every decade. Pathetic. If he'd really been convinced of Duclos' guilt, then he wouldn't have been so shocked as he read the words, felt suddenly cold and desolate, his stomach sinking still further as he forced his eyes open again and read Christian's description of the car turning and heading back, the rough farm track and him pointing to where his bike was hidden among the long grass, Christian's growing panic as Duclos reached out and touched him . . .

Or was it his own guilt at staying silent suddenly hitting him? Machanaud's innocence and the long years he'd spent locked away? Until a moment ago that too had been no more than a nagging doubt.

V-A-R-N? Marseille-based truck? Nothing immediately sprang to mind. Dominic read the remaining page of the transcript, then went back, honing in on where Christian was with Duclos, rereading individual lines for finer detail and small nuances. Then he went back to the beginning of the transcript and read it through for anything else he might have missed.

At length he looked up, rubbing his eyes. The elation that he had something that put Christian in Duclos' car, finally after all these years, rose slowly above the shock and emptiness, and he clung to that, forcing it home stronger, *yes!* He rapped one hand sharply against the desk, urging himself on. The possible start of a new case where before he had nothing. Something he could send a prosecutor. He drew on that new energy over the next hours.

Immediately after dealing with the Saint-Étienne inquiry, he tackled the mounting stack of papers from Lepoille at the corner of his desk – Manson, Hurkos, Joseph Chua, Geller, Berkowitz – sifting through the murky depths of murder cases involving psychics. Searching for the few key points that might entice a prosecutor's interest. By late afternoon, he had finished his notes and put them into a five-page covering letter to Henri Corbeix. After giving the background of the original case and trial, much of the letter was exploratory, questioning. Seeking the best way forward, procedural process, what they should look for in the sessions remaining and requisite validation beyond Monique's confirmation and the credentials of Marinella Calvan and David Lambourne. His reference notes to past cases involving psychics came at the end of the letter, and he attached the relevant files from Lepoille.

Despite the exploratory tone of the letter, it struck Dominic that his underlying aim had still shone through: convincing Corbeix that this most unlikely of cases stood some chance of successful prosecution.

33

Large eyes, full of passion, willing him on. Light hazel with grey flecks. The edges of the dream were less distinct, hazy, but the sensations burnt through strongly. Alain Duclos was excited.

The boy was quite young, not yet twelve. It was the boy he'd been with on his last trip to Paris. He couldn't remember his name, only that he was half Haitian, half French.

He could see the faint sheen of sweat on the boy's cream-brown skin, but the main excitement of the dream was that it was all so tactile – he could *feel* the sweat, feel its warm moistness as he slid back and forth and the boy looked back at him. Feel the smooth contours of the boy's body, the lean plane of his back, one thumb sliding slowly up the ridge of his spine. Then spreading slowly, out and around the stomach as he leant forward, feeling the warmth of the body tight against him . . . moving his hands slowly up the boy's ribcage and on to his chest . . . until he felt . . . *felt* something . . . something was wrong! The chest was too developed, too soft and fleshy. He recoiled suddenly in horror. The boy had breasts!

The boy's smile turned slowly to a leer, and as Duclos looked closer through the haze of the dream, he could see that the hair was not dark and wavy but short and blonde. It was Bettina. She'd tricked him!

She slowly pouted and blew him a kiss, but he felt suddenly repulsed. Sweat that smelt now like acid and roses, its stickiness against his skin, her attempt at a look of burning passion little more than leering stupidity . . . she made him sick. A sour bile rose in his stomach, a sense of utter disgust, and he mouthed 'You tricked me!' as he went to push her away.

But suddenly she was below him and holding tight, looking up with big liquid eyes staring straight through him, not saying anything but silently pleading 'I want you . . . I want you. Give me a child!' Gripping tight with her arms and legs wrapped solidly around his back, pulling him closer into an embrace, her tongue darting out and moistening her lips . . . he couldn't get away. The stickiness of her skin clung all around him, the grip of her arms and legs like some slithering, repulsive reptile . . .

the musty, acrid smell of her sweat, the darting snake's tongue – and he started protesting, screaming, 'No . . . *no* . . . You tricked me! Let me go . . . let me go . . . let me . . .'

Duclos sat up in bed with a jolt, his eyes slowly adjusting in the dark. The sweat felt suddenly cold on his skin. He looked over. Bettina was still asleep, he hadn't disturbed her.

I want a child. The first time she'd mentioned it had been almost three years earlier. She would be thirty-six next birthday; if they didn't have one or two children by the time she was forty, by then it might be too late. *Two?* He was still struggling with the unthinkable of one. She'd misread his look, fought to be reassuring. 'I know it hasn't been easy for you with me at times . . . and mostly my fault because of my past problem. But this is important to me. I'll make an effort, I promise.'

A nightmare come true. He was sick with flu for over two weeks. Probably psychosomatic. But then he had to become more inventive: headaches, allergies, sprained muscles, sudden business trips, stress and overwork . . . the chain of excuses became laughable, pathetic. She wore him ragged, he virtually broke out in a cold sweat each time she smiled at him approaching bedtime.

Though between the various excuses and trips away, miraculously he managed to succumb to sex no more than once every eight to ten weeks. Even then he would fail the occasional performance halfway through, claiming that he was too tense or that he could sense she was nervous, was perhaps trying too hard. At most there would be three or four occasions a year where she could possibly conceive.

But it was probably the worst possible time for the problem to have arisen. The calls from Marc Jaumard had started at the same time. Five years with no calls, then one out of nowhere. Duclos could hardly believe it. Only months after Chapeau's death, he'd erased thoughts of any possible repercussions from his mind, felt confident he was free of the problem once and for all. All those years with no blackmail, the first years of happiness with Bettina, and now both problems were plaguing him at the same time. Duclos shook his head. It was like some ridiculous cruel joke.

Marc Jaumard didn't have the same abrasive, taunting style as his brother, but on several occasions he'd been drunk, as if he needed Dutch courage before making the call. Duclos didn't want Jaumard calling his office, so gave him his home number. Often the calls would come through at night, probably after Jaumard had staggered out of some bar, and with him having to subdue his voice and often leaving for an impromptu meeting, Bettina had become suspicious.

During one of their failed lovemaking sessions, she'd rolled over furiously and asked him if he was having an affair – who was it that kept phoning? The thought of him in bed with the unkempt, overweight Jaumard, invariably Pernod-breathed, made him laugh out loud. One time when Jaumard woke them up with a 2 a.m. call and Bettina was staring at him accusingly, he'd thrust the phone out angrily: 'See for yourself. It's just some drunken arsehole.'

A second's silence from the other end as Jaumard got over the surprise, then slurringly Jaumard apologized for phoning so late. 'It's jussst . . . jusst some business with your husband.'

He'd thought the jealousy, her concern that he might be having an affair, could have partly been behind her new amorousness – but removing that worry had made little difference. She was as relentless as ever. Finally, eight months later, she became pregnant. All his efforts had been to no avail. She was now in her fourth month.

When she'd first told him, a chill had crept up his spine. His reaction perplexed him at first. He should have been relieved. The ordeal was over. No more bedtime demands. She finally had what she wanted. What had worried him more? His loathing of their having sex or her getting pregnant?

But months later, when she suggested a scan to check that the baby was healthy, he found himself about to protest at the idea – before realizing he had no good, rational grounds against a scan. Except one. In that moment, the root of his worry suddenly hit him. He was afraid to know it might be a boy! A girl, fine, and even a boy in those early years. But as it became older, started to remind him of the boys he sneaked off to see in Paris and Marseille, he would feel unsettled. His own son. Those big, innocent eyes staring straight through him . . . somehow sensing his awful secret. He could hardly think of a worse nightmare.

Dominic spoke to Corbeix late on Friday. Corbeix had been busy in court most of the day, apologized that as yet he'd only had half an hour to skim through the letter and the files sent. 'It looks intriguing. But give me the weekend to look through it in more detail. Let's speak Monday.'

Shortly after sending everything to Corbeix, the questions started turning in Dominic's mind: what happened immediately after Christian was by his bike with Duclos? According to the original medical report, the first sexual assault. But where had Duclos kept Christian afterwards, between the two attacks? Tied up somewhere near his bike? Or did Duclos take him straight to where he was finally found, perhaps hidden in the woods somewhere upstream from Machanaud? Whichever, the café in between had obviously been meant to create an alibi. It never occurred to them that Christian might have been tied up and left alone for all that time; it was always assumed that his attacker had stayed with him throughout, wouldn't risk leaving him to be found by someone else. If the boy had been discovered, his attacker could have returned straight into the arms of a gendarme welcoming party. Duclos had taken quite a risk.

'But I didn't realize it till I came out of the darkness. The field . . .'

Darkness mentioned again on the tape. A period of darkness between the first and second attacks. Probably a blindfold. He'd discussed it on the phone with Marinella Calvan late on Thursday, linking details from the transcript with what was known from the original investigation. Guide points for the next session.

Green sports car? Christian hadn't said that it was an Alfa Romeo. It could be argued that there were other green sports cars in the area at the time. Already he found himself pre-proposing the points that Corbeix might raise.

By mid afternoon Monday, with no call from Corbeix, other concerns sprang to mind: perhaps Corbeix was staunch RPR and wouldn't dream of going near the case? He phoned Verfraigne and, at the end of a conversation about Corbeix's overall strength and track record as a prosecutor, asked casually about his political leaning. 'He's a socialist, I think.'

Surely he'd made allowances for the tenuous nature of the case in his opening letter? He was just seeking guidance at this stage, what they should be looking for in the remaining sessions, what might help turn the case from something purely tentative, exploratory, into something prosecutable. Surely Corbeix wouldn't just cast it aside at this first stage, surely . . .

Corbeix's call came through finally at just after five o'clock, suggesting a meeting for eleven-thirty the next day. Dominic remembered that at that time Marinella Calvan would be in the midst of the second session, and suggested a delay until two-thirty or three. 'By then, I could bring another transcript with me which might throw more light on the case.'

Corbeix agreed to three o'clock. No indication either way as to what he thought, reflected Dominic. It had taken him a moment to recognize

Corbeix's voice. Husky, slightly breathless, it was almost a different voice to that on Friday. Corbeix had kept things short and seemed eager to get off the line.

When the transcript arrived the next day, the period between the two attacks, the *darkness*, was no longer a mystery: '. . . *just a spare wheel. Space was very tight. I was curled up around it . . . I could hardly move.'* Dominic's hands were trembling by the time he finished reading. He closed his eyes and breathed deeply, fighting to settle his nerves. Forcibly tried to return to some calm and rationality before he left to see Corbeix.

Dominic had photocopied the transcript. He followed down in his copy as Corbeix read his:

'*Let's move on to after when you were by the bike. You mentioned a period of darkness. Why was it dark?*'

'*I was in the boot of the car . . . the man's car.*'

'*The same man with you by the bike?*'

'*Yes.*'

'*Was there anything else in the boot with you – any bags or luggage? Anything that you could see or feel?*'

'*No . . . just a spare wheel. Space was very tight. I was curled up around it . . . I could hardly move.*'

'*Were you tied up?*'

'*Yes . . . my hands and my feet. And a cloth around my mouth.*'

'*Could you move at all?*'

'*Just a little . . . backwards with my legs. But I only tried once – when we'd stopped and I heard some voices outside. I kicked against the side of the car.*'

'*Do you think they heard you?*'

'*No. After a second I heard a car door shut and the sound of a car starting and driving away.*'

'*Was it a woman or a man you heard?*'

'*Two women.*'

'*And while you were stopped, did you hear anything else?*'

'*Only traffic passing. Some other cars pulling up and leaving . . . but most were more distant. No other voices.*'

'*Going back before – before you stopped. Could you hear anything? Could you tell which way you were heading?*'

'*No . . . not really. After a moment I could tell that we were passing some buildings – but I wasn't sure if it was Taragnon or Bauriac. I couldn't tell which way we'd headed.*'

'When you stopped, how long did it seem you were there for?'

'At least half an hour . . . I'm not sure. I became tired. It was very hot inside there. At one point I fell asleep. I was thinking about my father as I fell asleep . . . I started dreaming about him.'

'What did you dream?'

'I dreamt that I was in my camp at the farm, and my father was in the courtyard at the bottom of the field. I leapt up to surprise him and started waving . . . but he couldn't see me.'

'Were you upset that he couldn't see you?'

'Yes, I started running towards him, waving more frantically and shouting . . . but still he didn't see me. And finally he just turned and walked back towards the house. I felt that he'd deserted me. I kept thinking, why doesn't my father come out and find me . . . why doesn't he . . . he . . .'

'Was the camp somewhere you used to play often?'

'Yes . . . it was one of my favourite hideaways.'

'And did you ever take your friends there?'

'Only Stéphane once. But there was another place we used to go together. A camp we made in a tree hollow not far from where he lived . . . we would . . .'

Christian went off at a tangent describing his hideaway games with Stéphane, which linked in turn to recall of other times Christian had hidden: the roof eaves at the farm, a stock cupboard at school. Marinella wasn't able to get him back to the car boot to discover what happened next.

The early part of the session had been general detail to settle Christian into the mood, then she had tried to continue from where Christian had left off last time: sitting by his bike with Duclos touching him. Christian's responses were mostly garbled, incoherent – and two aborted attempts later Marinella changed tack abruptly to after the bike, honing in on the period of darkness. As Corbeix came to that part, Dominic noticed him flinch slightly, his mood discernibly darker and more intense.

Dominic had felt his blood run cold at the thought of Christian tied like a trussed chicken in the cramped darkness of the car boot while Duclos sat in the restaurant and sipped at a glass of chilled Chablis. Was it just for an alibi, or was Duclos calming deciding, while he sipped at his wine, what he was going to do next with the boy? Kill him, or perhaps a bit more buggery beforehand? Perhaps he should choose his dessert first and then decide. *Bastard!*

Despite a conscious effort to calm himself during the previous two hours, Dominic knew his reaction might still be volatile if Corbeix started to propose soft options.

Corbeix rubbed the bridge of his nose and looked up. 'In your initial letter you mentioned that Duclos' main alibi was him being seen in the restaurant. How long was he there?'

'An hour, an hour and a quarter perhaps.'

'So in total the boy could have been in the car boot as much as an hour and a half?'

'Yes.'

As Corbeix went back to reading, for the first time Dominic glanced around the room: trophy for squash, Toulon 1988; three more trophies with inscriptions too small for him to read. Harbourside photo with Corbeix, his wife and two young girls, presumably his daughters, smiling proudly beside a speedboat that hardly looked big enough to carry them all. Family photo with Corbeix, wife and four young girls ranging from seven or eight to early teens. Corbeix the sportsman and family man.

In his late forties, Corbeix was a little shorter than Dominic, broad and quite lean, a squat bullish figure. 'A powerful presence in court', according to Verfraigne. 'Relentless' if he strongly believed in a case. He had thick wavy black hair swept back and piercing dark brown eyes, his eyelids deeply hooded. Eyes that seemed to tire slightly with the reading, or perhaps simply become more sullen and grave as Duclos' actions sank home.

Computer replacing the old black typewriter; air-conditioning instead of a fan; beige carpet over the tiled floor. Minitel and fax. Apart from that the Palais de Justice offices were much as they were thirty-two years before.

It seemed somehow surreal that all those years had passed since he sat in a similar office with Perrimond, Poullain and Naugier. A young gendarme merely washed along on the tide of events. This time he had the chance to make his mark. But despite that, he couldn't help reflecting ironically that today might not be that different. He would still be a passenger aboard the direction Corbeix chose.

When Corbeix had finished reading the transcript, he spent fifteen minutes going back between the two transcripts and Dominic's original letter and the files he had sent, mostly clarifying points with Dominic about the original investigation – timing of the attack, forensics, Duclos' reported movements before and after, and the prosecution path and trial procedure pursued with Machanaud – before finally returning to the current information and how it tied in.

When the files had initially arrived with Corbeix, he'd started reading the attached transcript as if it was from a new witness, before realizing it was meant to be the victim's voice gained through a past-life regression on a psychiatrist's couch. He'd almost sent the files straight back with a note: *'You must be joking!'* But then he read beyond the first page of the covering letter from Fornier and started through the attached files: Calvan's and Lambourne's credentials, medical and psychiatric evaluations, past authenticated PLR cases, past investigations involving evidence from psychics – struck not so much by the credibility they strove to lend the transcripts, but the strong plea he sensed behind. Fornier had gone to a lot of trouble to prove this case was prosecutable. More effort than most investigators went to from the slough of mediocre police paperwork which crossed his desk. And then he saw why: Fornier had married the victim's mother. The first hurdle to be tackled.

Not sure how to broach the subject tactfully, Corbeix went through the thought processes very much as they'd hit him. 'Someone else's name should be on the files as leading the investigation. If your name's there, it could be argued there's personal bias. Your judgement has been coloured.' Corbeix suggested a name: Gérard Malliéné, an Aix-based inspector. Dominic didn't know him. Corbeix quickly salved his look of concern. 'It would still be very much your investigation. It's just a name to head the files. It's his jurisdiction and he's detached from any personal involvement. You'll be named in an advisory capacity for input from the original investigation. In reality, the investigation will run the other way around: you'll lead, Malliéné will lend an impartial voice, advise where he can.'

Initially put out by the suggestion, Dominic understood Corbeix's rationale. At least it meant Corbeix had been thinking seriously about the case. 'So you think there's a chance of launching this case successfully?'

Corbeix held one hand up. 'That's not what I'm saying. There're grounds for an investigation, no more. Enough to reopen the case for a *commission rogatoire générale* which I'll get an examining magistrate to sign off first thing tomorrow. But a case for prosecution is another matter. We don't have nearly enough yet, and I'm still waiting on some outside input.' Corbeix glanced towards the files Dominic had sent. 'One of them is the prosecutor mentioned in the Petit Grégory case you sent through. The other a legal expert at the Sorbonne, apparently strong on "procedural structure for the unorthodox".'

A weekend of notes and two twenty-minute phone conversations earlier that day and the prospects looked dismal. Psychics were used, but their testimonies rarely featured in case preparation. In the Yorkshire Ripper case the suspect had already been interviewed and eliminated, but a psychic later described his truck and the police returned to question him. Final trial papers were prepared on other evidence uncovered and subsequently a confession. The psychic's lead didn't feature. The cases with the Petit Grégory, Stanley Holliday and 'Son of Sam' were similar. Final prosecution relied almost exclusively on other evidence or a final confession. As Corbeix delivered his stark summary, Dominic's expression clouded.

Corbeix grimaced apologetically. 'It's almost as if investigators are afraid to mention the involvement of psychics in court. I suppose going to a psychic is a sort of admission of defeat for them: all our normal investigative skills and channels have failed, so now we're coming to you. Investigators are reluctant to admit that. Or perhaps they're advised of the difficulty of convincing a jury by a prosecutor like myself.'

'But in the case of Thérèse Basta . . .' Dominic tried to recall the name from his file notes a few days back. 'I thought there was quite a lot of psychic evidence presented in court.'

'Teresita Basa. Joseph Chua recalling details of her murder through voices in his dreams. Yes, nearly all of his evidence was presented in court – but the first hearing resulted in a hung jury. If it hadn't been for the killer's confession and a change of plea to guilty, the case probably wouldn't have been successfully prosecuted.' Corbeix observed Dominic look down and to one side, as if searching for a thought just out of reach. 'I noticed a lot of your files were from Interpol General Reference.' Corbeix knew that only Central Reference carried official police and court records. General was from outside, mostly newspapers, independent reports or extra-curricular police notes. Corbeix patted the files. 'Newspapers are often keen to report on cases involving psychics. Good copy. In cases with no other leads, the police will also admit to speaking with psychics. But preparing for the trial, the psychics invariably get forgotten.'

'What about the Manson/Bugliosi case?' Dominic asked.

'Different. More thought transference and influence than pure psychic evidence, and even then still a very difficult case to prove. A landmark case at the time. The case was built mainly on the premise of one person strongly influencing others – which is quite widely accepted. Whereas what we have here – past lives and reincarnation – is not. There's never been a case like this before.'

'There has, apparently – two. Both in India.' Dominic relished the brief surprise on Corbeix's face. One small victory swimming against the increasing tide of defeat. 'Marinella Calvan will get more information from her colleague Dr Donaldson and let me know tomorrow.'

'Yes . . . yes. I'd be interested. But I'm not sure how much it will help us.' Corbeix shrugged. 'India. In a way it underlines my last point. There, reincarnation is accepted – here it is not.'

Initially Dominic thought Corbeix was hopeful; there was a case to answer. Now it seemed all the avenues were blocked. They were almost back to where he'd been at the outset: thinking that approaching a prosecutor was pointless.

'Many of the cases you've mentioned appear to have succeeded through the police requestioning suspects and gaining confessions,' Dominic commented. 'With this new evidence we might be able to confront Duclos from the perspective that we *know* how he did it, know that he sat in the restaurant with the child in the car boot between the two attacks. The position is surely now far stronger to achieve that.' Tone too venturesome, tenuous, thought Dominic. Sounded how he felt: clutching at straws.

'It helps. But in most of those cases, there was usually some other hard evidence in place before the police pressured for a confession. That's what we're missing. And in the case of Duclos, a wily politician and past prosecutor, we'd be lucky to get past his hot-shot lawyer who'd first review how we got all of this marvellous information. Even if we were lucky enough to get Duclos in for questioning, he'd either say nothing or deny; either way he'd know we couldn't pursue with what we had.'

Dominic gripped tight at the transcripts in his hand. To get this far and let everything slip? An image of Duclos raising his glass, gloating. A sense of loss, of despair that what before seemed almost within grasp was now slipping away. A cold sinking pall that jarred against his nerves, against every precept of true justice – however much he should have been hardened the past thirty-five years to the fact that the law and justice were so often at odds. However much he realized Corbeix was probably right.

At his crestfallen look, Corbeix felt the need to buoy his spirits. 'Hopefully in the next day or so we might get some useful input from the people I've been in touch with,' he said. Concerned that Dominic's personal links and absorption with the case might lead to false expectancies, he'd accentuated the negative so there were no illusions about the enormous obstacles faced. But now he feared he might have painted too dark a picture. 'I prepared this earlier – key points which I thought would help strengthen the case. Some are essential, others merely desirable.'

Dominic took the single sheet from Corbeix and read:

1. *Psychic evidence. Little or no presentation of it in trial papers or court. Strong angle required beyond purely authentication of PLR.*

2. *Fresh clues or tangible evidence, uncovered from the sessions, that clearly ties Duclos in with the boy and can be corroborated independently. Perhaps someone who saw the boy in Duclos' car.*

3. *Duclos' background with young boys. Duclos is apparently married. A claim that he has no history with young boys, yet this one day, totally out of the blue, he sexually molests and kills this particular young boy, would not appear credible to an examining magistrate or jury.*

4. *Authentication of sessions taking place in London. A French notary would have to sit in on one of the sessions, confirm that in his view it was real and was conducted correctly, within whatever guidelines prevail for hypnotic psychotherapy. In other words, not faked.*

Corbeix was leaning over, pointing. 'The first point we've mostly covered. The last is essential if we want to present any of the tapes or transcripts in court. I'll arrange it. When are the final two sessions?'

'Next Tuesday and Thursday.'

'Tuesday's too tight. I'll lay it on for Thursday, phone you tomorrow with the details.' Corbeix made a quick note on a pad. 'But the main key to the case will rest with points two and three. If you manage to get some background on Duclos and young children, then we might have a chance of pressuring him in an interview situation, as you suggested earlier. It's unlikely he'll confess to murder faced purely with child molestation – but if we get him on just that, he's facing up to five years. And even if he's finally cleared, with the surrounding publicity it will certainly mean the end of his political career.'

So they'd have a shot at destroying Duclos' career and possibly landing him with a few years in prison, *if* he could find something. Not the justice due, scant consolation, but a start. Minutes ago Corbeix had been a stone wall; now at least he was throwing down a lifeline, however thin.

'I'm sure you have your contacts to track down such things.' Corbeix opened his hands out. 'But our main hope rests with you finding some tangible clue in the remaining sessions. Something which can be corroborated. Then we might, just might, be able to prosecute successfully for murder. Go the full course.'

'A tangible clue . . .' Dominic mimicked Corbeix blandly, as if saying it to himself would help. And then the ludicrousness hit him: *thirty years?* What earthly chance was there? Even if they were lucky enough to uncover something, half the people who could possibly corroborate were no longer alive. But for the first time that afternoon Corbeix appeared hopeful, enthusiastic. So in the end – as they went through the final details and next contact times and concluded their meeting – Dominic rode that wave. Pushed his doubts and sense of hopelessness to the back of his mind. Applied a singular focus and let it shine through all else – the daunting odds, the potential drawbacks and obstacles – until finally it was the only thing left in view: a tangible clue. And only two sessions left to find it.

34

Limoges, June 1985

A boy. Bettina had gone ahead with the scan.

Duclos focused his attention back as the windscreen wipers swung across. The rain had been heavy earlier, but now it was just light drizzle. The wipers were on intermittently. The lights had turned green, but the car ahead was slow in moving off.

A charity function, the fourth already this year. Annoying but necessary. Bettina was beside him in a satin-blue evening dress which hid her five-month pregnancy well until she sat down. Baby blue.

It would be all right, he told himself. Any worries were years ahead. While the boy was a baby, he would be Bettina's responsibility, something to keep her occupied. She would be busy with nappies and feeding, and he could use the excuse of the baby waking and crying to sleep in the second bedroom. Away from the occasional night-time grabs that increasingly made his skin crawl. The pregnancy had been marvellous. She hadn't touched him in all of the five months. The first eighteen months would probably be just like an extended pregnancy.

Then when he was a toddler, she would be busy knitting mittens and running after him to make sure he didn't fall down the stairs or stick his fingers in the electricity sockets. Father would retire to his study with the excuse of a heavy evening workload and lock the door. Solitude. The whole sad saga might not be so bad, might actually provide some good opportunities for him to keep his distance from Bettina.

Traffic was moving faster along Rue Montmailler. Duclos picked up speed, keeping up.

It wouldn't be until his son was older, at least six or seven, that he might be reminded of other boys and events he'd rather not think about, the secret life he'd been so careful to keep away from home. He never went with boys while in Limoges and tried as much as possible not to even think about them. It was only on his trips away, to Paris or Marseille, that he indulged himself. Everything kept away, in thought and in deed, from his own doorstep.

Under his own roof? A questioning or quizzical look . . . and he would wonder if his son somehow knew. He would flash back on the various times he'd seen the boy changing or dressing from the bath or shower, and wonder if on any of those occasions his gaze had lingered a second longer than it should, unconsciously sparked off the boy's suspicion. And if he had been guilty of that, he would torture himself whether it was because in that moment he'd been reminded of someone else or some past pleasurable instant. Because surely he would never look at his own son in that way, surely . . .

The brake lights loomed suddenly ahead, blurred through the raindrops on the windshield. A moment suspended – and then he braked. The wheels locked and the car started skidding . . .

He remembered most about the incident looking back on it. He wasn't hurt badly, just a bump on the head which had given him a few minutes' blackout. Bettina's side of the car had received the brunt of the smash. And as he rode with her in the ambulance, in the moments she drifted back to consciousness, she gripped his hand, muttering, 'My baby . . . my baby. Please . . .' The bottom of her silk dress was soaked in blood and one of the medics had cut through it with scissors, swabbing away the excess blood and feeling her stomach concernedly.

The final moment of the accident replayed in his mind, and he kept wondering: why had he been so late in braking, and why at the last moment did he swing to one side – let Bettina's side catch the main impact? Preoccupation, the delay in detaching from his thoughts partly answered the first, and some dumb throwback reflex from being used to driving alone, the second.

But even in that moment, as his guilt was at its zenith and he clutched his wife's hand and she clung in turn to the life inside her, part of him – some small part in which nested the rest of the dark secrets and shadows of his life – was already coming around to recognizing the real reason. He pushed the thought away and clutched tighter at his wife's hand.

Tired, so tired. The afternoons were usually worse than the mornings. Henri Corbeix was still in his office, the light on the past half hour as dusk approached. Sitting in the same position for so long making notes, his back felt stiff. He straightened up, paced to one side to ease it. But even with that effort his legs trembled uncertainly with the fresh weight.

He looked ruefully towards his office cabinet. He hadn't played squash for more than two years. He'd battled on a year after the diagnosis before it had finally become too much. At first, he'd felt it just on stretching for the low balls – the ones almost beyond reach he had always previously been able to get. But soon his legs started to twinge and spasm on even the easy shots, and he would be breathless and exhausted after the first fifteen minutes. He gave up before it became embarrassing for his opponents.

The only thing he'd managed to keep up was the weekend summer outings on their boat moored at Les Lecques. A day's fishing. Bread, Brie and pâté. A bottle of wine and some soft drinks in the polystyrene cooler for the girls. Maybe head across the bay to Ile Verte.

But this summer, even that, he feared, might be out of the question. The last time out, he'd felt the twinges and muscle spasms come on increasingly, particularly if the sea was choppy. He'd hardly been able to brace his legs against the repetitive pounding, a staccato reminder of how the disease had ravished his body, bit by bit attacking his muscle tissue and nerves until finally the simplest action tired him. Moving around a courtroom. A period of concentration and making notes.

MS. Multiple sclerosis. The drugs to treat it were crammed in his bottom drawer: steroids, baclofen, oxybutin, methylprednisolone. There was no cure, but they would 'help him cope; ease the muscle spasms when they struck', according to the doctor. Some days were better than others. He wondered why he still hid the drugs under papers in his bottom drawer. Habit from the first period of knowing he had the condition. But now half of his department knew and had done so for almost the past year. Soon after he'd announced his staged retirement: he would work full-time up until the coming August recess in order to clear his current caseload, then would step down as chief prosecutor and work mornings only for a year in an advisory capacity to his successor, Hervé Galimbert, at present his assistant. Then he would retire completely, unless his illness went into remission.

Unlikely. The past few months had been the worst. He'd feel exhausted immediately upon waking up, then would gain a burst of energy from his steroids which might, if he was lucky, last through till late afternoon. But if he had a heavy day or courtroom appearances, he would start to flag earlier.

Often when he came home from a day's work his youngest daughter, Chantelle, only seven, would jump up in his arms and he'd hardly have the strength to carry her more than a few steps. The anguish of his disease would hit him strongest in those moments. He was denying them. His other three daughters he'd been able to happily lift and swing around at leisure. He would become increasingly a burden, until finally there was nothing left but to sit quietly in the corner and occasionally rub his cramped legs while his daughters asked him if he wanted another coffee or something else to read. His anger and defiance rose up strongly. They were going out on the boat this year if it killed him!

He sat down and looked at his notes. The next session was tomorrow morning, final session Thursday. Notary arranged to travel with Fornier to London.

He hadn't told Fornier about his illness and that he wouldn't be able to pursue any trial cases beyond August. No point. Whatever stage the case was at then, he would merely hand over to Galimbert who was perfectly capable. Fornier had enough on his plate with trying to track down paedophile leads and find tangible clues from the remaining two sessions without having to worry about a change of prosecutor halfway through.

Corbeix looked at his calendar: three weeks left in April. August. Even if something came up quickly and he was able to file charges within a month, they would be lucky to be through the first four or five *instruction* hearings by then.

Going back through his notes and Fornier's files, the enormity of the case struck him. Leading politician. Murder. A landmark procedural case – the first of its kind in France based on such unorthodox evidence. It would make the Tapie scandal look like a parking ticket.

But it was all so tenuous, out of reach. Too many obstacles, too many contingencies – which was probably another reason why he hadn't mentioned anything to Fornier. He doubted that Fornier would even overcome the first hurdle. There wouldn't be a case to prosecute. Yet a corner of his mind – where he also contemplated what he would do if he won the lottery or woke up one morning with his illness suddenly gone – realized that if Fornier defied all odds and found something, it would certainly be the biggest case of his career. A fitting curtain bow. It would be tempting to see it all the way through.

He shook his head. He would file and put it in motion, set it on the right track, then hand over to Galimbert in August, as he'd originally planned. He didn't have the energy left for glory.

The tape rolled silently. The sound of Marinella Calvan tapping on the computer keys and then Philippe's voice. With five of them in the room looking on expectantly at the lone figure of Eyran Capel on the couch, the atmosphere was tense. Or perhaps it was because Dominic knew this was their last chance.

'Did you go into the local village with your parents often?'

'Yes, but mostly at the weekend. Hardly ever in the week when I was at school.'

'What sort of places did you go to in the village with your parents?'

'Mostly the shops with my mother . . . sometimes we would stop at a café for a drink. And there was a farm-provision store four kilometres beyond Bauriac where I would sometimes go with my father. At the back they . . .'

Dominic tuned it out. Marinella had mentioned the first moments were normally general background to settle Christian into the mood. Dominic looked back at the transcript from the last session and his own notes in the margin:

'. . . *When you finally came out of the darkness of the car boot and your eyes adjusted to the light, what did you see?*'

'*The field . . . the wheat field and the lane by the river.*'

'*Anything else? Was there anyone that you could see there apart from the man who'd taken you there in his car?*'

'*No . . . there was nobody.*'

'*Tell me what you heard there. Could you hear anything out of place?*'

'*No . . . not really. Just the river running in the distance . . . the sound of the wind through the trees.*'

'*Think hard. Was there anything else? Even the smallest sound at any time while you were in the wheat field?*'

'*Some other water running . . . spilling on the ground . . .*'

'*Anything else?*'

'*Some bells, faint, in the distance . . . but the light was fading. And another light . . . reaching out . . . but I couldn't feel my hand . . . the pain . . . the . . .*'

(Garbled and incoherent here. Words mostly unintelligible. Eyran moved on.)

Dominic had scribbled in the margin: *Church bells? Sound of water: how far away?* He brought his attention back as he heard Marinella mention church. She'd moved deftly from other places Christian regularly visited in the village to church visits.

'And while you were there with your parents, either before or afterwards, do you remember the sound of the church bells ringing?'

'Yes . . . sometimes. Usually before we went they were ringing.'

'Can you fix that sound in your mind and remember it clearly now?' Muted 'yes' from Eyran. 'And going back again now – back to when you had come out of the darkness of the car boot and into the light – you mentioned the sound of a bell ringing. Was it the same sound you remember from the church, or something else?'

'No . . . it was different. Not so distant . . . and higher-pitched, a tinkling sound.'

Goats' bells! Dominic remembered Machanaud in his statement leaving at that moment because a farmer was moving his goats into the adjoining field. The same farmer had probably disturbed Duclos, and Christian was obviously still conscious in those final few moments. Dominic was suddenly hit with a thought. He scribbled a hasty note and passed it to Marinella Calvan.

She was halfway through tapping out a fresh question, but realized it would be difficult to backtrack later to his. She back-deleted and typed: *About the same time, did you hear the man's car starting up or moving?*

'No . . . I don't remember that . . . I didn't hear anything else . . . I . . . th-there was nothing.'

So Christian had blacked out between the farmer approaching and Duclos moving his car. A minute or two at most. Dominic had noticed Lambourne look over sharply as he'd passed Marinella the note. Lambourne had appeared uncomfortable at the introduction of the notary, Fenouillet, who made periodic notes while observing the interplay between Marinella, Philippe and Eyran Capel. Dominic had claimed a desire to file some of the transcripts along with other official papers about the murder; for that, notary authentication was necessary. It was the closest Marinella felt they could come to the truth. Fenouillet didn't speak sufficient English for Lambourne to question him directly, and thankfully Philippe had kept in the background.

'Before that, you recalled clearly the sound of water running and splashing. Not the river running, but something else. How far away was that sound? Could you tell what it was?'

'It was quite close . . . only a few yards. Water spilling from something on to the ground.'

'Was the sound coming from where the man with the car was standing?'

'Yes . . . I think so.'

343

Memories of Perrimond claiming Machanaud had washed down the blood from his apron front with a bucket of water from the river. But where had Duclos got water from? He hadn't left the boy long enough to go down to the river and back.

Silence. Marinella flicking a page forward in some notes before tapping out again: *After those moments in the wheat field, do you have any recall of incidents with your parents?*

'No . . . can't remember . . . rememm . . .' Muted mumbling that faded away. Eyran's eyelids pulsed and he strained slightly, as if images were there but he couldn't see them clearly.

'And do you think that's why the wheat field has come to symbolize separation from your parents? Why you keep returning to it in your thoughts?'

'No, no . . . it's not that . . . not . . .' The pulsing settled, images clearing. 'It's just that when I try to think beyond it, I can't . . . I can't.'

Marinella pressed while she felt the advantage. The first gambit had perhaps been too hopeful: getting Christian to admit the influence of the wheat field on Eyran's dreams. 'And your friend, did the field become a symbol of separation from him too?'

'No . . . I used to play there with Stéphane, that's all. It reminded me of that. That was all I thought of when I saw the wheat field. Playing . . . us playing there together.'

'Do you go back to the wheat field in your thoughts to play with Stéphane?'

'No . . . no more.' Eyran swallowed slowly.

'And since? How do you feel about it now? What do you feel when you think about the wheat field?'

'I don't know . . . somm . . .' Eyran looked away slightly. Muscles tensed at his temples. Christian's thoughts clawing up through three decades of darkness, fighting to surface. 'Something warm . . . bright . . . but I can't feel the warmth . . . can't feel . . .' Eyran's head started shaking slowly from side to side. 'I . . . thh . . . there was nothing after . . . only a faint light beyond the darkness . . . but I can't feel . . . can't feee . . .'

Dominic noticed Lambourne sit forward sharply. Marinella had told him about Lambourne threatening to end the sessions if Eyran looked in danger of verging into a catatonic state, and she had already come close a few times. Now again she was walking the tightrope.

'Let's go back . . . back. Break away!' Marinella could sense Lambourne's hand hovering on the desk beside her, about to reach out for

344

the keyboard. She didn't dare look around, kept her eyes fixed between Eyran and the keyboard.

Dominic knew from Marinella that the field was central to Eyran's therapy, and she'd explained that she hoped to leap from there to a vital element he'd related from Corbeix: getting Christian to admit that the man with the car, Duclos, had killed him. 'If not, the defence could wriggle out by claiming culpability only for the sexual assaults. That the boy was left unharmed after that.' But as Marinella had warned, it was the hardest possible thing to get the boy to admit. And now any possible opportunities to make the leap had probably gone.

'I understand that those memories are unpleasant, that you don't wish to recall them. But beneath that – beneath the detail that I know is painful for you – you know that something bad happened to you that day. You know that, don't you?'

Eyran's brows knitted. A slight swallow. 'Yes . . . I . . .'

'And you know that somehow the man in the car was responsible, was the reason why you weren't able to see your friend that day. You know that the man hit you and stopped you from going.' Marinella knew the word 'kill' would produce another rush reaction. 'Do you remember the man hitting you?'

Dominic tensed as he realized she was going for it after all; he'd felt sure she would move Eyran on to another memory. He saw Lambourne look incredulously between her and the computer as Eyran's brow knitted harder.

'If it wasn't the man with the car,' Marinella pressed, 'if it was someone else – then tell us. Was it someone else who hit you?'

Eyran's head started shaking again. Small beads of sweat popped on his forehead. 'No . . . no . . . it was him.'

Lambourne's voice came almost immediately. 'I can't believe you did that!'

Eyran's head tilted, his brow creasing again. He looked suddenly perplexed.

Marinella tapped out on the screen: *And I can't believe you did that either! Broke the one-voice rule.*

Philippe looked up from the screen and shrugged, smiling. She'd forgotten to put it in brackets, but he knew not to translate.

Marinella continued tapping: *We've already got the problem of non-acceptance with two children. Let's not add another to the list: that you can't accept I might be right.*

Lambourne's expression was thunderous. He looked frustratedly between the screen and her. This was great, she thought. Argument by computer. Except that Lambourne couldn't answer because she was hogging the keyboard, and he couldn't risk speaking again. Just the sort of argument she liked.

Dread gripped Dominic as he expected Lambourne suddenly to stop the session, quickly overrode his brief amusement and admiration at Calvan's feistiness. Philippe was still beaming, and Fenouillet had merely paused in his note-taking, had no idea what was going on. But finally Lambourne just shook his head and waved one hand dismissively, as if the whole argument was suddenly unworthy; though some last fleeting shadow in his eye, the way he looked quickly between Marinella, himself and Fenouillet, made Dominic suspect Lambourne might already be thinking: so many questions around the murder, and was a notary really necessary for just a filing?

'Going back to where you left your bike – the other field and farm track. Did you hear anything there? Tell me what you heard.'

'There was nothing, really. Just the wind slightly.'

'Anything else? Are there any sounds in the background? Anything you can hear at all?'

Dominic noted the change from past to present tense: *Are* there? After the last session, Marinella had told him about a special New York-based FBI unit which specialized in hypnotizing crime witnesses to gain more accurate descriptions. The present tense put the witness directly back at the scene. Detail was usually far more accurate and in depth. Marinella had used the same technique in the last session with Eyran, but the results had been disappointing. Apart from the segment with the water running and the bells ringing, they'd gained little of value. She'd asked Christian if he remembered any shops they'd passed in the man's car, if he saw anyone on the way to where his bike was, if he saw anyone in the field or on the track by his bike, if any other vehicles passed apart from the Marseille truck. Nothing, nothing, nothing.

He'd banged his desk and kicked filing cabinets in frustration reading the transcript. Now she was asking if he *heard* anything by his bike: again nothing. They were fast running out of areas to explore. Marinella went back to the Marseille truck, asking Christian to concentrate on the letters on the side. 'Are there any other letters or words you can see?'

'L-E. Le something. P-O-N . . . T . . .'

'Anything else?'

It was hopeless, thought Dominic. Fragments of words from a truck from over thirty years ago. Even if by some miracle they traced it – a driver flashing by just for a few seconds all those years back – what on earth would he remember? *Goats' bells?* They'd interviewed the farmer shortly after Machanaud'd mentioned him, but he'd seen nothing; tree coverage was too thick by the river. What else was there: *water splashing? A woman's voice in a car park?* Pathetic!

Dominic looked anxiously at the clock: twenty minutes left. The letters had fizzled out with an *E-I. Pontei*: Not even a full word. Marinella was flicking back in her notes, as if searching desperately where to head next – and in that moment the realization finally struck him, dissolved his anxiety and clinging expectation to a sinking hollowness. Concrete to jelly: they weren't going to find anything! She'd exhausted all the main avenues and now was just scrambling around the edges at fragments. He could almost imagine Duclos smiling at them, *gloating* . . .

Marinella moved back to the subject of separation: this time other people Christian had felt separation from that day apart from his parents and his friend. Probably best, Dominic conceded dolefully; with no new clues forthcoming, at least she could satisfy the main aim of the therapy.

. . . *Gloating* as he sat in the restaurant sipping wine . . . as he untied and assaulted Christian for a second time . . . as he smashed down the rock repeatedly on Christian's skull, bludgeoning the life out of him. Dominic shook his head. The images were unbearably intense, because now they *knew* that Duclos had done it, but would have little choice but to sit back and watch him slip clear again. And Dominic would feel the same sense of loathing and disgust each time he saw Duclos' face in a newspaper, smiling, *gloating* . . . as he opened some new industrial park, smiling from a campaign rostrum, gloating at them that he'd got away with it . . . his arm coming down repeatedly to strike home his campaign points in the same way that he'd brought the rock down on Christian's head that day. And he would hardly be able to bear to look, *knowing* . . . knowing that . . .

'Grandpapa André?' The name cut abruptly into Dominic's thoughts. One name among Christian's recital of separation that he hadn't heard before: father, mother, Clarisse . . . but not Grandpapa André.

Dominic read the full line on the computer screen: *I remember thinking about Grandpapa André. I clung to the luck he gave me.*

Dominic scribbled a frantic note: *What luck? Why? Where is he?* – and handed it to Marinella Calvan.

She typed: *What luck was it that Grandpapa André gave you?*

'It was a coin . . . a lucky coin.'

'And were you holding the coin when you thought about Grandpapa André?'

'Yes . . . I was gripping it tight in my hand before I fell asleep. And then I realized suddenly when I awoke that it had dropped from my hand.'

'Where were you when it dropped?'

'In the boot of the man's car.'

'And were you able to find the coin?'

'No, it was dark . . . I felt around. But there was only the spare wheel . . . I couldn't feel it on the wheel or around the sides. I was still feeling for it when the boot opened . . . the light stung my eyes.'

'And when you realized you'd dropped the coin, did it make you fear that something bad might happen?'

'Yes . . . yes. In the darkness, it helped me. It was something I knew, a reminder of home. But then when it had gone . . .'

As Marinella returned to attachment and loss, Dominic touched her arm lightly, silently nodded his excuse, and left the room. Nothing else of interest was likely to come up and he couldn't bear waiting the ten remaining minutes to know. He went through Lambourne's reception and out into the street, dialling out on his mobile to Monique in Lyon.

On the third ring she answered, and he cut quickly through the preambles. 'A coin. A lucky coin that Christian's grandfather gave him. Do you remember it?'

'Yes . . . I do.' Hesitance; flustered by the sudden jump to a memory from over thirty years ago. 'But why?'

'It's important. Something's come out of the sessions in London. I'll tell you later.' Sudden chill as he realized he wouldn't be able to delay any longer; that night he would have to tell her everything: his buried doubts, the car sighting, Machanaud, Jean-Luc's wasted suicide. 'What sort of coin was it?'

'An Italian twenty lire, silver. Nineteen twenty-eight.'

'Was it rare?'

'Fairly. Jean-Luc's father had brought it back from Italy years before. He gave it to Christian on his eighth birthday.'

Dominic was silent, thoughtful: if Duclos had seen the coin, he'd have thrown it away straight away. But Christian hadn't been able to feel for it: what if it had dropped behind the spare wheel or in with some tools out of sight? A chance. Just a chance.

He confirmed that Monique hadn't found it later among any of Christian's things. 'With all the confusion – with the investigation and Christian in the hospital – it got forgotten. I didn't notice it was missing till months later. But it's obviously important now . . . very important. Why?'

And again he assured her that he'd tell her that night, diverted quickly to pleasantries before ringing off. A generation of hiding the truth from his wife and still he was playing for time.

Lucky coin? Dominic reflected ruefully. The only luck might be, thirty-two years later, it finally bringing some justice for Christian Rosselot.

35

Limoges, June 1985

A miracle. Duclos looked at the pathetic figure of his new-born son through two layers of glass: the first separating the observation room from intensive care, the second the glass of the incubator. Scrawny, hardly an adult's forearm in length, and purplish blue – all that was keeping him alive was the oxygenated, sanitized air of the incubator and the mass of pipes feeding and monitoring.

A miracle that would probably only last a few hours, according to the doctors. His son would be lucky to make it through the night. Those few hours strongly etched in his memory: a glass case. How he would forever remember his son, timelessly preserved in a glass cabinet; a freak of nature, an exhibit.

Bettina still hadn't come round from the anaesthetic. The only option left to save her and the baby had been a Caesarean section. Horrifically rushed, the anaesthetist had hardly finished his countdown and response tests before the surgeon made his incision. Some monitors were still being attached as he cut.

Bettina had begged and pleaded for her baby's life as they'd wheeled her frantically on a gurney towards the operating theatre. The attending emergency medic had gripped her hand and assured, 'Don't worry, you'll be okay.'

But entering surgery, the graver atmosphere and more concerned expressions made her panic that everything might not be okay. 'If there's a choice, save my baby first. Put his life before mine.'

'We try our best not to make choices,' the surgeon commented, 'unless God forces our hand.'

Bettina was still struggling with the significance of this, was about to press the surgeon for a clearer assurance when the anaesthetic bit.

She probably wouldn't awake for two or three hours yet, Duclos reflected. What was he going to tell her? 'He's alive, but he'll be dead soon. Doctors did their best. Shame.'

Or perhaps he would spend an hour's more bedside vigil with his son, then sneak away on the promise of returning a couple of hours later, but get delayed. Leave it to the doctors to tell Bettina. Avoid the drama of seeing her in tears, in the same way he had avoided every other drama and confrontation with Bettina through the years. Besides, they were more expert than him, were used to choosing the right words in this sort of situation every day. He'd be hopeless. Worse still, if the boy died before Bettina awoke, it was best if he wasn't there; he couldn't possibly face her given that circumstance. At least with a few hours of life remaining, she'd cling to some hope, some solace.

They'd even talked about a name: Joël. 'Hello Joël,' he murmured, and saw his breath mist the glass as he pressed his face closer. The frail figure, so pathetic and defenceless with all the tubes and monitors attached, reminded him in that moment of Christian Rosselot in the hospital . . . of him reaching out to stifle the last life from the boy. He shivered involuntarily. Had he really been so desperate? How could anyone . . . *anyone?* And in that moment, as his eyes welled uncontrollably, a tear trickling down, it hit him that it might just as well be his hand reaching across and stifling Joël. He realized that his turning the wheel at the last moment hadn't just been instinctive self-preservation; in part he'd responded to some dark inner fear, however irrational, of future complications he wouldn't be able to face.

Was that why he was crying now, he thought? Tears of remorse, the first he could remember, flowing freely because the sight of his son – an actual life rather than a shadow of shapes on a scan from his wife's womb – had reached out and gripped him hard? Or was it because he knew now with certainty that his son would die as he was now, would never grow beyond the pathetic, shrivelled form before him? The tears could be safely shed; all worries, whether real or ridiculously imagined in his own mind, were over.

It hardly mattered now. When all that remained was a few hours of life preserved in a glass case, what else was there but pity, sorrow? He was a politician. He knew the right emotion for every occasion.

In the midst of his other work, Dominic's occasional glances towards the phone in the past hour had become increasingly anxious. After his initial call to Lepoille, they'd spoken again an hour later, then nothing since. Almost half the day had gone now for Lepoille to find something. What had happened?

Seven months? Duclos had obviously been keen to dispose of the car. Unpleasant memories. The papers were strewn across his desk: faxed pages from an Alfa Romeo owners' club in Paris: *User's Manual. Alfa Romeo Giulietta Sprint, 1961.* Car registration for the next owner after Duclos: Maurice Caugine, an address in Saint-Junien, thirty kilometres from Limoges.

Details of the car boot and position of the spare wheel and tool kit were on the seventh page faxed through. The spare wheel had eight oval holes around its perimeter, each one double the length of a large coin. Easily large enough for the twenty-lire coin to have fallen through. He'd gained a photocopied picture and details of the coin from a collectors' catalogue: *Italian 20 lire, 1928. Silver. 15g. Emanuele III on head, Lictor hailing Roma on reverse. Edition minted between 1927 and 1934.*

The spare wheel took up half the boot space. As Christian had described, space would have been cramped. Even curled in almost a foetal position, part of his body or at least his arms must have been pinned above the wheel. If he'd fallen asleep and dropped the coin, it could easily have landed on the wheel and through one of the oval holes. Or at first have fallen on top of the wheel, then, with the vibrations and movement of the car or Christian shifting position, found its way to one of the holes.

If the coin had fallen to the side of the wheel, Duclos would have spotted it easily and pocketed it or thrown it away. But if it had fallen through one of the holes . . . *seven months?* What were the chances of Duclos not changing his wheel in that time? Whoever had been the first to change the wheel would have seen the coin.

Maurice Caugine had kept the car for over three years. The chances of him not changing the wheel in that time were remote. Either he'd seen the coin or their only chance was probably gone.

Lepoille had called back within the hour: bad news. Maurice Caugine had died eight years ago. 'But it looks like he was survived by his wife. I'm trying to track her down now.'

Since that call three hours ago, nothing. Dominic's spirits had slumped at the news. Another hurdle: now they were dependent not only on Maurice Caugine having noticed the coin, but him having mentioned it to his wife. And forcefully enough for it to have stuck in her mind to recall over thirty years later.

Corbeix had been initially enthused by the coin lead. 'Sounds rare enough to argue that it couldn't have got there any other way than by the boy being in Duclos' boot that day – *if* you can find someone who saw it there. Let me know how it develops. Meanwhile I'll send a note to Malliéné about the case.' They'd already discussed the procedural details: Dominic would provide a report every week or two weeks, as the case dictated, and would pass it to Malliéné to add any comment before he signed it off. Purely a safeguard so that Malliéné wasn't signing off anything he disagreed with. 'I'll ask him to contact you the next day or so to tie up the details.'

Corbeix finished by mentioning he was hoping for more information the next day or so on cases involving psychics from a specialist prosecution division in Paris. Dominic was encouraged by the fact that the case was increasingly commanding Corbeix's attention. But still it struck him that Corbeix hadn't even contacted Malliéné until he heard about the coin lead, and the examining magistrate who signed off the *commission rogatoire générale* Corbeix probably wouldn't call again until he was sure the case was prosecutable. There was still some way to go.

Dominic stared again at the phone. Although he had built up his own and Corbeix's hopes, it could all be over with a single call. Madame Caugine could have died as well, or gone abroad and be practically untraceable, or be senile or in a mental asylum. Couldn't remember anything from the day before, let alone thirty years ago. The possibilities spun through Dominic's mind.

Pierre Lepoille was on the home straight. He tapped in Jocelyne Caugine's identity-card number. Hopefully the office where she cashed her pension would come up with her current address.

Tracking Maurice Caugine had been easy. His identity-card number had been on the car registration papers, and from there Lepoille traced where he last drew his pension before dying: La Rochelle, on the coast from Saint-Junien. But Madame Caugine had been a different matter. He'd had no record of her identity-card number, nor even her first name. The few papers he found for Maurice Caugine didn't feature his wife's details. Tracking was therefore more tedious. He tried all Caugines drawing pension for that year in the area: two men, one woman. The woman was at a different address and her husband had died twenty years ago. So Caugine's wife had probably moved out of the area after he died, but where?

He tried several general searches and combinations before giving up. Some areas brought up far too many Caugines for him to search effectively. Stumped for an immediate answer, he went back to some other urgent work he'd pushed aside when Dominic's query had come in. Almost another hour had passed before the thought hit him: credit cards! Not current, but any applied for within three years after she had moved. Most credit agencies had a stipulation of the previous address being noted when the current address was less than three years old.

He searched 1989, entering 'Caugine' and 'Dourennes', the name of their previous street in La Rochelle as keywords. Bingo! Seven choices, mostly Paris, only one in La Rochelle. Jocelyne Caugine had applied for a store card in Arcachon, south of Bordeaux. Two more key strokes and he was able to call up her full details and identity-card number. He checked the current cashing address for her pension in case she'd moved, then called Dominic.

It took Dominic over two hours finally to get Jocelyne Caugine on the phone. When he'd first called, he was informed by another woman with the same surname, Josette Caugine, presumably her daughter, that she was out shopping, 'Shouldn't be too long.' The murder case of the decade on hold while this little old lady picked up courgettes and cat food at the local Leclerc, Dominic mused. He left his name purely as Fornier, no inspector. Didn't want to frighten her off. He'd call later.

The second call Jocelyne Caugine answered directly. This time Dominic introduced himself with his full title. She sounded quite alert, attentive, showed no hesitance with recall. Yes, she remembered the car quite well. 'We often used to drive in it from Saint-Junien to La Rochelle, particularly at the weekends.' Then her voice wavered slightly, sounding concerned. 'We're not in some sort of trouble, are we?' The 'we' as if her husband was still there partly to shoulder responsibility.

'No, no . . . not at all. You or your husband have done nothing wrong. But it is nevertheless a very important investigation we're conducting, and any assistance you can offer could be vital.'

'I see. Certainly . . . in any way I can help.'

The perkiness was back in her voice. A little old lady helping out on a Maigret-style inquiry. Probably the most excitement she'd had all year. 'I want you to remember back, Madame Caugine. Back to when your husband had the car. Do you ever remember him mentioning finding a coin in the car?'

'A coin?'

Dominic let the silence ride a second. Her tone was mostly rhetorical, self-prompting. She was thinking. 'Yes, a silver coin from Italy.'

'From Italy, you say? Not some French money left there?' she queried.

A quick mumbled 'no' from Dominic, and she asked, 'Was it particularly valuable?'

'No, not particularly. But as I say, it's very significant in a case we're handling now.'

'I don't know . . . I don't seem to recall anything.'

Dominic could almost feel her at the other end grappling through the years, straining for memories out of reach. He sensed that she wanted to help. He prompted, 'It was quite a large silver coin. Twenty lire, 1928. Do you remember your husband finding *anything* unusual in the car boot?'

Brief silence as Madame Caugine thought deeper, then a sigh. 'I'm sorry. No . . . I just can't think of anything. I haven't been much help, have I?'

Dominic felt the first twinge of alarm. It was slipping away. But how likely was it that her husband hadn't changed a wheel in three years? He was sure that the memory could be drawn out if he hit the right chord. 'Your husband would have probably only seen the coin when he changed the car wheel. Do you remember him changing the wheel at any time?'

'Yes . . . yes. I do.' Faint hope returning to her voice.

'When was that?'

'We were on the way to Paris to see his brother. We got a flat tyre on the way there.'

'Did your husband mention seeing anything in the car boot when he took the new wheel out?'

'No . . .'

'Or over the next few hours or days?'

'No, not that I recall.'

'Was it in the daytime? Was the light good?' Dominic could almost hear the clinging desperation in his own voice.

'Yes – it was mid afternoon.'

Dominic's mind spun desperately through the other options. 'And do you remember your husband mentioning changing a wheel while he was on his own?'

'Not that I remember. No . . . I'm sorry.'

'Perhaps when he changed the wheel a second time, he might have mentioned something? Perhaps doing it before, seeing something unusual?'

'No . . . nothing I'm afraid. As I said, I really can't recall my husband mentioning anything like that.'

Her voice was once again flustered, now with just a hint of defence. Dominic felt guilty: an image of him pinning the old lady back with increasing interrogation. He eased off. 'I'm sorry, yes. You did mention it already.' Dominic looked up: people busy on the phone, keyboards clattering, someone scanning the new roster on the notice-board. Dominic's gaze cannoned frantically around the squad room in search of inspiration for what he might say next. But there was nowhere left to go. He'd covered everything. 'Perhaps you might recall something later.' Stock phrase, his mind was still desperately panning in case there was something he'd overlooked. Nothing. *Nothing*. He left his number.

'If I do remember anything, I certainly will, inspector.'

Dominic thanked her and rang off. But he knew she probably wouldn't call, was just being polite. She'd had perfect recall of the wheel being changed; if the coin had been mentioned, she would have remembered. Maurice Caugine hadn't seen the coin. It was all over.

Dominic stayed late just in case she called, packed up finally at almost 8 p.m. But as he suspected, nothing. It was already dark as he headed out, the spring night air fresh. His shoulders were slumped in defeat, though in a way he also felt strangely relieved. The past two weeks had brought his nerves to the very edge. He'd hardly slept a full night since hearing the first tape. A nightmare of juggling psychiatrists, transcripts, police and court files with the ghosts of his family's past that he should have known at the outset were best left alone. He let out a deep breath, felt it all suddenly washing away from him. It was over. A stiff brandy, then he could mentally file it along with the other deep and bitter experiences through the years. His life could go back to how it was before Marinella Calvan had called.

The phone was ringing as Duclos walked in the house. No lights were on. He flicked on the hallway and lounge switches on the way to picking it up.

'Oh, it's you.' *Jaumard*. The disappointment came through in Duclos' voice. 'I was expecting a call from somebody else.'

'Anything important?'

'Yes – I'm waiting urgently on a call from the hospital. I don't have time to talk now.'

'What's happened?'

'It's my –' Duclos stopped himself. He didn't want to share the accident

356

saga with Jaumard. Curtailed version: 'My wife. The baby's premature. There've been complications.'

'I didn't even know she was pregnant.'

'You wouldn't. It's none of your business.' Flat tone, impatient.

'Is it a boy or a girl?'

Duclos cringed; he wished now he hadn't even said anything. 'Boy.' He could pick up Jaumard's slurring. As usual he had downed a few stiff ones before phoning. 'I must go. Keep the line –'

'That's good. You like boys, don't you? Well, I hope mother and son are both fffine.'

Duclos' jaw set tight. Was this just standard drunken, oafish Jaumard, or some attempt at his brother's line in acid banter? He felt like leaping down the phone and battering out what few brains Jaumard had left. He should have had him killed years ago, taken him out the same way as his brother. Except he was sure that, brainless or not, Jaumard had taken a leaf out of his brother's book and left a similar insurance letter with a lawyer somewhere. 'Look, as I said. I don't have time to –'

'I know. Sssorry. I only called now because I'm shipping out in a few days.'

Always the same, thought Duclos. Jaumard would hit him for some money just before a voyage. The only compensation was that he wouldn't hear from him again for six months, a year. 'I see. Call me tomorrow night when you're sober. We'll make the arrangements then.'

'What's his name?'

'Eynard. Justin Eynard.'

The name meant nothing to Dominic. The world of Parisian vice was strange to him. His two years at Interpol in Paris had been devoted to international cases. Marseille would have been more familiar territory, but nothing had come up through Bennacer. Only this one lead now from Deleauvre in Paris.

'What's his background?'

'Started off with girlie bars, then later a couple of sex accessory and video shops with under-the-counter material, a lot of it paedophile magazines and videos. Then finally he opened up a gay disco. But a lot of the boys there are under age, fourteen, fifteen – sat in dark corner booths heavily made up so that you would hardly know. And if you approach the barman and comment that they "look a bit old", he'll give you an address. Eynard runs a 'discreet' house nearby. He also started supplying some of his kids to paedophile porn-makers.'

' So, what have we got on him?'

'We're close to nailing him through one of his men. A recent bust on a paedophile porn ring has led back to Eynard. The contact, Ricauve, spends a lot of time in Eynard's disco. Says that he's not only seen Duclos there, but seen him go off with one of the barmen who normally escorts clients to the nearby 'house'. We're cutting a deal with Ricauve for information, so we should be able to land on Eynard like a ton of bricks. He's got a lot to lose, so we're pretty sure he'll roll over and finger Duclos.'

'Sounds encouraging.' Dominic could feel his enthusiasm returning. After the disappointment of the coin, some hope. Duclos gets away with murder, but they nail him for molesting under-age boys. Drag him through the system, ruin his career, anything from a two- to four-year sentence. It was something at least. 'Let me know how the Ricauve interview goes.'

Dominic signed off. Lepoille had also tried to pep him up, suggesting that it was worthwhile tracking down the car owner after Caugine. He'd get on it right away. Dominic wasn't hopeful. The coin not discovered until almost four years later? Escaping the notice of both Duclos and Caugine? Unlikely.

But the strongest encouragement had come from Monique the night before. 'If you really believe in this, so strongly in fact that it's haunted you for over thirty years, how can you give up now?'

Dominic's single brandy after work had turned into three. It took a while for Monique's comments to cut through his despondency. 'Perhaps I'm just tired,' he offered lamely.

Or was it their sudden reversal of roles from the night before which had thrown him? Except for his complicity over the car sighting, he'd told her everything – his doubts about Machanaud, his suspicion of Duclos, how he had just gone along with the investigative flow, Machanaud's long prison sentence. He hadn't mentioned anything through the years because it would have underlined that Jean-Luc's suicide had been in vain. Too painful. Besides, it was just a suspicion. Even when he saw the possibility of gaining fresh evidence through the sessions, the same reasons prevailed, and he was also sceptical that anything tangible would materialize. 'Again, there was no point in upsetting you if it was all to come to nothing.'

Until the coin – the first time he realized he had a chance of proving something against Duclos.

Shadows returning, shifting clouds in her eyes: doubt, disbelief, slow acceptance. Sensing her mood – the fact that in a few short sentences he'd torn down so many of her long-held beliefs about the crime and Jean-Luc's suicide, compounded now by doubts about the openness of their own relationship, the secrets harboured over so many years – he felt the need to be dramatic: 'It's almost as if Christian is guiding us through this other boy. Giving us the clues to track his killer.'

'Yes, uncanny, Dominic. Uncanny.' She was silent for a long while. She asked a few mechanical questions about the procedure and the state of play, then went to bed soon after. Her mood was sullen, thoughtful; little indication of how she felt. He was sure it still hadn't fully hit her.

But when the night following his own mood was grey and he felt the case was at a dead-end, she threw it all back in his face: 'So Christian's voice is guiding you, as if it's all somehow ordained. Meant to be. But now you're telling me it's impossible. I've never accepted what happened, Dominic. But at least I've been able to come to terms with the justice, such as it was. Jean-Luc was never able to do even that. And suddenly everything that happened then is meant to be wrong. You've harboured the doubts for thirty-odd years – but you told me just the other day. Then you tell me it's all over. You've hit a dead-end. "The possibility of justice I mentioned the other day – forget it." No, Dominic. It's not going to end like that.'

Dominic stressed the legal complexities of the case, mostly stock lines repeated from Corbeix: that psychic evidence presented in court was virtually non-existent in France; without tangible evidence corroborated by a third party they were lost; despite the accuracy of the tapes and transcripts and Calvan's and Lambourne's credentials, they just wouldn't stand up in court on their own.

Monique's eyes darted frantically as he spoke: 'But there must be something, *something!*'

To her this new situation was just one day old, he realized: she was invigorated by its freshness. To him it was the end of a thirty-year trail. She had no idea how tired he felt. He told her of the few weak options remaining.

She'd knelt in front of him, her arms on his thighs, her eyes imploring him. 'If that's all that's left, Dominic, then grasp it with both hands. Chase the next car owner, however remote the possibility. And if you fail, go for whatever remains: try and prove Duclos' background with young boys, drag him through the courts, ruin his career. Do whatever you can. You've waited thirty years – don't give up now!'

First thing, Dominic called Bennacer, Deleauvre and Lepoille. Things were starting to move again.

But just before four o'clock, Lepoille called with bad news: the car owner after Caugine was dead. 'He was a bachelor when he bought the car, didn't marry till much later, and his wife's dead now too. There's a sister he shared an address with for a while – though two years before he even bought the car. I don't think she'll be much use.'

Hardly any numbness this time; with the events of the day before, he'd already half accepted that all chances of prosecuting Duclos for murder were gone.

Two days later, Deleauvre called to tell him that their initial visit to pressure Eynard hadn't gone well. 'He was very cagey, defensive, didn't want to say anything without his lawyer present. We've arranged another "unofficial" meeting in one of his clubs with his lawyer present. But getting him to roll over for a deal might not be as easy as we first thought. Depends how his lawyer reacts.'

Dominic had visions of even this last hope with Duclos slipping through his grasp.

Dominic's spirits were still at a low ebb three hours later when the call came through. The desk sergeant announced a woman and 'something about a coin'. Dominic's first thought was Lepoille tracking down the second owner's sister.

It was Jocelyne Caugine. 'Sorry to trouble you, inspector. But I did remember something. I don't know whether it's useful or not. My husband bought the car from a garage near Limoges – they apparently did some sort of trade-in with the previous owner. Perhaps they changed the wheel and saw the coin you mentioned.'

Dominic felt his spirits soar. 'Do you remember the name of the garage?'

'Something-*beau*. I can't remember exactly. But it's the only garage for quite a while: about four kilometres out of Limoges on the Saint-Junien road. Left-hand side as you approach Limoges.'

'Madame Caugine – you're marvellous. *Marvellous!*'

'Well – I just hope it's useful.' Slightly flustered by his enthusiasm.

Useful? Dominic smiled incredulously. He wanted to hug Jocelyne Caugine until her cheeks flushed purple.

Dominic ordered the biggest food hamper he could find – cognac, champagne, select cheeses and pâtés, truffles and chocolates – and had it messengered to Jocelyne Caugine with a note:

From your favourite inspector.

Then he phoned Lepoille.

36

The TGV train hurtled across the flat plain of the Sologne.

Three names left to trace. Dominic called Lepoille on his mobile. 'Anything yet?'

'Just bringing it up . . . here we are . . .' The sound of Lepoille's fingers on the keyboard. 'One more found so far. Still alive. Limoges address . . . and, yes, a telephone number.' Lepoille read it out, enunciating clearly so that Dominic could hear above the noise of the train. 'Nothing as yet on the other two, I don't think . . .' Lepoille's voice drifted as he swung away, calling out across the room, some mumbled background conversation, faint echoing clatter of the computer room imposing . . .

. . . The room where Dominic had spent so much time the past two days: late evenings, endless chains of coffee in plastic cups, looking expectantly over Lepoille's shoulder while he waited for the next Internet or ASF link, instructions bouncing across the room as quick as the key strokes between Lepoille and his two team helpers, and then finally the names and telephone numbers . . .

Lepoille was back. 'Nothing yet. Found a relative on one, but nothing more. We'll phone as soon as we get something. What time will you get there?'

Dominic calculated: just over an hour more to Paris, then the connection to Rouen. 'About six o'clock.' He could have shaved fifty minutes by flying, but it was vital he maintain contact by phone throughout.

Dominic called the new number straight after signing off from Lepoille. It was engaged.

Madness. A boy under hypnosis mentioning a coin from over thirty years ago, an old woman remembering the name of a garage . . . and half of Interpol Division II's computer team had been tied up for two days.

Hundreds of computer records searched. Nine names and matching identity numbers of the workers in a Limoges garage from thirty years ago. Four traced. Three dead. Two left to find. Any casual workers not on the 1964 garage pay-roll list would be virtually impossible to track down.

Of the four so far traced two were still in Limoges, one in Narbonne and one in Rouen, not on the phone. Dominic decided to head to Rouen while Lepoille continued his search. With the train he could stay in touch, plus call directly any new traces which came in.

Dominic dialled the number again in Limoges: Serge Roudèle. He answered. Dominic introduced himself and confirmed with Roudèle that he had worked in the Mirabeau garage in 1964.

'Yes, I did . . . why?'

'It concerns an Alfa Romeo. An Alfa Romeo Giulietta Sprint.' The other two workers Dominic had spoken to earlier hadn't remembered the car. Among the hundreds of cars seen by a garage worker over the years, how to throw a spotlight on this one car? 'Now I know that you probably saw a lot of cars, but maybe not so many Alfa Romeos. This was the coupé version, quite a classic. Dark green.'

Brief silence, then: 'No, sorry. I don't seem to remember it.'

'Owner was a young lawyer, Alain Duclos. Went on to become your local MP, RPR party.'

'I'm afraid I was just on the works floor, I didn't deal with the owners. I hardly knew whose car was whose.'

'Quite a distinctive car.'

'Sorry – we dealt with so many classic and sports cars. They were a strong line for the garage, so I saw a lot of them. I just can't place it.'

As with the others, thought Dominic. But still he asked about the coin. One car among so many might be hard to place, but it wasn't every day that a rare coin was found in a car boot. 'An Italian twenty lire. Silver. Quite large. It would probably have fallen down and been concealed by the spare wheel.'

A pause. A long pause. The sound of a dog barking somewhere in the distance. 'I'm sorry, inspector. I really can't remember anything like that at all.'

'Or do you remember anyone else in the garage finding such a coin – any talk about it at all?'

'No . . . nothing, I'm afraid.'

'Well – if you do happen to recall anything later, give me a call.' Dominic gave his mobile number. 'It would help us enormously in a very important murder case. There's no possible recrimination against anyone who might have taken the coin, and there's even a small reward: 5,000 francs. About double what the coin is worth on today's market.'

The script was practically the same each time: setting the scene, the car, the coin, the seriousness of the case, the assurance of no recriminations in case of worries about a theft charge, the reward as incentive.

Dominic left a marked silence in hope of response, but Roudèle merely repeated that unfortunately he didn't remember anything. Dominic thanked him and rang off.

Madness. Hopeless. Thirty-five minutes left to Paris. Hurtling across France on a futile paper chase, pursuing a few fragments of memories from decades ago. One more lead to check and two more names to chase. But despite the odds against them finding anything after all these years, Dominic felt this strange sense of control: of him connected to Lepoille and Interpol's central computer room while speeding towards their next lead at over 300 kmph, of Lepoille in turn linked to networks of computers the length and breadth of the country, searching, sorting, feeding the information back to him. A web of control so wide and powerful it would somehow defeat the odds stacked against them. Modern France. Tracking down the clues to Christian Rosselot's murder in a way that was impossible thirty years ago.

Though just over an hour later, sitting in a Rouen café and sipping hot chocolate with a calvados chaser, watching through the rain for Guy Lévêque to return to his house, once again it felt like good old detective work. How it used to be.

'Pardon.'

At the sight of her boss with two other men in the cubicle, the girl pulled the curtain closed again and went to the next cubicle with her client.

'Okay, so what have we got?' asked Sauquière. 'My client names this Alain Duclos. Says that he comes to Perseus 2000 regularly and asks for young boys. What does my client get in return?'

Deleauvre looked between Sauquière and Eynard. Eynard with his ponytail and ridiculous purple satin shirt over his Buddha-like figure, Sauquière with his Armani blazer, furtive, darting eyes and greased-back hair. It was difficult to decide who looked seedier. The start of the meeting had been difficult, until Sauquière realized what cards Deleauvre was holding: a clear testimony from Ricauve implicating Eynard in supplying boys to a child pornographer. Sauquière suddenly showed interest in the benefits of his client in turn rolling over and naming somebody else. Deleauvre sighed. 'He's still going to have to do some time. But we'll make sure it's only two years rather than what he'd face normally, four or five. With remission, he'll be out in fifteen months.'

'And the clubs?'

'Perseus will probably have to close for six months.'

Sauquière threw his hands up. 'That's ludicrous. It's hardly worth cutting a deal.'

Deleauvre smiled tightly. The closure had hit a sore spot: the threat of Eynard's income squeezed, fat retainers being reduced. They argued the toss for a while, three months, one month, and then Deleauvre thought of an angle: gay activists. Closing Perseus could be sensitive. 'If the claim arises that this whole thing has been engineered just to close down one of the main gay night spots, it could become politically awkward. Something the judge would be eager to avoid . . . given pressure from the right quarter.'

Fifteen minutes later the foundation of the deal was decided: eighteen months to two years maximum for Eynard, Perseus stays open or, at worst, a one-month closure purely as a gesture. Current 'house' for young boys to close; if they wanted to open up discreetly elsewhere, then Deleauvre didn't want to know. But no supply of boys for paedophile magazines and videos.

Sauquière looked at his diary. 'I can't do tomorrow, busy day in court.'

They arranged for ten o'clock the following morning. Session room at the police station, taped interview, sample statement to be pre-prepared. 'You check it over, then your client gives a statement along those lines in his own words. Everybody's happy.' Deleauvre smiled, and they all shook hands.

Eynard had hardly spoken throughout. Sauquière had him well trained: a few words at the beginning, then later a brief confirmation that his term would be in an open prison. 'I've heard they're practically like hotels. I can still run my business from there. Catch up on my Rabelais.'

Deleauvre weaved back through the bar and the girls plying their trade. Some wore silver satin shorts and black see-through halter tops, others nothing but a tanga. One caught his eye as he passed, dipped one finger in her champagne glass, pulled her halter to one side to expose a breast, and teased the droplet around one nipple provocatively. She smiled. She was beautiful and very sensuous: a young Deneuve. Tempting. He smiled in return as if to say 'next time' and made his way out into the street.

Outside in Pigalle, a half-smile lingered on Deleauvre's face as he took out his mobile. Fornier would be pleased: they had Duclos' head on a platter.

Dominic was scanning the ground as the voice broke through . . . *Tails you lose* . . . and he looked up to see Duclos standing there. They were on the path by the wheat field. But it wasn't a young Duclos, it was Duclos from the last press photo he'd seen.

Duclos had the coin in his hand. He opened his palm for a second, allowing Dominic a tantalizing glimpse of it. Duclos smiled. Dominic made a desperate lunge for it, but Duclos closed his palm tight and swivelled around quickly . . . *You lose, Fornier!* In the same motion, throwing the coin high and wide . . .

Dominic watched it sailing high over the bushes and trees bordering the lane . . . realizing in sudden panic that if he didn't follow it, see where it fell, he wouldn't be able to find it later. He started running, following its path, bursting through bushes and foliage, feeling them lash across as he frantically ran down the river bank incline. 'Please, God . . . don't let it reach the river.' If it fell there, they would never find it. Lost for ever among the glint of rocks or beneath the river-bed mud.

The coin sailed high ahead of him as he thrashed frantically through the bushes . . . *You lose* . . . *You lose* . . . Breathless as he ran, a feeling of desolation as the coin soared almost out of sight . . . *Monsieur, coffee?* . . . a feeling that he couldn't possibly catch up with it before it fell. He wouldn't see where it fell, wouldn't be able to . . .

'Monsieur, coffee?'

Dominic woke up. A female attendant was pouring a cup for the man across the aisle. Dominic rubbed his eyes, caught her attention and nodded. 'Yes, please.'

He eased the stiffness from his back as he sat up straight. The past few days' activity and tension, the late nights with Lepoille, were catching up with him. He felt permanently tired. The coffee cut through his dry throat, cleared his thoughts.

Perhaps that was how it happened. Duclos saw the coin and threw it straight into the woods, or went to the edge of the bank so that it would reach the river. Or disposed of it later, dumped it along with Christian's shirt and the bloodied rock.

Only one lead left now. One hope remaining out of the original nine. Lepoille had phoned with another name while he waited in the Rouen café for Lévêque's return home. He'd called straight away. Nothing. Lévêque had been just as hopeless, hardly even remembered the garage, let alone the car or the coin.

Portions of the five conversations spun randomly through his mind. The man on the second call had commented: 'A coin, you say . . . now that's interesting . . .' Dominic's pulse had raced, only for the man to continue with a story about his nephew being a keen coin collector. 'I think he has one of that type in his collection. Bought it not long ago . . .'

Dominic shook his head. Nearly all of them had appeared more alert at the mention of the coin: 'Was it valuable?' . . . 'What type did you say?' . . . 'Was it from a robbery?' Cars they expected to be asked about, they'd handled little else for decades . . . but a coin linked to a murder inquiry? Something different from their daily grind. He had been so sure that one of them, just one of them would have . . . *Roudèle!* The thought crashed in abruptly. The pause. The long pause when he'd asked Roudèle about the coin and a dog had been barking in the distance. Roudèle hadn't asked any questions about the coin, showed no curiosity. Almost as if in that moment it had all come back to him, he knew exactly what Dominic was talking about. He didn't need to ask.

The thought settled. But then it could have been anything. A distraction: someone walking in the room, something interesting on the TV, Roudèle wondering why the dog was barking outside. Perhaps he should have visited each one personally, read their expressions, the look in their eyes.

A distraction, or did Roudèle know something? Dominic closed his eyes momentarily, sighing. Nothing underlined more strongly how little hope he placed in the remaining lead: a woman. Probably a secretary or receptionist. Certainly she wouldn't have worked on the car herself; the only hope was if she'd logged or recorded something found by one of the mechanics. Perhaps one of the three now dead. But what were the chances of her knowing something which nobody else in the garage had shared?

Dominic rested back, tried to get back to sleep. Catch another hour before they arrived at Lyon. He was exhausted.

When his mobile rang twenty minutes later, he was still drifting on the edge, revolving thoughts preventing him from falling fully under.

It was Deleauvre. 'We've got Duclos. Eynard's going to name him!'

The excitement suffused slowly; he was still half asleep. So tired. 'That's great. When's it happening?'

'Day after tomorrow. First thing in the morning.' Deleauvre summarized the deal with Sauquière.

'Will any children come forward in support?'

'No, too sensitive. A lot of them are illegals or runaways. It's complicated.'

Eighteen months, two years, thought Dominic. The maximum of four or five could only be gained with a child testifying and the claim of abuse. Poor consolation for murder, but at least Duclos' career would be ruined. 'Oh, how the mighty fall,' he commented, smiling. He thanked Deleauvre for his help, and they arranged to speak again straight after Eynard's statement.

Putting down his mobile, Dominic caught his own reflection in the train window: eyes dark-circled, haunted. The face of a man who *looked* like he'd been chasing the same case for thirty-odd years. But intermittently electric sparks from the train cut through the darkness outside and his reflection. How the investigation felt: hurtling through darkness with just a few flashes of hope.

Serge Roudèle remembered the coin straight away. He'd forgotten it had been an Alfa Romeo coupé, hadn't read where Fornier's questions were heading early in the conversation.

At the time, he'd been left his father's coin collection, but wasn't conversant himself with rarity and values. The coin had simply looked nice and could have had the potential to be rare. But when he'd checked, it hadn't been that valuable. Even when he'd sold it along with the rest of his father's collection just over ten years ago, he doubted it had garnered more than 500 or 600 francs.

And at today's rate? The offer of 5,000 francs was probably nearly four times its worth. Inspector Fornier was obviously valuing it at almost mint condition. His first thought had been theft – but would the police really pursue someone after over thirty years for a coin of such value? And then Fornier had mentioned murder, and he'd felt his blood run cold. He'd been eager to get off the line, let his thoughts clear.

Reward. No recriminations. But did they want the coin itself back, or just to know that he'd seen it? What would they think when they realized he'd sold it? And could he really believe Fornier's assurance of no recriminations? He remembered seeing a programme once about a police unit in America luring bail jumpers with letters promising lottery prizes. Part of a policeman's job was to trick, outwit criminals. How would they get people to come forward without some enticement?

The reward was tempting, he could do with the money. But would he be walking straight into a trap? His greed in taking the coin in the first place had caused this problem now, he reminded himself. A second bite at the same cherry was probably tempting fate.

37

Strasbourg, April 1995

Alain Duclos' hands shook as he addressed the EU assembly. The medical debate of the decade, and he was central rapporteur. It all rested now on this final stage of the debate: the case of John Moore and the ruling of the California Supreme Court.

The vote taken today was vitally important. The earlier call had come at the worst possible time: *'There's been a few questions with your name arising. Somebody's curious . . .'* It was Bonoit, a young Limoges prosecutor now with the Paris Palais de Justice. Bonoit had initially called Duclos' Brussels office, mentioned it was delicate. Duclos had phoned him back ten minutes later from a call box.

Reports were before each MEP, and Duclos summarized the key points. The University of California Medical Center had developed a unique cell line from a cancerous spleen removed from John Moore, filed for patent, then sold that development with resultant rights expected to yield over $1 billion from the pharmaceutical industry. 'Mr Moore subsequently sued, claiming ownership of the body part from which the cell line had been developed, but lost the case. The main premise of that ruling was that as soon as the organ left Mr Moore's body it ceased to be his property, and so was patentable.'

'I understand, though, that in a first action taken by Mr Moore, a court ruled in his favour?'

Duclos looked at the bank of interpreters beyond the MEPs' semi-circle: PDS, Italy. 'Yes – but this was overruled by the California Supreme Court. Another factor which weighed was the many years of genetic research taken to develop the cell line. A case of "added value" uniqueness, if you will.'

'. . . It's not directly my office – but because of the offbeat nature, it's being bounced around a few departments: questions about past cases involving psychics. Something to do with an original investigation back in 1963, apparently . . .'

Another voice rose. German Green Party: 'That "uniqueness" I believe was quite evident when Mr Moore's spleen was first removed. Mr Moore's argument is not only that he contributed the larger part of that uniqueness, but that he was not even consulted. That this was developed without his permission, and he was – as he described in his own words – "essence raped". His body part had ceased to become his own and was suddenly an industry commodity.'

Low mumbling: mixture of support and protest. The Green Party had invited Mr Moore to speak at a Brussels press conference during conciliation, Duclos recalled. If he couldn't get justice in America, then he could at least make history by influencing the future of European patent legislature. But every possible interest group – medical ethics, body and science rights, earth friendship, mainstream and fringe religious groups – had also come out strongly in support. Ownership of body parts was an emotive issue.

As the debates and arguments for and against flowed, Duclos rode the waves. His role as rapporteur was to take an impartial stance, merely present the facts and the varying arguments clearly, though he knew already what he wanted: rejection. At first a daunting if not seemingly impossible task. The EU Commission had already strongly backed a patents directive. The bill should sail through. If it didn't, it would be the first time a bill approved by the Commission at the plenary session was rejected by the Parliament. The whole conciliation process could be brought into question.

He'd pressed Bonoit for more information about the renewed invest-igation, but Bonoit knew little else; he promised to dig some more and suggested Duclos should call him back in a couple of days. The waiting to know was killing Duclos, and now the tension of the current debate. Incredible that the years of blackmail had brought him to this: swinging a key debate. But with the size of the coup, this one was as much for himself as for Jaumard. His retirement fund.

No trace of concern hopefully showed now in his face; his hands were pressed firmly on his folder to control their trembling. Enigmatic geniality as he tackled the various questions. The strength of the Greens' argument had laid a useful card in his hand.

Closing his presentation, Duclos provided a distilled summary of the arguments aired: a man whose cell line, he claims, is in itself unique. A laboratory claiming its three years of cell-line development was the largest contributor to that uniqueness. 'But at what stage do research and industry expertise give the new claimant predominant rights?' Duclos paused for emphasis. 'Yes, research and industry do need due protection in order to flourish. And the ruling in America should provide strong pre-eminent guidance to the assembly in that respect. But the many controversial issues raised by that decision need also to be taken into account. With the main question now: can the assembly rest easy with such a ruling in Europe and discard the arguments against, based purely on the fact that industry requires due protection for its research? Furtherance of science or furtherance of the rights of the individual? Thank you.'

Duclos closed his folder. He was sweating profusely. Hopefully he'd struck the right tone without being too obvious, but he couldn't be sure. Reactions looked mixed. Nothing left now but to wait for the votes to come in.

Metz, April 1995

Duclos never felt comfortable calling Marchand from either Strasbourg or Brussels, so invariably he would stop at a call box halfway in between. He found one on a quiet road eight kilometres beyond Metz. Georges Marchand answered almost immediately.

'What progress?' Duclos asked.

'The transfer was made three days ago. It should be in the account now.'

'Did you see the press coverage?'

'Yes, very encouraging. They were very pleased.'

To anyone listening in, a totally unidentifiable conversation, Duclos reflected. No names, no subject discussed. Only the two of them knew the gaps to be filled in: the EU Parliament had rejected the bio-technology patents directive. The Commission and industry lobby groups had cried 'Outrage', and had started talking about tabling a new directive. But the present directive had already been five years in preparation; a new one, even if successful, could take up to three years.

A remarkable coup. Better even than they'd anticipated. They'd agreed a month's grace after the decision to let the dust settle, then the transfer would be made. Additional transfers would then follow for each successive year without a successfully approved bio-technology patents directive.

'Looks like we might be in for a good run on this one. Anything from two to four years,' Marchand commented.

'Let's hope so. I'll probably do some Christmas shopping in Geneva this year.'

'Yes, certainly. It would be nice to see you again.'

Probably not, thought Duclos. At their one meeting, he'd sensed that Marchand hadn't liked him, nor had he particularly liked Marchand. A Geneva- rather than Brussels-based lobbyist – to Duclos, Marchand typified the breed of self-serving industry lawyers and lobbyists who constantly snapped at his and other politicians' heels. In return lobbyists were often resentful that politicians hadn't dealt with their clients' 'issue' effectively, labelling them incompetent at every turn. But the pecking order was always clear: politicians looking down, disdainfully; lobbyists looking up, resentfully.

Except that Duclos had broken from the mould, was a corrupt politician. One of the few Marchand felt he could look down upon. The air of mutual disdain could have been cut with a knife. The only common ground arose from the money they were both gaining through their association. Strange how money of that size created its own inertia, Duclos reflected: it cut across so many social divides.

Duclos shook off an involuntary shiver. Telephone boxes. The third in as many days. More information at last from Bonoit.

'Who's leading the inquiry?' Duclos asked anxiously.

'Corbeix. Aix-en-Provence-based chief prosecutor.'

The name meant nothing to Duclos. 'What stage is the inquiry at?'

'As far as I know, just the initial *commission rogatoire*.'

'Who's heading it?'

'There's two names: Mallié and Fornier. They've also been doing a lot of digging with pimps and gay establishments in Paris and Marseille for some reason.'

Duclos sensed the unspoken questions. 'Strange,' he commented. He felt his skin prickle. *Fornier?* The name rang a bell from somewhere, but he couldn't remember from where.

'What's going on, Alain?' Bonoit sounded suddenly concerned. 'You know, I shouldn't even be phoning you like this. It's just that, well, in the past . . .'

'I know, and I appreciate it.' Was Bonoit fishing, or seeking assurance? Duclos had given Bonoit strong support during his fledgeling years with the Limoges prosecutor's office. Eagerness for Bonoit not to see his mentor's image shattered, or repayment of favours? 'It's nothing. I was questioned for something several years ago and cleared. They found and charged the real culprit. Sounds a bit like a political witch-hunt to me – old enemies coming out of the woodwork. Probably this bio-tech dispute.

Seems to have upset a lot of people. I'm not exactly flavour of the month right now.'

Bonoit muttered an agreement which hardly registered. Everything suddenly gelled for Duclos. *Paris!* His pulse started racing. He couldn't wait to get off the line and make another call.

He quickly thanked Bonoit, and Bonoit promised to call again if anything more came up. Duclos leafed through the back of his address book for the number. It took him a while to find it, he hadn't called the number for almost fifteen years. The digits were jumbled and out of sequence, with each set of two in reverse. A number from the past he had long forgotten and didn't think he would ever have to call again: a Marseille back-street bar which would pass a message to Eugène Brossard.

Corbeix's body invariably told him it was time to go home an hour before twilight. As the effects of the steroids wore off, the cramps and muscle spasms returned to his legs. He'd been free from them for almost five days, then suddenly they had flared up again. About the time that Fornier had phoned to tell him all the coin leads had come up blank.

Fornier had put in a lot of work on the case. He also seemed to be able to pull favours at short notice, getting half of an Interpol department to back up his frantic nationwide search. Nine people from thirty years ago traced in just three days. Corbeix was impressed. But despite Fornier's effort and ingenuity, in the end, nothing. To have lived with the case for so long, to get so close and then see it slip away. Cruel fate. Corbeix felt for Fornier.

Raking through what meagre hopes remained, Fornier had asked him if he'd uncovered anything useful on past French cases involving psychics. He didn't have the heart to tell Fornier he'd hit a similar dead-end, said that he was still waiting on news. While five days of probing various departments in the Paris Prosecutor General's Office had uncovered eight cases with relatives or the press involving psychics, some of which had been entered in police files, none of them had ever made it into trial evidence. The consensus was that even if a prosecutor believed he could convince a final jury with such evidence, the examining magistrate was a different matter. Most dropped it for fear of jeopardizing the case through *instruction.*

A Sorbonne law lecturer who advised on unorthodox cases had raised some useful points from relevant trials in America, but still the bottom line was that psychic and PLR testimony could only successfully be presented in France as background and texture. 'Without at least some hard evidence from the living rather than the dead, I don't see any foundation on which to build.'

With the last coin lead now gone, their last hope of prosecuting Duclos for murder had disappeared.

But at least from what Fornier had mentioned, there appeared to be strong hope in one area: Justin Eynard, a Paris red-light club owner. If nothing else, their chances of prosecuting Duclos for child molestation looked bright. Some silver edging. Ten o'clock tomorrow morning. No doubt by eleven or eleven-thirty, Fornier would have a result, would phone him and then the fax machine would start whirring with Eynard's statement. At least he could start moving things positively on one front.

Justin Eynard lay back on the bed while the girl undid his shirt buttons. She smiled up at him lasciviously. A sunshine smile with a hint of mischief. Juanita from Santo Domingo was all he knew. An enticing mixture of negro and Spanish: dark *café au lait* skin tone and large brown eyes. Exquisite.

She watched his every emotion as she kissed slowly down his chest and stomach with each fresh button undone. Sampling the merchandise: executive benefit of running a hookers' bar. Eynard insisted on testing out all new girls and judging their fighting weight for clients.

Eynard tensed as she went lower. A few slow licks, and then she took him fully into her mouth. Eynard gasped. *God*, she was good. She wore a white satin evening dress slit to the thigh which contrasted wonderfully with her skin tone. As she sucked and rubbed him into her mouth with one hand, the other reached back and pulled aside the lower part of her dress to expose her bottom. She arched it higher. Underneath she wore a peach-coloured tanga. Two coffee ice-cream scoops separated by a peach slice.

Eynard watched in the mirror to one side as she deftly pulled the tanga aside and started rubbing herself in time with the motions of her mouth. Her fingernails were long and turquoise varnished with star bursts, and intermittently she would slip a finger inside herself.

Eynard was in heaven. His breath started to come in short bursts and, sensing his growing excitement, with one last loving lick the girl rolled away. Peeling off her dress, she bent away from Eynard to accentuate her bottom, then resumed playing with herself while sliding one finger in and out of her mouth in time. Eynard groaned in anticipation.

Slowly she peeled down the tanga, stepped out and leant back over Eynard. Her breasts were firm and cantaloupe-sized with large brown nipples the size of cookies. Coffee ice-cream and chocolate cookies. All Eynard could think of.

With a few more licks to resume acquaintance, Juanita swung one leg across and slowly sank down on Eynard. She reached back and grasped him gently by the balls, as if to push him firmer inside. As she started to get into the rhythm of the motions, she closed her eyes in abandon, sucking on the little finger of her other hand.

Eynard felt his excitement mounting, a raw tingle rising from the back of his heels. *Jesus*, this girl knew what she was doing. His clients were in for a rare treat. He reached out a hand and stroked her breasts, tweaked one nipple.

She writhed slowly and determinedly, picking up the pace gradually. Control. A virtuoso performance. Eynard felt his senses floating, the tingle rising higher.

'Close your eyes. I haff big treat.' The Spanish came through in her accent. A pleasant lilt.

Eynard smiled and closed his eyes obediently. He felt her finger slide into his mouth, teasing his tongue. And then the other hand was behind him again, gently stroking, urging him into her with each thrust.

So good . . . *good*.

Eynard felt something slide in beside her finger, cool and longer . . . plastic or metal? The finger slipped out. *Oh God*, a vibrator, he should have told her he wasn't into that sort of thing.

His eyes snapped open, and he went to shift his head away from the object . . . but a hand clamped tight on his forehead. The object suddenly came into focus: the silenced barrel of a gun. The girl's arms were still on his chest. Someone was behind him! Panic seized Eynard. Fear and the repellent feel of the gun metal against his tongue made him almost gag. The girl lifted off and moved away. He was already half limp, the excitement gone.

Eynard looked longingly towards her back as she headed for the bathroom, knowing in that moment it was probably the last girl he would see.

'It's done.'

'I see. Fine. I made the transfer as arranged.'

Brossard had already checked but didn't pass any comment.

Another call box, another conversation with no names or details. Duclos could imagine Brossard at the other end in a similar call box in Paris. They hadn't even met this time to set everything up. Just a voice on the line. He wondered what Brossard looked like now? Then realized he hadn't even known what Brossard looked like then, seventeen years ago in his blond wig and thick-rimmed glasses.

Duclos had called Eynard's bar only days before to set up a weekend in Paris and one of the barmen apologized that Justin was a bit pressured lately but that he should try again later. 'Anything serious?' Duclos had asked. 'No, just some stupid mix-up with the police over some child porno videos.' Duclos knew as soon as Bonoit mentioned the police hunting for background on pimps that Eynard might be a problem.

But if the police kept digging for something on himself and under-age boys, eventually they were bound to find something. Next time he might have to be more inventive.

Wheat. Shorter than Dominic remembered. Spring; over the next month or so it would no doubt grow alarmingly before being harvested.

Thirty-one years since he'd stood in the same field: the day of the reconstruction. The wind had been high then, the wheat shifting wildly, unkempt and hardly harvested from one season to the next. Now it was neatly trimmed and cared for, a half-metre short from its full harvesting height. And today there was no wind, the air still, a thin grey cloud layer with some diffused sunlight filtering through.

Stillness. Sterile. The crime scene washed clean by the shifting seasons and years, the many different families who'd owned the farm since. No trace left. Only distant images struggling to replay in Dominic's mind.

Originally Dominic had intended just to stay in Vidauban. A half-hour after hearing the news about Eynard, he'd gone to the nearest bar for a quick brandy. He'd called Guidier on his mobile from the bar: 'I'll be gone the rest of the day. I'll phone in for any messages early evening. Anything urgent, get me on my mobile.'

Time to think, clear his thoughts. He would spend probably a day or two down at Vidauban. He needed the rest, had hardly slept all week. He was exhausted.

Arriving at the farmhouse, he'd headed straight for the bedroom and lain flat on the bed. Solitude. Jérôme was working, probably wouldn't be back until six or seven. Monique was at the flat in Lyon, no doubt thought he was still at work. He would phone later to tell her he was staying overnight. Perhaps he would take Jérôme to a local bar to help him drown his sorrows.

But he'd been unable to sleep, had stared blankly up at the ceiling with too many thoughts jumbling. Coin leads all gone. Eynard gone. Nothing left. But that conclusion wouldn't settle, just didn't feel right. Monique's words from a few days before: 'There must be something, *something!*' Some small detail that perhaps he'd overlooked from the hours of tapes and transcripts from Eyran Capel. He felt angry this time; could feel it coursing through his veins, driving him on.

Though it wasn't until two hours later, after lunch and a chain of discarded notes headed *Coin? Truck? Restaurant? Lane?* – questions with few answers – that something useful finally came: *bottled water!* He'd been in the shower when the thought hit, the water swilling around him as he stood stock still for a moment . . . *Some other water running . . . spilling on the ground* . . . Duclos had just come from a restaurant, he didn't need to go down to the river where Machanaud might have seen him!

Dominic decided to head out to Taragnon and the field. He stood where he thought Duclos must have been after the final assault on Christian: a few paces into the wheat, his car parked just behind. Dominic summoned up the picture in his mind: Duclos' clothes are off, perhaps on the car seat or draped over the open boot. The bloodied rock is in his hand, his body splattered with blood. He knows he can't stay on the lane long for risk of someone passing.

Back to the car . . . Dominic walked the few paces, his feet crunching on the wheat . . . takes out the bottled water, swills down. Dominic imagined the heat of the day, a heat haze perhaps rising off the field.

Then dabs dry with . . . *with?* A cloth or towel from his car, or Christian's shirt? Perhaps that explained why Christian's shirt had been missing. Whichever, Duclos had obviously dumped it along with the rock somewhere.

And then the coin. Had Duclos discovered the coin? Was that why none of the garage workers or neither of the Caugines had seen it? And if so, had he thrown it away immediately or later with the rock and Christian's shirt? Or had he been stupid enough to hang on to it as a memento? A trophy. Dominic shook his head and smiled wryly. A sudden image of a dawn raid on Duclos' house – the coin found in a drawer under his underwear and silk cravats, Corbeix slapping his shoulder in congratulation – bringing home how far he was reaching.

Dominic crossed the lane and headed down the river bank. The river was grey, silent, reflecting the mood of the sky above. No glints reflecting from the rocks and shale; Dominic could hardly even make out the bottom.

Then he was back looking past Molet's shoulder at some leaves drifting past. The first realization that Machanaud's case was slipping away. Three decades melted away in an instant.

He looked down the river to where Machanaud had stood that day, then up the bank to where Duclos had parked his car. *Fourteen years in prison?* An afternoon's poaching, a few fish for Machanaud's supper. Dominic shook his head.

He decided to backtrack on everything else. He timed it to the restaurant: four minutes. It was now a hardware store. Dominic stayed in the car park, closed his eyes and imagined Duclos playing for time inside, making sure he was seen for his alibi, selecting from the menu and eating at leisure, sipping at his wine. Christian in the darkness of the boot, probably only metres from where he was now, trapped and afraid. Dreaming about his father and the farm . . . wondering if he was going to be harmed. Dominic shuddered.

The two women come out of the restaurant. Christian hears their voices, kicks out. But a truck passes at that moment, drowns out the sound. Their car doors open, close, they start driving away. Duclos settles his bill, asks for a bottle of water to take away.

Dominic drove out, headed back towards where Christian's bike had been left. A Citroën passed, followed soon after by a Mercedes van. Christian's truck superimposed: MARSEILLE, V-A-R-N and LA PONTEI . . . ? There was a small industrial park called La Ponteille in Marseille, but they hadn't looked hard. A driver recalling a young boy in a passing sports car thirty years later? Desperately reaching again.

Where the bike had been was now planted with vines, only two rows of peach trees remained at the back of the field. Perhaps if only forensics had checked here as well, Dominic reflected. No semen had been found in examining Christian, only ruptured vessels indicated a sexual assault. Duclos had obviously pulled out to ejaculate. Nothing was found by the wheat field, but what would have been the chances here? Christian's bike had by then been found and moved – Dominic wasn't even sure if he was standing in the right spot now. *Between what might have been and what had come to pass* . . . Dominic sighed. Probably they wouldn't have found anything.

He headed towards Bauriac. On the edge of town the tanneries were closed and derelict. A sign announced the development of industrial units to be completed in April 1997. No more acrid fumes . . . *Stinging his eyes as he drove out to see Monique, to tell her . . .*

Dominic stopped in the square and looked across at Louis' old bar. Louis. Dead these past seven years. He'd married and had three children with Valérie and sold the bar almost twenty years ago. Bought a small hotel on the coast near Mandelieu. Dominic had holidayed there *en famille* quite a few summers, spent days out fishing and reminiscing on Louis' speedboat. Jérôme had struck up a friendship with Louis' youngest, Xavier, and they still kept in touch. Valérie still ran the hotel, though they'd only been down to see her twice since Louis' death.

Dominic got out and walked across to the bar. He realized he hadn't been inside since Louis sold it, had hardly been back to Taragnon or Bauriac in all those years. Too painful. Even when they'd bought the farmhouse in Vidauban and might pass through on the way to Aix, Dominic would make sure to choose an alternative route.

Black and chrome: black velvet chairs, black smoked-glass table tops with chrome trim. The bar counter was black and had three thick chrome strips on the facing support. It was almost empty, with just a few stragglers at the bar and one table. The new owner obviously went for the evening cocktail crowd. Or perhaps this is what teenagers and bikers liked nowadays.

Dominic ordered a brandy. No jukebox. A powerful sound system played Brian Adams' 'Run To You'. Some French rap followed. The barman was young, slim and had a ponytail. As far removed from Louis as you could get. Dominic smiled. He drained his glass and ordered another brandy. Suddenly the alcohol felt good, cut through the images: Louis dancing with Valérie to the jukebox, him driving out to tell Monique, *tell her that* . . . the lorry flashing past, Christian trapped in the car boot, *the coin* . . . Duclos raising his wine glass, *gloating*. Dominic gripped his glass tight.

He knocked it back sharply, ordered again. Some heavy rock followed. Dominic headed for the toilets to escape. The images were too vivid, too harsh. He wished now he hadn't come back. He splashed some water on his face to freshen up. Catching his reflection in the mirror as he straightened, suddenly it struck him: he hadn't returned just to hunt for clues, but for himself. To relive the memories, then bury them once and for all. At heart he knew it was all futile, hopeless. No startling revelations would be sparked off just by him being there again. Duclos had outwitted them all thirty years ago, and he'd done it again now. Had somehow got to Eynard before them. It was over. *Over!* Even if they did find something, Duclos would no doubt beat them to it yet again, would . . .

'*Ça va, Monsieur?* Is everything okay?'

Dominic focused past his shoulder. An old man turning from the urinal was looking on concernedly. Images of Machanaud raising his eau-de-vie: '*How's the investigation going?*'

'Fine, just fine,' Dominic muttered. Suddenly he had to get out. He paid the barman, knocked back his brandy and headed back to Vidauban. He slotted in a CD to drown out the heavy rock still ringing in his ears: Simply Red. Jérôme had introduced him. His generation's soul music. Years before he'd introduced Jérôme to his own time-warped soul collection.

Dominic felt the music soothing him. The images and emotions started to settle. He should never have gone back . . . *never*. He banged the wheel in annoyance. Simply Red was singing about nothing past feeling good yet still holding on. Holding on? And as the words and rhythm flowed through him, mouthing silently to some of the verses, he wondered whether he'd chosen it because it was one of his favourites, or because subconsciously it just seemed to . . .

He bit at his lip. Tears welling suddenly gave him the answer. And the rest of the emotions and images he'd been fighting back, bubbling like raw acid beneath the surface, suddenly broke free: Monique in the hospital with the candle burning, him calling at her door and saying that Christian was dead, *dead*. The gendarmes' tapping through the wheat field. Jean-Luc's solitary figure at the back of the field. Louis smiling, pouring him another brandy, winking as a pretty girl passed. His mother smiling in the fading light at the beauty of the garden and the tangerine tree. All gone now, *all gone*. Old friends, loved ones, the endless chain of work colleagues long buried with heart attacks or liver failure. Even the memories now dull and faded with the years.

All that was left now was a voice. The lost and lonely voice of a small boy murdered over thirty years ago.

The welling tears stung his eyes, and Dominic thought stupidly, 'I'm too old to cry. Seen too much, buried too many friends. *Too many*.' But the long years of holding back the memories, of fighting back the tears, biting at his lip with each friend lost, each funeral, had built a veritable tidal wall. And as his last defences were stripped away, the barricades suddenly broken by that lone pathetic voice, by the week's activities and now the sudden recall and memories, it all flooded in a rush behind, the wave crashing down relentlessly. His whole body was suddenly racked with sobbing.

The road ahead blurred as his eyes watered, a pastel abstract. He had to pull over to the side and stop.

He cried at the injustice, cried for the lost years, cried for the loved ones and friends long since buried and forgotten, cried and cried and cried until his whole body started to tremble; a ridiculous, pathetic shaking that gradually struck him as amusing as much as sad and distressing. And he found himself half laughing between the sobs as it continued, as he glanced up and noticed a passing young man looking towards him concernedly.

He wiped his eyes hurriedly as he fought to recover, regain his composure.

For the rest of the drive to Vidauban, he felt strangely relaxed, calm. As if the sudden catharsis had washed away all the past bitter memories along with his false hopes and the frustrations of the past week. It was in the past. It was gone. How could he have ever deluded himself that he could solve some past problem with something now, thirty years on? That barrier was probably never even meant to have been crossed.

His life put in order, everything at last in perspective, when Dominic hit his bed back at Vidauban, the wave of exhaustion of the past days finally caught up with him. He fell into a deep sleep almost immediately. Though some faint memories still replayed: the tinkling of goats' bells from the next field, the church bells announcing the service for Christian Rosselot . . .

All that broke through his subconscious from his mobile ringing in his jacket pocket.

At the other end, Serge Roudèle counted off the third ring. He decided to wait three more rings before giving up. Ever superstitious, if it didn't answer by then he would read that as a clear message that he wasn't meant to make contact, confirming his first assumption about Fornier's call: it was a trick. He wouldn't call again.

38

The tape-recorder red light flicked on as the small bleep sounded. The operator, Lassarde, glanced up. Third recording of the night, must be approaching the hundredth now over the past five days. How long did Bennacer intend to keep the line tap running? He sipped at his coffee, stared numbly at the reels turning.

'*What time will you be here?*'

'*About nine, nine-thirty on the Saturday. Pretty much as usual. You mentioned a new boy. How does he compare with my usual, Jean-Pierre? Is he as young?*'

A pause, faint clearing of the throat. '*Look, let's discuss all that when you get here. Don't worry, you won't be disappointed.*'

Lassarde sat up. *Young boys.* Aurillet, the child pimp they'd tapped, sounded nervous talking about their ages over the phone. But who was at the other end? From what he'd been briefed, he doubted it was Duclos. This sounded like a regular, someone who visited practically every weekend. Duclos was apparently more a seasonal visitor. But because Duclos called rarely, hopefully he might announce himself – even though they might wait weeks for the call. Patience.

Lassarde looked at the digital monitor as the number came up: Toulon exchange. As he thought, the caller was a local regular. Brussels, Strasbourg or Limoges were what they expected with Duclos. The call finished with a few pleasantries, nothing significant. Lassarde got Bennacer's attention from the main squad room and brought him in, replayed the short segment.

Bennacer looked up as it finished. 'How many is that now with young boys mentioned?'

'Seven or eight. The rest has been just day-to-day stuff: bar stock, social calls, accountant, arranging builders to lay some new tiling in his main club, Nuages. Pretty mundane. And this is the first call where anyone has got close to talking about the age of the boys.'

Otherwise Aurillet could claim that 'boys' referred to sixteen or above, thought Bennacer. The legal age of consenting homosexuals. It would be that much harder to nail Aurillet and subsequently Duclos. Even if a call came through linking the two.

Three more days passed before another call came through which made Lassarde sit up.

'. . . *he's a runaway, looking for a secure place. He should be ideal for you. Can't be more than twelve or thirteen.*'

'*I don't know . . . I don't know if I can get involved.*'

'*What's wrong? You have before.*'

Lassarde smiled. A street pimp supplying to Aurillet. Aurillet's attempts to step back had put him in deeper water. The rest of the conversation was stilted, Aurillet non-committal before he signed off. '*Bring him around. But I really can't promise anything.*'

Though fourteen hours later, Lassarde once again disturbed Bennacer urgently in the squad room. Reading the anxiousness in Lassarde's expression, Bennacer broke short his telephone conversation and followed Lassarde hurriedly back into the small room. The recording was halfway through.

'. . . *probably three weeks from now. I just wanted to make sure that Bernard would be there.*'

'*Yes, he will. Everything will be arranged as usual. Do you know which day? Will it be the weekend, as before?*'

'*Yes, I think so. Probably the Saturday, late afternoon.*'

Bennacer looked at the digital display: 32-2-236521. Brussels number. Then sharply at Lassarde. 'Is it him?'

Lassarde merely nodded, drew hard on his cigarette.

'. . . *Fine. Look forward to seeing you then.*'

A click. The red light went out as the tape stopped.

'Okay, let's hear it from the beginning,' said Bennacer. Rewind it.'

Dominic hit 'play'.

'*It's Duclos. Is it all right to talk? Are you with anyone?*'

'*No, it's fine.*'

'*I'll be coming down soon.*'

'*When will that be?*'

'*I'm not totally sure yet, but probably three weeks from now. I just wanted to make sure that Bernard would be there.*'

'*Yes, he will. Everything will be arranged as . . .*'

A car horn blared to Dominic's side as he swung around the roundabout.

Somebody filtering in from the right. Coming out of the roundabout, traffic was slow, a long tail-back ahead.

Dominic had already heard the cassette briefly. When Bennacer had called, Dominic had asked him to play it over the line so that one of his radio officers could make a cassette copy. He was heading out urgently for a meeting with Corbeix and he wanted to take it with him.

Dominic hovered over the operator anxiously while the tape was being made, replayed it quickly once, then grabbed a portable cassette player and the tape and headed for his car. But he was worried that with the extra ten minutes' wait and now with heavy traffic heading out of Lyon, he would be late for Corbeix.

Three weeks? No, it wasn't worth waiting. Everything else on Duclos was practically in place. Dominic made the decision there and then. The traffic started to move ahead as he dialled Bennacer on his mobile. Brief routing through the Marseille station desk, then Bennacer's voice.

'Go for it,' said Dominic. 'We can't afford to wait. Raid Aurillet's place now and haul him in. Grill him as hard as you can on Duclos.'

'Do you think we've got enough?'

'Let's hope so. I just don't think we're going to get much more. We've got under-age boys on one call, Duclos on another. Let's just try and forge the two together as best we can. Good luck.'

'We were meant to service the car, give it a thorough check-over, clean it up for display.'

'What particular duty were you given?' Corbeix asked.

'To check all the tyre treads and pressures, check the wheel balance and alignment. Which included checking the spare-tyre pressure.'

Dominic walked in, nodded quickly to Corbeix. 'Sorry I'm late.' He took a seat at the end of the table on the same side as Corbeix and the notary.

Corbeix leant over the tape machine. 'Chief Inspector Fornier enters the room at 3.12 p.m. Interview resumes . . .' Corbeix looked briefly at his notes. 'Now. Checking the tyre pressure and wheel balance – what would that involve?'

'It means taking off all the tyres and spinning them for balance and then testing with a gauge for pressure. Including the spare tyre – which in this case was located in the boot.'

Dominic realized they had obviously already covered most of the preliminaries, including the year Roudèle worked in the garage and the type of car. Details he had already gained on tape the night after Roudèle's initial call.

Eleven days and the whole nature of the case had changed. Surprise and elation with Roudèle's initial call had brought him quickly alert from his sleep. A quick call to Corbeix, and he was booked on a flight to Limoges the same night. He taped an interview with Roudèle and a date was arranged for an official statement with Corbeix and a notary. Two days later, Bennacer's precinct received an anonymous tip-off about Duclos and a local child pimp, Vincent Aurillet. Within twenty-four hours they had a line tap arranged with France Telecom. Now that too had paid off.

The only drawback was that Roudèle's initial call had disturbed him barely an hour into his sleep. And due to the renewed activity, his sleep pattern had been poor since. Three weeks on a frantic rollercoaster bouncing between hope, despair and back again. His nerve ends were frayed raw. He'd never felt so tired. Only wild adrenalin drove him on.

'And after removing the car's spare tyre, what did you find that day?'

'A coin, a silver coin.'

'Can you please describe it to us?'

'It was from Italy, dated 1928. A silver twenty lire.'

'Do you know if it was particularly rare or valuable?'

'Reasonably rare in France. It was the first time I had come across one here, at least. But they're obviously more common in Italy, because the value wasn't that high.'

'What did you do with the coin when you saw it?'

'I put it in the pocket of my overalls.'

'Did anyone else see you take it?'

'No . . . not that I was aware.'

The atmosphere in the room was tense. Only Corbeix's and Roudèle's voices and the notary silently observing. The sound of the tape whirring in the gaps between questions. Dominic noticed his hand rested on the table shaking slightly. Build-up of tiredness and nerves and the traffic rush getting there.

'Having taken the coin, what did you do with it? How long did it stay in your possession?'

'I kept it with my father's coin collection until ten or eleven years ago. Then it was sold along with the rest of the collection.'

'Do you remember the name of the place where you sold it?'

'Yes. A coin shop in the centre of Limoges – Bagoudet.'

Corbeix leant forward again. 'Let the record show that the coin shop in question was visited on 26 April by Chief Inspector Fornier. An entry record was found for the coin in question, dated 18 October 1984. A statement was taken from the coin shop's proprietor and entered on form . . .' Corbeix leafed through the papers before him, found the statement form and read out the number. The notary checked the statement form briefly, passed it back.

After seeing Roudèle, Dominic had stayed overnight in Limoges to visit the coin shop. Corbeix felt it was essential to back up Roudèle's statement in case Duclos' defence tried to rip holes in it, suggest that he was fabricating purely to collect the reward offered. The coin shop provided that last vital link.

The coin brought originally from Italy by Jean-Luc's father, passed to Christian, then Duclos' car and the garage worker . . . the trail had finally ended in a musty basement in Limoges with an aged coin-shop proprietor leafing through dusty files. Somehow appropriate.

And then suddenly everything was in rapid motion: line taps, statements and notaries, a frantic flurry of paperwork crossing Corbeix's desk, the strands spun wide weeks ago now fast pulling in. Everything converging. Dominic drew a slow breath, trying to ease his jaded nerves. Aware that now as he sat with Corbeix and Roudèle, at the same moment in Marseille, Bennacer and his men would be bursting into Aurillet's office . . .

'I really can't help you. I'm sorry, I wish I could.'

'Oh, but I think you can.' Bennacer had arranged the three most incriminating conversations in a loop so that they ran in succession. He pressed play and sat closely observing Aurillet's expression.

The only other person in the small interview room was Moudeux, a lumbering DI whom Aurillet had been handcuffed to in the back of a black Citroën on the way down to the police station. A head taller than Aurillet, Moudeux had spent much of the journey jibing: 'You into bondage, are you? I understand you guys sometimes sample the merchandise. Do you test the boys yourself? What do you do, put these on them?' Moudeux raised the handcuffs. 'I suppose with an ugly shit like you, they'd come in useful. Stop them getting away.'

Aurillet had stayed silent throughout. The first few questions from Bennacer he met with blank denials, and now Moudeux stayed silent, just contemplated Aurillet with his slow, doleful eyes and smiled menacingly. As the tape ran, Aurillet stared nervously down at the table.

He looked faintly puzzled as the Duclos segment came on; unlike the other two conversations, children weren't mentioned. Just a name: Bernard.

'Fine. Look forward to seeing you then.'

Bennacer stopped the tape. 'So. We've got you clearly on supply of under-age children *and* your connection with Alain Duclos. What we want to know is how far your association goes back with Duclos. All the details.'

'I don't understand. Why are you so interested in him?'

'It concerns another investigation we're running. You're not the main focus here. What we're mainly concerned about is your involvement with Duclos. The wheres and whens of you supplying him with young boys through the years.'

Aurillet shook his head. 'Young boys?' He laughed nervously. 'That Marcus is crazy. Twelve and thirteen. He knows I never take them that young – but he keeps trying his luck. Keeps phoning.'

Bennacer stared at him blandly. 'I don't have time to sit here while your credibility and my patience are stretched. We know you trade in under-age boys. But as I said, you are not – I repeat *not* – our main interest. Duclos is.' Bennacer exhaled. 'So let's try again. Once more: Duclos and young boys. What do you know?'

Aurillet contemplated his shoes. Then the tape machine. 'It's awkward. I'm not sure where all of this will lead. I might incriminate myself. I don't think I should say anything without my lawyer present.'

Bennacer lifted his eyes to the ceiling. Strained effort to keep his voice calm: 'That's your prerogative. If that's your wish, then I'm afraid there is really nothing more for us to discuss at this juncture. I'm going to break this interview for ten minutes and leave you to decide fully. If when I return your decision is still the same, then you'll be held over until your lawyer's arrival.' Bennacer faced the mike. 'Interview suspended at three-eighteen p.m.'

Bennacer stopped the tape. Aurillet's eyes followed Bennacer to the door, darting back briefly to Moudeux: a 'surely you're not leaving me alone with him' look.

Moudeux smiled. He reached over and touched Aurillet's hand. 'Don't worry, I'll keep you company.'

Aurillet recoiled sharply, pulled his hand away. The door shut.

Bennacer stayed out of the room for sixteen minutes. When he returned, Aurillet's expression was strained, haunted. He got the impression that there had been silence between Aurillet and Moudeux for several minutes. Aurillet had reached his decision a while ago.

'Okay. I agree to help. What is it you want to know about Duclos?'

Bennacer started the tape. He didn't ask what had happened while he was out to make Aurillet change his mind. Moudeux's smug smile told him that everything had gone more or less according to their earlier plan.

'Was Aurillet difficult?'

'No, not too bad. There was a sticky moment when he wanted to see his lawyer. But I left him with one of my DIs, Moudeux, for a moment to contemplate the error of his ways. Moudeux explained the relative advantages of him co-operating.'

'Official or unofficial? Was it recorded as part of the interview?' Dominic asked.

'No. When I left the room I stopped the tape. I don't think I'd like any of Moudeux's usual vernacular recorded officially. But thankfully he usually doesn't have to say much. He dwarfs most people and he's got this great smile. Makes Jack Nicholson look like Mother Teresa.'

Dominic laughed, swirled the whisky in its tumbler. Bennacer's call had come through on his mobile fifteen minutes after the session with Roudèle, while he was still in Corbeix's office going through final notes. Corbeix had taken a bottle of Southern Comfort from his desk-side cabinet and poured them both a third tumblerful. Interim celebration: the successful conclusion to one stage, *santé* to the stage ahead.

Dominic signed off and filled in the details for Corbeix on Bennacer's call. 'I've asked him to fax over a copy of the statement to both our offices once it's typed up. 'Should come through in an hour or so.'

Corbeix raised his glass. 'Another piece in place.'

They sat silently drinking for a second. Dominic was exhausted. He felt somehow awkward, at a loose end. With the past weeks of hectic activity, it felt strange that now there was nothing left for him to do. Now it all rested with Corbeix. 'When would you hope to file and get a warrant?'

'Let's see.' Corbeix flicked through some papers. 'I checked MEPs' timetables the other day. I don't want to serve in Brussels – administrative nightmare. The next time Duclos is in Strasbourg is in nine days. I'll need six in any case to finish up paperwork and advise an examining magistrate. So – third or fourth of May.'

'I'd like to be there when he's arrested.'

'You don't have to. Two Strasbourg Judiciary policemen will go, serve, and transport will be arranged for Duclos' transfer to Aix.'

'I'd still like to be there.' Dominic smiled. 'Outside of the press, it's been quite a while since I've seen Alain Duclos. I was but a young gendarme. Should be quite nostalgic.'

'I know it's been a long time for you.' Corbeix grimaced as he swallowed another shot: pain and sympathy. 'Are you sure you'll be okay accompanying?'

'I'm not going to slug Duclos on the Parliament steps, if that's what you mean. As tempting as it might be.' Dominic shrugged, his smile subsiding. Thoughtful. 'So much of this has been dealt with from a distance. Often it's felt intangible, unreal. I need something physical to end the process. The warrant being served, the handcuffs being slapped on, the expression on Duclos' face. Then I'll know: we've got him! Right now I still have to pinch myself that it's all over.'

And I'm only just starting, Corbeix thought. But it wasn't the moment to remind Fornier of the difficulties ahead. That Duclos' heavyweight lawyers would bombard the case from so many angles, he'd hardly be given time to draw breath. Hopefully he'd shored up all their main areas of vulnerability, but what if he'd overlooked something? One foot-fault and Duclos could walk after the first few *instruction* hearings. 'Well, at least there's nothing more for you to do now for nine days. Probably you can do with the rest. You look tired.' A grimace that this time went awry. For someone with MS, bold comment. Ironic. He looked down and away as he remembered his own plight, the fact that he probably wouldn't even have enough energy to see the case through.

'Yes. Eight days of sleep. One day of pure bliss. After thirty years on this one case, I daresay I deserve it. *Santé!*'

Dominic leant forward and they clinked glasses.

But beyond Corbeix's smile, Dominic could see the strong shadow of uncertainty. His own sense of suspended belief with these closing stages he'd answered with the fact that the case so far had been fraught with so many obstacles and difficulties – that now with none in the way, it was no longer familiar ground. After so long, it still felt somehow unreal that it was all finally within grasp. But now, looking at Corbeix and downing the last slug of whisky, he wondered whether it was because reality lurked just around the corner. Something else would arise, Duclos would pull another rabbit from the hat to destroy their case and escape justice.

★

'They're pressing ahead with the case.'

A part of Duclos had feared they might, had prompted the safeguards he'd put into action. But another had clung to doubt: they would lack both the evidence and the audacity! And it was this part that held sway, wrestled with acceptance. Duclos went cold, rigid. He was in a call box on Rue Archimède, two blocks from the Parliament. He watched blankly the traffic and people passing.

With the long silence, Bonoit was suddenly hesitant, awkward. 'You know, I shouldn't even be calling. Certainly it will have to be my last call.'

'Yes, yes – I understand.' Duclos snapped out of his reverie. 'What earthly basis is there? What evidence?'

'I don't have all the details – but something about a garage worker and a coin found in an old car of yours. And still some background with psychics which I mentioned earlier.'

A coin? A coin left in his old car? Impossible, surely invented? He'd searched every nook and crevice straight after the incident, had driven the car for seven months afterwards without seeing anything. 'Sounds ridiculous to me. As I said before, some misguided political witch-hunt that will probably blow over before it's even started.' But Duclos could hear the nervousness, the strain in his own voice. The sudden worry that he might have overlooked something, would be facing the unknown. For the first time he was frightened. His hand shook, his palm clammy on the receiver.

Or was it sheer outrage, anger? Twenty years of serving his country, of fighting for bills and statutes for the benefit of all, and they had the cheek to drag this up now. That upstart Fornier and a ragtag bunch of Provence police and prosecutors. *Outrageous!* Two days of searching his memory after Bonoit's initial call, and he finally recalled. Fornier: the young gendarme assisting! Dour-faced and doubting in the background when Poullain had visited him at the Vallons. How on earth did someone like that rise to become chief inspector?

'There's something else,' Bonoit commented. 'Fornier was apparently involved in the initial investigation . . .'

'I see.' Duclos feigned surprise.

'His involvement now is meant to be purely because of that. Only someone involved then would know the gaps to fill in now. But it goes deeper.' Bonoit paused heavily. 'A couple of years after the murder, Fornier married the victim's mother – Monique Rosselot. They're husband and wife.'

Duclos was numbed, a tingling hollowness. A void struggling with the ludicrousness of what he'd just heard. He wanted to shout: 'But she was already married: Jean-Luc Rosselot. I read it in the papers at the time!' But he realized that might raise the question of why he had shown such strong interest in the case. He sensed the need to say something beyond just another 'I see'. Then it struck him: *personal involvement?* 'Given that background, should Fornier really be involved now?'

'Debatable point. Apparently, that is why Malliéné is down as leading the investigation. Fornier's meant to be just assisting and for background – continuity between the old and new case. But word has it that Fornier's doing most of the legwork. Malliéné is merely checking and signing off – possibly to avoid any claims of bias through personal involvement.'

The smile came slowly to Duclos' face, his concern dissipating. Something else that could probably be turned to advantage! 'Interesting.' He thanked Bonoit. 'I appreciate how you've stuck out your neck to try and help me.'

Bonoit said it was nothing. 'For old friendship.' A quick *'bonne chance'* before he rang off.

In the immediate silence following, it struck Duclos that he probably wouldn't hear from Bonoit again. When the arrest warrant came, there would be a lot more old friends and colleagues who would suddenly want distance, he thought ruefully.

Coin? The one thing that nagged disturbingly at the back of his mind. Everything else – garage workers, psychics – sounded like the sort of nonsense Thibault, his lawyer, would destroy in short order. He would phone him tomorrow. Start shoring up his defence before the wolf pack arrived.

Duclos could almost imagine Fornier rubbing his hands together. The incompetent hoping for final glory. But with everything with Aurillet already in place, and now with this new information, Duclos still felt confident of winning through – at the same time hopefully teaching Dominic Fornier a lesson he wouldn't quickly forget.

Perhaps he shouldn't have had the whisky. The effects of the steroids wore off in the afternoon; the drink had probably only heightened the problem. Corbeix could feel the muscle twinges rising in his right thigh. He'd planned to stay at least an hour after Fornier left and structure notes from the afternoon session, but already he could feel the warning signals. If he stayed more than another ten minutes, he might have trouble making it even to the car park. And in addition there was the twenty-minute drive home.

A recurring worry was that his legs would seize up in mid journey, he wouldn't even be able to operate the clutch or the accelerator. On bad days, he'd take a taxi in and back. But this morning had started off good, no twinges, then shortly after the session with Roudèle he'd felt the first. Almost as if his body was reminding him that the day had been gruelling. While the session had been in full flow, the adrenalin running, he'd hardly felt a thing.

Was that what it would be like in the *instruction* hearings ahead? Sailing through on a sea of adrenalin, and then completely demolished soon after? But today had started off well, he reminded himself: what about those days when he felt exhausted just with the effort of getting out of bed and having breakfast?

Corbeix packed his files in his briefcase and headed out, locking his office door. The corridors were quiet. Most of the staff had left an hour ago.

All to do. Fornier's road had ended, his own was just starting. And he knew now with certainty that he'd get little or no help from Galimbert. He'd sounded out Galimbert a week before, then again when the coin lead came through: sounds tenuous. Exploratory. 'Too much ground-breaking that could go wrong – especially against such a high-profile figure.'

Objections, objections, with no hint of support in sight. Galimbert wasn't keen on the case. If he handed it over to him to conclude after the summer recess, Galimbert would throw in the towel at the first serious onslaught from Duclos' lawyer.

Corbeix shook his head as he started down the Palais de Justice steps. RPR. He recalled soon after their first discussion about Duclos that Galimbert was a staunch RPR supporter. They were prosecutors, functionaries of the law, politics weren't meant to come into it. Governing parties changed, but they were always there, serving, holding the mantle of justice. But he couldn't help wondering if Galimbert's lack of enthusiasm had been largely swayed by Duclos' RPR status. One of Galimbert's heroes.

Corbeix grimaced tautly. It hardly mattered now. He was on his own. Fighting one of the largest cases in French criminal history when he felt he hardly had the energy to make it to the car park.

At the bottom of the stairway, he paused to regain breath, looking up briefly at the high-ceilinged entrance vestibule of the Palais de Justice and the motto above the doorway: *Liberté, égalité, fraternité*. Then he continued, his faltering step echoing starkly from the tiled floor and stone walls.

Echoing feet on marble floors. Dominic followed the two Strasbourg Judiciary DIs through the Parliament vestibule from the lifts. As they turned into the corridor leading to Duclos' office, thick pile carpet met their feet. Their steps became cushioned, silent, as if to mask their final approach from Duclos.

But a rather concerned guard at the entrance desk had spent time with badge-checking, register-signing and phoning through to Duclos' secretary before letting them pass. Duclos knew they were coming.

They walked into the main office: a secretary, a clerk behind. But no sign of Duclos. Dominic stayed in the background while one of the DIs, Paveinade, explained the purpose of their visit to Duclos' secretary. His sidekick, Caubert, just nodded as she looked between the two.

Halfway through, the adjoining door opened and Duclos stepped out. He was open-mouthed, and stared Paveinade up and down quizzically. 'What on earth is all this? What is the meaning of this intrusion?'

The same supercilious, condescending expression, thought Dominic. Except now there were few remnants of Duclos' previous round-faced, pretty-boy look; the face was puffed and jowly, lines and bags under Duclos' eyes betraying his age.

Paveinade started again, more hesitantly this time: the warrant issued from Aix, the notification that morning in Strasbourg for them to take him into custody. 'I have the papers here. I think you'll find them all in order.' Paveinade held them out, but Duclos just stared at them contemptuously.

'What are your badge numbers?' he snapped. 'And who is your commanding officer? Give all your details, along with the arrest warrant and your commanding officer's name to my secretary. I'll have her call him straight away and sort out this mess.'

Obediently, Paveinade took off his badge and showed it to the secretary. Flustered, slightly red-faced, Caubert started to follow suit.

Dominic glared at Duclos. He'd agreed with Corbeix just to stay in the background and observe. He might too easily lose his temper. He'd hoped to catch up on sleep in the nine days' wait. But with the build-up and expectancy towards the final issuing of the warrant, it had still been fitful. Four, five hours a night at most. His nerves were still frayed, and now Duclos was trying to steal the thunder from his moment of glory. Suddenly it was as if *they* were under suspicion and arrest! An inch more rope, and Duclos would reduce their visit to complete circus. Dominic saw red. Duclos' arrogance in trying to reverse the tables and take control reminded him just why he had escaped justice for so long.

Dominic put his hand over Caubert's badge as it was laid on the secretary's desk. 'That won't be necessary. The arrest warrant is in order, duly signed off by Inspector Malliéné of Aix-en-Provence and an examining magistrate. And as the most senior officer present, it falls upon me to observe and ensure that these officers are allowed to do their duty and execute the warrant without impediment.' Dominic stared at Caubert, his tone sharp. 'Now put away your badge, and get on with what you came here for. Read the prisoner his rights, and handcuff him so that he may be escorted to the car.'

Duclos looked between Dominic, Caubert and Paveinade. A battle of wills – though Duclos looked suddenly uncertain which next action would have the strongest effect. 'This is ridiculous, absurd!'

Sensing that Caubert and Paveinade were still hesitant, Dominic prompted, 'Who has the handcuffs? Let's get on with it.'

Duclos' eyes darted between them a moment more before turning to his secretary. Slow exhalation: exasperation. No energy left to argue with proles. 'Call Jean-Paul Thibault – his number is in my database. Tell him what's happened.' Then he rounded on the two DIs and Dominic. 'One of the first things he'll be doing is speaking to the Strasbourg police commissioner. I don't think you have any idea of the magnitude of error you're making here. I wouldn't hold your breath on any future promo –'

'Save the speech, Duclos,' Dominic cut in, damned if he was going to allow him this last frantic scramble for moral high ground. 'I'm not one of your electorate. Nor, if I have my way, will you be soap boxing to any more electorate.' Dominic nodded to Paveinade and Caubert. 'Now take the prisoner.'

As Paveinade raised Duclos' arms for the handcuffs, he muttered a quick, 'I'm sorry, sir.' Still observance of authority, albeit now reluctant. Dominic couldn't imagine Paveinade saying sorry to a street vagrant as he slapped on handcuffs.

'This is outrageous,' Duclos hissed. 'You are making a tragic error.'

Dominic leant closer. 'Yes, well. You pay for your tragic errors, and I'll pay for mine.'

They marched Duclos away. Stares of curiosity, surprise from people passing on the corridor. Whether because they recognized Duclos or just at the sight of a man in handcuffs, Dominic wasn't sure. Two people were in the lift down from the third floor; hesitant sideways glances at the handcuffs.

Dominic enjoyed every minute. He hadn't had so much fun since the Taragnon bank manager. Duclos was subdued, silent throughout. Eyes mostly downcast, embarrassed, not meeting those of people they passed.

He spoke only once more on their way out, as they headed down the Parliament steps towards the car. 'You know – I remember you, Fornier.' Duclos was staring at him directly; up until then, he'd been careful to avoid eye contact.

'Yes, and I've never forgotten you.' Dominic smiled tautly. 'I'll send you flowers in prison.'

Dominic sat in the front and stared resolutely ahead as they drove off. He wished now that he'd kept to his original plan, stayed in the background and kept quiet. His hands were clenched tight in fists on his knees. He could still feel his anger bubbling. The long years of waiting, the intensity of the past weeks of investigation – and all he could finish off with was a cheap jibe about Duclos' sexuality. But there was a momentary flinch in Duclos' eyes that at least gave some satisfaction, albeit slightly delayed – not a recoil reaction of shock or surprise. As if the jibe had prompted some past, unpleasant memory, and it had taken Duclos a second to link the two.

39

Jean-Paul Thibault pushed through the throng of reporters on the courtroom steps. Cameras clicked, microphones jostled for position. At first
they concentrated on Duclos, but as Duclos held one hand up and
Thibault's assistant clerk Madeleine led him hurriedly to the car, they
swung back towards Thibault. The lawyer touched his steel-rimmed
glasses, moistened his lips. The microphones moved in closer.

'As you can appreciate, my client doesn't wish to make any comment
at this stage. I can only say that I will seek to demonstrate my client's
innocence in short order: that these charges against him are totally
unfounded and without merit.'

A confused barrage of questions returned: *Match . . . Le Monde . . . Le
Provençal . . .* 'When will . . .', 'What do you propose . . .', 'Will Monsieur
Duclos now . . .' Thibault picked out one question: 'Why do you think
these charges have arisen now, so many years later?' Girl at the back: *Le
Figaro*.

'Good question. Why now? Monsieur Duclos provided a full unflinch-
ing statement when this case was originally heard. He has nothing to
hide. A suspect, I might add, was found, fully tried and convicted. A
reopening now is a complete legal sham, especially on the evidence
presented. I think that Monsieur Duclos' recent political involvement
might prove more of a clue as to why it has arisen now. Thank you.'
Thibault started moving down the steps towards the car.

The pack followed: more questions. They'd taken the bait. Again,
Thibault picked out just one: 'Which particular political involvement?'

Thibault turned just as he opened the car door. Reluctant admission,
as if the press were dragging it out of him. Thibault sighed. 'As you
probably know, Monsieur Duclos has recently been rapporteur in a patents
dispute which has gone the wrong way for the EU bio-tech industry.
If he's discredited, the case could be reopened. Also, I'd like to remind
you that all of this comes rather soon after a scandal involving a certain
Socialist politician from Marseille. Rather convenient, one might
say'. Thibault smiled. 'If I were you, I would look no further than

Monsieur Duclos' political enemies for those behind this ridiculous fiasco.'

Thibault held a hand up behind him as he stepped into the car, ignoring the continuing barrage of questions. It had ended on the note he wanted. Madeleine drove off.

He smiled across at Duclos. 'A good day's work, I think. Should be interesting press tomorrow.'

'Yes, I think so. Well done.' Though Duclos' smile in return was more hesitant. He had half an eye on the black police Citroën following. His shadow for the next few months.

Two days after the bail hearing came the first official RPR statement from the party general secretary and acting Prime Minister. 'We have spoken at some length with Monsieur Duclos, who completely repudiates these charges as false and unfounded. He will fight them vigorously, and the party will offer its moral support. However, it is Monsieur Duclos' personal opinion that it would be improper for him to continue in his duties representing the party as a regional representative or in Brussels while this case remains unresolved. His resignation of today has been accepted with due regret by the party President.'

The statement was as expected. 'Moral' support meant that the party could offer no tangible support, but their thoughts were with him. Good luck and *bon voyage*.

Eight days. All that Duclos had spent behind bars before being bailed. Quite a contrast to Machanaud, Dominic thought sourly. The system at work. *Égalité* its middle name.

But it wasn't full bail, Corbeix was eager to point out. More house arrest, with a gendarme permanently in Duclos' shadow, posted by his front door in Limoges or his hotel room in Aix when Duclos travelled down for *instruction* hearings. His passport had been surrendered, his bank accounts frozen, and practically all his assets tied up in bail funding. 'It was the best we could hope for in the circumstances.'

Two days since the bail hearing. A more sober meeting this time with Corbeix. No whisky. Not much to celebrate. Corbeix's desk was strewn with the main newspapers: most carried the story on the front page.

The bail decision hadn't been entirely a surprise. As soon as he had heard about Duclos' appointed lawyer, Jean-Paul Thibault, Corbeix had at least been forewarned as to what to expect: arrogance, brashness, cries of 'outrage' at every opportunity. Thibault's firm was a leading Paris *cabinet* with associate offices in Brussels and Washington. Heavy on corporate law, their criminal law division was smaller, but nevertheless competent and aggressive. Thibault was one of their youngest partners and had risen to prominence in the eighties representing a leading Paris *haute couture* director's wife charged with murder. A number of similar high-profile cases had followed, making Thibault's mark as a good 'celebrity lawyer'.

Thibault's steel-rimmed glasses, gelled-back hair and double-breasted suits had cut a good, clean, up-and-coming yuppie lawyer image a decade ago. But his image hadn't changed with the years, and now that he was in his late forties it made him look shady and sharp.

Dominic was thoughtful as Corbeix covered Thibault's background. 'Doesn't sound too far removed from a younger Duclos.'

'Perhaps that's what endeared Duclos to Thibault. Sees a bit of himself in him.'

Predictably, Thibault had come in all guns blazing for his client at the bail hearing: Duclos' status, his long years as a publicly elected official, his strong commitment to France. Corbeix had answered with the seriousness of the charges and the fact that Duclos had money; he had the means to escape.

They argued the toss for almost an hour before the examining magistrate, Claude Barielle, ruled: bank accounts and assets frozen. Passport held. House arrest. Counsels to be advised of the order of play for *instruction* hearings within ten days.

Corbeix had initially been enthused with Claude Barielle's appointment. Only thirty-two and with a sharply inquisitive mind, Barielle, he felt, would be more open-minded to the background of PLR than some of the older examining magistrates. But during the bail hearing, he began to worry that Barielle might turn out too much of a lightweight faced with someone like Thibault. A master manipulator, Thibault was used to ruling the roost in the main courtrooms of Paris. In a provincial Aix courtroom with a young examining magistrate, Thibault could have Barielle carrying his luggage in no time.

In most *instruction* hearings, defence lawyers were mainly passengers aboard an examining magistrate's inquisitorial flagship. Present only when their client was called, defence could only demand presence when witnesses were called by posting a 'request to confront' notice. Prosecutors too could, if they wished, coast along during *instruction*, merely make notes and suggestions, appear at only half the hearings, generally let the examining magistrate do the running.

Corbeix grimaced. Given his current condition, such a stance would have probably suited him. But he could see by the spread of newspapers on his desk that it wasn't going to be that type of *instruction*. Thibault was going to be posting a lot of 'request to confront' notices, calling foul at every turn.

'I think we're in for a rough ride. And possibly earlier than I thought.'

Dominic, too, glanced at the newspapers. One had already nicknamed Duclos 'the bio-tech MEP'. The rest made strong reference to his involvement in the bio-tech ruling somewhere in their article. The murder case and the bio-tech dispute had already been successfully fused in the public's mind. 'What do you think is Thibault's tactic?'

'On the surface, just a convenient smoke-screen. A distraction. But beneath, it's a very clever manipulation. The bio-tech ruling is pro–life, pro–rights of man. At the same time we are expected to believe that the man responsible is also a murderer. Thibault is trying to paint Duclos as a saint before it has even started. He's going all out for an early kill.'

'Any particular reason? He has his client bailed, so why the time pressure?'

'Think about it. Thibault has made the bold claim that this whole case is unfounded. But as the *instruction* drags on, not only will people begin to doubt such a claim but, win or lose, Duclos' political career will be over. Only if Thibault can get the case thrown out quickly does Duclos have any chance of bouncing back.'

They'd discussed the daunting task ahead at the last meeting, shored up the final barricades, Dominic reflected. Now Corbeix was raising the portent of an early defeat. Was Corbeix just hardening him up against a possible let-down, or did he really see losing as a strong possibility?

Twelve days later, with the agenda for the first six *instruction* hearings in hand together with Thibault's 'request to confront' notices, Corbeix's fears were confirmed. It was going to be a gloves-off fight at every stage. Though one confront notice surprised him. He stared at it long and hard before laying the papers aside, and wondered: bluff, or did Thibault know something they didn't?

Marinella Calvan cradled the phone to her ear with her shoulder, turning the top page of the official notice she'd received. 'Yeah, yeah. The sixteenth. Just over three weeks from now.' Her agent, Stephanie Bruckmann, was at the other end. 'That's right, yep. The expense this time is on them. No more pleading for departmental funding.'

'Who told you what the notice said?' Bruckmann asked. 'That cute French tutor you mentioned finding on campus?'

'No. Inspector Fornier phoned me directly. Went through it with me. I use Tom just for the newspaper articles. There was something else just the other day.' Marinella flicked through the copy of *Le Figaro* to one side. 'First *instruction* hearing, whatever that is, next Tuesday. Bit more about this Duclos' involvement with the bio-tech case.'

'The bio-tech stuff's good for us. The John Moore case was splashed across most of the papers here. Generated some great headlines. "Spleenless in Seattle" was one of the best.' She heard Marinella chuckle at the other end. 'So it should help build up some national exposure.'

'Let's hope so.'

Stephanie Bruckmann was thoughtful. She'd spent the last month setting up lecture tours, book deals and chat shows – then held back. The preliminaries done, the market primed – far stronger impact would be gained once the case hit the press. And stronger still with the confirmation of Marinella testifying at trial. She'd asked Marinella to phone her as soon as she received trial notification from France. 'Look, I think I'm going to go for Larry King straight away. His office were on just a couple of days ago, right after the *Washington Post* story. Let's save Oprah and the rest till later. Right now it's a strong international-political story – but not yet a strong American story. Let's give it a couple more weeks to brew on that front. But it's great for King right now. I'll call his office first thing tomorrow.'

Thibault behaved himself at the first two *instruction* hearings. Sat for the most part taking notes with his assistant Madeleine at his side, peering imperiously above his glasses at anything questionable, but generally saying little. Few objections or interruptions.

Corbeix hadn't been sure what to expect. Because Duclos' presence was necessary at both initial hearings, Thibault didn't need to post confront requests in order to be present.

Barielle sat with a *greffier* tapping notes into a computer to his left. Despite his years, Barielle had strong presence. He was receding prematurely and had sharp, piercing blue eyes. Brooked no nonsense. The hearing room was no more than eight metres square.

The main purpose of the first hearing was for overall presentation of the case: the main prosecution foundations in support and general aims – followed by defence rebuttal. Corbeix started with the background to the 1963 investigation and trial, though only the key points – the main details would be presented by Fornier at the third *instruction*. Then he came quickly on to the link between the two cases: Eyran Capel and the final PLR sessions. Corbeix was careful not to dwell, he wanted to get swiftly to the coin – the main tangible evidence – without attracting objections and interruptions from Thibault over PLR. Thibault raised his eyebrows to the ceiling at its mention, half smiled and leant over to whisper something to Madeleine – but no objection came.

Still, Corbeix was keen to push PLR as far out of reach as possible. 'Much evidence will be presented about the authenticity of PLR work. Not just with this case with Eyran Capel and Christian Rosselot – but hundreds of authenticated cases stretching back through the years. Countless eminent psychiatrists and psychologists all bearing testament to its authenticity. Hours of tapes and reams of transcripts available. Marinella Calvan, the main psychologist who conducted the sessions, one of the world's leading PLR experts, will also appear before us – as will the initial psychiatrist who recommended PLR sessions for Eyran Capel. And finally a French notary who witnessed one of the closing sessions.' Corbeix rested one hand firmly on his trial folder. 'But despite all of that, the prosecution case will not, I repeat not, be fought on the basis of such evidence. All of that will be purely texture and background to the main evidence: a coin discovered by a garage worker in the boot of Alain Duclos' car.

'PLR is therefore only a means to an end – but not the end itself. And the coin is significant because it is not just any coin: it is a relatively rare Italian silver lire given to Christian Rosselot by his grandfather, who brought it in turn from Italy. Christian Rosselot left his house that fateful day with the coin in his pocket, and it was subsequently found in the boot of Monsieur Duclos' car – albeit only coming to light all these years later.'

Corbeix held out a hand towards Thibault. 'I'm sure, your honour, that much will be made in argument against PLR by the defence, purely because of its unusual and speculative nature – especially in trial evidence. But I can only emphasize again that in this case it is purely for texture and background. However much the defence try to discredit or throw doubt on PLR, there's no escaping the simple, irrevocable fact that the coin was there. A physical, not a mythical discovery. And the only tangible explanation for it being there is that the boy – Christian Rosselot – was in the boot of Alain Duclos' car on the day of his murder.' Corbeix nodded abruptly to Barielle, then to Thibault, and sat down.

Thibault spent the first ten minutes mainly with character references for his client – almost a repeat of his bail pleas. How it was unthinkable that anyone of Duclos' stature who had contributed so much to the community at large could commit such a crime. A ludicrous travesty of justice that charges should have even been brought to bear. Thibault jumped deftly to the background of PLR and psychic evidence.

'Nothing else demonstrates more strongly just how ludicrous this has become. Shows fully the pathetic desperation of the prosecution's case.' But to Corbeix's relief and surprise, Thibault spent little time on the subject. 'These elements are so obviously questionable as to hardly be worth my time in trying to discredit them.' As if already half assuming that Barielle would also consider them obvious nonsense. Or perhaps saving his big guns for the hearing with Marinella Calvan, thought Corbeix.

Thibault emphasized the sensitivity of his client's political position and the rather suspicious and convenient timing of all this now arising hot on the heels of a controversial bio-technology ruling. 'Every politician has enemies – but when industry at large has been hit to the tune of fifty billion francs – the incentive is suddenly there to crush those enemies. So *why* this charge has suddenly materialized against my client should be very clear – emerging out of the blue after over thirty years. But the *how* is far more interesting. How a ragtag collection of coincidences and falsehoods have been strung together by the prosecution, with a few mystics thrown in for good measure – in support of this ridiculous political witch-hunt.' Thibault stared resolutely at Barielle. 'Certainly, your honour, in all my years I have not seen a more blatant case of fabrication of evidence and bias in support of a prosecution – and I will see it as my pleasure to expose this for what it is: a case totally without substance or merit.' Thibault cast his eyes down for a second, drawing a tired breath. 'Unfortunately for my client, regardless of the outcome, politics being what it is, his career will probably be over. His enemies will score their victory in any case. Which I think has been their intention all along – knowing full well that such tenuous evidence would be thrown out in short order. But let us hope at least that justice will be seen to be done on one front. Thank you.'

Thibault's only bout of band-standing. Bold claims, Corbeix thought.

Bias? But overall tame by Thibault's normal standards. There was obviously much worse to come.

As Thibault sat down, Barielle smiled. 'Yes, well. I think your aims in this case, Monsieur Thibault, have already been made clear to anyone reading the newspapers. In future, I would ask you to address your aims to me first before telling the world – not the other way around.'

Thibault was red-faced, but just nodded with a slight shrug. Couldn't quite wrap his tongue around an apology.

Corbeix smiled in turn. Perhaps Barielle wouldn't be such a walk-over.

The first part of the second *instruction* hearing was taken up with Serge Roudèle: confirmation of his name, the dates he worked in the Limoges garage, and then the reading of his statement about the coin.

Duclos was present because later he would be asked to testify. He looked uneasy as he listened to Roudèle's account. And so he should, thought Corbeix: it was the main physical evidence that could convict him. Duclos would have already known about the coin from the trial papers, but not all the details. Corbeix felt a twinge of pleasure at Duclos' discomfort. Duclos probably thinking of the many times he'd opened the boot in those seven months without seeing the coin. Or wondering why, *oh why*, couldn't he have had a flat tyre?

Thibault waited for Barielle to finish his questioning, and then requested the right to confront, but with only three questions. Barielle nodded, and posed them: 'Did you steal the coin in question?'

'Well, yes. I took it, at least.'

'Would you consider this an act of theft?'

'Yes . . . I suppose I would.' Slight fluster. Uncomfortable.

'And was there a reward offered for coming forward with information about the coin?'

'Yes, there was.' Roudèle was defensive. 'But not excessive in comparison to its normal value.'

Thibault made no concluding remarks and Roudèle was dismissed. But the points were in the file, and Corbeix was sure that Thibault would make much of them later: try and discredit Roudèle. Corbeix summarized with the statement from the coin-shop owner, reading out key segments – then passed it to Barielle and the *greffier* to note.

Duclos' testimony predictably stuck to the original account given in 1963: travelling through Taragnon, calling in at a restaurant, a quick stop-off at a garage, then on to Juan-les-Pins.

When Duclos had finished, Barielle asked, 'Did you at any time meet a young boy travelling through Taragnon?'

'No, I didn't.'

'Did you at any time have a young boy in your car? Either in the passenger seat or in the boot?'

'No.'

'How long did you spend in the restaurant in total?'

'An hour, an hour and a quarter . . .'

Barielle continued with a series of straightforward, mechanical questions, eleven in all, making short notes after each one. He would ask the same questions from a dozen more angles before the *instruction* was over, each time sharpening the angle or confronting with conflicting testimony from witnesses – the main skill of an effective examining magistrate digging for the truth. But Corbeix could hardly imagine Barielle commenting that according to the voice on tape of a boy long since dead, a different account had been proposed: *'What do you say to that, Monsieur Duclos?'*

A reminder to Corbeix, listening to Duclos' account, that his claim at the last *instruction* that PLR was just providing background and texture was in part inaccurate: the case hinged on the physical evidence of the coin, but Eyran Capel's PLR transcripts provided the complete picture of what had really happened that day.

All the details Duclos was now carefully omitting.

Jean-Paul Thibault had purposely coasted through the first *instruction* hearings. First of all he liked to listen, tune himself to the mood of the proceedings: the sensitivities and nuances of the prosecution and the examining magistrate, their strengths and vulnerabilities. Where to hit and what to avoid. When he knew where he would have most impact – then he would start striking out.

But there was another strong reason for him biding his time: research and background. Uncovering the most vulnerable areas of witnesses. The day after receiving the main file, he'd assigned two of his best researchers to get information on Roudèle, Fornier and Malliéné in France, Lambourne and the Capels in England, and Marinella Calvan in America.

Day by day the threads of information filtered in. Unfortunately, there was nothing on Roudèle. No past convictions for theft; the coin was possibly an isolated incident. He'd decide later if he would press the point. But with Dominic Fornier, they'd struck gold. Enough threads to weave a blanket. A shroud hopefully to smother Fornier, nail him with in grand style at the next *instruction*.

'How did we fare?' Dominic tapped a pencil on his desk. Papers and files, telephones ringing, interruptions. The normal morning. Dominic had hardly been able to pay any of it strong attention. He'd phoned Corbeix's office twenty minutes before to learn that he was still not back: still in *instruction*. On the second call he was put through to Corbeix.

'We're probably ahead after the second round as well. Thibault tackled Roudèle over the theft of the coin, but nothing serious. And Duclos gave the same lame, ridiculous account of his movements that day as when you first took his statement back in 1963.'

'I suppose we didn't expect any less.'

'Suppose not.' Corbeix was thoughtful. Voicing the ease with which they'd sailed through the first two hearings reminded him of the onslaught he feared was coming. He'd already warned Fornier about the 'confront' notice posted against him and Malliéné for the next hearing. Dominic had joked, 'So either Thibault is booking his ringside ticket and will just sit it out – or we'd better warn Malliéné what he's in for.' Corbeix too had laughed, but nervously. They both knew who Thibault was gunning for.

'Can I talk? Is your line secure?'

Duclos' heart sank. It was Jaumard. Thibault was due out of court soon. He'd hoped it might be him: news of how his assault on Fornier and Corbeix had gone.

'Yes, it's fine. You can talk. No bugs.' Bettina downstairs, gendarme at the front door. The phone was probably the *only* secure place. Thibault had made a big issue of it at the bail hearing. Emphasized that because his client was under house arrest, by necessity many of their conversations would be by phone. A secure line was therefore essential. Any line-tapping would breach client–lawyer confidentiality, and he would immediately call for a mistrial. Barielle agreed: no line-tapping. Duclos suddenly pinched himself. Perhaps he should have said, 'No, it's not safe.' The last person he wanted to hear from right now was Jaumard. But yet another part of him was morbidly curious. 'Still, you shouldn't be phoning me here. What do you want?'

'Isn't it obvious? I've read the papers. You're going down for this, aren't you? That's my old-age pension straight out the fucking window!'

'No, no – it's all complete nonsense. The whole thing will get thrown out quickly. Maybe even at this *instruction* – by the next at the latest. My lawyer's in court nailing them right now.'

'I've only got your word for that. And I'm not prepared to wait just on the off chance. As soon as you know you're going down for it, you'll stop paying me.'

No point in a clumsy denial; Jaumard's claim was patently true. 'You've phoned early. Normally you phone at night.'

'Yes, well. I wanted a clear head. This involves my future. I might only have one shot at it.'

Duclos sensed what was coming, but he didn't want to ask, invite it; as with everything else, delaying the ultimate – though part of him also clung to the hope that he was wrong.

Long breath from Jaumard. 'I want to cash in my pension now. Half straight away – the rest a week before your trial. That way if you go down I've got something put away.'

'And if I don't get convicted?'

'You won't hear from me again for three years.' Jaumard paused. 'Three hundred thousand francs now, three hundred thousand just before the trial.'

Duclos spluttered. 'That's outrageous – I can't get you that sort of money. In fact, I can't get you any money at all. All my bank accounts and assets have been frozen.'

'Don't give me that shit. People like you can always get their hands on money somewhere.'

'Not when they're on trial for murder. I've had bail bondsmen and court officials crawling over every account and asset – I can't shift a thing.' But Jaumard was right; despite everything, he *could* get his hands on some money. Though the money in Switzerland from Marchand's bio-tech people he dared not let anyone know about: $400,000 at the outset of conciliation, another $400,000 when the ruling had come through. $120,000 for each successive year without a new patents ruling, to a maximum of seven years. His escape fund if all went wrong. Jaumard was the last person he'd let in on such a secret.

'I don't care how you find the money – just find it! Because I'm not waiting. I'll call you tomorrow and give you a bank account number for the transfer.'

Duclos' stomach sank. This was a new Jaumard: tense, irrational, but for once sober. Abstaining Jaumard: high-octane mix of DTs and raw tension. 'It's impossible. I told you, if I try to –'

'Find it!' Jaumard snapped. 'If by the time I call you haven't worked out how to get three hundred thousand transferred to me within twenty-four hours – then the very next day I'll be on the phone to the police with my brother's little folder. Aix Palais de Justice, isn't it?'

Jaumard left a brief silence, then the line went dead.

Corbeix saw where Barielle was heading from the first few questions, saw the problem approaching like a truck aimed head-on. More pre-hearing pressure from Thibault.

'And how long have you been married to the victim's mother, Chief Inspector Fornier?'

'Twenty-nine years.'

'Was this involvement made clear to Prosecutor Corbeix when you first approached him with the case?'

'Yes it was.'

Corbeix raised a hand to interrupt. Barielle broke off from asking questions and nodded.

'Much of this was entered in my initial file folder, your honour.' Corbeix half raised. Thankfully no pains had hit at the previous *instructions*, and the last few days had been clear. But now he could feel the first onset of muscle cramps. 'We have made no secret of Chief Inspector Fornier's involvement with Monique Rosselot.'

'I appreciate that. But if you indulge me a moment more, or, in this case, defence counsel' – Barielle gestured towards Thibault – 'hopefully all will become clear.'

Barielle had already cleared the small hearing room for ten minutes' private consultation with Thibault before resuming with the questions. All *instruction* questions had to be posed by the examining magistrate to avoid direct intimidation of witnesses.

'What initially caused your involvement in the reopened investigation?' Barielle asked Dominic.

'The fact that I was one of the only people still traceable connected with the original investigation when Marinella Calvan first made contact.'

'And the reason for your continuing involvement?'

'Very much the same reason: knowledge of the original investigation. I was therefore in a far better position to piece things together from any new evidence uncovered.'

'At what point was the case handed over to Inspector Malliéné to head?'

'After my discussing the case with Prosecutor Corbeix.'

'And what were the reasons for this?'

'Partly because Inspector Malliéné was under the Aix jurisdiction, from where the case would be prosecuted, and partly because Monsieur Corbeix was concerned about any possible bias that I might bring because of my attachment to Monique Rosselot.'

'I see.' Barielle's tone was flat. 'And not purely as a smoke screen, a cover for any perceived bias?'

'No. Inspector Malliéné had full signing-off powers. He was fully at liberty to discount or discard any portion of the investigative inquiry with which he didn't agree.'

'Inspector Malliéné was controlling the investigation?'

'Yes.'

'So as the chief investigative officer, let us see: what exactly did Inspector Malliéné do in this case? Then let us compare with what his normal duties as someone leading the investigation should be . . .'

As Barielle continued with a chain of questions tying down Malliéné's and Fornier's respective investigative involvement, Corbeix looked down. He doodled absently on a pad. Concentric, diminishing squares: everything closing in. A cold tingle ran up the back of his neck. The rest of his body was too numbed, too cramped and bombarded by steroids to feel anything. Either Thibault suspected Malliéné had been just a front, or he'd been tipped off internally. And now he'd convinced Barielle, who was like a fox with a rabbit now that he'd gripped hold. Corbeix's fist gripped tight on his pen. *Damn Thibault.* He'd hardly been able to give Thibault even a decent run for his money. Any minute now Thibault would cry bias, Barielle would probably agree, and Thibault would call for a mistrial. It could all be over before he'd finished doodling.

At one point, Fornier fought back: 'Because so much of the later evidence linked to earlier findings, obviously it fell upon me to do most of the legwork. To run things any other way just wouldn't have been practical.'

But it did little good. The overriding image was that it had been Fornier's investigation with Malliéné just a nominated figurehead. Barielle wasn't happy.

Barielle asked Fornier's political persuasion, and then dismissed him. Odd question, thought Corbeix, looking up briefly. Malliéné, who had already appeared before Fornier, was recalled.

Malliéné tried to beef up his own role and involvement, but as the questioning focused on what exactly he'd done at each stage, it was easy to read between the lines.

At one point, Corbeix half switched off. There was nothing he could do. He rubbed his eyes, felt them stinging as the muscle spasms gripped harder. Often the two came together: blurring of vision and extreme vertigo and dizziness. But now it was just a faint haze and a watery stinging. Through the haze, the proceedings washed around him. Barielle would finish his questioning, a quick summation and demand for a mistrial from Thibault, and Barielle would rule. Hopefully, Fornier's small fight back and Malliéné's attempts at claiming stronger involvement, however transparent, might at least cast some doubt. If not . . .

Corbeix looked up sharply as he heard his name called. That was quick, he thought. Malliéné had been dismissed, but surely Thibault was just starting his summation? He nodded and raised himself up, but he could feel the pain jarring his legs, the spasms biting sharper. It took him a moment to refocus on what was being said.

'I find this all highly irregular,' Barielle commented.

'Under normal circumstances, yes,' Thibault agreed. He held out a palm to indicate Corbeix without looking across at him. 'But as I think has already been clearly demonstrated, these are not normal circumstances. This is merely an extension of the earlier points raised about bias against my client. Though, as I think you will see, equally as valid.'

Barielle looked awkwardly towards Corbeix and waved Thibault towards him. After a short spell in the clinches with Thibault pointing to a page in his folder, Barielle waved for Corbeix to sit down and shrugged apologetically: sorry this could take a while, or for what might be coming?

And suddenly it hit Corbeix: Thibault was trying to get Barielle to question him! Outrageous. What on earth did Thibault have up his sleeve? What could he hope to achieve? *Bias?* One chink of clarity struggling up through the haze.

At length, Thibault returned to his seat. Barielle looked up at Corbeix. 'I'm sorry, Monsieur Corbeix. I know that this is somewhat irregular. But some questions have arisen regarding your involvement which require clarification.' Barielle scanned the typewritten sheet Thibault had left with him a moment longer. 'I understand that you are ill, Monsieur Corbeix. Can you tell me, what is the nature of your illness?'

'I have multiple sclerosis.'

'And has this been diagnosed for very long?'

'About three years now.' Corbeix glared at Thibault, outraged that his illness should come under attack. 'But this is no particular secret. I informed the *garde des Sceaux* as long ago as last October. My semi-retirement aiming towards full retirement has already been planned. I just don't see the relevance of all this.'

'I know. I know.' Barielle held one hand up, calming. 'I know that your semi-retirement has already been planned.' Barielle read from the sheet. 'And as part of that semi-retirement, you had planned to hand your case-load over to Prosecutor Galimbert, I understand.'

'Yes, that's correct.'

'Except this case, I believe.' Barielle stared at Corbeix directly. 'This is the only case you're not handing over to him.'

Corbeix blinked heavily. Suddenly he could see where it was all heading. *God*, was there anything that Thibault hadn't discovered? 'Yes.'

'What is the reason for that?'

'I discussed it with Galimbert, but he just wasn't keen. I decided to continue myself.'

'Even though you had previously decided that you might be too ill to continue with full case-loads in court after the summer recess?'

'Yes. The final decision was perhaps against my better judgement. But if Galimbert wasn't keen, what choice was there? Also, there were the extreme complexities of the case.'

Curt nod and tight smile from Barielle. 'Of what political persuasion is Prosecutor Galimbert?'

'RPR – why?'

Barielle rode the question. 'And of what political persuasion are you?'

'Socialist.'

Suddenly it hit Corbeix in a rush: himself Socialist, Fornier Socialist, Thibault complaining about political bias against his client; and now them both clearly spotlighted as having bent the rules. Give Thibault his due, bastard as he was, he'd sewn the package together well.

Thibault raised one hand. Barielle acknowledged him. Corbeix expected Thibault's summation, his *coup de grâce*.

But Thibault was holding out a booklet. 'Some interesting facts I think are also worthy of note about this particular illness, your honour.' Thibault started reading from the booklet: 'In severe cases, during episodic attacks, this will lead in turn to eye strain, vertigo, and may affect vital functions of the brain, causing memory loss and temporary fugue states.'

Corbeix felt his blood boil. He'd accepted that in a year or so he might be in a wheelchair, accepted that increasingly he'd lack the strength to lift his youngest daughter, that he'd have to soon sell his boat because even a short day trip would be too tiring – but what he wouldn't accept was this smarmy Paris advocate preaching what his illness entailed, what he might or might not be facing.

'And given the effects of this disease on the brain, I think severe questions must be asked about Monsieur Corbeix's mental competence.' Thibault paused for effect. 'Or indeed, in this case, if he has allowed a combination of bias and mental impairment to colour his judgement in continuing.'

But Corbeix knew that to hammer home the point effectively, he'd have to stand, and he could feel the spasms biting deeper as he rose. He steeled himself against the pain, feeling it raise beads of sweat on his forehead. He was determined not to let it show – provide a physical demonstration to support Thibault's claims. Fully upright, the spasms in his legs screamed to drag him back down. 'Monsieur Thibault is not a doctor. And I resent him taking up *instruction* time with amateur diagnosis. Particularly when it's my health that is at issue.'

'I was just trying to bring some clarity to –'

'I know what you were trying to do,' Corbeix cut in. 'You were challenging my mental competence to continue with this case. As it so happens, my mental competence is not affected. The effects described are only in extreme cases. I am far from that stage yet – and perhaps, God willing, I might never be at that stage. Your pathetic, amateur diagnosis is about as ridiculous and assumptive as me suggesting that three genera-tions of inbreeding have made you the idiot you are today.'

'Gentlemen, please . . . please!' Barielle fought to regain order.

Corbeix threw in one last point. 'And as for Monsieur Thibault's suggestion of political bias, if your honour please, this is as ridiculous as me challenging Thibault's right to represent Monsieur Duclos, purely because he too is RPR.'

Corbeix sat down. A last-second, scrambled flourish, but would it be enough? Certainly earlier Thibault had done enough to convince Barielle of sufficient bias to call a mistrial.

Thibault quickly summarized the 'confronts' he'd raised: personal bias through family ties, political bias. Bias at every turn. And finally a question of physical competence: had Corbeix's judgement been sound, and would it still be so in three months? Alain Duclos' rights to a fair and even-handed trial had been severely compromised. Under the circumstances, Thibault would fully expect a mistrial to be ruled. Thibault sat down.

Barielle nodded curtly and continued for a moment with some notes. Corbeix's throat was dry; he found it difficult to swallow. Finally Barielle looked up to give his deliberation.

40

'When is it that you are due to testify in France?'

'Tuesday week.'

'I understand that the trial procedure is very different there, and in effect this will be one of a series of preliminary hearings.'

'Yes, apparently so. I'll be asked to provide the background of PLR to support the link between the two boys. And later, if the case goes to full trial, I'll be called to provide pretty much the same information in front of a jury . . .'

Lunchtime at Boehmier & Kemp, Washington DC. The only quiet time of the day. Jennifer McGill decided to have a quick sandwich and use the time to catch up on the morning's paperwork. CNN flickered on a 16-inch screen in the background, the sound on low.

A name on the TV suddenly struck a chord, but she couldn't remember from where. She looked up abruptly from the file she was reading and turned up the sound. Larry King was on with a Mary Elizabeth Mastrantonio look-alike whom she hadn't seen before.

'Even the pre-trial run-up is apparently turning into something of a media circus in France. Claims of political bias have been made, and of course then we have Alain Duclos' central involvement with a landmark bio-technology case. Given this intense spotlight, no doubt you will face quite hostile challenges regarding the tenuous nature of PLR in evidence: how will you answer these?'

'By keeping firmly to the evidence and the facts in hand. The sessions I was involved with alone produced almost ninety pages of transcript, and over sixty pages of notes and transcripts were prepared by an associate psychiatrist even before my arrival . . .'

And then the name hit: Calvan. It wasn't one of her cases, it was being handled by Gerry Sterner. But she remembered a researcher from Paris being on to Gerry just a few days back.

She picked up the phone and buzzed switchboard. 'Susan? Is Gerry still there?'

'I think he's in the library. I'll ring through.'

Seconds later Sterner's voice came on the line. 'Yeah.'

'Gerry, Jennifer here. Get to the nearest TV – fast! Your Calvan woman's on with Larry King.'

Garbled thanks as Sterner darted two doors along to the coffee room. Two secretaries were watching *Pacific Drive*.

He grabbed the remote. 'Sorry. *Sorry*. Emergency!'

Larry King's image flicked on in profile. Trademark red braces '. . . *to your knowledge have there been any previous incidences where PLR evidence has been presented in a murder case?'*

'Two in India – though only one made it to full trial. But this is the first case of its type in a society which inherently rejects the concept of reincarnation and PLR. And so in that respect . . .'

Sterner rushed from the room, grabbed the first telephone in the adjoining office. His secretary was out to lunch, so he raised reception. 'Susan, can you get me Jean-Paul Thibault at Guirannet & Fachaud in France. They'll be winding down for the day there, so you'll have to be quick.'

Could it be . . . *could it really be?*

Monique had decided even after the second tape, *yes*, purely because she couldn't think of any other rational explanation. Nobody else but Christian could possibly have known such depth of detail. Though still that initial wall of resistance; berating Dominic that she might accept some vague psychic link, nothing more.

But with the continuing sessions and tapes and then the trial, though never mentioning anything to Dominic, her view had slowly changed. At first just through attaching Christian's voice to the descriptions on tape . . . the many poignant memories flooding back. But then she'd become curious about Eyran Capel.

Initially only casual questions when Dominic talked about the progress of the sessions and the case: what does the boy look like? Is there a resemblance to Christian? Does he remember anything while awake? No on every count, no image or magic picture in her mind to cling to, nothing except the voice on tape. Playing them repeatedly, asking for each additional tape equally as casually, trying not to give away the mounting intensity of her curiosity.

She'd have asked to sit in on some sessions, but that too might hint of growing obsession – and Dominic had complained about the difficulties of personally attending, telling her about the secret game between him and Marinella Calvan. He'd only been able to swing one final session with himself and a notary.

Then only a few days ago, Dominic had mentioned Stuart and Eyran Capel travelling down for the next hearing – they'd agreed to meet up beforehand. She was sure in that moment she'd have said, 'I'd like to come', if it wasn't for where they were meeting: *the wheat field!* The wheat field at Taragnon. Suddenly her curiosity and everything she'd pushed away for so long were in conflict. She couldn't go back there, she could *never* go back there.

And so she told herself it wasn't important, clung to Dominic's earlier words that he was just a fresh-faced English boy, light brown hair, a few freckles across his nose, no resemblance to Christian, remembers nothing while awake . . .

What would she do? Stand next to this boy she didn't know and ask questions he couldn't answer, her heart and soul ripped apart again by the memories? Perhaps she was never meant to meet this boy. It was meant to stay a private thing. Just her alone with the tapes . . . *alone with Christian's voice* . . .

She focused sharply back over the top of her wine glass at Dominic. Dinner had been cleared away. He looked as thoughtful as her for a moment.

'Problems?' she asked.

'I don't know. Possibly. It didn't go well today. But we won't know the outcome for a few days yet.' When the doors to the hearing room had finally swung open, Corbeix's expression had been thunderous. He explained to Dominic the grilling he'd been subjected to and what Thibault was demanding, breaking off briefly as they both watched Thibault pass. Barielle wanted to consult the *greffier* notes before ruling: counsels to be advised in four days.

'What might happen?'

Dominic sighed. 'It's bad. A mistrial could be called – the whole case thrown out.'

Monique's eyes softened. She grimaced tautly and reached out and touched the back of his hand. 'I'm sorry, Dominic. You've put so much into this case. Fought so hard for it.' But beneath his hesitant smile in return, she could read the pain and anguish. It was little comfort. She gripped his hand tighter. 'Look, Dominic. If the case fails, you shouldn't feel bad about it because of me. We've had a great life together. You've given me two beautiful sons. You've made me very happy. Nobody could ask for more. I don't expect it of you to set the record straight on Christian as well.'

'Thanks.' Dominic squeezed her hand back, though he knew it was probably just to make him feel better about possibly failing. Like him, she would no doubt like to see Duclos nailed to the side of the Arc de Triomphe for what he'd done to Christian.

'You don't need to do this for me. I got over the ghosts of Christian long ago.'

But he was doing it as much for himself, he thought. To set the record straight; though she would probably now never know his guilt over Machanaud. She was right: they'd had a great life together. Shared everything. *Except a few secrets.* 'Does it bother you, everything coming back now? In any way awaken the ghosts?'

'Obviously a little.' Momentary flinch. She didn't want to admit how much it had obsessed her. He had enough worries and pressure. 'But we shouldn't let it rule our lives. If Duclos is meant to be convicted, then so be it. If not, the same applies. Whatever is meant to be is meant to be. Don't torture yourself trying to change it, Dominic. Don't punish yourself. You've done everything you can on this case. If it's still not enough, then let it go. Nobody would blame you, think less of you. And certainly not me.'

As ever: soft, understanding. Her eyes too implored him, added depth to her words. Soulful brown eyes that had melted him the first day he saw her, had glimmered and sparkled at him across countless candle-lit tables through the years, at the birth of Yves and Jérôme and the numerous birthdays and celebrations since. A good life. *God*, how he loved her.

But beyond the softness and compassion in her eyes, he could still see the pain. See the shadows that had haunted her with Christian through the decades. Shadows that belied her compassion, that screamed, get him, *get him!* Bring Christian justice. Don't let him get away.

Bettina's voice drifted from the kitchen. 'I'm bringing in the cake now.'

Joël smiled. Duclos smiled awkwardly in return. They sat at opposite ends of the dining table. Distance between them. Always more acute when Bettina wasn't present, as if she was the only link between them; they couldn't communicate effectively without her presence.

Bettina came in with the cake and the atmosphere eased. White icing with blue piping: HAPPY BIRTHDAY, JOËL. Ten candles.

A miracle. Five days' skirting with death in an incubator, then remarkably Joël had started to gain strength. Another two months with worries about healthy bone formation, and Joël had never looked back.

Delayed congratulations from colleagues once Joël was out of danger. Cigars. 'You must be overjoyed!' 'Yes, yes, of course.' His best politician's smile. Inside he was too numbed to know what he really felt. At least Bettina would be happy, had been the overriding thought. It would keep her occupied, away from him. Some advantages.

Blond hair, mop style. Blue eyes. Joël looked like his mother, took after her in every way. He could see very little of himself in the boy.

Bettina smiled appreciatively at the two of them above the cake. 'It's good to have you at home, Alain. Especially for occasions like this.'

'Yes, it's nice to be back.' Duclos forced a smile, but thought: Stupid bitch. Gendarme posted at the front door, his life and future hanging in the balance. It was hardly the ideal homecoming. But he knew what she meant: between Brussels and Strasbourg, the various business trips and weekends sneaked away – also covered as business trips – he hardly spent any time at home. Often he would see them only two or three days in as many months. Duclos laughed inwardly at the irony: such was their relationship, their sham of a marriage, that it had taken a court order to get him to spend some time at home.

Birthdays? Despite Bettina's comment, one of the few times he was actually present. He could remember missing only three of Joël's birthdays: two he'd forgotten and Bettina had barely forgiven him, and another had clashed with a vital business trip. He'd left a present and phoned from Prague to wish Joël 'Happy Birthday'. A seven-year-old's sweet lost voice on the line: 'Thank you, papa.' Probably hardly remembering from one month to the next what his father looked like. He was hardly there.

And when he was: *distance.* He could feel it in the boy's eyes whenever they settled on him. Perhaps he could expect no less with the time he spent away; or was it the strong bond Joël had with Bettina making him feel like a stranger, an outsider to their activities, outside their precious little circle? But in his darker moments, the boy's gaze would unnerve him. He would wonder if it wasn't just a questioning look because of his long absences, but more knowing: as if in that moment – as he'd feared through the long years – the boy had seen through to his soul and guessed his dark secret. But he'd been so careful, had consciously made an effort. He'd never looked at Joël in that way, *never.* The boy's blond hair and fair skin had made it easier. Not the type he was attracted to. But apart from that, it was his son, *his son!* He would never, *never . . .*

'Are you okay?'

Yes, fine. Fine.' But he could feel his pulse racing, his hands clenched in fists beneath the table.

Bettina's expression was contemplative, concerned. 'I know that all of this isn't easy for you. But you should try and relax for just a moment. You're at home now, with your family. Among people who care about you.'

He let out a long, slow breath. 'Yes, yes, you're right.' Tried to let the tension ease away, slowly unclenching his hands. Three more days to know if the case had been thrown out. If not, then their next chance was with Marinella Calvan. Thibault had phoned just the day before to tell him of some juicy new leads he was tracking on Calvan, was confident that he'd be able to crush her in grand style. Perhaps he shouldn't worry. If it wasn't all over with good news from Barielle in three days, then it certainly would be by the next hearing.

But that wasn't the only worry, he reminded himself: later that afternoon no doubt Jaumard would call again, and he'd have to spend time on the phone to Geneva to arrange a transfer. The court case; Jaumard; his name in every newspaper; a gendarme at his door; a clutch of newspaper reporters beyond, clicking and jostling at the first appearance. At times it felt like everything was closing in.

With the first headlines, he'd assured Bettina that it was all ludicrously fabricated. None of it true. 'My lawyer will have the case thrown out in no time at all.' She hadn't asked, but he'd wanted to answer before any questions possibly came. Bettina had accepted his answer without visible reservation, but he couldn't help wondering if a part of her suspected: the business trips, the long weekends away, his rarely sharing her bed. Just the pattern that would fit in with such a secret life.

Bettina was lighting the candles and smiling. And Joël was smiling too, bright eyes above the gleam of the candles.

Eyes that *knew*. Duclos shook the thought away. As Bettina had suggested: relax. He was among family. People who cared.

But through the years, how much had *he* cared? A son who felt at times like a stranger. A wife whom he hardly slept with. Eyes that sparkled with warmth and understanding – and all he'd done was spend the long years trying to avoid them.

And now he had been welcomed back. *Family*. The tight family circle of Bettina and Joël which he'd stood outside of for so long. Self-exclusion. He let the new feeling of welcome wash through him, bathed in its warmth as he watched Bettina light the last candles. Bettina smiling;

419

Joël smiling. Family closeness and warmth he could hardly remember experiencing before. But slowly beyond, he began to see something else: all the other smiles through his weeks at home. Tight smiles, anxious smiles — tension so acute that at times it could be cut with a knife. Moments when it had flashed through his mind uncharitably that he'd be better off in prison than stuck at home with the two of them.

And the falseness beneath their smiles suddenly struck him, the thought resurged: they *knew*. They both knew. And here he was firmly embraced within their syrupy little family circle, surrounded by candles and sweet smiles. Trapped.

Sweet icing smiles, blue piping: ten? *Oh God*, the age Christian Rosselot had been when he'd died.

The candles glimmered. Joël's smiling face was above them, eyes wide as he pouted . . .

But all Duclos could see was the single candle burning in the hospital with Monique Rosselot's face in profile, Christian Rosselot's eyes pleading up at him, don't kill me . . . *don't kill me!*

And as his son blew out the candles, the rock came down . . . he saw himself smashing the life from Christian Rosselot, extinguishing the light. *Feeling the small skull crush as the rock connected . . . spurts of blood warm on his chest.* And then he was in the car with Bettina, turning the wheel sharply . . . *her piercing scream just before they hit the truck . . .*

Duclos bit at his lip sharply and rushed from the room. He headed for the bedroom and slammed the door shut behind him.

After a moment, Bettina came in. She sat beside him on the bed, one arm across his shoulder in comfort.

Duclos looked down at the floor, found it hard to meet her eyes. 'If things go badly, it just hit me: this could be the last of Joël's birthdays I'll be here for, for a while,' he lied. Tears would have been fitting, but none came: dry well of emotions.

'I know. I know.' Bettina soothed.

But he wondered at heart what she did know or suspect. Perhaps they were both lying.

Corbeix phoned Dominic's office within minutes of the ruling coming through from Barielle's office. 'We've got it. But by the skin of our teeth. Barielle has made a strong reprimand which will be entered into the notes for full trial — may still be used by Thibault to rap us over the head then. But for the moment, we're still alive. Just. Though I'm sure if anything else comes up that even remotely smacks of the same, Barielle will throw the case out.'

'Well, hopeful news at least. 'Thanks.' Putting down the phone, Dominic wondered: Marinella Calvan? Thibault would no doubt give her a battering over PLR, but at least there should be no claims of bias. Calvan probably had little or no knowledge of French politics, nor cared.

Duclos picked up the phone after the first ring. He'd put down the phone from Thibault only minutes before: news of Barielle's ruling, strategy for Marinella Calvan at the next hearing. He thought Thibault might have forgotten something, was phoning back. But it was George Marchand from Switzerland.

After the preliminaries of 'can we talk freely' and 'how are you coping', Marchand got to the purpose of his call.

'I had a call a few days back from my people. They're not happy about all the talk in the papers bringing up the bio-technology ruling. They're extremely uncomfortable about the linking of your case to that – and with obvious reason.'

'It's just a ruse by my lawyer. They shouldn't worry.'

'What's his aim?'

'The bio-technology ruling provides good background for his claim of political bias against me. Strong incentive for political enemies to start coming out of the woodwork. We almost got the case thrown out at the last hearing – but almost certainly it will be at the next. Then the whole thing will blow over quickly. Some new scandal will hit the headlines.'

Brief silence from the other end. 'A few days ago they were merely worried. But when news from today's *Figaro* reaches them, they're going to panic. Remember Lenatisse?'

'Yes.' Jules Lenatisse was a French Socialist MP strongly outspoken about the bio-tech ruling, making caustic remarks about Duclos' handling favouring the Greens.

'One journalist seems to be linking your lawyer's comments with those of Lenatisse. Have you seen it yet?'

'No, no. I haven't.' He didn't get the papers early, hardly ventured out with the gendarme and the press at the door. He waited till later in the day for Bettina to bring the papers in with the shopping.

'I'll read it for you: *"Bold claims indeed from Defence Counsel Thibault of a political witch-hunt against his client stemming from the bio-technology dispute. But this raises other more intriguing issues: in particular Jules Lenatisse's earlier comment, however flippantly made, that Alain Duclos might be in the pocket of the Greens. Because certainly, if Alain Duclos is finally found guilty of murder, then it doesn't take too extreme a stretch of the imagination to believe that he might also be a corrupt politician. Perhaps Monsieur Lenatisse's comments might have some substance after all."* '

'I see.' Duclos went cold. Yet another dimension to his problems. 'I can see why they're worried. At least it still only points to the Greens – your people would be the last to come under suspicion.' Then realized it had sounded offhand. 'But point taken. I'll ask Thibault to lay off. No more mention of the bio-technology dispute. And, as I say, the whole thing should be quashed soon anyway.'

'Let's hope so.' Marchand wouldn't be surprised if the journalist too was playing an angle for some industry lobby group. At present, if Duclos was convicted of murder, the bio-technology ruling would still stand. Only if a connection was successfully made to possible corruption could the debate be retabled. 'There was another reason for me making contact at this stage.' Marchand sighed. From his client's last call it was obviously a prime concern, but the words just didn't sit right, felt out of place with the relationship he'd so far established with Duclos. 'I know that your lawyer is confident of clearing you. But if anything should go wrong – if you should feel the need for additional help – just call. It's just so that you know that if the worst comes to the worst, you have friends out there. People who will help you.'

'Yes, yes. Certainly. I'll remember that.'

Marchand rang off. Duclos had sounded suitably nonplussed by the gesture; probably its significance wouldn't hit him for a while. Or perhaps he was so confident his lawyer would clear him, he hadn't even considered other possibilities.

Not an entirely altruistic gesture by his client, Marchand realized. The last thing they wanted was a convicted Duclos, eager to make deals and turn state's evidence, sink some industry big fish by telling all about his years as a corrupt politician.

41

Stilted three-way conversation: questions from Barielle through the translator to Marinella Calvan. And in turn back again with Calvan's answers.

It reminded Marinella of the sessions with Philippe and Eyran.

'What is your preferred method of conducting sessions?' asked Barielle.

'Hypnosis.'

'I understand that your colleague, Dr Donaldson, prefers conducting sessions while people are awake. What is the reason for this?'

'He feels that sometimes hypnosis could be suggestive. Could spark off unwarranted imaginings if used the wrong way.'

'I see. So hypnosis could be used to suggest imaginative scenarios that weren't real?'

'Yes. But as I say – only if misused.'

Corbeix looked up. The first hesitation from Calvan. The first half-hour had already covered much of her background at the University of Virginia and her working relationship with Donaldson. Corbeix had spent almost an hour going over points in file notes in private chambers with Barielle the day before. He imagined that Thibault had spent a similar time. As it was the most unusual element in the case, it was important that Barielle gained a full grasp of the subject. But equally its unorthodox nature would target it as the main area for Thibault to try and discredit. Corbeix tried to pick up on his own questions and those influenced by Thibault. Sometimes the dividing line was vague, or there might be additional questions posed by Barielle. Except now: throwing doubt on hypnosis. Thibault's hand was on the rudder.

'Donaldson works almost exclusively with children, and I felt that many would have vivid imaginations in any case. Particularly in India and Asia where he so often works, where reincarnation is an accepted part of the culture.'

'And you generally have avoided working with children from those regions?'

'Yes. My main work has been with children in America and Europe.'

'Any particular reason for this?'

Marinella thought for a moment. 'Challenge, I suppose. It's more of a challenge to delve into past lives with children from a culture where reincarnation isn't normally accepted, rather than one where it is. And, of course, this makes hypnosis all the more essential – to drag out buried or heavily repressed memories.'

Fresh breath from Barielle. 'Can you tell me: what are the percentages of people who believe in past-life regression in Europe and America?'

'In America the figures are going up all the time. As much as thirty, thirty-five per cent, I now believe. But in Europe I understand that it's slightly less – twenty, twenty-five per cent. But among the rest, there's a lot of "not sures" and "don't knows".'

'I see. But in general, in America and Europe, is it fair to say that most people do not fully accept or believe?'

Marinella cast her eyes down slightly; reluctant admission. 'Yes, it is.'

'In your own work, has this been significant? Something you have seen as an obstacle and, if possible, would like to change? Get more people to believe?'

Marinella shrugged and smiled. 'Yes, of course. It's something that everyone working with PLR and related fields is continually fighting for – wider acceptance. That's why we spend so much time building up strong case histories.' One eyebrow arched, as if to say: stupid question. Days and sometimes weeks spent compiling tapes and transcripts. Ninety pages alone from Eyran Capel's sessions, with her and Donaldson up until 2 a.m. solidly for over a week to knock it into shape for a publishable paper for the university. 'It's a constant battle against scepticism – much of it from within our own profession. From the more staid and conventional areas of psychiatry and psychology.'

'So, it would be true to say that your desire to convince a wider audience about the relevance of past-life regression has been a strong driving force behind your career to date?'

'Yes.' The first warning sign; Marinella felt the need to quickly redress the balance. 'It was the main reason I specialized so strongly in xenoglossy: use of a foreign language unknown to the main subject. Probably the strongest possible support for real regressions – particularly with young children who've had little or no opportunity to learn the language in question. This was the main reason why Dr Lambourne contacted me in the first place with the Eyran Capel case. My work with xenoglossy.'

'Eyran Capel has been a particularly large and important case for you?'

424

'Yes.' Unequivocal: she'd had nothing else even nearing it.

Barielle flicked through some notes. 'But I understand that you had some relative success with a xenoglossy case a few years back. A young boy in Cincinnati. Can you tell me what happened there?'

Marinella looked sharply at Corbeix. She hadn't told him about this in her briefing that morning nor, she was sure, had she mentioned anything to Fornier. Then her gaze shifted to Thibault's tell-tale half-smile. He quickly averted his eyes to something indicated in a folder by his assistant. Jesus, they *had* been digging. 'I had a paper half published, announcements prepared for a forthcoming full paper, when the boy's father pulled him from the sessions.'

'What were the reasons he gave?'

'That he didn't feel his son would benefit from continuing regressionary sessions. Was worried even that they might harm him.'

'I daresay this is something that you would not like to have happen again: a subject being pulled away from sessions prematurely.'

'No, I suppose not.' Faint annoyance at the obviousness. 'I don't think anyone would.'

Barielle's blue eyes glared across purposefully. 'So tell me: what was the reaction of Dr Lambourne or Eyran Capel's uncle and guardian, Stuart Capel, when you told them that the final sessions would be used to track down clues on Christian Rosselot's murder?'

Marinella's mouth went dry. She felt as if a trap door had suddenly opened. She fumbled. 'Well – we just didn't know straight away that was what we were looking for. That didn't come out till later.'

'But I understand that Chief Inspector Fornier was present at some of those final sessions?'

'Yes, once early on, then one later session –' suddenly the fire exit was there and she bolted for it – 'when he saw the possibility of vital details coming out about the murder and decided to attend again.'

'And for the other sessions?'

'I sent him transcripts and tapes.'

'So he nurtured and maintained an interest in the case throughout – but didn't reveal the purpose of that interest until the last moment?'

'Yes.' Marinella shrugged. 'I don't think he was even sure himself until the last moment.'

'I see.' Barielle was brooding, thoughtful. He didn't look satisfied. He flicked through some notes, then looked across at Corbeix. 'What do you have in your file for the date the notary Fenouillet was first contacted about travelling to London? You might be able to find it more easily than me.'

Corbeix was slightly flustered at the proceedings swinging suddenly to him. He leafed quickly through his own notes. 'Here it is: 3 April.'

Barielle asked for the session dates in London and Corbeix flicked through more pages. Finally: '30 March, 4 April, 6 April and 11 April.'

'So . . . just before the second session. It would certainly appear that Fornier was aware of the possibility by then.' Barielle turned again to Marinella Calvan. 'And Chief Inspector Fornier mentioned nothing to you at that stage about using the information to possibly further his investigation?'

Marinella changed tack, realizing that if she stuck to her guns it would reflect badly on Fornier. 'Well, nothing directly. But he certainly intimated it.'

'Intimated? Could you possibly elaborate on exactly what was and was not said?'

Corbeix cringed as Barielle and Calvan argued over semantics of language: was she aware that those final sessions were aiding an investigation or not? After a few moments, the most he was able to get from her was that she was made 'vaguely aware'. But certainly she didn't know for sure until the sessions were drawing to a close.

'And this "vague awareness" – was this at any time passed on to Dr Lambourne or Stuart Capel?'

'I might have hinted at something,' Marinella fumbled. 'I don't remember exactly. We had quite a few conversations, some elements of the case were extremely complicated, as you appreciate.'

Barielle stared impatiently at Calvan. 'It's a straightforward question, Madame. Did Dr Lambourne or Stuart Capel know that these final sessions might aid a murder investigation?'

'Not directly.' Marinella bit back. 'How could they if at that stage I didn't even know for sure myself? As I mentioned, even Chief Inspector Fornier I don't think was totally sure until the final session.'

Barielle sighed. Calvan's ambiguity was wearing him down. The three-way nature of the questioning made it all the more tedious. 'Well, thankfully we'll soon be able to ask Dr Lambourne and Stuart Capel directly if they knew. But to dispense with you for the time being, Madame: your final word is that you did not know for sure the sessions were being used to aid a murder investigation until the final session?'

'Yes, that's correct.'

'And for a moment presuming that you had known and had informed Dr Lambourne and Stuart Capel – what do you think would have been their reaction?'

'I'm not sure. I don't know.' But she was trembling inside: she did know, she was sure.

'Then let me suggest something: given your past experience with the Cincinnati boy, isn't it likely that your first assumption would have been that they would have pulled Eyran from the sessions prematurely – they wouldn't have agreed to continue?'

'I don't know.' Marinella was flustered. 'That's purely speculative. The thought never even really . . .'

Barielle steamrollered over her protests, didn't even wait for the translation. 'Or certainly, even if that wouldn't have happened, that's what you would have feared. Which is why you ensured that nothing was mentioned to either Dr Lambourne or Stuart Capel. You were afraid of losing one of the largest cases of your career.'

Corbeix cradled his head in one hand as Barielle continued, now emphasizing just how big a case this was for her: speeches, book contracts, chat shows, a spot on Larry King just the other week which Barielle had viewed on videotape. Thibault's people had been busy. Very busy. Thibault had fed Barielle a particularly juicy rabbit this time, and Barielle obviously wasn't going to be satisfied until he'd stripped the last inch of flesh.

'It has been suggested by defence counsel that the enormity of this case and your pursuit of the possible fame and fortune derived from it have severely tainted your judgement. That if Dr Lambourne and Stuart Capel had been informed of the purpose of those final sessions, they would have never agreed to them. And by not providing such information, in effect, you gained the final sessions with Eyran Capel under false pretences. And consequently, none of the evidence gained therein should be accepted.'

Corbeix noticed Barielle glancing at his folder. Perhaps referring to the exact text provided by Thibault. No doubt another mistrial demand.

'And on the evidence so far before me, I'm inclined to agree. But before I reach my decision, as I say, I will hear first from Dr Lambourne and Stuart Capel.' Barielle flicked forward a page in his folder. 'Finally, Dr Calvan – when was it that the possible potential of this case struck you? When did you start arranging lecture tours and chat shows?'

An easy question at last, thought Marinella. 'Well obviously, not until after the last session.'

'So, mid April sometime?'

'Yes, about then.'

'Then I would like you to listen to this.' Barielle produced a small cassette recorder from beneath his desk top. 'I will ask for your comments afterwards.' Barielle ceremoniously pressed play. The sound was faint and tinny, and Barielle turned it up to ensure it carried across the room.

'. . . it's a story we're preparing for next week's edition.'

'What paper did you say?'

'Miami Herald.'

Marinella recognized the voice straight away: her agent, Stephanie Bruckmann. Stephanie had mentioned the *Miami Herald* calling.

'We're hoping to combine a short bio on Marinella Calvan with a human interest piece on this case in France. I saw King's interview a few days back. Sounds a fascinating case . . .'

A man's voice. Whoever it was, he was good, the mood settled with general questions to start with before honing in on finer detail. Answers were teased thick and fast out of Bruckmann, the two voices singing tinnily across the room.

Marinella felt as if she had been raped. She'd come fully prepared for PLR to be put on trial: its credibility questioned and pummelled from every angle. But in the end they'd attacked mainly her own credibility. And now this was the final assault. One of Thibault's Stateside goons posing as a reporter. She felt as if he'd broken into her home and rifled through her bedside drawer, had picked out her private diary and was now reading it aloud to the courtroom. Underhand shit.

'And when was it she first contacted you to start setting up possible speeches and interviews?'

'Sometime in April, I believe.'

'Do you remember the exact day? It's important, you see – to get the biography accurate.'

Pause. Faint flicking of paper. 'Yes, here we are. I started setting things in motion on the . . . the twenty-fourth of April. But she initially made contact, what – about three weeks before. She phoned me from London, told me what was in the pipeline with PLR and the murder case. Then we talked a couple more times in between as the sessions progressed.'

If Marinella hadn't already guessed what was the crucial point on the tape, she would have known from the way Barielle that second stared up at her. Searing blue eyes. She read it all in Barielle's face: three weeks before the twenty-fourth. Third of April! Only days after the first session. *Crucifixion.*

She wanted to scream: *It's not fair; it wasn't just for myself, but for the acceptance of PLR at large.* Scream at the injustice and the tactics used to gain the tape. At Thibault and his goons and the slimy murderer of a politician who had hired them. But the image that overrode everything was that of Dominic Fornier walking away from her that day in Covent Garden, shoulders slumped. A lifetime of tracking down Duclos, and now her stupidity had let him down. Destroyed the case.

And now there was probably nothing she could say that Barielle would believe; it would only make matters worse. So she just listened as the tape droned to a finish, stood red-faced, feeling powerless and cheated as the last of her credibility slipped away.

Cold marble. Dominic could feel the chill of the corridor. Unlike the individual rooms, the corridors in the Palais de Justice had hardly changed through the years. Timeless. Memories of Perrimond, of Machanaud; of every bold prosecutor and the many poor condemned souls who had sat in the cavernous hallways the past thirty years, awaiting their fate.

Sat as Dominic was now on a wooden bench, staring down at the floor. Dirt ingrained in marble tiles, the only remnants left of those who had waited for justice. Stained memories.

Marinella Calvan had come out only moments before and recounted the catalogue of disasters that had taken place inside. 'I'm sorry. It all went so terribly wrong. I just don't know how they got hold of half the information.'

Dominic could see she was distraught. She could have just rushed past him and headed straight down the Palais de Justice steps without taking the time out to say anything. He placated. 'It's okay. We gave it our best shot. If it's not meant to be, then so be it.' Monique's words. 'Even the publicity to date will have done Duclos no good.'

As Marinella had come out, David Lambourne was called in. She commented, 'I don't think he'll do us any particular favours.'

Beyond Dominic on the bench were Stuart and Eyran Capel. Stuart would appear straight after Lambourne, then Eyran to close the afternoon's proceedings. Since the boy had no direct recall of what took place under hypnosis, he would be asked only his name, date of birth, and to confirm the times and dates he attended the sessions in question.

Dominic wasn't sure how much Stuart Capel had overheard of his conversation with Marinella Calvan, but when she went over in turn to talk to Stuart, Dominic noticed that Stuart looked concerned. A few words with both Stuart and Eyran, a quick ruffle of Eyran's hair, and soon afterwards she was gone. Dominic recalled that she had a boy of her own about Eyran Capel's age.

Noticing Dominic stare thoughtfully at the floor, Stuart commented, 'I suppose it must come as something of a blow?'

'I don't know if it's fully hit me yet.' Dominic sighed. So Stuart had overheard something, or Marinella had mentioned it. 'It just seems to have been such a long haul. The past few weeks have felt like thirty years. I've had to relive my past all over again.' Pained smile. 'All my sins.'

They sat in silence for a moment. Respect for the dead trial. Stuart Capel was the first to break it.

'When is the hearing with your wife?'

'Two hearings' time. Probably about a month or so.'

Stuart nodded. Lambourne had sent him copies of the transcripts two weeks after the last sessions with Calvan. When Eyran's condition started dramatically improving, Stuart had been curious as to what had led to that turning point. There was a haunting, almost surreal quality to the transcripts which Stuart had found hard to relate to Eyran. Hardly any of that netherworld had broken through to Eyran's life outside of the dreams. Stuart hadn't let Eyran read the transcripts, but had recounted the main foundations of the case. Eyran's first main excitement was that he had been helping out on a real-life murder case. Then later the deeper relevance dawned: that it was a past life, and in that life, he had been the victim. Pieces of a dark puzzle slotting finally into place. The last stages in a long healing process. Acceptance.

And as part of that final closing of the book, they'd arranged to go to the wheat field with Fornier earlier that morning. They were staying in Cannes, Fornier in Lyon: they met at a café by the Bauriac main square and drove out. Thirty minutes of walking through an empty field, some extra texture and shapes put to the voice on tape – but no real answers.

But part of Eyran's rising curiosity had been Monique Rosselot, and Stuart had asked about her then: 'Will she be at the later hearing? Eyran had hoped to meet her.' And Dominic had explained the sequence. Monique wouldn't appear until a couple of hearings' time to confirm the details on tape and corroborate the coin evidence: that Christian left that fateful day with it in his pocket.

They'd followed in a separate hire car to Aix, so hadn't discussed it further. But now with its mention again, Dominic commented, 'With all this happening – I doubt her hearing will even take place now. Look, give me your number before you leave. I'll talk to Monique.'

Stuart took out his wallet and fished out a card. 'That's my work number in London.'

Dominic took it and tucked it into his own wallet. When he had mentioned the meeting at Taragnon to Monique, he'd left a long pause, half expecting a response. He hadn't wanted to ask directly if she wanted to go: insensitive. But she'd just bitten her lip and looked away. Her curiosity obviously didn't go that far. It could have been Taragnon, or what memories the boy might stir. 'How many sessions left now?' Dominic asked. Stuart had earlier mentioned them winding down.

'Only three more, then that should be it.'

Dominic smiled at Eyran. Coy smile in return, hesitant. Stuart said that Eyran had improved a lot, but he was probably anxious now about testifying, thought Dominic. 'Don't worry, the magistrate's quite tame really. They feed him fresh bananas and nuts every hour.' Wider smile in response from Eyran, all reservation gone. The boy looked well. At least one good thing to have come out of the whole mess. 'Just remember that he was also eleven once, and you'll be fine.'

Stuart too smiled and nodded. Appreciative of the brief pep talk. 'There was a bit of disagreement between David Lambourne and Marinella Calvan about the root cause of Eyran's problem. But in the end it appears Calvan's theory was right: Eyran's accident and period of coma linked to that previous period of coma, opened up the past.' *'Until the events that led up to that previous coma are fully confronted and exorcized, Eyran can't start getting to grips with the problems from his own life. Facing and tackling his own grief.'* But recalling Calvan's theory reminded Stuart of the calamity that had now resulted. 'Shame about what just happened with her. Nice lady – I like her. I'm sure she meant well.'

'I'm sure she did.' Feisty, well-meaning Marinella Calvan. One woman with a PLR banner against a world of disbelievers. Her cause was obviously far grander and nobler than his. All he'd wanted was to find justice for a ten-year-old boy.

Dominic shook off his anger quickly; she wasn't to know the lengths that Thibault and his henchmen would go to. Just another in a long chain of calamities. Though they'd scraped through the last hearing, Corbeix had admitted what had caused one of the main stumbling blocks: his illness.

431

They'd been kidding themselves all along, Dominic mused: the lost voice of a ten-year-old boy on tape, an ageing detective trying to prove one last big case before late retirement – a case that had haunted him through three decades – and a half-crippled prosecutor. Up against one of the top Paris law firms and a leading politician. They'd never even had a chance.

Corbeix felt the cramps bite deeper as he saw the case slipping away. But he felt powerless as he watched Barielle question Lambourne. Nothing left to do but to sit and nurse his painful legs.

'So, to recap: at no point were you informed by Dr Calvan that information from the sessions might be used for a murder investigation?'

'No, I was not.'

'We have heard earlier from Dr Calvan that in fact this was intimated or suggested by her. Was even this perhaps done?'

'No. I don't remember any such sort of suggestion.'

Lambourne had made it patently clear that he wasn't aware, with some earlier displays of annoyance: other objectives put before his client's interests he considered a serious ethical breach. His patient's progress could have been adversely affected.

Recalling the comment, Corbeix saw a last-minute chance to fight back. His leg muscles protested as he rose. A few minutes back and forth with Barielle, and the questions were posed:

'As Prosecutor Corbeix has suggested, Dr Lambourne, in regard to your comment about the possible adverse effects on your patient: is it not true that this tactic of getting Eyran Capel to face events surrounding this past-life murder finally led to a breakthrough in his treatment?'

'Yes, it did.' Reluctant admission. 'Though I think this might have been more by good fortune than design.'

'You were also, I believe, clearly informed that Inspector Fornier and a notary would be present for one of the final sessions.'

'Yes, but I was told that this was purely for "filing" of possible additional information about the murder.'

'Did it at no time occur to you that this "filing" might have also included a reinvestigation of the murder?'

'No, I'm afraid it didn't.'

Lambourne's final tone had been lame, tentative, thought Corbeix. A couple of weak strikes back, but Corbeix doubted it would be enough. Lambourne was dismissed and Stuart Capel called.

As Corbeix watched Stuart Capel go through the preliminaries of his name, age and relationship to Eyran Capel, his earlier sense of hopelessness settled deeper. Barielle would ask Capel if he'd been aware that the final sessions were aiding a murder investigation – and Capel would say he hadn't. A few small points and objections could be raised, but would it make any difference? He doubted it. They'd been lucky to scrape through the last hearing, and Barielle had warned that if any such circumstances arose again . . .

'You and your wife were given charge of your brother's son as god-parents, is that correct?'

'Yes, it is.'

'And at what point did you become aware that Eyran might be mentally disturbed and need treatment?'

'About two to three weeks after I took him out of the hospital in California.' The questions brought back the memories. *Vapoured breath on mist as Jeremy was lowered into the ground. The first bad dreams. Racing upstairs as he heard Eyran screaming.*

'The first indication that the boy might be disturbed, I understand, was a series of dreams. Is that correct?'

'Yes, it was.'

'And as a result of the disturbing nature of those dreams, you finally entered the boy into sessions with Dr Lambourne?'

'Yes. Dr Lambourne had been recommended by Eyran's surgeon in California, Dr Torrens.' *Christmas in Oceanside, just him and Eyran.* Taco dips and turkey. Distant, hesitant looks. The first moment it struck him: *this isn't the Eyran I remember!*

Barielle made quick work of the reasons why Calvan was finally called in, the switch from conventional to regressionary therapy. This was ground he'd already covered in detail with Lambourne and Calvan.

But at the mention of her name, Stuart's overriding thought was that she'd come up with the main theory for the breakthrough with Eyran, brought back the Eyran he remembered, and yet now . . .

'There were two stages to the sessions with Calvan, I understand,' Barielle confirmed. 'The first was just generally exploratory. But in the second, coming just over a week later, Dr Calvan apparently proposed a theory that she thought might help Eyran's progress.'

'Yes, she did.' And she was right, thought Stuart. Her theory had worked. And now they wanted him to betray her . . . *plunge home the final knife!*

'And as those final sessions were approached – did Dr Calvan at any

433

time make you aware that they might be used to further a murder investigation?'

But all Stuart could think of was Calvan's expression as she'd come out of the courtroom. Fornier crestfallen as she told him. *Betrayal.* It was wrong. He fumbled hesitantly. 'I'm not sure. I believe she did.'

Thibault looked up sharply, adjusted his steel-rimmed glasses and squinted. Barielle stared at him intently. Doubt, disbelief.

'Are you sure about this, Mr Capel? This is quite a crucial point.'

Fornier looking despondently at the floor. The distant, hopeful light he'd seen in Fornier's eyes earlier in the wheat field suddenly gone. Defeat. Sat now on a bench in the coolness of the corridor next to Eyran. Two survivors. The last fleeting image before he'd entered the hearing room. More confidently: 'Yes, I'm quite certain. She mentioned it at the outset of those final sessions.'

Thibault was on his feet. 'But this is preposterous! We have heard from both Dr Lambourne and even from Dr Calvan's own mouth that this in fact was not the case.'

'If anything is indeed preposterous, then it will be for me to suggest,' Barielle admonished. He asked Thibault to sit down and refrain from further interruptions. Then he couched the same question to Capel less confrontationally: 'Can you explain these apparent discrepancies in testimony?'

'As far as Dr Lambourne is concerned, I'm afraid it might be my fault. Perhaps I did neglect to mention it. But if Dr Calvan claims not to have said anything, then she's selling herself short. Perhaps she truly forgot that she'd mentioned it to me. A lot of other issues at the time were far more pressing – not least of all finding a cure for Eyran. It's easy for something like that to get buried.'

Corbeix observed Thibault's silent fury, and gloated. Due desserts for his tactics. Initial disbelief from Barielle, then finally acceptance. As a functionary of the law, his first duty was to record testimony, not interpret it. Regardless of any doubts Barielle still harboured, the file would show that Marinella Calvan had pre-advised of the final sessions being used in a murder investigation. No mistrial!

Corbeix was almost sure that Stuart Capel had lied, but why? Perhaps best in the end if he didn't know; no possible later self-recriminations that he'd nailed Duclos partly through unfair advantage. All he knew was that the cramps in his legs were suddenly gone. He was steering his boat towards port, and all he could see ahead was clear flat water.

42

'*Un Coca-Cola et une bière.*'

The waiter put down their drinks. Stuart Capel nodded and he walked away. Eyran sipped at his coke and looked towards the beach.

'Are you okay now?' Stuart asked.

'Yes, fine.'

Stuart had promised Eyran a visit to the beach after the ordeal of testifying, and Le Lavandou was one of the first they came to on their way back from Aix.

Eyran had been fine at first. Swimming, floating on his back, feeling all the tension drift from his body. But as he'd come to sit next to Stuart on the beach, the outline of the harbour and headland somehow seemed familiar. A sense of *déjà vu*.

'Have we been here before?' he'd asked.

'No. Only to the beach at Cannes. But you came with your mum and dad to the South of France a couple of years before you went to America. You'd have been, what, five or six.'

'Maybe that's it.' But Eyran knew in that instant it wasn't. He remembered other things from that holiday, but not this beach. The voices around, people talking and calling out, the excitable screeches of children playing and splashing in the shallows echoed and rattled inside his head. And then the other familiar images suddenly flashed through: the wheat field, the nearby village square, some men playing boules they'd passed. It was almost as if his nervousness with the trial had blocked everything; then as soon as he relaxed, the gap in his mind opened.

Stuart had asked if he was okay, and he'd fluffed that it was probably just the trial and having to speak in front of the judge. But seeing his eyes dart anxiously at the people around, Stuart seemed keen to get him away. He suggested they get a drink. Now, again, he was checking.

One thing at least with which he'd been fortunate. He'd always liked his uncle Stuart, and he could tell that his uncle really cared; his fostering wasn't just an obligation felt to his father.

'It was something about the beach. Something I . . .' Then Eyran stopped himself. Even his recall now of the wheat field was pleasant. Perhaps that was why he'd had a block before: the emphasis had been on him remembering anything bad. Yet all he felt was warmth; it reminded him of the fields by Broadhurst Farm where he played when he was younger.

Stuart was looking at him with curiosity, one eyebrow raised. 'Are you sure everything's fine?'

Eyran nodded hastily and sipped at his coke. He got on well now with Tessa, he'd settled in at his new school and made some new friends, the nightmares had stopped, and only a few sessions remained. Everything *was* fine.

Yet he knew that if he mentioned some fresh recall, Stuart might start to worry and think about extending the sessions. And probably that would bother Stuart more than himself. Whatever images still replayed after the sessions remaining, he'd just have to sort out himself; they'd remain his own private domain, like the copse at Broadhurst Farm.

'Yes. I feel better now,' Eyran said. And quickly turned away from Stuart searching into his eyes for the truth, looked again towards the beach he recalled from another time.

Dominic was on the A7 heading south towards the fourth *instruction* at Aix-en-Provence.

Clear water. Corbeix's view from the two meetings Dominic had with him in the twelve days leading up to the next hearing. Thibault had fired his main ammunition and failed. There would obviously still be some obstacles ahead, but Corbeix saw them as more clearly flagged. He knew what to expect. It should be more or less plain sailing now through the remaining *instruction* hearings towards full trial.

In particular, the next hearing should be an easy run: Vincent Aurillet and Bennacer on Duclos' background with young boys, then later Barielle with a summary of evidence to date from Dominic and Corbeix. The main feast would be Aurillet. 'Thibault would be wise to keep his head down,' Corbeix commented. 'Aurillet's evidence is unshakeable. Duclos' voice is on tape, and Aurillet will spill forth chapter and verse about Duclos' sordid history with young boys. I doubt we'll see a "confront" notice.'

But at the last minute, just three days before the hearing, one was posted.

The only thing Corbeix could think of was Thibault possibly attacking

Aurillet's seedy background. 'Trying to discredit him through that. I can't imagine he'll get much else worthwhile.'

But Dominic wondered. All the other 'confronts' had been posted at least ten days in advance. This time it was almost as if they'd only discovered something new at the last moment, or purposely wanted to post late so as not to allow time for the shoring up of defences. The thought preyed on Dominic's mind.

Dominic glanced at his car clock: 1.56 p.m. He wanted to give himself at least twenty minutes before the 3 p.m. hearing with Bennacer and Corbeix. Bennacer was escorting Aurillet up from Marseille. After losing Eynard, they'd taken no chances and had kept him under police guard in a hotel room.

Press coverage had gained momentum during the previous two weeks. A copy of *Le Matin* was on the seat beside Dominic, Duclos' haunted face staring out of the front page, snapped through a car side window. One of the few occasions Duclos had ventured out during house arrest.

It was one of the more considered articles, though still it ran along similar lines to those of the rest of the press: comparisons to the Tapie case and to Médecin, the ex-Mayor of Nice self-exiled in Uruguay due to corruption charges. New France against the old. The North against the South.

New France. Thirty-two years ago in Provence, it could take up to a year to have a new phone installed. Now a new Minitel system could be installed in twenty-four hours. A train then took ten hours to Paris, now a TGV sped through in less than half the time. But France was proud also of its political evolution in that period: past bureaucracy had been streamlined, the past 'old boy' networks of favouritism and protectionism torn down, corruption combated – particularly in the provinces, with the South always considered as one of the worst offenders.

The fact that Duclos was from Limoges was conveniently overlooked: the crime had taken place in Provence, and the original trial and now the retrial were also there. Crime and corruption in the South slotted into a popular and familiar image. Good copy.

Only this time it had been given a slightly different spin: the old trial and the failure to prosecute Duclos, the fact that instead a poor vagrant and poacher had been convicted, were seen as typical of the protectionist attitude to officialdom endemic then. A symbol of past corruption. And the new trial was seen as the fresh broom, part of the new tide that had swept away past corruption increasingly over the last two decades – a shining example of just what had been torn down in rebuilding the new France.

The trial of the decade. It had all the ingredients: a leading politician, a detective stalking him through three decades, regressionists and psychics on chat shows, a multi-billion dollar bio-technology dispute, and endemic corruption and political side-taking. No doubt he and Corbeix were both now viewed as champions of the new France, battling against endemic southern provincial corruption. Dominic shook his head. At heart, the issue should have been so simple: could justice finally be found for a murdered ten-year-old boy?

Dominic eased his foot down, touching 165 kmph. That justice was surely now closer. He pushed his concern about Thibault's late 'confront' notice to the back of his mind.

'I thought you said that it would be over at the last *instruction* hearing?'

'If it wasn't for something that came up unexpectedly at the last minute, it would have been,' Duclos defended. 'But it certainly will by the next.'

'First the last – now the next. My people are becoming anxious, and with good reason.' Marchand's tone was impatient. 'Despite the fact that your lawyer might have stopped mentioning the subject, the bio-technology dispute has come up again. As they say in the media "one of those stories that will run and run".'

Panic. Everyone panicking, everything closing in. Duclos rubbed his strained eyes. His sleep had been poor for weeks now. Even he'd panicked after the last hearing collapsed, begun to worry that this would be the pattern at *every* hearing: hopes built up of winning through, getting the case thrown out – then at the very last minute everything crushed. He'd started to think of last-ditch options if all else failed, and had finally put through a call to Brossard: 'Two more people who might need to go the same way as Eynard.' He would phone again if he finally had to go ahead with the action. In the end, he doubted it would be necessary; but it was comforting to know there was a final fail-safe option if all else went wrong – Brossard already checking the movements of the people concerned, primed and ready to move if he had to call again.

The only one not panicking was Jaumard. He'd called Duclos at five o'clock one morning from Tacloban in the southern Philippines. 'Thasss amazing, it's almost lunchtime here,' he'd remarked to Duclos' complaint about the time. 'It's just to let you know your transfer arrived okay. I'm busy spending it here with a couple of friends.' Duclos could tell that

Jaumard had been drinking, could hear a couple of girls giggling in the background. 'Well, it's nice to hear your voice, Monsieur Duclos. Nice to know that you're still alive, they haven't guillotined you yet.' A quick guffaw, and Jaumard rang off.

The call put Duclos in a foul mood for hours; he was unable to get back to sleep. Jaumard off in the Philippines spending his money with a couple of tarts, while he was trapped in his own house with Bettina, Joël, a gendarme and half the nation's press at the gate.

Finally, he'd managed to calm himself: it would soon all be over. He reminded himself of the strength of the ace card they were holding with Aurillet at the next hearing. This time there was a virtual guarantee.

He placated Marchand. 'Don't worry. The hearing coming up now is a completely different situation. We have almost total control over what's going to happen. But if you want to wait till after the hearing to assure your people, fine. We should know in a few hours.'

'What makes you so sure of success?'

At first, Duclos wasn't going to tell Marchand. He could have just glossed over the issue, avoided answering. But he felt the need to put Marchand's mind at ease once and for all. And he was also proud, found himself almost gloating over the ingenuity of the scheme as he explained it to Marchand. At least one touch of genius among the whole mess.

Marchand's reaction was almost as breathless as Thibault's when he'd explained the ruse four days earlier. 'What – you mean Aurillet is practically in your pocket? When in fact the prosecution thinks he's one of their most important assets?'

'Got it in one.'

Marchand at least seemed more settled and assured as he signed off. In contrast, Thibault had been quite agitated. At the sheer audacity of the scheme, or its implications? The fact that as his lawyer – unless he wanted to drop the case – he had little choice but to ride along with it? 'I'd better post a "confront" notice straight away,' he'd said.

'Do what you have to,' Duclos had commented flatly, but thought: if Thibault had delivered what he'd promised earlier, he wouldn't have even had to play the ruse and tell him, worry his delicate legal sensibilities. Thibault should have been thankful it had all been laid on a plate for him. All he had to do was sit back and watch the case explode in Corbeix's face.

Dominic's hand trembled on his mobile phone as he dialled. *Please God, let me be wrong . . . let me be wrong!*

Past thoughts flashing as he'd sped past traffic. Snippets of conversations. The phone started ringing. Motorway lay-by. The first Dominic had come to. Large trucks passing rocked his car slightly.

Bennacer answered after two rings. Background noise of traffic. Bennacer was on his mobile, obviously en route to Aix.

'*I'm surprised in a way that his pimp is Aurillet.*' Part of a conversation from over a week ago that Dominic hadn't pursued at the time. Dominic asked Bennacer about it now. 'What led you to make that comment?'

'It was just that looking at the details of the case, the boy killed in Taragnon was dusky – mixture of French and North African. Also Eynard in Paris specializes in a lot of that type. But as far as I know, Aurillet mostly deals with fair-skinned boys.' Bennacer glanced back towards Aurillet handcuffed to a sergeant in the back seat. Aurillet looked uncomfortable, possibly at the conversation taking place as if he wasn't there. He turned away, glanced through the side window.

'Is there a Marseille-based pimp who specializes in dusky boys?' Dominic asked.

'A couple. But the main one that springs to mind is François Vacheret. Place in the Panier district, used to be run by his father Émile. You should remember the father: we investigated his murder together back when you were on our patch. Looked like a *milieu* hit.'

'Yes, yes. I do.' Hazy memory from twenty years ago.

'That's the other thing: Vacheret's was one of the few places also operating back in '63.' Bennacer turned again to Aurillet. 'Too far back for you, Vince, huh? Still in nappies.' Aurillet sat tight-jawed staring through the window. Probably stung by the jibe, though Bennacer thought for a moment he saw something beyond: Aurillet looked genuinely perturbed. 'So if Duclos did have a pimp back then, it wasn't Aurillet.'

'Have you got a number for Vacheret?'

'Not on me. But if you call my assistant Moudeux, he'll pull something up from the file.'

'Thanks.' Dominic rang off, dialled straight out to the Marseille station and was put through to Moudeux. Thirty seconds of Moudeux tapping through a computer file and he had the number. Dominic dialled it straight away.

A man's voice answered after the second ring. Dominic asked for François Vacheret.

'He's on the other line right now. Who may I say is calling?'

'Victor. I'm an associate of Alain Duclos. Acting as liaison between him and his lawyer, Jean-Paul Thibault.'

'One moment.'

Dominic felt his nerves racing in the wait. If anything had been done to disguise Duclos' activities, then it was a strong bet it had been arranged through his real pimp. But Dominic knew that he'd have to be bold, take the initiative to get to the truth.

'François Vacheret. Can I help you?'

Dominic announced himself again. 'I'm phoning on behalf of Alain Duclos. He doesn't like to use his line at home too freely while he's under house arrest. We're just going into the session with Aurillet – and we wondered if there's anything we need to know from your perspective?'

'I don't know. Not really.' Vacheret sounded vaguely perplexed. 'My name shouldn't even come into it.'

'We understand that.' Dominic's heart was pounding. Vacheret hadn't denied knowledge of Aurillet. *He knew something.* 'It's just to make sure that Aurillet has everything straight to ensure that your name is kept clear.'

'He should do. Since one of the main aims was to make the police look bad, I made things pretty clear on that front.' Flat tone, as if: stupid question. 'Besides, I understand he has a tape. That should be the main thing to swing it.'

Tape? Dominic went ice cold. 'Yes, yes. Of course.' Fought to keep his voice nonchalant. 'So, from your point of view, nothing in particular that we should know.'

'No, not really.'

'Thanks for your time anyway. Just thought it was safest to check.' Dominic rang off. A juggernaut went close by, its air rush buffeting the car. He shook off a faint shiver and phoned Bennacer back.

'It's a set-up,' Dominic said. 'I don't know how yet, but whatever you do don't let Aurillet go into the hearing. Find Corbeix straight away and get him to arrange a half-hour postponement and a private room for Aurillet. I'll be there as soon as I can.'

'You've already been told. You're not our main interest – Duclos is.'

'Well. I've only got your word for that. I'd rather wait until I can be represented by my lawyer.'

'We can do this a couple of ways. To start with, I can bounce you off every

wall in this room. I'll claim that you became hysterical, started throwing yourself and furniture around – so I had to restrain you.'

Silence. No response from Aurillet.

Dominic sat with Corbeix, Bennacer and Aurillet listening to the tape. It was a small flat memo tape, the type that slots neatly into a wallet. Aurillet had taped the time when he was left in the questioning room with Moudeux.

'Then we can start contacting your clients. Inform them you're under police surveillance.'

'You can't do that!'

'I don't know – public duty, I would have thought. They wouldn't want to get caught up in your mess. We've got five days of clients on tape. Then we can spread the word through our milieu *contacts . . .'*

'You bastard!'

'By the time we're finished, whether you want to talk to us or not will be immaterial – you'll be out of business.'

The few minutes remaining on the tape were in a similar vein: threats, intimidation, protests from Aurillet before his reluctant agreement to co-operate. Not far different from what they'd had to employ in the first ten minutes with Aurillet to now get him to come clean, Dominic thought sourly. The fact that they already knew from Vacheret that a tape existed gave the initial advantage. Threat of prosecution for deception and perjury on one hand with immunity on the other tipped the remaining balance.

'So what was the plan?' Dominic asked. 'Getting a strike against the police for intimidation?'

'Not only that,' Aurillet said flatly. 'The voice you have on tape that you think is Duclos – it's not him. Close, but not his voice. His lawyer was going to contest that evidence too, call in a voice analyst. It wouldn't have passed the test.'

Dominic was incredulous as the full details of the plan unravelled: Duclos was desperately afraid of his background with young children emerging. Vacheret was also concerned about being implicated, so had agreed to help. Aurillet had a gambling debt of 180,000 francs which was troubling him, and in the end that was the fee agreed for his part in the plan. They knew that the police had been trying to unearth a child-pimp background on Duclos through *milieu* informants – so it wouldn't come as a surprise when an anonymous tip-off came through about Aurillet.

With that, they knew it was likely that Aurillet's line would be tapped, though made sure by having their own sound-engineer check. A decent gap of a few days, and then someone posing as Duclos phones. Aurillet is hauled in for questioning, but doesn't admit anything until unduly pressured.

'When the case comes to court,' Aurillet concluded, 'I deny everything and produce the tape. Duclos' lawyer has already been claiming that the case against his client is falsified – and all of this then ties in perfectly.'

Dominic was breathless at the audacity of the scheme. It would have appeared that the police had manufactured the tip-off *and* the taped call from Duclos, with a curtain call of intimidation of Aurillet. False tip-off, false tape, intimidation. Game, set and match. They'd only just scraped through the recent hearings with claims of bias – there would have been no possibility of surviving this last onslaught.

Last-minute reprieve. Dominic let out a long breath and looked up at the ceiling. *Jesus!* He looked back sharply at Aurillet. 'Was Thibault in on this?'

'I don't know . . .'

Stupid question, thought Dominic. Certainly, Thibault had to have been aware before the hearing now. Dominic stormed out into the corridor. He looked its length: three or four people milling, Thibault beyond them at the corridor's end on a wall pay phone.

Dominic felt his anger boil over as he paced towards Thibault. They'd been in the small room with Aurillet for over twenty minutes, and now Thibault was on the phone – no doubt warning Duclos that something had gone wrong.

Seething anger at Duclos' manipulation through the years. Manipulating the evidence and his timing in the café thirty years ago, fooling Poullain and Perrimond that he was straight-laced and squeaky clean, manipulating an electorate through all the years since. And now Aurillet and Thibault. Good, upright Duclos. Champion of the people! It was the police and all around him who were manipulative, *dishonest . . .*

Thibault didn't see him approach until the last minute. All Dominic overheard was: 'Good question, but I really don't know. It could be that . . .' Thibault glanced around, saw Dominic, muttered, 'I've got to go now', went to put the phone down.

Dominic grabbed it before it hit the cradle. 'Who were you speaking to . . . Was it Duclos?' Thibault shuffled nervously, looked down, didn't answer. Dominic spoke into the mouthpiece. 'Duclos? *Duclos . . .* is that you?'

Faint sound of breathing. Some background noises. Then the line went dead.

Dominic slammed down the receiver and pushed Thibault back against the wall. 'You were in on this seedy little scheme, weren't you?' Dominic grabbed Thibault's jacket by the shoulder, balled it tight so that it pulled against his neck. 'And now you were on the phone to Duclos, warning him it might have all gone wrong!'

'Haven't you heard of client–lawyer privilege?' Thibault spluttered. Mixture of fear and outrage.

Pathetic. Just like Duclos: clinging to the moral high ground to the last. Dominic thought of Thibault's assault on Calvan, the attack on both his own and Corbeix's credibility. And it was suddenly tempting to bury his fist in Thibault's face, wipe away his self-satisfied smile once and for all. But in the end he just gave Thibault a last push against the wall and let him go. He wasn't worth it.

Bennacer had followed out only seconds later, was now behind him, looking concerned. Corbeix had stayed in the room with Aurillet.

Dominic's main worry was that Thibault *had* managed to warn Duclos. They had Aurillet, but now they also knew that Vacheret was the main link to Duclos and young boys. Something Duclos would be eager to remove at all costs. If he'd been desperate enough to take out Eynard, then . . .

Suddenly it hit Dominic that even if Duclos hadn't already been warned by Thibault's call – he'd have guessed something was wrong by him suddenly snatching the phone and calling out his name.

Dominic turned to Bennacer. 'Call your station. Get a squad car out to Vacheret's. And fast.'

'Duclos? *Duclos* . . . is that you?'

Duclos recognized the voice immediately. A cold shiver spread through his body. Something had gone wrong. Desperately wrong.

Duclos went over to the window and looked out. Joël was in the garden, kicking a football. The view from the front was probably much the same as it had been twenty minutes before: gendarme by the front door and thirty metres beyond two reporters by the gate. Life *chez* Duclos. Fewer reporters than a couple of weeks back, but no doubt the rat pack would increase again closer to the full trial.

Joël's movements in the garden hardly registered beyond his thoughts. But he'd hardly noticed the boy anyway through all the years, he thought ruefully. Why should now be any different? *Especially now.*

Full trial? With everything now fallen apart, his last ace card destroyed, there would almost certainly be a full trial. And nothing to stand between him and conviction but two people. Two key people around which all else hinged.

Duclos' fists balled tight. His face was flushed, raw acid anger surging beneath. It was hardly believable that Fornier and his ragtag bunch had got this far, would end up pushing him to these limits. Had they forgotten who he was?

He'd already half guessed something was wrong twenty minutes before Thibault's call. Vacheret had phoned, mentioned he'd just had a call from someone called Victor. 'Said that he acted as liaison between you and your lawyer. Just struck me afterwards to check he was kosher.'

Arsehole. 'The time to check is beforehand. It's a bit late now.' When pressed, Vacheret claimed that he hadn't said much, but Duclos had sensed his defensive tone, his nervousness. With Thibault's call, Duclos knew that whatever it was had been enough: the police had woven the strands together.

The problem was, Vacheret probably also now knew. He might panic and do something foolish at any minute.

Duclos picked up the phone and dialled Brossard's number.

François Vacheret stared at the phone for a full minute after his call to Duclos. Jesus, he *had* put his foot in it.

Though hopefully he hadn't given away to Duclos just how badly. His mind grappled for other possible options: perhaps it hadn't been the police, just some obscure clerk in Thibault's office Duclos wasn't aware of. *Victor?* But as Duclos had protested, Thibault knew that his home line was secure, they'd spoken several times on it. And for anything as sensitive as that, Thibault would have phoned directly.

No, it had been the police or someone in the prosecutor's office. There remained little doubt. Once they'd uncovered the full extent of his little ruse with Aurillet, they'd be at his door in no time. And once Duclos knew . . .

Vacheret shuddered. He recalled one of his last conversations with Duclos when he'd discovered through the *milieu* grapevine about the hit on Eynard. He'd protested that if he'd known about the hit, he'd never have offered to help with Aurillet.

'What is this – paedophile pimps solidarity week?' Duclos had teased. Duclos went on to assure that he saw Vacheret in a totally different light:

reliable and trustworthy, whereas Eynard had been a rat ready to tell all at the drop of the first wad of notes.

'Very comforting. But no more killings.'

Duclos had assured that there would have only been one more planned in any case, and only then as a last-ditch fail-safe. 'Now with this little scheme in place, that won't be necessary.'

Vacheret cradled his head in his hands. He wished now he hadn't asked that one last question, asked out of morbid curiosity who that intended person had been. But Duclos almost seemed to relish telling him, remarked that in a way it was only fair he should know. 'After all, you recommended me to the hitman yourself all those years back. Eugène Brossard.'

Butterfly nerves danced in Vacheret's stomach. With the scheme fallen apart, that target would no doubt be back on Brossard's hit list. With his own name now probably alongside.

Vacheret jumped up and hurriedly packed a briefcase. He wasn't going to hang around to see who got there first: the police or Brossard!

He mumbled to his barman on the way out, 'Any calls, I've gone fishing. You don't know where I am. I'll phone you later.'

A quick stop-off at home to pick up a suitcase, then he would head straight for the airport. As he came to the junction with Rue de la République, a police car with Moudeux and a sergeant passed, heading towards the Panier.

Brossard called back within forty minutes. As before, Duclos had left a message at a bar for him. Duclos picked up the phone on the first ring.

'Those two names we discussed. I want you to move on them now,' Duclos said. 'There's no time to lose.'

'Which one should I aim for first?' asked Brossard.

'I'm not sure, let me think for a second.' Vacheret was probably more urgent, but he wondered if there was something he'd overlooked. Brossard had phoned him back the day after his first call; already he knew the movements of both targets the next few days. As ever, efficient.

Brossard chuckled at his hesitance. 'Decisions. Decisions. Not like shopping, is it? Deciding which shirt to choose. Not quite the same when you're deciding on someone's life.'

Memories of Chapeau and Jaumard. The many jibes through the years. Hit-man's revenge: how often did they get the chance to rib establishment figures? Duclos ignored it. 'Vacheret's more urgent. But you should try and take out both within hours of each other, if possible. Because once one has been hit the police will tighten everything on the other.'

'Fine. I'll aim to do both tonight.'

They made money transfer arrangements, and Brossard rang off. But Duclos thought he heard a faint echo on the line, and then a second click. As if someone else had been listening in. His heart froze. He thought that Thibault had assured the line wouldn't be tapped!

'*. . . Vacheret's more urgent. But you should try and take out both within hours of each other, if possible. Because once one has been hit, the police will tighten everything on the other.'*

'*Fine. I'll aim to do both tonight.'*

Bettina had picked up the phone not long after it rang. She thought it was strange that it had only rung once, then stopped. Wondered if there might be a fault on the line. But picking it up, she heard Alain's voice. She was downstairs in the drawing room; he'd obviously answered it upstairs. She was about to put it straight back down, when part of the conversation grabbed her: '*Not quite the same when you're deciding on someone's life . . .'*

An icy hand gripped her stomach as she listened to the rest of the conversation. At its end, she stood stock still, numbed, frozen. Too shocked to admit the reality of what she'd just heard, but the futility of grasping for other explanations also dawning: her mind trapped between the two. She shook her head. Too many years already spent fooling herself.

Telling herself that the trips away had just been business, nothing more. That his rarely touching her had been in respect of her past problem, her frigidity. But part of her had always suspected. The first thought had been that he was having an affair. He wouldn't be the first politician to keep a mistress. And perhaps given her past problem, she'd in part brought it on herself. Not acceptable, but at least understandable.

Bettina walked towards the stairs, started her way up. But even that chink of realization she'd in the end pushed away. She'd hidden behind her love, her absorption with Joël. The day that Alain told her that he was leaving her and wanted a divorce, she would worry about it.

Then with the first newspaper reports, she'd pushed it even further away. Young boys? Alain? *Ridiculous!*

Bettina reached the top of the stairs. But now she knew: Alain had done it! He *had* killed the boy . . . *and now he was sending a hitman to remove the key witnesses*. All the past denial came suddenly crashing back in: the trips away, him cringing at her touch . . .

She shuddered at the thought of the monster she'd lived with for fifteen years – under the same roof with her and Joël! *Joël*. She'd read the papers. *My God*, that poor boy had hardly been older than Joël was now.

Her heart pounded as she reached for the bedroom-door handle. Her mouth was dry. With a final swallow of resolve, she turned it and opened the door.

It took a second for Duclos to notice her standing there. He was still wondering about the click on the line.

He heard her say, 'It's true, isn't it? All true. You *did* kill that boy.'

She was ashen-faced, and Duclos saw that she was trembling. It had been Bettina on the line! She'd overheard his conversation with Brossard.

His mind spun. Judging from her expression, the stock lines of defence and denial that had tripped off his tongue since the first newspaper reports just wouldn't wash this time. If she'd overheard him with Brossard, she *knew*. She knew everything.

He looked down at the floor, blinked slowly, in the end said nothing. His panic waned. He owed her no explanation.

'All a lie, wasn't it? The boy, our marriage. All the weekends away, the nights when you shrank at my touch.' She moved closer, but stopped a metre away. As if bridging that last distance between them would somehow contaminate her. Her voice was rising. 'A pathetic sham, a lie! And I thought at one time that you loved me . . . if only for those first few years.' She shook her head, her face contorted.

Duclos looked up at her. Pitiable. Clinging to the hope that he might have once loved her. A few measly years among their lifetime together. As if reconciling that might make the rest not so bad. Acceptable. He didn't feel like giving her even that satisfaction. He sneered. 'Of course I never loved you. You just looked good at all the dinner parties and functions. And your ridiculous problem with frigidity from a date rape was ideal – the last thing I wanted was you touching me!'

She moved closer, then. Her eyes darted.

'You're pathetic,' he taunted, and felt the stinging slap strike his face a second later. If he'd said nothing, she'd have probably just stared a second longer, eyes searching for an explanation that wasn't there, then turned away. But perversely a part of him wanted the confrontation, a catharsis for his own anger and frustration. Take it all out on poor, pathetic Bettina. She was such an easy target. 'My skin crawled at every single touch through the years. I'd rather have fucked Mitterrand!' But this time he caught her arm in mid flight, wrenched it hard and levered himself up. He lashed at her face with the back of his free hand.

Bettina flew back, crumpled quickly to the floor. She glared back, eyes wild. Raw hatred. A red welt and speck of blood showed high on her left cheekbone.

'What about Joël?' Her voice trembled. 'It took a woman to give you him. Not buggering young boys!'

'Exactly.' Duclos smiled crookedly. A decade too late she'd finally got the message. 'He was the last thing I wanted!'

The images crashed in on him unwarranted: *her scream as the car crashed, Joël in an incubator . . .* The intensity of her stare unnerved him. He looked away.

He felt suddenly claustrophobic, stifled. He had to get away from her, away from her clinging eyes – searching deep for something that had never been there. Some remnant of fondness for her and Joël so that she didn't have to believe that her whole life had been wasted. *Pathetic.* He headed for the door.

Some movement behind him, rustling in a drawer. He was in a half-daze, hardly paid any attention to it until he heard her call: 'Alain!' A harsh, chill whisper that made him turn.

He saw the half-open bedside drawer at the same time as the gun: a Beretta .25 automatic they kept in case of burglars. Bettina pointed it at him shakily.

Bettina's eyes were stinging and bleary as she looked at her husband above the gun. She fought to control her trembling. *Her husband?* He was a monster! A murderer of young boys. She'd be doing everyone a favour if she pumped him full of bullets. Her finger tensed on the trigger.

It would feel good, *so good.* Repayment for the years of betrayal of her and Joël. Revenge for the little boy in Taragnon. But she should see him squirm a bit first. 'So do you still claim you don't love me? Or is begging for your life more appropriate? Perhaps they're one and the same.' But instead of moving away, he took a step closer. She shook her head, the trembling biting deeper in her arms. It was all somehow wrong! She'd seen it in the films: this was when they started backing away, holding one hand up and pleading.

Duclos smiled as he stepped closer. Perhaps she would be doing him a favour. The end to all his problems. 'Why don't you? I'm sick of it all. You can face it all then: public humiliation, the police at your door, a trial, a murder conviction hanging over your head! Yes, go on,' he taunted. 'Pull the trigger. You sit in my seat!'

Bettina's finger trembled on the trigger. *A monster!* He deserved to die. But he was smiling, almost as if he welcomed it. And what would happen to Joël while she was in prison?

Duclos saw the hesitation and leapt in, took the last two steps quickly, jolted her gun arm away. The gun flew free, fell a few metres to one side. He cocked back his arm and smashed his fist hard into her face.

Bettina fell back heavily on the floor. Her eyes were startled, a gout of blood spreading from her nose.

Duclos dived on top of her, straddling her thighs. Anger coursed red hot through his veins. She'd pulled a gun. The stupid bitch'd actually had the guts, the audacity! *She was going to kill him!* He cocked his arm to punch her again in the face, then decided against it at the last minute — shifted down and hit her in the stomach.

She screamed and groaned. He hit her again, her screams only driving on his frenzy. The long years of pent-up anger and frustration washing away as he struck out: for all the times he'd cringed at her touch, for the boring predictability and monotony of her conversation, for the son he'd never wanted . . . for the little clique of her and Joël excluding him through the years. He hit and hit at her stomach until . . .

Footsteps pounding up the stairs.

Barely broke through his consciousness, his frenzy. Then it struck him how loud Bettina's groans and screams had been. *The gendarme.* He'd heard the screams and run around to the open back door.

Duclos scanned frantically around. The gun was not far from his right foot. He kicked it further away, just out of sight under the bed. He straightened up as the gendarme burst into the room.

The gendarme's eyes darted between him and Bettina. His hand was poised by his gun holster, but the gun wasn't drawn.

'She became hysterical,' Duclos spluttered. 'I was trying to calm her. She fell and hit herself badly on the bedside drawer. Give me a hand to lift her up on the bed.'

The gendarme's gun arm relaxed. He came over, half stooped to lift Bettina. Bettina's eyes were clearing from her daze, settling on the gendarme. She was about to speak.

Duclos saw his only split-second chance, lunged for the gun under the bed. He turned and trained it on the gendarme. 'Now give me your gun. Left hand . . . ever so slowly. Just two fingers on the butt.'

450

The gendarme reached across and lifted the gun out awkwardly, held it out. Duclos grabbed it. 'Now turn around!'

The gendarme turned uneasily, trying to keep one eye on Duclos. Duclos raised the gun and smashed the butt against the base of the gendarme's head – but the first blow didn't connect properly, and it took a second to fell him, knock him out.

Duclos rustled in the top drawer of the dressing table for car keys and his wallet, then bolted for the door.

Joël was standing in the doorway, taking in the scene with his mother and the gendarme. *Those same searching, knowing eyes which had haunted him through the years.* The boy moved as if to block his exit.

Duclos sneered at how ridiculous and pathetic the boy looked, just like his mother – and barged brusquely past him, almost knocking him over.

Down the stairs, out of the front door, feet on the gravel of the driveway. One of the reporters by the gate noticed him, was looking over curiously.

Duclos ran to the garage, past Bettina's Renault parked to the side. He would have taken the Mercedes, but it was too distinctive. He'd bought a Peugeot 505 on leasing not long before leaving Strasbourg. The registration was probably still going through. Perfect.

Duclos jumped in, started it up and swung around.

He was shaking heavily, raw adrenalin surging, a dull pounding in his head. After-rush of Bettina and the gendarme. He felt it powering him on: foot hard on the accelerator, out of the driveway – a last sharp turn through the gate.

Cameras clicked and flashed as he sped past the gate on to the road, catching his crooked and desperate smile. But Duclos was past caring. *Freedom.*

43

Dominic spread out a map of France. Where? *Where?* Two of them now to find. Vacheret *and* Duclos.

No registration. Two gendarmes taking it in turns to guard Duclos the past weeks, and neither had taken Duclos' car numbers: 'The garage door was always closed', 'Our station commander never asked us to', 'The only number we know is the car they used regularly when going out – the Renault'.

Dominic shook his head. He'd put out a registration search through Lepoille and Interpol National over an hour ago. No answer yet.

Duclos could be halfway to Paris by now, or to the Swiss border, or heading due south, to one of those sleepy Pyrenees border posts with Spain where guards just wave people through. Without a registration number, they couldn't conduct a national search or a border alert.

And Vacheret had been on the run almost two hours longer. No trace yet either on where he was headed.

Two hits planned, Bettina Duclos said she's overheard. Vacheret was mentioned as one – explaining his sudden flight – but the other hadn't been named.

They'd put additional pressure on the only other person in hand: Aurillet. Two hits. What did he know? Aurillet said that Vacheret had voiced concern following the Eynard hit and about another planned, but no name; it was more in the vein of at least some good coming out of their plan. 'Now at least that hit won't be made. One life saved.'

But Vacheret obviously knew. It could be another child pimp like Vacheret or Eynard, but what if Duclos had sent a hitman after Roudèle to bury the coin evidence, or to England after Eyran Capel?

Dominic clenched a fist tight. Twenty minutes passed with no return calls, and his impatience grew. He could have phoned his Lyon station, but he had no wish to hear the day's panics and emergencies. Only one thing now that he wanted to know.

He called Monique to ease his tension. She was at Vidauban, spent more time there now in the summer months. She'd travelled down by train the night before, Jérôme had picked her up at the station.

'I'll be quite late tonight,' he said. 'Could be a long one.'

'Will you go back to Lyon or come here?'

'Probably Vidauban.' He was better off staying near Aix or Marseille for news on Vacheret. Vidauban was closer. 'But don't expect me much before ten or eleven.'

She started some small talk about Jérôme, but he was only half listening – and cut her off early, anxious in case calls were trying to get through.

Unsettling silence again. The phone inert. Dominic's thoughts fighting to move, but in the end equally inert. The clock on the wall provided an ominous, pulsing reminder that things elsewhere were in motion while he sat there: Duclos racing across the country, a hitman heading for his targets. Ghosts skittering across a map with no discernible form or direction.

But how far could Duclos get? No passport, assets frozen, money perhaps just for food, petrol and a few nights' pension.

Seven minutes before the phone rang again, though it seemed far longer. It was Lepoille.

'We've found something on Vacheret. Air France flight to Corsica.'

'Can we get the Ajaccio airport police to stop him?'

'Too late. He landed over twenty minutes ago. He's in a taxi and away. Could be anywhere on the island.'

Momentary hope fading. Perhaps Bennacer could dig something up from the lead. 'Anything yet on Duclos and car registration?'

'Nothing yet. Could be a long haul. There's nothing in his name, and apparently he got the car recently on leasing through a company. We've got to find the company and hope that the registration's already through. Otherwise we'll find nothing.'

A quick 'good luck' and 'keep hunting', and Dominic phoned Bennacer. 'Vacheret's in Corsica. Anything spring to mind?'

'Not immediately. Let me see if anyone else here has any ideas . . .' Dominic could hear Bennacer calling out: 'Vacheret – any friends or contacts in Corsica?' Mumble of background voices. After a moment: 'Doesn't seem so, I'm afraid.'

'Maybe Moudeux could go to Vacheret's. Say that we know he's in Corsica, explain that a hitman's chasing him. If we've got the information of where he is, then it's a good bet so has the hitman. Perhaps with a bit of pressure on his barman or manager, then –'

Bennacer cut in. 'Wait a minute, Dominic. One of my people working the Panier has remembered another club owner that Vacheret's friendly with . . .' Bennacer's voice faded: second conversation in the background before returning. 'Guy called Courchon. Owns a villa in Bussaglia on the north-west coast. Long shot, but it might be worth a try.'

Dominic thought things through quickly. He was in a temporary office in the Aix Palais de Justice that Corbeix had arranged for him. 'I'm going to start heading for the airport – and get someone your end to head there too. The extra half-hour jump could be vital at this stage. Meanwhile get the Bussaglia police to head out to Courchon's villa, and check the next flight time to Ajaccio.' Dominic glanced at his watch: 6.52 p.m. He gave Bennacer his mobile number for anything urgent coming up on Duclos en route, then left a similar message for Lepoille.

Nothing Dominic could do sitting where he was to aid the search for Duclos' registration. That was a game now being batted between the nation's network of computers.

Duclos headed east towards Saint-Étienne and Givors. He was unsure at first where to go, in the end deciding to join the A7 near Givors. It was the busiest and most faceless of France's motorways, and from there he could head north to Paris, south for the Côte d'Azur and Spain, or east at Valence for Switzerland and Italy.

He'd been left one current account unfrozen for monthly expenses. He stopped at the first cash machine outside of Limoges and drew the day's maximum. Together with what he had in his wallet, 3,260 francs. With food and petrol, enough to keep him going for five days or maybe a week if he stayed in cheap hotels. He knew he couldn't risk stopping again at a cash machine. Even if they hadn't by then frozen the account, his movements could be tracked.

His car was inconspicuous, just one of countless thousands of blue Peugeot 505s nationwide, and the police probably hadn't been able to trace the registration. But he felt conspicuous, self-conscious himself, was desperately afraid people would recognize him. He'd stopped only once for petrol just after Saint-Étienne and kept looking down as he went to pay at the counter. At the last moment he saw a baseball cap for sale to one side and grabbed it along with some sweets. The cap's peak would at least shield part of his face at future stops.

He hit the motorway again and at the Givors junction headed south. Speed steady between 120–130 kmph. Not too fast to avoid attention, but not too slow either. Still the occasional truck would push him over to the slow lane and rumble past.

Then it hit him: 6 p.m.! He glanced at his watch: 5.38 p.m. At six, the main news bulletins would come on. The case had been in the press, but the only recent photo had been hazy and distorted through a car window. Few people would recognize him.

But for the main news that night, they'd probably have a full-face portrait shot. From then on, he'd hardly be able to stop anywhere without being recognized. He'd planned originally to stop to eat later – but suddenly changed his plan. He pulled into the first motorway service station.

He chose a burger and chips at the self-service grill counter. The girl looked up at him, smiled and said, '*Merci.*' A baseball cap not too dissimilar to his own. A 'Have a nice day smile', or had there been a glimmer of recognition?

Duclos' nerves were racing by the time he paid and took his tray over to a table by the far wall. He took a seat facing the wall, his back to the restaurant. It was a large sprawling complex with supermarket, shops and a bar on a bridge structure spanning the motorway. A television was on in the bar area beyond the restaurant, but hardly anyone was at the bar counter paying it attention.

He let out a slow breath, tried to relax, eat his burger. It felt dry, difficult to swallow. His nerves had killed his appetite. But he forced himself, realizing that it might be his last meal for several hours. He laboured over each mouthful; it was like trying to chew and swallow cardboard.

He'd made the decision to head south just after Clermont-Ferrand; he had to get to Provence before Brossard made the hits! If Brossard made the hits, he was sunk: Bettina had overheard him order them!

Minutes after the thought hit, he'd stopped and phoned Brossard's number. Fifteen minutes later, when he'd stopped for petrol, he'd phoned again. Still no Brossard or message. Brossard was probably already heading towards the targets.

'*I'll aim to do both tonight.*' Obviously Brossard didn't want to risk the hits in daylight. Duclos looked at his watch. Two and a half hours of daylight left. If Brossard wasn't contactable, would he make it down there by then?

If he could get there in time and they never happened, he could claim it had been Bettina's neurotic imaginings. Faced with the rest – the tenuous coin and psychic evidence and the questionable testimony of two pimps – Thibault could still pull a few rabbits out of the hat. Perhaps Brossard could make a deal with Vacheret: his life for silence. Faced with just Aurillet, their chances in court were good.

Options, angles. Play, counter-play. Duclos' thoughts bounced between hope and desperation, skittering along a tightrope of possibilities as a *bleep-bleep* crashed in abruptly. Two kids had started playing on a nearby space wars machine. Duclos was nervous with them so close, but they paid him little attention. *Bleep-bleep . . . zap . . . crash. Bleep-bleep . . .* It was more the noise that grated, bringing his already fevered nerves to boiling pitch.

His hands were shaking uncontrollably. He'd eaten two-thirds of the burger and a third of the chips. He put the burger down; suddenly he couldn't stomach another bite. He remembered another restaurant from thirty-two years ago, staring out at the boot of his car . . . *wondering what to do with the boy inside . . .*

And suddenly everything else around flooded in: the space wars machine, the clatter of plates and cutlery, the noise and bustle . . . the news report coming up on the TV. People standing up and pointing, shouting: it's Duclos . . . *Duclos!* He's there . . . over there! *The child murderer!*

Duclos stood up abruptly, turned away. He was dizzy, disorientated for a moment, wasn't sure what he should be doing next. He felt like screaming help . . . *Help!* . . . out loud above the *bleep-bleep* of the space wars machine and the general clatter and commotion.

He was shaking, chilled sweat and goosebumps on his skin. He started making his way out hurriedly, away from the noise, the people . . . then stopped abruptly by the prepared-food display. He knew that he couldn't go through this ordeal of sitting in a café with people around again. He grabbed five packs of wrapped sandwiches, three bags of crisps and a large bottle of water and dumped them on the check-out counter.

Wry smile from the girl at the mountain of food as she totted it up.

'Large family in the car.' He smiled back. But he was sure it came out wrong.

He could feel her eyes still on him as he moved away. He looked at his watch: 5.57 p.m. In a few minutes the news item would come up . . . *and then everyone would be staring!* A moment's recognition and the girl would reach for the phone, start dialling the police . . .

Help. *Help?* It was then that he remembered Marchand's words: '. . . if

456

you should feel the need for additional help – just call. It's just so that you know that if the worst comes to the worst, you have friends out there. People who will help you.'

But he knew that he couldn't risk making the call to Switzerland from there, risk the news item coming up and someone grabbing his shoulder while he was on the phone. And still he had to hope that he could make it down to Provence in time to stop Brossard.

The view along the Bussaglia coastline was breathtaking. Rugged and undulating mountains, a rich green shroud of Mediterranean pines clinging to sheer rock against the azure sea.

But François Vacheret hardly looked at the view from the villa's front terrace; his eyes were pinned to the short snake-like stretch of road far below. The only warning of a car approaching.

The road led to only nine villas. Courchon had already told him all the regular cars to expect: he'd written them down on a piece of paper. Any cars sighted not on the list and he would race in and warn Courchon – then head across the road. Twenty metres along steps meandered down the cliffside to a small shingle beach and a boat house cut in under the rock. Courchon would greet whoever it was, then come down and tell Vacheret when they had gone.

Vacheret had mentioned his concern about the other hit to Courchon. Duclos was out of control, partly unhinged.

Courchon hissed in breath sharply when he heard who the target was. '*Jesus*. Could be trouble. Duclos doesn't have to live in Marseille, you do.' Courchon went on to explain the problem wasn't just with the police, but with the local *milieu*.

Vacheret's heart sank as he envisioned years on the run, of him having to sell his clubs and property without returning to Marseille. *If* he lived that long. For now, his main worry was surviving the next few days. Being stalked by the hitman he'd originally introduced? He might have found the irony amusing if he wasn't so desperately frightened. Brossard was an unstoppable killing machine. As far as he knew, had never failed to fulfil a contract.

He jumped at practically every noise or car sighting on the road below. Only three had so far approached: all local villa owners. But what was he going to do as it became dark – sit out there all night? Even if he did, the road was unlit: there would be no warning except noise, indiscernible from any of the other owners' cars.

But seeing his concern, at least Courchon had offered one ray of hope. 'I've got some good contacts in the *milieu*. I can certainly clear your name on that front of any repercussions. They'll be pleased too of the warning.'

Great. So Brossard might still get to him, but at least he'd die with a clean bill of health as far as the *milieu* were concerned. Comforting.

Vacheret's nerves tensed. A white car was snaking its way along the road below. He trained the binoculars: Citroën BX. There was only one on the list: metallic grey. Vacheret darted inside to warn Courchon.

'Where is he now?'

'Heading down towards Provence,' said Marchand. 'Apparently he's hoping to meet up with someone there urgently.' Marchand hadn't asked why, nor did Duclos offer any explanation. Duclos' call had come only minutes after Marchand had seen him on the Geneva news: fifth item on, though he was sure it was the top story in France. French MEP on the run.

Marchand had spent the last few minutes explaining the sorry mess. At the other end, Miguel Perello was thoughtful. They'd only met once before, in Panama. Perello ran the Panama associate office of a California-based law firm. That was what had made Marchand suspect it was a consortium of California bio-tech companies trying to throw the EU debate. Though it could equally be the Japanese using a California-linked company as a smokescreen. All Marchand knew was that they were happy when the finger was pointed at the Greens. Industry protectionism at its best: knock an $8 billion hole in a rival market by swinging a crucial debate.

'Sounds messy,' Perello said. 'Duclos could be too much of a loose cannon now. Too dangerous.'

'I thought that was the whole idea of offering him help if things went wrong. Get him away from the whole mess.'

'Yes, of course.' Moment's silence. Crackling on the line between Panama and Geneva. 'But how long can we effectively ensure a safe haven for a prominent figure such as Duclos? It might be worth considering again the other option we discussed.'

Marchand went cold. The subject had come up at the same time they'd discussed offering Duclos help to get away. Marchand had voiced his protest strongly: Duclos suddenly killed in the midst of such a high-profile investigation, however well disguised as an accident, could rebound badly. Too risky. He reiterated the protest now.

458

'I know. But now look at others like Médecin,' Perello commented. 'Every so often he makes the threat of coming back to France and telling all, bringing everyone else down with him if his hand is forced. I'm not sure my people would be happy with that sort of threat hanging over them indefinitely.'

'I still don't like it.' But the protest now sounded lame.

Perello sensed Marchand's discomfort with the thought of Duclos being hit. Swiss lawyers: watches, chocolate and money. No blood. He shifted its portent to one side. 'It's certainly not a decision that would be taken lightly, or right at this moment. And whatever's finally decided, it should in any case appear that we wish to help Duclos escape. So let us keep our eye on that for now.'

Marchand was once again a willing participant. They discussed a few options before deciding: private aircraft to Portugal, scheduled airline under new identity from there. Perello confirmed fund lines and they divided duties for the final arrangements.

When Duclos phoned forty minutes later as arranged, from somewhere near Avignon, Marchand gave him a name and time: Aérodrome du Luc et du Cannet. 10 p.m. 'The pick-up will be quick. Three minutes at most. You'll know it's him because he won't show lights the last few hundred metres of descent.'

Moudeux tried to shield his mobile from the echoing bustle of the airport and the intermittent tannoy. 'I see. Yeah. Yeah ... So no show on Vacheret? Yeah. One moment.' He turned to Dominic, sensed his eagerness to be brought up to date. 'The local police called. Courchon met them at the door. Said he hadn't seen anything of Vacheret. They searched the villa anyway, asked a few questions such as was Courchon aware of any other friends Vacheret had on the island – but blanks at every turn. They left. Bennacer's asking what you want the local police to do next – if anything.'

Dominic nodded and held out his hand. Moudeux passed him the phone. 'Did the police believe him or do they think he was covering up?'

'They thought he acted a big cagey – but nothing too suspicious.'

Dominic glanced up at the flicker board. Fourteen minutes left to boarding. No Duclos. No Vacheret. Deafening tannoy bombarding what few clear thoughts remained. Hustle, bustle. Everyone heading somewhere – except them. Yet another dead-end. Dominic's eyes darted, searching for inspiration; but all that crashed in was people, noise, suitcases, cameras, flight bags. Finally: 'Get the local police to head back out to Courchon's and park fifty metres down the road. Sit there a couple of hours – then knock again on Courchon's door. Vacheret might yet show, or at least it might rattle Courchon into remembering something.' But it was mainly because it felt wrong just giving up on Vacheret, and Dominic couldn't think of a better plan.

'Okay. I'll phone them back. Are you catching the flight still?'

'I don't know yet. There's still a few minutes to decide.' Though Dominic knew the answer already. They'd headed to the airport because if positive news on Vacheret came through, there'd be very little time to catch the next flight. But Corsica without Vacheret had little appeal. Too remote if . . .

Cameras! The thought suddenly spun back. Dominic's eyes fixed on another passing tourist with a Pentax slung over one shoulder. He was only half listening as Bennacer signed off. 'Yes, fine,' he mumbled. Thoughts clearing, focusing. His breath caught slightly in his throat as they finally gelled. Fresh adrenalin rush after the disappointment of Vacheret. Fresh hope. He tapped out straight away to Lepoille's number.

Lepoille had phoned while he was en route between Aix and Marseille: company traced that Duclos had leased under two years ago, but nothing registered since. He would keep looking.

'Still nothing,' Lepoille confirmed. He sounded resigned, defeated. 'I just don't think it's been registered yet.'

'Don't worry. I think I might have hit on a solution. Cameras!' Silence from Lepoille. Dominic explained, 'Apparently Duclos' home has been dogged by the press the last few weeks. When he made his break, no doubt a few will have tried to get a clear shot of him. One of them might at the same time have caught his registration number. Quick enlargement, and we've got it!'

Lepoille agreed: chances were reasonable to good. 'I'll get on to it straight away.'

Five main national papers. It shouldn't take long to find out who was outside Duclos' gate that afternoon.

Milieu crime boss André Girouves listened carefully as his lieutenant related the message from Courchon in Corsica.

'And this other club owner, his friend Vacheret, is the one involved with Duclos and Brossard?' Girouves clarified.

'Yes. Vacheret apparently recommended Brossard to Duclos for something else years ago.'

Girouves pondered. Everything was clear so far: Duclos had involved Vacheret in a scheme which had backfired, and now Duclos was using Brossard to bury the traces. Standard practice. Even high-flying politicians weren't too different to himself, he mused. He'd seen the Duclos items on the news. Politician fallen from grace. Loved it.

They were in one of Girouves' favourite cafés on Quai de la Tourette. To one side was his main business adviser, to the other a lumbering lieutenant serving as bodyguard. Business talks over late-afternoon coffee and pastis.

'But it's the other hit planned which was the main reason for Courchon's call,' his lieutenant said. He shuffled nervously, looked down slightly as he told Girouves who it was.

Girouves' eyes closed for a moment. He rubbed his forehead with one hand. Courchon was right to have warned them. *A chief inspector's wife!* The repercussions could be enormous.

Part of the strength of the crime empire Girouves had built up along the coast the past two decades had been its stability. A departure from the muddied dividing lines and power-vacuum struggles of the seventies. And part of that stability had been gained through not crossing certain lines with the police. No more Bar du Téléphone massacres.

Even among their own was the strict rule of never involving family in hits. A chief inspector's wife hit by a regular *milieu* freelancer? Favours would be cancelled, clubs and bars raided, licences revoked, all suspected *milieu* businesses would come under brutal scrutiny. The clock could be set back years.

Brossard? If it had been practically anyone else, he could have just picked up the phone and said, 'Don't go ahead.' But Brossard prided himself on fierce independence, wouldn't swear allegiance to either side. No gang-war hits, only internal enforcement or external contracts – Brossard worked all sides with equal ease. A true independent professional.

Girouves asked a few questions about the hit, but his lieutenant knew little beyond what he'd already passed on. 'Okay. Phone Courchon straight back. Try and pump him for more information.'

Girouves took a quick slug of pastis as his lieutenant dialled out on his mobile. If they didn't learn more from Courchon, he'd have to get a few men busy phoning around. Monique Fornier? Shouldn't be too hard to find out where she was. Then he would probably have to call

Tomi, the only person he knew who would stand any chance against Brossard.

Brossard rapped his hands on the steering wheel to the pounding beat of Seal's 'Crazy'. He particularly liked the organ backbeat, the way it seemed to slip away . . . *finger tensing on the trigger, shadows of figures falling back as he fired . . . slipping away.* But he could never picture any of their faces. Probably best. No ghosts.

Dented and rusty Citroën Dianne which had seen better days. Nobody would pay him any attention. He'd chosen a blue workman's overall which was worn and slightly stained from field work. He'd used it for a hit six years ago, though this time he chose a white cap instead of a beret, turning the peak so that it covered the back of his neck. Favoured uniform of so many field workers. He planned to stay low in the fields, but if by chance somebody saw him, he would blend in.

Brossard pulled the Dianne into a track in the woodland that bordered the back of the field; to anyone passing a farmer or someone having a woodland picnic. He turned off the cassette player, took a knapsack out of the car and headed deeper into the woods. Instead of sandwiches, inside the knapsack was a Llama .357 Magnum with silencer, binoculars and infra-red night goggles. After eighty metres the woods cleared and the field lay ahead.

To one side were a few olive and carob trees, but most of the field was long grass, now starting to yellow with the summer heat. At the end of the field, 200 metres away, was a short stone wall, and beyond that the farmhouse.

Brossard walked ten paces into the long grass and sat down with his knapsack. As soon as it was dark, he would move in. The sun was already low, threatening to fall behind the westerly ridge beyond the farmhouse. It would be dark soon.

Vacheret watched the gentle surf lapping against the beach. Half pebble, half sand, it was no more than fifteen metres wide, nestled under the sheer rock face above.

He sat inside the boat shelter at the back of the beach. Under a heavy rock overhang, he was completely concealed from the road above.

Lap, swish. Lap, swish. Soothing at first, now after more than half an hour, the sound was driving him mad. What could have happened with Courchon? Fifteen minutes after Courchon had first come down to give

462

him the all-clear, the same police car was snaking its way back up the road again.

What was Courchon doing – letting them camp for the night? Or perhaps they'd taken him down to the station for questioning. Vacheret sighed heavily. The first grey and red wisps of sunset were showing on the horizon. He could end up on the beach half the night without knowing what had happened.

He pictured the police pacing around, firing question after question at Courchon . . . at the villa or down at the station? It was immaterial. The police were obviously determined, and in the end would catch up with him. Courchon might have cleared the slate with the *milieu*, but with the police it would be a different matter. He would have to stay away for months, longer if . . .

The realization suddenly hit him like a hammer. At first, he'd clung to the hope that Brossard would head first for Monique Fornier. That might at least give him a bit more breathing space. But now it hit him that he could be implicated. He'd recommended Brossard to Duclos! Being involved with the ruse with Aurillet was one thing – but conspiring to murder a chief inspector's wife? They would throw away the key.

Perhaps if he helped them, warned them in some way. But what if Brossard had already made the hit, and his call merely confirmed his knowledge of it, his involvement?

Vacheret came out from his hideaway below the rocks and looked thoughtfully at the steps winding up to the road above.

'What time was he there?' Lepoille asked.

'Got there about ten in the morning. Normally the time they might show to do some shopping – *if* they're going to come out at all. Which has been rare.'

Third on Lepoille's list: Gaston Contarge, Picture Editor at *Le Figaro*. He'd already crossed out *Le Matin* and *Libération*. 'So he was there when Duclos made his break?'

'Yep. Got the whole thing. It'll be front page of tomorrow's edition.'

A tingle of anticipation ran down Lepoille's spine. He told Contarge what he wanted, and why.

Contarge was quick to mirror Lepoille's excitement. Breathless, slightly hoarse: 'Amazing. Look, I'll check with the editor – but I'm sure we'll help. The only thing he might ask is an exclusive for our part in all this. Any objections?'

'No. Not as far as I can see. I've got three more newspapers on my list. Whoever comes up with the photo first gets the story. Seems fair enough.'

Lepoille smiled as he hung up. He knew that Contarge would be sprinting for the darkroom.

He phoned Dominic straight away with the news. 'Three more to phone, but at least we've got one hopeful already.'

Dominic was on the motorway just approaching Gardanne, fifteen minutes out from Marseille. He'd stayed at the airport bar with Moudeux for a coffee and brandy while waiting on news, then decided to head back to Vidauban. With Duclos and Vacheret by now anywhere in France, it was as good a command centre as any. 'That's great news. Let me know the minute anything comes up. I'm heading back to Vidauban, but you can ring at any time. I'll be up till late waiting on news.'

Eight minutes later when his mobile rang again, he thought it might be Lepoille with an update. But it was Bennacer. His voice was urgent, frantic.

'Dominic! We just had a call seconds ago from Corsica. We now know the hitman's second target. And brace yourself, Dominic. It's Monique. Your wife, Monique. She's the other target!'

Numbness. Then blind fear, rage. 'When?' Dominic asked tremulously.

'Vacheret didn't know. Any time – it could have even happened already. Look – I'll mobilize the nearest station straight away, get someone out there . . .'

But Dominic was hardly listening. A quick mumbled 'Fine', a pounding in his head drowning out all else as he pushed his foot flat to the floor . . . *150 . . . 160 . . . 170 . . . 180 kmph.*

As he flashed past cars and trucks at break-neck speed, he dialled out his home number at Vidauban. But it was engaged.

Bennacer looked briefly at a wall map, and phoned the station house at Draguignan. It was on an answerphone. He slammed the phone down and dialled Toulon.

Girl's voice: *'Un moment. Ne quittez pas.'* Then a radio operator checking positions as Bennacer explained what he needed and stressed the urgency.

'The nearest car we have is just outside Cuers. They're engaged now, but should be free in five or ten minutes. Otherwise we'll have to pull someone up from the motorway section this side of Solliès-Pont.'

'How many men in the Solliès-Pont car?'

'Two.'

Two rookies up against an expert hitman? 'Send both cars. Dispatch them now! And warn them: they could be up against some heavy firepower.' Bennacer glanced back at the map. In fifteen, twenty minutes they should be there.

Dominic's speed held steady at just under 190 kmph. With any luck, he should be there in just under fifteen minutes. His lights had been on for the last ten minutes, and now he flashed wildly at anyone in his way.

The last grey-red remnants of twilight faded over the hills in his rear-view mirror. Beyond the beam of his headlights was pitch darkness.

44

As the grey skyline turned to black, Brossard moved in closer. Fifty metres from the short stone wall, he could see the farmhouse clearly.

One light on downstairs. He trained the binoculars, and after a while saw a woman come into their frame; brief profile: late forties, first wisps of salt in black hair, attractive. She moved out of sight again after a second, going deeper into the drawing room.

Brossard's anticipation surged, but only a trace of what he felt when going up against experienced guns. A woman alone in a remote farmhouse. A cakewalk. He'd put on the infra-red goggles, switch off or cut the mains electricity from the garage, and break in through a downstairs window. The woman would still be fumbling for candles and night lights when the bullet hit. One head shot, maybe two, and out. It would all be over in seconds.

Brossard kept low as he moved through the last fifty metres of grass towards the stone wall. Then he stopped again, studying the farmhouse closer and trying to work out the likely position of rooms. He quickly checked his gun and silencer, then took out the night-time goggles and put them on.

Waiting a moment for his eyes to adjust to their grey-green light, he slid over the wall and started on the last distance towards the farmhouse.

'What time would you hope to get here?' Monique was speaking to Yves, her eldest son. He'd phoned to tell her he would be coming up from Marseille for the weekend. She hadn't heard from him for almost two months, so they'd spent a few minutes catching up on news before returning to when he would be arriving.

'I'm on a late shift at the station tomorrow night, finishing at ten. I'll leave straight after that. So probably close to eleven. But I've got Saturday and Sunday free.'

'That's good. Jérôme will be here; he's not going anywhere this weekend as far as I know. It'll be nice to have a full house.' Already she was thinking of food and preparation: steamed C'ap Roig with couscous, *pâté en croûte* to start. A few bottles of wine on the terrace. It was going to be a good weekend. 'Jérôme should be back soon. You might get a chance to speak to him.'

'It's okay. I've got to go now. But I'll see him tomorrow anyway.'

'I'll try and make sure your father relaxes a bit as well. At least one full day without calls. See you tomorrow.' Monique looked thoughtfully at the phone as she put it down. Family. New family . . . *Old family*.

With the tapes she'd played repeatedly, she'd found herself thinking more about Christian and Jean-Luc. Memories that had plagued her the first few years, sapped her strength before she'd pushed them harshly away: self-preservation for the sake of both her sanity and her new marriage. She couldn't give all to her new family while burdened by ghosts from the past.

The only vestige Dominic had complained about, at times pointedly, had been her obsessive protectiveness with Yves and Jérôme. The ghosts of the past might have been buried – except for Clarisse and her family, whom they still saw every few months – yet a shadow had remained. She could never face losing another child, going through what she'd suffered with Christian again.

But the tapes and transcripts had brought it all back. With each playing, images of Christian and Jean-Luc had grown stronger. She'd resisted going out to the wheat field the day Dominic had met Eyran and Stuart Capel. She'd always vowed she'd *never* go there. The memories were too harsh. But knowing the three of them had stood in the empty field, searching for long lost answers, had raised her curiosity about Taragnon. Perhaps the farm would be different: the memories there happy as well as sad. Alone at Vidauban that afternoon, looking out across the farm fields at the back, she'd finally made the decision. She'd taken the old Simca left permanently at the farm for transporting garden pots and plants, and driven out to Taragnon.

Though it was only thirty-five kilometres away, she hadn't been back to the area for over twenty-five years, since they'd finally sold the old farm.

She parked in the road outside the old farm and looked up. Apart from some modernization with new windows and doors, it had changed little. The outside stonework was much the same.

As she looked, a small boy of no more than four or five came out of the back door and started pedalling a toy car around the courtyard. And in that moment, as she closed her eyes, she pictured Christian in the

467

courtyard at little more than that age, laughing and playing, his gentle high-pitched voice echoing slightly from the walls. And Jean-Luc coming in from the fields, picking Christian up on his shoulders and swinging him around playfully, smiling. The proud father.

Tears streamed unashamedly down her face as she drove back to Vidauban. She'd cried bitter tears for both of them for so many years, but not recently.

And then not long after returning, at six o'clock, the news item had come on about Duclos. She'd found herself honing in on the face flashed up on the screen as if drawn by a magnet. A face suddenly put to this new suspect Dominic had talked about almost incessantly the past weeks – *Christian's real murderer!* A rounded, slightly bloated face with thinning black hair and dark green, almost black, eyes. Thirty years? She tried to imagine in that moment what he looked like then, when he'd murdered Christian. But it was the one leap back through the years her mind wasn't able to make.

As it grew dark, she took out a night light and lit it in the small alcove by the telephone at the back of the drawing room. In the first glow of its light, she'd seen Christian's face clearly, the memories of those last nights of hospital vigil flooding back. She could almost feel his presence; as if he was partly with her now, guiding her actions, willing her to light the night light.

She hadn't prayed for Christian and Jean-Luc for years, but she would that night. She felt that by purposely casting them from her thoughts, she'd also in a way abandoned them. It was time to make some amends.

Now, putting down the phone from Yves, she looked thoughtfully towards the light. She remembered the night that Yves was born, the joy she'd felt. The doctors had told her later she'd been lucky to live. At least she'd been given a second chance of happiness. Some people didn't get even that.

With a last slow sigh, she knelt down before the light, gently closed her eyes and started to pray: for Christian's and Jean-Luc's souls, for the many memories, for the happiness that once was . . . *for the final justice that might now be so close . . .*

Suddenly the lights went out.

The quietly murmured prayers caught at the back of her throat. Her eyes flickered open. A sound outside the house, faint rustling, or was she imagining it? She listened harder, but could hear nothing more. Only stillness, silence. Pitch darkness beyond the weak glow of the night light.

She wondered what had happened with the electricity. Sometimes there were power cuts when there was a storm, but the weather had been fine. She straightened up, deciding to take the night light with her to investigate.

But barely two paces away, the phone rang, startling her. She turned to pick it up.

Dull grey-green light. It took a second for each shape to become clear.

Brossard moved stealthily away from the garage after switching off the mains. He'd already worked out the geography of the house. Drawing room with an office leading off, centre hallway, then a kitchen and dining room the far end. Bedrooms upstairs.

The woman was in the drawing room, but he didn't want to enter from that side, possibly alarm her while he fumbled to break in. He would go in at the far end. The kitchen window was too small, so he chose the dining room.

Looking through, he could see that the connecting door to the hallway was closed; sound wouldn't travel easily. He took the glass cutter and sucker from his knapsack, cut a neat hole, reached in and turned the window latch. He was in within twenty seconds.

Eyes adjusting, orientating. Objects became clear quickly, but it took a second longer to judge distance. Long table. Six chairs. Cabinet. Side table. Archway through to the kitchen. He focused on the door ahead. The door to the hallway and the drawing room beyond. Only the sound of his own breathing as he moved.

Sudden noise, alarming. Deafeningly loud among the silence and darkness: phone ringing! Beyond the hall, in the drawing room where the woman was, Brossard judged.

It stopped. It had been picked up. Good. She would be talking, he could move into the hallway without worry – and he made the last distance swiftly, turned the handle and went through. And waited again, crouching, listening.

But as he fought to pick out her voice and movements beyond the door, another sound came without warning, drowning it out. A car swinging into the courtyard, its lights flashing briefly across a small window by the front door.

Brossard's nerves tensed. An anticipatory thrill rose up from his spine and bunched the muscles at the back of his neck. His jaw set tight, every nerve end suddenly alive, tingling. This was more like it: two targets and only seconds to decide which to drop first!

The woman's voice beyond the door was staccato, alarmed. '. . . You mean now? . . . This minute? . . .'

Car door shutting, footsteps approaching, key in the door . . .

'But that's probably Jérôme now. I could go straight off with . . .'

As the door swung open and the figure took a step forward, Brossard took his first clear shot towards the centre of its chest, and saw the figure fall.

Brossard jumped up quickly from his crouch – no time to lose, the woman would have been alerted by the noise – and burst into the drawing room. Quick flash image: the woman, the phone receiver held out slightly in defence, her panicked expression, a night light beyond searing his eyes slightly . . .

Five seconds more and he would be finished and away.

'Monique. You're in grave danger. Get out of the house now!' Dominic flashed furiously as a car stayed obstinately in the fast lane. He'd phoned at two-minute intervals, and on the third try had finally got through. The pent-up frustration and fear came through in his voice.

'What's happening, Dominic . . . what's going on?'

'No questions, Monique. Just go!'

'You mean *now* . . . this minute?'

'Yes, *now!*' Dominic screamed. 'Get out quickly and run to the nearest neighbour's house.'

Sound in the background. Car engine, wheels turning. 'But that's probably Jérôme now. I could go straight off with him.'

'Whatever, Monique. But just go, get away from there as soon as . . .'

Another sound then: a dull thud and something dropping, as if Jérôme had dropped a heavy kit bag in the hallway.

A sharp intake of breath from Monique, then a shriek as Dominic heard movement in the background, the door bursting open.

'Monique, get out of there . . . *get out!*' Dominic's voice was shrill, his throat almost bursting as he screamed into his mobile.

The sound of scuffling and light banging, as if the receiver had been dropped for a second at the other end. Then a man's voice, deeper. Not Jérôme's. 'It's too late.'

And in that moment – with searing pain and lights bursting through his head in rhythm with his now almost constant flashing of the road ahead – the hollow, nauseating reality hit Dominic that the voice was right. He *was* too late to save Monique's life. He knew it even before he heard the gunshot and the sickening thud of the body hitting the floor. Then the line went dead.

Duclos was in a panic. He'd gone down to Vidauban with half an hour of daylight to spare, and had spent the time since scouting vainly for Brossard.

He'd looked first a kilometre in each direction along the road leading to the farmhouse. Nothing suspicious, out of place. Then he'd decided to park a few hundred metres along the road leading to the motorway junction – the most likely direction that Brossard would approach.

After a few minutes, he realized that a bend in the road obscured the entrance to the farmhouse, and became concerned just in case Brossard approached from the other direction. He moved closer, to within a hundred metres of the entrance – the closest he dare park – and waited.

The hit had seemed a good idea originally: without Monique Fornier, there was no case! She was the only one who could vouch that the boy had left that day with the coin in his pocket, or that the tapes and transcripts bore any relevance to the life of her son. Without the coin or the tapes and transcripts, the case collapsed.

But now he just felt foolish, standing on a remote Provence lane hoping to stop the hit he'd ordered in the first place. He didn't even know which car Brossard would be driving. Though of the three cars which had so far passed, he'd been able to catch a fleeting glimpse of their drivers. No Brossard yet.

With the last dusk light fading, he realized that even that would be difficult. Another car approached, and he was hardly able to discern anything beyond the glare of its headlamps until it was almost past him.

He shuffled anxiously. Was this how he wanted to spend his last hour in France? He knew that all of this was only because one day he might want to return. He might be happy sitting in South America for a while, but for ever? Times changed: the trial would slip from prominence, Corbeix would retire, a new prosecutor might not be so keen, might see through the evidence for the tenuous nonsense that it was.

Faced with no more than a weak, exploratory case against him, he might be tempted to return. But if Monique Fornier was killed, he would *never* be able to come back.

Another set of headlamps. Glimpse of a young man in profile as the car passed. The car slowed – it was turning into the farmhouse! Probably Fornier's son or a family friend, Duclos thought. With him there, would Brossard still make the hit? Perhaps Brossard would delay till the next night, and he could then reach him tomorrow from Portugal and tell him not to go ahead.

Listening to his own wheedling, pathetically hopeful inner voice, it suddenly hit him: apart from his own neck, what did it matter? What did he care if Brossard dynamited the whole farmhouse with them all inside? *Damn Fornier!* Damn the lot of them! They'd brought him to this: standing on a lonely backwater lane in the dead of night, tired and afraid, his nerves frazzled, his career and life in ruins, running for his life from half the nation's police to catch a flight in just over an hour.

And now he was almost as worried about saving their necks as his own! His anger brought back his earlier pounding tension. His hands were shaking, and he rested back against the Peugeot bonnet to try and steady them. But after a few more minutes with no cars passing, standing alone in the darkness with only some crickets breaking the silence, he couldn't bear it any longer. He slammed one hand on his bonnet. No! *No more!* He'd waited long enough. As far as he was concerned, Brossard could . . .

A set of headlamps appeared suddenly, startling him with the speed of their approach – and for a second he was caught in their glare. Quick flash glimpse as the car sped past, but enough: it was Fornier!

Duclos jumped in the Peugeot and started it up. His heart was pounding hard. Fornier had probably seen him! A moment for the realization to hit Fornier, and then the car would do a U-turn and head out after him.

Duclos bit hard at his lip. What a fool he'd been to come down here. He swung the Peugeot out quickly and put his foot down hard. He kept his eyes glued to the rear-view mirror as he sped away, fearful that at any second Fornier's headlamps would reappear at the farmhouse entrance and turn out.

Six minutes. All it had taken from the phone going dead for Dominic to reach the farmhouse.

He screeched to a halt, leapt out almost before he'd stopped, taking his gun out in the few quick paces to the front door. It was slightly ajar.

He pushed it, but there was a weight on the other side keeping it from opening. His nerves jumped; he thought for a moment that the hitman was still there, pushing from the other side – before his eyes adjusted to the dark and made out the ghostly white face on the floor. *Jérôme!* He recoiled in horror.

He couldn't risk forcing the door, moving the body, in case Jérôme was still alive. He ran around the house, saw the dining room window open, and scrambled in.

Dominic realized he was probably following in the path the hitman had taken. *Alive?* He'd accepted in the last few minutes of frantic driving – fragments of hope and desperation fighting against hollow bewilderment – that Monique was probably already dead. But Jérôme as well? He felt as if his stomach had been scooped out by a cold claw. Salt tears stung his eyes, his vision suddenly blurred.

But fear overrode, his hands trembling as he held his gun out, double-beat pulse skittering across his cold dark sea of bewilderment.

Six minutes? A lifetime for a professional hitman. But still he might be lurking in the shadows, waiting. Dominic part of the contract along with Monique. Dominic moved stealthily, cautiously, alert to the slightest movement. Across the dining room, through the half-open door, into the hallway . . .

Eyes adjusting, taking in the crumpled figure of Jérôme at its end. He bit hard on his lip . . . *Please God, don't let him be dead!* But he knew it was little more than a wishful, desperate prayer. Most professionals finished off with head shots.

To the side, the door to the dining room was open. Dominic kept very still, consciously holding his breath, listening for sounds from the room. Nothing. He eased up, turned into the room quickly, gun held straight out.

His eyes fell on Monique's sprawled figure immediately: to the right, by the telephone.

Then with sudden panic, as shapes became clearer in the darkness, he realized that it was two figures . . . and one of them was rising!

The hitman was still alive – he'd used Monique's body as a shield . . .

Dominic aimed square at the figure, started to squeeze off the shot.

'Dominic . . .'

The voice and the shape hit him at the same time. *Monique!* He lowered the gun, rushed towards her.

He hugged her tight, kissing her cheek repeatedly. 'You're all right . . . *you're all right.*' Breathless, tone disbelieving, the tension washing away from him. He felt dampness, stickiness on her cheek as he kissed her, and touched with one hand. 'You're bleeding. You've been hit!'

473

'No, no . . . I don't think so.' She reached up to her face, still partly dazed. 'I think it's his blood. It happened so . . . so quickly. While you were on the phone . . . He grabbed me . . . said something into the phone.' Monique fought for breath, words gasped on staccato exhalations as the thoughts hit her. 'Then the shot . . . us both falling back. Then I don't remember anything until I heard you moving in the hallway.' She shook her head, looked back at the body behind her.

Dominic would have checked the man's pulse, but he could see bone fragments among the dark patch spreading out from the head. Half the skull had been blown away. 'Did you see anyone else come in the room?'

'No . . . no, I didn't . . . I . . .' Monique touched her head thoughtfully. She could feel a bruise, a dull ache to one side. 'I must have . . . have hit my head or fainted. I thought I heard Jérôme's car. But it was all confusing . . . everything happening so . . . I . . .' Then the dam of her emotions finally broke. She burst into tears. Heavy racking sobs as she clutched back tight against Dominic. 'It's so good to see you . . . *so good.*'

Dominic felt her body quaking against him. Who had fired the bullet to save her, where had it come from? Though no time to find out now. *No time! Jérôme!* But it felt wrong to just push her brusquely away, or was it more that he was dreading breaking the news, destroying her while she was still in shock from her own ordeal. *Telling her the one thing he knew she'd feared most through all the years.*

It felt like a lifetime, but in the end was only seconds before he muttered, 'It's Jérôme.' He felt her pull back. Her eyes were darting, searching, and even in the darkness he could see that she had read the panic and apprehension in his own eyes. He gripped Monique's shoulders briefly, a gesture that said 'Please be strong' – and bolted into the hallway with Monique following.

Tomi straightened up from crouching in the field, detached the telescopic sights and slid the rifle back into its long case.

Everything had come through late, at the last minute: the location, his instructions. It had been a mad rush up from Marseille, with very little daylight left in which to scout the area. He'd almost missed what he believed was Brossard's Dianne parked deep in a woodland track – realizing with a shock that Brossard might have been there for some time, it might already be over!

It was fully dark as Tomi ran across the farm field and positioned himself by the short stone wall. Light on downstairs. Tomi attached the sights:

clear view of the drawing room, a woman kneeling down by a small alcove at the back.

Seconds later the light went out. Toni panned the sights sharply to each side and up to see if any other lights had come on – but there were none. The electricity had been cut.

He had no night sights – he would have to move in! And Brossard was no doubt already there and would have prepared with . . .

It was then that he noticed the faint glow at the back of the drawing room in his sights: a small night light.

He could just pick out the silhouette of the woman. She was standing, talking on the phone. Then only seconds later, another shape came swiftly into frame – gripping the woman around the neck with one arm, taking the telephone.

Tomi focused his sights, saw the man say something into the receiver, and then the gun in his hand raised to the woman's temple. Tomi trained the cross-hairs at the centre of the man's head and squeezed off the shot – saw it connect cleanly, both figures falling back.

He packed up the rifle and ran back across the field to his car. Girouves would be pleased. Harmony kept with the police, and quite a favour they owed Girouves if ever he had need to call it in.

Contarge looked at the photo developing in the trough of liquid: 30 cm × 22 cm print, the car number plate looked quite clear. Bit more . . . *bit more* . . .

The darkroom assistant yanked it out, pinned it on a wire next to two smaller prints. Contarge put his eyeglass close up to the damp, dripping paper. Even in the faint orange light of the darkroom, he thought he could make out the first five numbers. 'It's probably the best we'll get.' He'd picked it out from three possible negatives of Duclos' car heading towards the gate, then they'd worked through a succession of frame croppings and enlargements.

The assistant nodded. 'I think so. Any more and the resolution will start to break up.'

Contarge gave it a quick pass-through under the blow-dryer, then headed out of the darkroom and back to his desk.

In daylight, it was even better than he thought. All but the last two numbers could easily be read. He picked up the phone and dialled Lepoille.

45

The police siren screamed through the night.

Still alive. *Alive!* Dominic had shrieked the word above Monique's wailing cry as she'd looked on over his shoulder at Jérôme's crumpled body. The chest and lower part of the neck had been a mass of blood, and it had been hard to find the pulse at first.

Dominic knew that he would need light for what he had to do, and rushed to the garage to switch back on the electricity. Then he took a large bed sheet from the linen cupboard. He felt for the entry wound: through Jérôme's right breastbone, a few centimetres off centre. Slightly more to the left and it would have hit his heart.

But he knew that shattered bone could still have severed vital arteries or be sitting close to the heart. And blood loss was so heavy that Jérôme could easily still die from that alone. Ripping the sheet in two, with one part he'd mopped up the excess blood and with the other tied a bandage and part tourniquet around the upper chest, wrapping it under the right arm.

A police car with two gendarmes had arrived at that moment. It would have taken too long to get an ambulance, so Dominic arranged that one gendarme drive the police car as a lead, while the other drove Dominic's car following behind. Dominic would meanwhile tend to Jérôme in the back of the car.

The second police car arrived just as they had Jérôme in and ready to go. Dominic suggested they stay and phone for a meat wagon and forensics for Brossard.

Dominic grabbed another sheet to help stem any extra blood flow. Monique was meant to go in the lead car, but she'd insisted on staying close to Jérôme. She'd stayed turned from the front seat constantly, her eyes darting concernedly with each movement as he tended Jérôme – blood stark against the white sheet binding in the intermittent flashes from the police car lights ahead.

The pulsing glare and the siren added urgency to every movement. *Don't die . . . please don't die!* Dominic made sure to keep the airway free, kept Jérôme turned slightly to one side. He hardly took his eyes off him the whole time – not only because there was a constant need to tend and watch for any changes in breathing and pulse, but because he didn't want to meet Monique's eyes: frantic, pleading . . . *Surely it couldn't be?* All the years she'd feared something like this happening, though mainly with Yves because of his work, and in the end it had been Jérôme.

Dominic could almost feel her thoughts coming across in waves without looking up. And it had all been due to his obsession with justice for Christian. No . . . *No!* It was unthinkable. He couldn't let it happen. Jérôme *wouldn't* die. Yet from the blood loss and the weakness of Jérôme's pulse and breathing, he knew that they would be lucky to save him. It would be a desperate race against time.

'How far now to the hospital at Draguignan?' he asked the gendarme driving.

'Fourteen, fifteen kilometres. Five, six minutes at most.'

Jérôme hadn't at any time regained consciousness, and Dominic started to think of the many equally unacceptable alternatives: coma, mental impairment, paralysis . . . a pall of hopelessness descending as he took in the full horror of his son's shattered, bloodied body. He scrunched his eyes tight, and suddenly he had an image of Jérôme as a young child, playing in the sea, and of him lifting Jérôme above a wave that threatened to swamp him . . . lifting him clear of danger and planting kisses on his smiling face as Jérôme shrieked with excitement, feeling the slight tremble in Jérôme's small body. And he wished he could do that now, just lift him free of the danger. But as he opened his eyes he was back with the stark flashing glare and horror, blurred now from his tears welling.

Seeing his anguish, Monique commented, 'We'll be there soon.'

Her first words since asking, 'Is he going to live? as her initial wailing panic had subsided. Dominic had responded hastily, 'Yes', not even thinking whether he might be lying – reflecting his wish in that moment more than what he believed.

Minutes later, as they burst through swing doors at Draguignan hospital with Jérôme alongside on a gurney led by two medics, Dominic's mobile phone started ringing. He didn't answer it. His other life as a policeman could wait a while. All that mattered was Jérôme.

Pierre Lepoille viewed the photo sent by Contarge at *Le Figaro* on his computer screen. He'd asked Contarge to send through a scanned image by modem to Interpol's X400 server so that he could pull it up.

A few keyboard taps and he blew it up to 4× image enlargement, cropping in on the number plate. As Contarge mentioned, all visible except the last two numbers. He deliberated for only a second before deciding to put out the nationwide alert first. He phoned through to NCB Division II, from where it would be routed through to Interpol National and within minutes would be broadcast to regional stations and police cars throughout France.

Then he dialled Dominic's number. Tell him the good news: everything was already in motion, the hunt for Duclos was on in earnest. But the number rang without answering.

Lepoille looked back thoughtfully at his computer screen as he hung up. Those last two numbers bothered him. Some impressive image recognition equipment had been installed the past few years by Division 4, primarily for counterfeit bills, or art theft and fraud detection. If he put the image through its paces, he wondered if he might pull up the last two numbers.

A 1 or a 4, a 3 or an 8? All Lepoille could make out were vague shadows. He enlarged to 16× magnification and started piecing together the likely shape that the blurred dots remaining might have taken. Then he asked the computer for percentage likelihoods for each suggestion. After seven minutes, he had an 83 per cent on a 4 on one number and 74 per cent on an 8 on the other, with all other choices scoring less than 10 per cent. *Full house!* Got the bastard. Lepoille let out a little yelp and clapped his hands, causing a few people in the computer room to look over.

Lepoille put through an update to the NCB division, then tried Dominic again.

Duclos sat in the car park of the motorway services at Brignoles-Cambarette.

As he'd raced up to the N7 junction only two kilometres from Fornier's farmhouse, he'd had to decide quickly what to do. He didn't want to head straight for the airfield, there was almost an hour to spare and, besides, if Fornier was following, the last thing he wanted to do was lead him straight there!

But which way to head? He hadn't seen any lights behind him, but what if the realization hit Fornier a minute later and he decided to give chase?

He decided on west, heading deeper into France; east towards Nice and the Italian border would be the more obvious choice for anyone following. Five kilometres along some headlamps looming up quickly in his rear-view mirror worried him, and he took the A8 motorway turn-off. They didn't follow. He continued heading west and a few kilometres further on pondered what to do. He didn't want to head too far away from the airfield, yet didn't want to stop on the hard shoulder: too open, too conspicuous for any passing police cars. He also needed a main junction turn-off in order to turn and head back the way he'd come.

It was then that he'd decided on the next motorway services at Brignoles-Cambarette. Another twenty-one kilometres, it would take him less than ten minutes to get there and he would be only fifteen–sixteen minutes away from the airfield.

Duclos looked at his watch: 9.23 p.m. Sixteen minutes into his thirty-minute wait in the car park. It had felt like a lifetime. He'd parked at the very back of the car park where few people passed and might notice him. Only two cars had so far come around the back in search of parking spaces, and he'd ducked down out of sight.

He could see the hub of activity of people parking and entering the service complex of shops and restaurants forty metres ahead. He'd parked facing it so that he'd be forewarned of anything suspicious, any out-of-place movements or cars approaching. His nerves had bristled as a police car approached – but it went straight through without pausing.

Looking on at the activity, the hustle, bustle ahead, brought home to him more acutely the fugitive, the outcast he had become. Mothers and fathers with their children, young couples, old couples, teenagers, people on holiday from the North – dining, buying souvenirs and gifts, grabbing a few snacks and groceries. A tableau, a microcosm of life in France – and he was sitting outside it all, alone in the dark at the back of the car park.

Sitting outside their merry little circle . . . *in the same way that he had sat outside Bettina's and Joël's life all through the years.* Damn them! Bettina. Joël. Corbeix. Fornier . . . *especially Fornier!* 'Damn the lot of you!' Duclos shouted, sure that his voice had carried no more than a few metres away; nobody had heard him.

Perhaps that was why Fornier hadn't reappeared to chase him. Brossard had been lying in wait, had already blasted the wife and then the son – and then put a hole clean through Fornier as soon as he appeared. The thought put a thin smile on Duclos' lips. The first all day.

Ker-vrooom . . . bap . . . bap! Duclos jumped, his heart pounding, eyes darting sharply towards the sound: five cars to the right, battered old Opel, bad exhaust by the sound of it. His nerves slowly settled back as he watched it pull out and away, but he was still anxious that he hadn't noticed anyone approach. They must have come from the petrol pumps to one side and circled around the back. He would have to be more alert. He could have looked up to see a gendarme standing by his side window.

But in the remaining minutes, though he was more vigilant in keeping an eye on all directions, he realized how much the incident had unnerved him. The events of the day had slow-boiled his nerves, but it was as if the car starting had suddenly turned the flame up high.

Each sound – leaves rustling, a car door slamming rows away, footsteps on gravel in the distance, voices by the main service entrance – cut straight through him, his nerves thrumming like taut piano wire. His hands were shaking, his palms sweaty. He steadied them on the steering wheel only to discover that his whole body was trembling.

Duclos slowly closed his eyes. The sounds ahead, the people milling around, the succession of cars passing in and out – everything seemed to be closing in. There was a ringing in his ears, a dull ache at the back of his head. Even when he opened his eyes again, he could hear his own pounding pulse.

He suddenly felt the way he had earlier in the service café – that someone among the throng ahead would see him, pick him out sitting in the shadows at the back of the car park, and start walking towards him, pointing. And suddenly there would be a crowd following, all pointing, shouting: *Duclos! Duclos!*

His face would have been on news bulletins at least twice by now. He shook his head, tried to shake off his clawing fear. The only thing which helped was looking down upon them, clinging to the moral high ground which he felt had separated him from the masses over the years. Look at them! Nondescript rabble. He'd done so much for them, for France. And now they'd turned their backs on him. As far as he was concerned they could all rot. Perhaps he *would* be better off in South America.

But within minutes the trembling was back, a pounding in his head that said, Go, Go . . . *Get away!* As far from the rabble as possible. As if they might be unpredictable – a Bastille mob that could suddenly turn and steal away his escape at the last second.

He hastily started the Peugeot and headed away – four minutes earlier than originally planned. He looked at the people receding in his rear-view mirror and let out a long slow sigh, fighting to relax again, swallowing back the butterfly nerves and nauseousness rising in his stomach. Picking up speed on the slipway to rejoin the motorway, he didn't notice the police car he'd seen earlier, now parked on a ramp to one side – he was busy looking at the approaching traffic.

One of the gendarmes only noticed the blue Peugeot at the last minute – they too were more preoccupied with the oncoming traffic. But he was unsure, and by the time he'd confirmed the registration with his central dispatch as the one broadcast earlier, the Peugeot was out of sight. Dispatch would radio ahead.

'What here . . . *here* near Vidauban?'

Dominic's tone was incredulous, disbelieving. The second time his mobile had rung he'd answered, and Lepoille had told him about them coming up with Duclos' car number: the newspaper photo ploy had worked and a nationwide search was already in full swing. *Great.* Good news. Well done.

But now with this second call from Lepoille twenty minutes later it hit him that the chase had been brought to his doorstep! '*Why?* What on earth is he doing down here?'

'No idea. The sighting we have, the only one so far, was from near Brignoles.'

'Which way is he heading?'

'West – towards you. He's on the A8 motorway and should hit the junction down the road from you just past Le Luc in no more than eight or nine minutes.'

Perhaps some sort of meeting to pay off Brossard was the only explanation Dominic could think of. And then the image suddenly flickered back from his subconscious: a blue Peugeot parked up on the road side, a distant face caught for a split second in the stark glare of the spotlights – *Duclos!* Duclos had been waiting by the approach to his house while Brossard was inside! The fleeting image so totally out of place at the time, it hadn't registered. The last place he'd expected Duclos. But why was Duclos now heading back towards him rather than away?

'That's why I'm calling now,' Lepoille said. 'You're the nearest car north of the junction.'

Suddenly it hit Dominic with a jolt what they wanted from him: to join the chase, help apprehend Duclos! At any other time, he would already be running for his car, but not now. Not while his son's life was still hanging in the balance in the next room. 'But I left a squad car at the farm at Vidauban. What about that?'

'I don't know. The closest cars that could be raised apart from you were one heading south just past Puget-Ville – which was turned straight around – and another seven kilometres into the A8 heading east from the Le Luc junction. They've been told to stay where they are. The next turn-off is almost eighteen kilometres away – they wouldn't get back in time to cover the junction.'

Either one could be the cars sent earlier to Vidauban, Dominic reflected. But Lepoille obviously didn't know about the drama at the farmhouse. On Lepoille's first call he'd mentioned where he was, but not why: too personal, the conversation would have become maudlin.

Dominic had been sitting next to Monique on the nearest hospital corridor bench to Emergency. But after Lepoille's first few words, he stood up, started pacing away. With what she had on her mind now, insensitive for her to be bothered with police logistics. 'But the Puget-Ville car – won't they make it up to the junction in time?'

'No – they'll be about five or six kilometres short. You won't make it to the motorway junction by then either, but you should be able to make the N7 junction easily. That will effectively cut Duclos off from heading east on the N7 or north through Grasse. With the motorway and south already covered – we'll have him cornered!'

Impossible choice. Desert Monique and Jérôme at such a moment, or let the man who had wreaked these horrors on his family escape? The thought of Duclos so close made his adrenalin surge with a mixture of anger and excitement: the prospect of personally hunting down Duclos felt somehow fitting. Right. But he couldn't . . . *just couldn't.* 'Isn't there another car you can send?' Dominic's voice was pleading, desperate.

'No, afraid not. We've already checked all the options.'

Dominic was half turned away, and glanced back as he sensed Monique looking over more pointedly. Seeing the pain and anguish etched deep on her face made the decision for him. Long sigh. 'I'm sorry. I just can't do it.' Dominic briefly outlined the events at the farmhouse. 'Jérôme's still in Emergency – we're waiting on news any minute. I just can't leave now.'

'I'm sorry, Dominic. If I'd known, I wouldn't have asked.'

'It's okay, how could you know. Look, let me know how –'

'If you don't go – will he get away?' This from Monique, cutting in.

'I'm sorry, I –' For a second Dominic was confused, not sure whom to address first. Then: 'Pierre – I'll call you back in a second.' Monique's expression was taut. Fobbing her off with a lie seemed pointless: the N7 was one of Duclos' main escape route options. Dominic shrugged. 'Yes, I suppose so. He might.'

'And this is the man responsible for Christian and now Jérôme?'

'Yes.' Flat tone. One word denoting so much of her life's anguish.

Her jawline tightened. She contemplated the floor for a second before looking back at Dominic. 'Then I think you should go. I'm here for Jérôme, and the doctors are doing their best. There's nothing you can do for him by staying.'

Dominic shook his head. 'No . . . no. I couldn't possibly leave you and Jérôme at a moment like this. I wouldn't be able to face either of you squarely again, or myself for that matter. I can't go.'

Monique looked at him steadily, eyes piercing. 'And if Jérôme should die – do you think it will be any easier to face me knowing that you've let the man responsible get away?'

Dominic felt the words like a knife. If she wanted to punish him for what had happened, that was it now: those words. But as he met her eyes, he could see that she was resolute, determined. Beyond the barb, she wanted him to go. Arguing looked futile. The same message he'd read before: get him, *get him*. Don't let him get away!

Dominic started to hit back with more protests, but Monique was insistent – practically screaming at him to go as she became frantic that vital seconds were being lost. With a last defeated shrug and an elicited promise from Monique that she'd call him the second there was any news on Jérôme, he turned hastily away, already dialling out to Lepoille.

Monique closed her eyes, a tear rolling down one cheek. Jérôme near death, and it had sounded as if she partly blamed Dominic. But she knew that if she hadn't taken that stance, he wouldn't have gone. She could live without seeing justice done – had already done so for many years – but Dominic? Despite his protests, she could see that part of him desperately wanted to track down Duclos, exact justice. She'd seen it in his indecision on the phone, in the hunted, frantic look in his eyes when he discovered Duclos was so close, the plea in his voice: 'Isn't there another car you can send?' She knew that until he caught Duclos, the past would never be fully laid to rest.

Monique looked thoughtfully at the closed doors of the Emergency room. A desolate chill crept over her. Once again she would be alone praying for the life of a son. Though this time at least the choice had been hers.

The first thrill, the anticipation of the chase, hit Dominic as he felt the surge of his car engine powering away from the hospital. Then it built layer by layer as he continued his conversation by mobile with Lepoille and switched on his police radio to patch in and make contact with the other two vehicles: BRN 946 east of the Le Luc motorway junction, and TLN 493 heading north from Puget-Ville. Lepoille had already confirmed the Le Luc car was in position, so Dominic asked TLN 493 its current location.

Hoarse voice through airwaves surf: 'We're just about running parallel with Pignans – we should make it to the junction in about seven minutes.'

Dominic glanced at the map he'd spread out on the passenger seat. He spoke into his mobile. 'When do you expect Duclos to reach the junction?'

'About four or five minutes.'

Then back to the radio: 'Expect him to pass you at about four or five kilometres your side of the junction – if he's heading your way. Keep your eyes sharp then.'

Dominic clicked off the radio but kept his mobile on to Lepoille. He checked his speed: 152–154 kmph. Parts of the road were winding and it was difficult to go faster. 'I should reach the N7 in about five minutes.' And Duclos was eight or nine minutes away from that point, he estimated: eleven kilometres beyond the motorway junction. He should be able to head him off in plenty of time. 'I'll phone you again when I reach there.'

Dominic glanced again at the map, picturing their triangular formation as dots closing in. They had him! There was no way out. Almost unreal that after all these years he was finally so close. And now there was nothing tentative, venturesome about the case – they had Bettina Duclos' testimony! They would throw away the key with Duclos.

So close. He felt the earlier rush of anticipation grow stronger as the trees and hedgerows flashed by in the stark beam of his headlamps . . . shadows marking his progress. *Tombstones for Duclos.* He hit a flat stretch and edged his speed up to 160 kmph.

The past weeks of activity had left him tired and jaded. But now the adrenalin rush made him alert again, he could feel it touching every nerve end as he sped on, the kilometres starting to zip by . . . *seven . . . six . . .*

Dominic flicked the radio back on. He raised the motorway car, aware that Duclos would probably reach them first. 'He should be passing you

484

in no more than two or three minutes if he's heading straight on. If so, give immediate pursuit and we'll radio ahead. Keep the airwaves open throughout.' He left a similar message with the second car heading north, but with a four-minute timing.

Less than a minute later, as the N7 junction loomed ahead, he called Lepoille and brought him up to date. 'About two minutes now on the motorway, three if he's heading south.' Dominic turned at the N7, heading towards the motorway. Closing the triangle tighter. 'And maybe four minutes for him to pass me if he comes this way.'

Dominic tapped his fingers on the steering wheel, anxious as it came up to the minute mark for Duclos to pass the motorway car, then looked towards the radio as he silently counted down . . . fifty seconds . . . *forty* . . . *thirty*. At ten seconds over he prompted: 'Anything yet?'

'No.'

Beats of silence: *Forty . . . fifty . . .* a minute over! Duclos must have headed south or was coming north towards him! 'TLN 493 – he could be heading down towards you. If so, he should be passing any second.'

'Okay.'

But his radio stayed obstinately silent as the seconds passed: a minute over heading south, two heading north. The chances that Duclos was heading his way increased, and Dominic slowed – honing in closer on each passing car: type, colour and finally number among the glare of oncoming headlamps.

Still silence from the radio.

Duclos *must* be heading towards him, he'd have reached either of the other points by now. Dominic pulled over at the first farm turning on a flat stretch and backed in so that he was side-on to the traffic, ready to turn quickly.

Dominic's nerves tensed. Any second now: scrutinizing each passing car, looking two and three cars ahead at the first hint of shape and form on the horizon – lights and shapes becoming a blur, headlamp star bursts as his eyes watered . . . Come on . . . *come on!*

He knew that if he saw Duclos now, there would be little subtlety left: he'd just ram his car broadside and yank him out at gun point. But with each car that at first looked hopeful, yet when closer turned out not to be Duclos, his panic rose another notch, and he sank deeper into despondency – Duclos' smug face seeming to rise up increasingly out of each set of passing lights . . . *fooled you . . . fooled you again!*

Dominic made a final check with the other two cars: nothing. Then looked at his watch: 9.57 p.m. Duclos wasn't going to show! Dominic became frantic. He banged his fist on the steering wheel. Where? *For God's sake . . . where?* He stared blankly at the map. They'd had Duclos cornered, and he'd disappeared into thin air!

There was hardly anything in the triangle left worth Duclos heading for: Le Luc and small nearby villages such as Le Cannet, a few small roads leading to farms. Unless Duclos had taken the N7 doubling back so that –

Dominic froze. *Airfield!* The small yellow square to the right of the triangle suddenly leapt out at him.

The TB20 Trinidad banked at 9,000 feet as it passed over the last stretch of the Alpes-Maritimes.

There was a thin cloud layer, ghostly mist racing towards them and clinging to the windscreen. Then after a minute they were through and the lights of the Côte d'Azur were ahead. The pilot started a descent to 6,000 feet as he prepared to bank again.

His passenger had hardly said a word throughout, and his presence had increasingly unnerved him. A stocky man in his late thirties named Hector whose Swiss French had an Italian or Spanish accent, wearing a padded leather jacket which made him look even bulkier. The only bit of good news was that Hector would be staying in Portugal with his pick-up. At least he would have the journey back without his company.

6,000 feet . . . *5,600 . . . 5,200.* He dropped in stages following the lights along the coast, then as he saw the lights of Toulon ahead, banked sharply for the final descent.

Darkness. All they could see was the shape of three grey hangars at the far end of the airfield and another two to their far right by a small office building. Nine aircraft in total: two to their right, four spread between the more distant hangars, and three on a flat tarmac area at the end of the main runway. But there were no lights, no movement or activity.

Dominic had arrived at the airfield at 10.02 p.m., a minute after the Le Luc car with two gendarmes. The driver, a sergeant named Pierre Giverny, informed him that it was much the same now as when he had arrived. 'Total darkness. No sign of activity.' What Giverny hadn't noticed as he'd pulled in was one of the three planes on the tarmac beyond the runway taxiing slowly, starting to move into position to take off. It braked and stood motionless as soon as his lights appeared. Duclos' car was out of sight, tucked behind the back of the furthest hangar.

Dominic was parked next to the gendarmes' car: two sets of headlamps on full beam, probing expectantly into the darkness, though most of their effectiveness faded less than halfway along the main runway. Everything beyond was just vague, grey shadow.

'Perhaps I was wrong,' said Dominic. He looked thoughtfully towards the distant hangars and planes.

In the darkness of the plane's cockpit, Hector commented, 'Give them a moment more and they'll probably go.'

The pilot nodded with a pained smile. Hector had suddenly found his voice: police and night-time raids. Probably familiar ground.

Duclos consciously held his breath as he looked at the figures in the distance, shadowy silhouettes alongside the headlamp beams. His nerves were racing out of control. One of the cars, he was sure, was Fornier's!

He saw the figures huddled together talking, looking towards them. A shiver ran up his spine, his whole body suddenly shuddering. Then after a second they turned, seemed to be making their way back towards their cars.

'See!' Whispered, almost breathless exclamation from Hector.

Duclos thought Hector might have been a navigator, until he'd slipped in the back when Duclos had first got in. Hector's presence behind him made him uneasy. A final soupçon of tension he could have done without after the mounting panic of the day. Duclos felt his stomach knotting, his nerves breaking close to the edge.

Dominic got back into his car, starting it up. He moved forward, starting to turn . . . then suddenly stopped. He looked thoughtfully back at the runway fifty metres ahead, its long expanse of darkness and the planes and hangars at its end.

'What's he *doing?*' Duclos hissed. A frozen silence with no answer between them in the confined darkness of the cockpit; only slow breathing, waiting. Then: 'Oh God . . . *Jesus!*' as Duclos saw the lights straighten, start to head towards them.

'Go . . . Go!' Hector shouted. 'Get going!' He took out a gun and waved it, though the pilot was unsure if it was as a threat or to fire at the oncoming car.

The pilot started up and jolted forward, completing the turn quickly so that they were in line with the runway. Then he throttled up high, starting to roll forward furiously.

The car had almost covered the fifty metres of tarmac beyond, was approaching the beginning of the runway . . .

The plane shook and rattled as they picked up speed. The pilot knew that once the car had covered half of the runway, it would be too late, they would be blocked from take-off. He bit at his lip. It was going to be close.

Eighty . . .90 . . . He watched the speedometer climb quickly to over 100 kmph. But he could see that the car had already covered almost quarter of the runway.

'Are we going to make it?' asked Duclos. He was trembling, though he wasn't sure if it was more fear of collision or of them not getting away.

'I don't know.'

As the reach of the car's beam hit them, the pilot switched on his own lights. A stronger marker of their own presence, hopefully intimidating, a deterrent. The car seemed to falter slightly before picking up speed again. The second car had also now started following, was just touching the start of the runway.

'Don't worry,' Hector said. 'As soon as he sees we're serious, we're not stopping – he'll back off.' But his undertone wavered; even Hector now wasn't sure.

As the airplane lights hit Dominic, he'd braked slightly on impulse – it suddenly appeared more ominous, threatening – before steeling himself again.

His first intention had been purely to investigate the planes and hangars ahead – so one of the planes moving suddenly from the group had surprised him. Sliding quickly into panic as he realized it was turning, positioning, was starting along the runway. Making a bid for escape!

He knew in that second with certainty that Duclos was inside.

If he could get close enough to block their passage, they would be forced to abort take-off. But he could see now that they weren't easing back. His own speed was edging over 90 kmph, and the plane was probably nearing 170, 180 . . . rolling furiously towards take-off.

The first twinge of fear gripped him. If they collided at that speed, there would be little chance of survival. But Monique's words rang in his ear. '. . . *do you think that it will be any easier to face me – knowing that you've let the man responsible get away?*' But it wasn't just Monique . . . the other faces long etched in his mind burnt home stronger in the glare of the plane's lights . . . *Christian, Machanaud* . . . as if they too were somehow depending on him. No! . . . *No!* He'd chased Duclos for too long, too many lives affected – he couldn't let him go now! He kept his foot down hard, powering on . . .

'He's crazy!' Hector screamed as the car lights raced towards them.

Duclos said nothing, was too afraid, his simmering panic of the day reaching a crescendo – a nervous dribble crept from the corner of his mouth, his whole body seeming to tremble in time with the shuddering of the plane as it screamed forward. The engine's roar, the fast-approaching lights, the shaking and rumbling – a cacophony of sound and light which suddenly made him realize it was all going to end here. Here on this runway in a ball of flames! His whole body was bathed in sweat. But part of him perversely almost welcomed the oblivion – an end to all the panic and madness, the running and hiding and chasing. He couldn't go on any more! Nerves screaming: *End it . . . Yes, end it! I can't face another second . . .* A crooked smile crossing his face as it dawned on him that Fornier would also be consumed in the fireball.

'We're not going to make it!' the pilot screamed.

'Keep going . . . *keep going!*' Hector shrieked, pointing his gun. This time it was a threat.

Ninety metres . . . *eighty . . . seventy . . .* The distance closed rapidly between them.

Jérôme . . . Monique. Duclos standing outside his house waiting to give the assassin his blood money! Dominic gripped the steering wheel tight.

The pilot suddenly saw a niche, a slim chance. If he turned a fraction at the last second, the car would hopefully sweep past under the wing. He looked to the side, judging height quickly. It would be close – but probably their only chance now.

A monster! All those lives. So much destroyed. Duclos escaping was unthinkable. Dominic headed straight for the airplane's searing lights.

The pilot tilted the wheel slightly to the right, and felt the first lift under the wings practically at the same second.

Forty metres . . . thirty . . .

Dominic saw the veering in direction almost too late to react, sudden panic that the plane might sweep past him and escape – and he turned the wheel sharply. *Too sharply.* He felt the back swing around and the car slide into a spin, tilting heavily. It skidded inexorably forward with tyres screaming for almost ten metres before the tilt finally verged into a sickening roll – and Dominic saw everything spinning . . . the plane's lights, the car roof and side window, the seat and floor, shards of glass suddenly showering down around him and swirling as he thought: *Jérôme . . . Monique!*

The first roll of the car cut sharply into the side of the plane's windscreen view, but with the second roll the pilot could see the car was heading straight for them, its frame starting to fill the windscreen . . . but they were lifting . . . *lifting* . . . the nose edging up above the dark ominous shape.

The pilot felt the thud as the car hit something below them, then the violent shuddering and shaking through the joystick, fighting to keep control as the plane dipped and wavered. He thought for a second they were going to nose-dive straight down and crash, but the wavering quickly righted, they started to lift again.

Oh God . . . Monique! Dominic's last thought as darkness finally swallowed up the cataclysm swirling around him. If anything happened to Jérôme and now him, she could never face it. She would be practically alone.

Five hundred . . . 1,000 feet. Steadily climbing, the lights of the coast starting to appear in the distance below. The pilot looked out briefly for damage. He could see fuel dripping back from below one wing and checked his gauge. It was probably only a slow leak, but was it enough to stop them making it to Portugal? They might have to put down beforehand. But the thud had been one of the struts or possibly the landing wheel. If damage was bad, they might not be able to put down.

An electrical spark caught on the fumes from Dominic's carburettor, a small fire starting . . . but in his inner darkness all he could see was the single candle flame burning, flickering across Monique's gentle profile. And as the flames became more intense, starting to catch the dripping petrol all around him, he was back in the wheat field searching for Duclos. *The gendarmes were tapping forward with their canes, but Poullain had ordered them to torch the wheat field ahead. He was sure that Christian's murderer was still hiding in the field, and the flames and smoke would help flush him out. But Dominic was also concealed among the long sheaves, on his knees searching for the coin as the flames came close, starting to lick all around him . . . growing panic as he felt the searing heat and realized the fire had surrounded him, there was no way out.*

As the plane touched 2,000 feet, they saw the car's explosion in the distance below, as if someone had lit a runway bonfire to mark a landing point. A slow smile crossed Duclos' face.

As the explosion came, a jolt went through Monique's body. A feeling of dread, as if something terrible had happened to Jérôme in the Emergency room at that second.

She looked up anxiously towards the Emergency room doors, expecting a doctor to come out with a drawn face at any moment.

But with the passing seconds and nobody appearing, she went back to her silent prayers of the past hour, thinking: please . . . *please. Not this second time. Surely God couldn't be so cruel as to let another of her sons die.* It never occurred to her in that moment that her prayers should have been for Dominic.

Epilogue

Praia do Forte, Brazil, January 1996

Duclos sipped at the *caipirissima* as he swung on a hammock on the covered terrace. From the beach in front of the villa came the gentle swish of surf. Darkness had fallen almost three hours ago and it showed only as a white frothing line in the moonlight.

They'd finally landed over 300 kilometres further north than planned, close to Oporto, due to loss of fuel. A nightmarish, skidding landing with a damaged wheel – but they made it. Two days in Portugal with Hector to arrange a new identity and passport, and then he was on a scheduled flight to Salvador, Bahia. He was met there by a local, Jorge Cergara, who drove him the eighty kilometres north to Praia do Forte and the beach villa. His new identity was Gérard Belmeau, a Swiss French businessman taking early retirement. His hair had been dyed a red sandy blond, and he had started cultivating a moustache which was tinged every few days to match.

The papers for the house were already prepared in the name of Belmeau, and Praia do Forte was increasingly popular with foreign tourists. No eyebrows would be raised, Cergara assured. And if at any time they were, both the mayor and police chief were in their pockets from pay-offs on their hotel and resort investments in the area.

Gérard Belmeau? His new life. Duclos had rolled it around his tongue for days, tried to force it into his mind so that if anyone called out his new name he might actually respond. Except nobody did. Nobody knew him. He was just a shadowy quiet figure who shuffled into town occasionally to eat and buy groceries and visited the beach some weekdays. At the weekends it was too crowded and invariably he'd stay on his terrace and nurse a *caipirissima*, catch up on the latest news from France in the newspapers.

There was only one place in town he'd found where he could get them, and normally he'd buy *Le Figaro* and *Le Monde* – the only two available – at the same time. He'd filled the French press the first two months after his escape. Front page at first, then later further back with background and new angle items: rise and fall in politics or thrown in with a soup of other political scandals – Tapie, Médecin, now Duclos.

Duclos had smiled at the articles attacking the general bungling surrounding his escape. Barielle for allowing house arrest, Corbeix for not protesting more strongly against it, the entire examination process for not uncovering the fact that he very obviously had funds outside of those frozen, and finally the keystone collection of Provence cops who let him slip through their grasp.

A circus of finger-pointing and mud-slinging. Sitting halfway across the globe on a palm-fringed beach, Duclos found it all laughable, pathetic. A lot of ranting and political rhetoric, his name used primarily for ministers to score points off each other as they grasped at air with empty hands, screaming for justice. Duclos sneered. *Justice?* What did they know.

They had no idea what he'd suffered through the years for those few dark moments three decades ago. Plagued for years by blackmail from Chapeau, then in turn his brother; his secret life away from Bettina and Joël. Sometimes it had felt like a hell on earth in repayment for what he'd done, one incident linking to another through the long years. That was why he'd felt so outraged when the case had resurfaced – he'd felt as if he'd already done his penance, served his term!

Except one part of the link in the chain of fateful circumstances through the years had finally led to his salvation. If it hadn't been for the blackmail, he probably wouldn't have taken political bribes – the slush fund and contacts which had finally allowed him to escape. He raised his glass to an imaginary France and smiled crookedly. At least he'd had the last laugh there. *'Santé!'*

The first few months had been particularly idyllic, almost like an extended holiday. Any sense of isolation didn't set in till later, perhaps coinciding with him slipping from prominence in the French press. He decided he was sick of Brazilian TV with its endless lambada and game shows with scantily clad hostesses, and invested in a large satellite dish to get French TV. It helped, but also in part felt like nostalgic voyeurism: he was able to look at all that he loved and was familiar with – food, fashion, lifestyle – from a distance, but couldn't touch it, feel it. Not long after, he discovered the *caipirissimas* – white rum with lime, sugar and crushed ice. When Brazilian TV became too painful or French TV too nostalgic, he would retire to the terrace and his cocktail shaker.

His name had come back into prominence with the news that Corbeix was continuing with the case *in absentia*. As he watched the proceedings from a distance, it suddenly hit him why he felt such satisfaction when his name was in the news: it was not only a reminder of what he'd got away with, but a sense that at least he was still in France in spirit, if not in body.

He'd also been into Salvador a few times recently and made a contact for young boys, and Cergara had phoned and invited him to the Rio Carnival the following month. His next annual bio-tech payment was due soon and some new banking arrangements had been made. Their lawyer thought it was best to meet him in person to explain the new arrangements, and he could take in the carnival at the same time. All expenses on them. Things were looking up.

The effect of the four *caipirissimas* that night began to bite, he could feel their warmth coursing through him. A distant glow on the beach slowly pierced his blurred vision. As he focused, the four candles became clearer – a woman and small child silhouetted kneeling before them. Probably a Candomblé ceremony. He'd seen one before: candles and a collection of seashells on a white cloth, flowers and rice thrown into the sea to appease their gods Exú and Iemanjá. But in the distant flickering flames, he suddenly saw Monique Rosselot's face, her reflection in the glass as she prayed for her dying son . . . *the receding flames of Fornier's burning wreckage as they'd climbed up high above the lights of the Côte d'Azur.*

He shook his head. Freeing the ghosts was easier now: it all felt so far away in time and distance. Almost another lifetime.

Duclos closed his eyes and let the lapping surf and the night-time pulsing of cicadas and crickets wash over him as he thought ahead to the Rio Carnival. Drums and dancing and colourful star bursts of costumes gradually matched the rhythm, lulling him gently into another *caipirissima-*induced sleep.

'*Tudo Bem? Você gosta de Carnival?*'

Among the clatter and riot of noise and movement, Duclos would have hardly noticed the young boy if he hadn't greeted him almost as soon as he walked out of the hotel after meeting Perello. Not unusual. The street kids, *abandonados*, regularly worked the tourist hotels.

Seeing Duclos' quizzical expression, the boy switched to broken English: 'You want guide for carnival? I very good. Only five dollars 'merican. Show you everything.'

Duclos noticed then how beautiful the boy was. One of the most exquisite mulattos he'd ever seen: coffee-cream skin, brown curls with a tinge of light gold, soft brown eyes. The thought of spending an hour or two with the boy made his mouth suddenly dry.

The boy was right. He *was* a good guide. They took in the main Ipanema processions at Praça General Osório and heading along Avenida Visc de Pirajá, then ended up at Il Veronese where he bought the boy a pizza. The boy, whose name he'd discovered was Paulo, tucked in as if hadn't eaten in weeks. Duclos smiled. He felt a warm glow in the boy's company; it felt gratifying to spend his money like this. So much pleasure gained for so little. He ended up giving the boy almost thirty dollars to ensure he stayed in his company. The boy was still looking longingly at the menu after his pizza, so Duclos treated him to an ice-cream.

As the boy finished the last few scoops, he looked up thoughtfully, directly. 'You want spend longer with me. Alone?'

Duclos stared back into the boy's innocent eyes. Except they weren't so innocent, they were knowing. Senses honed sharp by years of street life. Perhaps the boy had guessed with him being so kind and attentive, or the fact that he'd hardly paid any attention to the writhing tanga'd bottoms and star-nippled breasts of the carnival girls. His eyes had hardly left the boy throughout. The boy knew. But at least he could now dispense with the subterfuge. 'How much?'

The boy thought for a second, plucking a figure out of the air. 'Sixty dollars.'

Duclos smiled. It was probably twice what the boy normally charged, but Duclos would have gladly paid double. This was great. Perello had just confirmed bank transfer details for his next $120,000 payment, and here he was in the middle of bargain-basement street-kid heaven. Perhaps he'd make a trip back to Rio every few months. Exile was starting to look better by the day. 'Where?' he asked. Sneaking an *abandonado* past his hotel reception was too risky.

'I know somewhere near.'

Duclos contemplated this briefly before nodding, though he'd known what his answer would be from the second the boy had made the proposal. He paid the bill and they left.

The frenetic activity of carnival hit them again outside. Fifty metres along they turned and the noise started to recede. Then another turn away from the main processions, and finally into a small back alley almost three blocks away. Carnival activity was now no more than dull background drumming and whistling. Crowds and people had also diminished with each successive turn: the back alley was deserted.

Paulo indicated a small door almost halfway along and led the way in. It was a deserted storehouse; old packing crates served as tables and chairs and some makeshift beds had been made with cardboard on the dusty concrete floor. It was obviously where some of the *abandonados* spent the night.

Paulo wedged a long block of wood between the floor and door handle. The only light came in from a high dusty window. Duclos handed over the money, and the boy tucked it in his shoe and started taking off his clothes.

Duclos was slow in taking off his own clothes, enjoying watching the boy strip: the lean, taut lines of the boy's body, his slim hips. An indefinable colour somewhere between teak and copper. Duclos' pulse raced with anticipation.

And then the boy was leaning over, going down on all fours, one finger beckoning. The blood pounded through Duclos' head.

Positioning himself behind the boy, he saw the faint film of sweat covering the body, and slid one finger measuredly down the groove of the boy's spine, then slowly caressed him with his whole hand, spreading around and up again. *Exquisite.* Duclos closed his eyes, felt himself sailing on a wave of pleasure.

Jahlep . . . Jean-Pierre . . . Pascal . . . the many boys who had pleasured him through the years.

But as he opened his eyes again, the boy was turned back towards him, his eyes caught in a shaft of light from the window above. Tan brown with small flecks of green, soulful, imploring – and suddenly they reminded him of the boy in the wheat field. *Sweet acid sweat mixed with the smell of peaches and ripe wheat. The wind rustling gently through the trees behind . . .*

Only as he looked deeper, he could see that the boy wasn't looking back directly into his own eyes, but at something beyond. Slightly behind him. And the boy's body was suddenly tense. Something was wrong. *Terribly wrong.*

A faint shuffling was the only other warning as the man stepped from the shadows behind and ran the blade deftly across Duclos' throat, severing his jugular.

The boy scampered up quickly and grabbed his clothes, eager to get them clear of Duclos' blood spilling. The man wiped his blade on Duclos' shirt draped over a packing crate, and took the wallet from his trousers alongside as the boy dressed. He watched as Duclos slumped to the ground, as if ensuring that the wound had been fatal, and then he and the boy left together.

As Duclos clutched at his throat, his life blood ebbing away, the image of the boy's soulful brown eyes stayed with him. Only in his mind's eye they were staring straight at him, not beyond.

Miguel Perello made his call from an Ipanema phone box. It was picked up on the second ring. The person answering in California was expecting the call.

'It's done,' Perello said.

'Any complications?'

'No. None. He took the bait and it went smoothly.'

'Good. Take care of the rest of the clean-up with the bank accounts and transfers, then that's the whole thing wrapped.'

'Fine.' Hanging up, Perello decided to join the carnival procession he could hear a block away. He felt like celebrating.

They could have kept Duclos hidden for a while, but eventually someone would have traced him and Duclos' first option would have been to trade juicy secrets in return for a lighter sentence. Not worth the risk when at stake was the bio-technology coup of the century. But it was Marchand who had unconsciously given them clues to the best game plan.

Marchand had been right. Duclos was too prominent a figure in France – and killing him in the middle of a high-profile murder trial, well-planned accident or not, would have attracted far too much attention. Letting the dust settle for a while and removing Duclos far from the central spotlight had been a much better plan. Now he was just Gérard Belmeau, a Swiss tourist mugged and killed in a Rio back alley during carnival. It happened every year.

Provence, August 1996

Dominic felt the late sun on his back as he inspected the tangerine tree. He'd originally bought it not long after coming out of hospital. Part nostalgia, part symbol of his and Jérôme's survival. Christmas past, there had been only four tangerines on the tree; now he could count eleven blossoms.

The day had been busy. The Capels had left just over an hour before. He'd been in the garden when they'd arrived, and now returned to do a bit more tending before it got dark.

The last skin graft for the burns on his arm had been that February, and his leg had been out of plaster now for over three months. Even his small limp had now gone. Giverny and his partner had been racing up the runway not far behind him and had managed to drag him free only seconds before the explosion. His only injury was a broken leg and burns to one arm.

Jérôme's condition had been more serious. The initial operation was successful, but he'd spent another two weeks in hospital for monitoring. Then two months later had returned for reconstructive surgery to his breastbone and the insertion of a plastic plate. Yves had ribbed him: 'At least you'll probably be the only *man* on the coast with an implant. Not a bad novelty line for chatting up on the beach at Cannes.'

There was a period of convalescence for them both at home, but despite Monique's fussing and small complaints that at times it was like having two babies again, Dominic could see her silent pleasure. Her prayers had been answered this time.

After another two weeks Jérôme went back to work, but Dominic stayed at home. The incident had been a stern prompt that it was time to take retirement: the pension was good, there was an invalidity top-up, and he had enough money put away. He was getting too old to chase villains along runways.

A month before he'd seen a bar in Juan-les-Pins for sale and made contact with Valérie, Louis' wife, for advice: she knew the bar and hotel scene on the coast. Themed bars were popular, and his idea was the late fifties and early sixties with period memorabilia such as an old jukebox and pop and movie posters. He had nearly all the period soul records for the jukebox already. In the end Valérie was so enthused she offered to go in with him. The thought of the *milieu* possibly visiting one day for protection money particularly tickled her. 'Just leave it to me.' Dominic had winked.

Papers were ready to sign the next month, and the refit would see the bar open just before Christmas. It was mostly summer trade, but weekends were good with another slight spurt at Christmas and Easter. The only cautionary note from Monique was that while behind the bar he should stick mostly to Perrier. Dominic wasn't sure what was his main motive: reliving his youth, keeping himself occupied or making some money. If he got two out of three, he wouldn't complain. Sipping Perrier while listening to Sam Cooke with the lapping waters of Juan-les-Pins less than fifty metres away. Heaven.

In early March Lepoille had phoned him to tell him the news about

Duclos in Brazil. The Swiss embassy's efforts to trace and contact relatives of Gérard Belmeau had unearthed the false identity, and photofit and dental-chart checking through Interpol had brought up the Duclos match soon after.

Corbeix had by then finished the *instruction* process of his *in absentia* case against Duclos, with a final trial date set for July. Corbeix had claimed that his main reason for continuing was the case's complexity and to prove to himself that he had the ability and stamina to see it through. 'A good note on which to finish my career. And prove that bastard Thibault wrong at the same time.'

But Dominic suspected that an equally strong reason was something Corbeix had mentioned before posting for an *in absentia* continuation. Corbeix had made an application to the *garde des Sceaux* for Machanaud's old conviction to be quashed, but when it was passed to the *Cour de Cassation* for review they'd decided that such action could only be taken 'if a conclusive case was proven against an alternative suspect'. Corbeix wanted to set the record straight. Reparation for injustices past.

'*C'est prêt!*'

Dominic was disturbed. Monique was by the lounge door, calling out: dinner was ready.

Duck *pot au feu* with spinach, asparagus and white beans. Yves and Jérôme were already at the table when Dominic sat down. He opened the wine and poured: Côte Rôtie, Les Jumelles '91. Amidst the clatter of cutlery of Monique serving, he raised his glass. '*Santé!*' Just two weeks before Corbeix had phoned him with the trial verdict on Duclos: *guilty*. 'Nice to see everyone.'

Raised glasses in return, awkward smile from Yves. He was usually the one absent, but had made the effort knowing in advance the Capels would be visiting that day. The only one missing was Clarisse; her family were due to visit at the end of the month.

Conversation was light at first: small talk from Yves and Jérôme about their work, a bar in Sainte-Maxime that they were planning to head to later. Monique was never happier than with her family around her, and Dominic basked in her glow.

Then after a brief lull she looked across thoughtfully. 'Eyran seems like a nice boy. Quite talkative.'

'Yes, he is. Very much so.' Monique had asked him a few questions after the Capels had left, but a lot had been relayed during a frantic three-way conversation while they were there. Jérôme's English was limited, Monique's and Yves' non-existent, and so Dominic had ended up as interpreter. Sudden flashback to the small room with Calvan and Eyran and Philippe translating. But Dominic knew why Monique was making the comment now.

Though Stuart Capel first let him know of Eyran's interest in seeing Monique the previous summer, the accident and period of hospitalization had pushed back the moment when he might mention this to Monique, and then when he had finally broached the subject, Monique had taken almost another month to answer. Slow acceptance. He'd told her before that the boy bore little or no resemblance to Christian, but still the same questions came, this time helping her fill in more detail: is he talkative, friendly? Does he know any French? Dominic had answered that he was a nice boy, but shy, reserved. That although he was out of therapy now, losing his parents had obviously left its mark.

When she finally agreed to the meeting, he'd phoned Stuart Capel. Stuart arranged that they would visit one day in the summer, combine it as part of their holiday. But the Eyran Capel who arrived that day was almost a different boy: talkative, attentive, eyes sparkling, questions every other minute: which is the nearest beach? Do you go there often? Do you have a boat?

'He's improved a lot since I saw him,' Dominic commented. 'Or maybe it's just that he's that bit older. More confident.'

Stuart had arrived alone with Eyran, leaving his wife and daughter on a Saint-Tropez beach. During the three-way conversation, Dominic had noticed the way Monique had at times looked intently at the boy. He'd never been able to see anything of Christian in the boy, but maybe in that moment she had.

At one point, as Stuart brought Dominic up to date on events with Marinella Calvan, Monique tried conversing directly with Eyran. A lot of stilted half-sentences with the few English words she knew, arm-waving and eye contact. Finally, she invited Eyran to look at the garden: safety of the universal language of trees and plants with some occasional pointing and smiling.

Calvan had phoned Stuart to thank him for saving her neck in court. She also had a proposition: she was writing a book which would be far stronger with some personal interviews with Eyran. She would pay 25 per cent of the royalties. She was taking the same, with the rest going to the university's PLR studies section. Stuart had agreed. It would help pay Eyran's school fees. The book was due out in seven months. 'I'll send you a copy.'

In turn, Dominic brought Stuart up to date with Duclos, the trial and Corbeix. When they'd caught up with Monique and Eyran, they were standing at the back of the garden with Monique pointing out over the low stone wall towards the field and the woods in the distance.

After they'd left, Monique had asked more questions to catch up on what she might have missed. Since the accident, she'd hardly mentioned Eyran and Christian, and he had the feeling that she'd purposely pushed the thoughts away as a form of self-protection. Now it was as if the visit had brought it all back and she was frantically assimilating everything anew. Again she'd asked the question: 'Are you sure he doesn't recall anything while awake? Only under hypnosis?' Sudden concern that she might have been struggling to communicate while everything was already half familiar to Eyran.

The conversation returned to light incidentals for most of the rest of the dinner. Then with the dishes cleared away, Yves and Jérôme having left for Sainte-Maxime and Dominic sipping at a brandy, Monique asked, 'When did Eyran finish therapy?'

'When I saw him with Stuart last year at the Palais de Justice, apparently he had just three more sessions to go. So perhaps a month after at most.'

Monique was thoughtful. 'From what you've mentioned, he's obviously a lot happier now. More settled. The past year has made a big difference.'

'It looks that way.' And suddenly looking back at Monique, Dominic realized why it was important to her. She'd initially pushed away full acceptance of a PLR bond between the two boys, 'some vague, unexplained psychic link' was as far as she would go. But if she was now finally going to accept it, it was important for her to know that Eyran was also happy. Her pain and grief – as with any mother who had lost a young child – was not only the personal loss, but the thought that that young life had ended with so much ahead, a tragic waste which flew in the face of all precepts of balance and order in life. Yet if she could believe that there was some continuance, some hope beyond, then it might help salve some of the pain and sense of loss.

A single night light flickered on the table between them. In the background crickets clicked softly. A calm and balmy night. Almost surreal that just a year ago the house had been the scene of so much mayhem. He reached out and gripped Monique's hand, and smiled. He could see how desperately she was now clinging to that hope, and he knew that if she could finally believe, it might lay to rest the last lingering shadows in her eyes. 'Yes,' he said. 'I think you're right. He is very happy now.'

That night, as Dominic started to drift off to sleep, the events of the day all jumbled together: the Capels, Yves and Jérôme, the news swapped about Duclos, Corbeix and Calvan, and Monique's final fight with acceptance.

But the image that lingered strongest in his mind was of Monique and Eyran standing by the back wall looking out over the field beyond. For a moment he had been concerned – as he had been the year before standing in the wheat field with Stuart and Eyran – that future nightmares might be sparked off in Eyran's mind, that the field might somehow unlock past buried memories of Taragnon. But the images that flashed through his mind were from his own past dreams: *the gendarmes tapping across, the field alight and burning around him, the assassin stalking through* . . . Bright, burning lights which seared at the back of his eyes.

As the stinging light faded and he pictured clearly again the two of them standing by the wall, now beckoning towards him, he knew that there was finally nothing to fear. And in that moment, looking on, he saw Monique's hand join with Eyran's. Or was he already dreaming?